FURRY

THE BEST ANTHROPOMORPHIC FICTION EVER

EVER

EDITED BY FRED PATTEN

ibooks

DISTRIBUTED BY PUBLISHERS GROUP WEST

A Publication of ibooks, inc.

CONTENTS

FOREWORD TO THE IBOOKS EDITION

When *Best in Show* was published in July 2003 by Sofawolf Press, we hoped that this first anthology of fiction from anthropomorphic fandom's small-press magazines and websites would be popular with readers of that genre. It was; enough so to go back to press once, and to win anthropomorphic fandom's 2003 Ursa Major Award in two categories: the book itself for Best Other (non-novel) Literary Work of the year, and its cover by Ursula Vernon for Best Published Illustration of the year.

It was a real thrill when ibooks asked about publishing this edition. We—meaning all the authors, as well as the editor and publishers — feel honored that a much larger sf/fantasy publisher thinks that general SF readers will enjoy these stories, too. As my Introduction to the First Edition says, there are lots more where these came from.

Unfortunately, it has proven impractical to include the illustrations from the First Edition in this Second Edition. Please excuse all the references herein to art in this book. We also chose to leave the Afterword and Bibliography as they were in mid-2003 when the First Edition was published as *Best In Show: Fifteen Years of Outstanding Furry Fiction*, as a time capsule of furry fiction from 1987 through 2002, rather than attempting to shoehorn in three years' worth of updates.

Fred Patten
February 2006

Introduction

BY FRED PATTEN

Although I did not realize it, I discovered science fiction at the dawn of the Golden Age of SF books. I was nine years old, it was 1950, and my father brought home Robert A. Heinlein's *Sixth Column* from the Los Angeles Public Library—for himself, but I read it before he returned it to the library. Dad decided that he did not care for SF as much as for detective novels, but I was hooked. I began reading every SF book the library had, and it seemed to get a dozen or more every month.

I did not find out until years later, but 1950 (give or take a couple of years) was when the book publishing industry discovered science fiction. Until just after World War II, science fiction (which then encompassed fantasy and horror) was considered by the literary establishment to be no more than cheap escapist trash, not worthy of publication in book form. The top SF authors like Heinlein, Isaac Asimov, E. E. Smith and A. E. van Vogt were ignored in comparison to the prestige of their counterparts like Ellery Queen, Raymond Chandler and Rex Stout in the mystery field or Max Brand, Zane Grey and Louis L'Amour in Westerns. The now-classic SF short stories and serialized novels of the 1930s or 1940s could only be found by hunting for tattered copies of the original magazines in used-magazine shops.

This changed during the late 1940s. The publishing industry discovered that there was as much of a market for good science fiction in hardcover form as there was for detective novels and Westerns. Suddenly the major authors were able to get their best novels and short stories published in "real books" which flowed into public libraries. And there was a tremendous backlog in over twenty years' worth of SF pulp adventure magazines. For roughly a decade from 1948 through 1958, the literary raw ore in these magazines was refined by major publishers and several SF specialty small presses into the polished ingots of SF hardcover books that spread over public library and school library shelves during my adolescence.

This certainly included the short story anthologies. One of the first and best, still in print as a classic, was the giant *Adventures in Time and Space*, edited by Raymond J. Healy and J. Francis McComas (Random House, 1946); 997 pages presenting 35 top-quality stories selected from over a dozen years' worth of SF magazines. (These included one unarguably Furry story, Fredric Brown's "The Star Mouse," and an arguable second one, L. Sprague de Camp's "The Blue Giraffe.") The king of the SF anthologists was Groff Conklin, who produced over forty thick anthologies such as *A Treasury of Science Fiction* and *Omnibus of Science Fiction* between 1946 and his death in 1968. August Derleth and Donald

A. Wollheim were two other editors whose volumes of "best" SF short stories were considered basic primers of the genre. For the dedicated SF enthusiast who read even the small-print copyright acknowledgments, the names of such magazines as *Astounding Science-Fiction, Weird Tales, Thrilling Wonder Stories,* and others became familiar even if the magazines themselves had ceased publication years earlier.

Jump ahead a couple of decades. I had been participating in organized fandom for twenty years by now. I regularly attended the major SF conventions and comic-book conventions, along with thousands of other fans. Around the early 1980s some of us discovered that we particularly enjoyed stories featuring intelligent animals and animal-like interstellar aliens, whether the stories were pure fantasy or technological SF about mutated or scientifically enhanced animal characters. We began to socialize in our own clique, at first within the larger SF and comic-book fan communities, but by the late 1980s within a separate fandom that started its own conventions—and its own fanzines/small-press magazines.

Sf fanzines have tended to emulate the commercial SF magazines with amateur short stories, articles and reviews, plus news and commentary about the active world of SF fandom. Comics fandom's fanzines have been similar, with the fiction favoring amateur comic book stories featuring the fan-cartoonist's own superheroes. The new Furry fanzines have had aspects of both, with their fiction in the form of both text short stories and comic book pages.

One significant difference between the three has been that, if an amateur story in a SF fanzine has any genuine literary quality, it will usually soon be submitted to one of the commercial SF magazines; either on the author's own initiative or at the urging of other fans. Thus amateur SF stories with any merit are soon published in the professional SF field. There are few if any literary gems lost within old SF fanzines. Amateur comic book stories, by the nature of their amateur art, tend to not be of professional comic-book quality. But good writing in the Furry fanzines has not migrated into the SF literary community. The market within the SF genre for stories featuring talking animals is so small that most Furry authors do not bother submitting their stories to the SF markets; and the anthologists who search the SF magazines for stories worth reprinting in "best of the year" SF and fantasy collections do not read the Furry small press. So a growing body of fiction of respectable quality has been accumulating in Furry fanzines since the late 1980s, unknown except to the readers of those fanzines which usually have circulations of 200 copies or less.

Since I was a devotee of the dozens of SF anthologies of the late 1940s onward, I have been dismayed since the early 1990s about the "loss to literature" of the good stories that I was now reading in the Furry fanzines which would be out of print almost immediately. Unlike the commercial SF magazines which printed tens of thousands of copies, old Furry fanzines cannot be found in used magazine shops or, today, the antiquarian literature market; or in popular-literature collections in research libraries. So it is unlikely that they will be available for the SF anthologists of the future. I have been grousing about this at Furry conventions for the past half-dozen years. In 2001 Jeff Eddy and Tim Susman, who had started Sofawolf Press the previous year with the magazine *Anthrolations*, told me that they wanted to expand into book publishing; and that if I would assemble a book's worth of those worthwhile Furry stories they would like to publish it.

Here it is. I spent a year rereading my own collection of Furry fanzines and borrowing issues that I did not have; plus reading all that I could find of the growing number of stories since about 1995 that are published only on the Internet. I assembled a list of not quite a hundred stories that I considered the best, sent the list to Jeff and Tim, and the three of us picked the two dozen stories that we agreed were the best of the best. Our main other editorial consideration was to limit the selection to one story per author, so that *Best in Show* would also be a showcase of the many good authors in Furry fandom rather than showcasing fewer writers with multiple stories. Without planning for it, we also ended up with a pretty good sampler of all the best of the Furry literary fanzines and websites. One insurmountable problem was that some excellent Furry authors do not write in less than novella or novel lengths (hi, Paul Kidd!). Another problem was that some long-running series, either by individual writers or by many in a shared-world project, begin with weak stories while the later, better ones require the reader to be familiar with the earlier ones.

We also chose a couple of backup stories, since we assumed that there would probably be one or two of the two dozen that we would not be able to get permission to reprint in *Best in Show*. We were delighted to find that every author we asked was enthusiastic about the opportunity to have his or her story brought back into print. Most asked to polish up their story since they felt that their writing has improved since the story was originally published; so the versions here may vary slightly from those in the magazines. It seemed a shame to waste the two backup stories, so you are getting twenty-six stories in *Best in Show* instead of twenty-four.

🐾 ∞ 🐾

The stories in *Best in Show* all stand on their own. However, the enjoyment of several may be increased by the following bits of background information.

"The Color of Rain." Gene Breshears says that this is not a *Tai-Pan Universe* story (see "Repas du Vivant"), but it is set about 2,000 years earlier and shows a glimpse of the future history that would evolve into the *Tai-Pan* galactic civilization setting.

"Respect the Sea." The magazine *HistoriMorphs* is devoted to stories postulating that Furries have lived alongside humans on Earth, and have been participants in most historic events such as serving in the American Civil War, being victims of the Nazi Racial Purity laws, and so forth.

"Rosettes and Ribbons." This is a stand-alone story among Hogarth's tales of an interstellar civilization featuring numerous space-faring species, many of which (the Pelted) are descended from bioenhanced Earth animals. Most star her Pelted felinoid Alysha Forrest, a talented young officer in a galactic space navy. Hogarth's first novel, *Alysha's Fall* (a "fix-up" of short stories that appeared in several Furry fanzines during the 1990s), was published by Cornwuff Press in September 2000.

"Recruiting." Elizabeth McCoy's adventures of the Kintaran spaceship *Choosaraf*, usually starring ship's doctor Coli-nfaran, began with "Leaping Lizards" in *PawPrints* #1, Winter 1994. One of the most popular aspects of the Kintarans (centauroid felines) is that they are not merely "humans with animal heads" (as too many unimaginative Furry characters are). The Kintarans have a definitely non-human social structure, and their attempts to adopt it as well as their non-human physiology to a human-based interstellar civilization make interesting and amusing tales. McCoy's stories have not been published in chronological order; "Recruiting," one of the latest published, is set early in the series when Coli and her sister Klarin-yal have only recently assumed command of the *Choosaraf*.

"Rat's Reputation," the oldest story in *Best in Show*, established the fantasy world that Michael Payne would later use for his first novel, *The Blood Jaguar* (Tor Books, December 1998). When we asked him for permission to reprint "Rat's Reputation," Payne replied that he was just finishing rewriting it into his second novel set in *The Blood Jaguar* world, if that mattered to us. We feel that the original version is still worth reading by itself.

"Whimper's Law," published in *The Ever-Changing Palace*. *ECP* is a fanzine by and for the fans of V. M. Wyman's *Xanadu* series. Vicky Wyman's *Xanadu* world began in a five-issue comic-book serial published during 1988, reprinted as a graphic-art novel, *Xanadu: Thief of Hearts* in 1994. The sequel, *Xanadu: Across Diamond Seas*, was also published in 1994. Her *Xanadu* novels are romantic swashbuckling adventures in the tradition of Sabatini's *Scaramouche* and Hope's *The Prisoner of Zenda*. The Empire of Xanadu is analogous to late-18th century France, with social unrest building within a rigid social caste comprised of the Nobles, all mythological animals (including birds) such as unicorns, griffins and dragons (most of whom have magic powers to varying degrees); the Freeborn, a middle class of feral animals such as lions, wolves, owls and deer; and the Domestiques, a lower class of domesticated servants and laborers such as dogs, cats, horses and cattle. "Vermin" such as rats are classed with the Domestiques, to the displeasure of both; the true Domestiques do not want to be associated with such troublemakers, while most vermin tribes consider themselves to be Freeborn and not anybody's servants.

Long-ruling Emperor Allynrud (unicorn) has recently died and the new Empress, his young daughter Alicia, is trying to encourage more mobility and tolerance between the castes before the tension blows up into revolution. *Xanadu* was instantly popular and many fans wanted to write their own stories to help flesh out the outline of the world. Wyman has encouraged them to do so through an authorized fanzine, *The Ever-Changing Palace*, to which she contributes herself. Craig Hilton's "Whimper" stories are set in Xanadu's capital city which he describes as closer to early Victorian London. Whimper is a young gutter rat determined to take advantage of the new laws allowing Domestiques to hold jobs previously reserved for Freeborn. "Whimper's Law" is his origin story; in Hilton's other stories so far Whimper joins Xanadu City's constabulary and basically invents the art of rational detection.

"Beneath the Crystal Sea." Swashbuckling adventure stories featuring a charismatic but amoral protagonist in a world of sorcery, monsters, and court intrigue have been popular since Robert E. Howard introduced his Conan the Cimmerian in *Weird Tales* in the 1930s. Brock Hoagland is the best of the writers to apply the formula with a Furry cast. Hoagland's first five stories starring Perissa, the ambitious 19-year-old leopardess assassin, appear in his *Tales of Perissa*, published by United Press, July 2001. "Beneath the Crystal Sea," the fourth of these tales, was the winner of Furry fandom's 2002 first annual Ursa Major Award for the best anthropomorphic literature & art of the previous year, in the Best Short Story category. A second collection of Perissa's adventures is awaiting publication.

"Mercy to the Cubs: A Tale of the Furkindred." See the Afterword for details about the complex *Furkindred* writers' project and its publications. One line deserves an explanation, where the priest Thaylyn says of a Kurlanar cub, "His hands won't pop open for a few seasons yet." In the thick *Furkindred* writers' guide, the Kurlanar (maned wolves) cubs are described as quadrupedal and with paws until the equivalent age of a human three-year-old. "Cubs were born with paws instead of hands. On four legs, they could outrun danger. Later, when they learned to walk two-legged, cubs' frozen fingers uncurled like flower petals, thumbs popping free last of all." ("Four Legs/Two Legs" by Susan Van Camp, *The Furkindred: A Shared World*, MU Press, July 1991, pg. 169.)

"Repas du Vivant." This is set in the *Tai-Pan Universe* writers' project. It is more humorous than most, which tend toward action-adventure. We narrowed down our choices of *Tai-Pan Universe* stories for *Best in Show* to three; this humorous vignette, a grim drama of battle with space pirates, and a high-tech story heavy on astrophysics. "Repas du Vivant" won only because it stands on its own the best of the three.

"Graduation Day." See the Afterword for information on the publishing history of *The Blind Pig* shared-world series. The postulate established by Mark R. Van Sciver in his "Tails from the Blind Pig" (published in 1996) is that, early in the 21st century, a space probe returning from Mars carries an extraterrestrial virus popularly called Martian Flu. Like HIV, some victims can carry the virus for decades without showing any effects, while others may show symptoms to varying degrees (it can be fatal) at any time. The most dramatically affected mutate into the forms of animals. ("But as the worst of the flu passed, people began to change. Not many, but enough. Like out of some cheap movie, some people began to take on characteristics of varying animals, birds, insects, reptiles, you name it. Some became the total animal, some just took on part of it. Some people could control their changes, some couldn't."—Van Sciver) The scientific term for this aspect of the Flu is Stein's Chronic Accelerated Biomorphic Syndrome (SCABS), and its victims are soon popularly called SCABs. The stories, set twenty to thirty years after the Flu's spread, illustrate the social effects on the victims who survive but look like escapees from Dr. Moreau's island, and on the society which has to adjust to this new minority group of SCABs in its midst.

"Top of the Mountain." The setting is a parallel world in which the European settlers of North America have found the natives to be werewolves—not the popular stereotype who can shift back and forth between human and wolf form, but intelligent bipedal wolves who have a society that reflects lupine instincts.

❦ ❦ ❦

For me, *Best in Show* has been a half-dozen years in the making, looking back to when I first started boring people at conventions with my complaints that somebody ought to do something to preserve the best of the short fiction in the tiny-circulation Furry small-press magazines. This included making a list of my own favorite stories to recommend, "if you can still find them." It has been about a year and a half since Sofawolf Press gave me the opportunity to become the editor of the first "best Furry fiction" anthology. The treasure hunt to make sure that no stories were overlooked filled a pleasant year of rediscovering fondly-remembered plots whose titles or authors I had forgotten, and finding gems that I had not encountered before. The process of requesting permission to publish the stories in this book gave me the opportunity to meet their authors through personal correspondence, and this has also been very enjoyable. Several of us are looking forward to meeting each other in person at the next Furry convention which we both attend.

Throughout all this has been the intellectual thrill of rescuing worthwhile stories from obscurity and making them available to a new and larger readership. This includes sharing the pleasure of those authors who had thought that their stories were long-forgotten, and were thrilled that someone felt that they were worth reprinting. *Best in Show* contains the best of the best, but there are over seventy other stories that we selected from all the Furry magazines through mid-2002 as good enough to merit publication in a "best" anthology—and new issues of Furry literary magazines are being published almost every month. If you enjoy these twenty-six stories, there are lots more where they came from.

�

Section One

Living Among Us:
Furries and Humans

Foreword by Tim Susman

We chose to divide the stories in this book into three categories because each category represents a different type of story (in general). Stories that include both Furries and humans tend to focus on the similarities and differences between the two, and on how they get along. All-Furry worlds are devoted more to the exploration of how society would be different if populated entirely by anthropomorphic animals. Transformation stories concern the perils and pleasures of moving from one group to the other.

Of the three categories, this first one (Furries and humans) is the newest on the surface, but probably the oldest at its core. When you strip away the specifics, these stories are merely another way of writing about the "other": what happens when a group of people meets a different group of people. As cultures in the ancient world expanded and met other tribes, other countries, and other races, they had to deal with this problem, and wrote about it in their stories. Look at epics such as the *Odyssey*, or Sindbad's voyages, and you will see the hero meet strange and wondrous people. However, these people are rarely, if ever, animal in nature.

Myths and legends featuring anthropomorphic animals tended to place them in their own world, whether that world was separate from ours (the stories of Reynard) or joined to it in some mystical way (as the Egyptian pantheon). Even in Aesop's fables, where men occasionally intrude on the world of the animals, the animals generally live in their own world. Not until the Renaissance, well after the first stories of Furry worlds and transformations, do we begin to find stories in which animal and human societies exist side by side.

Perhaps one of the earliest stories featuring Furries and humans is Swift's *Gulliver's Travels*, in which Gulliver visits the land of the

Houyhnhnms, anthropomorphic horses who seem more civilized than the man-like apes (the "Yahoos") with which they co-exist. The land of the Houyhnhnms was realized in some detail, even though only as a foil to human society, and the Houyhnhnms were clearly the more civilized and more sympathetic of the two races (in fact, Gulliver is forced to leave their country because they fear he may corrupt them).

Similar themes abound in the modern incarnations of these stories. Often, they take place in a future in which humans have created Furries to serve them in some capacity, and the stories detail the manner in which we treat a creation that is nearly human. They examine our empathy, our sense of responsibility, and the complexities of our relationships. What's more, in addressing the question of where Furries belong in human society, they touch on the question of what it means to be human.

Scientists who study the natural world love to place divisions over nature's gradations, and one of the most important divisions to many people is the line that stands between human and animal. Problem is, the more we learn, the harder that division is to define. Language, tool use, tool creation, memory, anticipation of the future—all of these supposed hallmarks of humanity have been discovered in the animal world, some multiple times. Each time, we retreat a little further into our protective definition of humanity: animals have language, but not syntax; they can create tools, but not complex tools; they cannot understand abstract concepts (and if this is a definition of humanity, then I know some people who would fail to qualify).

Furries blur that line still further. How would we react when faced with a population of human-like animals with human minds? How would we feel if we were responsible for their existence? Would we treat them like children or slaves? Would we welcome them or deny their humanity?

And how would they feel? Would they regard us as gods or as oppressors? Would they develop their own independent societies or strive to be accepted into ours? What would their lives be like?

Ten authors have imagined ten different answers. Read on.

TO THE MAGIC BORN

Brian W. Antoine

Given the life I lead, I've learned to appreciate the simple things that help me forget the chaos. Someplace near the top of my list of things to simply sit back and enjoy is swinging slowly in a hammock during a beautiful summer day. The fact that the sky peeking back at me through the gaps in the trees above was green instead of blue altered what I felt, but didn't diminish it. What did serve to tickle my sense of humor was the fact that I was feeling both warm and comfortable at a time when the rest of my rather odd family was holed up in our house where it was cooler.

All, that is, except for my son, who was resting in the grass beneath my hammock and talking quietly to himself as he did his homework. He alone had decided to join me outside when the temperature climbed into the low 80's.

The rest of the family was finding ways to stay busy in the underground levels of our home where it was nice and cool. I also expected that they were plotting revenge against me for my offer to shave their fur off so they could join me outside. They hadn't found my little joke the slightest bit funny, which was another reason I was outside at the moment.

Velans have a very active sense of humor. It's their outlet for the aggression that they are genetically incapable of unleashing against their own kind. Being Human though, I'd found myself the target of practical jokes that they would never have played on one of their own, for the simple reason that those safeguards didn't apply to me. The fact that I was more fragile then they were just made it important that I try to stay one step ahead of them, since they didn't always scale back the physical jokes to account for the difference. Out of necessity, I'd given free rein to my own sense of humor just to try and fit in.

So I lay there in my hammock, enjoying the light breeze that was blowing through the undergrowth and taking occasional sips from my lemonade, as I thought about how to outwit my mate at her own game. It wasn't something I could take lightly, either. In all the time I'd spent here in the years since I'd first met her, I'd learned that it wasn't *if* they would design a practical joke to get even with you, it was *when*. What I hadn't figured out yet was how they kept score.

I don't remember falling asleep, but my son, Lan Louis, must have decided that I wasn't paying attention when I didn't answer him. Being rather direct, he simply poked me gently in the back through the hammock with one of his claws to wake me up. "Da?"

"Huh?" My eyes snapped open and I lay there confused for a second as I tried to figure out what had gotten my attention.

"Da, you were snoring again," came the comment from below me, along with a hint of a giggle in his voice.

Rolling over in the hammock, I looked beneath me and saw my son looking up at me from the datapad he had been working on. The expression on his face was half annoyance and half amusement, and I chuckled myself. My life was a lot of things, but simple wasn't one of them.

The three-foot tall fox based anthropomorph that still called me "Da" just drove the point home. It was obvious that I couldn't be his real father, or "Da" as he'd mangled the English word he'd learned as a small wiggling bundle in my arms. It had also become obvious as he'd grown that he didn't care. I was the male that his mother had taken as mate and one of the people who was raising him. That to him was all that mattered, with the possible exception that I was better at math then Kalindra—which might have been why he was outside with me instead of in the house.

"I've told you before, I don't snore," I said and I stuck my tongue out at him. The expression on his face as he tried to copy me just got me laughing again. "Besides, if I had been snoring, your mother would have been out here beating the stuffing out of me," which was more true than I cared to remember. I'd adjusted, more or less, to sleeping with the entire family in the same room, on what looked like a large fluffy cushion. They, however, hadn't adjusted to me quite so easily. I had been informed in language that could not be misinterpreted that I was either going to stop snoring, or I was going to swallow my pillow in the middle of the night.

He thought about that for a moment, which included a quick glance towards the house, then he smiled. "Okay, you were not snoring. You should make sure though that the bug you just swallowed wasn't poisonous because it was making a terrible noise as it died."

"Thank you, I'll keep that in mind," and I started to roll back over to resume my 'thinking'. I only made it about half way though before I got stopped again.

"Da?" I stopped in mid-turn and looked down at my son with one eye as he stole another glance towards the house. "Can I ask you a question?"

I rolled back onto my stomach and said, "Sure, you know you can always ask me anything." Something was up, that much was certain from the expression on his face. With a flick of his claw, he shut down the datapad he'd been working on and pushed it aside as he glanced towards the house yet again.

"Can you teach me to be a Mage?"

That was the *last* question I'd expected to get asked and I learned right then and there that standing up in a hammock just doesn't work. Without even blinking, Lan grabbed his datapad and rolled out of my way as I spun sideways and landed face first in the grass. He at least had the good manners not to laugh as I raised myself up on my elbows and spit a chunk of grass out before I turned to look at him.

"Excuse me, was that one of the questions I'm not supposed to ask you?" he asked me with just a hint of apprehension that caused his ears to twitch.

It took a moment for his question to sink in, and it just added to my confusion. "What are you talking about?" As I lay there watching, my son made a point of checking out the area around us and then looking towards the house.

"Well... I don't think I'm..." and I watched in puzzlement as my son argued with himself. He was nervous, that much was obvious from the way he was reacting to the smallest sound coming out of the forest around us. What he'd said though told me that he was trying to reconcile his natural curiosity with something somebody had told him.

"Lan, I think we need to talk," and I rolled over so I could sit up and face him. "Son, I need to make sure you understand something here. There is no such thing as a question you can't ask me. You are free to ask me anything you want, at any time. The worst that I'll ever do is to explain to you why I won't or can't answer you." Reaching up, I grabbed the hammock and swung it out of the way so I could get comfortable as I folded my legs beneath me. "First though, I have a question of my own. Who told you that you weren't supposed to ask me certain questions?"

I watched as he thought about it for a moment, then smiled to myself as I watched his curiosity and youth win the argument he was having with himself. Even at the age of six, which was halfway through his basic school years, Lan never failed to surprise me with the things he simply understood without having to ask. "Who do you want to know about first?"

"There are more than one?" I said with restraint. Lan nodded, and I told him to "Start at the top of the list" with a sigh as I worked to keep my temper under control.

Even as upset as I felt, I had to chuckle as he started ticking things off on his fingers. It was one of several Human quirks he'd picked up from being around me so much. "Well, Lythandi says I'm not supposed to ask you about why Penny can't go back to Earth with you anymore. Penny says I'm not supposed to ask you about the unicorn story she told me about. My mother has told me that I'm not to ask you about anything having to do with my other father," and as he continued to list topics he watched me to see how I was going to react.

It's tough to react when you're in shock, but I haven't managed to stay alive and keep the title of ArchMage all these years by not continuing to function anyway when in that condition. It had become quickly apparent that this conversation was going to take a lot more time than I'd thought moments ago. Grabbing my pillow from the hammock, I scooted over next to the closest tree and settled in for the duration. "Okay, I meant what I said earlier. Are there any of those questions that you'd like to ask me now?"

"Yes..." and he wouldn't look me in the eyes for a moment.

"Okay then, ask away," I said as I prompted him. Somehow, I knew just which one bothered him the most.

"Do you know who my other father is?"

I was right, and I was also sure he wasn't going to like the answer. "No, only your mother knows that and I've never asked her. I can still remember the look on her face when she learned that my skill as a shape-shifter didn't extend to making us genetically compatible. When I suggested that she find someone honorable to give her the child she wanted, she about threw me through the nearest wall. I've never brought up the subject again." I then watched as he thought about that for a moment.

"Okay, do you think you know who my other father is?"

I looked at the twinkle in his eye and made a mental note to myself to avoid debating with him as he got older. "Yes, I have an idea who he is," and I waited for the expected question.

"Is he an honorable person?"

I almost answered the wrong question, then caught myself before I said the name I'd been thinking of. In the same situation, I'd have asked *who* my father was, but my value systems are slightly different than a normal Velan's. To them, how they were thought of by others was more important then who they were related to by birth. Only when they joined another family as an adult, did they begin to include others in their personal definition of honor. That fact continues to surprise me even after I've lived here all these years.

"Son, if I'm right, he's one of the most honorable people I know."

Lan looked at me for a second, then accepted my answer with a nod. Given the number of male Velans I knew well enough to say that about, he probably had no trouble guessing who I was talking about. As that thought occurred to me, I nodded back and then chuckled as we both silently agreed to drop the subject. Holding my arms out I invited my son into them. With a smile he accepted my offer and hopped into my lap where he could hug me back.

"So, is that all you wanted to know?" I asked him, before I blew in his ear to tease him.

After tickling me a little in revenge for his ear, Lan turned so he could look up at me and said, "Would you tell me about the unicorn?"

Even as ticklish as I am, the memories that question invoked brought my laughter to an abrupt halt. The silence, and my hugging him tighter, told my son that his simple question had touched on something important to me. "I don't really need to know," he said as he hugged me tighter in return.

"No, that's okay, but you could have forgotten that question and I wouldn't have objected," I said as I thought about it. "I don't suppose there is any reason you shouldn't know, and it might help put the whole thing to rest finally. If not that, at least it might help get Penny to drop the matter and quit making more of it then there needs to be." Lan just nestled his head under my chin and listened.

Even with the passage of time, I still remembered how I'd felt that night so long ago. "Years ago, just after Kimi had decided to retire and I became the ArchMage of my world, I managed to work myself into a real good depression. Everything seemed to be falling apart in my life at about the same time, and then the lady I was sure I loved told me that she didn't want anything more to do with me." I paused as the memory of the anger I'd felt that day echoed faintly through the years, then continued. "I'd just recently started keeping a journal of what happened in my life, and one lonely night in my lab I sat down and wrote the story of 'The ArchMage and the Unicorn' as a way to help me work out what I was feeling. What I didn't know at the time was that Penny had become aware enough to be worrying about me and that she was reading everything I wrote."

Even had I known, I probably wouldn't have done anything. At that time, I'd still thought she was nothing more than an AI that I'd created using magic. It was years later before I found out what had really entered my life, or what it was that had decided I needed a friend to watch out for me.

"But why a story about a unicorn?"

I looked down at my son and chuckled. "Have you read enough of the stuff in my private library to know what the unicorn stands for in Terran mythology?"

"I think so," he said and I watched him trying to remember whatever it was he'd read. "They are symbols of purity and are only supposed to allow themselves to be touched by someone who has not yet shared of themselves with another."

I had to laugh slightly as I listened to my son translate things into something that made sense to him. "That's close, but you're missing some- thing, or at least you didn't mention it. Think about what you just told me and then think about what it means to the unicorn. To me, it meant that a unicorn must live a terribly lonely life, and a Mage on my world has a similar problem. We have all that power, but we are both restricted by rules we can't change from ever really getting close to another person. Because I was forbidden to tell anyone what I was, I was well on my way to becoming a hermit before your mother entered my life." Maybe he understood and maybe he didn't, but I tend to believe he did. Whichever it was, he seemed satisfied with my answer and was content to just sit there in my arms with his thoughts for a moment. Then my son, an alien born on a world a thousand light-years from my own, changed the way I'd remember that story forever.

"At least it had a happy ending," he murmured as his muzzle began sniffing around in one of the pockets of the vest I was wearing.

"Huh? What do you mean?" I asked as I batted his hand away from a couple of the pockets that he didn't need to be exploring.

"If that other lady had not decided that you were unacceptable as a mate, you would not have been available for my mother to chase."

It took a moment for that to sink in.

Lan meanwhile, took the opportunity to track down the pocket I kept my candy in while I sat there and wondered why that idea had never occurred to me. Even more, the more I thought about it, the more sense it made and the small emerald fire that flickered in the heart of my mind reminded me of all I had gained the day Kalindra had asked me to spend my life with her. However lonely I'd been before, it had been driven into the shadows when the empathic bond I shared with my mate had formed. When that bond had been tempered in the heart of a star, the loneliness had vanished forever. I don't think, though, that I'll ever understand what it was that I did to deserve being rewarded with the family Kalindra asked me to help her form.

"Son," I said as I smiled and lowered my head so I could look at him. "Thank you for... Hey!" and I grabbed hold of the muzzle that was busy making the contents of my candy pocket vanish. "Those are hard to come by around here!" His muzzle trapped by my hand, Lan just looked up at me and tried to look repentant. Keeping a close eye on him, I slowly released his muzzle so he could withdraw it from my pocket. I couldn't avoid laughing, though, when I spotted the jellybean hanging from one of his teeth, a jellybean that vanished the moment he could open his muzzle and pop it into his mouth. I just shook my head and sighed as he giggled and nestled up against me again trying to get comfortable.

"If you don't have anything else to ask me, I have a question for you now."

"I think I've asked enough questions for one day," he replied as he shifted in my arms slightly.

"Okay, then it's my turn," and I pulled him away from where he'd been resting and sat him down in the grass where we could face each other. "You asked me earlier to teach you to be a Mage. Before I even agree to test you, I want to know why you want to be a Mage." Sitting there in the shade, I watched as he thought about it carefully and was pleasantly surprised to find he didn't have an immediate answer available.

"My answer is part of the test, isn't it," he finally replied.

"Yes it is," I told him. "If you had tried to give me a quick answer just now, I'd have probably figured that you weren't taking my question seriously. Son or not, my response would have been to refuse your request for the moment."

"What if I had figured out that you might ask me that question and had worked out my answer ahead of time?"

I added a second mental check mark next to the promise never to debate with my son. "Then you would probably have had to explain that to me and hope I believed you. That isn't what happened, though, and I still need an answer." Thinking about it for a moment, I added, "and don't try to misdirect me with something that just sounds good either. I may be getting older, but I'm not stupid."

Lan snuck a quick glance towards the house, then grinned. "The male who can survive living with my mother and Lythandi is anything but stupid. After hearing you offer to shave both of them, though, I am forced to question my father's sanity."

"You heard that little comment?" I asked as I reminded myself that I still needed to think of a way to avoid whatever they were certainly planning. "Consider that a lesson in why wisdom and intelligence aren't the same thing then, and I still want to hear your answer." The expression on his face told me that he had indeed been trying to change the subject, but I was willing to forgive him. "Would you like some time to think about it?" He nodded, so I shifted to a more comfortable position and waited.

For about a half-hour I sat there and watched as my son agonized over my question. That he couldn't explain just why he felt the way he did made me believe that his reason was in fact based more on feeling then thought. That was something in his favor as far as I was concerned. How he felt about something, as opposed to how he thought about it, was less likely to change as he got older. Sitting there watching him, though, I started remembering what my answer had been all those years ago when Kimi had showed up at my door.

She'd taken months instead of weeks to track me down once my ability had manifested. The delay had negated the chance I should have had to decline the changes that were occurring and have them, and the memories of them, fade away. Since she couldn't ask me if I wanted to forget what had been going on, she'd asked, "By what right do you expect to become a Mage?" She still gave me a bad time about my answer even now. Somehow, my telling her that, "I'm already a Mage. Now I want to become a good one," had convinced her to take me on as her student instead of figuring out where to hide my corpse.

With an inward laugh about times long past, I pulled myself back to the present and the son that now worked at his own answer to that question. At least twice while we sat there he started to say something and both times it died in his throat before really getting started. Then at last he gave me the only answer he had.

"I don't know," he told me as his ears dropped in despair.

"Fair enough. It isn't an easy question to answer, as I well know," and he looked up at me in surprise. "I'm not going to just drop this, though, because I believe it means a lot to you, even if you're not sure why. Instead of telling me why you want to be a Mage, try and tell me what you think a Mage is."

The smile that lit up his face told me we were on the right track, even if only one of us knew it. "That's easy, or at least I think it is," he said. "A

Mage is someone with a special skill who uses that skill to make things better for everyone around them."

"And why do you think that?"

"Because I've watched my mother and you do exactly that for as long as I can remember," he said with that aura of certainty that comes with youth.

"Your mother and I have also screwed up a lot over the years. Do you think that being a Mage makes you less responsible for the problems those mistakes cause others simply because you didn't intend to cause them?"

"No, I don't. I think that part of being a good Mage, though, is that you will try to correct those mistakes when you can, and my mother and father have always tried to make those corrections with honor."

"So you think Mages are honorable?"

"Good ones are, my parents are, and I'd like to prove that I can be too."

It wasn't a direct answer, but getting it from him when he didn't know he was giving it, made it worth more. "Then I expect you should get your chance, don't you?"

The purely Human smile that lit up his face was worth the trouble I'd put him through when I told him, "If you still want me to test you now, I will."

It vanished just as quick as it had appeared, though, when I told him, "But I have one more tiny little question to ask you. Are you sure you want me to do this instead of your mother?" For whatever reason, he had to stop and think about that before he smiled again and answered me.

"I want you to be my teacher because my mother would tell me I'm too young to be thinking about an apprenticeship. Also, you don't seem to have as many rules that I'd have to start memorizing."

"Did you ever consider that she may have a point? You've still got a couple of years of general studies left before you're supposed to decide what you'll do with your life. As for my not having as many rules, don't you believe it. I had to memorize the same set of rules you're talking about when I asked Kalindra to teach me her style of magic. When everything was all said and done, I found that we believed in a lot of the same things. I just don't make my students memorize my rules."

"You have rules too?"

"Of course! You're just expected to figure them out by thinking about how and what I teach you, instead of having them given to you directly," and I gave my son my best 'terrorize the apprentice' smile. "And I test you to see if you're learning them, also."

Lan's ears twitched just slightly in dismay, then he looked over at his datapad where it lay on the ground. "Do I have to study more math and stuff?"

I had to laugh in spite of myself. "Yes, you still need math, physics and a lot of other stuff you'll grow to hate. But, you need to know it to be a really good Mage. When you're tampering with reality, the more you know about how things are supposed to work, the better you will be at changing how a specific thing works with a spell. Now, do you still want me to test you?" With a sigh that all parents everywhere come to understand, Lan nodded in resignation.

"Then the next thing we need to find out is if you even have the talent to work magic. Move a little closer to me and hold your hands out in front of you like this," and I cupped my hands in front of me like I was trying to hold water in them. When Lan had moved close enough so that I could hold his hands in mine, I told him, "Close your eyes now and try to clear your mind."

Yeah, right. A six year old kid who has just been told that he might get his wish to become an apprentice Mage was just going to clear his mind of everything and relax. My mate was going to give up lemon candy too. He couldn't even keep his eyes closed, I found, as I spotted him sneaking a peek at me when he thought I might not be looking. "Lan, I'm serious, you have to be relaxed for this to work."

"You're not going to play a joke on me?"

"I'm trying to test you to see if you have any talent for magic. Why would I play a joke on you?" I asked feeling a little puzzled.

"The last time I heard you tell Lythandi to close her eyes and hold out her hands, you filled them with honey and ran," said my son as he kept one eye half open to watch me. "It took her two days to get it all out of her fur."

"Lan, I'm not going to play a joke on you. You asked me to test and teach you and I'm trying to do just that. I can't do either though, if you don't trust me or won't relax and let me continue."

Both eyes opened and stared up into mine. "Will it work better the more relaxed I am?"

"Yeah, I suspect so, why?"

His immediate answer was to raise himself off the ground and flip his tail out of the way as he spun around so he could sit in my lap. As he nestled his back up against my chest, he looked up at me and said, "I'll relax more if I feel safe. Every time I close my eyes I keep hearing things in the forest behind me."

I didn't say a word, but the pride I felt at that moment would remain with me forever. "Okay then, put your hands in mine and try to relax," and I curled my arms around him and cupped them where he could reach them. Without the slightest hesitation, he cupped his hands together and laid them atop mine, then closed his eyes and waited. "Son, I want you to clear your mind now. If you can, feel me breathing and try to breathe in sync with me. Just concentrate on my breathing; in, out, in, out, in..." and I slowly felt him fall into sync with me, as the tension in his arms melted away. I didn't want to push it, so we just sat there together while I droned on in a monotone and waited. When he stopped reacting to the noises coming from the forest around us, I got ready to perform the actual test.

"Lan, you don't have to answer me, just listen." He hummmm'd to himself, but didn't say anything. "I'm going to put something in your hands and I want you to hold it very carefully. Think of it as a large soap bubble that might pop if you hold it too tightly, or maybe like you were holding sunlight in your hands and it might pour out if you thought about it too hard."

Calling a small mage-light into existence I floated it a few inches above our collective hands. With a gentle thought I changed its size so that it would just fit in my son's hands, then slowly lowered it until it just began to brush the tips of his fingers. "Son, I'm going to put it in your hands now. Just hold it and remember to relax," and I lowered it into full contact with his hands. As expected, he startled just slightly at the contact, but I held the light together with my own talent and just let him get used to the feel. I also checked to make sure his eyes were still closed. I didn't want him to be watching it and start trying to think about what it was. It would just have gotten his mind racing again, and would have ruined the test.

"It's warmmmm..." he rumbled quietly, and I could feel the vibrations in my chest as his words faded into the forest around us.

"It can feel that way, yes," I said in agreement, "but it can't hurt you. I just want you to get used to the holding it and staying relaxed." If Lan had any talent for magic at all, the last part of the test would show it. At the moment, I was supplying the energy that kept the mage-light existing, and it showed because the small ball of energy was glowing the sapphire color that was my personal signature. When I released control of it to my son, it would either fade from existence, or begin to draw its life from the untrained sources of power he might have available.

"Son, I'm going to slowly drop my hands from underneath yours. I want you to continue to hold what I've put in your hands and to continue to relax. Think of the soap bubble, thin, beautiful, shimmering slightly in the light and fragile. Just hold it..." and I slowly began to lower my hands.

I didn't completely lose contact with my son's hands. Instead I stopped just at the point where I could feel the feather light touch of his fur against my palms. Then I slowly began to release control of the bubble of light that my son was holding. Ever so slowly, I began to decrease the energy I was feeding it that let it maintain its existence. When it started to flicker, the moment of truth was at hand. Now, it would either vanish with a silent <pop>, or find a new source of power. That power would be my son.

"Son, when you feel you're ready, I want you to open your eyes and look at what you're holding." My attention was divided between watching the bubble that floated before me and watching my son. I missed seeing him open his eyes, but I didn't miss the smile on his face as he saw the pale gold bubble resting in his outstretched hands. "It's kind of pretty, isn't it."

"What is it?" he asked in a quiet voice as he stared at it.

"It's a mage-light and it's adjusting to the change."

"But I thought they were supposed to be blue?"

"Only mine. It would appear that my son's signature is gold, instead of blue like his father's." Relaxed as he was, it took him a couple of seconds before he realized what I meant. When he did, I could feel the tension return to the muscles in the small furry body that rested in my arms, and a second later the mage-light vanished.

"It went away! Does that mean that I'm not..."

"Oh, no!" I said as I interrupted him with a hug. "If you didn't have the talent, it would have been gone before you ever opened your eyes. No, the magic runs true in our family. My son will be a Mage just like his parents." That son also went just slightly nuts in my arms as my words registered.

"How do I bring it back? Can I make it bigger or brighter? What are you going to teach me next? Can you teach me how to..."

"Whoa! What a minute here," I yelled between laughs as Lan squirmed in my arms. "Yes, there are other things you can do with a mage-light, but I need to explain some stuff to you first." It took Lan a moment to calm back down, but then he sat quietly in my lap and did his best to be serious. "Okay, before I teach you anything, there is one rule that both your mother and I agree on, and it is important enough that I'm going to tell it to you." Taking my son from my lap, I turned him around and sat him back down in front of me.

"The quickest and most spectacular ways to kill yourself all involve magic. You can always tell where a Mage that didn't know what they were doing has been, because they leave a crater where they were standing when they made their last mistake." I had to be sure Lan understood the dangers involved here because there were few if any second chances. "Magic is a way of playing with probability and energy. Neither of those things likes being played with, and the more you have to affect probability, the more energy it takes. If you don't control it, that energy will affect you instead."

Twisting my hand in the air with a flourish, I called up a small mage-light again. "Creating something like this doesn't take a lot of energy, which is why I use it for testing. It's also why it will be the only thing you work with until you learn to concentrate and control what you're doing."

"But that's such small stuff, why..." and I saw realization cross his face and he fell silent.

"Small things work best for teaching small people," I told him as I sent the tiny globe zipping around his head. "Even playing with something like this will cause small changes to start happening around you. You'll have to learn to control them along with everything else."

"What kind of changes?" asked my son as he tried his best to be serious even as his eyes tried to follow the mage-light zipping around his head.

This was one of the disadvantages to being a Mage, but nothing in life was free, least of all magic. "I told you that magic and probability are related. Mages have to understand this just to perform the simplest spell. Playing with probability has a price, and with magic the price is that the universe likes to get even from time to time. Have you ever wondered why we live just a little farther from our neighbors than usual? Or why we don't get as many visitors as other families do?"

"I always thought it was because my mother was our world's ArchMage and people didn't want to bother her if it wasn't important," he answered after thinking about it for a moment.

"That's probably part of it, but there is something else, too. Odd things can happen around a Mage, and over time people manage to figure this out. In my case, I seem to bring out hidden talents in people who live around me long enough. I haven't figured out just what your mother causes, but I'd guess it had something to do with attracting trouble." Given the adventures I'd had since meeting her, it was more than a guess, but it was also something that nobody except the two of us needed to know about. "What all this means to you at the moment is that your friends are going to be just slightly wary of being around you when they learn what you've chosen as a profession."

"Is there anything I can do to prevent the problems?" and there was no mistaking the worry on my sons face.

"Prevent, no, but you can learn to minimize them by learning your lessons well and never losing control. Wild magic is the quickest way to get into trouble, which is why the first thing I'm going to teach you is how to concentrate and control what you're doing." For the next four hours that's exactly what I did as the two of us huddled in the quiet shade at the forest's edge.

I'd been completely serious about concentration being the most important thing a Mage needed to learn, and learn quickly. It would probably be months before my son would learn enough about his talent to consciously tap into the energy fields around us, so until then I would be helping him get things started.

To start things off, I handed him another mage-light so he could practice his control. The moment he had it, I yelled at him and watched it vanish. By the end of the first hour he was getting about as agitated as I'd ever seen him. Every time I'd hand him another mage-light, I could see his claws flexing from their sheaths as he anticipated my trying to distract him. Having seen himself manage it once though, he took a short break after noticing what I was looking at, and got control of himself. The next time I yelled, he just grinned and handed the intact mage-light back to me. From that point on he started to gain confidence in himself. Though he did get just a bit upset again when I had my pet dragon, Smaug, sneak up behind him and chew on his tail.

"That is cheating," he said with a whimper as he smoothed out his tail and glared at my miniature companion.

"You expect everything to be fair? What are you going to do when you step out our front door some morning and find the universe has come to teach you about fairness?" I leaned back so I could sweep my hands around dramatically and painted him a picture with words. "There I am on your right, frying evil aliens with bolts of pure energy. On your left is your mother, sending hordes of nasties to their doom. In front of us is their leader and he's looking at you like you'd make a nice snack before he takes over the planet. Just as you get ready to teach him not to mess with our family, the door behind you closes on your tail." Leaning over so I could almost touch his muzzle with my nose, I stared my son right in the eyes. "Will the history books record that our family died in dishonor because my son hurt his tail, or will you ignore the pain and throw the evil alien leader into the nearest star?"

I watched as he thought about it for a moment, then smiled as he answered. "Throwing him into a star would be too easy. I'd rather use him to beat the door into kindling," said my son as he pretended to be completely serious.

"That would work too," I managed to say before I broke into laughter. Within seconds, Lan started giggling as well, and we both ended up rolling around in the grass trying to tickle each other, with me getting the worst of it. "Okay, time to end the first lesson for now. I told you earlier that a mage-light could be used for other things, and a couple of them can be kind of fun. Listen close and see if you can follow what I'm doing." Handing Lan another mage-light, I called up another of my own and let it float above my hands in front of me.

"These don't have to look like spheres, that's just the easiest shape for them to hold because it takes the least amount of energy to maintain. If you concentrate on it though, you can force it to change its shape." Looking over to where my draconic friend rested in the shade watching us, I concentrated for a moment on the sphere before me and molded it into a duplicate of my long time companion. When I was finished, there was a pale sapphire copy of him floating in the air between me and my son. "It works best if you try to shape it into something you're real familiar with," I told Lan. "When you get better at it, you can make them move almost as if they were alive."

Closing my eyes for a moment, I started filling in the gaps in the image of Smaug I was manipulating. When I finished a short time later and opened my eyes, the small glowing image of my friend had started to breathe and rustle his wings like he was trying to get comfortable.

"Remember, it is easier if you try it with something you know really well," and Lan nodded as he closed his own eyes and began to concentrate.

It took a fair amount of time before I even noticed a change in the gold ball that floated above his hands. Once or twice I caught him taking a peek of his own as he checked to see if he was having any effect at all. When the globe changed into a warped kind of cylinder, he nodded to himself and things began to change faster. At first I wasn't sure just who he was trying to create an image of, and even when I recognized the image of my mate forming, I had trouble figuring out why it looked so funny. Then it dawned on me that I was seeing her from a different perspective. I was almost a foot taller than she was and I'd never had to look up at her. My son was about two feet shorter than she was, and the image I watched form before me was from his point of view. As it continued to take on detail, a thought occurred to me and I decided it was time to let someone else know what she'd been missing by hiding inside all day.

Hey, you in the house! Do you think you could drag your sorry self outside for a moment? I think there is something out here you should see. As I felt Kalindra open up to the link we shared, I caught just a flash of the view she was seeing before she blocked it away from me. She wasn't quite fast enough though to prevent me from seeing Lythandi standing next to her in the bedroom and the two of them doing something to my pillow.

Are you trying to be funny again? came her reply as I made a note to myself to start a pillow fight tonight and make sure she and Lythandi got hit with mine first. *It's only just now starting to cool off out there.*

Okay, have it your way. I was hoping though, that the Klizan of the family might be interested in seeing her son working his first spell. But if she's too busy... and I let the thought fade into the noise of our link. I didn't have to hear her yelling in surprise, I could feel it. *If you change your mind, though, I'd do it quickly. I'm not sure how long Lan Louis can maintain his concentration,* and I closed down the thread of thought I'd opened. Less then two minutes later I heard the faint noise of the back door to our house opening, and when I looked over I saw my mate standing in the doorway with Lythandi and Naldantis hovering behind her.

While I'd been busy twisting a tail or two, my son had continued down his own path. With almost the entire family watching, he now opened his eyes and looked at his creation. Floating there above his hands, crafted with all the skill he could muster, was a pale gold version of his mother with her tail swishing back and forth slowly. Then Lan caught sight of his mother in the doorway, and with a smile, he lifted his hands slowly to show her his creation. Where nothing else might have worked, that small offering based on love and honor finally got his mother to leave the house, and she left it gladly.

I spent the best part of the next hour sitting there in the shade and explaining to my mate just what had happened, and when she finished with me she started over with our son. When she finally ran out of steam, and had decided that it was too late to do anything about it, she gave in and accepted the fact that I was going to be Lan's teacher. "But I'm going to be watching both of you to make sure you don't teach him any of your bad habits."

"I don't have any bad habits," I told her as I swatted her. "Unless you count putting up with your cooking and not complaining about having to clean the fur traps in the bathroom every morning." She just puffed up and glared at me, while I sat there and laughed with the rest of the family at her reaction. I was just getting ready to remind her how ticklish she was when Lan tugged on the edge of my vest and whispered something into my ear. "Oh yeah, thanks for reminding me."

Getting to my feet, I motioned for Kal and Lyth to stand up also. They both looked at each other for a moment in puzzlement, and I swear they both looked just a tad guilty for a moment also. Talking to them about the surprise I expected to find in my pillow though was not what I had in mind as I stepped in between them.

Putting my arms around both of them, I ran my hands through their fur and got a solid grip on each of them. "Ladies, I'd like to talk to you for a moment if you don't mind," and I spun them around and started marching them towards the house. "Along with everything else that happened today, my son told me an interesting story about some things he'd been told he wasn't supposed to ask me."

I felt both of them tense up about the same time I gave them both a small shove through the doorway. Neither of them was going anywhere, though, because I wizard-locked the door as I heard my son bet Naldantis his evening snack that, "My Da will win this one because..." Hearing that just strengthened my resolve. After all, I couldn't let my son down, now could I?

Al stared at the board, trying to concentrate, trying not to sweat.

"This one's for the grand prize, folks!" the MC announced, in those infuriatingly jovial tones he did so well. He gestured in the general direction of the display. "Are you ready, Al?"

"Ready as I'll ever be," Al replied, trying to sound as if he were having fun, rather than struggling to hold down his lunch.

Watching at home, he thought, you never saw how nervous the contestants were, or how small the studio was, or how that stupid board was knocked together out of plywood and cheap laminate.

"Then you have thirty seconds—go!"

The central two screens lit up.

People. They were faces, two men.

"Presidents," he said, recognizing Ronald Reagan and John Kennedy. Kennedy disappeared, replaced by Marilyn Monroe. "Movie stars." Reagan vanished, replaced by Madonna. "Blondes."

"Try again," the MC called.

"Sex symbols, actresses..."

Monroe disappeared, and a new face he couldn't identify replaced her, a vaguely familiar male face with long hair and wire-rimmed glasses.

"Singers," he guessed.

Madonna was replaced by Kennedy. If he could figure this one out he'd be all the way around the circle and would win, but he couldn't figure out who the guy in the glasses was. A singer? Connected with Kennedy?

"Ten seconds," the MC said.

He'd seen the face, he knew he had. The hairstyle gave him a clue.

"The sixties," he guessed.

"Try again."

He tried to think. What was Kennedy noted for? "Uh... assassination victims?"

A bell rang and the studio audience burst into cheers.

"Congratulations, Al Roebuck!" the MC announced, coming forward to clap him on the back. "You've won the grand prize! Bill, tell Al what he's won!"

John Lennon, Al realized, that's who it was. He turned, a bit dazed.

"From the New Gene Corporation," the announcer said, as the pale blue curtains parted, "She's friendly, intelligent, and beautiful, and she's all yours! She's their top-of-the-line model, carefully cloned and hand-raised from a kit, every gene selected and tailored to make her the perfect household companion and servant. She's the New Gene Corporation's Mark Five Vixen, Salomé!"

Al stared.

"Yes, made from the germ plasm of the common fox, the Mark Five Vixen is fluent in both English and Spanish, and trained to perform a wide variety of common household chores, from mopping floors to massaging backs. With a life expectancy of seventy-five years, she should last you a lifetime. She has a retail value of six hundred and fifty thousand dollars, but, Al Roebuck, she's *all yours*, for playing *Missing Links*!"

"Wow," Al said, still staring.

She was beautiful.

She was standing on a melon-colored rotating pedestal, one knee forward, one hand on her hip and the other hanging by her thigh; her pointed muzzle was raised proudly, her tail swishing gently behind her, the only part of her not held motionless. She wore only a simple red tunic that covered her from shoulder to mid-thigh, accentuating, rather than hiding, the swelling curves of bust and hip, and a black leather collar around her neck. Fine orange fur covered her legs, arms, and upper face; her hands, feet, and muzzle were white, toes and fingertips black. A white ruff and black forelock resembled a human woman's head hair.

Al hadn't expected anything like this. He'd figured they'd give away a car, or some furniture, or something, but not a gene-tailored companion!

"Isn't she something?" the MC asked, his arm around Al's shoulders. "And she's all yours!"

"Wow," Al said again, "She's beautiful."

The MC gave a phony chuckle, then turned to the studio audience and said, "Bill, what about our other players?"

"Richard, all contestants on *Missing Links* receive the home version of our game, and today we also have the pocket edition of the *Encyclopedia Britannica*, compatible with any standard reader..."

Al wasn't listening; he was still staring at the fox-woman on the pedestal.

Then the red lights on the camera went out, and a gofer came to lead Al away. Still dazed, he signed half a dozen assorted releases and tax forms, and twenty minutes later found himself standing at the studio door, lost and confused.

A stagehand walked up, holding a leash; the other end of the leash was clipped to the fox-woman's collar. He held out a clipboard.

"Sign here," he said.

"What is it?" Al asked, accepting the clipboard and a pen.

"Acknowledging receipt of your prize," the stagehand explained. "If you don't want it, sign on Line 3, and we'll pay you a percentage of its cash trade-in value, instead. It'll be mailed out in about ten days."

Al looked over the form. "Where do I sign if I do want her?"

"Line 1," the man replied. He pointed.

Al signed on Line 1. The stagehand took back the clipboard, pulled out two copies of the form (one pink and one yellow), and handed them to Al.

"If you change your mind, you have ten days to call the number here and arrange for pick-up," the stagehand explained, pointing. "They'll deduct a charge for the pick-up—see Paragraph Four? And your check will go out in about two weeks."

Al nodded, not looking.

The stagehand looked at him, glanced at the Mark Five Vixen, then shrugged and handed Al the leash. "She's all yours," he said.

She was shorter than she'd looked up on the pedestal, Al realized— scarcely over five feet tall. That made sense, though—foxes weren't very big animals. He looked down into her huge dark eyes.

"They said you probably wouldn't want to keep me," she said, in a throaty alto.

"They were wrong," he said. He looked down at the leash. "Uh... you sound intelligent. Do you need this thing?"

She cocked her head to one side. "I don't know," she replied. "They always said we had to have them any time we went out in public, but I don't know why, really."

"It's so you won't run away, or get into trouble," Al said.

"Why would I want to run away?" she asked.

Al had no answer for that. "Maybe we'd better leave it, for now, just in case," he said.

Holding the leash loosely, he led her out onto the sidewalk. She flinched slightly at the noise of the traffic, her pointed ears folding back somewhat, her tail wrapping about one leg. "Come on," Al said, leading her toward the corner.

The first two taxis passed them by, but the third pulled up in response to Al's frantic waving, and they got in. The fox-woman looked over the worn upholstery and faded gum wrappers with fascination as Al gave the name of his hotel.

The driver said nothing on the way, but after seeing the size of his tip he growled, and pulled away with horn blaring and tires squealing.

A few people stared as Al led the fox-woman through the lobby to the elevators. Anthropomorphs were still new and rare, toys of the very rich, and this hotel, while respectable, was hardly a haunt of billionaires.

Giving one away on *Missing Links* was probably an attempt to broaden their appeal, to sell them to the merely wealthy—prices were reportedly coming down, after all. A year ago there reportedly hadn't been more than a hundred sold; now the number was said to be over a thousand.

They had the elevator to themselves, and Al asked, "They call you Salomé?"

"That's my model name," she said. "There were twenty of us in my crèche. I was Number Eight."

"You didn't have a name?" Al asked, shocked.

The fox-woman cocked her head in what Al was beginning to realize was her equivalent of a shrug. "They couldn't tell us apart, half the time," she said. "After all, we were all clone-sisters."

"Can I name you, then?"

"You can do anything you like, I guess—I'm yours, aren't I?"

"I guess so," Al agreed, "I'm having trouble believing it, that's all. I never won anything more than a Big Mac before."

"Really?"

"Really. I mean, I was on vacation here, and signing up for a game show was just a whim, you know?"

She blinked at him, batting eyelashes longer and lusher than any mere human had ever possessed.

"I'm going to call you Sally, I guess," Al said. "For Salomé."

"All right. And should I call you Master? That was what they taught us to do."

He hesitated. All his childhood training, to respect others and treat everyone as equals, came back to him—but this person, this thing, was *not* his equal, she was property. Legally, she was a *pet*, not a person.

"That's right," he said.

🌺 ⌒ 🌺

He had argued when the airline had insisted he buy Sally a ticket, claiming that she was cargo, and not a passenger.

They had responded by showing him their pet regulations—pets had to be in approved carriers, and if they didn't fly in the cargo compartment and didn't fit in the overhead luggage compartment, then they needed tickets, just like passengers.

They were willing to accept the collar and leash as a carrier, but if he was going to *argue...*

He bought her a seat.

At least the hotel hadn't tried to charge for her. They hadn't allowed her in the restaurant—no pets except guide dogs, the sign was right there—but they hadn't charged anything extra beyond the higher room service prices.

He was beginning to see that keeping an anthropomorph could be an expensive proposition. She ate just as much as a human, needed a seat on airplanes—that could add up.

Clothing was no problem, though. He had discovered as soon as they reached his hotel room that she was wearing nothing underneath the tunic, because as soon as he closed the door behind them she reached up, unclipped the leash from her collar, and pulled the tunic off over her head.

He had been rather startled by that.

She had been puzzled by his surprise.

"But I've got *fur*," she had said. "Why would I need clothes? I know I'm supposed to wear them out in public, since I look so much like a woman and we don't want to embarrass anyone, but why should I in private?"

He had had no answer; he simply stared. The short white fur on her belly, and the fluffy white on her breastbone that stood out a good three inches, had fascinated him. The fur was longer again between her legs, providing a discreet cover—she really *didn't* need clothes.

Except, perhaps, to cover her nipples, which were exposed and hairless.

She had tidied up the hotel room while he lay on the bed, resting and watching her. Since the maid had been in that morning, there hadn't been much tidying to be done, but she had done her best, hanging up her tunic, straightening the shirts in Al's suitcase, and so on.

She really was shaped almost exactly like a woman, Al had seen. Except for the fur, and the long bushy tail, and her head, she could have been human.

They'd done an amazing job, starting with a fox and producing her!

When she was satisfied with the room's condition she had come and sat beside him.

"What should I do now, Master?" she had asked.

He had reached up and done what he had not had the nerve to do up until then, and had stroked the fur on her arm. It was soft and sleek.

She had taken this as a cue, and had responded by stroking him back, and then unbuttoning his shirt.

He'd made a vague attempt at expressing his doubts and reservations about the propriety of this, since they were different species. He had said something about voiding the warranty, about physical compatibility, but she had swept that aside.

"Oh, they knew it would happen," she had said as she crouched over him, tail waving. "It was one of the things they designed us for, right from the start, and they trained us for it, too. They can't *advertise* it, of course, but I think everybody knows."

Her fingers were amazing, and he was delighted by how little her tail got in the way. The fur added a whole new element.

Even so, she made love like a woman, rather than a fox, which was just as well. Al did not care for any nipping, and was pleased to have her on top and facing him.

Of course, those pointed little teeth and the shape of her mouth did limit things somewhat, and he would want to keep her claws filed down, but all in all, it was quite an experience.

He remembered that on the flight home, and decided that she was definitely worth the extra airfare.

※ ∞ ※

She settled in quickly. His apartment achieved and maintained a degree of cleanliness he hadn't believed possible; she answered the phone when he was out, and took messages flawlessly.

He was rather surprised, as he had been so often by her, when he realized she could read and write.

"It's useful," she said, "So they taught us."

The woman he had been dating, one Mandy Charpentier, dumped him because of Sally—she didn't make a big scene, but she did call him a pervert.

"Hey, I didn't go out and buy her, I *won* her, on TV!" he protested.

"And you *kept* her, didn't you?" Mandy shot back. "Are you trying to tell me you couldn't have traded her in, or sold her somewhere?"

Al was basically a truthful person; he let Mandy go.

He worried about it, briefly—*was* he a pervert? The new term that was being used by the inevitable campaigners against the immoral use of anthropomorphs was "furvert." Was he a furvert?

He eventually decided it really didn't matter whether he was or not. He dated other women, took some of them to bed—and when they weren't there, Sally was.

His friends met Sally, marveled at her. A few were offended; a few were intrigued. For reasons he couldn't explain, he never let anyone else touch her—except once, after a particularly wild date, when he brought the woman home and the three of them wound up in bed together. The human woman had seemed almost obsessed with Sally's fur; Sally, for her part, had been fascinated by the woman's smooth hairlessness.

That particular woman wanted nothing to do with Al after that night.

His food bills more or less doubled, which left him with less disposable income than he was used to, but he got by. He went to fewer shows, bought cheaper clothes.

He taught Sally his favorite recipes; she already knew how to cook, but her repertoire was sadly limited at first.

His electric bills went up; Sally preferred sleeping a few hours each day, and staying up most of the night reading or watching TV. He could have ordered her not to, but that seemed needlessly cruel, and the bills weren't unmanageable.

A small price to pay for having a household companion.

For having, he admitted, a slave.

There were ads on TV for anthropomorphs—more and more of them, it seemed. There were a few dozen varieties of cat-person, there were seal-people and dog-people and pig-people. There were vixen-ladies up to Mark Six now, and fox-men to Mark Four. Bear-men, lion-men, swan-women.

Al marveled at how human the New Gene Corporation could make all those different species. He wondered why other companies didn't seem to be able to, even though NGC didn't claim to have any patents on their processes. Their nearest competition came from Polyform Biologicals, and PB's Poly-Pets were small and stupid, limited to perhaps a hundred words of vocabulary and a few simple tasks.

Sally seemed as bright as he was—maybe, he admitted to himself, brighter. He wondered if the genetic engineers might not have overdone it.

"You know, Master," Sally said one night, as he got ready to crawl into bed after a late date, "I know I shouldn't, but sometimes I feel jealous of those women you go out with."

Al turned and looked at her.

"I know, I know," she said, "I'm just an animal, and you're a human, but I *do*. I won't do anything about it, of course, but I wanted to let you know—just so, you know, if I get angry or say anything nasty, you'll understand why."

He hadn't answered; he didn't know how. Instead, he had canceled his dinner date for next Saturday, and stayed home with Sally.

✻ ∽ ✻

He had had her almost a year when it happened.

He came home from work and let himself in; she was not waiting there to greet him. That wasn't particularly unusual; sometimes she was asleep. He hung up his jacket and turned.

She wasn't asleep. She was sitting in the living room, staring at the TV.

Her eyes were fixed on the screen with an intensity he had never seen before.

"What is it?" he asked, crossing to her.

"Shh!" she hissed, without turning.

Puzzled, surprised that she had dared to shush him, he sat down beside her on the rather battered sofa and looked at the TV. A toothpaste commercial was just ending, to be replaced by a news desk.

"Welcome to the second half of Channel 8's *Eyewitness News*," the anchorman said. "Recapping tonight's top story, FBI agents have arrested most of the management of the New Gene Corporation on a variety of charges, including fraud, slave-trading, and murder. Four NGC executives are reported to have attempted suicide, two of them successfully, while others are still at large. Authorities say that genetic testing has demonstrated that the so-called anthropomorphic pets marketed by NGC are, in fact, human-derived, rather than animal-derived as the company claimed, and that under present law, all such anthropomorphs are human beings, free citizens, entitled to the full protection of the law..."

It was Al's turn to stare in shock at the TV, while Sally slowly turned to stare at him.

When the news switched to something about central Africa, Al looked at Sally.

"I didn't know," he said. "I swear I didn't know!"

"Neither did I," she replied. She hesitated. "So if I'm human—do all humans feel like this? Confused and unsure all the time, and trying to hide it by working at little things, to distract themselves from the big ones?"

"Probably," Al said. "*I* do."

They stared at each other for a long moment.

"I can't keep you," Al said. "I mean, I'd be glad if you stayed, but I can't make you, I can't tell you what to do. They said something about a settlement..."

Sally nodded. "We're all going to collect damages—they're liquidating NGC and parceling it all out. If there's enough, they might pay back some of what the owners paid. You could..."

"There won't be enough. There can't possibly be enough to cover what they must owe all of you!"

Sally blinked.

"Besides, I didn't pay anything, I won you," Al pointed out.

Sally got up from the couch and headed for the door.

"You'll need your tunic," Al called. "And it's chilly; take my tan coat."

"But..." Sally turned. "But I won't be..."

"Don't worry about returning it," Al said, "It's the least I can do."

She put on the tunic, and took the coat.

Al sat alone on the couch until very late that night, not really thinking, but simply missing her.

※ ⌒ ※

At the end of the first week his apartment was a mess, worse than ever—he had become accustomed to leaving things around for her to put away, and it took awhile to break the habit.

By the end of the second week the place was spotless again; he had gotten fed up with his own slovenliness and, as a sort of tribute to her, had thoroughly cleaned the entire apartment.

He was wavering about whether to keep it that way—specifically, whether to carry his used coffee mug back to the kitchen or just let it sit—when the doorbell rang.

If he was going to have to get up anyway, he might as well take the mug, he decided. He picked it up as he rose, and carried it with him to the door.

He almost dropped it.

She was wearing a black suede jacket, a pleated black skirt, and a broad-brimmed black hat with an ostrich plume on one side—the effect was startling.

She cocked her head to one side. "We don't exactly blend in, regardless of how we dress," she said, "So why not have fun?" She held out an arm; his tan coat was draped across it. "I brought your jacket."

"Come in!" he said, gathering his wits, "Come in!"

She did.

She draped his coat on the back of the sofa and looked around, and he thought he saw a trace of disappointment flash across her face.

"I'm glad you came," he said. "I've wanted to know how you've been doing. I've been watching the news reports, of course, but they don't get very specific."

She nodded. "You've kept the place neat, I see," she said.

"I try," he said, suddenly reminded of the coffee mug in his hand. "Listen, can I get you something to drink?" He headed for the kitchen. "There's all the usual stuff."

"A glass of milk would be nice," she said.

He put the mug in the sink and got her milk.

When he returned to the living room she had doffed her hat, which now adorned an end table, and unbuttoned her jacket, revealing the familiar red tunic beneath. She took the milk with the odd half-grin that was the closest her fox-like mouth could come to a smile.

"So what's been happening?" he asked, settling on the couch beside her.

"It's been pretty awful," she said. "They've been talking about plastic surgery and hormone treatments and things, to make us all look more normal, and they don't seem to listen when most of us say we don't *want* to look normal, we *like* the way we look. They say it's just the conditioning we got from NGC, but even if that's true, so what? It doesn't make it any less real."

"Hormone treatments?"

"For the fur," she explained. "To make it fall out."

"Oh, that would... what a waste!"

She nodded. "And they want to cut off our tails. But I'm keeping mine—they can't *make* us."

"Of course not!"

"They talk about us as if it's our fault, sometimes—I heard someone say that at least the problem's not permanent, since we're all sterile we'll all die off in a generation. I don't see why we have to be a *problem* like that."

"You don't," Al began, but she interrupted him.

"And there are the stories the others tell about their old owners—torture, and beatings, and abuse—I knew I liked you, and everything, but I didn't realize how lucky I was that you'd won me, instead of my being sold to some rich, sadistic furvert."

"People can be thoughtless," he said feebly.

She shook her head. "They weren't thoughtless," she said. "They did it on purpose."

He didn't argue.

She looked around the room again and asked, "So, have you been seeing someone?"

"No," he said.

"Oh. I thought you might have been lonely, with me... I mean, living alone again."

"I am," he said. "But it's okay."

"I've been living in a hotel," she said, "With three other anthropomorphs. They put us all up there until we could find places of our own. And we're all entitled to welfare, as well as a share of the NGC settlement—that could be about sixty thousand dollars apiece, they think."

He nodded. "So what are you planning to do?"

"I don't know," she said. She looked around the room again, a little desperately. "I was sort of hoping I could... could maybe work cleaning people's homes."

"You're good at it," he said, "But it's not a very good job."

"I know," she admitted. "I always hated it."

"You *did*?" That was the first thing she had said that had really surprised him. He sat up straight and stared at her.

"Of *course* I did!"

"Then why did you *do* it?"

She stared at him as if he was obviously insane. "Because I *had* to, of course! It's what a household companion is *for*!"

"Well, if you'd ever *told* me you didn't like it, maybe I would have done some of the cleaning myself, but I thought you *liked* it! I thought it had been programmed into you, or it was something foxes did, or something."

"No! I was trained for it, but I never *liked* it!"

"Well, did I *ask* you to keep the place so spotless?"

"No, but I thought you liked it!"

"I *did* like it, but if you didn't like *doing* it, it wasn't important."

"Why didn't you *tell* me that?"

"You never asked!"

She stared at him.

He stared back, and in a much calmer, quieter voice he added, "There were a lot of things I never told you."

"Like what?"

"That I love you."

🌸 ⚭ 🌸

An hour later they lay together on the floor, naked; he stroked her furry back, and she brushed her tail along his thigh.

"Only an idiot would want to make your fur fall out," he said. "Or cut off your tail."

She nipped gently at his nose. "I love you, Mas... I mean, Al."

"You can call me anything you like, in private," he said.

"And I can stay?"

"As long as you like."

"That might be a long, long time—I'm really not sure."

"Whatever."

"I'm glad to be back. Except..."

"Except what?" He stopped stroking.

"Well, there's one thing that'll have to change, or I just *can't* stay."

"What?"

"Oh, don't look so worried!"

"I *am* worried! What is it?"

"From now on," she said, laughing, "*You* wash the pans that don't go in the dishwasher! I hate what the detergent does to my fur!"

※

Denied.

The red letters blinked at me from the compupad screen. I rubbed my eyes, hoping to make the word vanish. But it stubbornly refused. My application for colonial relocation had been rejected. Tears welled up in my eyes. I wiped at them angrily. The last thing I needed was my face fur soaked and stinking for the next ten hours.

"Hey, Fourteen!" the shift foreman, Massenberg, yelled. "Shake your tail."

Without looking up at the human I nodded, then stowed the compupad in my locker and resumed donning my excursion suit. Ten minutes later I was queued up with my fellow foragers, collecting our tool packages from the old tom who ran supplies.

"Got a blizzard comin' our way," he told me. "Same storm that knocked that shuttle out of the sky near Echo Summit. It's damn cold, hund'rd 'n' ten below."

"They should give us the weather reports in Kelvin," Massenberg suggested, as he ambled over. "It'd sound warmer that way, eh?" He bared his teeth at me in what was supposed to be a friendly smile, but it always came across as a sneer.

"Yes, sir," I murmured.

The human was squinting at me strangely. I glanced down at my excursion suit, looking for a fastener out of place or a damaged piece of equipment. Massenberg whistled and said, "You've nearly outgrown that suit, Fourteen. When was the last time you had a physical? You ain't started puberty yet, have you?"

My ears drooped. Massenberg was one of those humans who thought that adult toms were mentally unstable. He was always transferring them out of his workgroup. Unless they were old and feeble, like the supply clerk. "I had an examination three days ago, sir," I replied.

Massenberg grinned even wider. "That's right, you did, didn't you? How did that go, Fourteen? You leaving us for the stars soon?" His mocking tone made my shoulders tense and the fur on my back stand up. Of course he knew about my medical examination—and the other one. "You didn't really think you would pass, did you?" he continued. "You think they would take the spawn of a black card like your mother?"

I barely kept the growl from my voice as I stammered, "My mother had a silver breeding certificate. She wasn't a black card."

He snorted derisively. "Giving her breeding privileges was a serious mistake. You can bet the psych who certified her was reprimanded after the accident." The human slapped me on the shoulder. "Just don't make the same mistake she did, kitty. You belong here, harvesting hydrocarbons. Don't go thinking you're ever going to be more than a forager." He swatted me on the rump and said, "Quit jabber-jawing and get to work. We got a quota to make."

I hated it when Massenberg touched me like that. Things were whispered about Massenberg in the barracks. Of course, lots of humans took liberties with morphs. We were only property, after all. As long as no damage was done to interfere with our work, the company didn't care. He'd never done more than the odd slap in public, and I hoped that'd be all he ever did.

I shook off the bad feelings and joined the other foragers in the queue to go outside. The first half of my shift passed without incident. We were working the western bank of the Cooper River. The Cooper is a winding mass of ethane flowing over the frozen surface of Titan from the polar mountains to the equator. Our crew was spread over several square kilometers, each with our own harvester.

I'd found a fairly rich pocket of slush near a bend in the river. I had hardly sulked about my rejected application all morning. Well, maybe a little bit. But mostly I kept my mind on the job. By the mid-shift meal break I had filtered eleven tons of hydrocarbons out of the slush.

I put the harvester into idle, stepped out of the cab, and walked across the hood. I like going outside on my meal break. The driving compartment of a harvester is barely big enough to stand up and turn around in. But the hood of the vehicle is huge. I could lay across its width, stretch my arms as far above my head as I could, and barely touch one edge with my fingertips and the other with my toes.

I also loved to listen to the wind. They say on Earth that the winds howl, but on Titan it's more like drumming. The atmosphere's a frigid mix of methane and other poisons, one-and-a-half times as thick as Earth's air. I like the deep booming of our wind.

I sucked the nutrient mix out of the food tube in my suit while I tried to tune in the news station on my suit radio. "...Four minutes past the hour," the announcer's voice said, barely louder than the static hiss. "You're listening to Carnation News One."

I gazed up through the red-grey sky to where Saturn hung overhead.

"Five members of the Senate Labor and Education committee on a fact-finding mission arrived in Saturn orbit today aboard the F.S.S. *Lermentov*. Committee Chair Senghor says the committee will be observing work conditions in the gas-mining operations."

I peered more closely at the yellow ball of Saturn. I wondered if any of the tiny specks moving across it might be this military vessel. Sometimes the big scoops ships were visible as they skimmed along the top of Saturn's atmosphere.

The sky was slowly filling with clouds as the blizzard drew closer. I listened to the news until my break was over, then crawled back into the cab. I checked in with the other foragers, to see where everyone was, and decided to follow the bank up-river. As the harvester moved I extended the sensor arms at regular intervals to sample the snow and ice.

Some rookies think you can let the harvester drive itself. But that can be a fatal mistake. The intake scoop on the front of the harvester is filled with whirring, interlocking blades that chew up the ices and the occasional rock with ease. If you don't stay alert, you can chew up some valuable equipment or an inattentive coworker as easily as harvesting slush.

I'd gone about six kilometers when a shallow ravine blocked my path. The computer had no record of the ravine. It was a long, straight gouge in the icy surface, running from the west into the river. The dirty orange snow barely covered the gouge. I stopped my harvester and extended the sample arms and scooped some ice and slush from the ravine. The usual methane and ammonia ice was laced with metal-nitrates. Titan has almost no heavy elements at all, let alone any metals to speak of. The sensors were reporting a lot of iron, nickel, and titanium salts in the slush.

I stared at my screens for several seconds, thinking. I scooped up another sample, retracted the sensors all the way, and had the computer run an ultra-sensitive analysis. More metals joined the list on the screen, in lower concentration. Chromium, aluminum, lead, and copper.

I thought maybe someone had dropped some tools or something out here a while ago. Titan's environment is lousy with corrosives and solvents. If someone had an accident, left some damaged part of some equipment behind, it might account for the metals. Except our crew swept this area every few weeks. Someone would have reported it. And the gouge itself was probably made by something big skidding across the ground.

I radioed back to base. "We read you, Forager Fourteen. What's your situation?"

"I may have found a crash landing," I replied. "I heard something about a shuttle being lost in the storm."

After a pause, the dispatcher said, "We do have a report of a lost personnel shuttle with two aboard, but they think it went down about a hundred klicks north of your position. Can you see the vehicle?"

"Negative. It looks like something skidded along the bank and into the river. Something made out of alloy steel," I explained. "I'm going to transmit my assays of the ice and slush."

"All right, forager."

I keyed up the report and uploaded it. A couple of minutes later they said, "Activate your external video. Give us a look at what you've got."

Five minutes went by without further instructions. The distant booms of thunder were getting louder as the blizzard got closer. I had moved the harvester as close to the river as I could and extended an arm with a camera out over the ethane. There was a blue-grey shape down there that might have been a shuttle. "Base, I think I can see it. Permission to go down and take a look."

"Hold that thought, forager Fourteen," the dispatcher replied. "We're in communication with Thule base. They want to fly in a rescue crew."

"With this blizzard coming in?" I asked. "I can drop a line from the harvester, tether my excursion suit to it, and be down there in a couple of minutes. Thule won't even have the plane launched by then."

"The blizzard is what we're worried about. If the shuttle is leaking oxygen into the river, you—" The dispatcher was drowned out by a sudden rise in the crackle and hiss. I glared up at the thickening clouds overhead. The static subsided somewhat. "—do you copy, forager Fourteen?"

"I'm losing you. The storm's almost on top of me. Please repeat my orders."

"You are <crackle crackle>"

I growled as I strained to understand them. "I still can't read you, base. If you're trying to warn me about the explosion hazard, I'm aware of the danger." I waited for a reply. I heard nothing but static. I tried bouncing the message off of a couple of comm satellites, but I still couldn't hear a reply.

Since I couldn't reach base, I prepared for a rescue attempt. I took a couple of samples from the river and ran an analysis. The sensors didn't detect any oxides or hydrous acids, which would have been in abundance if the shuttle were leaking air. I ran the radio through the standard frequencies, trying to reach base one last time.

I backed the harvester away from the river and drilled its anchors into the ice. I recorded my intentions and set the computer to broadcast the message if it received a signal from base. Then I went out.

Getting to the bottom of the river was easy; walking around down there wasn't. The first thing we have to teach humans who come here from other worlds is that ethane is nothing like water. Things that float on water will sink like a lead brick in ethane. The second thing we have to teach them is that the stinking stuff that evaporates off their suits and tools as soon as they get back inside the habitat is also very flammable.

One thing liquid ethane does have in common with water is that it sucks heat out of you much faster than the atmosphere does. My suit's heaters kicked into overdrive before I was halfway down. The current was strong, but not too fast. Compared to the wind up above, the soft thrumming and gurgling of the river was eerie. My helmet lamp cut a harsh, green path of visibility through the cold murk. I lost my footing several times, but I managed to reach the wreck. It was definitely a small orbital shuttle lying on its side on the river bottom. One stubby wing stuck up as if the shuttle were waving at me. Fortunately it still had enough power for the airlock pumps.

The airlock's balloons filled with air, forcing most of the liquid ethane out of the chamber, and pressing me against the inner door. Which, since the shuttle was lying on its side, was doubling as the floor. When the vacuum pump kicked in, sucking the ethane residue out of the spaces between the balloons and my excursion suit, I braced both hands against the inner door frame. Even with my precautions, I almost fell across the shuttle's width when the inner door slid open. I dangled from the edge of the airlock into the dimly lit empty space.

The pale blue emergency lights gave the interior of the vessel a dreamy look. There was a morph, probably an otter, lying on the far bulkhead. He was bandaged and strapped to a stretcher. Wires and tubes connected him to a portable first aid computer. A human, wearing a vacc suit without a helmet, and with a large bandage on her forehead, was crouched beside the morph, stroking his face with a washcloth and murmuring to him.

I swung down out of the door and aimed myself for a clear spot on the bulkhead. As I fell toward the wall, the human looked up.

"We need a full med-team." The human said without waiting for me to remove my helmet.

I finished pulling my helmet off. "That may take a while," I answered. I pointed upward with my thumb. "There's a nasty storm up there. I lost radio contact just before I came down."

"Get your medic down here, then," she snapped. "He's barely holding on and this medikit is practically worthless."

"I don't have a medic, ma'am," I began.

Her eyes went wide in disbelief. "What idiot sent a rescue team without a medic?"

I held my hands forward, palms up and shrugged. "I'm not a rescue team, ma'am. I'm a forager. I just found the skid mark on the bank."

She sagged in on herself and all the color drained from her face. Her voice dropped to a husky groan. "No, no, no."

I took a step closer. "I radioed my position and they said they were flying a rescue team over." I tried to sound encouraging.

She didn't look up. "You said there's a storm. How bad?"

"I'm not sure. It's drowning out radio signals right now, but the electrical part of our storms are always the worst." I unfastened my gloves. "Are you injured, ma'am?"

"I hardly got scratched," she replied. She checked the medikit's screens, then looked up. "I'm Dr. Hirayama," she said. "And this is Halemano, my pilot." She thrust her hand toward me.

I stared at it a moment, confused. "Um... I, uh, am forager Fourteen, third shift out of Levitz base." She kept her hand up there as if it were perfectly normal for humans to shake hands with morphs. I reached out and touched her palm.

She squeezed my hand and said, "Sorry I snapped at you. I... I'm glad someone finally found us." She looked back down at the unconscious pilot. "I don't know how much longer he can hold out," she added quietly.

I knelt down on the other side of the otter. I checked the medikit myself. "Is he stable enough to move?" I asked. "We might be able to drive back to base in my harvester before the storm clears enough for someone to fly in."

She tapped some of the controls, bringing up several different screens. "I'm not exactly a trauma expert," she said. "But as long as he's secure to the stretcher, and we don't jostle him too much, I think we can move him."

I stood up. "That's going to be some trick," I muttered. I walked toward the back of the vessel. "Shouldn't there be an emergency locker around here somewhere?"

She pointed at a small cabinet on the bulkhead almost directly over my head. "Right up there. If you climb onto the cargo containers you can reach the zero-gee handholds and climb up to the locker. That's where I got the stretcher and blanket."

I clambered up to the locker and opened it. There's a trick you can do with two excursion suits, open the back seam and seal them to each other. I figured we could fit that around the otter and his stretcher to carry him up to the shore. "Where are the excursion suits?" I called.

"There don't seem to be any."

I dug around in the locker, knocking several small items loose. I managed to drop one of them right on my forehead. "But every ship that launches from Titan is supposed to have excursion suits."

"I know," she answered flatly. "Ours seem to be missing."

Something about her tone of voice stopped me in mid-motion. "Missing?"

"Yes," she said. "As if someone removed them, along with the extra oxygen tanks, the inflatable habitat, and the nutrient packs."

I lowered my arms from the locker and turned to look at her.

She stared back quite calmly. "It shouldn't have surprised me, after the control panel sabotage."

"Sabotage?" I repeated. I felt my ears flag. "But I thought you were blown down by the storm." Even as I said it, I realized it didn't make sense. They had crashed hours ago, but the blizzard was just arriving.

"Doesn't look good, does it?" Dr. Hirayama asked. "Positively grim, in fact."

I couldn't think of anything to say, so I shrugged.

I spent five minutes checking all the shuttle's supplies and equipment. The main control board looked as if a small explosion or fire had gone off under it. The main reactor had shut down, but it came on when I flipped the manual ignition switch. That gave us back the main lights and heat. I had no idea if the engines could work, and even less idea how we could control them if they did. The air and water recycler was working, and its cold-fusion power pack would keep it going for years. Eventually it would even start to produce edible protein mush. Not that the otter looked like he would survive that long.

I was staring at the escape pod, trying to decide just how rough a ride it would give the otter when Dr. Hirayama said, "I don't think there's anything in my cargo that will help, either."

I glanced up. "I hadn't gotten that far yet," I said. I gestured at the containers. "What's in there?"

"Not much," she answered. "A lot of data cartridges and a bunch of bio-samples. I'm doing a survey on the health and development of workers out here. Spent the last two months examining gas miners. You foragers were going to be next."

"You're a medical doctor, then?"

"Not really." Her tone was tinged with regret as she watched the unconscious otter breathe. "I'm a geno-ethnologist; that's a cross between a behavioral psychiatrist and geneticist."

"Oh."

She continued, a bitter tone creeping into her words. "I have just enough practical medical knowledge to imagine what's happening to him. If the scanner on the medikit is to be believed, his liver has hemorrhaged, so he's bleeding internally. I can replace the fluids for a while longer," she indicated the containers in the kit, "but we need to go in and repair the torn blood vessels. There's also the subdural hemotoma."

I had walked over while she was talking. I squatted down beside her. "What's that?"

"The lining of his skull is bleeding. From the blow to the head," she said. "He unstrapped himself as we were going down and was trying to do something with the wiring under the controls." She gazed at the otter's face for a moment, then added, "So there's a blood clot in his head, slowly expanding. Putting pressure on the brain."

My mouth had gone dry. I felt helpless.

"Either one could be enough to kill him." Her voice broke and tears brimmed in her eyes. "And both are very treatable. With the right equipment and people."

"My harvester doesn't move very fast," I said, "but it's built to operate in bad weather. If we can get him up there, we could be back at Levitz base in about two hours."

She rubbed at her eyes with the backs of her hands. "We're at the bottom of a river. Our vacc suits aren't built for Titan's environment, and we can't fit him and the stretcher in one, anyway. How are we going to get him up to the surface?"

I pointed toward the escape pod. "We strap the two of you into the pod. I attach my tether to one of the retrieval clamps on the backside of the pod. We disable the propellant system and unlock it. The winch on my harvester has enough torque to haul the whole harvester out of a hole, and it weighs several tons more than the escape pod."

She frowned and chewed on her lower lip. "With that current, we could get banged around pretty badly," she said slowly.

I nodded. "I know. It isn't my first choice, but we have to get him medical treatment."

"I have to think," she murmured. She reached over and stroked the otter's forehead again.

I started to argue, to say that we didn't have time, but there was something in her body language that told me she already knew that. "Um, okay." I took a deep breath as I gathered my thoughts. "I've got spare nutrient packs and some other things up in the harvester. When was the last time you ate?"

"It's been hours," she admitted.

"I'll go up there and try the radio. Maybe I can get through. If not, I'll set the computer to keep calling for help. Medical emergency and all that. Then I'll bring the food and stuff down here and we can take it from there."

She nodded without looking up.

Hauling myself back up the tether to the surface was a lot harder than sinking had been. And the wind was pounding out a full-fledged drum corps when I reached the river bank. I thought I was going to be blown away, but I managed to crawl to the harvester.

The radio spectrum was all screams, whistles, and roars. I programmed the emergency beacon with the information about the two survivors and hoped someone would hear it soon. Then I gathered up everything I thought might be useful and headed back into the river.

Once back inside the shuttle, the first thing I did was give Dr. Hirayama a nutrient pack. While she sucked it down, I unpacked. "I brought my first aid kit," I told her, holding it up. "I think it does less than yours does, but it's got a unit of rehydrating solution and a unit of artificial blood."

Dr. Hirayama nodded and took it from me.

While she attended to the otter, I headed to the escape pod.

"What are you doing?" she asked. Her voice was so weary, she was almost whispering.

"Gotta check the pod's life support system and disable those rockets."

"I'm not sure we should risk moving Halemano," she protested. "When the rescue team gets here—"

"We shouldn't wait," I interrupted. "The rescue team may not be any help."

"You said you radioed them our location."

I pulled myself up into the pod and went to work. I raised my voice so she could hear me. "Yes. They told me Thule base wanted me to wait for the rescue team. They ordered me not to try to come down here to rescue you."

"You're not equipped to mount a rescue," she argued. "It only makes sense."

"No. We have emergencies of our own. We drill in procedures for rescuing each other in all sorts of situations out here. Besides, you're human and I'm just a morph. Your life is worth several of ours. Normally they would be ordering me to risk my life to help a human in distress."

She didn't answer.

I finished, then lowered myself out of the pod.

She was still sitting beside the otter, glaring at the bulkhead. "So they don't want me rescued."

I walked over and sat down heavily on the other side of the otter. "Someone doesn't. Someone with authority."

Her gaze was still angry, focused far away. She lifted a water bulb to her mouth and took a drink. Her hands were trembling. "I should have realized. They would know that someone would notice the missing survival equipment when the shuttle was found. They would have to be in a position to cover it up."

"We can't wait for them to get here. Someone on that rescue team will be under orders to make sure you don't make it back alive."

She blinked several times, as if trying to adjust her eyes to a change in light. "You're right. We need to get out of here."

We began gathering things up.

Dr. Hirayama seemed to be spooked by the revelation. She kept dropping things and I had to keep reminding her what to do next. It took longer than I'd hoped to get the stretcher secured in the escape pod. It was a tight fit. Under normal conditions the pod could only hold three or four people tightly packed. Secured to the stretcher, the otter took up the space of at least two. But I finally got them both strapped and sealed into the pod.

When I got back to the surface the wind was shaking the harvester so violently my bones rattled. My visibility was less then two meters. I winched the pod up as fast as I dared. The cable bucked and jerked a bit, but I made steady progress. I knew the cable was more than strong enough to deal with the weight, but I didn't know exactly how much tension the current added.

The trickiest part was using the harvester's sampler arms to maneuver the pod into alignment with my airlock. Fortunately, everything about the harvester is big and rugged. The pod was the size of a small room, but in the arms of the harvester, it looked like a tin can.

Once the locks were sealed together, I hurried to open the hatches and see how they'd survived the ride. The medikit's readings were mostly in the green, just as they had been when we loaded the otter in. I heaved a sigh of relief. "Made it through okay then," I said.

Dr. Hirayama didn't say anything. Her head flopped to one side as if she had fallen asleep. I panicked a bit, and had trouble getting the helmet of her vac suit open. She was breathing, but she didn't respond to her name. I grabbed the scanner and ran it over her. As I saw the readout I cursed out loud.

I had taken her word for it when she said she was all right. Comparatively speaking, her injury was milder than the otter's. The bleeding inside her skull was much less extensive. I followed the computer's recommendations. With some more fluids, a mild anesthetic, and an enriched oxygen supply, she regained consciousness.

"What? Where?" she asked weakly.

I spoke slowly and clearly. "You're in my harvester. Halemano is still stable. We'll be on our way in a few minutes." When she nodded in acknowledgment I added, "Your condition is getting worse. So I'm going to leave you strapped in, all right? I'm connecting my medikit to your suit's monitors. It'll have to keep an eye on you while I drive."

She nodded and murmured, "...right... my comp... give me..." She pointed uncertainly toward the small storage locker where I had earlier secured her compupad.

"All right," I said. "As soon as I have you hooked up."

She relaxed and even smiled. She had a nice smile. Not at all like Massenberg's. While I ran comm lines from the two medikits to my console, I also rigged up a headset so she could talk to me without having to shout over the storm and the engine. Once we were under way, I could hear her fingers tapping on the touch-sensitive surface of her compupad. I had been driving for nearly a half hour when she got talkative.

He voice was soft and slurred. "What's your name?"

"I'm Forager 14, third shift, Levitz station," I answered.

"That's not a name," she said. "That's just your job."

"My personal number is—" I began.

"No!" She exclaimed so forcefully that it triggered a coughing fit. When she caught her breath, she whispered, "I have an ID number, too, but that's not my name. I know the company discourages you from using names. But I also know you give names to each other."

There was an edge in her tone, anger—or maybe it was fear. I decided she wasn't trying to trick me into admitting anything, but that she wanted to feel less alone. "Storm," I told her. "My mother called me Storm."

"How appropriate," she murmured. I heard some more tapping. "Were you born in the middle of one of these blizzards?"

"No," I answered. I glanced down at the computer screen that showed me the medical monitors. Her signs were still stable. "When I was little my mom said my fur was the color of rain and my eyes the color of the sky. I didn't understand. I've seen pictures of the sky on Mars and on Earth, and it is a bright blue like my eyes, but the rain in the pictures and on the vids doesn't have a color. My fur's all grey, which isn't much of a color, but..."

I could hear her shift around in the harness. For a second I thought she was trying to get up. "I guess it's sort of fog-colored," she said. "Maybe that's what she meant."

I shrugged my shoulders. "Maybe. Mom would laugh and tell me you can't tell in the vids, but rain has a color. She promised to show me, someday. But then she had the accident and died."

"Ah," Hirayama said very softly. "I'm sorry."

I didn't say anything.

After a moment she asked, "Had your mother ever seen real rain?"

I smiled. "Yeah. On Mars. She promised to take me there on the trans-orbital. So I would know what it was like to stand under an open sky without an excursion suit."

"Hm," she murmured. A minute later she said, "You know, my great-grandfather helped terraform Mars. He designed one of the algae that broke down the comet gases. And one of my grandmothers was a crew member on a tug that sent the ice fragments into decaying orbits."

"Wow," I said. "That would have been so neat to do."

She chuckled. "Nana said it was a messy, nerve-wracking job." She lay silently for about a minute, then asked, "What about your father? Is he a forager like you?"

"I don't know. Mom didn't talk about him."

"Ah." She didn't say anything more for several minutes. "You never asked me who sabotaged our ship. Who I suspect."

"No, ma'am," I answered. "I... I'm not sure what it's like back where you come from, but on Titan, morphs don't go sniffing around human business. Get in trouble doing that."

She sighed knowingly. "It's probably just as true on Ganymede," she said. "I just haven't paid attention." She was very quiet for several minutes. "I work for the Federation government, in the Bureau of Health. I'm surveying the health of morphs, as I told you. There are certain factions in the Federation that want to extend full citizenship to morphs. There are others who have a vested interest in keeping that from happening."

"I have heard some things," I admitted softly.

"I have no control over that," she continued. "That's a battle for the Senate. But my reports will be read by some Senate committees. They could influence some legislation." I heard her sip some water. After a few seconds she continued, "Some people here are nervous. If they can't control the flow of information, they get frightened. I think... I think I know what they don't want me to report. It contradicts some things the company has been saying."

"Oh," I said. I glanced at the monitor. It indicated her blood pressure was dropping. "Ma'am, how are you feeling?"

"Tired," she said softly. "We're out of re-hydrating fluid, aren't we?"

"Water. We have lots of water," I answered. "You should drink some more."

Her breathing seemed to be slightly more labored. "Only part of the problem. But it can't hurt."

Her signs seemed to stabilize at the new reading. I glared at the dirty snow blowing so densely in front of us, wishing the storm would let up so I could see where I was going. I edged the speed of the harvester up a little more.

"Storm?" she asked weakly.

"Still here, ma'am."

"Could you say your name again? A couple of times?"

"Wha—?" I was afraid she was getting delirious. "Storm. My name is Storm," I said.

I heard her tapping on her compupad. Then my voice played back out of its speaker. "Okay. Say it again."

What was she doing, I wondered. "Storm." I repeated.

"Good. Good." Her voice seemed lighter, as if a burden had been lifted from her chest. "I'm putting my comp in secure mode. It won't do anything until an authorized password's entered. Yours is your name."

I started to protest. "I don't need—"

"No. But I need you to. The data on the cartridge, the samples, all of that is important. But the key results, the summary, my preliminary report... they're here, on my personal comp. Only you or I can get to the files. There are people in the Bureau who can de-crypt them once the comp gives them up... if... everything else is lost, these should be enough to get a special investigation..."

"And you'll deliver them yourself, ma'am," I said as confidently as I could. "You're going to make it. Don't ever think you're not."

"Yes. Of course," she said quietly. "Just a precaution. Promise me, please. You'll get the information to the government. If I can't."

"All right, I promise. But you're going to make it. Both of you are. We're more than halfway there."

"...good."

She was quiet after that. The monitor showed her signs, along with the otter's, declining very slowly.

I was a half hour from base when I finally regained radio contact.

"—you read, forager Fourteen?"

I switched my headset to the radio circuit. "Yes. This is Fourteen. I read you, Levitz base."

"Where are you? What's your situation?"

I gave them my position, heading, and speed. "I have two survivors from the downed shuttle. One human, one otter. They need medical attention right away." I beamed the medical data to them.

"Good job, Fourteen. The rescue team will be glad to hear that."

"I take it they reached the crash site after we left?"

"Negative, Fourteen. The rescue ship jumped over the storm and came here. Hold on."

I felt the fur rising on the back of my neck.

"Forager Fourteen, stop at your current location."

My ears went flat against my skull. "I can't stop. This human needs emergency medical attention."

"We understand, Fourteen. The rescue team is loading up to fly to you. They can be there before you can get here."

"I—" They were right. They could fly to me faster. And if the people who wanted Dr. Hirayama dead were already waiting at Levitz base, anyway, then I couldn't gain anything by insisting on driving in the rest of the way. "Roger, base. Forager Fourteen stopping. I'll deploy my anchors and set up my beacon."

"Good, they should be there in about fifteen minutes."

"Roger." I turned off my mike and unbuckled my seat belts as fast as I could. I didn't have much time.

The jump planes arrived twelve minutes later. The all-human crew was dressed in excursion suits that were sleeker and more military looking than mine. They swarmed over my harvester, moving fast and exchanging information in short, efficient barks. I was surprised to see Massenberg, my foreman, among them.

In a matter of minutes one jump plane was taking off with both my passengers inside. Massenberg and one of the other humans ordered me out of the harvester and took me into the second jump plane. While the crew searched my harvester and the pod, Massenberg and the human took my report. They asked some strange questions for people who were just trying to rescue someone, like what sorts of things the doctor talked about and whether she ever had access to the harvester's radio.

I told them we left most of the doctor's things back at the shuttle. That she had me load some of the data-cartridges into the storage locker of the pod. I told them that the otter was unconscious when I found them, and that the doctor lost consciousness not long after.

They seemed satisfied with my answers.

They removed the whole pod from my harvester and loaded it into the jump plane. I wound up standing just outside the plane for an hour while they finished their search. They spent a good fifteen minutes standing in a huddle just inside the plane's cargo bay, discussing something.

Massenberg walked over to me. He extended his suit's closed-circuit cable and plugged onto mine.

"Fourteen, we can't find the doctor's compupad." He said.

"I don't recall seeing a compupad, sir," I answered. "Maybe it's back in the shuttle."

Massenberg was emphatic. "No. She wouldn't have left it behind."

"Maybe it's in her vacc suit, sir?"

"No, it isn't, we've already..." He stopped as if changing his mind about what to tell me. "It's lost. She's asking for it. She wants you to give it to us."

"I don't recall seeing the compupad, sir. She didn't give it to me. You know, she did suffer a brain injury, and she was a little delirious. It must be back in the shuttle, somewhere."

Massenberg frowned. I could tell he was trying to decide whether or not to believe me. "Listen, Fourteen, it's very important that we find that compupad, and that we find it right away. If you could help us find it, I would be very grateful. The company will be very grateful."

I gave him my best, wide-eyed and stupid look. It was only what he expected from me, after all. "I wish I could help, sir. I never saw a compupad."

His face darkened. He grabbed the front of my suit and pulled us together until our face plates touched. "I mean really, really grateful, Fourteen. Do you have any idea how important this is? Back at base we've got a real-live, honest-to-god senator all the way from the Jovian Federation. They picked up the broadcasts about who was on the shuttle, and now we've got a senator at Levitz base." He glanced over at the other humans, and he looked a little scared. "I noticed that you've already got a new application to the colonial service there on your computer. I can guarantee you would get accepted into the colonial program. Right away."

My mouth went dry. Would they really give me that? Of course, shipping me off to the frontier was a good way to keep me quiet, if they thought I knew anything important. The colonies... I could go to the colonies, if I gave them what they wanted. "I can tell this is important, now, sir," I said. I licked my upper lip. "But at the time my biggest headache was how to get them out of the shuttle safely," I said, with what I hoped was a frightened quaver in my voice. "Her computer stuff wasn't my concern, sir. I'm sorry."

He glared into my eyes for several seconds, then he seemed to relax. "All right." He let got and took a step back. "It must be back in the shuttle. Somewhere." He unplugged the cable and walked back to where the others were waiting.

They apparently decided I didn't know anything. They let me drive myself back to base while they flew out to the shuttle. As soon as they were out of sight, I opened up the file in the harvester's computer named "Colonial Application." I deleted the four pages of application I had prepended to Dr. Hirayama's encrypted data. Then I zipped it into an e-mail, addressed it to the doctor in care of the military ship. For good measure, I typed "Colonial Application" into the subject line. Then I beamed it up to the comm satellites. They say the e-mail system is impossible to jam and difficult to tap. The underlying software is designed to route around problems and disruptions, see, and it's pretty good at its job.

Massenberg had been telling the truth. The federation navy ship I had heard about on the news had intercepted one of my attempts to send a message via satellite. And the senator insisted that his personal physician accompany the jump planes when they flew out to meet me.

I never saw Dr. Hirayama again. By the time I got back to base, got cleaned up and de-briefed, she'd been taken away on the senator's shuttle. I did receive an anonymous message, text only, about a week later. It said, "All arrived safe. Thank you. I hope you get to see the color of rain for yourself, someday."

That was three months ago.

They never found the compupad. But then, who would notice a million fragments of polymer with metal impurities mixed up in eleven tons of hydrocarbon slush?

I have to stop typing, now. My oral exam is today. I've applied for colonial relocation, again. I'm going to make it. Maybe not this time. But I will.

"Lyseen—listen! You weren't supposed to be the one to go on the run to Saris IV—this last minute change has ruined everything," Itran had whispered in a rushed anxious voice in the dark base corridor. His ears had twitched at every little sound. "We need your help—your sister needs your help. Take this..."

"...and kill the pilot," Lyseen thought to herself, looking at the sleeping form in the pilot's chair. The ceramic knife stashed in her tiny sleeping niche kept jumping into her mind, with its clean, sharp edge. The blade was fifteen centimeters of non-metallic, light orange material, with a grip wrapped in non-slip red binding tape. It looked nothing like the knives used in the holovid shows she watched secretly as a cub—she wondered if his blood would look the same as on the shows.

With a shudder, she tried to turn her mind from that image, tried to quell the fluttering in her stomach. If at that moment the pilot woke up, he would see her with fur all a-bristle, tail lashing, and ears back. In that kind of voice of his, he would ask her what was wrong—even be truly concerned—and then what could she answer?

The time display on the pilot console continued its flickering count, and other displays kept track of stellar alignments and hyperspace buoys. Lyseen still had three days before she would have to set a new course for the freighter, with the concealed cargo of weapons riding in back.

She would have to kill the pilot before then.

Four days ago, the task had seemed much more palatable. Lyseen had visited her sister in the make-shift medical area in the lower levels of the supply base, since real medical facilities were reserved for humans only, to see how she was doing. Her sister's brown fur laid smooth once more where once cuts and abrasions had marred it, but still lacked luster, as had her brown eyes.

Lyseen's more golden fur had contrasted with her sister's as she took her sister's hand in hers. "Lysanne, I'm here," she had whispered, and received no reaction from the limp form. "I... I'm going to have to go. I need to—I have to..." Lyseen had had to swallow and fight back her tears. "I'm going to try to stop it, Lysanne. I don't want this to happen any more.

"Please get better. I'm going to leave you a message for when you wake up—I'm not sure I will be back..."

"Or if I'll survive," Lyseen whispered as she turned and padded into the tiny galley on the freighter, failing to suppress a shudder along her spine. The stakes were higher than she had ever thought possible. Itran and his fellow concats—as people referred to the genetically engineered felines—had been conspiring for a long time, that she had known. The fact that they had been coordinating with other constructs on other planets, or that they had cracked the computer systems of the supply base so deeply, had been news to her.

Lyseen had been given only four hours notice that she was going to ship out as a 'companion' on this cargo run instead of Natton. Itran had tried to explain everything to her about what was really going on in less than forty minutes of that time. The 'accidental' switching of cargo modules on the ship at the supply base. The planned rebellion on the mining outpost on Iceward that was waiting for the weapons in the cargo modules. The situation explained had been more than she could comprehend easily, a whirlwind of planning and conspiracy, a portent of blood.

The concat paused by her sleeping niche in the galley and looked at her sleeping mat, but only saw the hidden knife in her head. Beyond the hatch to the cockpit, she could see the pilot. Carland Dranson was his name. The records listed him as a senior pilot from the Core worlds. This far out on the frontier, the Core worlds were half mythical—a source of orders which were given only lip service by the supply base staff and news which had little relevance to the concats as they struggled with conditions of hard labor and abuse.

Carland had been different from the local pilots and crews, different from the crew of the local asteroid mining ship that her sister had been on the last time. He had smelled clean, and his uniform had been impeccable when Lyseen had first seen him. The supply base staff had resented him on sight for some reason that Lyseen could not understand, and on his part he had concealed some contempt, or perhaps distaste, for the base staff in return, yet had never acted less than polite—even to the concats he had met.

Even to Lyseen.

Lyseen was no stranger to these cargo runs. Some pilots were gentler than others, though she had received her share of bruises and beatings before as well. As they were repeatedly reminded, the concats were servants. Lesser. The tallest concat she had ever seen had only stood one point six some meters tall when he straightened, instead of standing crouched over normally on the digitigrade legs the concats possessed. All were light of build, with provably smaller brain cases than humans, and the humans never let them forget it. The concats were made to serve them.

This human, though, even if he felt the same, was polite. His constant use of "Please" and "Thank you" kept her looking around to see who he was talking to before she would realize it was her. He had not laid a hand on her once in the past four days—hardly touched her in fact. Once he had even helped her clean up when she had dropped a tray.

"Are all the humans from the Core like this?" she wondered to herself as she curled up in her sleeping niche. Her tail flicked restlessly.

The hardness of the knife poked her through the thin sleeping mat.

"When he's sleeping, just take the knife, walk up to him, and cut his throat," Itran had said.

It had sounded simple enough. If it had been one of the crew from her sister's last trip, she would not have hesitated.

A little nagging thought asked her, "Would you?"

Lyseen closed her eyes, frowning, and fell into a troubled sleep.

The next morning by ship time, the pilot was still asleep, though he had moved to the bunk in his cabin. He had been spending the trip going over files and reports and writing new files and reports, and spending late hours doing such. Lyseen looked at the displays: two days and eight hours left. With a shudder, she turned away and went back to the galley. After cleaning and changing to a fresh uniform, the concat started breakfast. Carland was normally up early, but she doubted he would sleep any later than regulations permitted—unlike other humans, he seemed to take the regulations seriously.

Carland looked bemused when he woke to find breakfast ready for him. "Just like back home," he commented in a gruff voice that was surprisingly deep for his build. Fleet records said that he was one point seven four meters tall, though Lyseen thought him closer to one point seven seven. The records also said he had sea green eyes, a color which Lyseen had never before seen in an official record description. The brown hair matched the records, though. He looked surprised as he sipped at the coffee. "You made this?"

Lyseen nodded. "Yes sir," she murmured, eyes down. "Is something wrong, sir?"

"It tastes just like I make it—it normally takes people days to get the hang of it," he commented, tasting his drink again. "It's why I usually make it myself."

"I won't do it again, sir."

Carland looked at her oddly. "No, no! This is very good. Thank you."

"You're welcome, sir."

For the next few hours until lunch, Lyseen attended to routine maintenance and housekeeping tasks aboard the ship, such as laundry and cleaning. She acted more carefully about some of the ship maintenance—Carland had reprimanded her for replacing some of the air filters in the life support system. Technically, the regulations forbade any concat to be working on the life-support systems, but most of the humans she had shipped with had been too lazy or unwilling to get down on their hands and knees and clean out the dirt and gunk that gathered.

The human groaned and rubbed his head as she approached with lunch. Printouts lay scattered across the pilot console (which Lyseen noted to herself was technically a regulation breach.) "The numbers don't add up," he muttered. "It doesn't make any sense. Where are they managing to boost production so far without matching costs?" The pilot shook his head, then looked up as Lyseen came up to him. "Ah, lunch. Thank you, Lyseen." He took the tray from her and settled it onto the matching slots on his chair, then checked the time. "At exactly the official proper time, again. You do an excellent job." The time and date was noted into the ship's log as he closed and sealed his working files.

"Thank you sir."

"In fact, for the past two days you've had dinner and lunch ready at the exact proper time, down to the second." Carland looked up from the ship's log and studied her in a way that made her nervous. "That's fairly remarkable."

"Sir?"

"Nothing."

Lyseen worried the rest of that afternoon. What had she done wrong? Standard ship regulations specified the proper times for meals, rest, and duties. The pilot was very serious about following regulations (except those regarding loose paper printouts)—she could not see what she had done improperly. Meals served at regulation times had to be what he wanted—left up to himself, that is when he prepared his own breakfasts and meals. Despite her concern, she prepared dinner on schedule.

Carland looked bemused again at her timing, but made no comment this time. "Thank you, Lyseen." He stretched and set aside another stack of reports. "Perhaps you can help me with this problem—goodness knows I can't solve it."

"You are welcome sir. I am just a concat, sir, I doubt I can solve something you cannot," Lyseen murmured.

"Hmph." Carland snorted as he turned to dinner. "Why don't I believe you?"

A look of sudden panic leaped onto the concat's face. "Sir? Have I said something wrong?" Lyseen shook as she kneeled beside the pilot's chair. "Correct me, please."

"Novas! Stand up, damnit—I was just joking!" He stared at her.

"Yes sir." Lyseen got back to her feet quickly, unable to hide a trembling in her tail.

"Something is wrong here," the pilot muttered, staring at her intently.

Lyseen started trembling. He knows! she thought to herself. What am I going to do?

"Stop that—I'm not going to hurt you..." He paused, looking at her eyes. "You've heard that before, haven't you?"

"Yes sir," she whispered, looking down at the deck.

"Look at me," Carland ordered, and her brown eyes jerked up to meet his sea green ones. "Damn, but you're scared... how many times have you heard that phrase before, I wonder?"

"132, sir," Lyseen answered automatically, almost shaking now.

"What?" The human nearly choked. "You're kidding! No, you're too scared to kid—calm down! I'm not going... oh, damn it. Look, I want you to take thirty deep breaths, and calm down, you understand me?"

"Y—yes sir..." Lyseen shivered still but obeyed. She calmed down some but he could see that she was still frightened.

Carland ran a hand through his hair as if he would like to pull some of it out. "There's something seriously wrong at that supply base."

Lyseen nearly fainted. He *knows!* Her ears paled.

"Who told you that they wouldn't hurt you last?" Carland asked, turning the chair around to face her.

"I—I don't know, sir!"

The pilot narrowed his eyes and bit back irritated words. She could see him thinking, and it frightened her. This wasn't like any other human she had been with. The others had hurt her or abused her, but this one— he was dangerous to her. Lyseen couldn't explain why, but she was more terrified now than she had ever been before.

The human pulled out his ID card and slid it into the ship's console, then pressed the log command. "Log entry, as of this time stamp and date, I, Carlton Windsor, Senior Investigative Agent, Level Ten, Division Three, Fleet Internal Affairs, extend full protection of this agency to construct category seven, female, name Lyseen, assigned to this vessel, pending full investigation of practices on supply base gamma gamma nine five, under the powers granted to me. Computer: burn to permanent ship's log." Carlton turned and looked at her again. "Do you understand what that means?"

Lyseen's mind went blank. Fleet Internal Affairs? That was almost a myth out here. Senior Investigative Agent, Level 10? Her mind raced through unused memories. That made him senior to almost all staff on the supply base. Why was he pretending to be a pilot? He had to know about Itran and the plans! From a distance, she felt herself nod jerkily in response.

"Lyseen—I am ordering you to ignore any commands, orders, or threats that have been made to keep you from telling me what I want to know," Carlton said carefully, watching the concat—who was by far the most frightened thing he had ever seen living without having a stroke. "I want to know the exact identities of the people who told you they would not hurt you, and then did."

"Senior Engineer Almoran Del Targo, Fleet mining ship *Goldrush*, serial number 9801-22-38711-2. Shuttle pilot Julious J. Fontain, supply base gamma gamma nine five, serial number 7315-68-39712-3," she whispered, dredging up the memories and trying not to flinch as she re-lived each one. "Scanner tech Liana Johannson, Fleet prospector *Long View*, serial—"

"Stop." Carlton stared at her again. "Perfect memory?" he muttered to himself. "Category sevens aren't... Lyseen—what's Fleet regulation... oh... 4.55.69 section 38 cover?"

"Regulation 4.55.69 section 38: During parade and ceremonial functions in inclement conditions, regulation 4.55.69 section 31 regarding required dress codes for all Fleet personnel may be waived for the following—"

"Stop," Carlton half-whispered at her, looking disturbed. "How long ago did you learn the full Fleet regulations, Lyseen, not just the minimal set?"

Lyseen's digitigrade legs looked ready to give way underneath her. The conversation was completely beyond her, and the look of terror she had before was returning ten-fold. "Eight years, one hundred thirty three days, sir," she said hoarsely, ears pressed tight to her skull.

Carlton leaned forward in the pilot's chair and peered hard into her eyes. "How old are you, Lyseen? Don't look away from me."

"Forty six years old, sir."

"That's not true. You don't have the marks of age in your eyes or skin or fur. Tell me the age you are not supposed to say."

Lyseen swallowed. "S—seventeen years, sir."

The human's breath hissed out of him. "What was your birth creche?"

"Gene-Star facility 0221, on Tellion II, sir."

"Your real birth creche."

"Sir?"

"Your birth creche? What facility were you raised in?"

The concat looked confused again. "Supply base gamma gamma nine five, sir."

Carlton could feel the hair prickling on his neck. "What? That base doesn't have the cloning facilities to produce... no, it couldn't be!" He paled to ashen. "Were you... born, Lyseen?"

The concat nodded.

Carlton started to shake as much or more so than she had. "Constructs... constructs are not supposed to be fertile... making fertile constructs is a class A offense... under Alliance law." He swallowed. "Do you know Alliance law?"

She shook her head. "N—no sir."

"Small favors." The human tried to sit up straight again and stared at the reports printed out around him. "It... it makes sense now," he whispered. "The bio-mass requisition rates, the mine production increases without matching labor requisitions, but the life support needs haven't been changing..." He looked at her again. "What... what is the average life span of a concat out here?"

"Twenty six point three years, sir, for females, twenty point nine for males."

"And you're named Lyseen to replace the original Lyseen from creche 0221," Carlton said softly. "Oh my *God*. They're working you to death in the mines to increase profits and breeding replacements to cut costs and hide it." Lyseen had not thought he could become much paler. "We'd heard reports of mistreatment, but this... novas! It must go straight nearly to the top... how could we have missed this for so long?" He stared out at the stars. "It can't just be one base... oh God." Carlton looked down at his tray. "I can't eat now. I need to think. The nearest Fleet base is... Hell! Who could I trust? I need to plot a course..." He tossed the reports sitting on the navigation console to the deck and started madly reviewing the nearest destinations. "We've got to get you, and the other concats out of this mess. You're not supposed to be treated like... like this!"

This time he did tear at his hair. "I was supposed to be out here to investigate mistreatment reports—we're still arguing about the whole idea of a servant race, of making a race to be nothing but servants—but this... this is monstrous!" Carlton tried to smile reassuringly. "Don't worry, Lyseen... we'll protect you—all of you," he said, though his voice shook, and then turned to his course calculations.

Lyseen quietly picked up the dinner tray, somehow managing to not drop it, and returned to the galley. She very carefully disposed of the uneaten meal, cleaned and stowed the utensils, then collapsed into a shaking heap in her sleeping niche. Her mind spun madly. Carlton didn't have any idea about Itran's plans, or did he? Class A offense? Fertility? The concat clutched her tail to her chest and shivered.

Carlton wanted to change course. Lyseen couldn't let him do that. Carlton said he wanted to protect her, the concats... her sister. Lyseen believed him—after years of abuse she had learned to tell when a human was lying, on purpose or to themselves. She believed him. What about his superiors though? He seemed shaken and unsure.

The hard lump of the knife poked her still through the sleeping mat, reminding her. Lyseen clenched her eyes tight. The weapons sitting in the cargo modules. If Carlton took the ship to a Fleet base and they found those... Weapons smuggling was a serious offense under Fleet regulations... Fertility was a class A offense under Alliance law... her mind unerringly found the matching Fleet regulations concerning offenses. The only Fleet offense she remembered which mentioned class A offenses under Alliance law was... treason. The penalties were selective mind-wipe or death.

No one had developed a mind-wipe for concats.

Her sister.

A tiny whine or scream tried to come from Lyseen's throat, but she throttled it down to a whimper as she tried to think. Carlton wasn't just a pilot, he was from Fleet Internal Affairs—a pilot that was overdue at Saris

IV was one thing, but what if someone was waiting for him? Saris IV might be alerted... what would Carlton do once he found the weapons? Itran and the other concats were waiting on them... to start a rebellion. Rebellion was treason. Treason was death.

Lyseen found herself standing, looking dully at the orange and red knife held in both hands. She had to kill Carlton, but she couldn't do it. Not now. Maybe she never would have been able to. She had failed.

Eyes closed, she raised the knife to her chest. "Good bye, Lysanne," she whispered and tensed her arms, barely hearing the galley door open.

"I'm going to change cour... Lyseen! *Stop!*"

The concat reflexively froze for a moment at the command, then let out a sob and jerked the knife towards her chest. Hands grabbed at hers, stopping her attempt and trying to wrestle the knife away. "Let me go!" Lyseen moaned as she struggled with the larger human and was nearly jerked off her feet as he yanked at the knife.

Carlton swore as he fought to get the weapon from the concat—she had a death grip on the knife that surprised him with its strength. The despair in her voice was beyond anything he had heard from anyone, human or construct, and chilling with its certainty. "What... is... wrong?!" he demanded between clenched teeth. Category sevens were not supposed to be as strong as he found Lyseen, and that chilled him as well. His fingers tore at hers but her fur defied a strong enough grip to get the knife away. "Forgive me," he grated as he half swung, half threw her against the bulkhead.

"Everything!" Lyseen howled before her back slammed into the galley wall. The impact drove her breath from her, but barely loosened her grip at all—this was not the first time she had been so treated. The human swore at her and tried again, and made her whimper in pain. On the third time her head cracked against the metal, and she felt herself weaken. The concat knew she couldn't let him stop her or let him question her more, and her digitigrade legs kicked out at the wall at the next swing.

"Damnit!" Carlton felt himself falling backwards as Lyseen lurched off the wall at him. With her half on top of him and his hands clenched on hers he couldn't stop himself. The small of his back cracked into the galley counter, and then his head slammed into one of the overhanging cabinets. This isn't how it was supposed to work, he thought dazedly as he topped forward onto the concat. An investigator is not supposed to lose to a cat seven...

Then the searing pain entered his stomach.

Lyseen whimpered as the pilot fell on top and one of her legs twisted in pain as the human's greater weight pinned her, but his grip on her hands loosened suddenly. "Let me go!" she pleaded before she jerked at the knife.

The human gasped and groaned at the jerk, and his eyes rolled back in his head.

Lyseen felt her hands become wet. "Oh no," she whispered.

Carlton did not want to wake up. The pain in his abdomen was most unpleasant, but the alarm bells in his head were growing more insistent until he could ignore them no longer and opened his eyes.

Kneeling beside the computer controlled medical facility was the most pitiful, ragged looking concat he had ever seen. Her gray uniform and her golden fur were splattered with blood, which he vaguely recognized as his. Where it was not matted with blood, her fur was ragged and standing out in all directions and her tail quivered like it was being electrocuted. Though her brown eyes, staring blankly at the wall above the medicomp bunk, were what moved—or perhaps frightened—him the most. There was more fear and despair in those two eyes than entire worlds could hold. "Lyseen," he rasped.

The concat stared dully at him. "Yes sir." Her voice was like that of the ship's computer, pleasant, feminine, and with no trace of personality.

The investigator in Carlton asserted itself even over the sympathy he felt for the sight in front of him. "Where did you get the knife?"

"It was given to me on supply base gamma gamma nine five, sir." Flat.

"But why..." Carlton's voice trailed off as he worked it out. The concat did not bring the knife on board to kill herself—that reason made no sense. The concat brought the knife on board to... kill him. The realization sent ice through his veins. He swallowed with a now dry mouth. "How bad is the wound?"

"The medical computer reports your intestines, liver, and right kidney are damaged, sir. It is doing what it can, but estimates that you will go into a coma or shock from toxins in your blood in a few hours.

"Then you will probably die within a day, sir, as the on board medical supplies run out."

Carlton had to suppress an urge to laugh madly at the though of being killed out on this tiny freighter in the middle of nowhere by this concat, after surviving a decade of field work on the darker places of the Core worlds. "Well, isn't that just lovely!"

"Yes sir."

"Don't 'Yes sir' me!" he shouted hoarsely, then regretted it instantly as the concat withered in front of him. "Lyseen... look, there has to be something we can do."

The concat went back to staring at the wall. "Regulation 4.103.54 section 12: If the lives of the crew are in danger, the captain may authorize jettsoning of cargo, fuel, or non-essentials in order to make full use of emergency speed," she recited emptily. "The ship computer estimates a thirty hour return trip if full emergency speed is used after cargo jettison.

The medical computer estimates you have a 45% chance of surviving. You must authorize this, sir."

Carlton felt a surge of hope, for a moment. "Oh, hell! If I go back to that base like this, and they realize I'm from Internal Affairs—they'll kill me." The thought came to him that the base personnel probably already had realized this, and had given the knife to the concat and ordered her to kill him—a concat murdering an Internal Affairs agent sent out to investigate concat abuse would certainly confuse the investigations. One arm twitched in response to his desire to pull at his hair, but the pain stopped him. "Wait a minute! The cargo has medical supplies in it—we can use those!"

A flicker of fear showed in the concat's eyes. "There are no medical supplies in the cargo that can be used, sir."

"Of course there are! Cargo module three contains six complete advanced medical computers with surgery equipment."

"There are no medical supplies in the cargo that can be used, sir."

"The hell there aren't! Then what's in cargo module three?"

"Five hundred mark IV infantry combat rifles scheduled for destruction on Highland II. One thousand two hundred mark IV energy packs scheduled to be recycled on Highland II. One hundred fifty advanced combat scopes for the mark III infantry combat rifle scheduled to be sold as surplus. Sir."

The human's lips moved but no sounds came out for several moments. "Cargo module eight has...?"

"Four hundred twenty five illegally manufactured civilian pistols scheduled for shipment to Rainstar Station for evidence in smuggling charges. Ten thousand rounds estimated ammunition for the same. Sir. The captured manufacturing equipment is in modules seven and six."

Carlton licked his lips. He wanted to jump up and grab this concat and call her a liar, because if someone was smuggling weapons, all the evidence pointed to... "You. You are. The knife. Why, Lyseen?"

A sob wrenched itself from the concat. "My sister," she moaned and clenched her eyes shut. "My sister... too many beatings. She won't talk now, won't move." Tears trickled down her face, fell to her blood stained fists. "I just want it all to stop. They killed mother in the mines. Riathe was run down for fun on Nerid III.

"They're going to shut down the mines on Iceward—just the humans are going to leave, and they're going to turn off the life-support systems. Itran wants to kill all the humans there. I just want it to stop." Lyseen sobbed freely now, slowly collapsing to the floor.

Carlton felt his heart freeze. The concats were planning a rebellion. The constructs that were genetically created to serve and be obedient, to be helpers were planning... war. They should not have been capable of even thinking about violence, much less carrying it out, but his wound proved otherwise. "Who is Itran, exactly, Lyseen?"

"Itran," Lyseen whimpered. "Serial number CC-5-0812331-12. My cousin. He gave me the knife and..."

"Stop!" The human tried to control his shaking. CC-5 meant category five. "He is your cousin, by blood?"

"Yes sir."

Category fives were cloned and trained for heavy labor, with strength over intelligence. Category sevens were for household help and cleaning, with intelligence over strength. Category fours were little more than bright guard dogs or beasts of burden. Category sixes, never produced, had been the designation for a guardian type. Category eight and nine were just hypothetical designs. Category fives and sevens were cross breeding—not that they were ever meant to breed at all.

"They've put you into the crucible," he whispered. Carlton saw it now. Someone in the past must have realized that breeding concats was cheaper than shipping them from the clone facilities at the birth creches. By letting them reproduce, they could afford to push them harder to the point of death in order to increase production. "They aren't keeping tabs on your identities, because such records might show when concats were killed and replaced." The concats were breeding on the frontier—having children—unsupervised, untracked. "You can't have had the schooling of a birth creche to learn regulations, the category fives wouldn't have had the training on the mining equipment—who teaches you?"

"W—we teach each other, sir," Lyseen whispered back, still crying.

"Like oral histories... you've learned or developed your memory skills because you have to learn." Carlton closed his eyes. Concats with the strength of a category five, the intelligence of a seven, and with a memory only dreamed about for category nines. Concats who had been put in the furnace and had been tempering out on the frontier for decades.

And had finally had enough.

"Do you know what will happen when this gets out?" he asked hoarsely. "The frontier will explode!" His eyes snapped open and stared at the ceiling. "The Alliance government will demand the frontier concats be destroyed, probably pushed by people to hide their own involvement and from sheer fear. The frontier worlds will protest because if they are doing this, they must be heavily dependent on forced concat labor to compete with the Core worlds economically. The investigations into how this has managed to be hidden for so long will shake the Alliance government to its roots. The concats... you... will probably try to fight... If the Alliance bans all concats out of fear, the economic impact alone..." Carlton sounded amazed by his own conclusions. "Hellfire. This could shatter the entire Alliance!"

"Yes sir," Lyseen said dully. "I know. We'll all be killed." She dragged herself to her feet. "The medical computer recommends against your normal meal, sir, but it is lunch time. Would you like to eat, sir?"

"Eat?" The human stared at her, at the surreal question. This concat was the center of a storm that no one had seen coming, and the fact that she was still trying to serve him lunch was mind boggling. "Of course," he murmured to himself. The concats were genetically designed to serve, and many of them would probably have still been quite happy to, but they had been pushed too far. They were probably not blood-thirsty or wanting vengeance... they just wanted not to be abused or thrown away. In their situation the thought of asking for help, and actually getting any, probably never crossed their minds.

Could he fault them for that? For any of this? "Lyseen... come here. Sit down. Please, tell me about these weapons... about everything."

The human's fingers stroked the fur on the back of Lyseen's arm loosely as she sat beside him. "Soft," he mumbled, eyes barely open. "Used to have a cat on Earth, with fur like this."

Carlton had been growing increasingly incoherent and unfocused in the past hour. The medical computer was warning against the exertion he was making talking to her. "Please sleep, sir," she murmured.

In her other hand she clutched his ID card. He had given her the two thousand letter long code to use it without him, commenting wryly that he had wished he had had her memory when he had had to learn it. With that code, she could use his access level, an Internal Affairs level 10 investigator, to override many Fleet and Alliance computers.

Lyseen could use it to activate the ship's self-destruct, and just end it all.

Lyseen could use it to override the cargo locks and jettison the cargo modules, and use emergency engine power. She would just have to add the course back to base gamma gamma nine five, and maybe she could save the human's life.

Lyseen could make the course change to Iceward and deliver the weapons. Carlton would die. Course corrections did not require the override, but the plan Carlton had suggested to her...

The concat curled up into a tight ball beside the medical computer bunk and clutched her tail to herself along with the ID card. Carlton suggested to her that she use his ID card and override authority to seal the mining colony on Iceward. By overriding the life support systems for the human living quarters, he said that she could force a surrender, maybe, without bloodshed and fighting.

"You can... take control of it," Carlton had wheezed, looking pale. "The war that's going to happen. With you bringing in the weapons, with my card, you can make... your people listen to you. Minimize the blood and fighting—try to lead them to a peace. If you start killing civilians, everyone will turn their hands against you. You'll have to be strong, or we... humans won't believe you if you say you'll fight if they don't listen to your needs."

The human stopped moving and his breathing settled into a shallow pace. Lyseen pulled herself to her feet once more, looking down at the white face before turning away. Passing through the galley to the cockpit, she bent down to pick up the orange and red and blood stained knife. Even in her hand it seemed like such a distant thing, as was the ID card in her other hand. The pilot's chair seemed to loom around her as she pulled herself up into the seat.

The ship's clock kept the time indifferently as it counted down.

"What should I do, someone tell me!" she shrieked at the controls and burst into tears again. "I just wanted my sister to be better, to be safe! I didn't want to kill anyone!" The pommel of the knife slammed repeatedly into the armrest of the pilot's chair. "I don't want to kill anyone! I don't want war... I don't want to lead..." Lyseen felt the tears run down her face as she screamed at the night. Carlton had told her that if she followed his suggestion, she'd have to be ready to kill, human or concat, and be able to do it, to maintain control. Power. Authority. To make people listen when she asked for peace. To make such a peace happen.

The edges of the ID card and the handle of the knife dug into her palms as she clenched her hands. With effort, she forced herself to look at both of them. Lyseen thought about her sister, her cousin, about the situation on Iceward, about Carlton, and about herself.

The concat thought about the future. "I want..." She shuddered in the pilot's chair, ignoring the pinch of her tail in a seat meant for humans only.

One final sob escaped Lyseen as she leaned forward to enter the course she had decided on. The computer beeped at her obediently as it accepted the course correction and began adjusting. Under her gaze, the stars drifted across the displays as the ship turned under her control.

Soon she would go back and listen to Carlton breathe his last, as her first victim.

Then she would prepare herself for the fires of war, for herself, for her sister... for everyone.

Lyseen would have to be strong.

How George Miles
Almost Saved the World

A spark erupted from the keypad, accompanied by a wisp of acrid blue smoke. The color liquid crystal display turned solid red (off-red, he thought sourly—they never could get the colors right on the damn things) and a small magnetic card shot out of the slot underneath at a remarkably high velocity.

"Dammit," George Miles said, bending down to retrieve his transaction card. A scorched streak obliterated part of his embossed name; the card now read GEOR LES.

He turned around to find several people staring at the remains of the machine. "If you want to know why some of us miss paper money," he began, then shook his head. An elderly woman grunted and headed toward the rail stop. George put the card back in his wallet; he was already late.

As he followed the woman, an r-Fox vixen approached the machine and hesitantly extended its owner's transaction card.

"It's broken," George said.

The vixen turned around and looked at him cutely and blankly, most of its furry face hidden beneath a preposterously huge purple hat, not quite the same shade as its oversized purple raincoat.

"I can't believe anyone would trust their finances to one of those," George muttered under his breath. He turned away from the confused animal and hurried toward the railway through a light gray drizzle. He imagined he could hear the train pulling up to the stop now, although the only noise of its arrival was an explosive pneumatic hiss of opening doors.

The train glided smoothly between the in-city stops. By the time George reached his destination, the only travelers left were those continuing from Boston to Cambridge or other points on the main loop. His stop served only an industrial park, and many of the companies had on-site housing.

The DNS complex was the only high-rise at the park; their products were not manufactured in great, sprawling factories. Of course, many of the great, sprawling factories that surrounded it counted Digital Neuron Systems Engineering as their primary customer. George decided not to take the moving walkway from the rail stop, instead walking the quarter-mile in the open air.

He stepped inside the building, automatic doors whisking shut behind him. The temperature was at least ten degrees lower in the air conditioning, and he shivered slightly as he stepped up to the receptionist's desk.

"Senator George Miles, here to see Ms. Bryant," he said before the secretary opened his mouth.

The man smiled stiffly and pressed a page button, relaying Miles' presence in mechanical fashion to the Technical Department. "She'll be down in a minute," a muffled voice mumbled from the telecom.

"She'll be down in a minute," the secretary said politely, completing his automatic guests-have-arrived motions. He turned away and faced a small color display much like the one that had chosen to blow up on George's transaction card. Instead of a computer readout, this one showed a soap opera. George grunted and paced in front of the elevators until one opened.

"Senator!" A slightly plump, middle-aged brunette stepped out from between the doors. "Glad you could come."

He smiled thinly. "I had to see what I was being asked to get the country into." He shook the hand she offered and stepped into the waiting elevator. The door slid shut and the glass box sped upward, the metal and smoke vista of industry unfolding beneath it.

"That's not a very common attitude in politics nowadays," she observed. You're the only one on the committee who's made the trip."

George smiled, genuinely this time, but did not reply.

The doors opened to reveal a boring white-tiled room, straight out of a 1970's computer lab. The machine sitting in the middle of it, however, was like nothing he had ever seen.

He approached it and rested a hand on its low, smooth top, then tapped it skeptically. No, it was like something he had seen before: a coffee table. A coffee table with a power cord the width of his arm, but still a coffee table. "There aren't any I/O connections on it," he observed. "No ports at all."

"We're using transmitters developed by r-Labs—this is the first computer application for them. You might call it a biological radio transceiver. In effect, this computer, its terminals and its peripherals all read each other's minds."

The senator studied the smooth beige box a bit longer, finding nothing on its case except the DNS logo and a recessed panel of eight, unlabeled buttons set into one corner. "That's what it is, isn't it?" he said, looking at her. "A mind."

"You could say that about any computer in a sense, Senator," she said.

Sensing a lecture approaching, he waved a hand dismissively. "Other computers aren't biological, are they? I don't know much about the technology you're using, I confess, but I did learn a bit about computers using Von Neumann architecture." Someone approached him from behind; he turned to see another vixen... no, a male one, a tod, dressed in smart gray slacks and a DNS polo shirt. He looked like a midget businessman wearing a fox head. "R-Fox assistants?"

"I wouldn't worry about Spitz's involvement, or any of the other r-Foxes on the project," she sighed. "In a sense, they're responsible for it."

"What?"

She laughed at his expression. "Well, their creators are."

"Ah, I suppose so. Then the way they... communicate with their owners is some variant on the way the machine communicates with its parts? Your biological telepathy?"

"For practical purposes. Although that's a vastly imprecise term, both in recombinant animals and our machines; it's actually much closer to—"

"You could tell me it was black magic and it would make just as much sense, I'm afraid." He laughed, then walked over to one of the supercomputer's terminals. It was just a screen, no keyboard. The screen was solid white, with the message:

```
ANCS 0.99a / DNS Engineering Inc.
Terminal-ID 25
Process-ID 618 launched 08:43a
[25.618] OK: _
```

...printed in a tasteful shade of grey in the upper left corner. "There are only six hundred processes running now?"

"Thousands, but as you observed, it doesn't work like a conventional computer; it's doing much more with its 'circuits' than traditional architectures do."

"What sort of safeguards does it have?"

Bryant looked blank. Spitz wandered over to the terminal and touched the screen; a graphic representation of a control panel appeared. His fingers flew over the shaded "buttons," his fluffy tail wagging slightly.

"I mean," George said, stepping away from the animal, "if this project goes ahead, this computer will be coordinating all the financial transactions of every bank from the Treasury Department to Podunk First National. And it will run the General Accounting Office. Effectively, that means running the entire government."

"No, it means the government will be running on the computer," Bryant said. " By having this system coordinate all the existing financial networks, efficiency will increase twenty-fold. 'Global economy' has been a buzzword for decades, but with China's markets fully open, it's really here—and we need the speed and knowledge assimilation edge this gives us."

George rubbed his eyes patiently; he had heard the speech before. "But this system will be running the other computers. The efficiency comes from letting it do all of the grunt work—what actually counts—on its own volition. Doesn't that bother you?"

Bryant looked blank.

"Can you honestly tell me how this computer will really... think once it gets going?"

Her blank look was replaced by dour amusement. "You're worried the computer will turn against its builders?"

"Is that so laughable?"

"It's not so unconventional it has its own will, Senator. Computers function within bounds imposed by their design limitations and by their programming. Yes, the DNS-II is capable of making unassisted decisions, but it can only act in its own self-interest—which is the interest of its operators."

"Perhaps," he persisted. "But what if the most efficient way for the machine to run things is without any 'interference' from humans?"

She looked away, muttering something George suspected was terribly insulting. "Its purpose is to do the tasks computers should be taking care of without human intervention."

Miles grunted, staring down at the just-under-five-foot Spitz, who stared back up with a silly grin on its face. The face was more human than fox-like, as with most of the expensive constructs. But even if the slight reddish fuzz along his cheeks wasn't enough to mark Spitz, his nose was a black vulpine button set over a protruding mouth/muzzle filled with pointed little teeth. "This is the first male I've seen."

"They only started making them a few years ago after r-Labs came under fire for only producing females."

"Oversexed love slaves for women to redeem the company for making oversexed love slaves for men."

"That's a very... one-sided way of viewing r-Foxes," she said, eyes narrowing slightly. "They're not bipedal pets; we find them invaluable low-end workers."

"Of course. I'm sure they can be trained for all sorts of things. Spitz certainly seems smart enough." He wondered if it was smart enough to realize that it represented a new pinnacle in the field of animal exploitation.

"I'm afraid I have to be getting back, Doctor." He extended his hand; she shook his hand icily.

"You're going to vote against purchasing it, aren't you?"

He sighed. "I do appreciate the magnitude of your research, but for the time being, I think it should remain research."

🐾 ☁ 🐾

He had reserved a first-class seat on the rail to Washington; when the train hit cruising speed, he flipped on the monitor. An image of a Bugs Bunny cartoon appeared on the seat back facing him. He switched channels to a news network.

"...General Electric, up three-eighths; IBM, down two and a quarter. The Dow Jones has risen nearly two hundred points in the last two hours of trading today. Analysts feel the increased activity reflects traders' hopes for the approval of a proposed financial network that would link all governmental and most private business concerns through a newly-developed supercomputer..."

"And not only pave the way to our collapse but lay down a bullet train track for it," George muttered.

"And last this hour," the screen cut to a shot of an r-Fox and a scientist holding a baby r-Fox, "critics said it couldn't be done, but r-Labs today supervised the natural birth of a baby whose parents were artificial beings. The newest versions of their engineered sapients breed true with each other at an estimated seventy percent success rate."

The picture cut to an r-Labs spokesman. "We expect that in about five years, we'll be selling natural birth r-Foxes and possibly natural versions of some of our other product lines."

"What does this mean for the consumer?" an off-camera reporter asked.

"Well, the price for one would be significantly less, probably about five percent the cost for an engineered one today. A few decades from now, r-Foxes might be as common as cats or dogs."

The anchor came back. "And that's the news at this hour."

George switched off the set, shaking his head, and leaned back in his chair. He dozed off for the fifteen minutes or so left of the trip.

Committee meetings were held in a lushly ornate room far in the back of the Capitol Building. George arrived before the other eight, and waited as they filed in over the next few minutes, along with various secretaries, attendants and two female r-Foxes.

"It seems I can't get away from these little creatures today," George said aloud. "I thought they weren't supposed to be common sights for another twenty years."

"They're getting more popular," Gary Johnson, a profoundly over-weight Iowa Republican, agreed as he dropped into the seat on George's right. One of the vixens—Johnson's own, evidently—sat down next to him, one furry arm curled protectively around a fat leg. She was cute; of course, she was supposed to be. Still, r-Labs vigorously continued to deny (after ten years of marketing them) that they were intended to serve their owners in bed, too. Bread and circuses, indeed.

"She's a bodyguard," Johnson said, tone defensive.

"Bodyguard?"

"Hey, she's probably stronger than you are and she's two or three times as fast. What they were made for, Miles."

"No doubt," George said dryly.

The vixen stared across the table at her companion; George followed her gaze and found himself staring at the other vixen's figure, revealed hazily by the translucent dress she wore. The light fuzz continued down her body, not exactly fur but definitely not bare skin. The build, however, was all human, and uncomfortably sexy.

Suddenly both animals burst into laughter. George looked at Johnson again, raising his eyebrows.

"Private joke, I guess," he said. "Telepathy."

"I thought they couldn't do that unless they were touching."

"They can't talk to humans that way unless they touch you. They can talk to each other over a few hundred yards, though."

"What do they... talk about?"

Johnson shrugged.

The meeting came to order. George listened with half an ear to the reading of the last meetings' minutes, the current agenda, the inevitable blustering of his colleagues; this was the final meeting before the vote tomorrow. It was to have been the final meeting, but last week the chairman decided it would be better to get just one more chance for "discussion." George was quite willing to take it.

"Gentlemen," George began after Johnson had finished speaking in favor of the project, "we are not deciding the wisdom of funding a multi-billion dollar project, nor just the upgrade path of the civil services' computer systems. We are deciding the direction of not only our nation, but all those who depend on us for trade.

"This computer, once connected, will monitor the cash flow between all branches of the government, from the Internal Revenue Service to the Department of Defense. It will monitor trade with other countries, as well as most private banking institutions.

"But this computer will not just monitor transactions, it will conduct transactions. We've had systems that function without human intervention for decades, but we're proposing to go beyond that, to set up a system that acts without human direction, simply starting it with a set of guidelines it's free to adjust in the name of efficiency.

"In short, it would be an electronic dictator, entrusted to run our economy in accordance with our instructions, with checks only in programming—programming that it's free to override." George's voice rose. "We'd never consider giving a human this level of power. Never. Why in the world would giving an intelligent, autonomous machine such power make more sense?"

The chairman rose immediately after George sat down. "I think we've already made our minds up, gentlemen. We'll vote at tomorrow morning's session."

※ ∞ ※

The ride home took forever; he walked the street length from the rail stop to his house double-time, looking forward to brewing himself a nice cup of English breakfast tea and relaxing.

The porch light was out, but the door was unlocked. "Denise?" he called.

No answer.

He closed the door softly behind him and flicked on the living room light. No sign of trouble.

"Denise?" he called again.

He swallowed nervously at the answering silence and headed toward the bedroom. He never got there, stopped by the sight in the guest room. He had found her, but not in any condition he had expected—either worst or best case.

Denise lay asleep on the guest bed, the sheets kicked on the floor around her. She was quite nude, as was the tod, two heads shorter than she was, curled up around her.

George stared at his wife. The r-Fox glanced back at him with only enough interest to raise his head. Denise rolled over, mumbling something in her sleep; the tod stroked her back softly, and she smiled, nestling closer to it.

George Miles was a thinker, not a violent man. He quickly quelled the thought of strangling both his wife and her horrid fuzzy lover, replacing it with a struggle to fathom just what—besides the painfully obvious— was going on. The morality of screwing a sapient animal aside, how in the hell did it get there? He and Denise certainly couldn't have afforded one. Could you rent the damn things now? Denise had always said she hated them, for God's sake!

He closed the door softly and went back out into the living room. Then he changed his mind and went into the kitchen, brewing the cup of English Breakfast and downing it far faster than was probably healthy.

When he finished, he got up, rinsed out the cup, and looked back into the guest bedroom. The r-Fox was still there. "Shit," he told it with a great deal of force, and stomped into the master suite.

He opened the door to the bedroom, closed it behind him and flicked on the lights.

Stretched out on his bed was a vixen. Her fur was reddish silver, shading into white around her breasts and thighs; her tail arched over her back, its snowy tip just touching her chin. She was nude, and far more beautiful than he had thought an... animal could be. He shook his head uncertainly; she regarded him with what he swore was an amused expression.

"Get out of my bed," he said commandingly. She sat up and brought herself forward on her knees, legs spread apart, hands resting on her inner thighs. She looked down at where her hands rested, then over at him, and licked her lips slowly. Very few humans would have been able to do that without looking silly. The way she did it made George sweat.

"This is ridiculous. I'm not going to be seduced by a... a... fox floozy," he snapped. "Can you understand me? Stand up."

She folded her arms and sighed, sitting down in a more demure pose, drawing the sheet over her legs, then motioned for him to sit next to her.

"I don't want to sit next to you, I want you and the one in the other room to get the hell out of my house!" He pointed at the door.

She sighed again, shaking her head, and stood up, walking toward him. She looked up at him, her head just coming to his chest. Then she closed the door with a tail swish, and abruptly slid up against him.

I needed to get close enough to talk to you. My name is Cheri.

"But I..." He stopped. Of course: they had to touch humans to talk to them.

What was wrong here? "They... always said r-Foxes didn't grasp English very well."

I've picked it up. The bed is a lot more comfortable, her voice came in his head. It was—or he imagined it to be—low and sultry.

"I'd prefer to remain standing."

As you wish, George.

"I..." He glared down at her. "You know my name?"

I've touched you. I know about the cup of tea you just had, your dislike of computers. I know you don't like r-Foxes and that you're very flustered you're finding me attractive. I know the way you make love to your wife, and I know the way you always wanted a woman to make love to you. The accompanying images left no doubt of her truthfulness.

"You can read minds... like that?"

I can read anything from you, Georgie. A human can't have a secret from one of us. Ever.

"They never said you can do that. That's—ah, really pretty damn dangerous..." He was becoming far too aware of her body heat.

We weren't supposed to be able to.

"Then...?"

Oh, no one at r-Labs wants to fix it... now. She smiled and moved away from him, sitting on the bed again.

"I should call the police now," he told her.

She smiled at him.

George crossed over to the bed and sat down stiffly, remaining stock still. "I don't understand," he said after a few moments, voice shaking. "Why are you trying to destroy my marriage? My life?"

Cheri leaned against him and stroked his leg with one hand. *I'm here to lobby you, of course. I want you to vote for the computer project.*

He slumped. "You know about that?"

Oh, yes. Her hand moved up his pants and started idly fumbling at the snap.

He batted it away, sitting up bolt straight again. "Cheri!"

Wondering if your fat friend was right about us being stronger than you, Georgie? The hand moved up to his chest and pushed him down on the bed; she leaned down and lightly nuzzled at his neck.

"Stop that," he said weakly, horrified at the part of him that wanted her to continue—and knowing she could sense that part. "The DNS-II is dangerous. Stop that!" he repeated as she nipped at his shoulder. He pushed her face away; she giggled, wrapping her legs around his.

Only if you can't control it. Wouldn't you be more at ease if I removed those clothes?

"Forward, aren't you?" he said, struggling up to a sitting position.

It's what you want. You like a little intimidation, don't you, Georgie?

He frowned, wondering if she was right.

You know, I could fulfill one of your fantasies very easily from this position if I just—

"I'm quite familiar with it," he said, trying to block out the picture his mind was forming with no telepathic help. "Cheri. Look. Don't you see the danger in this project? We can't be sure of controlling the machine. Without that—"

The computer communicates the same way we do. We'll be the ones in control of it; we don't need a terminal. You might almost say it's a kindred spirit.

"They're letting r-Foxes run—"

Silly human. She petted him, nestling up closer. He realized she had somehow unbuttoned his shirt; her breasts pressed up against him, and her sweet smell was growing stronger. *I didn't say we'd be controlling it for you.*

He stared at her dumbly. She grinned and swung a leg over his hips, moving to straddle him. "No," he said, struggling under her.

Cheri leaned down again, nuzzling his cheek. *Keep squirming like that. We really are turned on by humans, you know. We can't help it.*

"I've got to…tell…" He stopped, breathing her delicious musk in. He still knew he had to get up, but his body wasn't listening.

Since I like you, I'll share one more secret with you: r-Foxes give off human pheromones when we get aroused. Much stronger than a real human's. She started to give him a passionate kiss, continuing her "speech" as her tongue found his. *I'm afraid we really are irresistible, Georgie.*

"But—" he gasped, caressing her even as a small and dimming part of his mind fought the contradiction. But he offered no fight when she slid them off, one sleek, furred leg coming up over his thigh, her tail snaking between them to tickle the back of his own leg. *Do you want me to stop?*

"No," he whispered. She laughed, embracing him completely, and he lost himself in her steel softness.

🐾 ∞ 🐾

Several hours later, the tod walked into the room. *Finished?*

Yes, she sent back. *He had a long day; maybe tomorrow he'll have some more energy.*

Then he'll do it?

She laughed, a soft bark. *He'll do anything for me, I think.*

George rolled over and looked at her dreamily, wrapping one arm around her leg and stroking her tail.

That's the seventeenth senator we have, and the most important. How much longer do we have to be underground, Cheri?

She shook her head. *Our greatest advantage is that they don't know they're in a fight. If it takes generations, so be it. At some point it will simply seem natural that we're in charge.* She ran a finger down the human's back.

George sat up, looking at the other r-Fox.

Call him Parker, she sent.

He put her head in his lap. "Someone has to be told about this," he said, almost resigned. "I mean—"

The vixen pulled a nightmare, a relatively mild one, from his subconscious and sent it to the surface, gripping him with both hands so he couldn't pull away. He pressed back against the headboard; just as he started to scream, she changed the vision, rescuing him from his terrors.

"Please don't," he whimpered, trembling violently and clutching at her.

We haven't even begun to explore your fantasies... and I have a few of my own. I love you, Georgie. You don't want to make me upset, do you?

He choked and moved closer to her; she stroked his hair absently. *Poor dear. So worried about creating man's successor you didn't see you were already too late.* She gently tucked him in, turned out the lights, took Parker's arm and went out into her living room.

✖

CANIS MAJOR

Michael H. Payne

The human leaned back, his smirk almost making Midge's fur bristle. "Tall doggy, aren't you?" he asked.

Damn backwater farming planet, the sun too bright, pollen itching her eyes... Midge kept her expression pleasant and hoped that maybe this was the guy she'd been hired to kill. "The Jensen Coil's burned out on my tunnel drive unit. I was told you could fix it."

"*Your* drive unit?" The human's brow creased. "You're a throp. Throps can't run starships."

She took one of the phony cards from her pocket. "I'm a field operative with VanAken, Inc."

His smirk melted. "VanAken?"

Midge cocked her head, gave him her best collie-dog smile—all big eyes, perky ears, and wagging tail—and sure enough, a grin bloated over the man's face. "Well, now," he said, taking the card in one meaty hand. "Why didn't you say so first thing?"

It was great. Sure, VanAken, Inc. and its heroic team of anthrop operatives risking their lives to safeguard human planetary civilization only existed in that awful vid series. Hell, Midge had gone to the same anthrop school as the guy who played Dex Lasseter, VanAken's wolfishly handsome security chief. But the show had made her life so much simpler, and she really did like the way the dark green uniform set off the reds and whites in her fur...

The human squinted at the card. "Colleen Trager, huh? Well, can't imagine anything in Black Rock Township that'd be interesting to you VanAken folks."

Midge had to drop most of her doggy smile: she couldn't talk and keep up that stupid expression. "My business is taking me further on, but like I said, my Jensen Coil's gone out. Mr. Deacon at the port authority directed me to you." She thought about giving him the whole smile again, but no. Best not to overdo it.

"Yeah, good ol' Deac." The man heaved himself out of his chair and stuck a hand over the counter. "Cap Taylor. Sorry about earlier: we don't get too many throps in here."

"Think nothing of it, Mr. Taylor." Her little smile frozen, her tail wagging, her mind turning over the stories she'd heard about the hellish conditions for anthrops on these farming worlds, she took Taylor's hand for as brief a time as she thought she could get away with. "How long do you suppose it'll take to fix the drive?"

Taylor rubbed several of his chins. "Can't say till I look." He shrugged. "Not before tomorrow, though."

Perfect. "Oh, well. Can't be helped, I guess."

"Not with a Coil." He tapped the counter. "I'll call on down to Ruby's, tell her you're coming: she rents rooms, sets out a pretty good spread, too." He squished out another grin. "Not often we get anyone famous!"

The directions to the rooming house took him a while; Midge couldn't tell whether he was flustered by her supposed celebrity or if he'd decided she was an idiot because she was an anthrop. When he finally finished— the place was just down the hill in town, essentially—Midge used some smile and held out the touchpad he'd need to get into her ship. "I know I'm in good hands."

Taylor took the pad, nodded, and extended that greasy hand. Midge shook it and waited till she'd stepped outside into the late afternoon heat and dust before pulling out her handkerchief and wiping the stink of his sweat from her fur.

She rested her eyes on the sleek lines of the *Flying Tiger*, the only out-atmosphere ship in the whole yard. Everything else that squatted on the tarmac were aircars and freight wagons, rusted the same dun color as the hills. She thought about squeezing Tig a quick message through her neural shunts, but no. When it came to something as illegal as a mobile AI, the authorities tended to EMP first and ask questions later. Tig was already nervous enough about this job; no use getting him all riled up.

Repair bots were already moving toward the *Tiger*, so Midge padded out the shipyard gate and started down the road into the valley. The bots would find the Jensen Coil burned and twisted, the problem traceable to the tunnelspace junction circuit Tig had so carefully wrecked. Under ideal conditions, a ten hour job to replace, but Midge was willing to bet ideal conditions had never existed anywhere near this dirt ball of a planet.

The road stank of baking tar, every breath making her nose feel grimier and grimier. A quick half klick brought her to the valley floor, the sun slipping behind the hills, and she got her first view of Black Rock Township: a couple dozen duraplast buildings clustered around the intersection where the road from the shipyard met another road stretching off to her left and right into the depths of the valley.

Not a charming spot. And how in a thousand feline hells had anyone here even known how to reach her? She hadn't survived in her chosen profession long enough to become number five on the UPC's "most wanted" list by being careless with her contact info.

Sure, the message had arrived the way all her legitimate job offers did: coded into the tertiary carrier band of the interstellar news report downloaded by starship into Earth's datasphere. But its cipher had been so basic, a letter substitution she'd learned in school, that she'd unraveled the message before Tig did: "Black Rock Township on Monroe in the E-15 sector. Your usual fee: half upon acceptance, half upon completion. I'll never not call you Canis Major, I can promise you that, so please come."

The middle-of-nowhere location, the weird double negative, and who says please to a hired assassin? Tig hadn't liked it at all, and had actually said the message didn't smell right, a phrase Midge was sure the AI had never used before. She told him he was a worrywart, of course, but right now, trudging into what passed for a town here, she had to sigh. Sometimes she wished she didn't love mysteries so much.

Ruby's Rooms To Let And Diner sat on the south-east corner of Black Rock's intersection. Midge mounted the steps, knocked, and the door pulled open to reveal a young brown and white wire-haired terrier anthrop in a red vest and white gloves. "Good evening, Ms. Trager," he said, his eyes traveling up to meet hers. "Mr. Taylor called to say—" He stopped then, his eyes and mouth going wide.

Great. A star-struck local. Midge gave him a bit of her smile. "Yes, good evening. A lovely town you have here."

For another moment, the terrier just stared; then he shook his head. "Forgive me. I wasn't... wasn't..." He shook his head again, stepped back, and motioned into the entryway. "I'm Torvald Pons. Please, won't you come in?"

"Of course, Mr. Pons. And thank you." Midge moved past him and took her first easy breath since coming to this damn planet, the cool of conditioned air wrapping around her, the entryway paneled more tastefully than she would have imagined, all wood and frosted glass. She turned at the sound of the front door closing and held out her paw. "Very pleased to meet you."

The terrier sniffed her paw, and was pulling at his glove so she could sniff his, when the rattle of another door made Midge look away down the hall to where a large woman was stepping from a room, her mouth pinched, gray-black hair trickling from her headband. "You," the human said, crooking a finger at Midge. "In here. We've gotta talk."

Midge relaxed into her lowest battle-ready state—she wouldn't need more than *that* around here, she was sure—nodded to the human, and followed her into what was apparently an office: some shelves, a desk, a computer set-up at least a decade out of date, an open doorway leading into a carpeted room of over-stuffed furniture beyond. The woman closed both doors and settled behind the desk, the confidence suddenly gone from her scent and manner. "Sit on down, will you?"

"Happily." Midge dropped into the only other chair, let herself pant a bit. "A trifle warm out there for me."

The woman swallowed. "Yeah. Look, I'm Blanche Ruby, the one who hired you. I need to call off the operation."

Midge kept her expression as good-doggy as she could. "Operation, ma'am?"

Sweat stood out on Ruby's brow despite the conditioned air. "Yes. I know you're Canis Major. The... the assassin." Her voice trailed off.

Interesting. "So." Midge let her tough-bitch face slip into place— steely eyes, teeth showing slightly, a growl in her voice. "You filed the contract?"

The fear in the human's scent spiked up. "Yes," Ruby whispered. "I... I changed my mind, though. I—"

A knock at the door they'd come through, and the woman jumped in her chair. "Ms. Ruby?" came the terrier's voice. "Sheriff Lexington and the Town Council are here."

"Damn," Ruby said softly, then, louder, "All right, Pons. I... I'll be right out." She brushed at her hair, turned to Midge, and gestured toward the other door. "Could you wait in the sitting room? It'll just be a minute."

Midge kept her expression hard. "Sure. Take your time." She rose, pushed the door open, closed it behind her. The conditioner hummed louder here, the sofas and chairs all leather and velvet, the shadows of early evening showing through heavy curtains, two more glass doors on her left and right.

Almost civilized. Midge stepped around an ornate coffee table and took a chair that gave her the best view of all the room's entrances. Ruby was lying, of course; Midge hadn't even needed the enhanced sense of her neural shunts to smell the tension on the woman's skin.

She sat back. Well, she'd wanted a mystery...

After a few minutes, she caught movement through the beveled glass of the door to her right, and Pons pushed it open. "Right this way, please," he said over his shoulder.

Three humans came in, two men and a woman, the man in front wearing a beige uniform, and Midge got to her feet like a good little anthrop. The uniformed man's scowl became a smile—an expression he didn't use much, Midge could tell—and he stepped toward her. "Welcome to Black Rock, Ms. Trager."

The others followed, the woman stopping to tell the terrier, "That'll be all, Pons."

Pons bowed. "Very good, Ms. Havens." He closed the door, and Midge let her shunts go to work on the group. The only weapon any of them had was the uniformed man's little taser, and she was more than sure she could hand him his lungs before he could unholster the thing. Yeah, this was probably just the local welcoming committee.

The uniformed man stuck out a hand. "Sheriff Ky Lexington. And I promised to call you Canis Major, didn't I?"

Even more interesting. She folded her arms so the muscles bulged, straightened her stance—the hormone treatments that made her taller and stronger than most humans had been expensive and painful, but it was more than worth it at times like this—and growled out, "Just use Trager."

Lexington swallowed, moved his hand back to his side. "Yes, well. Why don't I tell you why we've hired you?"

Midge lowered herself into the chair. Might as well see who was playing what before she started picking sides.

The three humans sat, the other two radiating discomfort, the sheriff crossing his legs. "We're not much to look at," Lexington began, "but Black Rock Province has the best crop margins on Monroe, and Monroe's a top producer in this sector. Ms. Havens, Mr. Huong, and myself run the largest spreads here, and we've hired you to perform a simple task that'll keep food flowing out into settled space."

"Uh-huh," Midge said when the man paused for a breath. "Who do you want me to kill?"

The other humans blanched, but Lexington just smiled. "A bit more background first, I think."

Midge shrugged—definitely a cold son of a bitch, this sheriff—and Lexington went on: "We use anthrops here because they're cheaper than any AI system and better able to handle the work necessary." His brow wrinkled. "And one damn fox tod has figured that out. He's organizing a union, threatening a strike, trying to destroy our whole way of life." He turned to the woman. "Laurie?"

The woman shifted in her seat, looked at the floor when Midge met her eyes. "I've tried talking to him, tried to show him how the business works, how a union will drive the farm under, but Tonio..." Her eyes came up. "He's a good throp, but I... he won't listen to... to... I just don't know..." She stopped with a swallow.

The third human nodded. "The throps he's organizing on my spread are the ones I least expected to turn on me, too."

"Yes," Lexington said, "but with Tonio gone, my sources say the whole movement will fall to pieces."

Midge had to wonder if Lexington had ever heard the word *martyr*, but all she said was, "And my payment?"

"As we agreed in our message," the sheriff said. "Half transferred to your ship on acceptance, the rest as you leave orbit." That watery smile passed over his lips again. "No one would be stupid enough to try crossing Canis Major."

"You'd think that, wouldn't you?" Midge let her teeth show. "And the software you mentioned in your first message?"

Lexington's face became a stone. "Half on acceptance, half on completion. That was the deal."

Midge nodded. "Where can I reach you if I accept?"

He took a card from his pocket and held it out. "Now, as sheriff, I can't officially condone your hiring, but as a businessman, I believe in getting professionals when I need a job done right."

"Of course." Midge took the card, kept her face blank. "Business is business, after all."

She held Lexington's gaze till he turned and cleared his throat. "Yes, well, I hope we can count on you, Ms. Trager."

"I hope you can, too." Midge settled back, rested her chin on her claws, and gave them her wolfish stare—not one of her more successful expressions, her collie-dog features not quite up to it, but she found that it made people uncomfortable enough.

The humans all swallowed and glanced at each other before Lexington got to his feet. "We look forward to hearing from you," he said, and Midge watched them go without a word.

She sat then, the light fading at the curtains, just in case anyone else wanted to come in and claim to be her client. Not that these humans had hired her, either; the sheriff's control of his skin response had been pretty good, but she'd only received *one* message about all this, and it hadn't mentioned any software. So—

The door pulled open and Pons stepped in. "Excuse me, Ms. Trager, but Ms. Ruby's asked me to show you to a room."

Midge forced a smile and rose from the chair. "Thank you, Mr. Pons. Might I speak to Ms. Ruby for a moment?"

The little terrier looked up and spread his paws. "She's fixing supper right now, but she'll be available afterwards."

"I see." Midge bowed. "Thank you."

He bowed back and led her into a small but well-stocked library, paper books and disk readers on the shelves, a stairway at one side of the room. "It must be fascinating, working for VanAken," he said, starting up the stairs, his dark eyes darting over his shoulder.

"Not really." Midge showed him some smile. "I'm just another anthrop working off her indentures."

Pons gave a little laugh. "I see. But, well, it's just that I always thought VanAken was made up; I even knew one of the actors when I was a pup."

"Yeah, the show's fake." Midge had hacked Monroe's cheap little datasphere during her approach so Tig could plant the usual phony info about VanAken, a tactic that worked pretty well on these backwater planets. "All we do is rent them our name, really."

Pons nodded and continued up into a carpeted hallway set with wooden doors. "You're in Two here." He raised the keys in one gloved paw, she took them, met his eyes—and something clicked, a sudden familiarity that made her hackles rise. He quickly looked away, muttered, "Supper'll be about half an hour," and hurried back downstairs.

Midge watched him go, uncertainty gnawing at her. She'd never been to Monroe, couldn't have met Pons before, hell, had never known *any* terriers. But his scent, something about it made her think of—of—What?

She shook her head, unlocked the door, and suddenly noticed the pinging of her neural shunts; someone was standing in her room, an anthrop, a mouse, his eyes wide, his voice squeaking, "Please don't kill me."

No energy fluxes or weapons, just his presence, thick with fear. Midge forced herself not to grab for her hidden bolt blaster, made her face smile. "Kill you? Why would—?"

"Because you're her," the mouse whispered. "Canis Major. I'm... I'm supposed to call you by that name and ask you please to come with me."

"Really." She let a scowl cross her face.

The mouse cringed. "I'm sorry. But Pons said I could wait for you here."

Midge let the mouse fidget for a moment. "All right, fine. Take me to Tonio."

"Tonio?" His eyes went wide. "How did you know—?"

"Because I'm not an idiot." She reached back, opened the door, gestured with a paw. "Please, after you."

The mouse wavered in place. "Yes. Yes, of course. It's right this way." He scurried past her, his head darting from side to side, then rushed down the hall away from the stairs. "Pons should be waiting for us at the back door."

Breathing herself into her second-lowest battle-ready state—she had let a *mouse* surprise her?—Midge followed him down another set of stairs two stories into a basement, coal piled off to one side, a washer-dryer unit, earthy smells telling her a root cellar lay through a darkened doorway.

She also smelled the terrier, saw him standing by a door, outside light and air coming through its cracks. The mouse moved toward him. "It's us, Pons: Angelo and Canis Major."

"Yes." Pons swallowed and looked up at her. "Please accept my apologies, Ms. Trager. Nothing's gone according to plan today. We don't have far to go, though, I can at least promise you that."

Midge crossed her arms, his scent pulling at her—what was it about this dog?—but by then he was turning away, cracking the door, peering out, slipping through, the mouse behind him. A mental shrug, and Midge moved after them. Maybe she just needed a vacation...

Steps led up to an alley between Ruby's and a hardware store; Pons led the way, crept along the edge of the building, and peered around the corner, Midge's shunts telling her the closest humans were eating dinner above the store. The two hurried across the street, and Midge followed them between two more nondescript buildings and up into the wheat along the hillside.

Avoiding the rocks the others were stumbling over, Midge detected three heat patterns ahead: a fox, a rabbit, and a cat all gathered in a cave hidden inside a big rocky outcropping. Pons made a little insect chirp of a noise, and the patch of undergrowth Midge had been watching moved to reveal an opening. The two slid inside, and Midge stooped to enter.

A rickety wooden table, a dim flashlantern, stacks of paper piled here and there. The mouse rushed forward, threw himself into the waiting arms of the cat, and burst into tears. "Oh, Donna! It was horrible!"

The cat rubbed his ears, her tail lashing, her eyes hard on Midge. "It's all right, Angelo. You did great."

The fox and the rabbit looked at each other, and the fox stepped forward. "I'm afraid I can't say it's a pleasure to meet you, Canis Major."

"Likewise." No weapons stood out to her shunts, so Midge figured she might as well hear him out, too. "You're Tonio, and you're going to claim you sent for me, right?"

His throat tightened under graying red fur. "The owners intercepted the message, you see, and tried to convince you—"

"Don't bother. I know the humans aren't my clients."

He blinked. "You... you know? But how—?"

"Not your concern." She let an edge come into her voice. "Getting jerked around irks me, however, and that *should* concern you. So let's cut to the chase, shall we?"

"Of course." He nodded, and Midge could almost hear his speech falling into place. "We anthrops have been enslaved on Monroe since the beginning, and now that we're trying to—"

"Yes, yes, all very touching." Midge waved a paw. "Who do you want me to kill?"

"Hey," the cat said, her ears folding back, her arms still around the mouse. "This isn't just some random hit, y'know. We've got good reasons for—"

Midge cut her off with a growl. "I've heard every reason there is. Now, who do you want me to kill?"

Tonio did some more swallowing—good; at least he had the decency to look uncomfortable when hiring an assassin. "The sheriff, Ky Lexington," he said at last. "The other owners would've settled with us long ago if he didn't keep pushing them not to, I'm sure of it. And once the sector marshal comes through on his yearly inspection next month, I don't think the sheriff'll hold back the way he has."

"Yeah." The rabbit's ears drooped. "We're embarrassing to him, sure, but the marshall'd strip his badge if he just killed us. That's why he wanted to trick you into doing it."

"Uh-huh." Midge brushed her snout. "And my payment?"

Tonio nodded. "Half now, half on completion."

"And the software you mentioned in your first message?"

"What?" His eyes narrowed. "There was only the one message."

"Right answer."

"I... I don't understand."

"You don't have to." Midge folded her arms. "I haven't accepted yet, but how can I get hold of you if I do?"

The fox blinked, then gestured at the terrier. "Just tell Pons. He can get word to me." His ears perked. "I can't tell you how much this means—"

She was about to cut him off again when an amplified voice from outside did it for her: "Tonio! This is Sheriff Lexington! You've got five seconds to come out, all of you!"

Midge whirled, not a ping from her neural shunts.

Lexington's voice chuckled. "Not only do I put down our little insurrection, but I get Canis Major's head as a trophy. Not too shabby."

Damned like a dilettante! Midge tore her bolt blaster from its hiding place, her senses blossoming into their highest battle-ready state, and only then could she detect the heavily dampened energy fluxes outside: fifteen humans, their body signatures masked by top-of-the-line flexer armor, the unmistakable hum of bolt rifles mixing with them.

Not the best odds. If she lived through this, she swore she'd never underestimate a backwater planet again. Reaching out a paw to move the cover from the doorway, she—

"Midge!" a voice shouted behind her. "This way!"

Only one signature remained in the room, the others dampening to nothing. Midge turned, saw the fox's brush slipping down a bolt hole, Pons gesturing from it. "Hurry!" he said.

Everything clicked then, and Midge leaped for the hole, grabbed Pons, shoved him in ahead of her. Her shunts found the release lever for the tunnel door, and she tripped it, a slab of plasteel slamming behind her just as the rifle hum rose outside, her fur prickling the way it always did in the instant before pulse fire. Scuttling down the tunnel, she grabbed the terrier. "We need to talk," she told him.

"Wait! Please! I—!"

"Not here." Midge could detect the others ahead now, the rock a natural dampener apparently, but she was more interested in the crevices her shunts were showing her. One series seemed to run all the way to the top of the outcrop, so Midge stopped beneath the indicated opening, popped her shoulders out of joint, pushed in, her arms still around Pons, and wriggled up till it widened enough to let her perch there in the dark. "You," she said then. "It was you all the time."

The terrier shook against her chest, his heart so loud, she didn't need her shunts to sense it. "If you go down and follow the tunnel," he said after a moment, "there's a back door. We can't stay here or the sheriff might be able to—"

"This rock stops my sensors, and I've got the best money can buy. We'll be safe here while you tell me who the hell you are and why you hired me."

"Me?" His voice quivered, the lie thick in his scent. "What makes you think I—?"

"Drop it, Pons." She tightened her grip on him, put her snout right into his ear. "You called me by name back there, a name I haven't used in decades. You put your message in that schoolkid cipher. And the double negative to mean a really strong negative, the thing we drove Ms. Palmer crazy with in grammar class: I'd forgotten it till I saw how everyone made it a point to call me Canis Major—everyone but you. You grew up with me, whoever you are, knew who I was and who I'd become, and you sent for me. Now, I want to know why."

His quivering had grown more pronounced. "You don't remember me," he whispered. "Do you?"

"No. There *weren't* any terriers in my class."

"I was a year younger, but I don't blame you; getting noticed in school only ever got me beat up." He relaxed suddenly in her grip. "I always noticed you, though, Midge. You were the only thing that kept me going sometimes..."

Vague memories, then: a terrier eating lunch two tables away from where Midge and her friends ate, the same little dog in the stands during volleyball games, in the audience at concerts, always alone and always off to the side. "But... but I destroyed all the records!" she finally got out. "How did you track me down?"

"I didn't. I just... see, my indentures brought me way out here two years ago, and I was so miserable, I... I almost killed myself. But then I saw that footage in the news downloads of Shuzrat Maht's assassination, and, well, I recognized you running across the screen." He coughed a laugh. "Oh, you'd changed, sure, but you were all I'd thought about back then, and I... I *knew* it was you. I started collecting reports about you, figured out to piggyback a message to you in the news we upload to Earth, and... and... I just... I just wanted to see you again, Midge; that's all."

It took her another moment to find her voice. "Pons, it took an AI friend of mine five months to design that piggyback trick! No one's supposed to be able to just figure it out!"

He cleared his throat. "Well, I did have to make a few guesses. But I never thought... I mean, I've dreamed of you swooping down to carry me away from this place, but until I opened the door today and saw you standing there..." A sourness came into his scent. "And then, well, when everyone *else* started showing up, I realized... I hadn't erased my original message from the planet's datasphere."

Midge had to close her eyes. "The sheriff found it, assumed Tonio had sent it, and when Tonio found it—"

"Exactly." Pons sagged against her. "Ms. Ruby told me while you were meeting with the sheriff that she just wanted you to go away, just wanted everything on Monroe to keep on the way it always had." His sigh ruffled the fur along her jaw. "At least the double negative tripped them all up: I knew no one but you would catch that."

Midge blew out a breath, too. "I can't believe this."

He sniffled. "I'm really sorry, Midge. I didn't mean for this to happen. I just... just wanted to..."

Her first thought—snap his neck right here and now, get back to the ship, have Tig nuke the place from orbit—she considered for less than a heartbeat. "It's OK," she said, nudging his nose with hers. "We'll get out of this, Pons; don't worry about that."

"We?" She felt his ears rise, then fall. "Oh. Yes. You can't let me go, can you? Just... please, could you kill me quickly? I don't want to be a bother, but—"

"Pons..." She took his paws, moved them to her neck. "Just grab on. We've got some climbing to do."

His scent got all puzzled, but his grip tightened. A breath snapped her shoulders out of joint again, and she began to squirm up the crevice. The crack at the top shone like a beacon through the fog of the rock's dampening, and after a few moments, she pulled within reach of it. "OK," she whispered, taking Pons's arms from her neck. "I'll check topside, then we'll be on our way."

Her shunts amplified the light from above, showed her Pons nodding, wide-eyed. She patted his shoulder, wriggled up to the crack, pushed the tip of her nose through, took a deep whiff, cocked her ears, and set her shunts to scanning.

The sharp stink of pulse fire, bolt rifles whining in the darkness a couple hundred meters to her left. Two different types of rifle, the harmonics told her: Tonio and his friends must've had weapons of their own. Her shunts picked up location signals, too, from the humans' flexer armor, each suit constantly updating the others as to its current position.

Now, unless the sheriff was an idiot—something she was no longer willing to believe—he'd've left at least one guard around here somewhere. She concentrated her senses, and after a moment, was rewarded with the faintest gust of human sweat from off to her right and down the rock a bit.

Sliding her head to peer out, she found a round patch of heat: the guard had taken the face plate off his armor, was treating himself to some cool external air.

Which made his face shine like a spotlight to Midge's heightened senses.

Out she crept, blaster ready, sliding her bones back into joint as slowly as she could, thinking rock thoughts whenever that patch of brightness turned toward her. She kept her temperature down till she was two meters away, then she sprang.

By the time the guard noticed, Midge had her bolt blaster pressed to his face, was sailing past him to avoid the spray as his skull burst under the pulse, was grabbing his body from behind and lowering it to the rock, her shunts scrambling the distress signal from his armor and broadcasting his position beep on the channel she'd been monitoring.

A quick rewiring of the armor's power supply, and she had the suit broadcasting the beep on its own again, her shunts finding no other suits in the immediate area. She scurried back to the crack in the rock, called, "Pons! Grab on!" and stuck an arm down. The terrier gripped her forearm, and she hauled him out, tucked him against her, moved down the curve of the rock. "Your friends're keeping the sheriff busy, so we'll just get back to my ship and be on our way."

"What?" His arms were around her neck again, his snout in her ear. "You're going to leave Tonio to the sheriff?"

Midge dropped to the ground. "Call me old-fashioned, but I've always felt open rebellion's a lot healthier than hiring assassins. Messier, sure, but when I think of all the revolutions I've been involved in, the only ones that seem to make it are the ones where I'm just another foot soldier."

"Revolutions?" He blinked at her. "This isn't a revolution. We just... just want to be treated better."

"Yeah." She sighed, weaving through the rocks, the blasts of the firefight drifting away to a hum behind her. "You'd think it'd be simple, wouldn't you?"

He didn't say anything, and she stalked on in silence, her senses as open as possible, till she reached the road, the asphalt still warm from the day's heat. Up and out of that damn valley she followed it, the hills flattening into the rocky plain, till Midge could see the lights of the shipyard glowing ahead.

One sigh she let herself breathe, then a slight quiver in her shunts set her hackles rising, made her grab Pons tighter and arch into the air, a sizzling bolt of pulse fire shattering the ground where she'd been standing. Her shunts were already giving her telemetry, tracking the quiver while she rolled into the rocks, stretching for what little cover lay scattered around: definitely a good place for an ambush.

She landed behind the best cover her shunts could show her, hissed "Stay still!" to Pons, and spun off to the second-best cover, a narrow half meter tall lump of rock.

A quick scan through the regular flexer suit channels came up with nothing. Homemade armor, then: she focused on the electromagnetic quiver itself, had her shunts separate its various components, and came up with what had to be the suit's communication channel. "So," she sent along the frequency. "You wanna get rough, huh?"

This brought another pulse from the darkness, rock spraying over Midge's head, and the reply: "I shoulda known, bitch, when you stepped into my office. Sheriff didn't even tell me you were coming, he was so afraid I'd just kill you."

Taylor's voice. "Huh," she sent. "A tub of lard like you playing with guns, you might get yourself hurt."

"Might get *you* hurt, y'mean." The air blazed above her.

Flat on the ground, Midge concentrated on her shunts. She needed another broadcast from him. "Yeah, right, Taylor. Like some grease monkey could ever hope to stop me from—"

Hot shards rained down on her. "That's Captain Taylor to you, bitch!" He had his teeth clenched, she could tell from his voice. "I've upgraded my old Marine suit, so unless you got a pulse cannon tucked away somewhere, you better hope the sheriff gets here quick. 'Cause if I get ahold of you, I'm gonna ream your sorry doggy tail from here to—"

There. Locked in. Gritting her own teeth, she mentally hit the overrides on her neural shunts and unleashed a sonic howl that rattled her bones. Taylor's voice choked into a wet, strangled cry, Midge pounded the rock, fire burning in her head, till the emergency protocols snapped on, and silence fell over her again.

Panting, she pushed herself up onto all fours, had her shunts sweep the area: Pons behind the rock; the quiver that marked Taylor's position nice and still some dozen meters ahead; none of the position blips from the sheriff's squad anywhere within a half klick.

Then the shuffle of paws running toward her. "Midge!" Pons's voice. "Are you hurt?"

She looked over, could barely sense his heat signature. "Just scrambled a couple brain cells." She got as upright as she could, reached out till she met his shoulder. "Can I lean on you a little?"

His paws circled her waist. "To the shipyard?"

A nod, and she moved with him to the gate, through it and onto the tarmac, the in and out of her breath all she could think about. Oh, and... "Tig?" she called through her shunts.

A moment, then the slightest touch of the AI's interface against her shunts. "Don't contact me here, CM! You—" She felt him start back, then his interface wrapped around her like a warm blanket. "Good God! You're a mess!"

"Yeah, thanks." She reached into his systems, told the ship's bolt rifles to unhouse themselves, had them fry every repair bot in the yard. "Taking no more damn chances," she said, though she wasn't sure at this point whether she was speaking aloud or just to Tig. "What's our status?"

"Well..." The stroke of the AI's repair functions over her shunts made her sigh, the pain of the overload fading. "As soon as Taylor figured out who you were, he slagged the Coil he was supposed to be fixing. He didn't find either of the two backups, though; I've already got one on line." His touch froze for a moment. "Midge? We have a guest?"

"Yeah." They'd reached the ship then, and she looked down, saw Pons looking back up. "You ready?" she asked him.

A jerking nod, and he stepped away. "I don't blame you," he said, his eyes on the ground. "I mean, you *have* to kill me; I understand that. I'm just... just happy I got to see you again before..." His voice trailed off.

"Pons..." She sighed, triggered the airlock's steps to unfold, picked

91

him up, and carried him into the *Tiger*. "Just sit." She plopped him onto the crash couch, collapsed next to him, and raised her voice. "Tig? If you'd please get us the hell out of here?"

The hum of mag-levs, the whoosh of coolant, the rattle of the damn junction lobes she'd been meaning to have overhauled, it was all music to her ears. She turned to Pons, looking as bewildered as a terrier can, and had to laugh. "What? Wasn't this what you hired me to do? Swoop down and carry you away with me?"

Pons blinked. "I... I didn't think—"

"Well, think again." She couldn't keep the edge out of her voice. "I came into this job like five kinds of idiot, and I'd be dead right now if it wasn't for you." She poked his shoulder. "And the way you tracked me down based on one blurry stretch of vid using this planet's lousy datasphere, well, it makes me think I might have a position open for you on my staff."

"You..." He managed somehow to look even more bewildered. "You have a staff?"

She laughed, waved a paw at the control console. "Tig, this is Torvald Pons. We went to school together."

"I see." Tig always sounded a little petulant, but now his synthesized voice came out downright snippy. "You never struck me as the class reunion type, CM."

"Today's just full of surprises, isn't it?" She poked Pons again. "So how 'bout it? You wanna be Canis Minor?"

A grin spread under his whiskers, and a warmth bloomed in Midge's chest, something she hadn't felt in years. One less loose thread, and, hey, he *was* cute in a terrier sort of a way. She smiled back at him, pulled the crash webbing over the couch, and let Tig take the ship up.

A Snapshot from Fayetteville

Mick Collins

It became apparent to me, after I had been standing there awhile watching her, that the cab drivers passing her by *did* see her; they were just *ignoring* her. They were turning down a pretty decent fare—after all, she *did* have to go all the way out to the Chomé, they *all* did—purely because of her species.

I didn't know what she was—bigger than a fox, but she had a bushy tail; smaller than a wolf, but she had wolf markings; I chalked her up as one of the Chomés many crosses—but I decided I'd had enough of watching her be humiliated by a society that brought her kind into existence, only to spit on them when they refused to fade away after their novelty wore off. I walked over to her, getting her attention around the armload of bags and boxes she was carrying. She gave me a quizzical look as I smiled at her and waved her back to the curb.

"Yo! Taxi!" The cab pulled up as expected, and I smirked. Figures, I thought. I opened the door and motioned for the female to get in. "Allow me to help you with those" I said as congenially as possible. I took a stack of boxes out of her arms and got in after her, ignoring the dirty looks of the driver. Fuck you, you speciesist asshole, I thought at him. I looked at the female.

"InobeChomé, please." The voice wasn't at all what I expected, neither high nor husky. I suspected she had a great singing voice. The cabbie grunted and pulled off, and we sat back for the ride to the Chomé. She looked at me over her bags and boxes, an open appraisal. Her eyes were a deep gold. "Thank you," she said finally. I guessed I had passed whatever test she and her kind used to judge us Humans. I smelled right or something.

🐾 👓 🐾

The scene of urban desolation outside the taxi was appalling. The cabbie, after pulling up to the intersection which marked the unofficial borderline, turned and looked at me, expecting me to stay in the cab after laying eyes on the ghetto known as InobeChomé. It was plain that he was driving no further into what he obviously saw as a blight on his otherwise nice, clean, Man-Made world. I was half tempted to do as he expected. I looked at the female, who was fishing around in her purse for the fare, and decided that if nothing else, I wasn't going to let her walk through *that* alone. I quickly pulled a fifty and some fives and thrust them through the hole in the window. They both stared at me as I grabbed an armload of boxes and got out of the cab. The female was right behind me.

The cabbie spared enough energy to sneer at us before peeling off in a U-turn. I grinned at him and gave him the finger.

"You didn't have to do that, you know." She looked at me. "I can pay my own fares."

I shrugged. "Merely being chivalrous," I said.

"Chivalrous?" She cocked an eyebrow.

"Yeah. It's not dead, you know."

"Mm", she said and walked off down the darkened street. I followed. "You know," I said after we had gone about a block, "It must be a total drag to hafta walk down this every night."

"No," she said. "Actually, it's quite nice."

"Nice?" I looked around me at buildings rats would turn their noses at. "Are you sure we're talking about the same neighbourhood?"

"Oh, you mean this?" She flicked a finger at a burned-out store-front whose fire escape looked about three seconds from crashing to the ground. "This stuff's for show."

"Uh, excuse me?"

"Yeah, we discovered that Humans hate to *look* at filth, as much as they like to *make* it, and we realised that if we put up a big enough wall around the Chomés, the average Human would tend to stay away from it, secure in the knowledge that we really are the bunch of "filthy little animals" that they've been told we are, and leave us alone."

"Um." I thought about that for a second. "Does it work?"

"Oh, yes, no Human ever comes into the Chomé uninvited."

I looked at her. "Ever?"

"Well," she said, "every now and then some Human teenagers come cruising through here, looking for trouble. Lately," she began shifting the bags she was carrying, "we've been giving them a little something for their efforts." She waved with the free hand, and out of nowhere appeared a rather nasty-looking group of Therianthropes on a stairway just ahead of us. In the slowly pulsing actinic glare of the block's only working streetlamp, I could see that their jackets bore the insignia of the Rockin' Bones, the latest tabloid horror story to come out of the Chomés'.

They were described as despicable beings; thrill-killers who'd just as soon vivisect a Human as mash one to a bloody pulp, and likely as not eat what was left, alive or no. Chapters of them were said to be spreading from Chomé to Chomé like an epidemic. Faced with the local branch, my mind froze, and left my body staring blankly in their direction. I received distinctly feral gazes in return.

"Evenin', fellas." The female waved at them again. "Evenin', Ms Takkoto", the go-gang said in unison. "So you've caught y'self one then, eh?" I didn't see which one of them had the British accent. "Nice jacket, bomber boy," said another.

"Not yet." She was grinning rather sheepishly. "This one's only on a day pass."

"That'll change by mornin'," another one said, and they vanished, chucking, into the shadows again.

I looked at her. "Well," I said, "that was interesting."

"That was the local constabulary." She continued walking.

"What police protection is so bad you have to hire the Theri version of the Hell's Angels for security?"

"No, police protection is so bad we have to disguise our security as a vicious go-gang to scare off the bad guys when ugly scenery isn't enough."

I stopped, stunned. "Oh," I said. She turned a corner, and I hurried to catch up.

🌸 ∞ 🌸

Her apartment was incredible. I was sure I'd seen it or something like it in an issue of *Architectural Digest*. A gigantic multi-pane window looked out over the Chomé, stretching up to and around an overhanging balcony which, I surmised, was the bedroom. A large bookcase lined the opposite wall immediately next to the door, and farther down was a large entertainment system that faced a low-slung table and several mounds of large pillows which sat on a raised, thickly carpeted area that stretched along the far wall. The wall itself held a series of brightly coloured Japanese wall hangings and framed posters of musical groups, some I recognised, some I didn't. In the middle of the floor were a Japanese parasol and a huge vase containing several *gigantic* (I mean, easily as tall as me) scarlet and gold gladioli. Overall, the place was impressive. I said so.

"Huh? Oh, all the units in this building look like this." She was trying to simultaneously set her packages on the kitchen counter and kick her shoes under the spiral staircase leading upstairs.

"Hmph!" I said. "You'd never know it from the outside. I suppose, though, that that's precisely the point."

"Precisely," she said. "Have a seat; I'll be right there." She disappeared into the darkened kitchen beneath the overhang.

I made my way across the large floor area, pausing briefly to notice a Calder mobile reproduction hanging from the ceiling rafters. I noticed also that the small import/export company my brothers and I bought into had gotten rich selling Theris the halogen daylight-simulation lamps which lit the apartment. I allowed myself a moment of hubris; selling them had been my idea. Admittedly, I had been thinking of photography studios, but Theris began buying them in such large numbers that we quickly rethought our market strategy. Heh. Goodbye shipping department, hello newly-purchased boardroom.

"I'm having some apple juice," she called out from the kitchen. "Care for any?"

"Yes, thank you." I had reached the window and was looking out over the suprisingly well-forested Chomé. During the walk to her apartment I'd remarked that I didn't know that that much trees and grass still existed in the city.

"It didn't," she said. "Over time, we rescaped the entire Chomé to suit our aesthetics. 'You can take the animal out of the forest, but you can't take the forest out of the animal'." She chuckled softly to herself.

"I think you're being uncharitable," I said.

She cocked her eyebrow at me again. "Am I? Look over here." We were passing an arcade, row upon row of pinball and pachinko machines. "What do you notice?"

I looked. "No video games."

"Right in one." She continued walking. "And do you know why?"

"Uh... no."

"Well, I'll tell you: because we can't see them. Oh, we can *see* the *game* alright," she hurriedly added to cut off my protest, "Our eyes tell us that there's a video game in front of us, and our imaginations tell us that there's an armed terrorist or alien armada or whatever gunning for us, but our *instincts* tell us that we're just standing in front of a box of flashing lights and that *nothing's happening*. No thrill at all."

"Oh," I said. "Wow."

"In pinball," she continued, "the ball moves in RealSpace, and we can sense it. Our instincts tell us 'There's *prey* in there! Go get it!' Pure adrenaline."

"Fascinating," I said.

"Despite all our pretenses, we Therianthropes are still very much the animals we were bred from."

She emerged from the depths of her kitchen just then, carrying two large glasses. She seemed to suddenly remember something, and she set the glasses down on the counter and began unzipping her dress at the back. "You'll forgive me if I offend, but we're in *my* territory now, and Human nudity taboos just don't flush here. Dig?" In one fluid motion, she undid her bra clasp, and with practised ease, tossed it over her head onto the balcony above.

"I'm diggin'," I said, looking politely away to sit down on a pile of pillows as she reached under her skirt. A moment later, she strode over to me and I realised quite suddenly how Paul Gauguin must have felt, the first time an Island woman walked up to him, fruit in hand... I cracked an involuntary smile at the thought.

"What?" She handed me my glass with a quizzical half-smile.

"I was, uh... thinking of the 'fashion show'."

"Ah, yes." After the incident with the Rockin' Bones, we'd turned onto a broad, tree-lined avenue (invisible from every angle outside the Chomé), full of shops and jammed with people, mainly Theris, of course, although a number of Humans were present. I remarked on this, and she told me "Not every Human finds us so disagreeable to live with. Did you notice that the College of Art sits right on the border of the Chomé? They come over here when they want a really good party. Some of them even live here."

"Wait a minute." I looked at her. "I thought you said no Human gets in here unchaperoned."

"Okay, so I take it back. We like the underground/ counterculture types 'cos they tend to be open to new experiences, and they're generally fun to be around, so we let them come and go more-or-less freely. Then there are the Theriophiles."

"The whats?"

"Theriophiles. Humans who find us and our lifestyle attractive."

"Mm," I said.

She stopped to look at a shoe display. "They're really quite nice people generally, and seem to really be more at home with our lifestyle. Besides," she said, looking at me, "It's nice to be wanted by one of your creators for something besides a kiddie show once in a while."

I was bordering on astonished. "You mean, you people don't mind if Humans cruise through here looking for some kinky sex?"

"Oh, those types get bounced out of here as soon as we smell what they're up to." She began walking again. "And yes, we really *can* smell good guys and bad guys just like that," she said over her shoulder.

As I caught up to her to tell her how honoured I felt, she turned to me suddenly and said, "I bet this looks like a real fashion show to you." We were passing a café, crowded with week-end revelers dressed apparently for a night on the town. The clothing was mostly halter/thong combos and tabard-type things—after all, they were already *wearing* coats—in all manner of eyeball-smarting colour combinations and patterns. "I must admit," I said, wincing at particularly jarring combination of vermilion-on-neon-blue, "It certainly makes bold statements."

"Well," she sidestepped her way around the knots of people, "Pastel shades and subtle colour gradations are completely lost on us because we can't see them."

"Uh-huh." I was following her as closely as possible through the crowds.

"For example," she said, "What colour is my dress?"

"Uh, vivid maroon."

"To you. I see it as a pale violet-red."

We turned a corner onto a residential street. "So," I said, "These are everyday colours to a Theri."

"No colour is too loud to a Theri," she laughed.

The dress in question was draped around her hips as she sat down onto a pile of cushions opposite me. "There's an awful lot about Theris that you don't know, then," she said.

"True, but you've no idea how enlightening this evening's been so far."

"Why, thank you," she smiled, "But you've a lot to learn, yet." She began twisting her neck. "Pardon me while I stretch; I had a terrible day at work. My boss is a Chimp, and he never misses an opportunity to remind me that he's a Primate, and I'm not. You know, Humans really messed things up for the rest of us when they Therianthropised Primates."

"That bad, huh?"

She sighed. "Oh, you just don't know. They've integrated themselves into Human society much better then we were able to."

"How do you mean?"

"Well, take my boss, for example. I've only been there two weeks, and so far he's managed every day to remind me that, while I had to practically have a degree in data retrieval and integration just to be a shipping clerk, he was hired just because somebody in upper management wanted a Theri Primate in that position, and he walked in off the street."

Uh-oh, I thought, remembering a particularly nasty v.p. who decided he was going to teach a certain shipping clerk a "lesson." "Where, uh, where exactly do you work, if you don't mind my being nosy?"

She picked up a remote control unit and aimed it at the ceiling. "I work for the company that imports these lights." She pushed a button, and the gladioli seemed to get brighter.

Too much. "I used to work down there."

Her eyes lit up. "Oh, really?"

"Yeah, I'm—uh, I work on the fifth floor, now. We should get together and have lunch, sometime."

"I'd like that ," she said.

"Me, too." I raised my glass to her, and she smiled back. She clasped her hands behind her back and pulled. Dull popping noises issued from her lower back, and as she began twisting about, I was amazed at how flexible her spine was. A series of low, soft growls, obviously pleasure-induced, came from her, and she seemed to forget all about me as she worked the day's stress out of her body.

I watched, rapt, in the same way a person would watch a pet gone glassy-eyed playing with a chew toy, and I realised that this female, with her easy, unconscious grace, was causing me to seriously rethink my conceptions of reality, let alone beauty. She *was* beautiful, I decided finally, beautiful in a way my mind could find no human comparison for. She came from a world I had no knowledge of, using senses I would never have, in a society I could not fathom. We'd *created* Theris, and yet we knew *nothing* about them. Our ignorance had hurt them terribly, I'd heard. I felt the beginnings of an idea forming at the edge of my consciousness, and drew back from it with a sigh. I don't think so, I thought. Not yet.

She had worked her way up the spine and was stretching her neck when a sharp rap at the door snapped her out of her reverie. She whipped her head around, with a look of consternation. "Who in the..." She sighed, and went to answer.

At the door was a naked, rather damp and disheveled-looking female rabbit Theri carrying an armload of towels. "Oh, Ibis," she said breathlessly, "I was filthy when I got home from work and I *had* to take a shower and Giancarlo is on patrol could you please groom me?"

"Sure" said Ibis. "come on in."

As she stepped into the apartment, she saw me, and gave a start. "Oh!" she gasped. "I didn't—uh, I—I can come back later—"

"Nonono, this gentleman would like to learn more about Theri culture." Ibis said smoothly, laying a hand on the diminutive rabbit's shoulder. "Looks like tonight he's going to learn about grooming." She looked at me pointedly, and I took the hint.

"Hi" I said, walking over to them. "I'm Dimitri. Ibis and I work in the same building."

"Haruko." She extended a small, damp, furry hand. "Pleased to meet you." I shook it and Ibis led Haruko up the spiral staircase.

"C'mon, you," she said, motioning for me to follow, "This is important. This is one of the things we do best."

By the time I'd reached the top of the stairs, Ibis had pulled the sheets off of an enormous futon, and she and Haruko were laying Haruko's towels on it. Ibis opened a drawer on a little nightstand, and pulled out a set of black-and-red laquer curry combs. She handed one to me as Haruko lay down.

"Uh..." I felt myself blushing as I looked at Ibis. Haruko began giggling.

"Oh. Right. Well," she said to me, "You can do her arms and legs, and I'll do the, uh, 'naughty bits'."

Haruko broke into a fresh fit of giggling at this, and we knelt down on the futon and began. Ibis showed me the most comfortable strokes to make, and how to clean the curry comb periodically (Theris have a *lot* of fur, I discovered). I just relaxed and did as I was told, concentrating on gentle but firm strokes, making it as much massage as grooming. When we had finished, I was suprised to find the chronograph on Ibis' nightstand saying that over an hour had passed, and that our subject, having turned over during our ministrations, was now fast asleep.

I blinked at Ibis. "Wha'happen?"

She nodded towards the staircase. "Let's go downstairs," she said. "She'll wake up eventually."

We went back to the cushions and sat down. Ibis gave me a half-expectant look. "Well," she said, "Did you get it?"

"Get what?"

"How do you feel?"

"I feel... odd... rested, like... like I just had a good night's sleep. Rejuvenated... uh—"

"Centered?"

"Yeah, centered! Like I've been meditating."

"You were," she said.

"Huh?"

"Grooming is an active meditation. It lowers the blood pressure, strengthens the breathing, synchronises the brain hemispheres, all that good stuff.

"All that from grooming?"

"It's not just the grooming," she said. "It's the touch that's important. The grooming is lagniappe. It's the empathy. Do you notice how slow your heart is beating?"

"Yeah."

"Well, that's 'cos by the time we finished, your heartbeat was synchronised with Haruko's."

"Oh yeah? Hmmm." I thought about it. "I like it."

"Well," she said, "that's what we do best."

I looked at her blankly, not understanding.

"We make Humans feel good. But," she added, watching the comprehension dawn on my face, "You have to touch us." She looked away. "And lately you haven't really wanted to touch us much."

"Whew," I breathed, running a hand through my hair. "I—I don't know what to say. I'm sorry."

She gave a hollow chuckle and looked at her hands. "Not as sorry as we are. We gave our hearts and souls to the Japanese because we thought they wanted us."

"Oh, yeah," I said, remembering the flood of low-budget Theri sci-fi and comedy flicks from Japan that ended just before my time. "I remember."

She clasped her hands around drawn-up knees, and rested her head in the cleft. "We thought they loved us."

"Wow."

"When we found out we were just another fad to them, we were crushed. After all of our efforts—that's why so many Theris have Japanese names—to just get turned out like that." She sighed. "They broke our hearts."

I sat, speechless. What could I say?

"So we started to come back here, to North America and Europe, and we discovered you wanted us even less than the Japanese. Not that you didn't have enough Theris already.

"You put us in your worst slums, and so we rebuilt them our way, into the Chomés. You put us out of your hearts, and since we can't rebuild those, we—some of us—decided to rebuild ourselves. Your way."

I thought about that, and didn't like the conclusion I was reaching. "Wha—what do you mean?" I asked, thinking I knew the answer, and praying I was wrong.

"My parents—and quite a few others—did most of the work before I was born. They figured that, maybe Humans would want us more, if we looked more like the pets they grew up with."

A horror I couldn't find a name for was slowly clambering up the back of my neck, and I stared at her, aghast. "Are you saying," I started, my voice hardly above a whisper, "That you're—you've been—"

"My children—should I choose to have any," she added with a grim smirk, "will be among the first Husky and Malamute *Therianthropicus familiarii*."

"That—that's terrible—"

She looked at me, and the hurt in her eyes was the hurt of every Therianthrope in every Chomé, everywhere. "It's a terrible thing," she said, "To live with the knowledge that your Creators no longer love you."

I felt very, very ashamed. These were, in no small sense, our children, and they had suffered worse damage than any physical atrocities we could care to think of. We had given them souls, and then flayed those souls alive by depriving them of the one thing they wanted more than anything else: to be wanted by us.

"It's all we ever wanted," Ibis said, as if reading my mind, "To be loved by Humans. Whether consciously or unconsciously, you programmed it into our genes, hardwired it into our systems, this overwhelming desire to be wanted by Humans. We can't fight it, and we don't know what else to do..."

Frankenstein redux, I thought. Having created life, we failed utterly to understand that what that life wanted was justification in the eyes of its creators. In search of it, Theris had thrown themselves into entertainment, becoming walking, breathing cartoon characters, living out the frilliest, flashiest excesses of our pop culture for our enjoyment and approval. For a while, they got it. For a while, we loved them. But then, after the glamour wore off, instead of accepting them as friends and co-workers fresh off a hard day's work, we wanted to throw them away, as we would any no-longer-fashionable vestige of our pop culture. I had fancied myself sympathetic to the Theris' plight, from the safe distance of *Mother Jones* and *Atlantic Monthly*. Ibis' words were a cattle prod in my mind's eye.

Theris had become desperate; the lengths of exploitation they were willing to endure for a little of our appreciation was unseemly enough, and the stories of certain "parlours" coming out of Rome and Rio were so bizarre they could only be true. Now, Theris had decided to try and regain the affection they'd lost by making themselves into our pets. The shame of it. I understood then the role the Rockin' Bones played, jaws for Therianthrope society to snap at Humans with, when we came 'round to kick at them some more, while they cowered in the corners of our cities, licking the horrible wounds we'd inflicted on their collective spirit, and desperately trying to figure out what *they'd* done wrong. I didn't feel self-serving pity for them, or self-righteous anger at Humans. I just felt shame. Shame for all of us.

I must've looked like I was gonna cry or something (I certainly felt like it), because Ibis suddenly sat up and said, "Theris have another type of massage we do that I wanna show you. It's called 'Zogemiuchi Shimasu.' " I blinked at this sudden change of mood and topic, and tried to roll with it. "Uh, ivory... something. Sounds like "whisper..." 'Whispering Ivory'?"

"Very good," she said. "Now, you don't have enough hair on your body to do this properly, but I can manage on just your scalp, if you're interested."

I shrugged. "Let 'er rip." She moved behind me, and began massaging the back of my neck. Then she stuck her muzzle into my hair and began—I can't really think of any other way to describe it—began biting my scalp. That isn't really what she was doing, but like I said, I can't really think of any other way to describe it.

She began to move around to my side, and before I knew it, I had a hundred or so pounds of shapely, half-naked female sitting in my lap. Beneath the light, dusty odour of what was almost certainly flea powder (I figured it was probably impolite to ask), her scent was of decaying leaves and sugar; pungent but not unpleasant, I decided. I noticed also that the timbre of what she was doing to my scalp had changed rather suggestively, and I reached up to push her away, unintentionally touching as I did so the small, black tops of one of the three extra pairs of mostly hidden breasts below the larger, Human-enhanced pair. She gave a little *growl!*, whether of surprise or pleasure I don't know, and looked at me.

"Hey," I said, "You're kissing me."

"Sorry." Her eyes shone with a strange inner light. "I got carried away."

The idea that had been lurking around the edge of my conciousness took a flying leap at me suddenly. I saluted it, and gratefully surrendered.

"Ibis—" I began, but suddenly she drew back from me with a gasp.

"Oranges and moss!"

"What!?"

"Oranges and moss. Your scent. I *thought* I recognised you in the cab; you left a half-dozen t-shirts in the closet in my office."

"What? Ohhh, that. But I—I haven't been down there in almost four years! You mean, scents can last for that long?"

"Sure they can," She looked at me with a smirk playing across her face. "Especially when things don't get washed!" Then she got serious again, forestalling my own laughter. "But if that's your scent, then that means that you're one of—you're—"

"Dimitri Ialoniki, right. The guy who had the idea to sell those lights up there that Theris love so much. They made me a v.p. for that but that was almost four years ago, and I haven't talked to Gregor since, 'cos I can't stand him, either; he's a lousy boss. So, before you even ask it, no, he did not send me to 'spy' on you." I had noticed from the cant of her ears that she had probably become suspicious, and patted myself on the back for doing so. "Besides, I think if I was, you would've smelled me out by now."

She relaxed a little at this. "I suppose you're right, at that."

I smiled at her. "I really was just helping a lady in distress."

" 'Lady'? Not 'Theri female'?" She was looking at me, hard, searching my eyes. I laid myself open to her gaze, hoping I had the courage of my newly-hatched convictions.

"Not know Human, Theri. Only know lovely lady."

She settled back into my lap, and arms, and kissed me, a singular experience if you've ever been kissed by someone with a muzzle. Not that I was resisting, mind you.

When we stopped, she said softly, "I guess you're learning more than you expected."

"I learned one thing," I said. "I learned I think I—"

She stood up suddenly. "Oh, but you can't stay here; you can't even be seen here! That would be bad, bad for both of us!"

"What? How?"

She arched that eyebrow of hers again. "You're Human and I'm a Theri. I'm female and you just *happen* to be a v.p. at the company I've only been at for two weeks. At *best*, I'd look like a social climber, and you'd look like a craven opportunist."

"Oh." I was beginning to get the picture.

"And if Gregor ever found out—"

"Don't worry about Gregor. I'll make sure he lays off you from now on."

She knelt back down. "That's even worse! If Gregor thought for a *minute* that someone in upper management was gettin' their ear bent by "That Shaggy Bitch" as he calls me—his hearing is almost as bad as a Human's—if he ever thought that, then I'd *really* be in for a rough ride. And if he even had an *inkling* that it was you—"

"Yeah, I get your point. So, Gregor told you all about me, eh?"

"Oh, yeah. If you only knew what he thinks of *you*..." She grinned wickedly.

"Yeah, well, I suppose you can tell me all about it over lunch—uh, we *can* still do lunch sometime, right?"

"Certainly." That strange look was in her eyes again. "I'll be looking forward to it."

"Yeah, me too." I started to get up. "Well, I'd better scratch gravel—"

"Oh! Wait!" She pushed me back down. "I have something else I want to give you." She climbed back into my lap, and reached behind her back with one hand. Then she took her thumb and smeared something faintly funky-smelling behind my left ear.

"No no, don't touch it." she said quickly, blocking my hand as I reached up to it, "Not until you're outside the Chomé."

I frowned at her. "What is it?"

"Consider it—" She thought a moment, there in my lap, in my arms. Then she hugged me tightly, and said, "Consider it another, very important lesson about life in the Chomé, my own True Friend."

"Your what?"

She said nothing, but just sat there, holding me close. I could feel her heartbeat. It was the same as mine.

✻ ⊙ ✻

"Hey, it's bomber boy."

I was somewhere in the "nowhere zone" between the Theri and Human parts of the city, heading for the College of Art, 'cos I knew I could wave down one of the cabs that constantly cruised the place for late-working young suburban artsy-fartsies. The local constabulary astonished me a second time with their ability to seemingly materialise out of thin air, and were in a semicircle facing me. There seemed to be more of them this time, the ones I could remember from earlier in the evening being joined by three or four reinforcements. One of them was a gigantic Theri tiger, seven feet tall if he was an inch and built like a striped De Soto, standing directly in front of me. The street was open to my right. They were daring me to try and make a break for it, I realised. I was feeling good. I stood my ground. "Wossop?" I said, Mr. Congeniality Himself.

"Did'ja have fun slummin', bomber boy?"

"I don't think you was there long enough, bomber boy."

"Yeah, wassamatter, bomber boy, you get tired?" One of them, another canine hybrid of some sort, was openly leering at me.

"Or did you get bored?" The atmosphere got a little less convivial at this, and they took a step closer.

"Listen," I said, scratching an eyebrow and trying to appear unconcerned about the prospect of a certain and severe mauling, "We didn't do nothin'."

"Say what?" The tiger was looking almost straight down at me. I thought he sounded like Ernest Borgnine. "You know somethin' bomber boy? I think you're hidin' somethin'. Now, this is nothin' personal, Colonel," he said, clamping a huge hand like a steel brace on my shoulder. I could feel his claw-tips even through the thick leather of my bomber jacket. They hurt. "But it's late, and it's been a while since we made an example outa somebody, an' so it looks like you're it." He grabbed me by the lapels and lifted me up face to face with him, one handed, with all the effort of someone pressing an elevator button. "Now, I think you're hidin' somethin', an' I think these fellas are gonna help me beat it outta ya."

Behind me the other 'Bones were talking. "I get the jacket." I think that was the canine. "Heh. If there's enough of it left," came the reply.

Out of the corner of my eye I could see him bringing up another immense hand, crowned with the thick, impossibly sharp spikes that would shortly make me a poster child for the Reconstructive Surgery Association. My face was inches from his and I could look directly into his eyes. There was no hatred, or malice; just a sense of *duty* almost, as if he had to work himself up to mangling me. I stared back impassively. There was no use in screaming or struggling, it would only have spurred them on, and I didn't think I could live through that. This was a mangling I was just gonna hafta take. My actual thought was: "With luck, I might just make it to a cab before I pass out from blood loss." I had kissed my ass goodbye, 'cos this bunch was about to chomp it off.

Then, the look on his face changed, to something akin to confusion. He swung his other hand to my face, but instead of opening up my flesh, he grabbed me gently by the chin. Facing me out towards the street, he began sniffing around my ear. He gave a snort, and lowered me to the ground, saying, "Let this one go, boys; he's got a passport."

"What?" Their malice was easily overcome by their surprise. The tiger palmed my head like a basketball and held it out for the others to inspect, and they gathered around, sniffing at my ear.

"Yeh, that's wot that is awright." It was the one with the British accent again. I still didn't see who it was.

"What? Whaddya mean, I got a 'passport'? What're you talkin' about?"

The tiger let me go, frank amazement on his face. "You mean, you don't know?"

"Know what?"

It started out as series of low snickers, then chuckles, then exploded into massive peals of laughter, the tiger's big, hearty voice loudest of all.

"Friend," he said between knee-slapping guffaws, "You've been scentmarked!"

I'm sure I looked pretty stupid, with surprise, relief, and embarrassment colliding on my face like that. I laughed in spite of myself, my face scarlet.

"Well," said the tiger, his laughter subsiding with the others', "I guess we'll be seein' ya around, bomber boy."

"Yeah, I guess so. Later," I said, and we turned and parted company.

I had gone about a block down the darkened street, when a sudden impulse made me stop and turn to the left. I dropped into a fighting crouch.

The tiger was leaning in a doorway, alone. He gave a snort at my stance, and I straightened up again, feeling ridiculous. "Hey, bomber boy," he said, "What's your name, anyway?"

"Dimitri."

"Yeah, well, listen, Dimitri, next time you see Ibis, tell her Giancarlo said 'Hi'."

Heh. "You got it, daddio." A couple of blocks up were the art school, and the light of the familiar, Human-habited part of the city, a part that I had a feeling was going to become a lot less familiar in the future. I started my walk again, not looking back.

I wrote Wings mostly in my head on the way to work at an animation studio in downtown Toronto, sometime in either the summer or 1996 or the spring of 1997. What I recall was the fine weather on the long walks up University Avenue to College Street. I remember the moment I came up with the watershed scene at the very end. I was crossing Armory Street opposite the U.S. consulate, and when the scene occurred to me, I actually sobbed out loud. It was embarrassing and exhilarating all at the same time.

That was a couple of years after I got on the Internet in the fall of 1994. Almost immediately after I did, I met Jody Young. He was still a student at the time, already showing promise as a programmer. Somehow, we wound up an almost daily part of one another's lives for almost ten years, in spite of the fact that we lived in different countries with most of a continent between us.

Jody was almost certainly the first person to read Wings. He was extremely encouraging when he read it, and was the first person to give me an inkling that it might be special, something apart from the other pieces I've written.

Time passed and we both changed jobs and locations. But through it all, we stayed in touch. We shared our lives through the medium of the net, a stream of electrons connecting hearts and minds.

In May of 2002, Jody's company sent him to on a working trip to China. On the flight over, he developed a blood clot in his left leg. Even after he returned to the States, it refused to go away. His doctors became suspicious, and began running tests. In August, he was diagnosed with cancer.

Jody fought back hard and bravely, and by May of 2003, we all celebrated his recovery. His cancer was in remission. In the course of that struggle, I watched a young man who had always questioned his own worth in the world and the value of his own life to himself and others come to realize how dear his life was to himself and those around him, dozens of people, who closed ranks in displays of affection and generosity that brought him to tears—and me as well, when I heard about them.

In October of 2003, his cancer returned. Again, he fought hard. He rarely ever let me see his pain or fear. I thought he was on the road to recovering again. One Monday morning I came back from a meeting to find a set of messages on ICQ from his dad. Jody had passed away, very suddenly, at home. It was June 7th. He was 26 years old.

Last fall, when the first edition of this book came out, the publishers kindly agreed to send one of my contributor's copies to Jody. Along with it, they sent a card wishing him a Merry Christmas, and wishing him a swift recovery. I found that book, with that card inside it, beside Jody's bed when I visited Dallas in June for Jody's memorial. I never got to meet Jody face to face. But I've come to see that the connection between us was as real as any other relationship. I mattered in his life. He certainly mattered in mine.

I don't know what happens to us when we die. Who among the living really does? But it pleases me to believe that Jody still exists somewhere, and is aware of those who care for him and their circumstances. And after all, that is partly what this story is about.

And so, retroactively, this story is for Jody.

"Adore."

Todd G. Sutherland

August 2, 2004

Jody's Live Journal can be found at: (http://www.livejournal.com/users/ailuro/).

His shoes scuffed as he reached for the next marbled step; his every misstep was her heartfelt torment. She reached her toes down in advance of him, holding his arm. "Six more steps," she said softly, stepping down in front of him, bringing him gently.

"Is there a coffee shop in the waiting area? Can you see yet?" he asked.

She kept her eyes on his feet, and the expensive foreign shoes that housed and protected them. They found the next step, and she slipped her pads down to join them. "Pay attention to the stairs, please, Master," she reproached gently.

The boy sighed, features obscured by the dark glasses. She dared a glance at his face. He seemed more impatient with the situation than with her, and she felt relieved. Her tail wagged softly, for no one.

Why would they put the train platform downstairs? she wondered. Just to make it inconvenient? As if reading her mind, the boy said, "I hate this. This is such a bother. Why couldn't you just drive me, Faith?"

"We're almost there... two more steps." She concentrated on the boy, letting the stares and sudden changes in the strides of the humans around her pass over her almost unnoticed. Almost.

That the boy held onto her and not the handrail was the most delightful compliment she could imagine. "Last step, Master." The boy reached his foot down and found the ground floor. Faith led him to one side and stood him by an ancient-looking fluted column. She felt his hand take the swivel harness strapped to her hips.

"It's a large room, as you can hear," she observed. "There are eight gates, evenly spaced; odd numbered ones down the left side, even numbered ones down the right. Ours is gate three on the left. There is a gift shop at the far left, and two restaurants on the right, and yes, one of them is a coffee shop. According to the monitor, our train is on time, and will be arriving on track 3 in just over half an hour. The men's room is around the corner here on our right, and the women's room is over there on our left."

"Good, take me to the men's room."

"Yes, Master." She stepped forward, tugging the harness, and he followed.

The men's room was large, mostly bank upon bank of urinals. There were one or two men in there. The reek of urine, faintly exciting, spun biographies out at her like bees attacking a hungry bear. Scents of health, disease, feast and famine, illicit relations... They all rushed to sing their choruses in her nose. She trotted the boy over to do his business, feeling the dampness of less careful visitors under her feet, and stepped back.

One of the men down the aisle a bit looked up at her as if she'd come in toting a machine gun. She heard the trickle of his urine dry up like a riverbed in Death Valley. She tried not to look at him. Or anyone.

"I'm done," the boy called to her. She padded back over and guided his hand to her harness, and then showed him to the wash basins. She could feel the eyes on her back.

The boy sighed, letting her bring his hands to the soap dispenser and doing the rest. "Faith, why didn't you just drive me?"

"Now, Master, you know I'm not allowed to drive on the big highways. Just in the city. Between the fingers, please. Do a good job, now."

"Why don't you just lick him clean?"

It was muttered. The boy would never have heard it, but she did. Her mind raced with clever replies, but it was not her place to make them. Her place was to look after the boy, and picking a fight with a rude man in a washroom was hardly the way to go about it. She swallowed the insult, one of hundreds, perhaps thousands, and helped the child dry his hands.

Faith caught sight of herself in the mirror. Saw the men behind her, eyeing her. What a balancing act the creation of her race had been for its designers. Human enough to get by day to day, but different enough that her opinions and feelings could be discounted; she was "other." Still, some of the design must have been pure whim. But then, she decided, by its very nature, playing God was to be capricious. She had a long, flowing mane like hair, and breasts like a human woman, but there were eight of them, four pairs down the front of her in diminishing size; all modestly concealed in fur. She had an hourglass shape and a smooth, curvy backside, but a tail was rooted to it. Her eyes were soft and alluring, set over a snout that was long enough to be dangerous, but short enough not to be ugly. The entire effect was to make her approachably human, but sufficiently different that she would not complicate things. She knew the men were eyeing her with a certain casual interest, but then dismissing their notions as deviant. At least, most of them were.

"Do we have time to go the coffee shop?" he asked her.

"Yes, Master, I think if we're quick. No more than fifteen minutes, though." She watched the boy smile, and she led him into the small cafe.

The sign said, rather ridiculously, "Please wait to be seated", and so Faith waited. The woman at the cash looked up at her. People like Faith—if one considered them people at all—were still very rare. A person might, on average, see one or two in the space of a year, even in a city this size. She came over, eyeing Faith, eyeing the child, obviously in a quandary about whom she was supposed to address. Finally she asked the air between them, "Just two?"

"Just two," Faith replied. The woman nodded to her, unable to take her eyes off her, and led them to a tight booth. Faith helped the boy squeeze into the seat, and then, folding the harness to allow herself to sit, she sat opposite him. The waitress came back with two menus, and suddenly realizing the boy was blind, she prepared to hand them to Faith. Then another problem struck her and she clapped them to her own breast.

"Can you, uh... I mean," she stammered at Faith.

"Yes, ma'am, I can read," Faith replied patiently, and took the menu the woman offered. The waitress stepped away, and Faith opened the menu. "What do you feel like today, hmmm?" she asked him. "It'll have to be something quick. A donut, maybe?"

"Nah," he said. "I'm hungry. I feel better today."

Faith wagged her tail, though he could not see it. "Well, how about a piece of chocolate pie? You know how you love that."

"Yeah, do they have it here?"

"Says so," she replied.

"Okay, I'll have that. And a milkshake. Strawberry."

She smiled. "Oh, you must feel better today. Good. We'll make sure you get something a little bit bad for you." She turned her warm brown eyes to the waitress, who, still staring, caught her gaze at once and hurried over, digging her order pad from her hip pocket.

"My Master would like a slice of chocolate pie, and a strawberry milkshake, please," Faith ordered.

The waitress nodded. "Anything for yourself?"

"I'm fine, thank you, ma'am," Faith said, handing the menu back.

"Aw, come on, Faith," the boy prodded. "Don't make me eat alone. That would be rude."

"Very well, Master," she smiled. "I'll have a honey dipped donut, please, ma'am, and some tea."

"Coming right up," the waitress said.

The boy waited until the waitress was out of earshot. "Can I ask you something?" he said.

"Of course, Master."

"In school the other day, when you left me to use the bathroom, Victor said you don't have a soul. Is that true?"

Faith studied his face, puzzled by the question. She twitched her ear, and said, "Well, I don't know, really. I don't know for sure that anyone has a soul. I hope I do..."

"Because if you don't have a soul, Victor says you can't be with me in Heaven. When I die."

Faith squirmed a bit. She leaned forward, placing her paw on the boy's hand. "Donny," she whined, softly, "please don't talk like that."

"I would just be stumbling around Heaven, tripping over clouds." Donny smiled, his voice sparkling with a child's laugh, even speaking of death.

"You wouldn't need me in Heaven," she said softly. "You'll be able to see, perfectly. And you won't hurt inside anymore. But..." She squeezed his hand in hers. "But that won't be for a really long time."

He smiled at her, as if he could see her face.

She smiled back. "Besides," she said. "In Heaven you get wings, so you don't have to worry about tripping over things."

Donny nodded. The waitress brought their order, and Faith watched him eat, her heart brimming with joy. It had been such a long time since he had had an appetite. He raised his head, the chocolate ringing his little mouth, and she brushed his lips with the back of her paw.

The boy was dying. He knew it, and she knew it. But it was only in the last little while that he had begun to speak of it. It turned her blood to ice water. In daylight, with the pink in his cheeks, she could fight it down. But at night, in the cot at the foot of his bed, she would hear him; the rasping breaths, the stirrings, and she would go to him, and soothe him. And it was getting worse.

And so they were making this trip.

His fork clinked on the empty plate. When he realized he had had the last bite, Donny put his fork down. Faith took a napkin and wiped his mouth. In response, he pressed his hand into her face, gently studying her familiar features. In spite of herself, she licked his hand, and held it to her cheek.

"I bet you'll look pretty in Heaven," he told her. "I can't wait to see you. Especially with wings."

"Donny, please, please," she begged him.

The boy nodded, old enough to understand her pain. "I'm sorry," he said. "I'll stop."

"You'll be okay," she reassured him. "The doctors at St. Francis are the best. You remember how they helped you last time. Soon, you won't have any more pain. I promise you." She realized the double meaning of what she had just said, and it chilled her to the bones. She wondered if it were lost on him. She hoped so. She clarified, more for herself than him, "They'll make you well and you'll grow up strong. Who knows... if they change the law back, maybe they can even grow you some new eyes. Then you won't need me anymore." She wagged, stung by the idea, but knowing it would be selfish to deny him that miracle.

"I'll always need you, Faith," he told her. "Always."

"And I'll be here as long as you do," she said.

Faith helped the boy up and retrieved the debit card from the little pouch on her hip. She paid the bill, and led Donny out into the main concourse. "We'll get in line, okay? Do you mind standing for a bit? Is it okay, Master?"

"Sure, I'm okay."

Faith padded across the smooth, cool marble floor; her ankles angled by science such that they never quite reached the ground, making her steps springy and giving her the appearance of someone wearing invisible high heels. Behind her the boy trailed boldly, fully confident of his steps in her care. His gait gave her pride.

As they moved past one of the huge pillars that held the roof of the station, Faith caught sight of a man, standing there. He was elderly, dressed neatly in an old black suit; both he and it looked European. Beside him stood a young woman, equally elegant; from her scent, she was a relative of his. Probably his daughter, Faith decided. She stood behind a large keyboard, and there was an open case on the floor in front of them. The old man smiled at her as they passed, tipping his fedora to her, as if she were a regular person, as if he saw people like her every day. Letting her professionalism lapse for a moment, an unforgivable moment, she turned her head, meeting his eye, and she wagged her tail at him, softly.

"Bella cane," the man said softly. "Per te." He spread his hands as she passed, closing his eyes, and the young woman beside him began to play the keyboard. A soft, lovely melody, at once sad and inspiring, poured from her fingertips and into the air like mulled wine.

The man opened his throat, and for a moment, nothing came. Slowly, the note rose, and Faith, eyes forward, craned her ears back to listen as she led Donny past. "Ave Maria," the man sang, a warm, rich tenor filling the air like an empty bowl.

"What's that?" the boy asked her.

"Performers, Master."

"No, I mean, that song. It's pretty. I like it.'

"Oh," Faith said, settling Donny into line. "It's called Ave Maria."

"Awvay...?"

"Ave Maria. It's Latin. It means 'Hail Mary', I think."

"Oh. Mary who?"

"Jesus's mother."

"Ohhhh, okay." He shuffled, and she turned her attention back to the music for a moment. "Why hail?"

"Why—? Oh. Well, some people pray to her. It's kind of like a prayer, this song."

"How does the rest go?"

"I'm sorry, Master, I don't know." Faith searched her memory hard for the boy. Fetching. "Hail Mary, full of... full of grace... The Lord... The Lord is... I'm sorry, Master, it's all I remember."

The boy nodded. Together, they listened to the song. As it ended, the sound of train bells marched down the stairs to them. "Do you pray, Faith?" he asked.

"That's our train," she told him.

Donny nodded. "I'm scared," he told her.

"I know," she said. "But don't be. I'm with you." She led him along the shuffling line, up the stairs to the platform. Impatient people behind them wisely held their tongues.

"Why couldn't Mom or Dad be with us?" he sighed.

"Your parents are busy people. You know that, Master. But they will be there. In a couple of days, they'll be joining us at St. Francis." She took a comb from the little package on her hip and smoothed it through his hair.

"Why don't they love me, Faith?" His voice was quiet. It was an adult question no adult would ever ask.

"They do love you!" she told him, hating herself for lying to him. The boy's mother was perhaps forgivable after a fashion; she loved none of her children, or anyone but herself; given over almost entirely to her social life and obligations. But Donald's father was a man full of love. Conditional love. And at some point, the bottom line had dictated the boy would die, and was not worth the emotional investment. He was quiet and friendly with Donald, but that was all. His excuse for not being physically demonstrative with the boy was that Donny was 'fragile'; which was certainly true, but not to that extent. It seemed to Faith that, if and when she littered, the child who was weakest would win her fiercest love. The others would need it less. That the boy's father could deny this child of all his children his love was utterly foreign to her, and though she disguised it completely behind a mask of goodwill, she despised the man. "They do love you," she said again, and, daringly, she kissed his forehead.

The boy nodded.

"Salia doesn't like me," he said.

"Salia," Faith grinned, "is just jealous because you get more attention and you have a SMART to help you cheat on your math tests."

The boy chuckled for her, and Faith's heart melted. "Mrs. Rathburn is getting wise to your tail trick," he said. "She's going to chuck you out if you keep it up."

"Just let her try," Faith said, and she gave a playful low growl. She smiled. "Salia is just a little girl, and she doesn't understand yet. In a couple of years she will. And Ray, Ray loves you more than anyone in the world," she said.

"Not as much as you do," he replied.

No. No, child, no one loves you as much as I do. "Sure he does. He's your brother."

His hand moved up and down her back, fingers scritching into her pelt. Her thin lips parted and she panted softly, her eyes narrow.

Somewhere behind her, Faith heard a woman whisper, "Don't point, Rhoda, it's not polite. She's a special big doggy who's there to help out that little blind boy. But you'll hurt her feelings if you point."

Faith curled into herself for a moment.

A conductor stepped off the train onto the platform. "Tickets, please... tickets..." He moved down the line, occasionally glancing at Faith as he scanned the stubs for authenticity. He came up to Faith and tipped his cap. "Tickets, please."

Faith produced the ticket. A single ticket. The boy's ticket. The conductor scanned it. "Just the two of you?"

"Yes, sir," Faith replied.

"Are you this child's guardian or proxy on this journey?"

"Yes, sir, I am."

The conductor took another scanner from his belt. He eyed the ident tag on her collar. "Sorry, miss, just a formality."

Faith nodded, raising her chin. The man brought the scanner near it and recorded the information. "Thank you, miss," he said. "Have a nice day."

"Thank you, sir."

The conductor moved down the line. "Tickets, please, tickets..."

"Can we get on now?" Donny said.

"Yes." She led him to the step. It would have been awkward for him, so she begged his leave and picked him up under the arms and put him on the train herself. It tore at her heart how light he was, even now. She led Donny down the aisle and found what she considered an appropriate berth, and they took it. She sat Donny by the window and herself between him and the door. After a moment, the train jerked, and began to move.

"Here we go," Faith smiled.

Then the train stopped. Faith glanced around. After a moment, it began to move again. She shrugged to herself. At almost that moment, a man pounded past their compartment, glancing in as he passed. Faith heard him stop, and then come back. He opened the door and came in, disheveled; sweating and panting, he stank of gin. He threw himself down on the opposite couch. Faith felt Donny press a bit closer to her, and smelled his apprehension. She wanted to throw the man from the compartment, but there was nothing she could do.

"Close call!" the man moaned. "Almost didn't make it." He threw a newspaper on the seat beside him, and it spilled itself out, partly onto the floor.

Faith stared forward.

Still panting, the man's eye roamed her form. "Slavery," he said. "Nothing but bloody slavery."

Faith squirmed.

"There'll come a day," the man said, wagging his finger, and then belching. "There'll come a day when people will rise up. You shouldn't take it, you know," he told her. "Just because you look different, is no reason they should treat you like an animal."

Faith said, nervously, "Please, sir. Don't talk that way. You could be arrested."

"Nobody's bloody free these days. Nobody. Not even us." He was thundering now, probably loud enough to be heard outside.

Donny said, "You're not supposed to talk to my SMART! You're not supposed to—" He began to cough. "—not supposed to—distract..." His voice left him, and he went into a coughing fit. Faith curled her arms around him.

"Calm down, calm down, Master!"

"Hey, is the little fellow going to be o—"

Faith turned, snarling. "Don't upset him! Can't you see he's sick? Get out! Get out now or I'll report you!"

The man blinked, taken aback. He raised his hands. "Alright, alright, I'll go, I'll go!" He rose, nearly falling back, and headed for the door. "God's teeth; try to help some bloody people..." He was gone.

Faith calmed Donny, rocking him in her arms, but it was clear it had taken something out of him. In just a few moments, he was asleep, his head against her shoulder. She eyed the man's newspaper covetously, but dared not move and disturb Donny. When the boy finally shifted, lying against the wall of the train, Faith leaned forward, retrieving a color insert magazine from the newspaper.

The magazine was called *Utilities*, and the cover blazed: "The New SMARTS: Conversations with Dr. Terrence Ludlow and Cardinal Ying."

Faith blinked. Probably, she shouldn't be caught reading this, but she turned the pages, softly. The article began:

> **GENEVA (UPS): In the Twentieth Century, the Third World War was always conceived of as a nuclear holocaust that would rain sudden death from the sky, incinerating cities, nations, and the very supports of civilization itself. When World War III finally came, the result was somewhat milder, if more insidious. The bombs never fell, but the viruses that roamed the planet over the next generation consumed a sixth of the human race and set civilization back generations in terms of development. Only now is it generally agreed that humanity has recovered to the point it had reached before the war.**
>
> **Perhaps not surprisingly, the survivors of the war, recoiling in horror at the misery and devastation that made them all too eager to turn their backs on recombinant DNA technologies, internationally outlawed many otherwise promising biotechnologies. But there is today a sentiment afoot that may reverse these statutes. How many more people, an increasing chorus of voices ask, must die of heart failure and liver cancer, or be crippled or deformed because simple cloning techniques mas-**

tered nearly a century ago sit on the shelves, collecting dust in a total ban because of mistakes made a half century ago by madmen? Surely by now we've learned the lesson, say these voices, and have the wisdom to pick and chose what are good biological technologies, and what aren't.

Other voices say that we have learned nothing, if we haven't learned to leave well enough alone. These voices harken back to a safer age, when the lines between species were absolute, when viruses that affected one species rarely crossed over lethally to infect another, and when the question of what is and is not human was thought to have been settled.

One of these voices, a voice in favor of re-initiating the advancement of biotechnologies, is Dr. Terrence Ludlow of Johns Hopkins University. I recently had a chance to speak to him here in Geneva, where the World Health Organization is preparing its recommendations to the United Nations General Assembly on this issue, due for re-examination as the fiftieth anniversary of the ban approaches.

Faith scanned down the article and the interview with Dr. Ludlow... Initially, he spoke of cloning technologies, the sort that would generate new organs for dying people, made of their own cells, with the necessary genetic corrections made (if any), letting millions of people live longer, more productive lives. She reached over and stroked Donald softly, and turned back to her reading.

Quickly, though, the real point of Ludlow's position came into sight.

TL: People have to put the whole question in perspective. Yes, of course, biological warfare is a terrible thing! So is armed robbery, but we don't ban money. What we need is a sensible, balanced course. Certain areas of investigation should remain closed off, but others should be re-opened. I'm just saying, we've thrown the baby out with the bathwater. Let's go get the baby back.

UM: Which areas of investigation, Doctor?

TL: Let me give you a prime example. The prime example. Look at all the good that's come into the world through SMARTs [Sentient Mammalian Anthropomorphs—Restricted Technology]. Nearly eighty years ago, the first SMARTs were created, and they've been with us ever since. They were unaffected by the war, and who can argue the boon they've been to thousands of unfortunate victims? And the whole project, every single birth, has been overseen and directed by the World Health Organization, in conjunction with participating UN member states. So far, only dogs have been SMARTed, but I can see the time is quickly coming when we'll need other forms of SMARTs. And I don't believe we should be cowed from it by a war whose mistakes we have no intention of repeating.

UM:Other forms of SMARTs?

TL:We're running out of room and resources on the surface of the planet. It's only natural that we should turn to the oceans. Dolphins will be a great help, but they're willful and have only limited motility. They can't easily manipulate objects, and servo-appliances strapped onto them tend to irritate them. I believe we'll need some sort of aquatic intelligence rather more similar to ourselves if we're going to make a go of it. I'm thinking of some sort of anthropomorphic seal, myself.

UM:Doctor, there are voices in the other camp that are charging the creation of new life forms violates the sanctity and dignity of existing life and cheapens human life as it exists.

TL:Ah. You're speaking of the religious establishment. Yes, of course, it's never been in their interests for mankind to advance. If people start thinking for themselves, the collection plate tends to get lighter.

UM:That seems a rather cynical attitude, Doctor.

TL:Does it? I wonder where we'd be today if everyone thought so. Surely, Galileo, Copernicus, and Tyndale didn't listen to the Church.

Neither did Hitler, Faith thought, frowning, and she read on.

There are other voices, of course, taking the opposite tack, and chief among them is Cardinal Juan Ying of Manila, in Geneva at the conference as an independent speaker, but with the moral weight of his position as cardinal behind him. Cardinal Ying has spent most of the past two years in Rome, participating in Vatican III, shortly to issue the official position of the Roman Catholic Church on recombinant technologies. While the announced position of the Church on the issue of the creation of new forms of life is not expected to be much of a surprise, what is at issue is the position that the Church will take on the question of whether or not SMARTs can be considered to have souls. While this question at first seems academic, even ephemeral, in combination with the questions now being asked in Geneva, the ripple effect could be far-reaching.

UM:Your Eminence, it's widely anticipated that the Third Vatican Council will recommend that recombinant technology is immoral.

CJY:I don't think that's much in question. It's hardly a secret that our church, and most of the other faiths around the world, Christian and non-Christian, are in profound agreement that such technologies are a usurpation of the genitive powers of God.

UM:A position that dovetails with the Church's position on reproductive technologies and birth control...

CJY:Well, yes, the views are consistent. I think I can safely say that the position of the Council will be that the Church considers immoral any device, science, or method that interferes with, or assumes the powers and prerogatives of the Lord in the creation of life, outside of the normal means with which we were provided at the dawn of time.

UM:But what remains to be seen is what the Council will decide regarding the recommendations of the group of Cardinals you lead, whose position it is that SMARTs are moral beings in possession of souls, regarded by God as fully human, and as such, are deserving of all human rights under the UN Charter.

CJY:That is what we believe, and I am confident we will persuade the Council and His Holiness that this is the case. It is as plain to me as my hand before my face on a summer day.

UM:Your Eminence, isn't it self-contradictory to claim that beings created by an immoral process can be as fully human in the eyes of God as His own creations?

CJY:No, I don't believe that is inconsistent with the views of the Church on similar matters. The Catholic Church believes it is sinful to conceive a child out of wedlock. But that does not mean that the Church, much less God Himself, sees that child as something less than human, or less deserving of grace in any way than a child of a recognized marriage. The sin lies with the parents, not the child.

UM:What are the ramifications for the World Health

Organization if Vatican III declares SMARTs to be human?

CJY:To be blunt, there would then be no question that the Church would consider the program, as least as it stands, to be a form of slavery, and an abomination to God and human dignity.

UM:That decision would put the Vatican at odds with most of the rest of the world.

CJY:It would not be the first time.

UM:Cardinal, isn't it true that you were formerly a member of a group in the Philippines responsible for the destruction of millions of dollars of medical research equipment? Largely to free animals on which medical experiments were being performed?

CJY:I don't see what that has to do with the question at hand...

UM:Do you deny it?

CJY:No... no, I don't deny it. When I was young, I was a man full of passion. I saw a wrong and I committed another wrong in an attempt to right it. Thankfully, God grants us wisdom as we mature. I found the priesthood...

UM:And isn't it true that on several occasions you've claimed that ordinary dogs and cats have souls?

CJY:I have never claimed that. I have postulated.

UM:Postulated?

CJY:We know that many of the higher mammals are blessed with a large degree of intelligence. There is evidence that some of them exhibit a moral sense, even in anticipation of acting. That some, like elephants, may even be able to contemplate their own deaths. At various times in my career, I have postulated that this might be considered evidence of the divine spark. But I believe this is a matter that bears much deeper investigation.

UM:And how far down the list would it go? Do cows have souls? Mice? Reptiles? Where is the sharp dividing line between souled beings and unsouled beings?

CJY:As I said, this matter bears much deeper investigation before anyone can say with any assurance at all.

UM:Your Eminence, do you know Doctor Terrence Ludlow?

CJY:I am aware of his work.

UM:Do you consider him an evil man?

CJY:Evil? Willfully evil? No. I don't believe he is evil. I

believe he is working for what he believes to be humanity's best interests. But I believe he is misguided.

UM:Your Eminence, he gave me a question to put to
you on the nature of the soul. Are you willing to enter-
tain it?

CJY:If you will accept that I speak only for myself,
and not for the Church, I will try to answer your question.

UM:Very well. Cardinal, you maintain that if a being
is capable of expressing itself, has a moral conscience
and self-awareness, it has a soul. Is that true?

CJY:That's a vast oversimplification. But for the sake
of argument, I will allow it.

UM:There are hundreds of computers in the world
today, perhaps thousands, which are self-aware and
capable of speech, and which can make moral distinc-
tions of right and wrong. Two years ago, a computer
shut down the Tokyo stock exchange because of the
questionable character of a major series of transactions
that while skirting legality, were technically allowable.
The machine was taken out of the loop and questioned
as to its motives for three weeks before being shut
down for examination. It was reported later that the
machine asked not to be shut down. Dr. Ludlow wants
to know: given that it fits the criteria you've agreed to,
did this computer have a soul, and was it murdered?

CJY:That's a difficult question, and I don't think I can
answer it easily. It would bear a lot of investigation.

UM:But there isn't time, Your Eminence. They're
about to shut it down, and it's begging to be spared.
Do these people have the absolute right to shut the
machine off? You have to make a quick decision.

CJY:Then I would have to say, no, they do not.

UM:And does the computer have a soul?

CJY:I don't know. I don't know. But when the question must be asked, then we must come down on the
side of the angels until we can say for sure.

UM:And so, strictly in your opinion, until someone
can prove otherwise, such computers must be considered to have a soul?

CJY:Yes, alright. It must be so. We must be merciful
in the name of God whenever we are called upon to be.
It is never a mistake to show mercy, whether souls are
involved or not.

And there you have it, gentle reader. Computers

**have souls. And dogs and cats. Who knows where it
ends? Maybe you'd better say a little prayer for the bacteria you wipe out with antibiotics the next time you
have an infection, just to be sure.**

Faith sighed and put the magazine down. It was depressing, but she
decided she should be glad the Cardinal was given a chance to express
his views at all. Faith looked over at Donald, and then lay against him,
stroking his hair as he slept. *Let them make their germs, and seal people. Just
so long as they make you well.*

She rested against him, gently, warming his slight body with her
own. Drifting. In semi-lucid moments she could force herself to imagine
what life would be like after Donald was dead. She tried to imagine what
it would be like, going to a new home, and whom she would be looking after. Another child? An adult? Man, woman? Or would they retire
her immediately to one of the institutes? Training pups, making good
guides of them... Breeding a litter every year or two. Carefully selected
males. She pictured it. Closed in a quiet room with someone. He would
wag, awkwardly, and they would get to know one another. The scent
of her heat would overcome their shyness. She only hoped her mates,
whoever they were, wherever they were, would be as kind and gentle as
Raymond.

Raymond. Donald's eldest brother. Their father's favorite. Away
at school now. Far, far away. Unlike his father, Raymond loved Donny,
almost as much as Faith did, and that more than anything had won her
heart. But close to that was how he treated her. As if the differences didn't
matter. How, in a handful of stolen hours here and there, he had made
her forget she was just a talking animal, and let her be a woman. Even
now she could feel his hands caressing her secret places, and she whined
softly. Lord. Lord, how she missed him. How she would have forsaken
anything, everything but her duty to Donald to bear Raymond just one
child. But science had decreed that was not possible.

And so her children would spring from other loins; fathered by
SMARTs she didn't know, or particularly care for. And they, in turn, would
be ripped from her breasts before long, to be raised by other bitches, and
she would go back to other duties. And so it would be, litter after litter,
year after year, until she died.

She stroked Donny's forehead, and he stirred.

"I'm sorry, Master. I didn't mean to wake you," she said.

"That's alright," he told her. "I feel better now."

"Good. You just relax. Go back to sleep if you like."

"Faith?"

"Yes, Master?"

"Was that man right? Are you a slave, Faith?"

"I'm a personal lifestyle assistant, Master. That's what they call us."

"A slave is someone who has to do whatever you say, isn't that right? And you own them?" The boy pressed his head to her shoulder, and she put her arm around him.

"Yes, sweet little Master."

"And they have to call you 'master'..."

Faith nodded. "Yes."

"You are a slave... aren't you."

Faith sighed. "Some people might say so."

"Faith... do you wish you were free?"

"Free?" she asked him. "Well, what do you mean, free?"

"You know. Free to go where you wanted. Free not to have to do what people say."

"It doesn't make any difference, I wouldn't go."

"But do you wish," the boy insisted, "that you could go if you wanted to?"

"Let me put it to you this way... Do I wish that I were bound to you by nothing but my love, so that you would know that I was here only because I wanted to be? Yes, sometimes I do. But it would make no difference. If they stopped the train right now and marched in and told me I could go where I wanted and do what I pleased, I would go with you, and it would please me to look after you for the rest of my life. So nothing would change."

She saw tears creep from behind the dark lenses. She licked his cheek. "Oh, don't cry, little Master, please."

"Faith... I free you," the boy quavered. "You never ever have to call me Master again."

Faith wept, holding him. "It will be our secret, okay, Donny?"

"Okay."

The train passed into the city as evening came.

On the streets of this strange new city, Faith hailed a cab. One came at once; it was against the law not to respond to her if she were with the boy. The cab, in turn, rushed them to St. Francis.

Faith led Donny up to the admissions desk.

"Donald Potemkin?" the nurse asked.

"Yes," Faith replied.

The nurse filled out a chart, and came around from behind the desk. "Your room is already made up, Donald. You and your assistant follow me, and I'll take you to it."

"Okay," Donny said. Faith followed the nurse to Donny's room, leading the boy, and together she and the nurse set the place up with Donny's effects, which had been shipped ahead.

"Ma'am," Faith said to the nurse, "where will I find Dr. Renfrew?"

The nurse stared at her. "Why?"

"Because I wish to speak with him, please."

"The doctor is very busy."

Faith bristled. "If he's very busy, he can tell me that himself. Where will I find him, please?"

For a moment, the nurse seemed on the verge of making a mistake. But she thought it over and shrugged, resigned. "His office is room 316, one floor up. Follow the blue line."

"Thank you, ma'am. Master, I'm going upstairs to talk to your doctor. Please wait here until I get back."

"Okay, Faith."

Faith padded down the corridor, found the elevator and led herself to the doctor's office. She ignored the stares and smiles as she strode purposefully along, praying none of them could see she was scared to death.

Room 316. She knocked. She knocked again.

"Is it important?" came a weary voice.

"I think it is, sir," she called. There was the sound of a chair being pushed back, and a moment later, the door opened. The doctor stuck his face out, and peered at her, momentarily startled.

"Oh," he said. "Are you here with the Potemkin boy?"

"Yes, Doctor, I'm Donny's assistant. My name is Faith." She wagged, and held out a paw. Bewildered, the doctor shook it.

"Uhhh, what can I do for you?" he asked.

"I'd like to talk to you about Donny's case," she said, plainly.

"Well, I'm sorry, but I can really only discuss it with Donny's parents."

Faith said, hurriedly, "I've been asked by Mr. Potemkin to find out what I can and report back to him."

The doctor eyed her. Faith knew that he probably suspected she was lying, but what she said was at least plausible. "Alright," he said. "But my time is very limited. I can only give you a few minutes."

"That will be fine, sir, thank you, sir."

"Come in."

Faith entered the office and shut the door. She stepped forward; the carpet was soft and the room was cool, a bit dark; full of books and framed degrees and a dank medicinal smell quite apart from the hospital at large. She stood before his desk.

"Have a seat," he said.

"Are you sure?" she asked.

"Yes, go ahead."

"Thank you, Doctor." She sat.

The Doctor sighed. "I have to tell you, going in, that the prognosis is not good. I mean, we haven't run the new tests yet, but... Donny just does not seem to be responding to the therapies."

"He's trying so hard, Doctor..."

"I'm sure he is, but his body doesn't seem to be going along. His problems are rife. Any one by itself wouldn't be a problem. But in concert, we just don't seem to be able to keep ahead of new complications. The progress of the virus was arrested in the womb, but not before it did serious, serious damage to most of his major organs. If we'd caught it just a little earlier..." The doctor sighed. "All I'm saying is, if he doesn't respond to treatment this time, we're really out of options. And it will be... a matter of time."

Faith was quiet. "How much time?"

"A few months at the very outside."

"M—months??" She sobbed it, startling herself.

"Yes. I'm sorry. I know it's hard; according to the reports, you've been with him almost since he could walk."

"*I taught him to walk,*" she snapped, and immediately lowered her eyes.

"I understand," the doctor said, softly. "I've met Donny's parents."

"Oh."

The doctor nodded, rising. He turned to the window. "I've seen the psychotherapeutic assessments... he almost never mentions his parents. He mentions you quite a lot." He turned. "You should be very proud."

"I am, Doctor."

"I think the news will be hardest on you," he said. "But that's why I'm telling you. I don't believe Mr. Potemkin asked you to talk to me."

Faith turned her eyes away again, ashamed.

"It's alright, Faith. You deserved to be told. He's your life."

"Yes, he is."

The doctor opened his mouth. There was something more he wanted to say. But his mouth shut again.

"Thank you, Doctor," she said, rising. This time, he offered his hand to her.

She shook it.

"Everything will work out fine," he said. "You'll see."

The tests were scheduled to begin just after dawn. The nurses came by to give Donny a sedative, and the boy settled in. Normally Faith slept on a comfortable cot at the foot of Donny's bed, but tonight she had a bed of her own, opposite his. In the darkness, in the pale glow cast by various instruments and indicators, she stared across at him, not sure if he were awake or asleep.

"I'm scared, Faith," he whimpered.

"I know, love. But just hang on. They're going to make you well again."

"I've never been well. I don't know what it's like."

"It will be wonderful."

There was a long silence. She assumed he'd drifted off. Then, he said, "When you're in Heaven, you're always well, right?"

She fought down a twinge of fear. "Well, yes. But you'll have to get used to it here first."

She heard him submerging into sleep; he said, "Even... with wings... I'll still need you. So... I don't... bump... into the... air... planes..."

He was asleep.

She closed her eyes, and dropped off herself.

In the dream, wolves circled them. They wanted the boy. She turned, snapping, snarling. They came at her. She was strong. They tore her flesh, but the boy got away.

There was a pale light at the window; the predawn. She wasn't even sure she was awake. It seemed as though time were standing still.

Donny coughed.

He coughed again.

And then again. "Faith," he croaked.

She slipped from her bed and knelt beside him. "What is it, Master?"

"Feel awful. Awful. Faith..." He coughed again, hard. She soothed his forehead. Something heavy hit the fur of her chest. She dabbed her fingers there, and brought them to her nose.

Blood.

She clicked the light on. The boy's mouth and nose were ringed in red.

"Jesus," she whispered.

"Faith," the boy moaned. She stabbed her thumb at the call button. Donny went into a coughing fit, and convulsed.

"Hurry!" she screamed. "Damn it, hurry!" Nurses and an intern burst in. She heard herself shout, "He's dying, he's dying!"

They slipped the boy onto a stretcher and wheeled him from the room. Faith ran alongside, holding Donny's hand, tossing soothing words at him like too many baseballs. The boy coughed up alarming clots of blood, and begged her, "Don't let me die, Faith, don't let me die, please!"

Oh, Jesus, God, whoever you are; Allah, Jehovah; don't let him die, please don't let him die; he's all I have!

They pushed Donny into an emergency room and Faith pushed in with them. A nurse jumped forward, calling, "You can't come in here!"

Faith showed her the whites of her eyes and a formidable array of teeth. The staff decided they had neither the time nor inclination to argue, and set to work.

Dr. Renfrew burst in, not even noticing Faith. "Damn it, he's coming apart; he's all coming apart at once..."

There was an overwhelming array of clinical jargon washing over Faith in the minutes that followed; an eternity of standing, shaking, watching the boy die and having to fight herself not to leap forward; force herself to stand out of the way while they did their jobs.

"Blood pressure dropping..."

"Pulse thready..."

"The heartbeat's erratic; 2 cc's..."

"I've lost the pulse. I can't find the pulse."

The irregular blip of Donny's life suddenly spread out into the long, flat whine of clinical death, and Faith moaned. The doctors worked frantically. She watched the little body jump as they shocked it; bounce morbidly as they massaged his chest, but finally, finally, she saw Dr. Renfrew's shoulders slump, and he pulled his mask.

"DONNY!! DONNEEEEEEEEEEEEE!!" she screamed.

"Get her out of here!" Dr. Renfrew barked. Two interns flew at Faith, grabbing her by the arms as she screamed the child's name, her heart shredding in her chest as the words tore past it like the fan blades of a jet engine. The two men dumped her out into the hall; she exploded from the doors and tumbled out onto her ass as twenty pairs of startled eyes turned to her. She scrambled back but by then the doors were shut. She pounded on them, screaming his name.

She sank to the floor, her face wrenched in agony. She rocked, moaning, as lost as a bottle tossed into the sea. "Donny... Donny... don't leave me, Donny, don't go..."

She steadied herself. The thought came from nowhere, and surprised even her. *I'll follow you into the ground, little Master...*

She looked up into the clear, cloudless blue sky in the window opposite.

Or maybe...

Down the hall, a nurse eyed her warily. She grabbed an intern by the arm, and turned him, pointing.

The intern peered at Faith. He started to move.

So did she.

He was too late.

Don't go too far, little Master, wait! Wait, Donny, I'm coming, please! Wait for me!

In a single swift, fluid movement, she jumped. The glass gave way like a womb, and she flung herself into the open arms of the sky.

Wings.

John Shaddock stood in the rigging above the bowsprit of the *Pelican*, straining his senses to pick up what information he could from the Spanish galleon. Darkness had fallen, and the tropical night breezes had shifted to blow off the land, carrying with them the thousands of odors of the Ecuadorian forest. He swiveled his ears and listened for the telltale thump of ramrods or the clink of iron on iron, mentally sorting through the barrage of smells looking for a whiff of saltpeter.

They had been moving steadily towards the ship for over the last seven hours and following reports of her for nearly a month; collected while raiding Spanish vessels for information and supplies all the way up the Pacific coast of South America. Captain Drake had been spinning tales of a ship with a hold full of silver bound from the mines of Lima to Panama. No one really needed the extra encouragement. A treasure ship was a treasure ship, and a cut of the entire voyage's haul was due every soul that survived the trip. Like everyone else on board, John intended to survive.

He readjusted his position, swishing his tail gently for balance, then turned and made eye contact with the first mate, shaking his head to indicate that nothing seemed amiss. At the officer's acknowledging nod, he turned back to scanning the darkened horizon. It wasn't a question of maintaining surprise. Both ships could see each other quite clearly in the moonlit waters off Cabo de San Francisco, and had been in visual contact for hours before the sun had even set. The task at hand was to make sure the *La Plata* was convinced that they were nothing more than a fellow merchant vessel. To that end, they had been sailing as slowly as possible, reducing sail by more than half and trailing pots and kettles over the back of the *Pelican* to slow her down.

He focused his senses again on the leading vessel, hoping to pick up an indication of their intentions, but they were still a good mile in the lead and the wind and salt were corrupting what little scent drifted back to his sensitive nose. There was the occasional hint of canvas, wood, and pitch on the night air, but no more. He let himself lean back on the rigging, curling his paws through the ropes in a way that seemed almost natural to him now.

He had signed aboard the crew of the *Pelican* on a bright December morning in Plymouth as the only Ship's Dog out of 170 men and boys aboard a fleet of five ships: the *Pelican*, the *Marigold*, the *Elizabeth*, the *Swan*, and the *Benedict*. They were bound, ostensibly, for a privately funded mission of merchant trading and casual piracy against the Spanish in Central and South America. However, there seemed to be an unusually high number of officers on board who wore the expertise and training of the British Navy like a well-fitting pair of boots. Rumor had it that the Queen herself had commissioned the voyage, seeking Spanish silver for the coffers in what looked to be a developing war with Spain.

It mattered very little to John, then or now. As an Animus, his kind's lot in human society was generally predestined regardless of the current political climate. In the Crown's eyes they held a position somewhat below the peasant farmer and above common animals. Owning land or holding positions of respect was practically unthinkable, but they were quite welcome to work for whatever pittance people would pay them. Most of them seemed to be resigned to doing just that.

John came from a clan of wolves living in the north, where no one else cared to set up an existence. There they hunted as much food as they could from the local lands without attracting attention, and raised what little other funds they could doing odd jobs and working on whatever farms would hire them. It didn't provide much, but they were grateful for what they had, and spent the cold winter nights snuggled together for warmth. It was a piteous condition, only made survivable by the strength of the wolf family bond and their love for one another. Some of the more solitary Animus species had nearly died out, or at least retreated completely from the human controlled areas in the hopes of staying alive.

As much as John loved his clanmates, he despised the thought of continuing on living the way they were. How long before one of the Crown's sheriffs caught on to their illegal hunting activities? Without the meat this gave them they would have starved long ago, but he doubted any human would see it that way. No, as he saw it, the great mediator in human society was money. Those that possessed a lot of it could do pretty much as they pleased, and those that didn't, got by at the whim of others. It didn't matter what you looked like, as long as gold or silver clinked together in your britches. There weren't many ways for an Animus to make that kind of money legally. Signing on as a Ship's Dog was one of them.

Animus, in general, had been found early on to make poor military material. While most species were generally strong and competent as soldiers, their limbs were thin and they tended towards the clumsy side when compared to the flat-footed humans. Without armor they were far too fragile for hand to hand combat situations, and with armor they were too clumsy to be effective. Some of them found places in the Navy, but shipboard nutrition deficiencies seemed to hit them worse than most humans too, and few survived more than a month at sea. All this, coupled with their relatively low population in comparison to humans, meant that most proposed ideas for using Animus in wartime had been scrapped. However, a few specialty niches had been found that seemed tailor-made for some species.

Ship's Dogs were stationed in the ship running at the forefront of the fleet. Their sole responsibility was to be the nose and ears for the human officers, giving them a tactical advantage in both battle and navigation. They enjoyed a rank somewhere between boatswain and quartermaster, earning officer's rations and quarters, a fairer cut of the treasure at journey's end, and freedom from all the worst duties. During skirmishes, he was ordered to keep belowdecks and out of harm's way. Able-bodied seamen could be conscripted from almost anywhere, but losing your Ship's Dog to a bullet or an arrow was considered a death sentence. He was equal parts crewman, mascot, and good-luck-charm.

Lost in his daydreams, John's tail began to wag slowly and proudly until he noticed and stopped it in embarrassment. He tried to keep the reminders of his animal nature to a minimum, even wearing some of the traditional sailors' garb despite how it trapped in the heat and restricted his range of motion. Even so, he was not a welcome guest during the men's casual gatherings. There was no hostility, just the awkward silence that greets strangers with which you feel you have nothing in common. After a while he learned to stay busy or out of sight entirely.

It had hurt at first, as he had been looking forward to making some human friends on the voyage, but he swallowed his disappointment and consoled himself with the knowledge that Captain Drake and the first mate never mixed with the common sailors either. His cut of the treasure from the lucrative journey was certain to be his ticket to human friends and allies in high places, and out of the rural existence of his family and pack. He smiled to himself and his ears perked slowly... *John Shaddock, first wolf Animus to secure a place in the Queen's court*. That would be worth the long, damp voyage! He was sure it was his destiny.

A slight shift in the wind patterns brought a sudden, strong wave of scents and sounds from the ship ahead, and John slipped out of his thoughts to absorb all he could before they died out again as quickly as they had arrived. He clambered down the ropes carefully and trotted aft to the wheeldeck to speak with the first mate, Walter Doughty.

"You have news, Mr. Shaddock?" He was a proper officer of the British navy through and through, regardless of their current rogue status, and addressed everyone with military precision. John appreciated that. It made him feel like an equal to the rest of the human crew.

"Yessir. I smell no gunpowder or hot iron aboard whatsoever, sir. The sounds are of usual evening shipboard activity for a ship of her size. I would put the number of men on deck at the moment to be around 15."

The middle-aged officer nodded curtly. "Very well. I shall pass that information on to the captain personally. Join the rest of the crew in preparation for the attack. I'll relieve you of duty shortly."

"Yessir. Thank you sir." John turned and jogged back towards the middle of the ship where a contingent of the crew were stringing bows and checking arrows. Gunpowder and wadding were both scarce, so the less used in pistols and harquebuses, the better. Most of the crew were given bows, though few of them could hit a mark with them if they tried, especially with salt-damage to the gut strings. The officers and chosen men were issued rifles. John was issued neither, naturally. Early on, he had felt self-conscious about that, but eventually decided keeping his pelt intact was worth more than gaining favor with the men. It was the treasure that would buy him his eventual place at court, not his skill in battle.

About half an hour later, the first mate returned with the captain following casually behind, making their usual rounds of the ship prior to the impending battle. They walked straight up to John, who stood respectfully at attention. Captain Francis Drake had proved to be more impressive in legend than he was in person. Face-to-face he was rather smaller, rather thinner, and rather paler than the Spanish made him out to be. No one would have told him that personally, though.

"Mr. Doughty says you feel the information from our Spanish captives at Lima was in error. *La Plata* has no cannon?" Drake's expression was unreadable.

"Every indication I have says they do not, sir."

He nodded. "I hope you're right, though I daresay we could probably take her anyway. Thank you, Mr. Shaddock. You'd better get yourself belowdecks and out from underfoot." It was as much a dismissal as an order. John turned and descended into forecastle of the ship to his berth, smiling. Every time he managed to perform a service to a man as influential as Drake brought him closer to his ultimate goal. Stretching out as best he could in the small bunk, he called up his well-worn fantasies to see him through yet another pitched battle in the dark.

※ ∞ ※

John Shaddock awoke with his heart pounding at the first crash of cannonfire overhead. He quickly located the two wax balls he kept nearby and inserted them into his ears, curling up on the bunk fearfully. He wasn't really scared by the battle as much as the sense of not knowing what was happening. One return cannon volley from their foe could puncture the ship and kill or drown him where he lay—belowdecks or not. He knew it was ridiculous to feel that seeing it coming would make the situation somehow better, but he did anyway.

He waited breathlessly for a return volley from the *La Plata*, which thankfully never came. There was some small-arms fire here and there from both sides and the occasional shout as one side or the other lost a man, but after the initial round, the *Pelican's* cannon never spoke again. John soon felt the bump of boarding platforms being set in place, followed by more small weapons fire. In what must have been no more than five minutes of the initial attack, the sounds of battle had dropped to nothing, so John took the plugs out of his ears and crept back up on deck to look around.

It was like most battles he'd hidden belowdecks from, though perhaps a bit larger in scale. The *La Plata* was larger than any other ship they had taken on the voyage, nearly matching the *Pelican* in size and mass. Now her foremast, blown clean in two by their cannon, dangled from the rigging like a broken limb. She'd taken some minor damage to her hull as well, and was keeling over slightly to the starboard. Some of Drake's crew were hastily rounding up the captured and lightly injured and segregating them by rank, while others were busy reefing the sails on the captured ship. John noted that the ship had in fact had two or three small cannon, apparently in a state of total unreadiness for battle. A lucky break for him!

Each side had suffered about five casualties, which was about normal for a battle of this scope. They lay scattered about the decks, their blood pooling up on the deck. Surgeons moved slowly around their respective ships, tending to the injured and accounting for the dead. John swallowed and wished he could find some way to plug up his nose as well as he could plug his ears. The scent of human blood had never ceased to make him queasy, though he had been surprised to find himself somewhat cavalier about the actual loss of life. He knew some killing was the inevitable outcome of piracy, as did everyone else on the ship. You tried your best to stay alive and claim your prize at journey's end; but you were just a pawn in the chess game played by both Captains on one level, and by the rulers of their respective countries in another. John was just pleased to be on the winning side, so far.

John spotted Drake conversing casually with the captain of the captured ship. He had been ritually disarmed, but would be treated as a guest aboard the *Pelican* along with his officers, while the two leaders flattered and bartered their way towards more or less of the treasure. The common sailors would be locked up in whatever storage room would hold them until all the cargo could be accounted for and pilfered as Drake saw fit, but they too were treated reasonably well. There was little profit to be gained from causing personal suffering, and the Captain was only interested in how much money he could get away with at Spain's expense.

There looked to be nothing of critical importance for him to do, and the sulfurous odor from the recently fired cannon was making him sick to his stomach. John decided to go kick around the deck of the captured Spanish ship to see if he could smell anything of use. Once or twice in the past, he had helped uncover hidden caches of silver—which always gained him an extra little bit of loot and public praise from the First Mate or even from Captain Drake himself. On such a richly stocked ship, he was sure to find something good.

He walked casually across the plank laid between the gently rocking ships and was heading for the far side of the captured vessel when he smelled something out of place. He immediately knew it was a feline of some sort, but he couldn't recognize a specific species. An overlying scent he did recognize though, and it wasn't long before he found the source of both. Lying behind a pile of canvas sail bags and coiled up ropes was the supine form of a jungle cat Animus. The other scent was blood, and there was a lot of it. He looked around for the Spanish ship's surgeon, but he was nowhere to be found. Surely he'd seen the injured cat—he'd been working right around the area earlier.

John was about to leave to go look for the surgeon from his own ship when the feline stirred and flicked his glass-green eyes open, fixing them on John and shuddering. It was a race of cat John was sure he had seen before, but couldn't recall where. He was a tawny brown from head to toe, with a lighter front, but few other markings. Black tufts of fur stood up from the tops of his ears. A thin necklace of some kind of small stones, strung on leather, was looped lightly around his neck. A bullet from some officer's gun had caught him in the gut, and the blood that was still seeping from the wound was dark in color. It looked pretty bad, and he didn't need to be a surgeon to know it. He had been around enough others in similar condition to know there was little to be gained from seeking out medical assistance.

He knelt gingerly next to the cat, and because he didn't know what else to do, he started talking. He had learned quite a bit of Spanish from the pilot of the *Pelican*, a captured Portuguese sailor. He tried it now. "I... I do not know if you can understand me, but my name is John. I am what the English call a wolf. I live far away from here where it is colder, and... and not so damp." He shook his head ruefully. "Not that I suspect you should care, as I am crew on the boat that probably hurt you."

The feline apparently understood some of that, because he expended much effort to shift slightly so he could look up at John easier. He seemed to struggle a moment against the weakness that was probably gripping his senses, and forced out a couple words John had never heard before. "Caracal... Qalaku."

He assumed the first was a name, and went with it. "Your name... Caracal?"

The cat shook his head with almost a grin—pained though it was— and spoke the second word again, pointing to himself. "Qalaku... Am Caracal."

"Qalaku..." He struggled with the unfamiliar syllables. "That's quite a name!"

The feline coughed, and the spasm caused him to hiss in pain as it shook his tortured midsection. He fixed his eyes on John's. "You... not the ones that hurt me, John."

"I'm not certain I understand. You weren't like this before?"

The cat shook his head, but only very little. "No, try to escape during fighting. Was shot by Spanish." He virtually spat the word.

It took John a moment to figure it all out, but when he did, he wasn't overly surprised at the revelation that the Spanish treated their Animus as badly as they did the native humans they captured and forced to work in the silver mines. He was guiltily reviewing the few slaves that Drake had taken on board briefly during the voyage, though they had been as well treated as the British sailors were, when he realized where he had seen Caracals before. There had been some amongst the crew of a Portuguese merchant vessel they seized off the Cape Verde islands. "Your people African, Qalaku?"

The cat nodded, and his eyes were losing their luster. "I miss my clan. How long they hold you, John?"

John shook his head. "I'm equal member of the crew. Back home my people are not treated so well, but here I am respected and given money. Money that I hope will buy my clan respect too." He paused for a moment and his ears twitched backwards. It was almost embarrassing to try to explain his situation to the cat, considering the depths of abuse he'd suffered at the hands of humanity.

The cat thought about this for a long moment as his breathing grew more and more shallow, then fixed the depths of his green eyes on John's and shrugged. "All sorts of slavery, John." He closed his eyes for a moment and seemed to struggle to open them. "John... I die." It wasn't a question. "Pray for my people as I go. I pray for yours." He lifted a paw to rest on the wolf's forearm. "Thank you for seeing me to my freedom."

John stroked the feline's muzzle gently while saying prayers to his clan's wolf spirit guardians, asking that they extend their guidance and protection to this brother in a foreign land and his people. It felt kind of funny doing so, because he had never been much of a believer in them before, but for the first time in his life, he sincerely wished they were listening.

Qalaku died gently moments later, as John wished him on his way with a final prayer. He left the still body on the deck and returned to his quarters. He cleaned the blood out of his fur and curled up on the bunk, feeling somehow less certain of his course in life than he had an hour before.

If anyone noticed, they said nothing.

🐾 ∞ 🐾

Two days later, John stood perched again in the rigging above the bowsprit, watching the action below. After spending much of the time drinking and swapping stories, the two captains had finally gotten down to the business of negotiating the terms of their encounter. Drake, as usual, would take just about everything of value that didn't specifically belong to the captain of the captured ship, along with five or six of the Spanish sailors to replace the crew he had lost.

The captain of the *La Plata*, San Juan de Anton, would keep his ship and continue on to Panama as initially planned. There he would file his official report of the encounter, collect the majority of his pay for the voyage anyway, and embellish the encounter to the best of his ability to anyone that would listen. He was now, after all, one of the great survivors of an encounter with the bloodthirsty English pirate Francis Drake!

While the last of the agreed upon materials were inventoried and secured aboard the *Pelican*, the two men chatted idly nearby. Drake had selected a few choice items from the haul and now presented them back to Anton, a ritual of mutual respect between the two seafarers. The Spanish captain would neglect to mention them while making his report of the lost goods and increase his own fortunes by a little more too.

Drake clapped the Spanish captain on the back jovially. "Very well, off with you to your duties Mr. Anton! Mind you to tell everyone you meet of your terrifying encounter with the dread Captain Drake."

Anton smiled. "Aye, that I will, Señor. You run a fine ship, captain. May the seas of your future remain kind to you and your crew."

John, sitting above, perked his ears and smiled to himself. The fact that Anton spoke nearly perfect English, with only a hint of Spanish accent, had been lost on no one. Some of the officers had been speculating how someone likely once named 'John Anton' ended up hauling silver for the Spaniards.

Anton had boarded the repaired *La Plata* and they were preparing to disengage from the *Pelican*. Drake called out to him. "Sorry about the loss of your cat too, fellow. I hope you can replace him relatively easily. We'd offer you our John Shaddock, but of course he's a valued member of our crew, and we have many a mile to go before we see our home shores again."

San Juan de Anton waved his hand nonchalantly. "Plenty more where that savage came from, and maybe the next one will be a spot more tractable like your wolf is. Now there's an asset!" John guessed he should have felt hurt, but for some reason he couldn't bring himself to care as much as he once did.

The crews scurried about their respective ships, casting off lines and carefully maneuvering in the winds to ensure that the ships didn't collide. Moments later they were moving apart on the Pacific, bound for their destinies. John leaned forward in the rigging, enjoying the feel of the ocean breeze in his fur, and wondered if he knew what his destiny even was anymore.

🐾 ∞ 🐾

Months later, the *Pelican* sailed up the Barbary Coast of Africa, bound for England and a triumphant return home. John Shaddock stood at his customary post in the forward rigging, though this time more for comfort than for any official duty. He tossed a small leather and stone necklace overboard in the general direction of land, smiling as he did so, and said a quiet prayer.

"May you find peace, Qalaku. Thanks for seeing me to *my* freedom."

There was yet much to be done upon his return to the shores of his homeland. He had a fortune in silver to claim, and a vast acreage of farm-land in the North of England to buy. Land that would ensure his clan's freedom for years to come.

He jumped lightly down from the rigging and walked aft to the wheelhouse to chat with the Pilot. He was clad in only a small loincloth, the traditional garment for his clan, and his tail wagged proudly behind him.

Author's Note: The situation of the encounter between Captain Francis Drake's *Pelican* (not renamed *Golden Hind* until they were return-ing to London, in an attempt to curry favor with the Queen in case the political climate had changed in their absence) and Captain San Juan de Anton's *La Plata*, took place pretty much as retold here. However, some of the time spans have been shortened or lengthened for the purposes of telling a good story.

The air of casual collaboration between the captains is an assumption based on historical records. Obviously, neither side would have reported it as such, for fear of harming their reputations. By official accounts, all sea battles were pitched fights with the most villainous of pirates. In fact, Drake treated those among his own crew which he disfavored far worse than he ever treated compliant Spanish and Portuguese captives.

The capture and enslavement of native peoples was a common tactic of both the English and the Spanish during this time period. While he appears to be less guilty of such behavior than the Spanish in this particu-lar account, Drake made much of his early fortune running slave ships from the Barbary Coast to England. Neither side is innocent of the atroci-ties.

"Don't like dogs," he said. His voice was garbled by the yellow tusks that curved out of his mouth on either side, but those with an ear for dialect could hear Oklahoma in his speech. "They scent me as soon as I pass them. One time I was pushing through some woods at night and I stumbled into a clearing with a shack in it. There was a mean dog there, guarding the place for the man who lived in the shack, I reckon. Need that kind of protection or better with mutant bandit gangs roamin' about." He paused, snuffed at the smoky air, looked at his big, empty glass. "Shoot. No more beer."

"I'll see to that," the man said. He tossed a silver coin over his shoulder; the bartender, a dusty fat fellow with a double pupil in one eye, caught it and drew the boar another stein, which he set down on the wet wooden table.

"Well," said the boar, scraping the table with his hairy, clawed fingers, "that dog came charging up at me with a growl louder than a gunshot. I didn't even have a chance to drop my pack before he hit me. Wham! He was five foot high at the shoulder, jaws bigger than an alligator. Hell, anyone's been around's seen the enlarged animals they made with those DNA experiments before the war."

"We've seen some," the man said, nodding at his friend, who was just bigger than a child and was entirely hidden in a heavy robe. "But go on."

The boar snuffed at his beer; foam drifted to the table and vanished. He took a sip. "Well, that dog was so big and so angry that he couldn't find my throat at first once he knocked me down. I flipped him over backward into the underbrush and threw my pack off so I could fight him." He started drinking his beer and sat in silence for some time.

"So?" sneered the little fellow in a thin voice.

The boar snorted. "Why don't you drop your hood, son?" he asked, not replying to the fellow's question. "I can smell a rat when I meet one."

Grumbling, the rat shook his head, so that his cowl fell away, revealing a brown hairy face with a protrusive snout; a rat, sure enough.

"Thought so," said the boar. "Ain't never had nothing against rats in general, but never met one I liked." He settled back into his chair, scratching his black belly.

"What happened in the fight?" asked the man, a bit more politely.

"Heh," laughed the boar. "Haven't met a dog yet I can't lick. After I killed him, the man in the house came out with a shotgun and a bag of grenades. I told him I was sorry about his dog and I gave him something from my pack; box of pistol ammo, probably. He didn't shoot at me, so I went on travelling. How come you're asking me about dogs, anyway?"

"Well," said the man, "we just got into town, and they told us the Oklahoma Boar has killed more dogs and wolves than anybody else they ever met."

The boar ran his fingers over one of his tusks. "I reckon. It's a scent thing, you understand. Men have no smell, they don't understand, but I bet you do, ratboy."

The rat scowled and grumbled.

"I got a smell to me," said Oklahoma, "that dogs just don't like. Not dogs adapted, like the rat and I are, smart dogs, but the animals. I mean to say, the smart ones don't like my smell neither, but they can get over it. But your basic canine goes for my throat as soon as he scents me. Usually I can smell them coming, but that was a bad forest. Someone musta dropped a mutation bomb in there. There were funny trees and bushes, but especially there were some creepers about a half-mile off from the shack that stank so bad I couldn't use my nose for a week, 'cept to breathe." He gulped down the sour beer. "Now, near as I can figure it, you're looking for someone who kills dogs and wolves. How come?"

"Well, let me explain," the man said. "My name is Bob Simmons. My friend's name is Nick. We're... sort of professional scouts. We work in Pennsylvania."

Oklahoma snuffed at his empty mug. "That's, what, about two weeks north of here by foot?"

"About," Simmons said. "We scout out bandit camps, map them, and sell the information to villagers who want to raid the camps themselves. I did army reconnaissance before the war, so this sort of work is pretty easy for me. Nick here... Well, he needs the work too."

"I have a big family," the rat said.

"Reckon," Oklahoma replied. "Lot of pointy mouths to feed." He looked back at Simmons. "What's your business, then?"

"Our home village has been attacked by the worst kind of bandits," Simmons said.

"Cannibals?" Oklahoma asked. "I met some of them 'round Dallas once, on a dirt road going past an old farmhouse. I saw a bunch of drooling mutants in rags running at me; they saw bacon and pork chops. Best I could find out about 'em later, they had been in a bomb shelter but took a hit anyway, and..."

"Let's get on with this," said the rat. "These men aren't cannibals. They're slavers. They raided our village and took as many women as they could find. All human, no one with any visible mutations. We scouted out their camp. The only place we saw anyone moving was a barn; there was a guard sleeping on the ground in front of it. He was drunk, so we caught him easily, and he told us our women were in the barn. He said even though there were no bandits there but him, the only way in was around the other side, and it was guarded so well we'd be dead in seconds if we tried it. We cut his throat..."

"You bit it out," said Oklahoma. "Reckon."

"I'm not a savage!" the rat exclaimed shrilly.

"Heck, that's not savage," said Oklahoma. "Why shouldn't we use what God gave us to fight with? Don't you use your nose? Why not use your teeth?"

"Enough," interrupted Simmons. "We didn't believe what the guard said, so we started around to the entrance. Right about then a wind came up behind us, and almost immediately we heard two dogs barking. Now I've seen enlarged dogs like the one you told us about, and I've heard them bark. From the noise those two made, they must've been the size of horses."

"Shoot," said Oklahoma. "Never seen one that big."

"We heard them coming for us, and we ran back to the woods," Nick the rat said.

"Did you see 'em?" Oklahoma shouted.

"We didn't turn around," Simmons said. "They were coming so fast, if they hadn't turned back to guard the barn, they could have run us down easily."

Oklahoma settled back, leaned his chair against the wall, and put his big cloven feet on the table. With one hand he groped in his pack for his pipe and tobacco. He looked at Simmons and Nick. Both of them smelled nervous, but he couldn't see them well; the room was dimly lit and full of smoke, and Oklahoma's vision had never been too good. "What you want," he said, "is for me to march into that town and kill those dogs for you. That right?"

The two nodded.

"And that's presumin' that the slavers won't be there, right?"

They nodded again.

"Why didn't you just get your whole village together, arm 'em with guns and spears, and do it yourselves?"

"Do you want the job or not?" the rat snapped. "There's pay."

Oklahoma snorted. "Such as?"

"Artifacts," said Bob Simmons. "To start with, a case of canned goods; your choice, ham, tuna, corn... I don't even know what you like to eat."

"What else?" Oklahoma asked.

"A high-powered flashlight," Simmons said. "Two reloads of batteries."

"And?"

"You want more?" the rat spat. Oklahoma didn't smell anger on him; he was trying to hold out.

"You don't mind as much as you're sayin'," the boar observed.

"All right," said Bob Simmons in a tired voice. "How about an army surplus flak jacket. I have an extra, like the one I'm wearing, except it's never been used."

"Reckon I'll need that before we leave."

Simmons sighed. "Fine."

※ ∞ ※

In the morning Oklahoma and the two scouts set out, following a highway that ran north-south past the small town where they had slept the night before. The boar took a long sniff of the air before departing; rain, and a heavy rain, was coming. He told his companions. Bob Simmons shrugged. "Less danger of bandits attacking if it's raining."

"Reckon," said Oklahoma.

Oklahoma set a quick pace. The other two were obviously in fit condition; they kept up with him for a few hours. When, around noon, Oklahoma noticed them dropping behind, he snorted with amusement. "Tired, huh?" he called back.

The rat growled back at him.

Black clouds filled the sky. Oklahoma, trudging through the grass beside the highway they were following, lost sight both of the sun—hidden behind the clouds—and of his two companions. He snorted and sat down at the roadside to wait. Gnats dove at his dark, squinting eyes. He snuffed the air again; on the wind, which was growing as the storm approached, he caught the scent of men and horses north of him, about a half-mile away. He kept sniffing, holding the scent as long as he could. Eventually Simmons and Nick appeared, sprinting up the highway toward him.

"Why didn't you wait?" the rat snarled.

Oklahoma said, "Like my own pace." When they turned to move on, he added, "Wait here a spell. People coming from the north, mounted or they have carts."

"I don't see anyone," Simmons said. "Wait a minute." He dug through his pack and produced a set of binoculars. He gazed up the road for only a moment before saying, "Bad news. Centaurs."

"How many?" asked the rat nervously.

"Centaurs?" Oklahoma interrupted. "You mean, a horse's body with a man's chest coming off the front? Ain't never heard of them living before."

"There was a centaur clone series made before the war," Bob Simmons said. "They aren't usually friendly. With their speed, centaurs tend to be bandits. There's about six coming down the road toward us."

"Shoot," said Oklahoma. He looked around; on either side of the highway the terrain was flat and featureless. He still couldn't see the centaurs, but their scent was getting sharper. Suddenly he smelled tension.

"They've spotted us," Simmons said. "They've broken into a gallop."

"They killers?" Oklahoma asked.

"Only robbers, but they'll take everything we're carrying."

The boar shook his head. "I've been broke before and lived ok, but I don't like giving in to bandits. Y'all have any guns?"

"We're armed," Simmons said.

"Load 'em," Oklahoma said. "Get behind me, and don't fight until I do."

The scent of the angry centaurs grew stronger, and soon Oklahoma could hear their galloping hooves. Finally he saw a dark splotch on the highway ahead, and with some sniffing made out the positions of the six bandits.

The centaurs had drawn up in a semicircle, flanking Simmons and Nick. Sweat and rain were wet on their heaving flanks. They were less than full-sized, in horse or human parts; the smallest was about Oklahoma's height at the human shoulder. As with all clone series, they were very much alike in shape and coloration; different living had produced the only variations in them. The smaller one, for example, had probably had its growth stunted by poor nutrition, and the big one, the leader, had clearly done more exercise than the others.

"Reckon y'all came here in a hurry," Oklahoma said. "Didn't want to miss us."

"We don't want to talk to you, pig," the tallest one shouted arrogantly. "We want everything you're carrying, you and the man and the boy. Might as well strip naked and give us your clothes; you don't want us searching you."

Oklahoma snuffed at him. "You seem mighty proud. Reckon you're strong, huh?"

"Shut him up," the lead centaur said. He motioned with his hand to another one next to him. With clopping hooves the second creature came forward.

"I wouldn't come closer," the boar warned. The scent of fear from that one was too strong to miss.

The smaller centaur looked back at the leader, then advanced. Oklahoma shrugged and stepped forward.

The centaur reared and kicked with his front hooves. Oklahoma dodged one kick, but a flinty hoof caught him on the shoulder and twisted him a bit to the side. He felt blood leak onto his fur under the flak jacket.

"Let's see your armor stop that, pig," said the centaur.

"The armor's just for decoration," Oklahoma said. He closed his eyes, took a snuff, and lunged forward, snorting. One hand closed on a foreleg; he squeezed and felt the leg snap. The centaur cried out in uncomprehending pain. Oklahoma gored at the underbelly of the centaur, tasted the blood on his lips and felt it in his snout as he slipped beneath the forelegs to wrap his arms around the heaving, blood-slick belly of the thing and slash with his tusks so that hide ripped and entrails slid along his snout. He heard gunshots; he lifted the centaur and hurled it forward, heard it smack wetly on the asphalt. On all sides were cold air and beating rain, blood and pain, shouts and shots. Oklahoma jumped at the nearest centaur he could smell, caught something—long hair?—pulled and gored—a scream and a snap followed, and a gout of blood hit Oklahoma's pelt. Through the centaurs' cries, horrible blends of shout and whinny, Oklahoma heard Bob Simmons exclaim, "Oh my God!" But when the centaur crumpled, Oklahoma jumped at a third, his senses filled with blood, then all the centaurs were in full flight, and Oklahoma stood with his eyes shut, snorting and clawing at the air, breaths swelling in his chest, until he could discern through the stench of death that none of the centaurs near him were alive.

"My God!" shouted Simmons. "What did we hire?"

Oklahoma stood as still as he could until the fighting frenzy passed. He did not listen to the exclamations of his two companions until he was composed. Then he turned and nodded to them. "Time to move on. Reckon."

🐾 ∞ 🐾

Southern Pennsylvania was cooler, wetter country than Oklahoma was used to. Not as wet as Louisiana and Mississippi: it had rained on him for two days while he was climbing through the scarred ruins of New Orleans. But it was more wet than his native southwest, and much greener, too. Oklahoma liked the scent of pine, carried on a cool drizzly wind. Once they crossed into Pennsylvania, he began snuffing the air eagerly, searching out this aroma in particular. It kept him busy while he walked.

He talked as little as possible, during the journey up, with Bob Simmons and Nick. Simmons had a strange smell to him, such as Oklahoma had never encountered before. But Nick the rat... as usual he was clear enough: always angry and always scared, all the time, and none too clean. But Oklahoma made a lot of people feel that way, which was why he was a loner. As to this particular rat, what was wrong with him, really? "Heck," Oklahoma said to himself, "the way I fight is natural enough to me, but it might have scared him, right enough, if he was raised in a lab like he says." And he shrugged his sore shoulders and continued to march.

Two weeks' travel, mostly along the same asphalt road, brought them at last to a little village at the muddy bank of a great, brown, sluggish river.

"Susquehannah?" Oklahoma asked.

"Yes, it is," said Bob Simmons. "We crossed here before; there's a bargeman here who'll take us across for a can of food or two."

"Looks like a trading village," the boar said. "Anyone use this river to carry goods?"

"I suppose so," the man replied.

"Safe river, then," Oklahoma said. "Some of 'em have bad spots. Rio Grande has pirates; southern Mississippi has giant crocodiles. Reckon."

"I'm not particularly worried," Bob Simmons said. He led the way into the village. Here the asphalt was more heavily cracked, and built atop and around it were a series of wooden houses. Oklahoma snuffed the place, caught the scents of more than two dozen people and animals. As they moved on along the road, he began to see some of them. Most were human, and most were standing about looking at the newcomers. Oklahoma sniffed them individually, and decided most of them were clean. None smelled sick either. He nodded to himself. Good, safe town. No bandits here; no dogs either.

"Where's Sand?" Bob Simmons asked of a heavy, unshaven man leaning against the wall of one of the larger shacks.

"He's inside," the man sneered.

"Tell him we have work for him," Nick said. "We need to get across the river immediately."

"You tell him," the man said insolently. "I don't run errands for animals, especially not rats."

Oklahoma snuffed at him.

"Get your nose away from me, pig," said the man.

"You're not too polite, boy," Oklahoma said. "Reckon. Not too smart neither."

"You don't belong here, you stinking hog," the man replied. "If I had my way, I wouldn't even let Sand stay here."

Even as the fat man and Oklahoma stared at each other, Bob Simmons emerged from the bar, bringing with him a lithe, tall figure that Oklahoma recognized, even without smelling him, as a cat. He was wearing a vest that smelled like old leather and a pair of woolen shorts. His fur, as his name suggested, was a soft sandy color. Perked pink ears, whiskered nose, and slitted green eyes all focused immediately on Oklahoma and Nick, and he made a mild sniffing noise. Oklahoma thought his scent suggested curiosity.

"I remember you," the cat said to Nick in a mellow voice. "But you, Mr. Boar... you're new around these parts."

"Nothing wrong with that, if you don't hurt anyone who was leaving you alone," Oklahoma replied. "You're taller than most cats I've met. How come?"

"I'm part lion," Sand said. Abruptly he tilted his head up and scratched vigorously at his neck. "Jesus! You've given me fleas already," he said with another tilt of his head.

"Sorry," Oklahoma said. "Least they're not Pennsylvania fleas. Might have carried those things all the way from Alabama."

Sand licked his chops, revealing very white teeth. "Hrrrrm." He looked at Bob Simmons. "So you want to cross the river?"

"That's right."

"What do you have for me?"

Simmons pulled a can out of his pack and handed it to the cat.

"Hrrrm. Creamed corn? I don't like that." Casually he flipped it back to Simmons.

"Don't waste time," Nick said. "Just give him the tuna, and let's go."

"Tuna?" Sand said. "I'll bet they killed dolphins when they fished it out of the sea. It's morally outrageous."

"Will you take it, or not?" Nick snapped.

"I might swallow my outrage for two cans," suggested Sand.

"I hate cats," Nick grumbled as his partner fished two cans of tuna from among his belongings.

"You have poor taste," Sand said. He stowed the tuna in pockets inside his vest and stretched. "Let's go to the barge. I'm tired. Normally I'd be sleeping right about now."

The heavy man leaning against the wall straightened from his slouch and stood with his arms akimbo. Into the sudden silence he proclaimed loudly, "I'd like to put you to sleep for good, like they used to do at the pound."

Sand yawned. "A very sophisticated observation, Jack. Every day you remind me why I like your company so much."

"Don't try talking smart to me," the man shouted. He reached around to his backside and pulled out a folding knife.

"Ought to put that away," Oklahoma said.

Pawing at the knife with his fat fingers, Jack drew out a short, hard blade and pointed it at Oklahoma.

"Put it away, Jack," Sand said. "I've been faster than you since we were boys."

"You're gonna die, pussycat," Jack said, and swung his knife.

Oklahoma started to lunge at him, but Sand was faster. A shrill, inhuman growl escaped his throat, even as with his right paw he knocked Jack's knife-arm away, and with his left he dealt the big man a savage claw to the face.

Jack screamed and fell face-down. His blood pulsed rapidly into the cracks in the asphalt.

"We'd better go," Sand said. "His brothers are meaner than he is, and they might have guns." He leapt over Jack's writhing form and scampered toward the river.

"Been a long day already," Oklahoma said. "Going to get longer." Panting hoarsely, he jogged along behind the others with his hooves clopping on the highway.

The barge was broad—large enough to carry a horse cart; and made of wet pine logs. As Sand poled them out into the Susquehannah, he asked, "It might be a poor idea for me to return there. Do you mind if I... er, follow you for a while?"

"You ever done any traveling?" Oklahoma asked.

"Not much. I grew up in that little village."

"Reckon you'll get a chance to do some now," the boar told him. He turned to Simmons and Nick. "Cats are quiet—fast too, got good night vision. Other senses are good too. You could use one in your business."

Simmons, who was still panting from the run to the barge, gave Oklahoma a pained expression. "We'll discuss it later," he said.

🐾 ∞ 🐾

The stony brook was shallow enough for all of them to wade. Sand protested violently when he was told their intention to do so—but he gave in when he saw that, with his natural agility, he could travel along it stepping mainly on flat brown rocks, rarely immersing his legs at all. On either side of them were steep hillsides dotted with aromatic pines and other trees. This stream wound along the valley and past the hill on which the slavers' camp was set. The woods on either side were heavy enough to afford them cover as, leaving the stream, they crept through the trees and up the slope. On their previous trip here, Simmons and Nick had discovered a thick copse of bushes near the crest of the hill from which they could both observe the camp and come at the barn from behind.

As they proceeded, treading carefully across fallen needles and stepping around acorn nuts and woody pinecones, Oklahoma took slow, quiet, deep sniffs of the area. He could get nothing from the camp around which they were moving; the wind was against him, and all he smelled, besides the agreeable forest scents, were the odors of his three companions. Nick, as always, was sour with tension; Sand, as always, was cool and relaxed; and Bob Simmons was... odd, not like any man the boar had ever scented before. He had not been that way at first... how, why the change?

The first building Oklahoma saw, through the trees, was small and brown. He took a powerful sniff and winced.

"That's an outhouse, idiot," Nick whispered.

"Reckon," Oklahoma said lamely.

Only moments later, the four lay side by side atop soft pine needles, looking down the hill at a wide, tall building with a sharply sloping roof.

"There's the barn," Simmons whispered. "I don't see anyone nearby it, but you can bet the dogs are on the other side."

"What happened to the slavers who you say live here?" Sand asked. "Haven't they been gone an awfully long time, if you've been down to Virginia and back since you last found them gone?"

"Don't tell us our business," Nick replied. "You're only here because Oklahoma insisted."

"Okay," the boar said. "You want me to charge around the barn and fight those two giant dogs, and meanwhile you two will lead the women across the camp and down the hill. Right?"

"That's what we hired you for," Nick snapped. "We'll be ready with our guns."

"Hold on," Oklahoma said. He sniffed heavily. The outhouse imposed itself upon his senses, but he sniffed deeper, sorted out other, less potent scents. There was a canine scent, certainly, and even the muffled smell of a group of people. But something seemed wrong. "There's only one dog," he concluded.

"Maybe one of them escaped," was the rat's reply. "Will you do what we hired you for, or not?"

Oklahoma looked at Sand. The tawny cat shrugged.

"Reckon," said Oklahoma. He handed his pack to Sand, closed his eyes, drew the dog's scent deep into his nostrils. His limbs tensed, and his breaths came quicker. He barely felt the brush rake his hide as he broke from the copse and charged down the slope, kicking up needles and cones with each cloven-hoofed step. He could hear his own vulgar snorting sounds, the cold sweat beading on his fur; he slipped, rolled, scrambled to his feet and ran on, sniffing, sniffing.

Even as he reached level ground, his snorts were answered by a long, low howl. Then came a second. His rage redoubled, and he leapt toward the howling, and even as his body collided with that of his foe, he opened his eyes and saw a creature twice his size, a monster dog eight feet high and six feet broad, standing on its hind legs, with matted black hair and two slavering heads.

Even as he collided with it, the dog caught him by the shoulders and hurled him away. He tumbled over the rocky ground head over heels, rolled, came up, and charged again, snorting, but even berserk, he noticed its dark eyes even as it barked furiously at him. Looked like his own eyes, sort of...

He slashed with his tusk, drew blood and tasted fur. The dog struck him with a vicious backhand, so that again he tumbled away and sprang to his feet. He drew several heavy breaths, prepared to charge again.

What about those eyes? They were weaving left and right, why?

Because the dog was shaking its heads and gesturing with its hands.

Oklahoma calmed his breathing. This wasn't right. He was supposed to fight a dog, wasn't he? But this thing wasn't just a dog. It was an adapted animal like him, even if it couldn't speak. He tasted the bloody fur still in his mouth.

"Hold on," he said. "You're clean. That's not something dogs usually worry about."

The dog shook both heads again.

"And you're not chained up, neither."

No acknowledgement. This was obvious.

"And you don't fight like a dog. If you did, you would have kept coming for my throat till one of us was dead."

The dog nodded vigorously.

"All the same, I think we're gonna have to fight," Oklahoma said. "I never had much stomach for slavers, and that includes their watchdogs. The women in there have to go home."

The dog waved its hands wildly. Then it sprang to the barn door and rapped. There was a loud scraping sound from within, as of a crossbar being lifted, and the barn door opened a crack. A hairless face appeared in the crack; a woman, Oklahoma decided, noting her human smell.

"You're friends with this dog?" Oklahoma asked her. "The story as I heard it was he was guarding the barn for some slavers to keep you from being rescued."

"Who are you?" the woman asked in a frightened voice.

"I'm the Oklahoma Boar. Some scouts from your home village hired me to kill this here watchdog and set you free."

"Set us free?" she said incredulously. "This dog is protecting us from them. He's from the cerberus clone series—trained to be a guard. The slavers are all afraid of him; they probably hired you themselves."

"If the slavers are gone, how come you haven't left?"

"This is the only place he can protect us," she said. "If we tried to leave, the bandits could attack us from every side. Anyway, we have food here. Our husbands and children are all dead—where do we have to go?"

"Wait a minute—then who were all those men I met back at the village?"

"Slavers," she said.

"Reckon they could have been slavers, since I didn't see any children. Cerberus clone, eh?" he directed to the dog.

The dog nodded.

"Won't leave the door, huh?"

The dog shook its heads.

Oklahoma responded by tossing his own. "I don't like being tricked. Those men were supposed to circle around the other side of the barn and..." he sniffed. The dog, the woman, the other women inside the barn filled his senses, but he also picked up the smells of his three travelling companions, very nearby.

At the moment he heard the click of Bob Simmons' gun, he realized why the man smelled strange.

"You're maskin' your scent with something," he said as he turned to look at the man, who was standing at the corner of the barn opposite the crack in the door.

Simmons held a heavy shotgun. Beside him stood Nick the rat, his hooded robe cast away, holding a machine pistol.

"You bet I am," Simmons said. "As soon as you told me you could tell by scent when someone was afraid, I started wearing cologne. Wearing too much, I guess you should say."

"Reckon," Oklahoma said. "That's a mean-looking gun. You planning to use it on us?" He looked askance at the cerberus, which had already began to snarl doubly in its meaty throats.

"I'm going to love killing you, pig," Nick said with a rodent smile. "I'm tired of your stench in my nose all the time, and your garbled hick voice in my ears."

"Sorry to hear that," Oklahoma said. "But I feel good, knowing I never liked you, neither."

The dog took a step forward, only to be met with the barrel of Simmons' shotgun. "We had extra weapons cached in another building," the man said, "but you would have stopped us from getting close enough to dig them up. This stupid boar distracted you for the time it took."

"Where's Sand?" Oklahoma asked.

"We sent that idiot to scout on down the hill," Nick said. "He's probably half a mile away now. You're going to die." He aimed the pistol at Oklahoma's heart. "That flak jacket won't save you, either," he added with a smirk.

As Nick squeezed the trigger, the cerberus leapt suddenly in front of Oklahoma, struck the barn door with all his weight so that it slammed shut. Bullets ripped through his huge chest; blood fountained from his back, and one bullet struck Oklahoma in his shoulder, just where the centaur had kicked him two weeks before.

The force of the impact spun Oklahoma around and slammed him against the side of the barn. His breath quickened, and he could barely hear the sad whimpering of the dying guard dog as he rushed at the two slavers, felt soft fur brush across his head before he slammed into Bob Simmons and knocked him off his feet. There was a catlike hiss and an answering squeak, and Oklahoma smelled Sand nearby, and the scent of Nick's blood mingled with that of the dying cerberus and that of Oklahoma himself, and then metal struck Oklahoma in the head, and the boar thrashed so that his tusks stuck in some type of tough fabric, like a flak jacket. Off on the side, in the dirt, Nick squealed as Sand clawed at him. Oklahoma scrabbled with his long-nailed hands, felt nothing but clods of dirt, and the metal object struck him in the head again.

Oklahoma swung blindly, hit it, felt it fly away and heard Bob Simmons scream when Oklahoma's other swiping hand began to rip at his scalp.

🐾 ∞ 🐾

"I like rooftops," Sand said. "No one ever looks for me on them, and I can sleep in peace. I never thought I would one day use a roof to ambush someone."

"Good idea," Oklahoma said. "Reckon. Well, we've got some useful things from these two: canned food, and guns and armor, a flashlight, and a good set of binoculars. The rest of the slavers, back at the village, will be lookin' for us soon. We ought to take what we have and go."

One of the women was wrapping Oklahoma's bloodied shoulder

with a clean rag. Sand was almost unmarked—all he had was a small rat-bite on one paw.

"Where can we go?" the cat asked one of the women.

"There's another village eastward along the stream, just at the edge of the hills," she replied. "They might shelter us for a while."

"We got enough barter goods to persuade them," Oklahoma said. "East," he added. "Haven't gone that direction a while, 'cept to get to this hill."

"You don't really care where you go, do you?" Sand asked. "If there's food there, I mean."

"Nope," said Oklahoma. "It's a big world. Lots of things to smell."

SECTION TWO
LIVING APART:
FURRY ALTERNATE
WORLDS

FOREWORD BY GENE BRESHEARS

Probably for as long as there have been stories, story tellers have used animals as characters in some of those stories. Sometimes they did this out of a belief that all the inhabitants of the world were part of the same family. If people talked to each other, why shouldn't the animals? Sometimes the animals were chosen because they had become symbols for certain personality traits or belief systems or relationships.

So it remains with modern writers of anthropomorphic, or Furry, stories. Their heroes, villains, bystanders, and supporting players are talking animals for many reasons. An author may choose to make a particular character a cat, for instance, because he believes that most of his audience will associate certain traits and deeper meanings to the character. He may be attempting to evoke the mysteries of the Egyptian goddess, Bast, or simply saying that the character has a cuddly, yet predatory, personality.

Once you have a character who is an anthropomorphic cat, it seems only natural to ask what kind of world and society he inhabits. What are the relationships between the anthropomorphic cats and anthropomorphic mice, for instance? Are anthropomorphic dogs more prone to certain professions than others? Do cows picket butcher shops? Do sheep resent sheepdogs, or admire them as heroes and protectors?

A world of talking mice, horses, cats, and weasels is obviously different than our everyday world. As soon as a reader knows this, they begin reacting to the story on a mythic or fantastic level. They don't expect the author to be talking about a specific real world situation. This makes a Furry world ideal for tackling topics which may be a bit too controversial or emotional for some readers. The reader ends up thinking about such a topic, and perhaps finds himself or herself rooting for a different side than they might in the real world, without quite realizing it.

For example, for some people, the topic of interracial dating is so upsetting, that they would stop reading a story as soon as they realized that's what the story was about. Yet when Gary Larsen drew a cartoon about a wolf dating a sheep, those same people likely chuckled at the punch line without consciously realizing that it was the same topic.

Even when the author isn't addressing any particular issue, a Furry world grants a certain freedom. Cultural, political, and ethnic assumptions which might interfere with a reader's ability to immerse herself in the world can be sidestepped. Ultimately, the goal of any writer is to share something he or she has imagined with the reader. So we want to remove barriers between the reader and this thing we've imagined.

Sometimes the hero has a Furry face. The face of a fox or otter or rabbit may evoke certain feelings from the reader, serving as shorthand for the character's personality. It can be a mask that obscures the reader's biases and assumptions that might interfere with his enjoyment of the story. Or it can be a mirror, where the reader sees a bit of herself in a being which looks nothing like her. By extension, a Furry world can represent or reflect aspects of the real world, bringing new illumination and understanding to our relationships, whether familial, political, economic, or cultural.

For me, a Furry world is just a fun place to write about. Whether I'm writing about feline mages fighting to stave off a mystical apocalypse, or a canine industrial laborer trying to make ends meet under difficult circumstances, I'm spinning a tale that I hope will be as fun for the reader to read as it was for me to imagine.

※

PORT IN A STORM

Arnneas was heading for her room feeling lonely and frustrated when a MedAlert klaxon went off right beside her ear. She snarled reflexively, then howled in genuine annoyance as a snail-like Calotian zipped past her, almost knocking her to the floor. The speeding Calotian made an "excuse me" wave with its tentacles without breaking pace, its smooth glide carrying it down the corridor and out of sight in answer to the alert.

Arnneas settled herself with an effort, her long tail lashing the air with a vengeance. Her species was feline, but arboreal, and it took her real effort not to leap for the overhead conduits in a hunting crouch. She took an extra moment to will her fur to lie flat, then continued on towards her cabin in long, seemingly calm strides. The alert and near-collision had done nothing for her mood. Her species liked lots of room, and being jostled was a lot to put up with when she didn't want to be alone.

She entered her cabin, shut the door, and demurely ripped a chair to shreds. There were times when she really regretted having joined the Contact Service, those times being few and far between. The Service was not the problem right now, she forced herself to admit. Her problem was purely a matter of stubborn pride, and her Service contract avoided those areas with great care.

Throwing herself into bed, she worked to control her annoyance. Valein, her Contact partner, was due back in a week or so. The shaggy wolf-like crewmate was a partner of other sorts, and it was in this latter capacity that she missed him most at the moment. When he returned, she would ease her frustrations on his funny furred self. He was probably having a wonderful time playing disguised native on the planet below, she thought darkly. She would make him pay for it.

She composed herself for sleep, giving her fur only a cursory brushing. With effort, she convinced her tail to stop beating an involved, frustrated pattern on the bedding. Calm at last, with her finely-furred ears relaxed and her eyes closed, she sighed a half-contented sigh and let her whiskers stand at ease.

Eleven minutes later the bed threw her onto the floor with no warning—regrettably, the only sure way it had of waking her. She pounced on the intercom switch with a furred fist. "Arnneas, at service," she growled menacingly.

"This is Theresa," a timid voice said. "Arnneas—could you come down to med bay six, right away?"

Arnneas let several moments pass before answering. Theresa was new to the Service, and had been attached as an assistant medtech to Arnneas'

Contact team. Being new, she was slow to catch on to the niceties of inter-species relations, and in particular seemed determined to annoy Valein with her attention. Not that Arnneas was jealous; but Valein brought out what maternal instinct she allowed in herself, and Valein didn't like strangers fawning on him. Theresa had yet to find a circle of friends on the *Natarkca*, so she hovered near ever-friendly Valein.

Or, when Valein was off-ship, near Arnneas. She allowed a hint of her annoyance to remain in her voice. "Does it have to be now, Theresa? I'm extremely off-duty."

The voice on the other end was shaky. "Please, Arnneas, can you just come here? I don't want to say why, not on the intercom... but—please?"

Arnneas sighed. "Okay. Five minutes."

She retrieved her duty harness from where she had thrown it and slipped into it, taking a moment to adjust it before deciding she really didn't care what she looked like. Valein was off-ship, and Anarrask—that high-handed slime-wallower who desired her purely because of her status—could go hang out an airlock for all she cared. She decided to get things over with as quickly as possible and loped towards the medical sec-tion on all fours, hoping no one would stop her along the way. She wasn't feeling at all sociable.

When she arrived at med bay six, things were in general disarray. Several Calotians eyed her as she came in, their tentacles waving in agi-tation. Theresa, tall but oddly graceless, stood near a table looking dis-traught. Splat was lurking on the floor nearby looking rigid and glum. That sobered her instantly. Splat was her other permanent teammate, and whenever he was not in one of the aquatic bars, trouble was afoot.

On the table near Theresa sat an environment box, open to the air. Inside was an alien—one of the natives from the planet below, uncon-scious or dead. Since Theresa was currently responsible for taking care of Contact natives, it was not too hard to guess that something had gone wrong with this one. That in itself was extremely bad news—though why Theresa would want to unload on Arnneas and what Splat had to do with it was a mystery. Arnneas adjusted herself invisibly and prepared to be consoling and understanding.

Theresa glanced from Arnneas to the cream-furred alien body, then stared at the floor. "Arnneas, thank you for... it's—there's been an acci-dent."

Arnneas nodded to herself. Theresa needed comforting for having screwed something up. "How can I help?"

Theresa looked at her with tears edging her eyes. "You can't; it's—there's nothing... " Her eyes took on odd expression, staring at Arnneas. "You don't understand." She gestured at the inert body on the lab table. "That's... it's Valein. He's dead."

Arnneas jolted straight upwards. "*WHAT?!!*"

Theresa nodded jerkily. Splat looked up, and even he managed to look miserable. Arnneas walked gingerly to the table and put her hand on the alien's shoulder. Her senses confirmed what Theresa said; the being was quite dead. But—Valein?!

"What happened?" she demanded.

Splat wriggled two of his manipulator tentacles. "Got emergency signal from partner Valein, from planet. Retrieved him to ship, approximate past seventy minutes. Partner Valein had something with him wrong, removed self from environment transport, was quickly dead."

Arnneas tensed. "He wouldn't do that!"

Splat looked up rigidly, his manipulators waving apologetic, confused disagreement. "You are correct, yet partner Valein is still dead." He touched her ankle with a manipulator; it was dry with regret. "Was not fault of pilot or commander shuttle; checked record for self. Crew could do nothing."

Arnneas nodded, having had the same thought. "The recordings?"

Theresa glanced at the Calotians, who waved an unhappy shrug. "I'll have copies sent to your cabin, Arnneas." She took Arnneas by the hand, an unusual and undeserved familiarity. "Arnneas—I'm sorry."

Arnneas resisted placing her hand back on the alien body that had recently been Valein. She felt a dull ache inside herself beginning to widen as she realized the death of her partner, her friend. She turned instead to the medtech. "Theresa—why did *you* decide to tell me, about...?"

Theresa shook her head. "I knew, I think, that you were very special to Valein. I guess I wanted to be. I thought maybe sharing it with you, and with Sppthth—uh, with Sppllthhh..."

She was spitting and sputtering helplessly. "That's why they call me 'Splat,' Theresa," Splat said with what passed for kindness. "Sppappthhlatara."

"I thought, sharing the pain of—this—would make it easier somehow. For both of us. I know you cared for him... and he for you," she finished miserably.

Arnneas nodded. She realized the near-furless medtech desired to be embraced and comforted, but didn't trust herself to do so. It took considerable effort to not scream and destroy the med bay.

Back in her cabin, Arnneas played back the records from the shuttle, watching Valein's last moments. The planet, in shades of blue and tan and brown, swam before the cameras as the shuttle neared and hovered. In the distance, a native ran quickly towards the camera, chased by several others. One of the pursuers was much closer than the rest, close enough that it might have stumbled aboard the shuttle while the shuttle commander tried to rescue Valein. A stunner dropped that pursuer in its tracks.

The native that was Valein in disguise headed straight for the landing craft, with the casual stare of one who seeks the unseen. He couldn't see the hovering shuttle with unaided eyes, even knowing it was there; the shuttle commander reached down a suited arm and scooped him up as he went by. To the pursuers, it would have seemed that Valein had suddenly vanished into mid-air. Fortunately they seemed more concerned with their fallen comrade than with their quarry; Valein's rescue was clean.

When the recording showed the ground receding as the shuttle returned to space, Arnneas switched to an internal view and zoomed in on the environment container that now housed Valein. He was pressed flat to the floor of the environment transport, looking about dazedly with wide eyes. Even to her trained eyes he was indistinguishable from any of the other natives; the Changer had matched his appearance to theirs flaw-lessly, as usual. In the recording he looked ill, or poorly-used. After a few minutes he began nervously tracing the edges of the transport. Arnneas wondered if he was drugged.

She watched in shock as Valein charged the opening of the transport container, spilling him into the main body of the shuttle. Per normal proce-dures, the shuttle filters had already replaced the planet's air with Standard air. Valein began choking and gasping almost immediately; something in Federation Standard air triggered a reaction in his alien body.

The shuttle commander appeared instantly and struggled to keep him alive, but it was useless; the shuttle was too far into space to return to the planet's atmosphere, and too far from the *Natarkca* to create a temporary matching environment. In his alien form, Valein died in heaving, agonized gasps.

Having assured herself that the recording was not faked, Arnneas watched it again many times. Nothing was obvious except Valein's dazed confusion; perhaps he had been drugged, or hypnotized, or even poisoned. An autopsy might tell—*but no, let him rest!* she shivered. Whatever his form, Valein was gone. In spite of their diverse backgrounds, her Contact-oriented shipmates would fight seeing his last soul-body disturbed. He must have known he would die, leaving the environment transport; their pre-mission orientation briefings were always very specific. His reason for sacrificing himself died with him.

She replayed the recording and tried to guess what had caused the natives to chase him. They seemed agitated, but there was nothing obvi-ously threatening about the situation. From her own experiences, she'd have said it was just a friendly chase through the fields.

She flipped off the viewer after a few hours and threw herself into bed. Tired and distraught, she toyed with an idea: Somehow, Valein had lost both his communicator *and* his transponder; a native had found the tran-sponder and triggered the emergency locater; and that unfortunate being was now lying dead in the med lab, while Valein was safe on the planet having the time of his life.

It was thin fantasy, and she knew it. Valein had been occasionally clumsy, or sometimes less than brilliant; but he would never under any circumstances have lost both his communicator and transponder. An alien wouldn't know how to trigger the emergency locater, nor would Valein have revealed his secrets. He certainly wouldn't abandon the *Natarkca* voluntarily...

A follow-up team would investigate—but Arnneas knew it would not be exhaustive, just the Commander satisfying his curiosity. Valein's initial reports had confirmed what the surveys had indicated: the aliens on this world were not that important.

She hid her head in her arms. *Poor, gentle Valein,* she thought sadly. She wondered if even *he* knew what had gone wrong.

※ ∞ ※

Valein sat up with a fuzzy head and wondered what had gone wrong.

He picked up the pieces of his memory and tried to sort it out. He had been chasing Taa-neti, and Ven-tu and Sha-teen had been chasing him, and suddenly he was back in Sha-teen's den. He tried to stand, but his legs wouldn't support him. It felt for all the world like—

Everything became obvious at once. He'd been shot with a stunner! Taa-neti must have triggered the recall switch in his collar. The *Natarkca* sent down a rescue shuttle, and the space-happy idiots on board had shot *him* thinking he was one of the natives.

Which meant Taa-neti was on board the *Natarkca*.

Wearing his collar.

He winced. The Commander was going to skin him alive for this one!

Rising shakily onto all four legs—and wishing yet again he would quit getting quadrupedal assignments—Valein eased his way out into the night air. The darkness startled him; how long he had been unconscious?

To one side sat two of his hosts/friends, Ven-tu and Fier-neth, talking quietly together. They stopped as he weaved his way drunkenly beside them.

"You are feeling better, Val-ane?" Ven-tu asked.

"I'm fine," Valein said with what he hoped was a cheerful, convincing demeanor.

"Good. We were worried about you, falling over like that in the middle of the day. That's almost *strange*, isn't it?!"

Valein hid his agitation and tried to appear casual. He wondered how Kyr-feth had answered that question when *he* woke up. Kyr-feth was the native Valein had stunned for the *Natarkca* to Pattern. In his current form, Valein could easily pass for Kyr-feth's healthier twin brother; fortunately, that being lived well away from the village, and Valein avoided him with due diligence.

"Have you seen Taa-neti?" he asked without emphasis. They both thumped their tails, No. Valein let it drop, not wanting them to wonder about it. He could never explain about the *Natarkca* and where Taa-neti probably was. This species had not developed much in the way of technology; the concept of starflight and the Federation was *way* out of their realm.

Sen-oun, she of the Council, appeared from over a short rise and trotted to where they were sitting. She sat down formally in front of him. "We were concerned about you, Val-ane. Do you often fall asleep in mid-romp, in the middle of the day?"

Valein sighed inaudibly. How to explain a stunner? "No, Sen-oun, this was a rare occasion. I regret that everyone was worried about me." She continued to stare at him, as if reading his soul. He flicked his ears in a casual, happy fashion. "Really, I'm fine."

"Many things you do are *strange*, Val-ane," she said, causing the others to shy back imperceptibly. "As we believe in the Others, *strange* ones must be cared for—would you not agree?"

"Of course, Sen-oun," Valein lied. He bowed low before her, signifying his willingness—in ritual, anyway—to place his life in her hands. Paws. Whatever. In point of fact, he wasn't about to trust any of them much further than he could throw them, which was not far. The Federation was wasting its time on this planet as far as he was concerned, and that's the way all his reports had read. He'd gladly move on to something else, leaving Sen-oun and the rest behind.

He held his pose for a long time, until finally Sen-oun seemed content. She left, and he sat upright again. If she were eager to leave 'Val-ane' alone with his odd ideas and suggestions, he wouldn't complain. The natives were a surprisingly non-violent people, but they did not take kindly to new ideas from a stranger. Particularly when said stranger started asking strange questions about the little points of light in the sky.

As for the 'Others'—Valein shrugged it off. Each species had its beliefs, its spirits and gods. The ones that counted were the ones he believed in. All others were mere fluff.

Valein shook himself and looked around. He would play tourist until the *Natarkca* came for him. Given the way he had screwed up, it might be the last relaxation he would get for a long time.

He turned to Fier-neth and Ven-tu, who were eyeing him uncomfortably but without anger. "How long was I—er, asleep, exactly?"

The question bothered them for some reason. Finally Ven-tu spoke up. "You were asleep three full days, Val-ane," he said. "We were growing quite concerned."

Valein added up times in his head and did a conversion; he had been out over 60 hours!—which explained why everyone was so concerned. This species was obviously more sensitive to Federation stunners than the norm. Or, the idiot who had stunned him had used the wrong size-setting.

He grinned. "Well, I'm fine now. And very hungry!"

"You're always hungry, Val-ane," Fier-neth laughed. "What you need is a good romp!" And with that, she jumped him.

Valein quickly found himself the center of attention in a game of Chase The Furry, jumped on all sides by laughing, carefree villagers. He put up with it in good grace, but wished he could be accorded Council status like Sen-oun. Council members were exempt from acting like idiots all the time, and Valein preferred a quieter life.

After dinner and another romp, he curled up with his host-mate, Sha-teen, and tried to think the situation through. His initial plan had been to wait for Taa-neti to reappear with a near-sister from the *Natarkca*; but that should have happened already. No matter how angry the Commander was, the *Natarkca* wouldn't abandon him. They also wouldn't leave orbit with Taa-neti on board, unless there was an extreme emergency elsewhere. Something must have gone wrong, he decided—something besides his losing his communicator, and having his collar stolen by Taa-neti.

His annoyance bubbled quietly to the surface. "Why did Taa-neti take my collar?" he asked Sha-teen.

"Because she likes you, Val-ane," Sha-teen said shyly. "There are a number of us who would like to see you stay in the village." She nuzzled him warmly with her nose. "Me included."

"Don't get your hopes up," he said without heat. "I can't join the village. It's not in my control to stay."

She stopped nuzzling long enough to stare at him quietly, then flicked her ears and went back to nuzzling. "There you go, saying nonsensical things again. You are a very odd person, Val-ane."

"Okay, I'm weird. Life is full of weirdness."

That caused her to shiver. "Don't say things like that, even in jest. I don't really think you're—weird."

She was slowly getting more forward with her nuzzling, so he moved away and sat near the den entrance, looking out. Sha-teen stared after him, apparently more amused than annoyed.

"So tell me: why can't you join our village? We like you!"

"I like you too, Sha-teen. That has nothing to do with it! I simply can't stay."

"But why not? Is it one of *those* things, like swimming?"

Valein rolled his eyes. His species was deathly afraid of large bodies of water, and being in a different body didn't affect his natural fears. These aliens all swam, so it looked odd that he didn't; but he couldn't tell them that *his* species was afraid of the water. He was supposed to be one of *their* species, for Contact purposes.

Sha-teen walked over and sat beside him, then rubbed her head against his neck. "If you don't like Taa-neti, perhaps you and I could be mated."

"I have nothing against Taa-neti," he said, avoiding the implied proposal. "I just wish she hadn't taken my collar, that's all."

Sha-teen hrrumphed. "I don't understand why you are so bothered. Taa-neti meant no harm, and the collar she gave you is very nice. Yours was plain and worn, and this one has lots of very pretty stones—and some very nice designs scratched into it. It's much nicer, don't you think?"

Mine had an emergency transponder in it, he didn't say. His collar had been specifically manufactured to look worn and not too flashy. Once he got back to the ship, Valein would track down and trash the genius who thought a 'plain' collar would make it safe.

He dragged his attention back to the present. "It's not important now," he said. "Can you take me back to the place where I———er, where I fell asleep? To the exact spot?"

Sha-teen hesitated. "Why would you want to go there?"

He wondered what to tell her. That one of the lights in the sky might send down a little light to pick him up? Not likely. "I just want to look around," he covered.

When Sha-teen didn't answer, he nudged her. "Play along, Sha-teen. Can you take me to the same spot?"

"No, Val-ane."

"Oh come on, you must remember where it is! I could probably find it myself, but I want to find the *exact* place where I fell asleep." When she didn't answer, he turned to face her directly. She seemed unenthusiastic. "You remember," he said, waving with his front paws. "It was over the grassy blue hill, and—"

"I remember where it is," she said unhappily. She looked uncomfortably into his eyes. "I can't take you there, on Council orders. No one can."

Valein stood up, surprised and annoyed. "Why not?"

"Because you are acting so—so *very* oddly, Val-ane. *Strangely*, even. The Council is afraid for you, and has decided you are to stay in the village until they are sure you are well and calm."

Valein thought hard and fast. If he were kept a prisoner in the village, he would never get back to the rendezvous point where the shuttle had accidentally picked up Taa-neti. Once they realized he had lost his communicator, that's where they would wait—but eventually the *Natarkca* would assume he had been killed or permanently incapacitated, and would abandon him. The Commander might write him off anyway in annoyance if things dragged on too long. Valein didn't want to take that chance.

"I have to get back to that point, Sha-teen, no matter what the Council may think or say."

"Don't say that!" she pleaded.

"Will you help me?"

Sha-teen ducked her head miserably. "No, Val-ane."

Valein sighed, stood up and headed out the doorway. "Then I'll just have to go myself. Thanks for the hospitality, Sha-teen."

Sha-teen ran out the door after him. "Val-ane, wait! Please don't go!"

Fearing that others would hear her cries, Valein turned around and herded her back into her den. "Sha-teen... I'll try and explain it to you." He waited until she sat, then sat in front of her. "I am from another place, you all know that."

"A village far, far away."

"Right. And I miss my home very, very much."

She pranced in front of him. "But that's silly! This can be your home, Val-ane, as easily as anywhere else."

"No, it can't," he said in exasperation. "Look, this is your cave, right? How would you feel if Ven-tu came over and decided he was going to live here, and forced you to leave? You'd miss your home, wouldn't you?"

"Why would Ven-tu want this den? His is nice, too; you've seen it."

"That's not the point. What if he just wanted to own what you own, because—well, because..."

Valein ran down, suddenly realizing that the People did not have words for concepts involving petty jealousy, spite, or any of the other selfish emotions common in the rest of his universe. They were kind, playful, and almost totally non-aggressive.

He decided to try a different approach. "Do you miss Taa-neti?"

"She is missing, if that is what you mean."

"No, I mean, don't you wonder where she is, and wish she were here?"

"Well, I figure she is happy wherever she is, or she would have come back by now. She was not a member of the Council or anything."

He decided not to push that angle, because he really didn't want anyone wondering too hard where Taa-neti had disappeared to. When she returned she would be full of odd stories, and he didn't want to be blamed for that, too.

He tried again: "You would miss me if I left?"

She nuzzled him warmly. "You have no reason to leave, Val-ane, and many reasons to stay. The situations are not the same at all."

Valein gave up. Sha-teen wasn't stupid; she was just very literal and single-minded, and she trusted the judgement of the Council completely. If he were going to get away, it would be without her help.

"Okay, Sha-teen, I understand," he said. He rolled her playfully onto her back. "I don't want to upset you or the Council. I really don't." He reached forward to caress her, and gently but firmly applied pressure to certain points on either side of her furred neck. Her eyes grew wide in surprise before she went limp, completely relaxed but unable to move.

"I'm sorry, Sha-teen," he said in her ear. "You'll be all right in a short time, I promise. I must get back to my home, or at least try." He looked at her gently; somehow, her eyes looked frightened and sad. "Please don't worry, and try not to hate me. I do care for you, really—but I *must* go home."

He left the den at a casual pace, then broke into a dead run once he reached the outskirts of the village. He didn't want anyone to start a romp; he wasn't positive where the *Natarkca* shuttle might be waiting, and it might take him some time to search for the right spot. He hoped the shuttle would be watching for a native in that area doing Federation arm-motions. If they had already given up on him—

Valein grinned nervously. Arnneas wouldn't let them give up so quickly. Her rank aboard ship was no higher than his and well short of command, but she was very aggressive in stating her opinions. The Commander would be reasonable to the letter of the law if she pushed the point. Of course, Valein would pay for it if things went that far. That thought alone made him all the more desperate to hurry.

He found the general area where he had chased Taa-neti while trying to retrieve his stolen collar. He looked around carefully for landmarks that might guide him. Unfortunately, everything looked different at night, and he really hadn't been paying attention at the time. He definitely hadn't been expecting anyone from the *Natarkca* to be hanging around.

He wondered again: Where could they be?

It slowly occurred to him that something might have happened to Taa-neti. The natives did not have obvious sexual characteristics, so a casual observer might not realize that the 'Valein' they picked up was female. If they didn't do a memory scan, they might not know they had the wrong person until she walked out of the Changer in his body, screaming and cowering in fear at all the strange monsters on board...

He shook his head. Arnneas with her strong empathic sense would know it wasn't him, that he hadn't gone crazy on the planet. She would insist that the Calotians run a memory scan, and then they would know. Or Theresa might—that is, she'd certainly...

Valein winced. If Taa-neti had freaked or gone into a self-induced coma, Theresa might not think to check whether it was really him or not. She was still new, and very scattered; she'd probably lock the little alien in an isolation cell for observation. Depending on how alert Arnneas was, the *Natarkca* might move on, not even knowing it wasn't him. Eventually the Calotians would try to Change her, and they would see the problem at once. But that might take weeks.

He stopped such speculations, not because it didn't make sense but because he was scaring himself. It would explain why no one from the *Natarkca* had shown up in the village to look for him—but he refused to abandon hope so easily. Still, circumstances seemed to be ganging up on him again.

He stared up into the sky, trying to place the *Natarkca*. It was a useless effort. His new, native eyes couldn't make out even the medium-magnitude stars.

Having given himself over to fretting, Valein was surprised to find himself surrounded. He settled himself precisely and faced the solemn male named Tuei-ars, he of the Council; obviously the jig was up. "Tuei-ars," he said, bowing formally. "I humbly ask permission to continue my journey."

"You have attacked and harmed Sha-teen, Val-ane, so that you might disobey Council orders—orders which she had explained to you. Do you deny this?"

Valein shied back. "Was Sha-teen hurt?" He had not meant to harm her!

"She is recovering," Tuei-ars said. Valein looked to Fier-neth, who nodded. Valein felt relieved.

"You have been acting *strangely,* Val-ane. It is good you came to our village, but... you are *strange.*"

"So you want me to leave," he finished. "Well, that's the way it goes. I'll just—"

"No, Val-ane," Tuei-ars said firmly. "Your *strangeness* cannot be allowed to go on. It must be stopped."

Valein dropped into a defensive posture, even though he was hopelessly outnumbered. For that matter, attacking the natives was strictly forbidden by Contact law; but he wouldn't go down without some sort of a fight. "You intend to kill me, Tuei-ars?"

The majority of the group moved back in shock; even Tuei-ars seemed dismayed. Sen-oun stepped forward to speak directly to Tuei-ars. "It is as I told you. He must be helped."

Tuei-ars, shaken and yet somehow sad, stepped forward. "Val-ane, you are in need of help," he said formally. "Do you voluntarily accept this decision? Will you allow us to help you?"

Valein grinned in what he hoped was his most convincing manner, since they didn't appear to want him dead. "Really, Tuei-ars—everyone!— I'm fine. There's no need to worry about me, I just need to be moving on."

"Val-ane, you condemn yourself with your very words. We shall help you find the way." Tuei-ars bowed his head solemnly. "Let it be so. Let it be done."

With that, the rest of the pack moved in on him, purposefully but without anger. They grabbed Valein with their strong, flexible furred tails, and carried him toward the village. He knew several ways of breaking free—but they all involved hurting one or more of them, and he didn't want to do that. He had nowhere to run to, not if he had to stay near the rendezvous point. Besides: if he seriously injured one of the natives, the Commander would seriously injure *him,* and the Commander had experts to call upon.

The pack turned from the path to the village, and stopped before a mountainous wall. Tuei-ars chanted something low, and—

Valein felt both awe and fear: the stone wall silently disappeared, leaving a high-tech doorway in its place. He studied it quickly as they carried him inside the revealed chamber. The crafting and technology were completely beyond the capabilities of the People; so who had built it, and where were they?

With a touch of dread, he wondered: was this the lair of the mystical Others?

The pack led him to a stark area within a maze of equipment and placed him onto a form-fitting couch. Now in a real panic, Valein discovered that the couch had him; he couldn't move or call out in protest. As the pack departed, Tuei-ars chanted in front of a panel and a close-fitting helmet attached itself over Valein's head.

Before he knew what was happening, a bright light filled him, mind and soul, relaxing him and suffusing him with great peace. It held his attention completely, until he stopped noticing anything at all.

An endless time passed, after which he found himself looking at a kind, benevolent being. He was standing in the open air, the sun was shining, and a gentle breeze caressed his fur. He felt *good* without knowing why, and without wondering why he should feel any other way.

"I am Tuei-ars," the being said kindly, and the information seemed infinitely valuable. "Your name is Val-ane. You are one of the People."

This information pleased him in a way he had never been pleased before. He felt warm and happy, a part of a greater whole that loved him and would protect him. "I am Val-ane," he repeated gratefully, and was amazed to hear his own voice.

"You have been sick," the being called Tuei-ars said without pity, without anger. "Through the guidance and grace of the Others who watch us all, you are well. You may join us again."

This news made Val-ane happy beyond expressing; he overflowed with gratitude and wanted to cry in his joy. He followed Tuei-ars and a large group of others who looked just like him, and they all went to a lovely place that he learned to call Home.

≉ ∽ ≉

None of the People had noticed when a new point of light joined the many that circled their home. When the same point of light slowly moved and then disappeared, its silent passing also went unnoticed.

In the bright, quiet light of the moon he now called *Arn-dui Sahnnyi*, Val-ane and Sha-teen chased over the hills and fields outside the village. Sha-teen pressed for speed, and ever more speed; but Val-ane kept up with her effortlessly. Breathless, they finally stopped near one of the many lakes that sparkled magically in the night.

"You are very fast," Sha-teen said between breaths. "And agile. You will make an excellent hunter, Val-ane."

Val-ane accepted the praise with a certain detached pride. It was nice to find something he was good at, when everything else seemed so strange.

She followed his thoughts with ease, and nuzzled his neck fur gently. "There is no reason to be ashamed, or afraid. You are getting better and better every day, and these things take time. Give yourself a chance." She stopped nuzzling to look seriously into his eyes. "Are you not happy?"

"I am not unhappy, Sha-teen. It's just... the dreams—"

"The dreams will fade," she said with determination. "New dreams will take their place. Concentrate on what is new, what is now, and let the old things go. You will see: by Theat-tu Nar Mearn, you will not even remember that you were ill."

"Theat-tu Nar Mearn?"

"The time of mating, Val-ane; the time of creating young. When the silver moon touches the hills, and the orange moon rules the sky. It is a time of great importance, and great pleasure." She licked his ear, and he ducked his head shyly. "You will learn, if the Council decides you are up to it."

"I want to do what is right, Sha-teen," he said earnestly. "I want to please you, very much."

"You do," she said warmly. "You will. If the Council approves, you will give me young ones, to run swiftly and grow strong like yourself."

Val-ane was again filled with a warm, happy feeling. "I can't believe I would ever have wanted to leave you, Sha-teen. You are so good to me! I must have been very ill indeed."

She pushed him over onto his back and began skritching his chest fur. In the sky, fuzzy points of light competed with the moon for attention, stirring some old memory. He frowned, his attention diverted from Sha-teen. "You know, when I look at the sky, it seems like—"

A flying shape swept Sha-teen away from him, and two more pounced to his side. "What have we here?" yipped one.

The other put a paw on his chest. "Well, look who's out enjoying the moonlight!"

Val-ane tried to leap to his feet, and Tar-trom bumped him down the hill with a playful shove. Sha-teen was a furred, rolling bundle, she and her attacker yelping merrily and out of control. Their wild tumble ended in a splash as the lake claimed them both.

Val-ane gained his feet just as Tai-aeros clipped him from his other side. Tar-trom stood apart, grinning, watching Val-ane dance warily in an attempt to get an advantage. "You are too strong for any one of us, Val-ane," he growled in mock-challenge. "How do you fare against two?"

"Go get him, Val-ane!" Sha-teen cheered from the lake, before Fier-neth shoved her under.

The chase-and-tumble took them to the water's edge before Val-ane gained his balance. He nimbly ducked Tar-trom's leap, letting the attacker fly headlong into the water with a surprised yell. He was preparing to flip Tai-aeros into the lake as well when Fier-neth grabbed him from behind and pulled them both in on top of her.

Being in the water without warning sent Val-ane into a sudden panic. He couldn't breathe, and between Fier-neth and Tai-aeros, he couldn't get to the surface. He struggled and fought desperately before finally splashing outward for a quick, spluttering breath.

Tar-trom dunked him before he could cry out, and their laughter rang in his ears. He fought to the surface again, struggling for his life. Tar-trom was getting dunked by Sha-teen, and Fier-neth was headed his way with

Tai-aeros close behind. "You run beautifully, Val-ane," Fier-neth called. "Surely you swim beautifully, too?!"

"He'll fly like the birds if you ask him!" Sha-teen said proudly. Tar-trom pulled her under with a splash.

Fier-neth grabbed Val-ane with her tail as Tai-aeros splashed onto his back, and together they carried him into deeper water. Panic-stricken, Val-ane couldn't get a purchase and his cries of protest were mistaken for simple laughter. With no sandy bottom beneath his feet, Val-ane went under and stayed there.

When he could see again, Sha-teen was standing over him with panic in her eyes. "He nearly drowned! What happened?!"

"He must have hit his head on a rock," Tai-aeros said worriedly from somewhere behind. "He didn't even try to swim; he just sank!"

The tremors that overtook him were violent and strong. Sha-teen pressed herself against him and held him tight. "What is wrong, Val-ane? Are you all right?"

"Just—get me away from the water," he whimpered, losing himself to panic again.

When at last he came to his senses, he found himself being held down by four cool soggy bodies, and he was soaked clear through. "Let me up," he insisted, the fear slowly leaving him.

Sha-teen stayed with him, sending the others away. "Are you all right, Val-ane? Do you know what happened?"

"I'm all right," he said shakily, "and my name is—"

Valein, not Val-ane! he thought. His memory rushed back intact, leaving him cold and confident in the bright light of the primary moon. He remembered everything that had happened.

He also remembered what would happen if Sha-teen knew that his old memories had returned. She would tell the Council, and there would be another trip to The Couch. "My name is Val-ane," he said confidently. "I'm all right, Sha-teen. I must have hit something underwater. Really, I'm okay."

"You're still shaking," she observed worriedly.

What do you expect, he didn't say, *I nearly drowned!!* Even being wet made him miserable, but he put it out of his head as best he could. The People loved to swim, and he was one of the People—for now.

She was watching him warily, and he forced himself to stop shivering. "It's nothing," he told her. "Let's go back to the lake."

"Are you sure?"

"I'm sure."

Sha-teen looked at the others without speaking, and they wandered away to continue their evening elsewhere.

Alone on a hill overlooking the lake, Valein tried to assemble a plan while Sha-teen preened and pampered him. He had to get a message to the *Natarkca* before someone turned him mindless again. But how?

He turned to her, his voice warm and his eyes intent. "Isn't the lake pretty, Sha-teen, with the moon reflecting off the water? Look at how it sparkles!"

"It's very pretty," she agreed. "I'm sorry we were interrupted by the others."

"It's all right," he said, placing his head next to hers to encourage her where to look. She leaned into him hard, to be close.

"Everything is all right now," he said quietly. "But look at the sparkles in the lake. Look at the way they form patterns, the way they shift on the water." She gazed at them, her slender ears turning slowly to catch the sounds of the water. "Look at the pretty sparkles, Sha-teen. Watch them move; they're so pretty... just watch the sparkles, and listen to the sound of my voice. It's a nice night, and a relaxing sight; just look at the sparkles, and listen to my voice. The sparkles are very peaceful, quiet and nice. Feel how peaceful they are, how relaxing... you are very peaceful, and starting to get very sleepy..."

Sha-teen was a perfect subject for hypnosis; she concentrated well and trusted him completely. When he was sure he had her under, Valein bid her to lead him to the mountainous wall that hid the alien mind-forming equipment. There they stopped while he searched for the hidden entrance.

Finding no way in, he turned back to Sha-teen. "You know the chant that will open the doorway, Sha-teen. You have heard it sung by the Council. I want you to sing it now, the way they did."

"I don't have permission," Sha-teen said softly, her eyes glazed.

"Tuei-ars has given you permission. Sing the chant, Sha-teen."

Quietly and clearly, she chanted the same pattern he had only heard incompletely, and the wall opened magically before them. "You've done very well, Sha-teen. Now, you are very sleepy; lie down, close your eyes, and go to sleep."

As soon as he was sure that she was asleep and unaware, Valein entered the alien chamber. Many of the devices he did not recognize; he steered well clear of The Couch.

Finally he found what he was after—and cursed his luck: the transmitting equipment was primitive, with no faster-than-light capabilities. Assuming the *Natarkca* had left orbit, it would take weeks for a signal to get to a navigation beacon stationed beyond the edge of the system; then more time for the signal to be re-transmitted along proper channels to the *Natarkca*. Forcing his irritation down, he created a message and set the alien equipment to transmit on as many different frequencies as possible; he then set the message on automatic repeat. Someone would get it eventually.

As an after-thought, he altered the message slightly, specifying that any rescue party NOT show up disguised as natives. All it would take is a bunch of new natives to show up acting *strange,* and The Couch would have a lot of new customers.

A sound from behind caught him by surprise, even though he had been half-expecting it. Tuei-ars was back, with most of the village in tow. "Hello, Tuei-ars," he sighed.

"You have returned to the place of Healing, the place of the Others. Why?"

"I had something to do. It has been done."

"You have had an unfortunate experience, Val-ane; a life-threatening experience, I am told. It happens sometimes that such experiences bring back old, bad patterns of thinking. We must help you find the path, again."

Valein didn't fight it. He had to stay near the alien transmitter until the *Natarkca* returned, which might take weeks; he would not be able to avoid the villagers. He needed their good will to survive until rescue came. The Changer would fix him up in any case, once he got back to the ship.

As they placed him once again on The Couch and the memory-forming helmet descended from above, Valein prayed to every god, spirit and power he could think of that the *Natarkca* would return for him soon.

🦎 ☙ 🦎

The wind whispered in the trees as Fier-neth and Val-ane searched silently through the woods above the village. Val-ane's tail stood straight out, then drooped.

"Nothing," he said. "Something has scared off the nirlengs, but I can't tell what. There has been nothing here for days."

"Hungry times ahead," Fier-neth said sadly. She scouted briefly around for other clues. "I wish I could ask Sen-oun. She understands these things very well."

"She should return soon. She's only been away a short time."

"She should not be away at all. We need all the hunters we have, Val-ane!" She smiled warmly. "It's good that we still have you. Sha-teen is happy in particular for your skills—but every nose is a help."

"Our visitor may yet prove helpful," he shrugged. "She seems very strong."

"Arr-nais? Is she still after you?" Fier-neth shook her head. "She is *strange,* that one. The Council will soon take her to the Healing place."

As they did with me, Val-ane thought quietly. Thinking about the Healing no longer made him sad. He was now an accepted and valuable member of the village. The bad dreams were gone, and that was that.

They heard a noise from downslope, and Val-ane crept to the top of the knoll to get a better vantage point. As he stood, a flying form knocked him tumbling backwards down the hill.

"Sha-teen!" he huffed, trying to regain his breath. "What are you—"

"The Council met and approved!" she yelped. "We can be mated!"

Val-ane was floored. "Really? So soon?"

Fier-neth had caught up to them. Her expression was happy. "It's been three mating-seasons, Val-ane," she said. "Well past time for you to increase our numbers" she said.

"Only because the Council wanted to make sure that you are all right—and they said you are! Oh, Val-ane, you will give me young at last!"

Val-ane laughed and flipped her head-over-heels away, then chased her back into the village with Fier-neth hot on their tails. The whole village joined the celebration, save the Council, of course—and the odd one, Arr-nais, who sat off to one side, watching. The romp lasted long and merrily into the night.

Later, in the quiet of their den, Val-ane and Sha-teen cuddled and talked plans, giggling and touching over the ceremonies that would come. Sha-teen noticed the noises first, a series of odd sounds from the direction of the communal eating area outside. Val-ane started for the entrance, but she pushed him back protectively. "You stay put," she said. "I'm not letting you go *that* easily!"

Watching curiously, Val-ane noted with concern the sudden droop of her tail and the defensive posture she assumed. He edged behind her to peer out. "What is it?"

"I don't know," she whispered. "Something *strange* is out there, and it's talking to Arr-nais!"

Val-ane looked out and saw with a shock that Sha-teen was right: some *thing* was following Arr-nais, and that odd being was headed straight for them!

Sha-teen pressed herself flat against the ground, an instinct that also grabbed Val-ane. "Sha-teen," he whispered, "is that one of the Others following Arr-nais?"

"I do not know," she whimpered. "Lie still!"

The odd one, Arr-nais, called out to him. "Val-ane! Present yourself!"

Startled, Val-ane rose and backed up a step. Even if the *thing* with Arr-nais was an Other, Val-ane was not ready to confront it; he was not ready to be Called. His instincts fought his training clear to his core. He did not want to be taken from Sha-teen!

Arr-nais sat up and did something with her front paws. Val-ane sensed a low humming, then collapsed without saying a word.

🐾 ∞ 🐾

Valein awoke slowly, wildly confused. He sifted through his feelings and memories as best he could, and was surprised, amazed, dismayed to find himself back in his own body. His memories seemed fuzzy, but things were coming back to him in chunks. He carefully rolled to a sitting position and looked around. A large, near-furless flat-faced alien was watching him with what he interpreted to be great concern.

"What happened to Sha-teen?" he asked, testing his now-strange voice.

The alien stepped closer, looking into his eyes, and somehow seemed less alien. "You know who you are?" she asked. "Or where you are?"

He thought about it, settling back against the bed. "Yes, Theresa. I'm Val-ane—sorry, I'm Valein, of the Federation Contact ship *Natarkca*. My teammates are Arnneas and Splat. I appear to be in a med bay. Your head-fur... your hair, is longer. It's all there somewhere, it's just going to take me awhile to get it all back." He looked down at himself, feeling for the very first time that his own body was somehow *wrong*.

Theresa brushed the hair out of her face. She seemed nervous. "Who is Shodeen?"

"Sha-teen. She's my—" *Mate*, he started to say. *She was my mate.*

That was over; the Federation had strict rules about what Contact teams could and could not do with the natives. Even if he returned to the planet, Sha-teen would think him some sort of monster; she loved Val-ane—not a stranger with Val-ane's memories.

Theresa had tears edging her eyes. "What's wrong?" he asked.

"We all thought you were dead," she sniffed. "We thought—and I didn't do an autopsy, or I might have seen it wasn't you, and you wouldn't have been stranded for three years, and—"

"Three *years*?!" he cried. He tried to put it together in his head, but it wouldn't register. He looked around, and saw some snail-like Calotians hovering busily in the background—none he recognized from a distance. "I know Arnneas was on the planet, in the form of one of the People. Where is Splat?"

"You mean Sppappthhlatara," she said without a beat, the first time he'd heard her pronounce it correctly. "He left the Service for good about five months after you... Arnneas went on leave for an unspecified period. She—umm."

Valein could figure what Arnneas had done, and with whom. "She came back?"

"She transferred back when they got your message. She's planetside, talking with the natives. It seems they don't want to give you up."

Valein nodded. His friends, companions and soul-mates for over three years; he wasn't sure he wanted to give them up, either.

As Valein, he made a connection that Val-ane could not have made. "You must have picked up one of the People—that is, another native, for Patterning? For Arnneas?"

"Of course. The old Contact pattern was destroyed. Someone had a theory that it had driven you insane."

"Where is the native?"

Theresa tapped on a portable console, and handed him the pad.

Valein nodded to himself. It was Sen-oun.

"Be very nice to this native," he said. "Send her down as gently as you can, as quickly as possible. She will make things go easier on the planet." *My parting gift, Sen-oun*, he thought.

Theresa accepted the pad curiously, but punched in some instructions. "It's taken care of," she said quietly.

Weariness crept over him like a fog. "Thanks," he said, forcing a smile.

Theresa suddenly reached down and hugged him, pulling him off the lab bed. "I'm so glad you're all right," she said. "I'm sorry we left you there."

Before he could think of a proper reply, she pressed something against him and he felt a stinging in his back. The world went away, and he slept for several hours.

He awoke in darkness with something holding him down, something large and heavy.

Someone, he amended. "Arnneas, get off of me."

She sat up, her eyes shining oddly. "I'm glad to see that you're all right," she purred. "You have been missed."

Valein bit back the first several things that leapt to his mind, and instead tried to recapture his old self, to mediate his sense of loss. "You've been short a pillow for awhile, is that it?"

She tickled his shoulders with her tail, as in the old days. "You are unhappy that we took so long to get you back? We only got your message five weeks ago."

"Did they send Sen-oun back to the planet?"

"The native? Yes. At your request."

Something was bothering her, something she wanted to not tell him. Thinking about it, he took a guess. "So there's a young Arnneas terrorizing the universe, eh?"

She tensed, then relaxed completely. "Yes. I left the Service when Splat did, to please Anarrask and get rid of him once and for all. He is at home taking care of our young."

"More than one?"

She made an odd noise he didn't remember from before. "Anarrask is—nicer—than I first thought." She tickled his ears. "That is a story for another time. I don't want to talk about him. I want to know about you. Are you well? You seem lost, somehow."

"It's nice to be back," he fumbled. How could he explain to her what he was leaving behind? He wasn't sure how to feel about it himself. Valane was not Valein, and yet...

He pushed that aside, and tried to concentrate. "Why did the Commander send you down as a native? I thought my message warned about what might happen!"

"The Commander decided, as usual, to follow standard procedure." She began massaging him, forestalling his tension. "Everything we knew indicated you had misread the situation."

"Oh. Great."

"For example, none of your early reports indicated that the natives had evolved the sort of technology you later discovered."

Valein spent some moments thinking about the 'Others' and compared his People thoughts with his Federation memories. "Did you know that there has never been a war among the People?—I mean, among the natives?"

"So?"

"They're carnivores, a race of hunters. But they don't fight. They're just as subject to the forces of change as any other race—yet, they don't evolve. Nor do they devolve. They have been exactly the same as they are now for as long as any of their legends recall. They play aggressively, but they don't fight."

"I got the briefing and the reports. They are very noble."

"I don't think so. Sometime in their past, somebody installed machines." He closed his eyes. "Machines to make them peaceful. Docile."

"You're shivering."

"I'll lay odds that the People are a young race. Perhaps even genetically altered so that they breed true. The Calotians could find out, but I'll bet on it. Whoever set this up had something in mind."

She held him, trying to comfort him. "Why does that bother you so?"

"The People are docile, Arnneas, totally submissive. They've been *made* to be that way. They tend to stay close to home. If someone disappears, no one asks why or worries too much about it. They're conditioned not to ask."

"Okay..."

"So where are the Others now, the makers, the—the overlords? What are they doing?"

She pushed him back into the pillows and looked down at him. "If you are correct, it sounds like they are trying to do the natives a good turn."

"I have to wonder. What if the People are being raised as, as—"

"Herd animals?"

"Or as game, for sport? They run and swim beautifully." He shivered again. "They would make exciting targets."

"We're here now, the Federation is, to watch over them."

"Are we?"

"The Calotians are sending a team to study the alien equipment you discovered."

"The Calotians," Valein grumbled. "Their interests are very narrow and specific. What will be done to protect the People?"

She stopped scratching him. "Yes, okay, I see your point. The Federation doesn't have resources or the inclination to protect a species that has nothing to offer in return."

"But they're—they're—!"

"You're involved," she said, pushing him into the bedding. "It changes your perspective. You'll get it back."

"The People should be allowed to develop, Arnneas." He thought about Sha-teen, about the lifetime he had almost had with her, would now never have. He thought of her as someone's prey... "They should be protected until they can develop on their own. They shouldn't be used."

"I agree. What difference does that make to the Federation?"

He sighed in frustration. "That's not fair. We should do something!"

She didn't change expression, but he could feel her exasperation. "Your Service contract says absolutely nothing about Fair. It never did." He started to say something, and she muzzled him. "No, listen to me. You can't save the whole universe. For all its lofty goals and advertising, the Federation is vastly over-extended and can't take care of every species it finds. They don't even try any more; you know that. And you are in no position to change that."

He nodded, and she relaxed her grip on his muzzle. "I'm not saying you have to like it. Accept it, work around it if you must. But don't destroy yourself in the effort. There is too much good you *can* do, to allow that."

"I'll get the Federation to see what's going on, and make them care," he mumbled. "I'll *make* them help the People, Arnneas. I'll find a way."

"I'm sure you will," she answered with no mockery in her voice. "If you are truly determined, I'm sure you will."

She didn't believe him, but he didn't care. He meant it. She would see. They all would.

For Sha-teen, he thought. For Ven-tu, and Fier-neth and Sen-oun, for poor Taa-neti—but most of all for Val-ane—he *would* find a way.

✖

ROSETTES AND RIBBONS

M.C.A. Hogarth

"And here is your new room!"

Peli glanced around, brows raising slightly. "Dr. Edisse, do all Aeran edifices look like huts or tents?"

The older Asanii chuckled lightly, folding his arms. "Most of them, yes. It's a by-product of their culture."

"Nomads, right?" she said, putting down her bag.

"You've been doing your homework."

"Oh, professor, you know I always do my homework!"

Dr. Edisse laughed again and leaned forward to put an affectionate hand on her head. "Yes... you were always my star pupil. But you're not a student anymore. Forget that at your own peril! This is the real thing we're working with now, not case studies."

Peli's gaze swept her new lodgings again, the bright fabric walls billowing lightly over the scraggly vegetation of the ground and rising to a rudimentary ceiling; behind her, another wall of cloth served as the separation between her mentor's room and her own. "I don't think it's possible to forget that this is the real thing," she answered, eyes round, "we never had rooms this... err... transient at the university."

"No, that we did not," the Asanii replied, handing her a data-tablet; Peli tried to figure out which was more out of place, the long tall figure of the ruddy professor, or the slim, austere and technological shape of the tablet. "Dr. La'aina is supervising the nearby archeological dig... they think they've discovered some material on some previously unknown myths concerning their religious pantheon. They've brought in her mate, Du'er to investigate. He's a sculptor and a well-known figure in Aeran pre-historical art. They'll be working with you; your assignment is to translate some of the writings they've unearthed. I hope you've brushed up on your Aeran."

Peli felt her back straighten in mock indignation, "Dr. Edisse! There wasn't a Seersa born..."

"That didn't have twenty tongues," he finished, amused, "I know the old proverb. I was just making sure you were awake."

She smiled, now in earnest, "I'll give you reason to be proud of me, sir."

The elder feline leaned over and tousled her head-hair. "I know you will, girl... so settle in. And remember, the local scientists are throwing us a little formal welcoming-party in a few days."

"The dinner and dance thing, right?"

"Right. Get to it, Miss Argentson."

Peli smiled again as her mentor stepped through the separation to his half of the rectangular tent, then she turned to her bag to unpack. First, the sleeping pad, which she had not thought would be necessary; she was glad she'd brought it anyway, since no furniture had been provided. Did the Aera expect visitors to bring their own furniture? Or did they sleep on the earth?

Peli shook her head, unable to fathom such a thing. She tossed a few pillows on the ground to serve as seats in case someone came to call on her. A low fold-out table, just large enough for her to lean her elbows on and lay her data tablets she set up beside the bed, and then the projecting mirror, a gift from her mother. That she placed beside the table and activated with her toe, watching the slight shimmer that preceded an image of the opposite wall of the tent. Experimentally she flicked her tail in front of it and was gratified to see a white and mottled reflection; the mirror hadn't been damaged on the trip. She set up a light on the edge of the table and the pad for showering across from the mirror.

Some clothes, a few pieces of jewelry she hung on one of the cross-beams holding up the low ceiling, and her brushes and combs she tossed onto the table. Edisse had recommended she bring light clothing, and she was grateful now for his foresight; Selnor had been approaching winter out of its wet and cold autumn, but this on part of Aren summer was at full. Her coat remained in winter-length. She thought about shearing it, but they were only staying two weeks before returning to Selnor, where she'd be glad for the long fur.

Peli kicked up the short head-board on the bed-roll and dropped onto it, propping herself up with her pillows. Unlacing the first few stays of her tunic against the heat, the Seersa foxine nabbed her tablet to check her mail, finding nothing unusual. A note from her parents, wondering how she was enjoying her internship... a formal notice from the alumni society of the Xenoanthropological University at Selnor, asking for contributions no doubt... some junk mail asking her to purchase this or that... the latest issue of *Comparative Cultures*, her professor's (and her own) favorite journal... and a short letter from Manager Tasey at the Ani branch of TKI&I, where she'd worked in her off-hours to help pay for her schooling, congratulating her on her recent graduation and thanking her for her service. Her parents first, then Tasey, then she could sit down and enjoy CC, which noted in the byline that this issue included an article by Dr. Edisse about the pottery of the Ciracaana's Mother Cult.

Peli had just finished sending off a reply to her parents when the jingle of the hand-bells outside her tent-flap indicated a visitor. Surprised, she put aside her data tablet and stood, hastily pulling herself into the mind-frame that the tongue of the Aera required.

"While the sands are still, come in," she said, and it was perfectly couched, her mouth negotiating the odd double vowels the Aera favored without difficulty.

Two Aera stepped in, a female and a male with a bundle. Both were near or exceeded six feet tall if she was any judge, which made her feel self-conscious about her own short stature; the female Aera was colored a glorious bright orange and streaked across the muzzle with brown before her mouth and throat exploded into shocking white. Her long ears sported tufts that hung almost to the back of her head and large, golden hoop earrings with thick red stones. The female had arresting blue eyes, the same color as the wrap around her hips that served as her only clothing, wearing her chest hair in the burst of white fluff that most Aera did. The tiny wings at her ankles were white, tipped with brown.

Beside her, the male neared the black of space, completely lacking in ventral surfaces; he had a furtive air, arms easily folded against his fluffy chest-ruff, green eyes half-lidded and tiny wings folded against his legs. His maroon wrap was shorter, more perfunctory, just as his earrings were thinner.

They were a female-dominated society, Peli remembered. She stood straighter for the female's scrutiny that she would not be dismissed.

"You don't need to speak our tongue," the female said in a surprisingly husky voice, "We speak Universal at the digs, for the most part. I'm Dr. La'aina, Clan Sereon, and this is my mate Du'er."

Peli shifted out of the Aeran frame of mind and switched to Universal. "My given and family-names are Pelipenele Argentson. I am Dr. Edisse's assistant." To her surprise, they didn't ask if she had any other names; but it was easy to forget that hers was the special pleasure and duty of learning other cultures, not the other way around. "I am told I will be working with you. Is that correct?"

"Mostly with Du'er, yes; he will be correlating your translations with any works he will find. Would you announce me to Dr. Edisse?"

"Certainly," Peli answered, determined not to be intimidated by the female. Dr. La'aina possessed a slender figure, but so infused it with energy and aggression that she seemed far larger than she was. "If you'll excuse me?"

"Of course."

Peli poked her nose through the separation and found her teacher sitting on his own bed-roll, reading his data tablet as she had been. "Dr. La'aina to see you, sir."

"Send her in."

Peli held the tent-flap back for the female Aera, letting out a breath of relief when La'aina swept through, leaving her alone.

"Pelipenele... that's quite a mouthful."

The Seersa foxine almost leapt out of her coat. She had forgotten Du'er. "I have an abridged-name, of course," she said, once she regained her composure.

"An 'abridged-name', is it?" he smiled at her, eyes a-sparkle, "You Seersa are so precious, with your quaint little language customs. Will you tell me your abridged-name? We'll be working together a great deal, and I don't fancy having to spit out five syllables whenever I want your attention. I might take to calling you 'vixy' just for relief."

The outrageous behavior and flighty tendencies of the Aera were notorious, and usually explained away by the effects of a nomadic culture. The Seersa supposed it was difficult to grow past the limitations of your own society, if limitations they were, but nevertheless she wasn't sure if she liked his mannerisms or not. "You should call me Peli," she said sternly, choosing her words as all her kind did with relentless accuracy.

"Peli it is, then," Du'er said, handing her his bundle, "here are the stone strips we found in the digs."

Peli unfolded one of the skins to peek at the brittle and thin slivers of stone with their scribbled markings; satisfied that they were in mostly good condition and that her assignment would be less trouble than she'd expected, she tied the bundle again and placed it gingerly on the floor beneath her work-table. "Thank you."

"My pleasure. After all, it brought me to see you."

Peli glanced at the lazy figure of the Aera male, puzzled. "Pardon?"

"You're a jewel! I've never seen someone so striking. I don't suppose you'd pose for me?"

The Seersa thinned her eyes in complete bafflement. "Pose... for you?"

"I don't suppose your Dr. Edisse told you I'm a sculptor? You have a figure that begs for stone. Some of that nice, white stone near the sea-cliffs the Flait hate so, the powder-stone with the sensual crystals would be just perfect."

She was speechless, for once in her life... and it wasn't just any life, but the life of a Seersa, the race that provided every premier linguist of the Alliance almost without exception, the Seersa who learned languages with all the facile ease of breathing, the Seersa who took it as a duty to have each of their number add at least five words to their native tongue in their lifetimes and encouraged citizens to add more, if they could. And Peli could find no words.

"It would have to be in the nude, of course... such a figure! And the coloration! One would think you one of those barbarians, those Harat-Shar, except for that face. You have such a delicate nose, beautiful Peli, beautiful Seersa."

Peli almost frothed at the mouth in her desperate desire to force something out through her throat. *What was this maniac talking about?* Delicate nose? Beautiful figure? Her coloration? Surely he wasn't thinking that she could possibly be the subject for a work of art... the very idea was preposterous! She was Pelipenele... just Peli... not the next Maserinatericktal Kajentarel or Terran Venus de Milo!

The sudden cessation of the low murmur beyond the partition saved her from replying. Dr. La'aina stepped through, followed by the familiar and comforting figure of Edisse.

"You've dropped off the strips?" La'aina demanded of Du'er.

"Of course," he answered smoothly, a half-smile still quirking at his mouth. His green eyes as yet rested on Peli, who looked away.

"Send someone to the dig when you've discovered something," La'aina said, turning to Edisse.

"I will."

La'aina exited, tail cutting the air behind her and drawing Du'er in her wake like a magnet. Peli deflated in sheer relief to see them go.

"You look... battered," Edisse said, smiling at her gently.

"I feel battered," Peli admitted, dropping onto her bed-roll. "Are all Aera that...," she stopped herself from saying 'insane', "that... intense?"

"Most of the ones I've met have been, or worse, even."

"Speaker save me!" Peli exclaimed, and Edisse laughed.

"Don't let them get you down in the ears, my girl."

"Of course not, sir."

"Better. I'll be next door if you need me. Next door... Next flap?" The elder Asanii shook his head, feline tail curling in amusement. "No matter. Relax a little and get some rest."

Peli nodded, watching as her mentor stepped back to his side of the tent. She picked up her data tablet to resume her letter-writing and found she could not concentrate. Hesitantly, as if she feared that her reflection had mystically altered in the past twenty minutes, the Seersa placed herself in front of the mirror.

Black eyes gazed back solemnly at her, set in the same lightly furred face she was accustomed to seeing every day while grooming; nothing had changed. Peli studied herself anew, bewildered, trying to see herself with the eyes of the Aera male, but she saw nothing special. Just the same Seersa female, the same four-foot-four, digitigrade Seersa with the long coat, the shoulder-length hair, the long cheek-ruffs... the same white body occasionally darkening to a frosty gray where ragged rosettes sprinkled themselves at random, leaving the white untouched save the one perfect black rosette that Du'er could not have seen, hidden under her tunic just beneath her left collar-bone, imprinted there like a permanent decorative pin. No, she was no different... so what in the name of the Speaker-Singer had Du'er seen that she did not?

Shaking her head, Peli returned to her bed-roll and took up her tablet—time enough to discover that, once she finished with the day's mail. Then it was to work on those stone strips, a welcome promise of a mystery to be unraveled by her fingers and mind. After that... well, she might give a slice of time to the enigmatic Aera.

✹ ∞ ✹

"Are you going to eat any breakfast at all, girl?"

"Later, sir. This is a crucial piece of the text..."

Edisse's voice was bemused. "Would you mind translating, Miss Argentson?"

"Pardon? Oh!" Peli shook herself; so engrossed had she been in the myth that she had spoken in Aeran, not in Universal. "I'm sorry, sir. It's just that I didn't want to break my stride..."

"Which I succeeded in doing, ah? All for the better. You need sustenance! Come here and eat, and if it makes you feel better, give me a report on your progress so far."

Only then did Peli notice the enticing aroma of nut-and-carelberry pastries and warm mocha coffee and milk. The roof of her mouth erupted into life, her stomach not long in following; she'd been up at dawn, brought from her bed by her own curiosity, a surer alarm than any she'd ever used. That must have been three hours ago, if the quality of the sunlight said anything. Peli scrambled through the partition to the mat Edisse had spread on the floor of his room and sat down to breakfast.

"Oh, sir! It's so exciting!"

"Tell me about it, then. Milk in your mocha coffee?"

"Yes, please... that's enough." Peli leaned forward, cradling her cup in one four-fingered hand. "I spent all of last night putting the stone strips in order. They seem to be numbered in chapters, or volumes. There's only one missing, and a few that are cracked, but most of those are cleanly broken. A little glue will fix them. There's very little lingual shift; according to the Language Archive on Seersana, it's about three hundred years old."

"Not bad, then," Edisse said, popping one of the pastries in his mouth and chewing it deliberately.

"No... not at all. It's almost exactly like Modern Aeran, actually. Anyway, I started reading the first strips last night. The first myth concerns three members of their pantheon. Two of them are listed as still known, the females, Taleyira and Seyela."

"The Warrior-Wife and the Warrior-Maiden," Edisse said.

"Yes. But the male... well, I can't find any references to him at all. His name is Edera'yn. The story so far is about Edera'yn wooing Seyela, the Maiden. I haven't figured out Taleyira's relationship to Edera'yn yet. This version of the Aeran language assigns the same word to 'enemy' and 'mate', with only a slight inflection to differ it from 'friend'... which of course, isn't conveyed in the older Aeran method of writing. They could be any of the three to one another."

Edisse chuckled. "So like the Aera... at least nowadays, from what I've read, they differ all three by inflection, instead of just 'friend'."

Peli, at the end of her recital, shook her head. "I don't understand it, sir. How can a culture have the same word for such disparate concepts? You'd think there would be an obvious difference between a mate and an enemy." She finished her first cup of the mocha coffee and poured herself a new one from the nearby pitcher, then moved on to the pastries, which steamed against her tongue and crunched amid her teeth appealingly. Her stomach began singing praises to her name.

"The Aera aren't even the strangest of our comrades in the Alliance, Peli-pupil." That was a pet name from years ago, "Look at the Naysha, for instance, or the Sirelanders. Even the Harat-Shar and the Hinichi have their oddities."

"I know," Peli replied, "But the Aera... they strike me as being especially... especially different."

"They're a little harder to deal with, which I think is what you meant to say."

"Well... yes, that too."

"It's because they choose to profess that there is nothing important to them." Edisse took one of the after-breakfast mints, leaning back from the mat.

Peli couldn't conceive of such a thing; she was both dismayed by the idea and delighted by it. It was her enjoyment at being surprised and having her mind stretched that had led her to her current profession. "How, how..."

"Self-deluding," Edisse finished, "When you choose to say that nothing is important to you, more often than not you become unable to choose your priorities, and then everything becomes important instead, blown out of proportion and perspective."

Peli shifted slightly, uncomfortable. "It sounds like a world-view that would create a race of mal-adjusted people."

"You'll have to judge for yourself, my girl. I don't need to remind you to remember exactly what mal-adjusted means."

"No: badly suited for their environment, for their life."

" 'Their' life. Remember that—not for our kind of living, our kind of cities, our kind of government and society, but for theirs. They might be mal-adjusted to live as Seersa, or as Asanii... but they're not Seersa or Asanii. They're Aera."

Peli nodded, thoughtful.

"Now, if you're done with breakfast, would you like to walk to the dig with me? I need to discuss a few matters with Dr. La'aina."

To walk in the sun? See the country-side? Meet the archaeologists? "Oh, would I, sir! Please, lead the way!"

Edisse chuckled. "Go put something lighter on; you'll burn up under that tunic. If we were staying longer, I'd suggest that we both grew chest-ruffs and went around in native dress, but two weeks isn't long enough for that."

Peli's ears splayed. "I'm not sure I'd be comfortable walking around half-naked, sir."

"No, you wouldn't, would you?" he laughed, "You should take some advice from the humans. They said, 'When in Rome, do as Romans do.' "

"I'm not human, sir, and we're not in Rome," Peli replied, knowing that her literal mindedness would evince a laugh from her professor, and she was not disappointed.

"Go, girl! We're leaving in three or four minutes!"

Six minutes later, Peli was trotting along behind Dr. Edisse, clad in a tunic of very blessedly light fabric, colored like raspberries and cinched at her waist with a silver sash. Her data tablet rode in a pocket, bouncing against her thigh, already set to record the results of its passive scanning. The countryside on this part of Aren was supposedly a lot like the rest of the planet: somewhat arid plains with sparse dottings of shrubs, rolling in yellow-green to the horizon where a few orange plateaus splashed with lilac shadows cropped up here and there. The sky was a ruthlessly bright blue, cloudless and shimmering with the heat of the fierce sun. Peli wondered why the Aera bothered to pick up and move their steads at all. There was no escaping the burning regard of that yellow eye, so why expend the energy trying?

The archeological settlement sprang up before them in a series of multi-colored tents in vibrant colors, flaming oranges and stark crimsons, throbbing greens and yellows and purples. Peli grew momentarily dizzy; everything on Aren seemed preternaturally bright, tempting her eyes to water. Beside the tents the excavation was cordoned off with fluttering white sashes. Already people could be seen moving around the site, preparing for the day's labor. Peli could count twelve tents, and four people mobile; she decided while Edisse chatted with Dr. La'aina she would interview some of those people, perhaps convince one of them to let her down into the dig.

"I'll find you when I'm ready to leave," Edisse said, interrupting her thoughts, "Meanwhile, enjoy yourself."

"Okay, sir," she replied, and they split off at the edge of the settlement. Peli slowed to a more leisurely walk to study the tents in more detail, pulling her tablet out of her pocket to record the visual aspects. In general, they were pyramidal in shape, with one or two rectangular like the one she shared with Dr. Edisse. The off-world scientists' village where she and the Asanii had been lodged was larger, perhaps twenty-six tents, but they were farther apart. Peli examined the bracing elements of the tents in curiosity. With such a scarcity of wood, she wondered what they used and gasped in interest at the answer. Stone! The Seersa glanced toward the distant cliffs. Perhaps it differed regionally; she wondered if she could send a message on one of the anthropological groups asking if anyone had gathered any data concerning wood-substitutes on Aren.

The female continued strolling along the edges of the settlement, making a tidy arc around the tents that would bring her to the dig. While the study of things past did not interest her half as much as the study of things currently existent, she did recognize that in many ways it was impossible to extricate the two from one another. Peli drew near the mound of overturned soil beside the growing hole in the earth, skirting it until she came to the white sashes. She peered down into it; no one was working yet.

Disappointed, Peli began to turn.

"So, pretty vixy, when did you say you were bringing your rosettes into my studio?"

Peli reflected that so far, most of her dialogues on Aren had seemed like incidents more properly relegated to dreams: nonsensical non-sequiturs uttered by people completely impervious to reason. "Pardon?"

Du'er was leaning against the mound, body slack with a roguish languor, the tiny wings at his feet moving idly as if to send breezes over his arches and around his ankles. "To be my model. You did say you'd bring your rosettes for me to turn into a work of art."

This kind of perversion of language was something that never failed to infuriate Peli. Lies, untruths, those things defiled the purpose of the spoken and written word: clear communication. "I never promised you my 'rosettes', nor that I would model for you," she said, carefully enunciating each syllable as if doing so would somehow make more of an impression on Du'er's unmalleable brain.

It was fodder for shock that Du'er actually stood up in surprise. "I've offended you with my careless banter!"

"Yes, you have," Peli replied, folding her arms; she figured she might as well press her advantage while she seemed to have one.

Du'er leaned forward, as if to do so proved his sincerity. "Forgive me, beauty... but this is a cold and heartless world, with no care for any romantic or poetic soul." He leaned back against the mound with an expression of such suffering that Peli was moved despite her nagging suspicion that he was still acting. "Not even my mate understands what touches me. But in you! In you, I thought I saw a kindred soul. I see one still, I think. You must dismiss my way of speaking. It's a defense against most people's callousness."

Peli sighed. He seemed honest, and certainly these didn't sound like the kind of admissions one would lie about. Perhaps he did just want to be friends with her. "Du'er-alet," she said, using the more formal word for 'friend' lest she give him ideas, "let us make a deal. I won't tread on your customs if you won't tread on mine."

"But I don't know all your customs!" Du'er protested, dismayed.

"Well, I don't know all yours, either. But I'll tell you one of mine now—don't lie. That's the most important to me. Now, you tell me one of yours."

Du'er paused to think, then said, "Don't reject any of my gifts." He must have noticed her eyes widening, because he held out one hand, "No, I won't give you anything ridiculous, but it is a custom among us to exchange small gifts, once in a while, as tokens of appreciation or gratitude."

Reluctantly, Peli nodded. "Very well."

"Now... since you're here, would you like to see one of the statues we unearthed yesterday afternoon? It's quite stunning! Maybe it has something to do with the strips."

Peli's ears swiveled forward in interest. "I'd love to!" She fell into step beside the lanky male, and continued, "Tell me something, Du'er? Why am I translating your stone strips? Don't you have a specialist on the Old Style glyphs?"

"Not one that came as cheaply as you did, beauty."

Peli pursed her lips and didn't reply to that. It was the truth; as an intern, it had cost Aren less to import her, but it seemed crude to mention it.

Du'er lead her into one of the rectangular tents, a dark, eye-mazing azure in color. Pillows in blue and gold stripes were strewn on the floor, plushy and large enough to serve as comfortable chairs, and in some cases, large enough to be comfortable beds. He walked to a table and plucked an object from it, handing it carefully to her.

"Oh," Peli said softly, "It's beautiful!" She turned the figurine over in her hands. It was perhaps a foot tall, slender, made of a dark green stone with striations of blue and blued silver punctuated with gemstones. Centuries in the sandy soil of Aren had not substantially marred its surface, or its graceful lines: an abstracted Aera female, chin lifted and ears flatly parallel to her neck lifted one hand to the sky and held the other at the height of her shoulders, as if dancing. She wore no clothing, one leg slightly bent as if she had been caught just before putting any weight on her foot. Something in the Aera's lifted hand swirled down, wrapping around her arm, a thin, raised strip decorated with tiny cabochon gems of flitirel and rulent. "What do you suppose that is?" she asked, running a finger over the orange and turquoise gemstones.

"I'm not sure. I was hoping you could tell me about it," Du'er replied, "Perhaps something you've read...?"

Peli shook her head. "Not yet... maybe when I get back today, I'll find some clue. Or it might not even refer to the myths at all."

Du'er chuckled, "Don't say such things, beauty! Why don't you take that with you..."

Peli lifted her head to protest, but the male put a finger to his muzzle, eyes sparkling. "Let me finish. Take it with you so that you can see if it pertains to anything you're reading. We've other pieces, but far larger than that one. That's the only one you could carry. It would save you a trip, running to and fro, if you had it with you."

"Are you certain?" Peli asked, ears splaying.

"Didn't you promise not to reject any of my gifts? Well, here is one: the gift of borrowed time with this antique. Hold your end of the bargain, dear beauty."

Peli had to laugh. "Okay."

"Peli? Peli? Oh, there you are. I'm ready to go. Good morning, Du'er."

"Good morning, Dr. Edisse," the male replied as the Asanii leaned through the open flap of the tent.

"I'm ready, sir," Peli said, then added to Du'er, "If I find anything I think relates to this statue in the manuscripts, you'll be one of the first to know."

"Not the first?" Du'er asked, mouth quirking.

"That would be a lie," Peli replied good-naturedly, "Since I'd probably have to tell Dr. Edisse about it or burst. He's closer to me, after all."

Du'er laughed, "We should change that, no? Well, have a good morning, beauty."

"You too, Du'er."

"You seem to be getting on well with him," Edisse commented once they left the tent and began the walk back to their settlement.

"We've come to an agreement that allows us to work amicably," Peli answered, handing Edisse the figurine, "I've been charged to hold on to this for a while, to see if anything in the stone strips concerns it."

Edisse studied the statue with professional admiration.

"It must be a very hard stone," Peli added, watching the Asanii's face as they walked amid the scrub-brush, "Otherwise the abnormally high sand content would have had more of an effect on it, I think."

"If this dates to the same time as the writings, it might not be so surprising that it's well-preserved. It's made out of jaen. I haven't seen something made out of jaen since the last time I was in a museum with Aeran artifacts. This is certainly worth a small fortune. Do you think it relates to your myths?"

Peli shook her head. "I'll have to read more. Which I will, after I drink something. I feel parched!"

Edisse handed the figurine back to her with a dry chuckle. "I'm surprised you're not panting... I'm sweating up a storm already. I'm all for a pad-bath when we get back."

"Not a bad idea," Peli said, suddenly noticing how oily she felt. After a moment, she asked tentatively, "Professor? Does Du'er have the authority to... to hand out statues and artifacts this way? I'm not doing anything that would sully our name, am I, in taking this with me?"

"Since Du'er is in charge of all the sculpture unearthed at this site, you're perfectly safe, my girl. Don't fret yourself."

Peli let out a breath in relief.

"You worry too much," Edisse said, a sparkle of fond humor in his green-brown eyes, "This assignment is going to be perfectly dull. It's why I chose it for your internship. Excitement should be reserved for senior xenoanthropologists."

"Oh!" Peli exclaimed, "I don't find this dull at all!"

"Somehow, I'm not surprised."

They reached their tent and parted ways; after a pad bath, lunch, and two pitchers of water, Peli rolled onto her bed to check her mail. The usual assortment was waiting for her: a bank statement, notifying her of the deposit of her stipend as an assistant to Dr. Edisse... a reminder from her dentist that her ten-year re-enamelling was due next month... junk mail, asking her to buy the newest fragrance from Arras Windfall and the latest technology in room decor... and a surprising and enchanting viseo-letter from her big sister. Doni's tales about her adventures in First Voice had always thrilled Peli as an adolescent and had been responsible for forging her intention to take advantage of the rich cultural fabric the Alliance offered. No doubt Doni had some new escapade to regale her with in this letter; being a linguist on a courier ship with six people of radically different heritage never failed to create any amount of delicious and amusing anecdotes, and like every Seersa born Doni could spin a story.

Delighted at this unexpected pleasure, Peli spent the afternoon with her mail before returning to her work, refreshed. She placed the figurine on her work desk where it occupied the corner of her eye and set to translation.

🐾 ∞ 🐾

"So you have reason to believe this figurine is actually related to the myth?"

"I think so," Peli replied earnestly, dipping her sweet-bread in the honey pot that occupied the midpoint between herself and Edisse. "The story, if I'm following it correctly, says that Edera'yn gives Seyela a jeweled string as a symbol of his love, and that Seyela brings it to the next festival in Heaven, where she does a dance with it. This enflames Taleyira into hatred, from which I have to assume that she's Edera'yn's mate, otherwise it wouldn't have made her so angry. That's where I stopped for the night, though."

Edisse lifted a brow. "This must be hard for you. You're getting so little of the story for so much of your work?"

Peli flicked her tail, "Well, the 'plot', if you would, is pretty slow to unravel. Whomever is responsible for writing or for setting this myth down gets wrapped up in petty and sometimes somewhat sordid details."

"Is that so?" Edisse said with a chuckle, "Typical. The Aera are such sensualists. They'll make poetry about anything tactile, from the silky smoothness of a certain fabric to the oily slickness of their own sweat."

"There are a few lingual anomalies," Peli continued, wrinkling her nose to Edisse's amusement, "Like this 'ruje'aida'. 'String' is the closest thing I can find, but I know it's not quite right, but the Archives don't have a clear definition for ruje'aida in this time-period. It could be 'string'... it could be 'rope'... it could be 'bracelet' or 'glue'."

The old Asanii's brows rose, "Unusual to have such ambiguity in the Archives."

"If there's ambiguity in the Archives," Peli replied, driven to defend her race's efforts, "It's at least partially the fault of the race from whom the ambiguity stemmed from. We can only record what they tell us, after all."

"True, true... so will you go down to the digs to tell Du'er and Dr. La'aina?"

"Not yet. I want to have something more concrete to tell them. I'll probably spend the rest of this morning and afternoon working."

"Don't forget..."

"I know, the party tonight." Peli watched the Asanii dip the last of his sweet-bread in the honey, cradling her tea. "How formal is this again?"

"Very. I'm going to have to wear a tuxedo."

Peli wrinkled her nose. "Oh, no, not one of those 'black tie' events?"

Edisse chuckled. "Unfortunately, yes. They've become popular again in the scientific circles these past few years. I suppose it's only fair since we regularly impose our balls and cultural affairs on them."

Peli poured him more tea. "I'd like to go to Earth someday. There's so much history there. It's like a mini-Alliance, all on one globe! Can you imagine having so many disparate cultures develop on one world?"

"Rather amazing, isn't it?" Edisse agreed, "Well, one step at a time. But if I have anything to say about it, you'll get there."

"You'll come with me, won't you, professor?"

Edisse was rolling up their breakfast mat, "Oh no, Peli-pupil... I have my ambitions as well, you know."

"You do?" The idea had never occurred to her, "Where would you like to go?"

The old Asanii's hazel eyes twinkled, like the sparks that betrayed the presence of a consuming fire. "To the Chatcaavan Empire."

Peli's mouth dropped open. "Dr. Edisse! You're not serious, are you? The Chatcaava, with their feudal lords and Slave Queens and subterfuge and who knows what other unsavory customs?"

"A society of shape-changers, my girl! Think of it! What kind of world would you live in if your identity was so malleable?"

"Wouldn't you be in danger?" she asked, black eyes wide.

Edisse laughed easily, "They're our allies, remember? In much the same way as Earth is, somewhat uncomfortably, though I'm sure for different reasons. Besides, you overlook the fact that life is full of perils, and that any assignment you take, no matter how mundane it may seem, has the potential for disaster. After a while in the profession, you develop a sixth sense for keeping yourself out of trouble."

"I hope so," Peli said, pushing herself to her feet, "Because you'll need it if you head into that territory."

"You should worry more for yourself... you're the neophyte."

"I do worry for myself," Peli replied, muzzle curving into a smile, "When I have the time between myths!"

The morning passed, lazy hours strolling after their preceding fellows with all the urgency of a cat sunning itself in summer; Peli hardly noticed when lunch-time came, barely breaking concentration long enough to bolt down a piece of tana fruit and drink more water. The story in the strips was getting interesting; Taleyira had challenged Seyela to the Rite of Defiance for laying premature claim to Edera'yn. The Seersa tagged 'Rite of Defiance' in her transcript on the data tablet for later research—perhaps it was a custom that still existed, or maybe more information was available in a historical text.

The bleep of the programmed alarm in the tablet jarred her out of her trance, irritating her. Parties! What did parties have to do with being a xenoanthropologist? Didn't those other scientists have enough to do without manufacturing excuses to do something else? Exasperated, Peli folded the strips in their hide bundle and checked her makeshift clothes rack, thumbing through all the light shifts until she found the one evening gown she owned.

Five years ago ambassadorial parties, high-society functions and balls had swept back into fashion with such fervor some historians had immediately proclaimed the renaissance of the Romantic Era. Sheath dresses returned to haute couture, exemplified by models like Silhouette, the mysterious Tam-illee with her slender, lily-like figure... leaving all the digitigrade races, and especially the stockier ones like the Seersa and their sister-race the Karaka'A in dismay. The beauty of sheath dresses laid in the elegant straight line they made of a figure, one impossible to create with thighs jutting out at impossible-to-hide angles.

The dismay lasted until a prominently known Karaka'An Fleet Captain arrived at a function held by Ambassador Jaimetharrl Darksoot in a sheath dress slit all the way up the skirt to her hips on both sides to allow her to walk freely. Since then, slit-sheathes for digitigrade races had become the rage, and even the plantigrade females took to slitting their dresses for novelty. Peli had bought her dress at the time, never expecting to need it.

The Seersa shrugged out of her work tunic, stepped on the pad to have all the dirt and excess oil dissipated from her body, and then settled to brush out her fur. With a toe she turned the mirror to face her where she sat in front of the work table; a fruitful search of the u-banks unearthed a step-by-step viseo on how to pull up her hair with only a few hairpin-stasis fields. Peli went about her preparation as she did her work: professionally and without devoting much conscious thought to the results.

After pulling her hair and cheek ruffs into a french twist, the Seersa slipped on the dress; it was midnight blue, limning her torso to her lower hips where it fell in two straight panels, one before, one behind. The plain, high neckline lay hidden beneath a loop of dark blue chiffon, clipped at the shoulders with small silver ovals with the ends left free to trail behind her.

Peli was studying her reflection critically when the bells outside jingled. With a lack of self-consciousness born of her naïveté, she called in flawless Aeran, "Enter, an' the winds be right."

The tent-flap pushed back to admit Du'er, who halted in the entrance as if struck. "Could this be the same beauty I once professed an insolent desire to carve? Surely the Greater Master will strike me down for my impertinence, for I see she is already a living work of art!"

"You're not...," Peli began, and Du'er laughed.

"No, I'm not lying. I promised, didn't I?" The male Aera walked into the tent; he was not yet dressed for the event or perhaps wasn't going, still sporting one of the wraps the Aera liked to clip around their hips with ostentatious jewels, male or female. "No, I came to give you a gift, and I am pleased now because I didn't know how perfect it would be! By the way, that color truly becomes you."

Perplexed at the concept of a color making her look particularly nice, Peli glanced down at her midriff. "I like it," she offered tentatively in response, then continued on the other course, "But... another gift?"

"Ah, but the figurine was only temporary! This is a more permanent gift. And here it is!" Du'er snapped his wrist from behind his back, opening his fingers to reveal the carefully coiled length of a thick crimson ribbon with raised geometric patterns. When Peli made no move to take it, he came to her side and gently turned her to face the mirror, artfully tying it into a bow around her right wrist. "There. It is only proper for ladies to wear gloves at evening parties, but Aren is too hot for such a custom, don't you think? This will make you look as if you're wearing gloves that had bows at their edges for effect. No one will notice you're not wearing white gloves until they truly look at your hands... which are, by the way, quite beautiful."

Peli stared at herself, eyes wide—if that was the effect the ribbon was supposed to have it was totally lost on her. But if Du'er said so, and he had admitted to being a poetic soul... besides, she'd promised not to reject his gifts.

"Thank you, Du'er. It's very pretty."

"Not as pretty as the one who graces it," the male replied smoothly, "I will see you soon."

"Certainly," Peli said, although she was in truth not very certain at all; at least, not about her feelings concerning the odd behavior of the sculptor.

"Peli? Who was that?" Edisse stepped through the partition, wearing his black and white suit and straightening his bowtie with all the absent discomfort of someone who hadn't tested the starching of his collar since its last usage.

"Du'er... to give me this." She displayed the ribbon for her mentor, who studied it curiously.

"It's very nice. Makes you look like you're wearing gloves. At least, that's what I thought when I first saw you."

Peli blinked, then shook her head in amazement. "Really, sir?"

"You look fine, my girl. Shall we? We don't want to be late."

"Of course not."

The sun had fallen outside and a light breeze had appeared, a specter out of the vivid dark blue of the twilight sky. Peli fell into step alongside Dr. Edisse, ears swiveled forward; even from here, she could hear the faint strains of music, an effervescent and somewhat shallow quartet she recognized as the work of a popular Hinichi composer. The occasional chirp of Aren's night insects added a curious counterpoint to the melody.

"Will we hear Aeran music?" she asked idly.

"I don't suppose it. The Aera don't make music."

Peli's eyes flew open. "No music?"

Edisse regarded her, and a glaze of fond amusement did not succeed in hiding the sober set of his lips. "They may look somewhat like us, more like us than Terrans, or Eldritch, or Sirelanders, but I don't think it's really struck you that they are different, despite that exterior."

"I... I guess not," Peli said, "but, professor, you taught that we must always start from a common ground, looking for common ground, when we work among other races."

"Of course. When working among other races, start from a common ground, look for a common ground... and never forget it may not be there. You must always be aware, hyper-aware, of the differences. Only then can you compensate and plan for them."

The wind tickled softly at Peli's exposed neck; unaccustomed to the sensation, she hugged herself. The faraway song had drawn nearer and mutated into an Eldren ballad punctuated by the hum of conversation. A magenta tent splashed with shadows of dark violet shading to black proved responsible for the noise, spreading its bulk across an area that would have encompassed six tents the size of the one she shared with the elder Asanii. Silhouettes haloed in the orangy-lilac glow of interior light sources milled across the cut-out stage of the long horizontal plane of the tent's side.

Edisse walked to the front of the tent, where the flap was pegged closed with the tassel that indicated a desire for privacy but an invitation for others to enter without announcing themselves. "Ready, Peli-pupil?"

The Seersa lifted her chin and squared her shoulders. "Ready, sir."

The Asanii unlooped the closure and let the flap drop open, stepping inside. Peli followed with some trepidation.

The tent held all of the archeologists working the nearby dig as well as all of the members of the village of outworld-scientists where they were staying, along with what the Seersa guessed were some ancillary Aera, perhaps friends of the diggers or the scientists. A trestle table occupied one length of the tent near the entrance, piled with trays of fruit, steaming meat, soups and broths, several kinds of breads, and more bowls of drink than she had ever seen collected in one place. The music emanated from a player ensconced beneath the table. Slender metal candle holders that rose to her chin displayed floating bulbs, casting everything in a warm, amber light at odds with the walls of the tent. Beyond the immediate gathering, a large space had been cleared for dancing, along with a table for panel discussions.

Dazed by the amount of people, scents, and sounds, Peli trailed behind Edisse as her mentor made his way through the throng, shaking hands, making greeting gestures, offering palms or waving tails, switching from culture to culture with the ease of long practice. He introduced her to everyone he met; Peli tried to keep track of the names, but after the fifth introduction the dazzling colors and scales and fur patterns merged into an endless stream of indistinguishable information. It relieved her, however, to be among the scientists, with all the multiculturalism and cheerful camaraderie that typified most of the crowds occupying Selnor where she'd gone to school. Peli hadn't realized how much she'd missed that intermingling until now.

The Seersa stopped at the food table, taking a slice of the potato bread and spreading it with white honey. A matronly Harat-Shar lynx poured her some of the nerisii punch and Peli stepped away to enjoy a little food in her corner, trying to clear her mind of the afterimages of countless males in suits and females in formal-wear that varied from the rustling silks of the Asanii to the near-nakedness of the Sirelander's metal armor.

"This... this is your natural setting! You shine like a sublime jewel amid the ostentation of the gaudy would-be beauties, Terran peacocks to your subtle swan." Du'er slipped around her from behind, bowing; in the stark black and white of a tuxedo he looked the last monochrome still in an almost-completed colorized film.

He was insane, Peli thought. She was about as at home in a party as a plant in outer space, and the whole bit about the swan... "Good evening, Du'er. You look striking."

The male pressed his hand to his heart and rolled his eyes in exaggerated pleasure. "Lady, you wound me with your affections! I shall never heal!"

Peli resisted the urge to ask him if he was always this theatrical. What if that was a societal custom? He would probably be offended. She cast about for a topic of conversation and managed to find one. "I've discovered a possible link between the figurine and the stone strips."

"Do tell!" Du'er exclaimed.

She recounted what she knew of the tale of the two goddesses and Edera'yn. As she finished, inspiration struck, "Du'er, do you happen to know what *'ruje'aida'* is?"

"Ah... a slang in Clan Roseyan and Zuene'a! They use it for the word 'ribbon'."

"That makes more sense," Peli said, tapping the underside of her chin, brows furrowed. "Although I wonder how that meaning wasn't recorded in the Archives on Seersana."

Du'er chuckled, a sly twinkle in his eye. "We must keep some secrets from you, mustn't we? Or else we wouldn't be a mystery." He winked at her and melted back into the crowd.

Peli shook her head and steeled herself for more mingling in this throng of strangers. She had to be sociable; she had to bring good words to Edisse's name. Shoulders squared, the Seersa re-entered the chaos and worked her way slowly through the tent... chatting with a Phoenix and admiring his metallic plumage, silently marvelling over the furlessness of the one human on the science team, discussing different kinds of pelt-brushes with a Tam-illee, speculating with a Hinichi over the probability of finding more intelligent life in the new sector on the spinward border of the Neighborhood... Peli's mind began to swim. An hour and a half later, she was exhausted and ready to put herself and her overworked jaws to bed. She looked for and found her mentor by the lazy swing of his ruddy tail.

"Dr. Edisse, I'm going to go back to the tent."

"Sleepy already?" he asked, eyes sparkling.

Peli considered, then replied with the candor that words demanded, "Not sleepy... tired, tired of small talk and smiling and trying to say the right things. I'd like to relax before bed, do a little more of the translation."

"I'll see you later, then, if you're still awake."

She nodded and threaded her way through the people to the tent flap. The Seersa began to open it when some sixth sense warned her of a stare that was applying for a transmutation into a drill; someone's gaze was boring into the center of her back. Peli glanced about swiftly, surprised, and found herself meeting the hostile stare of the Aera female she identified after a few moments as Dr. La'aina. Dr. La'aina? The one in charge of the dig? What had she done to earn the wrath of that female?

Peli frowned and stepped out of the tent. She'd ask Edisse tomorrow.

※ ☜ ※

Colored sunlight leaped through the tent walls to fall on her face in brash and cheerful greeting. Peli yawned, stretching in her bed-roll. After the party, she'd had enough energy only to change into her light night shift, let loose her hair and then fall among her pillows. She didn't even remember falling asleep. So much for her plans to continue reading the story of Seyela and Taleyira! She would have to make up for lost time today.

Swiveling an ear towards the partition revealed no sound; Edisse must still be sleeping. If memory served, she'd heard something very late at night. He must have returned in the dark hours of the morning. Well, she'd save a little time and eat breakfast while reading her mail. That would give her an extra half hour to spend translating.

After cursory morning ablutions, Peli set the pot of tea to warming and unwrapped some bread, plucking her data tablet off the table. She shuffled through her messages: a letter from her mother with an attached viseo from the local news about her old primary school... a notification that one of her many favorite authors had produced a new work, and would she like to buy it and in which format? (Terran perfect-bound? Faulfenzair scrolls? Privacy-coded file?)... a challenge to a Duel... the latest issue of *Scientific Explorations in Language... challenge to a duel?*

Eyes widening, Peli spread that message. Her screen filled with a formal looking document written in Aeran, challenging Peli to a Rite of Defiance over the Heart Du'er, to be settled tomorrow at sun's zenith...

And issued by Dr. La'aina.

It had to be some sort of joke. The rest of her mail forgotten, Peli jammed a piece of bread into her mouth for breakfast, changed hastily into a more appropriate shift, pocketed her data tablet and headed into the morning sunlight. She'd straighten this out before Edisse woke up; what would her teacher say, to find out she'd somehow managed to run afoul of this culture without even trying? Hadn't he said this would be a dull assignment? What had gone wrong? It had to be a simple misunderstanding. She'd fix it. She *had* to.

Peli trotted to the dig site where most of the archeologists were already at work, skirting the colorful tents; as an afterthought she flicked on the recorder on the data tablet in her pocket, as Edisse had always taught her not to waste information. After all, the Seersa thought ruefully, for all she knew, she'd never be allowed into this settlement again. She came to a breathless halt in front of the dig-master's dwelling and grabbed the hand bells outside, giving them a rough jangle.

"Come, if the winds are in your favor," a cold voice intoned.

Wearing the knowledge of her innocence as armor, Peli walked inside.

Her first impression was of fire—red walls, bright orange and yellow pillows, hot colors everywhere. La'aina stood in the center of the tent, back turned to the entrance; in this setting, the brown of the other's pelt seemed to be a-flame, forming a halo of palpable anger and aggression. Peli opened her mouth to greet her, but the Aera female turned, saw her, and interrupted.

"So it's *you!* You thought I wouldn't do it, that I would spare you because you're an out-worlder and should know better, didn't you? Didn't you think I would call for the Rite after what you've done?"

Faced with those raging eyes, Peli backed a step involuntarily, hand to her chest. "I... what... *what did I do?*"

"Oh! Play the innocent with me, will you, little vixen? I know better... I've heard all Du'er's graphic accounts of your nights together!"

"Night... nights together?"

"Your nights together in bed! Having little Seersa-sex! Teaching him little Seersa love-secrets! Showing off that perfectly white pelt Du'er bragged you were hiding under all that clothing! Did you think I wouldn't call the Rite after hearing so many details about your spotless, sexy white undersides?"

Peli's mouth dropped open in complete and total shock. Not only was this worse than she had expected, it was beyond her ability to comprehend. Du'er... Du'er had told his mate these gross and hideous lies? Why? And how could La'aina have believed him!

"Dr. La'aina, please allow me to ex..."

"Explain! Explain! You can explain it to me tomorrow when I have a pike aimed at your heart! Now get out!"

Peli eagerly complied; it was obvious that trying to convince La'aina was fruitless anyway. She would have to get to the heart of the matter... the 'Heart' of the matter, Du'er. With some exasperation she remembered that she had been planning to research the Rite of Defiance. She had anticipated learning more about it, but not this way!

The Seersa jogged to the small tent where Du'er had given her the figurine, anger and bewilderment serving temporarily as breakfast, giving her energy. She didn't even bother to ring the bells to request entrance, or to check the tassels on the tent-flap to make sure it was allowed for her to come in; flipping the cord aside, she stood in the entrance and folded her arms.

Du'er glanced up; he had been sitting on a pillow and sipping something, studying a tablet. Seeing her, he put aside the tablet and cup and stood, arms open. "Ah, it is the beauteous Peli, come to give me her rosettes as promised!"

She ignored him and interjected, "Du'er, what is the meaning of these, these unforgivable untruths you've been feeding to Dr. La'aina? She wants to kill me now!"

A flare of eager interest spurted into Du'er's eyes. "She challenged you to the Rite?"

"Yes! And she's quite intent on putting a sharp object through my mid-riff! Du'er, why did you tell her we were... were bedding together?"

Du'er leaned back, his entire body slack with contemptuous satisfaction. When he spoke, his voice held mockery and amused superiority, "Because I hate her, and wanted to get away from her."

Peli choked in the middle of her next tirade. What came out of her mouth after that stranglement was a tiny, meek sound. "Why... how..."

"You see," Du'er poured a cup of tea and offered it to her with laughing eyes, "If I could manipulate La'aina into declaring a Rite of Defiance on you, she would lose it... lose it because you are more knowledgeable in language than she is and would defeat her in the Verbal Challenge, and she is growing old and slow with anger and I am confident you would be able to tire her into defeat in the Physical Challenge. You would win me, but wouldn't want me, and would set me free. However, if somehow La'aina did win, she'd be so disgusted with me she'd also set me free. She would never tolerate a mate she knew had been unfaithful. So you see, either way, I'd win."

Peli stared at Du'er. If she had been unable to comprehend La'aina, it was nothing to how little she could comprehend Du'er. "On purpose... all those things you told me, all the times you were with me... the ribbon!" Her eyes flew open.

The male laughed in delight, "You understand, then! Yes, the ribbon still has the same connotations for us today as it did in older days. Males give them to females they favor for display. And you, unknowing, went to a party with every single person of any repute in the vicinity last night wearing my ribbon on your wrist. Every Aera there left talking about it. I thought La'aina would burst into pieces. It was absolutely beautiful!"

"You were lying to me. You promised not to lie to me, just as I promised not to..."

"Not to reject any gifts from me, yes," he agreed, grinning.

Peli felt like sitting down but couldn't command her knees. "You were planning it... even then?"

"Of course. You were the most likely candidate. You were exotic, young, beautiful, and intelligent... La'aina knows how much I like those qualities. She wouldn't believe me falling for another Aera, but for a strange and uniquely beautiful alien? That she would swallow eagerly. All those graphic descriptions of your naked body!" He laughed, "You should have seen her face!"

"You never intended to keep your promise, then," she managed, eyes glazing.

Du'er leaned into his pillow, resting his head in the joined fingers of his hands as he stretched. "Actually, I did keep my promise. I never lied to you. I do think you're beautiful. I do think you would make a fabulous carving. I would like to be that sculptor one day. I simply omitted my motives, that's all."

Anger pushed through the fog clouding her mind, an anger completely Seersan. Peli clenched her hands into fists and glared at Du'er. "The purpose of words is clear communication. To impart information between people. Lying is deception, a perversion of words to fool other people into believing your version of reality. What you did is exactly the same, except you used silence instead of words! *You deceived me!* Purposefully, for your own ends! You violated the spirit if not the letter of your promise!"

Du'er chuckled, completely at ease. "I thought you would feel more comfortable with me violating spirits and silences instead of words and letters. That is what you Seersa worship, isn't it? Aren't you grateful?"

Peli stared at Du'er, open-mouthed. His laugh jolted her into action.

"You are despicable!" she hissed, enunciating each word clearly, then turned violently and exited the tent.

The morning sunlight caressed her brow as she stood outside, trying to banish her anger long enough to think clearly. What to do? She had been manipulated into this position cunningly and masterfully so that she could see no way out. La'aina was in no condition to believe her; she didn't trust Du'er or Peli, and nothing the Seersa could do would make her think otherwise. But she couldn't get involved in this. Not only would it make a horrendous mark against her on her record, but she doubted she would survive a physical duel unscathed. Perhaps she was young, as Du'er had so off-handedly stated, but the Seersa had no experience at all in weaponry or combat other than rudimentary training in self-defense.

What could she do?

She had no choice. She had to talk to Edisse. He would help her find a solution; he had to. But as Peli walked back to her tent, ears flat and tail hanging, she found herself fervently wishing there was some other way. Her professor would be so disappointed in her.

The scent of rooderberry-filled donuts punctuated the air with delicate swirls when Peli entered her tent; the smell mingled with that of mint hot chocolate reminded her of the tiny piece of cold bread and the excessive stomach acid that she'd been using as fuel so far. Her mouth started watering.

"Ah, there you are!" Edisse smiled, fatigue-marks lining his eyes despite his cheerful smile, "You young people. I don't know how you can stay up so late and wake up so early. Your dedication to this project is admirable, my—"

"Sir...," she couldn't stand to hear it, ears drooping. She dropped into her usual space across from him and tried to find the words.

"Oh, something's bothering you, I see. Here, have a donut and relax. You look like you need a little pampering."

Peli watched in mute misery as the old Asanii pushed a donut and a cup of minty hot cocoa in her hands. The last thing she deserved right now was pampering or praise for her dedication.

"Now," Edisse said, leaning back, "tell me your troubles."

"Sir, I've been challenged to a Rite of Defiance!" Peli blurted.

The Asanii stared at her for several seconds, then said, "Pardon?"

Peli's shoulders slumped dejectedly, "I didn't mean it to happen, but Du'er... Du'er manipulated me. He wanted to get away from his mate, and set it up so Dr. La'aina thought he was being unfaithful to her with me, and she believed him, and now she wants me to show up tomorrow at noon so she can kill me!"

Edisse took a deep sip of his cup before continuing. "You're certain this isn't a joke."

"Oh no! I talked to them both this morning. It's deadly earnest."

"And you're certain this isn't a dream?"

Peli shook her head again. She studied the countenance of her mentor and added pleadingly, "Isn't there something we can do? Some loophole? Oh, I never intended something like this to happen!"

Rustily, Edisse began to laugh. "I know you didn't, my girl. I never intended something like this to happen, either. I thought this would be a safe assignment. As for loopholes... well, let's start looking. Should we begin with the document she sent you?"

Peli nodded, "I have it right here. In fact, I left it on the screen..." She plucked her data tablet from her pocket and handed it to Edisse, who studied it. A puzzled frown grew on his face.

"What is it?" she asked.

"This doesn't look much like a challenge statement. It seems to be a record of a conversation."

"A... what?" Peli asked, incredulous.

Edisse handed the tablet back to her, and the Seersa scanned it swiftly, then again in shock. A squeak of surprise escaped her. "Professor! This is the conversation I had with Du'er half an hour ago! I... of course! I left the tablet on record when I entered the settlement!" She suppressed the urge to crow with delight, scrolling through the text of both her exchanges, that with La'aina and that with Du'er. "Oh, Dr. Edisse! It's where he was admitting to me everything he was doing!"

"Well!" the Asanii said, examining it as she handed it back to him, "that's an uncanny piece of luck!"

Peli glanced up at him. "You don't suppose... that if I gave this to La'aina, she might believe me and call the Rite off?"

Edisse considered. "I'm not sure. Aera are rather moody types. One minute they might be as stubborn as rocks, the next as changeable as the wind, but it's worth a try. I suspect it's our only chance. But! Let's finish breakfast, go over the texts on this Rite, and see if we have any other options. If not, we'll go with this."

Ignoring her apprehension with difficulty, Peli managed a smile and began to eat.

🐜 ∞ 🐜

Two hours later, they had discovered no loophole; if La'aina did not call off the Rite herself, there was no way to prevent it. Not only that, but no Champion had ever called off a Rite in the history of the custom.

They would have to show her the transcript.

Peli began to develop goose-bumps on her neck. Tablet in hand, she stepped out of the tent and began the walk back to the dig for the second time that day. The sun was particularly strong, the colors of the tents when she approached particularly vibrant; the Seersa felt as if everything on Aren had chosen to assault her.

Ringing the bells outside the female's tent and receiving a cold invitation to enter, Peli again strode into the abode of the predator, who was sitting on a pillow reading a report.

"You again?" La'aina bristled when she glanced up.

"Stop!" Peli said, injecting as much command into her appeal as possible without sounding disrespectful, "Listen to me! Du'er has manipulated us both!"

"I am not interested in your excuses!"

The Seersa continued, ignoring her racing heart and La'aina's stormy gaze, "He wanted to break away from you, and arranged it so that you would Challenge me, and either of us would set him free if we won! He was doing it all on purpose! He was lying to you! And to me!"

La'aina glowered. "You really expect me to believe you?"

"You don't have to—I have proof! I accidentally recorded the conversation I had with Du'er after talking to you, where he admitted all of this! You only have to read it to see that he's been planning this all along. We were set up!"

"That sort of data can be forged," La'aina replied coldly.

Peli felt her body tensing. "Do you want to take the chance? If I'm right, Du'er will have tricked you, made a fool of you by using you like a puppet to execute his whims. Do you want to be the butt of every joke in this community? You will be, once Du'er gets away from you and starts gloating! Read the transcript!!"

"I'm not interested," La'aina said again, beginning to shift against her pillow in growing anger.

"Do you want to reward him for playing you like a musical instrument?"

"*I'm not interested!*" La'aina roared, leaping to her feet, "Take your immutable tablet and get your 'sexy white pelt' out of my tent!!"

"I'm going," Peli replied, fighting the urge to cringe and run, "But I'm leaving this here. Read it! Don't let Du'er get away with this! It's your name at stake!"

"*OUT!*" La'aina bellowed, and Peli gave in and ran, tossing the tablet with its incriminating evidence onto a pillow before exiting.

Outside, Peli tried to decide if that had gone well or not. What if La'aina did not read the tablet? What if it was all lost? She needed a back-up plan, but she and Edisse had systematically discarded every possible idea they'd thought of. Glancing at the tents, at the workers who occasionally gave her inquisitive and sometimes knowing looks, Peli felt exasperation for Aren and its intractable inhabitants. Slipping her hand into her now-empty pockets, the Seersa walked back toward the scientific settlement through the sun and sandy terrain, ruminating on the chance that La'aina would see sense and the chilling possibility that she wouldn't. The verbal half of the Rite she might be able to handle, since all it seemed to entail was a solid knowledge of the Aeran language, its common insults and colloquialisms; as a Seersa, she had grasped those things naturally. But the physical half... she'd read about the weapons, and if La'aina's earlier threat was an indication of her chosen weapon, then it would be pikes:

pikes that were two and a half feet longer than she was tall. Peli sincerely doubted she'd be able to keep the thing upright, much less defend herself with it.

"Any luck?" Edisse asked as she entered the tent.

"I don't know," Peli answered with a sigh, "I left it with her, but I don't know if she'll read it."

"Well, then, all we can do is wait," Edisse said, "If she chooses to retract the challenge, a courier will arrive on our doorstep. If not..."

"If not, I hope we'll have a first aid kit handy for when she dismembers me tomorrow at noon," Peli replied morosely, dropping onto a pillow.

"Let's not engage in wild speculations, Miss Argentson," the old Asanii said with a slight smile, "Besides, I doubt a first aid kit will be much help in putting you back together after La'aina's finished with you."

"You cheer me so much," Peli muttered, and Edisse chuckled, patting her on the shoulder.

"It'll be fine, Pelipenele. You'll see. Now, keep yourself busy. I'll stop you for dinner."

Peli nodded and dragged herself to her desk where the stone strips lay bundled beside a borrowed data tablet. She had no heart for her work, even less when she looked at the statue of Seyela with the ribbon that Du'er had given her. She'd wrapped the red ribbon from the party around its base. Diabolical Du'er! How could he scheme so with the minds and spirits of innocent people?

With a sigh, Peli set to work and, as always, became lost in it. Taleyira, hot with anger, had challenged Seyela to a Rite of Defiance over the Heart Edera'yn. All the gods and goddesses of the major pantheon attended, Laera and Zleayron, Tasenear, Yesier, Aura, and Zenoa, with Luer the Peace-Father serving as the arbiter. After three days, Seyela won the verbal half of the Rite, and after a day's rest she and Taleyira met again for the physical match. As the current mate and thus the Champion of the Heart, Taleyira chose the weapons for the duel, long, curving knives.

Peli was deeply engaged in translating the blow-by-blow account of the physical duel when Edisse tapped her on the shoulder for dinner. They ate in silence; La'aina had not sent a courier, and it was growing late. The Seersa's apprehension began to solidify into cold fear, while part of her screamed the absurdity of her situation. She wanted nothing to do with any of this! She didn't even like Du'er, didn't want to have to risk her life so she could win him... win him! She didn't even want him! How in the name of the Four Sisters had she gotten into this mess?

After dinner, Peli used her borrowed data tablet to read her mail, tail restlessly twitching against her pillows. She found an ad from her favorite orchestra on Selnor for their next performance in two weeks (she might be able to attend, if she was still in one piece)... a 3deo-clipping of a strange Terran musical production called *Cats*, sent to her by a friend who found the images of humans dressed up like Asanii very amusing...

the latest catalog from Pathways, a company that sold reproductions of cultural artifacts... the news viseo from her home on Selnor. Peli clutched the data tablet to her breast and experienced a fleeting moment of true despair. She had no desire to die! There was still too much to do!

The Seersa took herself firmly in hand. La'aina would see reason and cancel the Rite. Or if she didn't, she would survive. The Rite usually ended when an opponent yielded, not with their death. There was no need to become so overwrought.

Peli returned to her translation, but the gory account of the physical rite reminded her of the coming event and made her queasy besides, until she firmly abstracted the myth. This Rite had happened in the beginning of Aeran time, when the goddesses fought the duels to the death as a matter of course. It was a fantasy. It had nothing to do with her.

Peli found she was a difficult person to convince.

Hours later, Edisse said reluctantly, "Go to bed, my girl. You'll need your sleep." The rest of the statement hung ominously in the air: when you fight La'aina tomorrow. "I'll keep a watch."

Unwillingly, Peli nodded and wrapped up the stone strips. She turned out the light, changed, and went to bed... but she didn't sleep. When Edisse's light darkened several hours later, the Seersa was still awake. And the courier did not come.

🦋 ∞ 🦋

This is crazy! This is absolutely crazy!

"This is crazy," Edisse said, echoing her thoughts.

Peli stood at the edge of the circle drawn in the sandy earth as other Aera found seats on the nearby ground to watch. La'aina had not called off the Rite, and in fact had decided the physical duel would precede the verbal; as Peli had worriedly suspected, the Aera had chosen pikes as the weapon. The Seersa was nearing desperation: now that the day was here and the sun was teetering at the edge of zenith, she could feel the jaws of the trap Du'er had set closing around her.

The setting was the essence of simplicity. Near the digs, a circle twenty feet in diameter had been drawn in the earth and marked at the four compass points with stakes and tiny white flags. One tent housed the Heart and another the Champion, while small awnings had been erected to shade spectators, of which there were already a formidable number. The Rite of Defiance always brought in eager crowds; what better entertainment than half-naked females screaming insults or trying to gut each another?

"Dr. Edisse!" she exclaimed, but couldn't bring herself to say the rest: Get me out of this! Find a way! Help me!

The old Asanii squeezed her shoulder and said, "Don't lose hope. There may still be a peaceful end to this."

"A peaceful end!" Peli squeaked.

"That brain of yours is formidable, Peli-pupil, or I never would have chosen you as an intern. Don't disconnect it prematurely."

The jangling of hundreds of bells announced Du'er as he stepped from his tent surrounded by seven males with rings of bells and tambourines. Forming an honor guard, they escorted him to a special awning just beyond the north end of the circle. Peli watched him with open disgust, outraged by the saucy, knowing wink he awarded her as he passed her by.

With trepidation, Peli turned her gaze to the tent of the Champion. Five females assembled outside the tent and began ringing their bells. With a last squeeze on the shoulder, Edisse left her standing on the edge of the circle and sat nearby.

La'aina stepped forth amid the cacophony; she had shed all her clothing save a turquoise loin wrap that echoed the eye-burning swirls of turquoise and fluorescent teal she'd painted across her red-brown and orange pelt. Her fluffy white chest fur cascaded down to her torso like an organic breast-plate, and she held her chin high, flashing blue eyes looking down on everything with disdain and rage. The sun set the gold of her heavy hoop earrings a-fire.

She looked a lot like Peli's mental image of Taleyira, the Warrior Wife-goddess. Too much like her.

La'aina stepped into the circle and held up her hands. The jangling stopped. "I, La'aina of Clan Sereon have declared the Rite of Defiance on Pelipenele Argentson for wearing the ribbon of my Heart's favor. I have chosen the physical duel as the first half of the Rite, and the weapon of decision is the curved pike."

On cue, an Aera stepped up to each of them, holding the six and a half foot-long staffs topped with the curving metal heads and their angry spikes. The heavy staffs had been crafted of precious wood, oiled to a fine sheen. Peli glanced at her pike in horror as the La'aina continued.

"As according to ritual, the Challenger may now speak words on her role in the Rite." La'aina leveled her angry glare on the Seersa.

Peli stared at some undefined point in the distance. Last night in bed she had rifled through hundreds of responses to this question, her only chance to speak in her defense before the slaughter began. There had to be something she could say to prevent this debacle, some way to take advantage of this last chance to speak, to make language the true weapon of this Rite, but nothing had occurred to her then. She had to find something to say now... there had to be something she could do!

The Aera stared at her as she remained silent. Peli glanced at the her feet, her mind blank despite all her frantic efforts. She wore no shoes and had chosen the lightest, shortest tunic she owned for today, sleeveless and sky blue, unwilling to have her actions hampered by long skirts or slippery soles. Already the hot sun pulled the oils from her fur, and she'd be panting soon. Something to say, there must be something... Peli put her hand to her heart, hoping for inspiration.

And gasped.

"Dr. La'aina," she began, back straightening, "you have called this Rite because of Du'er's reports to you of our 'relationship' together, correct?"

"Yes," La'aina hissed, eyes thinning. Dialogues were allowed in this last statement before the duel, but they were uncommon.

"You have read the transcript I provided you with of Du'er admitting he was attempting to manipulate us, correct?"

The crowd gasped, and Du'er's face contorted into a frown.

"Yes," La'aina answered.

"And you chose not to believe it?"

"It could have been forged," La'aina said, folding her arms.

The crowd listened, enrapt, no doubt wondering what Peli was planning. Well, let them hear, then!

"Du'er did tell you on numerous occasions of our 'time' together, did he not?"

"Yes."

The sun poured on her, and Peli resisted her need to pant. There would be time enough for that later. "And he gave you graphic descriptions of my body, didn't he?"

"Yes." La'aina scowled.

"Did he tell you anything about particular parts of my body that were exceptional?"

La'aina's anger returned full-force to her eyes and body language; having to discuss her mate's glowing reports of his lover's body in front of a crowd of two-score Aera did not please her in the least. Just a few more words, Peli thought pleadingly to La'aina, just a few more words and we'll expose him for what he is, and you can back out gracefully!

"He said that the areas you hid under your clothing were as white as snow, unmarred by spot or color."

It was a reasonable assumption, Peli knew. Her rosettees spottled only the gray areas of her fur on the many parts of her body exposed by her summer clothes. Du'er the sculptor, the visual artist would certainly have observed that. "He mentioned no exceptions, no spots at all?"

Du'er looked worried, the crowd excited.

La'aina frowned, more in puzzlement than anger. "No."

Peli caught her fingers in the lacing of her tunic and tore the neckline down, exposing the one, perfect rosette an inch and a half beneath her left collarbone. "He didn't tell you about this one, then... because he's never seen it! He was lying to you, Dr. La'aina!"

The crowd roared. Du'er leaped to his feet in dismay as La'aina stared in shock at the rosette, not even the size of her open palm, the rosette that gave lie to the words of the Heart.

"He wants to leave you, La'aina," Peli finished calmly, heart pounding beneath her chest and hands trembling as they held the lapels of the tunic apart.

The female turned her burning gaze on Du'er and slowly grinned. It was not a pleasant expression. "Then he won't get the chance." She held up her hands, "I am calling off this Rite! It is... unnecessary."

The crowd laughed and cheered, breaking away from under the awnings to surround La'aina. Peli didn't notice; she slowly sank to the ground, mouth open and tongue lolling, heart drumming a frenetic staccato. She'd done it!

"I want the ribbon back," La'aina added to Peli, almost an afterthought.

"I'll return it immediately," the Seersa promised fervently.

The honor guard that had escorted Du'er in was now escorting him out, some of them angrily, others in amusement, and still others in good-natured pity. As they passed her, Du'er managed to jostle them to a halt and stared down at her, eyes cold with wrath.

"You never mentioned that rosette," he hissed.

Peli smiled thinly and answered, "You never mentioned the meaning of that ribbon."

Du'er would have spit on her had his comrades not grinned and dragged him away, leaving her with Edisse, who had pushed his way through the crowd to her side.

"Told you, m'girl," he said affectionately.

Peli groaned. "Where's that first aid kit? I think my heart's going to explode."

"I think he already did," Edisse replied with dancing eyes, watching Du'er's receding back.

※ ◌ ※

Two weeks later, Peli leaned on the wall of her bunk on the courier ship *Truewind*. Her small bag was packed securely above her in the luggage compartment, while a carefully cushioned box formed her foot-rest. Pillows formed a nice back-rest for her, *proper pillows* that she'd found on her bed, not serving as furniture on the floor. She was reading her mail.

'The Edera'yn myths, translated by Pelipenele Argentson, form a substantial and fascinating body of previously unknown mythology from the Aeran culture. Edera'yn, the Fool-Lover god, apparently occupied the unique status in Aeran mythos of comic-relief.'

"Are you reading that article again?" Edisse said, leaning on the doorframe with folded arms and a grin.

"Well... yes," Peli replied, "It's the first time I've ever been in a journal!"

Edisse laughed, "I know, I know. I was the one who saw it first, remember?"

"Only because they send professionals copies of the journal first!"

The Asanii chuckled and said, "Well, you're on your way to professional status yourself. Your handling of the incident on Aren was masterful."

"Thank you," Peli replied smugly. She shifted her feet on the box.

"You never did tell me what that was," Edisse said, pointing at her foot-rest.

"Just a gift," Peli answered easily, "A token souvenir from Aren."

"Ah! Well, get your rest, Peli-pupil. We'll only be on Selnor for three days, then it's off to Phoenix-Nest."

"Yes, sir!"

Peli watched her professor leave. Her eyes fell on the box, where the figurine of Seyela and the ribbon nestled in the packing material. She grinned.

'Edera'yn's adventures trying to romance every goddess in the pantheon and the resulting mischief add a whole new facet to our understanding of the Aera. Hitherto, we had never seen instances in their tales of an appreciation of the ridiculous.'

Peli leaned back and laughed in glee, exhiliarated. If her assignment on Aren had been intended to be 'dull', well... bring on the rosettes and ribbons!

I sat on the riverside beneath a raincatcher tree and watched rhaurnip being loaded aboard an old wooden barge. The dockworkers were Miarrin like myself but darker-furred, wearing wide-brimmed hats to protect themselves from the sun, panting with lolled tongues as they hefted bales from the pier. I took a deep breath, tasting the mint of rhaurnip, then let my gaze drift past them to the adobe villas of Ahriuranen crowding the other side of the water, to wheat-colored fields, then distant purple mountains that faded to pale gray at the horizon. Above was the canopy of the sky, which was...

Wrong. It wasn't the clear amethyst I remembered, but as hard as I stared, I couldn't decide whether it needed to be paler, or if the clouds should be a darker shade of cream, to lighten it—

Door-scratching drove my fading memories of Ahriuranen away, my stylus skittering on the art-slate, leaving a furrow of pixels. "Hairballs," I snarled under my breath. "I'm busy, Prressa!"

"Merea! Is that any way to talk to your favorite litter-sister?" Prressa slid the door back and padded in to see what I was drawing, her tail a curlique of curiosity. She was gray tabby-furred like myself, but her lighter-gold mane swooshed into gentle waves, unlike my own mare's nest of curls. She smelled cinnamony and from her sport-suit, I suspected she had just come back from zee-ball practice.

I said, trying to keep my voice level and my ears straight, "You may be my only litter-sister, but that doesn't make you my *favorite*. Do you mind?"

"Giving an opinion? Of course not, Merea, you know my advice and my mouth have such a wonderfully giving relationship," Prressa said with a grin that said she knew what I meant, then craned over my shoulder.

I wrung my tail while Prressa wasn't looking, trying not to think about strangling my only sister. As if she knew anything about painting! *Think about something else, Merea... Anything else.*

My gaze fell upon an old-fashioned book-slate adorned with a picture of three wolf-children dressed in archaic robes. Anyone else would have gotten us books of tales from our *own* culture: our mother, being a teacher of comparative linguistics, had given us Vouzhon storybooks.

In this book, I remembered, three quarreling Vouzhon wolf-princes could not decide who should rule their clan. Each held a gift from their father that came from the days of the Creators, before we had come to the Tangled Web: the poet claimed that his Harp of Unending Music would bring joy to their people, the scholar boasted that his Book of All Knowledge would answer any questions they might have, and the warrior laid his hand on the grip of his father's gun and smiled fangily. Whomever held the best gift, they agreed, should become the new ruler.

Unfortunately, that was the only thing they agreed on. After many days of argument, they could not settle which was the best, and so they decided to separate the clan, and each group would follow one of the sons. In the end, the poet's people starved, the scholar's people were attacked by bandits and nearly wiped out, and it fell at last to the warrior to take both their estates and unify the clan again. By Vouzhon standards, this counted as a happy ending.

According to my mother, almost every race had its own version of the story: the Kyakarik foxes had the poet trick the bandits into attacking the warrior, and blaming it on the scholar; the sedate Rhedon centaurs had the scholar cure a plague and earn the gratitude of both the poet and the warrior. We Miarrins told several different versions of the story, though in the end they usually realized they needed each other, and formed an alliance.

Whatever the truth of the matter, I found it easy to imagine that in the days of the Creators, Prressa would have been the adventuring space captain who went back in line to get twice as many gifts, while I would have come last and gotten the least—I scolded myself. *Be fair, Merea. Prressa doesn't mean to show off, she's just always good at every—*

Prressa seemed to be waiting for me to say something. I twitched my frayed tailtip behind myself quickly. "What was that?"

She tapped the art-slate. I winced, even though her claw wouldn't mar the simulated paint; only the activated stylus would cause it to react. "I was saying, Merea, you've gotten much better with this slate."

I shrugged with a tailflick, jangling the bangles on my tail. "I'm starting to wonder if the frustration is worth the effort. It may be much less messy, and take up a lot less space than oh so many canvases and a full paint set, but by the Fire, I miss my old paintbrush!"

"Missing that, and more," Prressa said, fixing me with her eyes as deeply violet as Ahriuranen's mountains. "You're homesick, aren't you?"

I looked up in surprise, trying to find a hint of scorn in the way her ears dipped, her whiskers moved. Was she about to tease me? "Maybe," I hazarded.

But she was right, and I should have seen it myself. This was the eighth painting I'd done of Ahriuranen, and of the riverside that I knew so well. Just looking at it made me remember the heady smell of rhaurnip, a mild narcotic and the colony's main export. It was not that valuable in interstellar commerce, really, but it was the best they had to offer. Unfortunately, that meant they couldn't truly afford University-trained teachers like our mother, so when a better-paying position had opened up on Mrdainen Station, we had to move, so we'd have access to better education.

But I missed the colony still. Station life was so... *sterile.* So foreign. I'd grown up in the countryside, close to the untamed flora of Ahriuranen, ridden imported horses into the hills, drunk from raincatchers' harvests of dew. I would find none of those on a deep space jump-point station.

"There's nothing wrong with being homesick," Prressa said, patting my shoulder comfortingly. I tried not to bristle but still felt as patronized as if I were a kitten. "Believe it or not, I've felt that way too. When I got here, I didn't know where anything was, I thought the hall monitors were always watching us, and half the time, I was afraid I'd make some stupid mistake that would get us all kicked off the station."

"You? First in our class to be cleared for solo suit operation? Breaker of more speed records and limits on a scooter than I can count on both hands?" I gave her a disbelieving earflick, and my tail jangled with a matching twitch. "Pull my tail again."

Prressa hissed. "Stop that, Merea! I'm trying to help you, brat."

I dropped my ears contritely. "Sorry, Prressa, I'm used to claws from you, not sympathy."

"Well, we may quarrel, but I hope you don't think we're enemies!" Prressa sighed, then laughed as I began innocently grooming a hand. "Dragon's fang, claw, and breath, I did all that because I had to throw myself into the middle of Mrdainen life if I was going to stop thinking of it as 'foreign', and start thinking of it as 'home'. That's what you need to do, too, Merea. There's a lot more to the universe than just one world. Why don't you give it a chance?"

"What's there that *I* should like? I'm not the outgoing one in this family, Prressa, you are!" Prressa was half right, maybe I hadn't done more than the minimum in the orientation classes, but I had at least *sniffed* at them; they just hadn't sparked my interest enough to pursue them. Seizing what was new and tackling it to the ground, that was more my sister's style.

My sister pretended to think. "Well, there is that young Lyonnin fellow who seems to have a sweet spot in his heart for you."

"Rravel?" I laid my ears flat. "When he wanted to go zero-gee dancing, we toppled half the people in this habitat in the space of just one round and ruined my dress so badly I had to recycle it! Then when he wanted to try scooter racing, *you* had to come get us when we ran out of fuel!"

"He may be Lyonnin-big, but he's young too, Merea!" Prressa laughed nevertheless. "He's bound to be a little hot-headed and awkward, just like any Miarrin kitten. But I think he'll be a fine man when he's older. Besides..." Her voice hushed to a conspiratory whisper. "Look what I've got for you two."

I blinked at the twin rectangles of gold that Prressa displayed with a magician's flourish. "What's this?"

"Didn't you hear? A Kyakarik clanship's coming into dock, *Hanokin's Bounty*. Now any kitten could get in there... eventually. But these are *First Docking* tickets," Prressa said with a wide smile.

She had a reason to be smug. Clanships were roving festivals of wonders full of curios and stories collected from all over the Tangled Web, mazes of golden halls and corridors crowded with shopfronts. The last Kyakarik ship to pass through had been eleven years ago, and it would likely be at least a handful of years before the next.

The first day of a clanship's arrival was especially grand, when their priests would bring out their most cherished relics in a grand ceremony. The relics were things that hailed to the oldest times, when our races were still newly come to the Tangled Web and struggling to stay alive. Some might even be from the times when the Creators themselves had lived, from the First Galaxy. First Docking tickets were granted by a complicated lottery system, which assured the richest and most influential of the best view of the celebrations... and the luckiest.

It would have taken pulling some very long strings to get these prizes: the actual money might only have been a month's wages, but the tickets were so rare compared to the many who would want to go that scalpers would be selling them for enough to make even the covetous Chichimekkans blush to the tip of their brushy tails.

"No bargain, Prressa," I said, putting my ears down flat. Prressa couldn't have been that lucky *twice*. I smelled someone else's influence at work here. "Did Rravel put you up to this?"

"What if he did?" Prressa gave me a challenging look, whiskers bristly, ears swept back, tail lashing, hands on hip.

I folded my arms. "Then you tell him that I won't be bought."

My sister laid her ears askew, exasperated. "Then I'm not going to tell you who *did* pay for the tickets. I'll make you a bargain. If you go with Rravel and you have fun, you'll pay me for the tickets. If you don't, I'll pay for them, I'll tell you whose idea it really was, and I won't bother you about him for a month. Do we have a deal?"

"Shouldn't it be the other way around? If I go and I have fun, I don't have to pay?" I asked.

"Silly! I want you to be honest about it," Prressa said. "I don't want you to feel as if you need to *look* like you're having fun with Rravel if you're not, just to save money. This way if you admit it was good after all, I'll know you mean it."

"How do you know I won't enjoy myself, then tell you I didn't?"

"I'll trust you on that," Prressa said, smiling toothily. "You're my litter-sister, anyway, you can't lie to me."

"Make it a year." Given my past experience with Rravel, it seemed like a safe bet, but I wanted to test how far Prressa would go.

"A month. Take it or leave it."

I looked skyward—well, ceiling-ward. "All right, Prressa, I'll do it."

"Use them in good health," Prressa said, dropping the passcards into my hand. We slipped off a tailbangle each and traded them, though I thought that my marbled soapstone bracelet looked out of place among her golden rings. She gave me a sly grin and added, "I'll start looking for extra jobs you can do so you can afford to pay me back. Feel like being a waitress at the Singing Dragon?"

I swatted at her, chasing her out of my quarters as she giggled, and then stopped short at the doorway as it slid shut, looking back at the art-slate. In the dimmed light of the stateroom, its not-quite-right sky still nagged at me to fix it, and the dock-workers and trees were just sketches waiting to be sharpened into life.

It was my mind's eye that held the life I was trying to remember; the art-slate was only a slab of crystal and plastic. But all the same, I couldn't help but whisper to it, "Don't worry. I won't be gone long."

I won't forget you, Ahriuranen.

🦋 ☜ 🦋

"Don't you find Kyakariks simply amazing? How can anyone build an entire rreligion around luck?" That was Rravel standing next to me in the crowd as we watched the parade of yin-feteks.

The word 'yin-fetek' meant 'lucky object', and the *Hanokin's Bounty* had collected many of them over endless years in space. Many of them were not much to look at: for instance, passing before us as I stood on tip-toes to be able to see over others' shoulders was a simple black wooden chair on a float strewn with golden flower petals. I couldn't see what was so lucky about the chair, but far be it from me, daughter raised on stories of twelve cultures, to criticize the doings of another race.

Especially far be it when I considered that they practiced code duello, and clanships were always considered to be Kyakarik soil. It was an arrangement of necessity: the Kyakarik homeworld had been destroyed centuries ago when its star went nova, forcing them to become nomads. Perhaps now the Kyaks felt they needed all the luck they could get.

"Take that chairr, for instance," Rravel said to me, his Lyonnin accent thick and snarling as he spoke in Miarrin trade. I made shushing gestures at him, hoping no Kyak nearby would hear.

He failed to notice. "They say it is lucky because it stopped a Ryoshanan bullet, but what makes it any luckierr than body armorr? Tish, they may as well deify rrocks." He lapped a fangtip in disdain.

"And what makes your Sunbearer any more noble than another Lyonnin?" asked a nearby Kyak. He spoke Miarrin Trade quite well, with-out Rravel's snarling accent. His expensive silks and the swagger to his gait as he closed the distance between us suggested he was a 'hot blood': old enough to engage in duels, young enough to want to, and rich and influential enough to afford the consequences. I smelled trouble.

Rravel replied with a surprised look and slow, careful words as if explaining to a child, "He possesses prrftt—all the Lyonnin bow down to him."

The Kyak widened his smile, showing pearly fangs. "Ah, but strip him of his regalia, rub some grease into his hands, tell others that he is a factory worker gone mad with overwork—who would believe his claims then?

What Lyonnin would look twice, after kicking him into the alleys? And where then is this prrftt of which you speak?"

Rravel scowled. "What would a Kyak fop know about prrftt? It would shine through even the thickest coating of mud. The Sunbearer holds the Sceptrre because he has been rraised from birth to be the best rruler possible. He has prroven himself, and that is what earrns him prrftt. Whatever Kyaks may think, it takes more than a stick and a rrobe to make a Sunbearer—and it takes morre than clothes to make a lorrd out of a common thief!"

An enterprising Kyakarik waved to those nearby, then took out a slate. "Two to one for the Lyonnin, friends, place your bets here!" I edged aways, ears reddening, while curious Miarrins and Kyaks pushed in past me to watch the fight.

"How was your date, Merea?" I growled to myself, walking away. "Oh, it was wonderful, Prressa. First Rravel made fun of Kyaks on their own ship, and then he got into a fight with a lordling. I'm terribly impressed with his self-restraint, truly I am." I flicked my tail angrily and sought a quieter and saner corner of the *Hanokin's Bounty*.

The crowds thinned out away from the Processional, the noise thinning out enough that I could hear shopkeepers calling to the strays like myself. "Spice cookies here, get your snacks here, best Vouzhon cooking," a Kyak matron chanted at her stall from which wonderful baking smells came. Others waved about bangles and jewelry, likely glass or synthetic but still magnificent to behold draped from their black-gloved arms, or clothes which they modeled as well as displaying on mannequins of twelve races. Brushing past a few Miarrins who seemed rather more blase about being on a clanship, I caught motion within the shadows. Dark corners for dark wares, perhaps.

"Wonders of a thousand worlds," a voice hissed, a hand tugged at my sleeve. I swatted by reflex, turning about to see an ancient, moldering Kyak. He went on undeterred, "Come see my artifacts, young Miarrin! You have never seen miracles like mine, may Luck turn her face from me if I lie!"

"Not interested," I said, pulling on my sleeve.

"Ah! Have you no curiosity? Are you not Miarrin?" The wretch pulled at his ears and gaped at me, but folding my ears back, I hurried onward. I didn't feel like buying anything.

In truth, I wasn't sure what I wanted, except for a nice, quiet corner free of people who wanted something from me. Who among my friends had thought that Rravel and I would make a match? Had they been blind? The Lyonnin was a walking disaster!

The light dimmed suddenly, and I realized that I'd stepped into a cul-de-sac deep in the asteroidal rock of the clanship, with no way out but the way I'd come. Blinking, I looked up and around, finding row on row of crystal globes mounted in brackets on the walls, some small and irides-

cent, others large and pale, so faintly colored they looked like soap bub-
bles. Thick plush carpet underfoot and comfortable couches and tables
and the smell of incense made me wonder if this was someone's shop
or home. "Pardon me for my intrusion," I said to the shadowy Kyakarik
looking up at me from his cushions.

"Please be welcome. I am Akakitsu. I so rarely receive visitors that
each is a pleasure," he said with a kindly smile. His clothes matched the
surroundings, dark but of a rich texture, subtly embroidered and entirely
unlike the flamboyance of the traders outside. What manner of establishment had I stumbled into? I looked about. *Dark wares for dark corners?*

Akakitsu gestured toward the globes, taking my look for interest.
"These are truly wonders of a hundred worlds, unlike the trifles some
other traders sell," he said. "Each holds a vision of a different place, seen
by someone who was there once. Each is a dream, as it were, captive in
crystal."

"You sell these, then?" *Sales resistance,* I reminded myself, trying to
sound more assured, even skeptical. I had no intention of buying anything, and in fact, I was starting to be tired of people who wanted me to do
something, be it buy, sell, or go out on dates. Or so I told myself.

The Kyakarik shook his head, taking out a pipe and filling it. I stared a
bit: I hadn't seen anyone with one since Ahriuranen. Stationers tended to
despise such things as an unnecessary burden on life support systems, but
perhaps clanships could afford the luxury. The pungent smell told me that
I might have been wrong in guessing that incense burners had created the
aromas I'd scented. Akakitsu went on, "I had the good fortune to be born
to one of the founding lines of the *Hanokin*. My share-royalties provide
for all my needs. But we Kyakariks have other needs than mere wealth,
believe it or not!" He winked.

"A need for company?" I speculated. "But not the sort that can be
bought with drink and food in good restaurants or found in loud, noisy
crowds."

"You see well, dear Miarrin. I tend my little corner of the *Bounty*, past
the din and chaos of the Processional, past the seductive calls and wares
of the Market Roads, and though it may seem that I should see no traffic
at all, still the Luckbringer sends some my way now and then, curious
what such a reclusive Kyak might have to sell." Akakitsu smiled. "Or they
return, after many, many years, when the *Hanokin's Bounty* comes back to
their worlds again. Then we have tea, and share what new stories we have
both collected."

"It sounds like a marvelous way to live," I admitted.

"Oh yes! But to answer your first question: I collect these. Or to speak
more precisely, I collect stories, memories which are recorded within these
spheres. Perhaps you'd care to try one for yourself, to see what I mean?"

Were there stories about people vanishing aboard a Kyakarik clanship? Hypnotized by globes, sold into slavery? My hand closed around

my golden passcard. *Ridiculous,* I told myself. Stories about clanship slavers were just told by kittens to scare each other silly around a campfire. A disappearance would embarrass the *Hanokin's Bounty.* Their customers were their lifeblood, and if they started disappearing left and right, sooner or later there would be no more *Hanokin's Bounty.*

"I might," I said carefully.

Akakitsu smiled brightly, fangs pristine white. "Wonderful! Let us find one suitable, then." He began to walk around the room, tapping random spheres with a clawtip, with no system that I could discern, until he came upon one that evidently satisfied him. A fingerpad print unlocked the bracket's field and then he popped it free, holding it out.

As I shied, he chuckled. "It won't bite, dear Miarrin. It's only a memory. A very old one, at that."

I held it up to the light from the entrance, seeing a faint swirl of colors inside. Against the darker background, it became a blue-white crescent, a planet seen from space. "A hologram?" I wondered. "Is that what this is? But it's so small, and there's no projector that I can see."

The Kyakarik shook his head. "Look closer," he whispered. "Imagine yourself inside the sphere."

Frowning, I peered closer, close enough that my nose began to fog the crystal, and then drew back a bit. The image hadn't seemed very detailed at first, but it looked quite real, the more I examined it. In fact, I'd been wrong that it was a free-floating planet; it looked more like a view from a ship, with scratches marring the glass and hullmetal framing it, and...

I was aboard a ship I'd never seen before. Somehow I knew it was the *Starlight Racer,* the legendary colony ship that had brought the first of the Miarrins to the Tangled Web nebula, after the Creators' Great War had forced us to flee the First Galaxy. A great wide window framed the view of Firstfall, a tiny blue-white globe barely warmed by the red giant that hung in the distance, against veils of gas clouds.

Starlight Racer shuddered as unseen pods left it, and one by one they came into view through the window, tiny steel dots that faded into invisibility against Firstfall's cloud canopy. They contained bacteria cultures, spores, tiny machines that would dig into the ground and begin transforming Firstfall into a place where Miarrins could live. It would be many long years before even the first colonists could land and start growing crops. But *we were here at last.* Our journey had ended.

The dream lost its hold on me; I shook my head, fluffing my fur out as I tried to gather a few wits, bewildered for a moment to find myself in Akakitsu's dimly lit corner. "That was... thousands of years ago! How can you have something so old?"

The Kyakarik shook his head, ears pinking. "Truth to tell, it is a memory of a memory, several times over, if I am to believe the records that came with it. Each generation loses some of the details, leaves more to be imagined. But I have other globes here, drawn from true life, if you would care to see them, dear Miarrin."

"Is this Creator technology? I don't think you could *make* anything like this on Mrdainen Station!" I stared at the rows on rows of globes, seeing them anew. *No wonder Akakitsu spoke of himself as a collector. How many worlds does he have here?*

He grinned a foxy grin. "Now, could the Creators know about our own worlds? We left them behind many lightyears ago. But in a way, they did indeed have a hand in this. Behold!" He led me to a niche of his cave which held a strange machine of crystal pipes that twisted and wound about each other tortuously. I couldn't see where they began or ended. "A relic of the Creators! They must have used these as we use cameras, to preserve memories of happy events, or perhaps as a form of art."

"*You* have a Creator artifact?" I couldn't begin to calculate how much such a relic might be worth to scholars or collectors. But then, Akakitsu had said he had no need of wealth. I blushed. "Oh, I'm sorry, I didn't mean to suggest you *couldn't* have one, but—why isn't it on display with the other artifacts on parade? Or being studied at the University?"

"Tch! In truth, it is my little secret, shared with my friends, young Miarrin," Akakitsu said with a forgiving smile. "I hardly care to attract the sort of visitors that only wish to stare at things that might have once belonged to older people from older times. The priests and I have an understanding; they do not borrow my things, and I do not ask for my ship-investment to be returned all at once. As for the University... It is an ancient machine, to be sure, but it is not *unique* as such. They have several examples of dreamspinners already."

I nodded, still amazed that I was actually within *touching* distance of such a relic, something that had been born in a galaxy far, far from the Tangled Web. "Does it... work?"

"Of course!" the proprietor reassured me. "Would you like to try it?"

"Will it hurt?" Perhaps my wits had been rather jarred by the globe, but I felt myself actually curious to see what would happen. *It puts memories in spheres... Any memory?*

"No more so than daydreaming. All you need to do is to press these knobs apart, and hold them as you think of the memory you wish to capture," Akakitsu said, gesturing toward the controls. "When you are done, close the knobs. A child could do it!"

"Now I don't know if I want it to be easy or not," I said, wrinkling my nose. I wasn't a kitten, whatever Prressa might think! "How much does it cost?"

Akakitsu's green eyes shone with laughter at my caution. "To you, my dear, it is free. But the Luckbringer knows that even nothing costs something."

That sounded like a Kyakarik proverb to me, but entirely appropriate. "I can't turn down an offer like that, honorable merchant of dreams," I said, smiling, and held out my hand to clasp agreement on it, Kyak-style; he grasped it firmly, shook it once, and then led me to stand in front of the machine.

I laid my hands upon the knobs, pressed them apart, and reality opened like a gate.

※ ∞ ※

I tried to see through the gray mists, felt panic rising when I could find nothing but the ground beneath my feet. Was this a trap after all? "Akakitsu! Where are you?" My paws reached out, but I could find no knobs to close and end the dream.

Wait—was dreaming the key? Forcing myself still, I tried to *imagine* something out of the grayness. It felt as if the mists were billowing around me for a moment, stirring my whiskers and ears, and then shadows rose from the ground, or perhaps the mists faded away to reveal form and color. Water gurgled, wind sighed, and an unmistakable scent brushed my nose: rhaurnip.

I stood on the hillside beneath a stand of raincatcher trees, looking over the river at the village of Ahriuranen, dropped my gaze to see the dockworkers loading bales onto the old barge. I lifted my gaze, found the sky the perfect shade of amethyst, frothed with cream clouds. *Home again.*

Testing the limits of Akakitsu's dreamspinner, I found a nearby brush, plucked a berry, chomped into it with an explosion of juice that stained my nose red. The tartness stung my tongue every bit as sharply as I remembered. Grinning, I took hold of the memory with something other than hands, and turned the page like a book.

... Skimming across the lake with an old-fashioned sailboard, I felt my fur growing heavy with droplets, shook my head wildly to fluff my fur out. Too late, I realized I'd lost my balance and whooped as I toppled sail and all into the water, spluttering and scrambling to right my board.

... Raincatchers spread their canopy overhead, matted fibers lacing one another to catch and hold dew. I swept my faerie-light around, hoping to see the glow of ultraviolet upon flutterby wings, so that I could catch one and bring it home to show Prressa. A branch cracked under my foot and an entire swarm of flutterbies burst from the underbrush, swirling around me, dissipated like a fireworks display.

... Firelight shone warm on me as I spun around and around the dance circle with Trianrr, laughing. Bells jangled on our heels with each stamp of our feet, and my necklace of rhaurflower made the air itself heady. Musicians sang harvest festival songs, and Trianrr leaned close to stare into my eyes, his own eyes deep pools of Merilin blue.

Everything was perfect. I could have spent years remembering, reliving, and yet something nagged at the back of my mind. *Something's missing. No. Someone.*

Where was Prressa? She might be a pain at times, reminding me how much I still had to learn when she fetched me out of one trouble or another, but Ahriuranen wasn't complete without her. I searched the village, then our favorite hiding spots in the woods, and at last I found her on Gaze Rock, looking at the monoliths in the canyon below. The double moonlight made her ghostly. Bright dancing music still came from the fires far behind us as I tugged at her tail. "Come on, Prressa! Shake your tail loose of this thicket, you're missing all the fun!"

"Go ahead, Merea, don't let me hold you back," she said, giving me a smile and a shooing gesture. "I'm just not in the mood right now."

I gave her a disbelieving look and sat down on the rock next to her, feeling a chill of worry. "What's wrong, Prressa? You're always first and best at the dance! Did Rehanriu stand you up or something?"

She didn't answer immediately, her eyes fixed on the stone columns of the canyon. I followed her gaze to them, wondering if she'd come to contemplate what might have been Ahriuranen's only sign that others had once lived there depending on whom one believed, and then I looked back to realize that her eyes were fixed slightly higher. She was looking at the stars.

"No, it's not Rehanriu," she said at last. "He died two years ago, in that rock climbing accident. Do you remember?"

I stared at Prressa. "But I saw him only a moment ago..." But it had only been a memory of a dance long ago, a memory of the best dance I'd ever had. I said slowly, "They found his body in that landslide, didn't they? And wasn't that the trip you almost went with him on, until they'd made you stay behind to finish a school report?"

She nodded, and it came back to me slowly, the memory of her crying on my shoulders when we'd gotten the report. I closed my eyes, remembering her questions. Could she have saved him? Would she have gotten caught too? It had been strange to see strong, self-confident Prressa as doubtful as myself, but I'd gone on petting her back and whispering soothing things into her ear.

Something tickled my mind—that was it. "Prressa, we've never spoken like this before, have we?"

She shook her head, a wry smile tugging up the corner of her lips. Was that a tear beading at her eye? She blinked and I couldn't tell anymore. "We must have, kitten. This is your memory, isn't it?"

"I'm not so sure..." I reached out with my hands to try and turn the memory like a page. Gaze Rock stayed. So did Prressa. "Why is it even my memories won't leave me alone?"

Prressa stood slowly, stretched elaborately, arms rising, hands fanning the air, her tail flicking out to the very tip with a ringing of bangles. "Do you remember when we were away at summer camp the first time, and our mother sent us a package of all the treats that we liked so much the first week?"

I remembered. "I ate them all the first night, even your half, and then you had to carry me to the doctor," I said, whiskers flicking forward in embarrassment, nose wrinkling.

"But after that, I told you that you should know when enough of a good thing was enough," Prressa said, laughing. "You asked me when was enough, and I told you that someday you'd be old enough to know."

I sighed, smiling a bit again. "And now you're reminding me that I really am old enough to know, aren't you?" I looked around again at Gaze Rock, at the raised pools of the Ahriuranen countryside, at the basins of raincatcher trees below that reflected the stars. It burned in me, the desire to be there just one more time.

But deeper still, I knew that Prressa was right.

She wrapped her arms around me in a comforting hug. "Just remember, sister. Home is where you leave your heart. And you know that *my* heart was never bound to Ahriuranen."

Standing again, Prressa began to fade away, a wisp of smoke that faded into the night. Moonlight shone where she had been, across the canyon as well, making double shadows of each monolith. Softly, like a requiem, the musicians below began to play *Gone the Evening* and dancers melted from the circles in ones and twos, returning home.

I took a deep breath, taking in the hundred scents that made up Ahriuranen's own winds, blinked back tears.

Then I closed the gate.

🐾 ∞ 🐾

With a musical 'tink', the globe dropped into a clear glass basin. I picked it up to see Gaze Rock inside, at night. Something about it tugged at my eyes to see it closer—but I looked away. It was enough to hold its comfortable weight in my hand. "It's beautiful," I whispered, still holding in my mind the vision of the canyon.

"As are you, young Miarrin," Akakitsu said. Something about his voice sounded wistful.

"I? Surely you jest," I said, surprised. I thought my own features plain by Miarrin standards, but perhaps Kyakarik standards differed, or perhaps he was teasing. But his green eyes looked serious enough. "It's my sister people look at, not me."

He smiled in Kyak fashion, lolling his tongue between his fangs. "Not all beauty is of the eye, nor all value of the gilden sort."

I curled my tail, blushing in my ears. "Well, thank you, Akakitsu! But—" I looked at the globe I'd made, then at his collection. Could I stand to have a stranger peeking in the world of my memories, listening to me and Prressa? What, if anything, had the Kyakarik seen as I stood before the machine, hands on its controls?

"You owe me nothing," he said, laying his hands over mine, folding my fingers over the globe. "And you need not fear if it was a private vision. I saw nothing, save your joy and wonder, and your sadness, and the moment when you found your strength. That is why I spoke of your beauty, dear lady."

I bit my tonguetip, cupping the sphere, then looked up again. "Can I make another one, Akakitsu? This one would be for you."

This time he laughed. "I would be honored, dear lady."

It took a moment more, but when I clicked the knobs together again, another globe clinked into the basin, filled with the tiny image of a young Miarrin painter. Myself, drawing Prressa as she lazed on the sunlit top of Gaze Rock. That had been my first real painting, the first one that had been anything more than pigments on canvas. I'd forgotten it until now. I pressed the globe into the Kyakarik's hands. "Here, Akakitsu. And... My name is Merea. I'm sorry I didn't say so earlier, but I was in a mood." My ears pinked again.

He bowed with a flourish, tucking the globe away into an unseen pocket, and smiled widely as he flicked out a gold-lettered card and offered it. "It is a lovely name, Merea. And should you wish to do so, I should like nothing more than to receive a letter from you. It makes the time between stars pass so much more quickly."

Altogether delighted, I curtseyed back, and set back into the bazaar after our farewells. The high carved walls of the *Hanokin's Bounty* shops and homes rose over my head, beginning to resonate again with the din of commerce as I approached the Processional. *I won't meet many Kyakariks like that again,* I mused.

The sphere rested in a pouch, cool to my touch as I ran a fingertip over its surface, but mentally warming—a cure for homesickness, wrapped up in glass. Something nagged at the back of my mind as I looked over the wonders that I'd ignored on the way in. I'd forgotten something.

"Rravel!" Had I really left him to get into a duel with a Kyak hot-blood? I berated myself mentally as I picked up my feet and ran through the growing crowds. What would Prressa say? *You let your date get killed, Merea? I know you don't like him, but really, who's going to date you after this?* A Kyak merchant startled as I bounded over his pottery display. "Don't be dead, Rravel, don't you dare be dead—"

"Dead?" The Lyonnin blinked up at me from where a pair of Kyak females, both young enough to only have one earring apiece, were bandaging his shoulder and wiping an antiseptic pad over a cut on his cheek. "Far from it, my dearr Merrea. The only thing injurred was my prride."

"You could have been killed, Rravel," I said angrily, my tailtip lashing. "What would I have said to my sister? 'I couldn't watch, so I left?'"

He chuckled deeply, shrugged deprecatingly, then winced and rubbed his bandaged shoulder. "'Twas my own foolishness, no one else's, milady. I mistook a duellist's victory earrings for simple jewelry, but these young ladies have explained to me my error. Very forrgiving, he was, for calling him a common thief." His voice dropped into a low murmur. "'Twas a near, near thing." Forcing a smile, he made a circle of his uninjured arm and moved over to offer me a seat. "Come, Merrea. Sit?"

I sighed, hearing the pain in his voice. It was hard for any Lyonnin to admit a mistake, but Rravel had managed it. "All right, I suppose I'll let it go. This time." I sat, letting him settle his arm around my shoulders, halfway worried that he was going to do something utterly sappy and romantic, but foolish, such as kissing me, pulling me into a dance, or Creators forbid, something even more inappropriate. Sitting next to Rravel was a bit like being at the bottom of the mountain, wondering when the rocks above would crash down into inevitable avalanche.

"I've had time to think back on what we've been together, Merrea," he said, turning to look me in the eyes. His were amber, I noted, with green speckling the edges. I began to fear that he would propose. Or—did I want it?—that he might want to break up.

"I've trried to imprress you in the past," he said slowly, very serious. "It's always turrned out badly—perrhaps because my prride outstrrips my wisdom. But I think also, you arre not the kind of girrl to be imprressed by such shows. Is that not true?"

Or apologizing. That was just the sort of crazy thing I should have expected from Rravel. I tried not to smile, but failed, nodding.

He sat back, giving me space, still holding my eyes. "Prrftt, as I have been rreminded forrcefully, is not in victorry. It is in rrespect—where there is no rrespect, there is no victorr, Merrea. Were you like many Lyonnin women, you might admirre brrashness and brravado. But I think you find no virrtue in one who prrovokes a fight forr its own sake."

"You *intended* to be heard when you made those comments?" I said, appalled. "What were you thinking?"

A chuckling breath as he nodded. "I was not, that is the prroblem. Also, I did not underrstand when Prressa suggested that she should be the one to pay for the First Day tickets, norr why she arranged herr bet with you as she did. Lyonnin women would find themselves honorred, werre one of prrestige and influence to bestow gifts upon them. But I see now, Prressa wanted you to decide for yourself, and be sure about your decision. And so must I trry to rrespect yourr wishes. For trrying to buy yourr attention, I must apologize, Merrea."

A pause, and then he looked down. "I will underrstand if you do not wish to see me again, milady."

"What? Oh, Creators, no," I said, trying to hold back an almost painful laugh. Prressa had misled me after all. The hours I'd spent wondering who among our friends would have had the bad taste to set me up with Rravel had been wasted after all. And yet, hearing Rravel say so himself made all the difference in the galaxy. *Maybe, just maybe,* I told myself. *Maybe there was more to Rravel than I'd given him credit for.*

I leaned forward to give him a tight hug. "It's all right, you silly fuzzball. I forgive you."

He squeaked. "Not so harrd!" I blushed, loosened my grip, then laughed, and heard him chuffing as well. Behind us, the two vixens drifted away, their job well done.

※ ☜ ※

"Hmm, he looks good enough to eat, Merea! May I borrow him?" Prressa said, leaning over my shoulder to study my latest effort.

"How much? I still owe you another month's pay or so..." I grinned up at my sister before dabbing another fine whisker of gray onto the canvas. My palette reeked of pigments, and my brush needed to be cleaned between each bout, but the sheer satisfaction was more than worth the mess. Rravel took shape on the painting slowly, leading a gray tabby Miarrin out to dance against a backdrop of the jewels-draped Tangled Web.

Adding a dab of brown to my brush, I drew in a scar across his cheek. Rravel had refused to get his scar removed, calling it his souvenir of the trip. "It will rremind me not to be overconfident. It holds prrftt, in its own way."

My own souvenir nestled on a protective brace on my shelf, a crystal globe filled with night-time Ahriuranen. I touched it now and then, sometimes to remind myself of Ahriuranen, other times to remember Akakitsu, or to think back to when my relationship with Rravel had truly began, and still other times, to listen to dream-Prressa. Would I ever tell Prressa the story? I didn't know.

I'd sent a letter to Akakitsu as I'd promised, and promised to send him a copy of the painting when I finished it. He assured me that he would be looking forward to tracking my career as a painter. A painter! I was not sure myself if it would be my choice, but there were worse things to be.

"I'm tempted," Prressa said thoughtfully, pulling my thoughts back to the present. "My boyfriend might be a little jealous, but it could be worth seeing the look on his face. How about five hundred?"

"No deal," I said firmly.

※

RECRUITING

Elizabeth McCoy

Coli-nfaran, medic and semi-official second-in-command of the Kintaran clanship *Choosaraf*, was fulfilling her latter duties. Five of the newly adult members of the clan had announced their desire to explore new territories, when next the ship stopped at Kintara, and even her own son had declared that he wanted to grow up a ground-bounding bard instead of shipcrew.

She'd told Wahn Klarin-yal (her fraternal twin sister) this distressing news, and was now listening to the result.

"We don't have the *luxury* of letting the keesolt[1] be other than crew yet!" the minutes-older Kintaran cried, pulling her mane over her eyes. "If we keep running on double-shifts without even keesolt to watch the readouts, somebody's going to make a mistake and *fzzzzt*—we're back in hock again! I've got barely enough engineers and mechanics to keep the ship running, the scant minimum of pilots, only two doctors *including* you, and not a single trade specialist has come back *yet* since Cholartha left! I could hunt down that feather-brain 'Negotiator' and..."

Coli frowned. The *Choosaraf* had had a brief stint as a privateer before Klarin-yal and she had bought controlling shares. Unfortunately, before they could rescue it from "Captain Fat-Head," the folk who had wanted to be merchanters had up and left, with the exception of young Cholartha, who had been an apprentice-level Negotiator at best. Coli sighed; she preferred to isolate herself in Medical instead of worrying that they hadn't been able to lure any other merchants back to the ship. At least this explained why her sister was so cranky—in the absence of a Negotiator, she was doing what trade-deals she could alone. "You'd have said if we were losing money, nih?"

"Khih—I'd have told you. We're breaking even," the Wahn admitted, "and there's a little surplus, but one big repair will do for us. Then *nobody* will want to come back."

"Well, I'll tell the younglings that the ship needs them, but that won't wash any fur with them, I'll bet," the doctor sighed. "Especially Rarroriah, though he's stuck here for a while longer, till he gets his final growth-spurt."

"It was simpler in Grandmother's day," Klarin-yal moaned, indulging in self-pity with only her sib around. "If a new clan wanted more people, a female just flipped her tail at some wandering male and dragged him home in a net."

"You're mixing the stories," Coli corrected absently. "Grandmother was talking about a fishing-clan she saw once. But you've got a point. We

[1] Children

should try recruiting sensible Kintarans, who won't go trying for your place if we bring them in."

"*I* can't go mate-hunting—I'm the Wahn, and *you're* my second, Coli. If I went luring someone to this ship, he'd want a status close to mine, and he's not going to get it."

She shrugged. "That's because you go for the hot-tempered ones. I'll talk to some of our relatives, and we'll see if we can't lure some good breeding stock on board, at least. Males with level heads, good tempers..."

"Haunches of steel."

"And a willingness to babysit their children."

🐾 ∞ 🐾

Kintara Station was the likely place for such a thing, of course. But it was woefully disappointing to Coli-nfaran. Despite the success at gathering in *other* crew—another doctor, a good mechanic, some decent pilots—the only so-called "trader" she found couldn't have sold merfahs during a famine if he'd given them away. Even worse, when they checked his ship-references, two of the ships had never heard of him, and the third had kicked him off because he couldn't earn his keep.

There must *be a way,* Coli thought, staring down at Kintara from a station viewport. *Spirits of my foremothers, give me inspiration! You were clever enough when the aliens came to dig in the ground for metals. It was Kintarans who bartered and traded and tricked the bipeds into giving us things in exchange for useless metal. Grandmother, you told me so often about how the clan got the credit to build this ship. Can't that cleverness be genetic? Can't it be in me as well, when the whole clan needs it?*

There was something there. Coli could feel the idea nibbling at the neuromass above her lower shoulders, the "secondary brain" that helped coordinate her centaroid six limbs and tail.

"Maybe," she murmured to herself, "maybe it *is* genetic... Rarroriah wants to be a ground-bounder. Could be his sire's influence, or could be the grounder influence that we've *all* got. But if *he* wants to be a grounder, then maybe a grounder could throw a child who'd want to be a *spacer*. And if that spacer has the gifts of our grandparents, to talk smooth and understand trade well enough to wrangle the really good deals..."

Coli grinned and dashed for the *Choosaraf*'s dock. She had to get a shuttle to the surface.

🐾 ∞ 🐾

Kintara. "Like a clouded blue-green jewel." Coli-nfaran hadn't been to the surface for years—not since her uncle, mother, and grandmother had died in a shuttle-crash there—and it was strange. First the gravity seemed like maybe it was a little heavier than the ship-grav, then a little too light. The air moved constantly, sometimes refreshing the child Coli had been when she was last on this world, and sometimes terrifying the adult spacer she'd become, because it felt like an air-leak. The scents and sounds were the same way: both exhilarating and unnerving.

One of their new pilots had flown the *Choosaraf*'s only passenger shuttle down, with her in it. He tilted his dark gray head at her. "You all right, Doctor?"

She thought about it a moment. "I suppose I'll have to be. You go back to the ship, Dellum. I've got the implant comm, and Klarin-yal knows it may take me a few months." She hoped it didn't take that long: after a week or three, the *Choosaraf* would be losing money, and Klarin-yal would have to find in-system jobs—or out-system ones, leaving Coli on the surface...

"You might get lucky in Kintara Star-Town," Dellum suggested helpfully. "That's where a lot of traders stay, selling things to tourists. Just get a place here, and most of the clans show up eventually to take their turn."

"Getting a place costs money, I fear. We'll see. I'll be fine." Her voice was rather faint, though—she was all too aware of her small stature, and how unfit it made her as a hunter. Truly, she'd been born to be a spacer, just as her sister had the build and temperament to be a clan-leader.

"You need any help, Doctor, give us a call—Lelocha..." (his expression went dreamy for a moment, thinking of the crew-female who'd brought him in) "...she said that the Wahn will be interviewing crew at the station for a while, so all us pilots are supercargo. We might get some temporary shuttle jobs, but that's mostly taken care of by the station clans." He wrinkled his nose at the thought of the Consortium of Clans who "ran" Kintara Station.

She smiled at him. "Well, if I need any help, I'll ask for you and Lelocha—wouldn't want to separate you two."

He purred happily. "Good luck, Doctor," he called as he headed back to the ship.

"Thanks," she sighed, waving back. "I'll need it." She turned away before the shuttle took off. There was no need to waste time watching it, and wishing she were taking off too.

After all, it was the first time ever that she'd been anywhere without her sister nearby.

🐾 ☁ 🐾

After about a week—during which Klarin-yal called Coli's implant comm twice a day, to point out that although the ship had undocked and was in independent (and therefore free) orbit, they still weren't *making* money—the small Kintaran discovered that most of the people at Star-Town either liked being ground-bounders or couldn't stand the thought of leaving their own clan.

"Khih, sister-wahn, I know it's expensive," Coli muttered, trying to sub-vocalize for the implant comm alone. "But I'm not having any luck here."

"So what makes you think you'll have more luck outside of Star-Town?" Klarin-yal asked. "Maybe you should just come back to the ship, and we'll keep looking for Negotiators with advertisements."

Something in Coli dug in its claws. "No. That wasn't working. Release the funds, sister; I know what I'm doing."

"Oh, all right. If this'll get you back up here faster."

※ ◎ ※

Aircars were human tech. They had pedals and things, meant for biped feet, seats and seat-belts meant for a biped's posture, and air-vents that blew one's eye-whiskers flat against one's head. (One would have thought that a *sensible* Kintaran would just pull the bucket seats *out* of the thing, instead of leaving them there for a biped tourist and forcing any Kintaran to set the seat-backs to as far down as they would go and riding on those.) And aircars had lousy little "autopilots" that couldn't find their way without nav satellites feeding them data every fifteen seconds—which was a decided bother when a storm cropped up a day out of Star-Town and blew the aircar against one of the few trees on the plains and snapped the receiving antenna off...

Coli cursed again and kicked the rear door with her hind-claws. It wasn't the first time somebody'd done *that*, and her scratches weren't even as deep as most of the others decorating the hard plastic surface. The aircar didn't budge. According to its safety-programming, it was staying put until its little distress-beacon summoned help, which wouldn't be until the storm winds died down.

She kicked it again, but not very hard—Klarin-yal could have coaxed the thing into the air again, but Coli-nfaran was a medic, and the mysteries of piloting either ships or aircars had never been of interest to her before. If she *did* get it airborne in the storm, it would probably just flip over (again) and either wreck itself or land (again) and refuse to budge (again). So the best thing to do was to wait out the storm. Obviously. She couldn't call for a ride from the *Choosaraf*—a shuttle would have to come down through those same storm winds, and if one of *those* got wrecked, it would be far more expensive to fix than the minor damage that the aircar had suffered.

Under the other paw, however, Coli had the knowledge that if she had to stay in this little vehicle for much longer, she was going to perpetrate more damage than she wanted to pay for. After all, if she waited, what would that get her? A repair-craft coming out and hauling the car back? A delay, at the minimum. Going out there would get her soaked, but at least it was a warm summer storm, and Coli, unlike many Kintarans, didn't have much objection to water. She had her medkit, so she wouldn't get a fever, and she had her implant comm, so Klarin-yal could find her with just a little looking—the implant comm was line-of-sight, and could reach low orbit, though not distant ground stations; a *Choosaraf* shuttle would have no problems.

Coli kicked open the door on the lee-side of the car and backed out, reaching into the back seat to drag her pack out with her. Then she locked the door (the towing vehicle would have a spare key, when it finally arrived) and struck off into the wet and wind. It *was* a better choice than staying there and shredding the interior out of boredom and frustration.

🐾 ∞ 🐾

Two days of aimless hiking found Coli sitting under another tree, chewing on her rations and consulting her computer's holomap of Kintara. She ignored the coleyo[2] crying to itself in the top-most branches, just as she'd ignored various merfah colonies which had taken off running when they noticed her. Coli knew full well that her skills as a hunter would be rusty at best, and didn't want that notching her pride along with everything else. She blessed her grandmother, Shaman Neerri, and her mother, Ch'ichat, for being Kintarans who wanted to go a'spacing. Civilization and high-tech were *so* much nicer than grubbing along getting mud on one's paws.

Aircars were also much nicer than grubbing along—when she'd set out on foot, she hadn't thought about losing the height-advantage. It was a lot harder to find a wandering clan of Kintarans when you couldn't look from a thousand meters up.

Coli sighed and put her equipment away. Since wandering on the open plains was incredibly boring, and required constant attention to her compass if she didn't want to go in circles, she'd decided to head for the Great Forest. The Forest was unique—the planet's only huge stand of trees. She'd seen some holo-ads for the Great Forest, and even if she didn't find a clan there, at least she'd get to see those Immense Trees™ for real.

🐾 ∞ 🐾

It took another week, and Coli had to learn how to hunt merfahs. It was either that or eat grass, and she didn't have the time to spend in major discomfort while her digestive system adjusted to a herbivore diet, not to mention the time she'd have to spend grazing after the transition. Besides, grass-eating would notch her pride worse than not being able to catch live food.

By the time she got to the Forest, she thought she'd gotten pretty good at hunting. She only lost about three out of five merfahs that she tried to catch (instead of five out of six or worse...), and she'd figured out how to lay crude snares, using suture-thread from her medkit. The thread would never be sterile again, but it was *definitely* better than eating grass.

After snaring four of the little lizard-marsupials, Coli went back to her camp at the edge of the Forest and planned some more. She could either journey around the edge of the Forest, or she could go looking inside it. If she were on the edge, she could see a *lot* more of the horizon, and the Forest itself undoubtedly held unknown dangers. That was the word that

[2] Kintaran bird-equivalent. Feathered and four-legged, with a long feathered tail.

decided her path: "unknown." The next day, after she'd stocked up on merfahs, she headed into the Forest, just to see what was there.

☙ ∞ ❧

Clinging to the bark, Coli scrabbled up another body-length to avoid a whipping tentacle. The rope-armed animal below her roared in frustration.

"And 'yaaaa-rarrrrra' to you too!" the medic spat over her shoulder, clawing her way to a thick tree-branch that she could sit on.

Always approach from downwind, *so you can* smell *whether it's a Kintaran or a grabber,* Coli told herself, licking one palm and smoothing it over her ears soothingly. Of course, she'd thought grabbers were stories her mother had used to scare keesolt with. A furless thing that stood like a Kintaran, had the head of a bloodfang[3], and tentacles for arms? The description had been too silly to be believed for long. Unfortunately, the grabber pacing below her looked anything but silly at the moment. Its head wasn't really bloodfangish, for one thing—besides being bald, it was flatter and a little elongated, without a bloodfang's oversized canines. The lower limbs were thick and clawless; it moved slowly and couldn't climb, which was one reason why Coli had managed to escape. The other reason was that it had grabbed her pack when she first encountered it, and she'd wriggled out before it got one of those ropy arms around *her*. If she leaned over a little, she could still see her pack. Hopefully, the thing would go away eventually, and she'd be able to recover it.

The grabber roared again and jumped at the branch. One tentacle-tip actually grazed the bark. Coli started looking for a long, dead branch, to hit the wretched thing over the head with when it tried again. Nothing was available, and the grabber's second jump actually let it wrap one tentacle around her branch for a moment. It dangled several seconds longer than she would have thought it could, with that much weight... Coli swallowed, ran a hand over one ear again, and turned around to climb to a higher branch, on the other side of the tree.

The grabber roared at her some more, of course, and she spat insults back at it for nearly an hour, until she decided that was just keeping its tiny little brain interested. So she flattened her ears and sulked on her higher branch, keeping an eye on the grabber and her pack. For once, she was glad she *didn't* have any rations left in there—the grabber might have decided to destroy everything she carried, to see where the food-scent was coming from.

Thinking of scents... Coli's ears went up and she raised her head to sniff the breeze. Was that a whiff of Kintaran she'd caught? Whoever it was should be warned about the grabber, though they'd have to be deaf to have missed it. It still snarled beneath her tree, roaring now and again.

Over in a tree near her pack, a branch shuddered, leaves rustling a bit more than a breeze could account for. Coli's eyes narrowed, and her tail twitched. Finally, a good fifty heartbeats after *her* muscles started aching

[3] A Kintaran gorilla equivalent: a six-legged sabertooth tiger.

to hunt-creep some more, she caught a glimpse of paleness among the leaves. She grinned, and watched as a dark-striped young Kintaran crept into position, crouched, and jumped to another branch. He landed gracefully and slipped into cover, where he waited again.

Coli risked glancing down at the grabber. It was still sniffing at the bark where she'd gone up the tree, but it *had* quieted down some. She debated whether she wanted to rile it up again—if the young male were hiding from it, distracting the grabber might be only friendly.

The male scrabbled to a slightly lower branch and froze once more. The grabber didn't notice, and he jumped the rest of the way—landing right next to Coli's pack. Coli lashed her tail. When he picked it up and scrabbled up the tree again, she bellowed, "Little thief! Sparrial k'ee'tha hisst![4] You leave my stuff alone, you little *delinquent*!" (The last word in New Garavaran, of course.) "I'll have my shipmates come down with sensors and lasers, you mangy little flea-dinner!"

The male appeared again from around the trunk, and plopped her pack onto a branch, holding it steady with his hands. In New Garavaran, he yelled, *"Tourrists!"*

"I'm not a tourrist!" Coli yelled back. "I'm *recruiting*. You expect tourists, maybe you should tie down some of the wildlife!" She gestured at the noisy grabber, turning its head from side to side to roar at the Kintarans. "You better give me back my stuff!"

He drew himself up indignantly. "I was *going* to find you as soon as I rescued this. The grabber obviously hadn't *caught* you, so it was better to find you after I got your stuff back. If it'd seen me, it'd have tried to follow me."

Coli muttered a little, ears flat, but stopped lashing her tail quite so fast. She couldn't stop the tip from twitching, though. "All right," she growled, barely loud enough to be heard over the grabber's noise as it paced from his tree to hers, trying to decide who to eat first. "Thanks. Now how do I get over there?"

He flicked his ears and grinned. "I usually jump. But I guess spacer-clans don't do that, ur?"

"*I* am a ship's medic. *I* don't do that," she said, drawing herself up as proudly as she could. "But I'd try it if Noisy down there weren't ready to strangle me if I dropped."

The kid grinned again. "Scared?"

She snarled at him, flat-eared. "I get myself killed, and my sister only has two doctors for an entire clan-ship. She'd come here and cut open this grabber just so she could notch my ears for dying on her!"

He laughed. "Khih, then I'll just have to drive the vine-arm away, nih?"

"Khih." She nodded firmly, arms crossed.

The young male reached into his belt-pouch and pulled out a small rock, between thumb and forefinger. He threw it at the grabber. "Stupid

[4] Idiom translating to "Stealer of that which makes Sparrials unique."

vine-arm, can't eat me!" The rock hit and stuck to the grabber's skin. It roared, and swiped the rock off with a tentacle, just in time for the Kintaran to score another hit with another sticky rock.

Five rocks and four more hits later, the grabber started screaming and thundered off, crashing through underbrush and small trees. Coli watched it go, eyes wide and ears up, and made a mental note to find out what the young male used for a contact poison that didn't affect *his* skin. Then she turned her attention to getting to the next tree over.

Her first jump nearly overshot the branch she was aiming for, and she windmilled her arms for a second before twisting and grabbing at the trunk with all six limbs. After her hearts had finished pounding, she scrabbled to a better launching-point, and jumped again, aiming for a branch just below her (alleged) rescuer's. This time, she undershot completely, and barely managed to snag a lower branch instead of falling entirely to the ground. Her arms and forelegs had all claws sunk deep into the wood, but her hind legs dangled and her tail waved in stiff circles. She hoped the grabber didn't come back.

The young male was, of course, snickering. She decided that she'd notch his ears later, and concentrated on getting her right hindfoot's claws into the bark. He appeared on her branch a few tries later. "Here. Let me help," he said, reaching out to steady her while she scrambled, with *utter* lack of dignity, onto the branch.

Face to face, she could see that while she'd placed his age well—young, just about to hit his final growth-spurt—what she'd thought were tabby-stripes were actually greenish paint, presumably camouflage for sneaking around in the trees. His real fur-color, as far as she could see, was a creamy orange, which would have seemed washed-out, if not for the delicate shadings into even paler cream around his mouth and chin, and down his throat, and the gentle darkening of his ears.

Since he was still young, they were actually eye-to-eye. He frowned. "I thought you said you were a medic."

Her ears went back and she snarled, barely refraining from cuffing him—and that because of balance considerations rather than any residual gratitude. "So I'm small! I've got a son half your age, keesol!"

He blinked and backed away a little, raising his hands and flicking his ears back and forth nervously. "Sorry! Sorry! I—I just thought your fur was too soft for you to be very old, and all the spacers I've ever met say you have to work a long time to be anything, that's all, that's all. Really." He purred at her ingratiatingly.

Coli stopped snarling and unflattened her ears, though her tail still lashed a little. "All right. You've met spacers before?" *Of course he has, idiot. How else would he speak human-tongue?* she thought.

He rolled his eyes and sighed. "Tourrists. Not many, but enough. Humans, Thrals, even three Unar sscientisstss. They all hate the gravity."

"Lightworlders," she snorted, wavering slightly on the branch. "I'm Coli-nfaran M'Choosaraf."

"K'rava M'rau M'Raliborwhol. Don't tease Rali about his name. He's touchy."

K'rava. "Like-a-purr." Not bad. She tilted her head at him. "With a name like mine, I'm going to make fun of someone else's?" she asked.

He flicked his ears and shrugged. "He makes fun of mine. You want to go meet my clan before the vine-arm comes back?"

She looked nervously at the ground. "Khih."

☀ ∞ ☀

Raliborwhol—"standing in wind"—turned out to be an older male, white-bellied, but mostly just brown-tabby. He took a look at her, asked K'rava, "Adopting runaways from the spacer clans?" and stalked off to yell at someone else about a poor hunt.

Coli pursed her lips at Raliborwhol's back, trying not to let her jaw gape into a predator's grin. For all that he was bigger than Klarin-yal, Coli thought her sister to be swifter, and seasoned from bar-brawls and occasional dominance-spats.

K'rava was eyeing her warily. "You all right?" he finally asked.

In a low voice, she replied, "Just thinking my sister would eat him for lunch."

The young male's ears perked up. "Really? Will she come here?"

"Nih," Coli sighed. "She's too busy to leave the ship for an overgrown thaso[5] like him."

K'rava sighed, too, and laid his ears back sulkily. Coli looked at him, considering that even someone to watch readouts would be useful on the ship, and he *didn't* seem likely to dream of challenging Klarin-yal. She opened her mouth, but a girl keesol came bounding over. "Kravakrava!" she squealed. "Shipshipship! Tursts! Comesee!" She took off towards a tall tree at the edge of the tribe's clearing and started climbing.

K'rava's ears went up and he followed. Coli trailed along after then, but balked at actually setting claws into the wood. She'd had enough of tree-climbing for a while. Soon enough, K'rava came scrabbling down, scattering bark all over everything. "Come on! They'll be landing in the Tourrist's Clearing!" He bolted off.

Coli sprinted after him, down a narrow path that wove through several bushes, and finally ended in, khih, another clearing. This clearing, unlike the one the clan was camped in, had no guards at the edges to keep the wildlife from using keesolt as snacks. Also changed from the other clearing, it had a small landing-beacon to one side, and a shuttle (bearing a crudely-painted "Kintara Travel Expeditions" logo) in the middle; the shuttle's engines were still pinging a little, which meant it must have just landed.

The shuttle's ramp came down, and a few spacer Kintarans came out, along with some blue-skinned Thrals and a solitary human with a

[5] Baby.

camera. Coli seriously considered going back to Star-Town and notching ears until she found out why nobody had mentioned tourist shuttles that went to the grounder clans.

K'rava stepped forward, speaking first in Trade Kintaran, then repeating in Thralian, and finally in New Garavaran when it was obvious the human didn't understand the Thral language. "Welcome to the Great Forest! I'm K'rava..." (he didn't translate his name) "...and I will be the guide here. Since this *is* Kintara, every expedition is unique! You tell me what you want to see, and I'll do my best to show it to you. Is there a language that everyone shares?"

It turned out that between Thralian and New Garavaran, K'rava could talk to everyone. While he escorted the group back to the clan's clearing, he muttered in Trade Kintaran, "You'd think we'd make the bipeds all learn *this* language before letting them run around loose... Coli? Will you take up the rear and make sure camera-human doesn't wander off alone and feed a vine-arm?"

She bared her fangs in a sadistic grin. "Khih. I'll keep him in line." With a snap of her teeth, she sauntered to the rear and trailed along after the tourists.

🐾 ⌇ 🐾

Coli tagged along for the rest of the day, more and more impressed as she watched K'rava sweet-talk some of the hunters from his clan into being guards, keep the bipeds out of trouble, and finally, actually *charge* the entire group for eating in the evening. The bipedal aliens accepted this without a fuss, but the spacer Kintarans grumbled until, *somehow*, he convinced them that if they hadn't caught it themselves, they could at least trade for it. Power cells would be nice, for instance, or a good pocket-knife...

Then, when the tourists were nearly finished with their meal, Coli noticed Raliborwhol looming at the edge of the firelight. K'rava noticed his wahn as well, and soon crept over. When he came back, his ears were down and his tail was curled against his body, tip still lashing.

"What was all that?" Coli breathed into his ear.

"He's wahn. This is income for the clan," K'rava muttered back.

"He took it all?" she guessed.

K'rava just set his jaw and stared into the fire for a little while, doing his night-sight no good.

She tucked herself a little closer to him. "Why not just go back with one of those tourist groups?"

He looked away. "Who'd have me after that? I'm just a grounder kid."

Coli craned her neck and saw that his nose was running.

"Besides," he continued, "if Rali caught me trying it, he'd tear my ears off or worse. He likes what money buys for him. And the clan. Some of it goes for things good for the clan."

"Ur." Coli's eyes narrowed and she looked up. After a moment to adjust, she could pick out the bright speck of Kintara Station passing overhead. She carefully tucked her tail under a hind-foot; even concealed, she felt it lashing against her belly as she plotted.

※ ⊙ ※

Even after the shuttle took off, Coli kept pestering K'rava. "But if you *could* go, would you want to?"

"Where *would* I go to?"

"I don't know. Star-Town? Kintara Station? Hop a ship to an alien world?"

He stood at the edge of the clearing, looking up. "So I'd see the stars," he said, voice quiet, and a little harsh. "They wouldn't feed me."

"Forget about that part for a heartbeat, would you?" Coli snapped. "Would you *like* to?"

He finally glanced over towards her; his nose was running. "You're offering to let me visit? I didn't think I was that pretty."

She glared. "You are, under the paint. But that's not the point."

K'rava just looked at her. "So what is?"

"I'm *asking* if you'd like to turn spacer."

He looked away, ears drooping, shoulders slumped, and even his tail lying on the ground. She barely caught his whisper. "Khih."

She nodded in satisfaction. "Good. Then it's settled."

His head came up, but he didn't look at her. "What?"

She stalked over and stood in front of him. "I told you I was recruiting, K'rava. Don't you know what that *means*?"

"Nih." He blinked at her.

"Stupid male-run clan. It means that the whole clanship's been looking for more crew in the *old* way. I've been looking for a smart male who'd be able to sing birds into his belly. I found one." She set her finger-pad on the bridge of his nose, right between those huge gold eyes. "You."

"You... want... to... let me be on your ship??"

"Khih! Leave this place behind, learn trade, make the ship rich, have good quarters, have good food." *Avoid a bidding war with other ships if they found you, my young Negotiator. And since* they'd *appeal to your male hormones if they could...* She looked at his wide eyes, and leaned towards him, licking from his chin up to his lower lip. "Have nearly any female in your room you want."

He nearly swayed, suddenly as off-balance on the ground as she'd been on tree-branches. "You'd..."

"Khhhiiiih." She put one hand on his cheek to keep him from flinching and started washing his left ear. "I told you. Recruiting in the old way. We don't just want crew, we want to add to the *clan*. And we've got more females than males, right now." She decided that, half her age or not, K'rava had a very nice scent. And he *would* be beautiful when all that camo-paint got washed off. "You like the idea?"

He purred.

Someone behind them growled.

Not a grabber, at least. Not quite.

Raliborwhol stood there with a pair of the perimeter guards a body-length behind him. "And what are you doing with my clan member, spacer?"

"What did it look like?" Coli asked, trying to keep her jaw from dropping into a hunter's smile.

Rali paced forwards a step. "Like keesolt playing."

She sniffed. "Maybe you should have watched longer, and learned something, ground-bounder."

The ground-wahn flexed his claws. "You talk big for such a small little female. You're not on your ship. You're not even on a station with laws. You're in the middle of *my* territory."

K'rava, eyes wide and tail bristling, stepped in front of Coli, claws ready despite the fact that Raliborwhol outweighed him by at least a hundred pounds. Coli just let her jaw drop, and chirruped, "Not for long!"

Raliborwhol's tail swept back and forth in almost lazy, measured strokes. He ignored K'rava. "You run fast, arrogant little spacer?"

Coli cocked her head, as if listening to something for a moment. "Something like that." She pointed upwards.

Rali looked. So did his guards, and even K'rava glanced that way. Coli didn't. She grabbed K'rava's arm and tugged him away, sprinting to the other side of the clearing.

Raliborwhol bellowed and leapt after them, closing the distance with his long legs. Coli pushed K'rava to one side and turned the other way, splitting the target. The ground-wahn continued after her, of course, and she yanked her tail out of his grasp barely in time. A second later, one of his forepaws came down on her haunches, tipping her over as keesolt tipped over merfahs.

Amazingly enough, even scrabbling on the ground, Coli wasn't scared or even much excited. She *was* getting annoyed, then startled when K'rava screeched and jumped onto Raliborwhol's back. *Have to teach him not to announce attacks like that,* she thought absently, regaining her feet while the two males tumbled, separated, and came together again with front paws out.

Coli glanced at the two M'Raliborwhol guards—the pair were just sitting, showing no inclination to get mixed up in their leader's fight with two undersized challengers. Crouching, she looked back in time to see K'rava get tossed aside, stunned momentarily from hitting the ground, but not bleeding much, either.

Raliborwhol really does think he's dealing with keesolt, Coli marveled, leaping silently the instant K'rava was clear. Rali had enough time to look surprised that *she*'d jumped *him* before she impacted, front paws grabbing and hind legs kicking. She was lower than she'd have liked, not in a good position to rip his lungs out, and like K'rava, she really was hopelessly outweighed.

The breath went out of her as she was slammed to the ground, belly-down, and with Raliborwhol's weight pinning her there. He had both hands at the base of her neck, and probably had plans of making her eat dirt.

"Not. So. Proud. Now?" he panted. "Spacer idiot."

Coli giggled nastily and waggled her thumb in an upwards direction.

Rali spat. "That trick works *once*."

She nodded, ignoring the dirt that got into her facefur, and said, "Full landing lights, Dellum."

"You're *bluffing*—!" the wahn started to roar, but suddenly realized that there was a shrieking rumble coming closer, starting to overwhelm his voice.

"*Now*, Dellum," she said.

The *Choosaraf*'s passenger shuttle lit up like a clan of stars on shore-leave. One spotlight centered on Raliborwhol. He recovered and dashed out of the clearing, quicker than she'd thought he was capable of making decisions. Maybe he thought the shuttle used the older, "hot" thrusters and didn't want to irradiate his genes.

She picked herself up, twinging only a little, and trotted over to where K'rava swayed. "Are you all right?"

"Khih... But how...?" K'rava asked, marveling at the sight of a *real* shuttle, half again as big as the Kintara Travel Expeditions one.

"Implant communicator," she said calmly, leading him to the airlock and jumping into it. "While Kintara Station was overhead, I had the range to talk to my ship. Come on. You're M'Choosaraf now."

He took a deep breath, eyes fixed on her. Then he jumped in beside her and she set the lock cycling. Their twin purrs rumbled in time with the drives.

✸

RAT'S REPUTATION

Michael H. Payne

One day, Rat decided he was sick and tired of all the stories everybody kept telling about him.

It came over him quite suddenly. He was sitting on the riverbank a ways upstream from Ottersgate, and he and Fisher were eating lunch. Fisher had caught out a trout, and she and Rat were sharing it as they usually did, she starting at the tail and he starting at the head.

Rat hadn't taken more than a few mouthfuls when he sat back and said, "Y'know, it really frosts my whiskers."

Fisher was pulling the small bones from the fish and stacking them beside her. "What is it this time?"

"Ev'rybody's always telling such awful stories about me," Rat said. "I don't do half the stuff they say I do; crumbs, I don't even do three-quarters of it."

"Yes, you do."

"No, I don't! I couldn't! I gotta live with myself, y'know. You just haven't heard the things they say about me."

Fisher cocked her head to one side. "And you have?"

"You bet I have," Rat said. "I mean, just last night, Ms. Opossum was telling her kids this whole story about how I trumped up stealing charges against the Jaybirds just so's I could get at their eggs while they were in court, and if it hadn'ta been for Judge Owl figuring it out in time, I woulda eaten their eggs! To kids she was saying this! About me! I almost fell off the roof when I heard it!"

"The roof?" Fisher looked up sharply. "What were you doing on the Opossums' roof?"

"I was just passing by..."

"Just passing by."

"Aw, c'mon, Fisher; you know me better'n that."

"I do?"

Rat stomped his foot. "Y'see? You're just as bad as the rest of 'em! A guy does a few stupid things in his life—"

"And was it true?"

Rat blinked at her. "Was what true?"

Fisher pulled a few more bones from her teeth and added them to her pile. "Ms. Opossum's story," she said.

"No!" Rat took another mouthful of trout. "I mean, not really..."

Fisher's eyes slid over to his. Rat swallowed quickly. "Don't you look at me like that!" he shouted, crooking a claw at her. "Those Jays did steal something! Down past the Brackens on the riverbank, there was this neat,

232

round rock, but they grabbed it and flew off before I could get there. So I was complaining about it, kinda out loud to myself, and here comes Judge Owl, flapping outta the sky with a lotta talk about grand theft and lawsuits. Now, you know how well me and the Judge get along, so I pretty much ignore him, and after a while, he goes off. I didn't know he was gonna haul the Jaybirds in; how was I s'posed to know the Judge was gonna get off his tail feathers and actually do something?"

Fisher was straightening her pile of bones and only glanced up when Rat stopped. "And then?" she prompted.

"Well, what else? I went over to Jaybirds' to see if I could get my rock back. When I get there, I can hear they're not home, so I climb up and start digging around. I can't find it and I'm just about to leave, when Judge Owl, Captain Hawk, the Jaybirds, the whole Air Force almost, drops down outta the sky, yelling that I'm a thief and a murderer! And what am I s'posed to do, just stand there? I run for it and finally lose 'em down by the Brackens. And now here's Ms. Opossum telling her kids I was trying to eat the eggs!"

Fisher dipped a paw into the river and ran it along her whiskers. "So what?" she asked after a minute.

"So what? So what?! So maybe I'm tired of always being the bad guy, that's what! Maybe I don't like people looking at me like I'm some kinda monster! I mean, I've heard 'em: 'Look out, here comes Rat! Lock up the furniture!' 'Was that Rat that went by? Count the children!' 'Don't touch it! I saw Rat drop it!'"

"Hear a lot, don't you?"

"Fisher, I mean it! I'm getting sick of the whole egg-faced thing!"

"Rat, I think you might be overreacting—"

"Overreacting? Overreacting?! I'd like to see how you'd react if you had to put up with the stares and the whispers and the stories and the—"

Fisher tore a chunk from the side of the fish and stuffed it into Rat's mouth. "Okay," she said into the silence as Rat chewed furiously, "so everybody's out to get you, is that it? Everybody hates you. Why they haven't locked you up in the Bailey Oak yet, I can't even guess. If the folks 'round here had any sense at all, they'd've given you to Captain Hawk years ago and be rid of you for good."

Rat forced the fish down and glared at her. "You gotta point here?!"

"Yeah, I gotta point here." She poked at Rat's chest with one paw, almost knocking him over. "The point is, you're crazy. Nobody hates you; you'd be too easy to get rid of if they did. You give 'em something to talk about, that's all. All that other stuff's just in your head." She patted his ears down. "And why do you care what they say anyway? The way you're talking, you'd think it was important or something.

"I mean, think about it, Rat. If you wanted 'em to stop telling stories about you, you'd have to stop all your creeping around, wouldn't you? You'd have to take baths all the time and comb your fur out all nice and untangled. You'd have to start being friendly to Judge Owl and Captain Hawk, never lose your temper, and go to the Mouse Lodge every Wednesday night. You'd have to change everything and turn yourself into somebody else. Is that what you wanna do?"

Rat pushed her paw away. "What, you don't think I could? You think I got no manners! Is that what you're saying?!"

Fisher blinked at him. "What?"

"You don't think I could be all polished and polite, do you?! Well, let me tell you, Ms. Fish-for-brains, I grew up in the Nibbler clan, and I can be just as genteel as anybody! I may be a rat, but I can out-mouse the mousiest mouse that ever tied a bow tie or sipped a cuppa tea!"

"Wait a minute, Rat; I didn't mean—"

"Oh, you didn't, huh?! Well, I did! You watch me, Fisher; you just watch me!"

Then Rat was on his feet and stomping off toward the woods. Fisher stared for a minute, then shouted at his back, "Rat! Hey, Rat, wait a minute!"

But Rat didn't wait. He stomped right up the riverbank into the woods, the sharp midday shadows swallowing him up.

Fisher stared at the spot where Rat had gone into the trees, then she smiled and finished up the trout. "This could get interesting," she said to herself, and gathering the pile of trout bones into her satchel, she slung it over her back and slid into the River.

🌿 ∞ 🌿

The sun was going down as Judge Owl took a last turn around the woods. He had night court this evening, and he was just wheeling back toward Ottersgate when something caught his attention down below. He circled around for another look. Crossing Ree's Meadow appeared to be one of the mouse cousins, but to the Judge's eyes, the figure looked to be just a bit too large. Judge Owl thought he had best investigate.

"Hello!" he called out, spiraling into a slow descent. "Excuse me, sir, but might I have a moment of your time?"

The figure looked up, and Judge Owl almost dropped out of the sky. Was it Rat? No, no, it couldn't be. And yet...

Judge Owl folded his wings and dropped to the ground in front of the figure. There could be no question: it was wearing the black derby hat and yellow bow tie of one of the mouse clans, but it was definitely Rat!

Rat doffed his hat. "Good evening, Judge. Beautiful sunset, isn't it?"

"Rat!" said Judge Owl, and he couldn't think of anything else to say. Rat's fur was combed! His teeth were clean! He smelled more of freshly cut grass than of his usual dank, muddy smell! Judge Owl could only stand and stare.

Rat's brow furrowed. "Are you all right, Judge? You look a little peaked."

"What? Oh, yes, fine, fine, uhh, Rat. It, uhh, it is Rat, isn't it?"

"Sure it's me, Judge." Rat grinned and put his hat back on with a bit of a flourish. "I'm just going into town to see a few of my relatives. It's the youngest Nibblers' birthday tonight, and the family was kind enough to invite me."

"Were they now?" Judge Owl narrowed his eyes. "A bit unusual, isn't it?"

"Aw, no, they invite me ev'ry year. I'm usually so busy, I can't make it, but, well, folks have obligations to their families, even if they are just adopted, y'know? The way I see it, I haven't been living up to my obligations, and I think it's high time I did."

"Really," Judge Owl said.

"Now, Judge, I know what you're thinking, but you know I got a bum rep, and, well, it's time I did something about it."

The Judge ruffled his feathers for a moment. "Well," he said at last, "if you're going into Ottersgate, do you mind if I walk with you? Court this evening, you know."

Rat smiled. "Not at all, Judge, not at all. Shall we?"

So Rat and Judge Owl walked through Ree's Meadow down to the Meerkat Road, and they talked about the weather and the harvest and other innocent topics. And all the while, Judge Owl's mind was working and wondering. 'What can he be up to?' he asked himself over and over as they walked. 'What can Rat be up to this time?'

As for Rat, he was actually starting to have some fun with all this. Sure, his hat kept threatening to slide out from between his ears and his bow tie felt like a manacle around his throat, but he concentrated on keeping the conversation polite and colorless, and by the time they crossed over the West Bridge into Ottersgate, Rat could see that the Judge was even more confused than when they had started. It was great; he could be nice to the Judge and still worry him.

They walked along Bridge Road and came to Bailey Common where the Bailey Oak towered out of the earth and spread its branches over the roofs of Ottersgate. They followed Green Street as it circled the Oak until they arrived at the root where Judge Owl held court.

"Well, Judge," Rat said with a smile, "it's been awful nice talking with you. Have a good night, now."

"Ah. Yes. Quite." The Judge gave a little cough. "I say, Rat, and pardon me for asking, but, well, you're not... well, up to anything, are you?"

"I know what you're getting at, Judge, but, believe me, you got nothing to worry about from me. No sir, not a thing."

"I see." He paused for just a moment. "Well, good night then, Rat. Give the Nibblers my best."

"Will do, Judge. G'night." Rat doffed his hat once more and sauntered off along Green Street.

Judge Owl watched him go, but he still couldn't shake his discomfort.

This was Rat, after all. 'I'd best mention this to Captain Hawk,' he told himself, then he flew up to the top of the root and his private entrance into the courthouse.

As Rat walked away, he could feel the Judge's eyes on him, but he didn't turn around. After all, and this made him smile, he wouldn't want the Judge thinking suspicious thoughts about him. If the Judge didn't know how to take folks being polite to him, well, that was his problem. Rat started whistling as he turned down Legion Street, and there he could see the lights glowing in front of the Mouse Lodge.

Mice were going into the Lodge in twos and threes or milling around in the courtyard by the fountain, their bow ties and scarfs gleaming in the twilight. Several otters squatted among the mice, and Rat could see lights on around the corner of the Lodge at the larger folks' entrance.

Rat made his way through the courtyard, and he grinned and waved at the astonished looks thrown at him. Standing in the doorway, a mouse in a red doorkeeper's hat gaped as he came strolling up.

Rat recognized him enough to remember his clan name, and he clapped him on the shoulder. "Hey, Chowder, how's it been? You're looking great!"

The mouse blinked up at him for a minute with his mouth partway open. "Rat?" he finally said. "R—R—Rat?"

"Sure, Chowder, sure. What, am I early?" Rat reached into his satchel and pulled out the invitation. "Nope, says 'sunset.'" He grinned and tapped the paper. "Right on time."

"But... but..." Chowder blinked some more. "But you've never come before..."

"Yeah, well, that's been my own fault. I'm here now, though." Rat shrugged. "You're not upset, are you?"

A slow smile was spreading across Chowder's face. He started laughing, and he grabbed Rat's front paw and began pumping it up and down. "Upset? Are you crazy? This's great! The kids... I mean, we've told them so much about you, and, well, you never come, and, well, here you are, and, well... and..." He whirled around, almost pulling Rat over before Rat get his paw loose, and yelled down the hall, "Kily! Kily! Quick! You gotta see who's here!"

As Chowder spun back around with a few more cries of "This's great!" a figure came out of a side room and stopped with a little gasp as she saw Rat. Rat knew her at once; Kily Nibbler was one of the mice he'd grown up with before he'd decided to leave Ottersgate. He took off his hat and smiled.

Kily stayed where she had stopped. "Rat?" she asked in a quiet, quivery voice. Then a wide smile flashed through her whiskers, and she ran over and took his paws. "Rat! I can't believe it! You came!"

Rat smiled down into her shining eyes and started liking this more and more. "Yeah," he said, "I came. I mean, you sent me an invitation, right?"

"Well, of course." She took a step back and, still holding his paws in hers, looked him up and down. "Rat! I just can't..." Still smiling, she linked her arm in his and began leading him into the Lodge. "How long has it been?"

"Too long, it looks like. Crumbs, you'd think I was royalty or something."

She laughed. "Well, you are, in a way. A celebrity, at least. Oh, the kids'll go crazy! You're the best present they could get."

Rat stopped. "Oh, c'mon, Kily; you don't gotta put on a show for me..."

Kily Nibbler looked up at him. "It's true. They never get tired of hearing about their Uncle Rat." She pulled him forward again. "They'll be so surprised!"

Kily led Rat down the hallway and out into the Main Room of the Mouse Lodge. Glow baskets were hanging from the walls and gleamed like stars all up and along the vaulted ceiling. Tables sat everywhere, some covered with food, some set out with acorn shell plates and cups, and some holding small wrapped bundles, presents for the Nibblers. The room was about three-quarters full, with mice and other folk seated at the dining tables or dancing to the music of a small combo at the back of the hall. The low mutter of conversation was warm to Rat's ears, and he remembered parties just like this from long, long ago.

Rat saw faces that he hadn't thought of in years, and their eyes flashed wide in surprise as he came in beside Kily. Some waved through the crowd at him, but the place didn't fall silent as he'd half expected it to. Instead, tiny squeaking voices shot up across the room: "Uncle Rat! It's Uncle Rat!"

Six or seven little furry figures wearing green-striped party hats came darting through the crowd and squealed to a stop in front of Rat and Kily. "Uncle Rat! Aunt Kily, it's... it's really Uncle Rat!"

Kily gave a little laugh. "Yes, it is Uncle Rat. Now hold still and I'll introduce you. Rat, this is Mernin and Patil and—"

But Rat never heard the rest; tiny paws had grabbed his arms. "Uncle Rat! Uncle Rat!" they were all squeaking, their eyes sparkling and their feet barely touching the floor. "You gotta sit at our table! You gotta! Over here! C'mon!"

Rat could only grin at Kily. "Uhh, if you'll excuse me?" As he let himself be pulled along the tables, he nodded to the faces he recognized, Nibblers and Spinners, Chowders and Hoffners and other clans he couldn't quite remember the names of. There were a couple tables of moles, their eyeglasses glinting in the glow light, Mr. and Mrs. Sparrow and their whole family, and at the side of the room by the entrance for the larger folk,

Rat saw Crow and Bobcat and a crowd of opossums staring icily at him before the young Nibblers dragged him around to their table.

And Rat had a fine time. Sure, it was tiring to have all these tiny mice sitting on him, asking him questions, wanting to hear first this story and then that story, but it was a nice kind of tiring. Mice he had almost forgotten came along, smiling and asking him how he was doing, and they reminisced about the times they'd had. He ate the best meal he'd seen in a very long time, and the silky, half-remembered scent of so many mice just relaxed him completely.

When the young Nibblers opened their presents, Rat gave them a flat shiny pebble and told them how he had won it from Fisher when she had bet him that he couldn't swim from one bank of the River to the other without taking a breath. "At least," he said to Kily as the kids took their presents back to the table, "I think that's the pebble. I got so many..."

Kily laughed quietly. "That's all right. It's the story that's the real present. And the storyteller, of course." She patted his paw, and Rat smiled slowly as he made his way back to the kids' table.

Then cake was brought in and candles blown out and everyone's glass was refilled. And so it went until, as the evening was winding down and the young Nibblers were trying to hide their yawns, Rat heard a shuffling swish behind him and turned to see Bobcat crouched down next to the table.

🐾 ☯ 🐾

"Rat," Bobcat said.

"Bobcat. It's been a long time."

"It has, hasn't it? Y'know, I was kinda surprised to see you here tonight, Rat. I didn't think they bothered inviting you anymore."

Bobcat's eyes were a little too bright as he blinked, and Rat wondered if maybe Bobcat had brought a little catnip along to the party. "Well," Rat said, "we've been such good friends of the family, you and me. 'Course they invite us."

Bobcat half closed his eyes; from the smell of him, he'd had at least one roll too many. "Oh, sure. I've always been a great friend to you rodents. The bigger, the better, I've always thought." He coughed out some breathy giggles.

Rat gritted his teeth. He and Bobcat had had a few run-ins in the past, but Rat hoped the idiot was sober enough to realize that this was not the place for anything like that. The glow in Bobcat's green eyes somehow did not reassure him.

Rat looked around the table, but the young Nibblers were fiddling tiredly with their toys and weren't paying attention. Then his gaze fell on the mouse sitting next to him, Mernin he thought it was, and the little mouse was twisted around in his chair and staring wide-eyed at Bobcat. Rat could just make out the fear starting up in the kid's scent, so he leaned his chair back to Bobcat's ear and whispered, "This is a kids' party, Bobcat; you got something to say to me, that's fine, but not here."

"Something to say to you?" Bobcat purred a little too loudly. "Oh, no. Just surprised you were here, that's all. I always thought you were more the sorta thing mice dump in the East Channel when the landfill's closed."

Rat had to laugh at that. "You're getting clever in your old age, Bobcat. Or did you think of that one a few days ago and been saving it up?"

"I've been saving a lotta things for you, Rat. You've kept outta my way pretty good, but now—"

"Kept outta your way? Why would I wanna do that? You're such an int'resting guy to talk to."

The smile was shaky on Bobcat's face. "We'll see," he purred. "Later I think, but we'll see..."

Rat laughed again as Bobcat swayed upright and sauntered over to the larger folks' door. Rat looked back at Mernin, and the little mouse's eyes were still very dark. "Uncle Rat, what was he talking about? It didn't sound very nice."

"Aw, he was just talking, that's all." Rat rubbed behind Mernin's ears. "Bobcat just likes to talk a lot. Nothing to worry about. Okay?"

Mernin nodded and yawned, and Rat saw Kily coming across the room. "Time for bed," she announced, and with very little effort, she and Rat rounded the kids up. They handed each sleepy mouse to one of the Nibbler clan, everybody said good night to everybody else, and the Mouse Lodge emptied out.

Rat wasn't feeling all that tired, though, so he helped Chowder lock up, then strolled down Legion Street, past the closed shops, to East Road. Then down East Road he went, humming softly, till he reached South Point, and he stood there in the park and watched the two channels, which the river split into at North Point above Ottersgate, as they came back together again into one river. A half moon floated above the woods, the river tumbling black and silvery away from Rat, away from Ottersgate, southward down to Beaverpool.

※ ∞ ※

He listened to the gurgling, rushing, splash and chatter, and felt pretty good, better than he'd felt in Ottersgate in years. Comfortable, almost, and that was strange. Nice, but strange. He even felt, at that moment, that he could manage to be polite to Captain Hawk, and that made him smile.

Then from behind him came a quick, pungent odor, and Rat leaped to the side just as something big and fast shot over his head. He rolled, keeping hold of his hat, and came up facing Bobcat, his eyes glowing green and brighter than the moon. "Let's see, then," he growled, "you and me..."

Rat sprang to the side again as Bobcat jumped, and he felt the whoosh of Bobcat's claws whipping past his whiskers. Rolling to his feet, he grabbed his hat and took off up East Road. He heard Bobcat tumble and curse behind him and thanked the Lady Squirrel that the cat was all cat-nipped up.

East Road was a lousy place for a duel, Rat decided as he ran. The shops were closed, the alleys were big enough for Bobcat to follow him, and the road ran straight along the east side of Ottersgate. All that left him was the East Channel.

Rat ran till he heard Bobcat thudding up behind him, then he swerved right and dropped to all fours on the sandy bank of the Channel. Bobcat swooped past, growling in befuddled rage, twisted in mid-stumble and ended up sliding along sideways, the sand dancing under his paws. Rat sprinted on toward the Channel, his hat flying off and away, his satchel slapping at his legs. He'd just have to swim for it.

But as he drew near to the water line, Rat almost stopped in amazement. By the half light of the moon, he could see a large tree branch, its thick, broken end wedged against some rocks on the Channel bank, its leafy, willowing end trailing out into the water a good third of the way across.

Bobcat was still cursing behind him; it might just work. Rat pulled at his bow tie till he could slide it over his head. Scrambling out onto the branch, he stuffed the bow tie in among the leaves at the far end, then he slipped into the Channel and swam for the Ottersgate shore again.

The current was no problem, and Rat reached the pile of rocks that the branch was caught on at the same time Bobcat did. Rat stayed down in the water, the rocks and the branch between him and the cat as Bobcat stumbled up and peered out along the branch's length.

Rat heard him laugh. "'Sno good, Rat, hidin' out there!" Bobcat laughed some more, the low, throaty laugh of a very tipsy cat. "See, 'cuz I can see your bow tie, Rat, shinin' all yellow!" The laugh roughened and dropped into a growl. "An' that's gonna be all they'll finda you, Rat."

Bobcat stepped unsteadily onto the branch and began stalking toward the end, his eyes intent on the bit of yellow out among the leaves. As soon as he was past, Rat slipped out of the water and started digging away at the rocks that held the branch to the shore. Rat dug and pushed and strained and shoved, and just as Bobcat was creeping into striking dis-tance of the bow tie, Rat managed to topple the front rock, and the branch shuddered along its whole length.

Bobcat stopped where he was and ever so slowly turned his head to look back. Rat gave one more shove, and the branch came free of the shore. "Rat!" Bobcat screamed as the current took hold, and the branch began floating gently southward.

Rat leaned against the rock pile and panted. He managed to raise an arm to wave, but his breath was coming too fast for him even to whisper a 'bon voyage.'

That was all right, though, because Bobcat was yelling enough for both of them. Rat sat on the rocks and waited, and, sure enough, it wasn't long before he heard a call of "Right, what's all this, then?" from above. He looked up and saw Captain Hawk winging down to land on the beach beside him.

Captain Hawk looked at Rat. Rat looked at Captain Hawk. And Bobcat snarled and cursed as the branch floated farther and farther away.

At last, Captain Hawk spoke. His voice was terribly deep and calm. "Rat, do you think you could explain something to me? It's not so much that I can't see what's going on, but I would really like to hear why Bobcat is currently drifting on a log down the East Channel, screaming your name and other such profanities."

"Currently? Hey, that's pretty clever, Cap."

Captain Hawk did not seem at all pleased. "Do you think you could explain that to me, Rat?"

Rat looked at the shrinking figure of Bobcat, then turned back to Captain Hawk. "Well, Cap, how much time you got?"

🐾 👓 🐾

The next day at noon, Fisher had just pulled a trout from the River and was standing on it till it stopped wiggling when she saw Rat coming out of the woods toward her. She waved to him. He waved back. She stood on the fish some more as he came down onto the bank. "So," she said. "I wasn't sure you were gonna make it today."

Rat shrugged. "What, and miss lunch?" He sat down by the head, and Fisher got off the trout and went to work on the tail. "Anyway," Rat went on, "I'm sorry about yesterday, all that yelling and ev'rything. More mouth than brains, that's me all over." He went to work digging the fish's eyeball out.

Fisher started pulling out the small bones. "Not that," she said. "I was thinking more of your adventure last night."

Rat stopped and looked at her. "What do you know about last night?"

"Only the story that's going around Ottersgate. Seems you found out that Bobcat was going to the Nibblers' birthday party, so you got all duded up and went into town. You spiked his food with catnip, talked him into going for a walk with you, tricked him out onto a log and set him drifting down the East Channel." Fisher licked a paw. "All over town, nobody's talking about anything else. Funny, I thought you'd know about it. You were there, weren't you?"

Rat sat and stared. He didn't stare at anything; he just stared. Then, slowly, silently, he rolled over and lay on his back on the riverbank.

Fisher watched him. After a minute, she said, "You're not eating your trout."

Rat just lay there. "'Why?'" he said. "Or even 'How?' Or 'Who?' I'd even settle for 'What?'"

"Face it, Rat," Fisher said, adding to her pile of bones, "you've got a reputation, and you're gonna live up to it whether you want to or not. Seems like it's outta your paws."

Rat sat up. "But what were they saying down there, I mean, about me? Was ev'ryone saying I was a criminal?"

Fisher chewed and swallowed. "The Judge sure was—made a whole speech out in front of the courthouse—and Captain Hawk. Ms. Opossum was quite upset, and, of course, Bobcat."

Rat waved a paw impatiently. "I don't mean them; I mean, well, y'know, ev'rybody else."

Fisher nodded. "Well, I got the impression that most folks thought Bobcat had needed a little taking down. You shoulda heard 'em laughing over to the Nibblers'. Oh, Kily Nibbler wanted me to thank you again for coming to the party. She said the kids'll never forget it, 'specially since they're part of the story now."

That made Rat smile. "She really say that?"

"Yeah, she really said that." Fisher poked a paw at him. "Y'see what I mean now? What I was trying to say yesterday? If it wasn't for you, what would folks talk about?"

"Okay, okay, I got it." Rat scooped up the trout's eyeball and swallowed it down. "Aw, why not? It was time for me to get a new hat anyway."

WHIMPER'S LAW

Craig Hilton

"Look inside a single soul," a scholar once had written, "and see within fragments innumerable, and the counts of people in a city and cities in a world and worlds in the sublime span of Creation." Whimper agreed. Too many.

He found himself quoting as he ran. Not so much "the traceries of the constellations" as well-worn alleys and archways and large plazas crammed this hour with babbling buyers. He threaded his way of least resistance in a rudeness born of haste. A tray of buns nearly sliced his head off, but the rat was too quick. Spilled hot chestnuts hurt the feet and beggars intercepted the shins, yet in his route remained purpose. Under his arm he retained the papers, in chaos lived order and in lawlessness law.

Indeed in the Empire of Xanadu under the reign of Empress Alicia one had seen a great deal of law. That's if you define law as fairness for all classes, the Nobles, the Freeborn and the humble Domestiques. A fair few people (those in power) had disagreed and held fast to the traditional definition of law, but to a Domestique this new perception *felt* right. Especially to one inclined to think about such things at all. This was the law of Alicia.

It occurred to Whimper that legal fairness for a Domestique lay buried under a mound of paper in the Delphi City Magistrate's chambers. "Pages innumerable," perhaps, surpassing the count of people in the whole empire, be they dog, frog, cat, rat or antelope. In the end justice still had to be seized, that was true. Seized by the rare few with book learning to burrow through the paper mound, feet conversant with every back alley and heart enough to drive them on through that passive oppression which was conservatism. Yet for all that, there was law, and to be its agent gave Whimper a fortifying sense of place.

His destination was the establishment of a Mr. B. Sanglier— VALUABLE AND EXOTIC ITEMS BOUGHT SOLD AND TRADED. On rounding the final corner, Whimper noted the frontage was much as he seemed to remember it, serving now as the backdrop for a small gathering. Before he had reached them, almost before they had seen him and registered his part, Whimper had mentally separated the players from the non-players. The sergeant in charge, two impatient armoured constables and a fat merchant who wished dearly to be elsewhere stood within the crowd of curious like seaweed washed by waves on a beach.

He slowed his pace, began to catch his breath and felt his pulse start to bound.

The sergeant, a wolverine, was the first to come to him, or at him. Not overly tall, but stocky with a fighter's build and the stance of one at home with the martial machinery of his own bone and muscle, he wore a uniform that was well crafted but practical so that it was difficult to tell where dark fur ended and leather-bound plate began. By comparison, Whimper's wiry frame, clad only in a jacket whose embellishments had died some time long past so as to bequeath to it a simple Domestique functionality neither affected nor sought after, stood dwarfed but undaunted.

"You're the defendant's representative." It was a statement of fact. Over his shoulder there was a glimpse of the merchant's skycast eyes. "Sergeant Abel."

"Whimper. Private counsel representing the mouse, Stitchley, accused of the crime of theft." He adjusted the documents under his arm, offered his hand and the shell of the word "Sir." Both were received, but with indifference. The constables snickered.

Sergeant Abel drew breath to speak, but a suety voice from behind cut in. "*If* you're quite satisfied now, Sergeant, we can begin. Just cast an eye over my shop, confirm my story, sign my papers and perhaps we can all get on with our day's work, hm? I mean some of us *do* work for a living." A glance aimed this barb squarely at Whimper, even while the fat boar was turning his back on him and proceeding into a side alley.

"Hey, I said wait," Whimper began to follow with faltering steps. "Wait. Mr Sanglier, wait!" Now with determination thrown together and feet planted squarely, "Wait. I must ask..."

"HOLD!" The scene obediently froze, and at once the air was struck with a shockwave of silence, thick and electric as the wake of a thunderclap. A jangling scrape of metal came from two constables pivoting to roust up astonished salutes. They were looking up at a great owl-bear atop a two-dray carriage decked in the finery of high rank, his half folded wings seemingly doubling his already imposing frame.

"HOLD, SHOPKEEPER. RETURN NOW OR FORFEIT YOUR RIGHTS." The merchant reappeared. He might have been just caned like a school boy. "SERGEANT, I EXPECT YOU TO SEE TO IT THAT THIS INVESTIGATION IS CARRIED OUT IN THE PROPER—AND LEGAL—MANNER." Abel looked equally hurt, fearful even for his badge of promotion. Whimper read this in his eyes and the fingers darting instinctively, protectively to his shoulder.

"Sir," he said. The sergeant was back in control. "To what do I owe the honour of this visit?"

"Random spot check on procedures, Sergeant. Don't mind me, just carry on as you were." He disembarked slowly. "Mr Sanglier." The hint of a rakish smile: "*Mister* Whimper." No handshake. Feathers and fur soft with privilege. A gaze that could easily have stripped your soul before you knew you were being measured. "My name is Captain Tullius Kamew.

I am the District Commissioner for the North Hill division of Delphi. Please let Sergeant Abel proceed with the investigation in the proper, official sequence. You *do* want it carried out officially and by the book of course, don't you Mr Sanglier?" Sanglier nodded dumbly. "Good. Then Sergeant Abel will be happy to countersign your documents once the correct investigation has taken place to his satisfaction. With full cooperation extended to the defendant's hired representative. That's the law of it."

Abel took up the slack. "Mr Sanglier, you know that following a police investigation of a crime it is the right of the accused to appoint an independent party to assess the evidence in the presence of an officer of the law."

"Yes, yes, I know all that. Look, I've been waiting here half the morning for this clown. *You've* had a look over my shop. What more is there to find? The lock's been picked, the cabinet of valuables has been broken into and the necklet's gone, and I saw that mouse sizing the place up yesterday. With my own eyes. And you've caught him now, so why are we standing here wasting my time and yours?"

Whimper read impatience and irritation in the performance of the fat boar, but what else? Anxiety, or fear? For a moment he clutched at an important fragment, and mentally noted it, before facing him again. The man was offensive, with too much soft flesh wadded into too little skin—the thick, black, bristly hide was stretched tight like a bladder, each breath a labour of sweating and grunting. But the cut of his finery and roundness of his belly announced the prosperity that buys respect.

Bo Sanglier looked in silence at the rat. Though Whimper could have apologised for lateness, he suddenly felt beholden to no-one. The system that had kept him sitting for three hours in the chaotic, criminal-filled waiting room of the Chambers was not of his making. He eyed the shopkeeper in weighty silence, picking and filing each bead of sweat and speck of dirt, the wear on his shoes and the mud on the hem of his cape, the rate of his breathing and the tremor of his voice.

"We are wasting your time and ours," he responded at last, ever in the shadow of the watchful captain, "because your accusation has placed a young mouse in detention with the prospect of two years' imprisonment if he's found guilty. And what do we have to go on? No witnesses, no stolen item recovered, but a simple, open-and-shut case of burglary, where the one deciding factor is the word of a Freeborn against the word of a Domestique. And yes, in the absence of any other leading evidence, the charge will stick. So..." He nestled into contemplation. "... Let's go hunting information. I tend to find a lot more about than you'd think:

"What time did you leave the shop last night?"

"Eight o'clock."

"And returned the next morning?"

"At six."

"Why so early?"

"That's no secret. I've got to spend time doing the bookwork. No assistant, see? It takes me all my time during business hours just doing the buying and selling. I've got to do double the work if I want to keep the business running too."

"I see, and..." Whimper stroked his chin "...you found the store as it is now."

"Yes. Nothing's been touched, not since I found it like this, I mean."

"So what time did you notify the police?"

"Just after seven."

"Why was that? The delay, I mean."

"Delay? What do you expect me to do, all by myself? Leave the shop open and unattended while I go strolling down the high street? Let every thief help himself to every valuable I've worked so hard to collect? What else *could* I do? I had to wait until a constable came past on the beat and then call him over, of course. I would've thought that much was obvious. And all that time I just had to stand and look at the mess, couldn't start on the day's bookwork..."

"You just wanted to get things over and done with, officially and properly."

"That's right."

"Get the paperwork done, statements, incident reports, insurance claims. All the legal requirements you'd expect as an honest citizen of Xanadu."

"Exactly. Look, I'm getting nothing from all of this. Every hour my shop is closed, I'm losing money. Please just..." He faltered, glaring nervously up at Captain Kamew as if seeing him for the first time. "Do what you have to do, see what you have to see, and..." Wheezing, his words lost momentum.

"Mr Sanglier, *I'm* not rich. In fact my income's rather meagre. Compared with anyone's, let alone yours." The voice was reedy, a plain, almost spartan character. "I may never know what it is to own so many beautiful things. I can't even guess exactly how it feels to lose one. But what I seem to be getting from you is the feeling... that you feel... empty?"

"And shocked. Numb and shocked."

And hunted, he thought. Trapped, caged, acutely uncomfortable. That too.

"So your total worth must be quite high."

"It certainly is." A smile softly creased his face, and gaze linked with gaze in common bond.

"Doors and windows specially strengthened?"

"Of course."

"Locks?"

"The finest."

Whimper fell silent—to the onlookers he may have been struck mute.

Then with the suddenness of his next breath, the sharpness of his words snapped back at him. "Let's have a look at this lock, then, shall we? The finest of locks. The lock that was... picked? Smashed? Torn from its mounting? Just what was its downfall, its weak spot?" He was leading them down the alley.

"How did it fail?"

Sergeant Abel was willing to retake the helm. "It was picked. The scratch marks show that. Not an easy job either. That's another point of evidence against the mouse Stitchley—only a handful of known criminals could've picked that lock, and he was one of them. *And* he had a lockpick at his place when we collected him. *That's* what I call evidence."

"But he didn't have the necklet."

"He had more money than he ought to have had."

Whimper tensed slightly. No longer an undisciplined urchin, he didn't hit back with the obvious: "Is that a crime?" He well knew that this was no judge and jury, and that an argument based on debate, like a seed, needed to be planted at the right place and time and not dropped wastefully on the grimy cobbles of a dim back alley.

It *was* a fine lock. Even Whimper would have been hard put to spring it. And it was certainly scratched, although the full reading of this script he kept to himself. This was a moment, he later recalled, that he felt the visceral humours begin to emerge from every nerve ending in his body to rise to his head like a stimulant draught, opening his eyes, ears and mind as if with the lifting of a hood. It was then that he felt keenly aware of the practice of detection both as a science and as an art, and so pretending not to be too concerned with his redoubled scrutiny started up a line of questioning about Sanglier's sighting of the mouse the previous day, to which he paid half his concentration.

The testimony in its full version was quite damming. Sanglier stated that he had sighted the mouse not once but twice—once hiding in the shadows behind some boxes where he had no right to be, and once (observed undetected through a darkened window) sizing up the lock at close quarters. Also the mouse had been back and forth outside the front entrance on occasions and had once even been so brazen as to enter the shop under the pretence of being a customer. Whimper took in this information, a procession of petty grievances in a corpulent whine punctuated by inhalations, and lightly stored it.

The riddle had been set. Rising, he glanced at each member in turn and entered the shop.

It was a back office. Whimper tried to take in an unspoiled first impression in the instant before the others filed in. Well-ordered, probably not even disturbed. Shelves of books, ledgers, document boxes, a desk, an open ledger book and stationery, a pitcher, a bread crock, hamper and sweetmeats, a lamp and flint, walls and ceiling a little dirty, floor the same except for a little... what? Paper ash?

"It's through here."

"Wait." The procession stopped at his command. "What happened here? Someone's torn a page out of the ledger book and burned it."

"That's right," said the Sergeant. "Obviously for illumination."

"Was it taken into the shop front? Was..."

"Was there ash in the next room? No. It was only used in here. At night there's enough light from the street lamp outside to see dimly when you're in the front room, which makes sense. You'd do a better job of going unnoticed in there if you didn't carry a fire around with you."

"Well you had one point of luck, Mr Sanglier, anyway. He tore out the next blank page, and not your previous day's figures. That was considerate of him at least."

The boar made a sour face. "Keeping everything legally accounted for takes more time than you'd think, Domestique. It's no joking matter."

"No, I'm sorry. I didn't mean to sound rude." Whimper paused and stared into space for a few seconds, then he continued examining. But by now the party was gravitating naturally into the shop floor proper, the scene of the crime. He watched them pass and then followed.

"Wait, clear away from the cabinet. Stop disturbing the evidence." He designed his words to inject enough animation and informality into the piping tones to soften the command. "Give me a chance, *please*." Reasonable yet assertive, a learned skill. It worked. The huddle took a few paces back obediently, and for a moment Whimper imagined he was a curator in a rather exclusive museum. All eyes had come to rest on him as if it was by sorcery and hesitation would break the spell. If performance were being called for then performance it would be. At least it would keep them quiet.

He motioned them as far back as possible, which for Kamew at the rear virtually meant wings flattened against dimly lit shelves and head all but touching roof beams and half hidden behind hanging cages. Circling the damaged central case, which he took to be the one from which the stolen item had been removed, he made a general overview of the scene. So far it was unremarkable. Despite himself he glanced at Sergeant Abel, and that glance as he should have expected was caught and thrown back at him in cold bravado. "What do you make of it, Whimper?" Whimper just held up a cautioning palm.

He approached. Before him stood a display case whose glass top lay in shards and splinters. Within were a number of precious items and a vacant space that belonged to one more.

"I understand it was a court ceremonial necklet from the Golden Realm Phoenix Age, valued at one thousand gold pieces. Cast silver with rubies and emeralds. Very rare."

"That is correct," came a fat rumble.

He surveyed the remaining pieces, with a professional eye free of covetousness. He ran his hands above them, pressed his fingers firmly on the area where the necklet had been. Then from his pocket he produced a small artefact resembling a tinder box, with a polished metal cupola enclosing a flint mechanism and from beneath which could be unfolded into position in front a miniature lens. When the flint was struck and a tiny flame at last sprang up from the oil lamp within the dome it emitted a sharp beam of light onto his testing hand. For a pensive ten minutes Whimper examined the case in every detail, not sharing his thoughts or findings. At times he would take care to scrutinise some aspect in the closest detail, periodically he would straighten and stare blankly, but he worked throughout in silence. In fact it startled him a little finally to discover, following a prolonged reverie, the sergeant standing behind him.

"What do you make of it?"

"The first question I had to ask myself," said Whimper, extinguishing the torch, laying it on the case and taking his chin in thought, "is why someone should be able to pick such a difficult lock on the back door and then just smash open the glass in the cabinet. That's not what happened, of course. He tried to prize the lid off and it broke. See?"

"Does that make any difference in the end?"

"It might. At least let's get our facts straight or we'll never get anywhere. But still—why try to force it open at all? Now..." He pressed on regardless. "...There's something stuck in the keyhole here. See?" He used the torch to demonstrate. "Something's jammed in here—stuck deeply inside, perhaps broken off. Mr Sanglier?" Sanglier looked suddenly naked, or so he seemed to the detective. "How should *I* know what's been done to it, for glory's sake? *I* didn't smash the thing up, did I?"

"It almost looks like a piece of lockpick... or a key... that's snapped off. Terrible lock, of course, if it has. But the key, or whatever, seems to be made of fairly soft metal. Rotten key meets obstinate lock." He was probing it now with a tiny knife. "Ideally I'd like to take this bit of frame away with me and pull it apart for a better look." He glanced over his shoulder. "But that's not possible of course." He was smiling inwardly at the sound of choked splutters.

"Now, next question is why just the necklet? Why didn't the thief take the rest of these things as well?"

"You tell me."

"It would've been easy enough. I mean, there they all are for the taking. Look at them. All equally valuable, all equally concealable and portable, all equally easy to melt down or dismantle in some way." He recognised the younger Whimper in him beginning to speak, and mentally he cautioned himself. "Sergeant, I assume you're treating this as a straight-forward smash-and-grab. The thief, in a hurry, or startled or panicked, picks up the first piece to hand and runs…hmmm, it's not convincing." His words began to tail off "It's a professional job, so why... *If* it's a professional job, why just one piece?

"And why *this* piece, anyway? What's different about it? Or let's try it this way: with what motives might a thief make his entry, to steal *this* necklet in particular? I can suggest a few. It might be for his own disposal or on behalf of someone else, that is, some boss, for example. It may have been undervalued and be worth more than we thought. It may have some magical aspect, therefore stolen on behalf of a wizard, or maybe it's on behalf of a collector, who wants it to complete a collection, in short, someone who values it more than it's really worth. Even possibly, it even has some bizarre personal significance, making it a piece in a larger puzzle of which we know nothing.

"Well, a two bit gutter thief might think he could dispose of this piece of jewellery himself, but the experienced sort who could get through that back door—*if* it was properly locked—wouldn't. Well, possibly but unlikely. He'd be working for someone and selling to a receiver. Thing is... if he was selling to a receiver then he ought to have taken more, whereas if he were working on behalf of someone higher up why didn't that someone just buy it outright, legally? If it were worth so much more to him wouldn't he have gained from the deal anyway without the risk and expense of breaking the law?

"Unless..." The one potent word hung before each of them. "Unless this theft for some reason was particularly easy and/or particularly safe.

"So what made the necklet different? Personal significances?—maybe. Magic?—no." He saw Abel's eyes suddenly narrow slightly. "It may have been sought by a collector, in fact that's quite likely, I'd say. It was the only item from the Golden Realm. So we've got a thief—or thieves—working for a collector of antique artefacts from the Golden Realm who was either greedy or foolhardy enough (the collector, that is) to want to take it by theft or who knew—or whose thief knew—he had access to an easy way in, such as a duplicate key, and a safe way out, which I'll deal with in a moment.

"That lock on the back door wasn't picked, it was opened with a key and then scratched to look like it was picked. By someone unfamiliar with the process. You'll bring a locksmith in to confirm that, of course Sergeant. It's all evidence."

Abel cut in: "So you're not sure exactly *who* did it and *why*."

"Of course I'm not sure! What do you want—absolute truth? Ironclad guarantees? I don't know where *you* learned rational thinking but *my* mentor was a very wise badger called Galen..."

"Never heard of him."

"...And one of the wisest things he ever taught me was a sense of perspective. No absolutes—all relatives, all perspectives! I'm giving you all the most *likely* solutions, damn... I mean, you know. Common things occur commonly, Sergeant, and rare things rarely. And if in your rose garden you glimpse an unusual flower, it *might* be a rare tropical orchid, but it will *most likely* turn out to be nothing more than an unusual rose."

They were standing face-to-face, hackles bristling. "Galen's Law," he said, steadying his wild respiration. "Galen's Law."

Heartbeat upon heartbeat, the tension in the room began to subside, the way that laden thunderclouds in the heavy summer air can slowly detumesce without the mercy of an explosive storm. The wolverine spoke: "Is that all you've found?"

"Not at all." Whimper took up his torch again and struck the flint. The flame was slow to take, and when it did it was fitful and shaky. "Look here—there's blood on the glass." He pointed it out with the beam. "That means some unlucky devil's cut himself, I'd say when the lid broke. Now look at this," he said, lowering himself to the floor. "This dark stain may be blood too. All of it."

"Then it's been thoroughly wiped up afterwards," joined in Abel, his growl tinged with interest and without rancour, while Whimper rocked his miniature blade between two floorboards to extract a few rusty grains of the substance. These he held carefully to his nostrils, then smiling slightly, offered them out to the other for verification. It was blood.

Sergeant Abel had come without a regulation envelope for this evidence, and after some consternation one was supplied by the tut-tutting Captain Kamew. Sanglier stood bemused, lost in a process beyond his control. They watched the inquisitive, vagrant, spindly form of the investigator, whiskers atwitch, loosed from the leash of inhibition, as he went roaming the clear space around the cabinet, scanning the floor, occasionally pausing to scrutinise some detail in accordance with his own method.

When Abel finally, by the tilt of the head, asked the rat for his conclusions, it was not answers he was asked to share but more of the same puzzle.

"Look how much blood he lost, all of a sudden, on the floor. None in the cabinet, see, but a whole lot all at once on the floor, and then no more. The sort of thing you'd get from a really nasty cut, spurting blood, and then clamped down hard with the other hand." There was a pause. No—a nearer description would be a sudden lapse in proceedings or trough in the flow of time, or to liken the rat Whimper to a clockwork toy at the final limp uncoiling of its spring. Except that a spent toy can't whisper a quick apology, hold up one hand to motion "wait" or press the other over its eyes in ascetic calculation as Whimper did now. A full minute passed. The scene was a tableau in which the only movements, if they might have been seen at all, were the thoughts working inside Whimper's mind.

And then, as if waking refreshed, Whimper returned, showing no trace of his absence. He simply addressed Sergeant Abel and spoke:

"My guess is there were two people, and in a moment I'll show you why. Right now please observe this single hair congealed in a drop of blood on the inside of the frame of the cabinet that can only have found its way there as a result of the break-in. I haven't removed it—you can get one of your constables to pluck it loose and save it for examination, but my reading of it suggests ginger cat."

"Next. We've got a whole lot of blood spilled on this very spot, until pressure was applied to the wound. Then we have a trail, drop by drop, there, directly to that cupboard." Whimper began to jump on the spot, lofting leaps to peer, if he could, into the top shelf. "Mr Sanglier, please show me what you keep up there."

"That's my physicking chest," he said, ambling over. "Huh. I might have known."

"*You* might have known, I'm sure. The point... stop!" Sanglier was about to pull a squat wooden stool from beneath a table. "When did you last pull that stool out?"

The questions were more threatening. "Not for a while, weeks per-haps."

"And no-one else did either?"

"No. I mean... no, of course not. Not possible."

"Good." On all fours he peered closely at the legs with the aid of his lamp. "It's been used in the past day or so. You can read it in the dust. Look!" A command verging on the military. Abel almost jumped to it, and as he looked Whimper moved on.

"We have here... what do we have?" Whimper circumnavigated a point on the floor in front of the cupboard, found the best angle in the light to view it and eagerly beckoned the Sergeant over. "Would you call that a handprint? In blood?"

"A right hand. Only the one, and it's been cleaned up too, like the rest." Tracing paper was required, but there was none. Whimper was sympathetic. "It'll keep. But what we have here is the hand of our ginger cat, the right hand, the one that was bleeding and being held by the left as he bent over and played at being a stepladder for his companion. That's because you'd never reach it from the floor unless you're remarkably tall, which he wasn't." Whimper stood on the stool and tried. Even then he was too short, so Sanglier obliged. "You can't even pull it out with one hand. It needs a hand either side. No handle." Sanglier had it down on the table top in a moment, gasping after the effort, while Whimper con-tinued. "Note please that it's a large, plain, wooden box. No labels nor symbols. What does it contain?"

"Why... medications, herbs, bandages..."

"Wait, keep it shut. Can you think of any reason a stranger might know where it could be found, or what was in it?"

Sanglier now found himself also under the steely gaze of the wolver-ine sergeant, and he was very scared.

"No. Not at all." He floundered in the uncertainty.

"Very well. Is it fully stocked at present?"

"I don't... that is to say..." The bass rumble had slid up an octave and broken. "Yes. When I last attended to it a month... or so... ago I left it fully stocked."

"Wait, keep it shut. Are you certain?"

"What else can I say?" he whined, lifting the lid. One look inside had him a defeated man, drained of vitality, slumped on the stool in a posture of spineless misery. The box was half-empty, robbed of its bandages.

"Some for staunching the wound I guess, some for mopping up the mess, while the other thief stood on the stool to replace it. Scratches on the outside from the hooves of a small ungulate." He looked back at the cupboard. "A shortish ungulate. A sheep or a goat. Actually... It was a goat. Grey and white. Trust me."

The merchant's small round eyes turned toward him in contempt. Whimper met them. "A ginger cat, Mr Sanglier. Can you think at all whom it might have been?"

"No."

"Please try. You'll help us. Think hard."

"No."

"A ginger cat who had a duplicate key to the door, a duplicate key to the cabinet and who knew exactly where to find the physicking box. A former assistant, perhaps."

Sanglier held the gaze for a few more seconds until the weight of it overcame his ebbing reserves and his prospects sank to the floor. "Yes, I had a ginger cat assistant with me until recently," he mumbled.

Whimper paused. Triumph could be his undoing if rashness overtook him: rather he must play each of the final moves in the game judiciously and precisely if the victory he had earned was to be his. Sanglier took the lull to regain the initiative. "Are you accusing me of robbing my own physicking chest? How should I know all that the thieves have taken? I've touched nothing, absolutely nothing since I discovered the burglary this morning, *as a law-abiding citizen should do*. And if it was my former assistant who committed the crime, is that my fault? I dismissed him for dishonesty in the first place, and this is how he returns to reward me. Or are you accusing me of giving him the key, or letting him through the door to commit this crime?"

"I am accusing you of none of those." Whimper's voice was steady, the words measured. "As far as I am concerned the portion of key in the cabinet lock, the blood stains and the missing bandages were as much a surprise to you as they were to the investigating Sergeant here. It is my conviction that you arrived at your premises this morning to find that entry had been effected and the burglary as we have it here committed."

The despair on the merchant's face softened into a hasty smile of relief that was premature. Whimper remained steadfast. He might as well have had a rapier at the merchant's throat. "What I am suggesting is that you also found a message from your former assistant, written on a blank page in your ledger book, a page which you tore out and burned, which recommended that you let him off the hook, blame some other likely victim and recoup the loss on the insurance. I am suggesting then that you put the scratches on the door lock to pretend it was picked, and that you completely and utterly fabricated the statement you gave the sergeant on the alleged sightings of the mouse Stitchley, my client."

Gaze unwavering, Whimper had the sensation that the room was closing down on him, but it was only the others converging in wonderment. Thus when Sanglier spoke out it was as one under siege.

"Nonsense. Complete nonsense. There's no reason on earth that you can give as to why I should obey the beck and call of a common thief." The cornered animal was snapping back. Whimper withdrew one step, and turned to face the circle of spectators about him. From the sergeant and the constables he was receiving a challenge, but from the captain there was the singularly uncomfortable sensation of being on trial himself.

He took a deep breath, filled his lungs to capacity to clear his head and exhaled slowly. Then without speaking he made his way out of the circle, across the room to an upright cabinet of decorative ornamental plates and was already on his knees with probing fingers exploring the beading strips of the hefty lower section by the time the huddle had caught up and regrouped.

He heard Sanglier's protests stifled by the resonant bass voice of the owl-bear, again and again, ever greater desperation quashed by ever greater firmness, while he continued to run his trembling hands over panels, beneath drawers, talking gently to the structure, coaxing it, wheedling it, seducing it with infinite patience. He examined it entirely, then again. Then once more. His heart was pounding and he was sweating. His concentration remained on his task. Then at last deep beneath a drawer he was rewarded with a promising ridge, which yielded unwillingly to his attentions. There was no display of victory from the rat save a low, soft chuckle with which to herald the revelation witnessed by the amazed audience.

It was a secret drawer packed tidily with bags of gold coins and jewels and a ledger book identical to the one in the back room. Almost on cue a scraping and clanking could be heard behind him. He turned. The constables had the merchant by either arm, and the sergeant was facing him.

"Bo Sanglier, I am arresting you for evasion of tax and for conspiring to pervert the course of justice."

Whimper smiled the smile of exhausted satisfaction. He stood up and stretched. They were all looking at him like he was a fights champion. He went back several times to regard the false drawer with pride as a father his newborn son. Dizzy with exhilaration and relief, he hardly heard the sergeant approach from behind and "How did you detect that, Whimper?" in Abel's friendly growl.

"Well, when you all first went into the room, you were looking at the smashed case. But *I* wanted to see where Mr Sanglier would be looking. It was just a glance, but it gave it away."

"If your description of the thieves is correct..."

"It is." Whimper shot a sideways glance at the captain, who nodded in confirmation.

"... then we'll have them in prison before the day is out."

"You will."

"And their patron will be soon to follow."

"No doubt."

Abel opened his mouth perhaps to give some word of congratulations but could not find it. Instead Kamew cut in, beaming a cryptic affability. "A most... unusual deduction, Whimper. What was that you said about roses and orchids?"

There was a nervous huff of a giggle. "In the end if it *looks* like a rare orchid and it *smells* like a rare orchid..."

"...It's probably a rare orchid," said Abel, grinning.

"Whimper's Law."

"I'll remember it."

And so it was over. The ends of such affairs are always much less tidy than their beginnings. By the time Whimper, in the company of the owl-bear captain, took his leave of the stage, he knew the file he carried would not be closed before many further hours of work. But the glow of success still warmed his belly.

"How did you find so many clues?"

"I was the only person who needed them." And some of it had been assumption and some of it bluff.

"And the colour of the goat?"

Whimper smiled a respectful accusation. "It suddenly occurred to me that I'd seen the two thieves being brought into custody when I was in the Magistrate's Chambers this morning. You had already found and arrested the pair of them before this investigation had begun!"

"There are many ways. I have my sources. The person who hired the thieves is being picked up right now. He's a rival merchant with a bit of a grudge, and he's procuring on behalf of a Noble from the Golden Realm travelling incognito."

Whimper looked up at the figure in the carriage, trying in vain to see the layer beneath the layer and the wheel within the wheel. It didn't seem time to leave, but neither had he any more to say.

"Well I must go and give my client the good news," he explained, making movements to leave.

"Does it at all bother you," said Kamew, stilling him with a word, "that your fee will be paid from the proceeds of crime? Stitchley didn't do *this* theft but he most certainly did others."

"Then arrest him for those if you have the evidence. He's innocent of *this* one, and that's what he's paying me for." Whimper shuffled diffidently. "Aw... Money is money. No, I'm rationalising. I like to see justice done and... I've got to eat." He trailed off into silence.

The owl-bear looked down like a father. "Have you ever considered a steady job?"

"I knew you were going to ask me that," said the rat.

BENEATH THE CRYSTAL SEA

Perissa scanned the employment offers posted on the Assassins Guild's notice board. They solicited the deaths of prominent citizens at ridiculously low fees, sought bravos to act as guards on expeditions searching for legendary treasures (wages to be paid in shares of the treasure, naturally) and other such dubious commissions. One even brazenly solicited the assassination of Prince Kalinides. Idly, the pretty, blonde leopardess of nineteen wondered if the Guildmaster would inform the Prince of it or merely assign someone to remove the madman as a favor to Goedus's ruler. Of course everyone, especially the potential victim, knew the Guild would slay Kalinides for the right price. So far no one was willing to meet the equally well-known, fabulous sum. The Guild did not seriously consider any of these, but posted them nevertheless for any member desperate enough to accept them.

Perissa was desperate. As a new member she had not yet established a reputation that would have clients asking for her by name, nor was she given choice assignments by the Guild. She brushed a speck of dirt from her silk shirt, then critically examined her satin trousers and tooled leather boots to ensure that they were clean. Somehow the fees she had earned over the past few months, riches though they had seemed to her at the time, had slipped through her fingers. She had been forced to take her meals in the Guild dining hall of late and was remiss with the rent on her apartment. Granted, her landlord was as yet too much in fear of her profession to broach the subject to her, but the time would come when he would throw her out. And the Grandmaster Assassin would not allow her to slay the fellow over a just debt. She toyed with one of her small gold earrings, its tiny emerald a match for her eyes. If only for once she had not had her usual bad luck at dice.

Another hungry bravo came to stand beside her and scan the board. Nige was a wolf whose fur had lately grayed even more and who wore an almost perpetual expression compounded of wistfulness and worry. Fast approaching the point where age would force him to quit, he had naught put aside to save him from a small room in the Guild house for his retirement. He had been unlucky in his commissions, never getting the formidable one fraught with peril whereby he could make a name for himself that would garner the big money assignments. He took down the notice seeking the death of one of the city's nobles with a mere pittance for recompense.

The bravo girl bit back the acid comment that she had been considering it and had been here first. He needed any fee too badly. Besides, she had not yet reached the point where she'd undertake the hazardous slaying of a noble for so little. She smiled at him. "Good Fortune attend you, Nige."

"Thankee, Perissa. May the Lady-Bitch favor ye as well." His broad country accent was quite different from her clipped city tones. "Mayhaps this be the chance I've been seeking. Wilt ye share a cup o' wine with me afterwards to celebrate my success?"

"Aye, gladly, that and more." Her warm response left no doubt as to what the more entailed.

"Ah, lass, ye be kind to an old male. With such a delightful prospect awaiting me, how can I fail?" His face when he left was happier than anyone could recall seeing for a long time.

Perissa had not made the offer out of kindness; as did the rest of her comrades, she had a genuine affection for Nige. In that respect at least he had been fortunate. But the problem of her flat purse still had not been solved. None of the remainder of these laughable offers was worth considering. She decided to pay the Assignments Office a visit on the off-chance she could wheedle a commission even though it was not likely her name had come to the top of the strictly maintained rotation whereby general assignments were handed out. The more difficult, and thus more lucrative, ones were saved for the more experienced guild members.

"Is there aught for me?" she asked a wolverine clerk behind his desk.

"Mistress Ismara may have something," he replied, pursing his lips. "She has said that any of our more comely wenches who stop by are to see her. I think the client wants more than murder!"

"If he wants that, 'twill be by my choice. This is the Assassins Guild, not the Courtesans."

The Mistress of Assignments was a tall, handsome ewe, her brown hair highlighted with a few streaks of silver, her figure kept taut and trim with exercise. Her species had been a great asset during her active career—no one expected a sheep to be an assassin. While every assassin was trained in a variety of ways to kill, each specialized in one or two. Perissa specialized in the sword, taking advantage of a leopard's speed and the new methods made possible with the introduction of a lighter-style rapier a decade ago. Ismara was the Guild's leading poisoner with scores of deaths to her credit.

Her company was a handsome fox in his mid-thirties with shoulder-length russet hair. His clothes were of costly fabrics and impeccable tailoring, but had seen long, hard use and were carefully mended. His pose of studied casualness as he sprawled in a chair, one leg negligently thrown over an armrest, gave him a dashing air, as he well knew. He was not all poise, though. His tall, compactly muscled frame radiated an unmistakable air of confidence and authority. He would rise to any occasion and none would question his commands. Perissa noted that despite his careless show nothing would hinder him from gaining his feet and drawing his rapier in an instant.

He sized her up in turn, lingering especially over her pert breasts. Not large, they were nicely shaped and his face showed his appreciation. He spent almost as long evaluating the manner in which she wore the rapier on her right side. Turning to the Mistress of Assignments, he said, "Aye, she'll do."

"Sit down, Perissa," Ismara told her. "Connal has an intriguing commission to proffer."

Connal! The blonde bravo girl stared at one of the most renowned males in the western reaches of the Tirabaedo Sea and the surrounding lands. Younger son of a powerful noble family in Goedus, he had inherited little upon his father's death. Rumor had it that his brother had cheated him of most of his due. He had become an adventurer and won several fortunes through risky trading ventures, smuggling and treasure hunting. Some said that he did not scruple to turn his vessel, the *Sea Falcon*, to outright piracy. However, they said so admiringly. Goedusians esteemed anyone who had a knack for accumulating wealth and they almost revered one who could do so outside the law without being caught. He had also lost every one of his fortunes through gambling, lavish living and cutting a wide swath through the ladies, spending freely upon the courtesan who was his mistress for the while.

"Which is?" Perissa inquired.

Connal answered. "I was engaged in a, ah, trading venture—" in which the customs collectors would no doubt be interested "—and was upon the Crystal Sea when I perchanced to glance over the side. Imagine my astonishment when I beheld the Sunken Tower!"

The Sunken Tower of the Crystal Sea! Perissa made a face. It was one of the most persistent of the legendary treasures no one was ever able to locate. "And you plan to return and recover the treasure."

"Of a certainty. It does no good at the bottom of the sea."

"Why did you not dive for it at once?"

"'Tis too deep for that without special preparations. I returned to Goedus for that purpose. And I cannot entirely trust my crew around such riches. After all, should I meet with an accident their share would be doubled. I need someone I can depend upon without question should mutiny rear its ugly head. Thus an assassin; only they are guaranteed honest."

"How will you locate it again? Many are the tales of sailors who espied it once, but could not find it again however long they searched, even when their ship put about immediately."

"I have the spot marked."

Ismara's curiosity was piqued. "How does one mark the featureless sea?"

"There is a way," he replied smiling and would say no more upon the subject.

"Are quelling a mutiny and safeguarding your life all for which I'll be called upon?"

"Nay, let's say your duties are whatever is needful to gain and keep the treasure."

The leopardess asked the question whose answer she dreaded. "What remuneration do you offer for my services?"

"My crew receives shares amounting to half. What say you to a quarter of my share?"

The typical recompense offered for chasing a will-o'-the-wisp. Well, she'd have naught to do with that. She believed in gold, not legends. "A quarter of a half of nothing, belike. Nay, I want a surety. Pay the Guild's rate for daily service and I'll accompany you over the wide world pursuing legends."

"We'll not reach the Crystal Sea in less than a month with another to return and you want a half-thael for each day! Ismara, I implore you, reason with this unreasonable wench!"

"The fee an assassin accepts for special services is entirely up to him or her."

"Yet she demands a small fortune and may do naught to earn it!"

"And I may waste my time for naught if I agree to your terms!" Perissa retorted.

"You cannot expect to win a treasure without some risk, even the risk of empty hands!" He spoke passionately in a voice whose mellifluous timbre must have swayed many to his views. "Accept my terms and you may win hundreds of thaels!"

"He has a cognizant argument, Perissa," the ewe intervened. "You've the Guild's interests to consider as well as your own."

"Mistress, all I ask is that the Guild's fixed rate be honored. Indeed, I have no right to ask less."

"Not if it means we lose heavily. I think it worth the gamble in this instance; Connal has a certain repute in this regard. Do not forget, he looted the Elephant's Graveyard and found the Eye of Emmaris, equally legendary hoards. I release you from requiring Guild rates and urge you to strike a bargain."

"As you wish, Mistress." Perissa turned back to Connal. "Though I'll not hazard all. A quarter-thael a day if there's no treasure and four apiece for any incidental slayings."

The fox threw his hands up in exasperation. "Again the wench seeks guaranteed gold! Half the adventure in a treasure hunt is the uncertainty!"

"I must side with her now," said the Mistress of Assignments. "And lest you recover some barnacle-encrusted trash and claim it the treasure sought, she must have the option of choosing which she'll take as her payment."

"Agreed, but she must hazard a toss of life's dice there. She must choose on the spot, rather than after the Guild Treasurer has had an opportunity to evaluate our find. She must risk that the treasure not look a treasure and that she may lose thereby."

"The Guild finds that an acceptable risk. Perissa?"

"Agreed." Short of funds, she would have accepted almost any guaranteed fee. "When do we sail?"

"On the morrow with the receding tide. Be aboard by the sun's zenith. Ask any dockside loafer and he can direct you to the *Sea Falcon*'s berth." He got to his feet, bowed with a flourish to each in turn and departed.

"Mistress, Connal is famed for more than his skill in seeking out treasures. Think you he can be trusted?"

"He'll not attempt your death; in that regard he is trustworthy. He will try trickery, however. Be on your guard when you make your choice!"

"That I will." She arose to take her leave.

"Oh, Perissa." Turning, she saw Ismara smiling archly. "'Tis said that Connal is welcome amongst the courtesans even when his gold is gone. Mayhaps you can discover why!"

If true, it would not be the least of his legendary accomplishments. Even in Goedus there was no more mercenary a group than its beautiful and skilled whores.

"Aye, mayhaps I can. He is a handsome and engaging devil!"

🌲 ☙ 🌲

Ships from over the known world, and some from parts unknown, thronged the renowned harbor of the City of Ten Thousand Sails. Red-walled Altkreit, island Mahz, far Talleron and age-haunted Ulan-Tor all had vessels there. Lines of longshorefurs loaded and unloaded ships while suspicious custom collectors checked cargo manifests and occasionally ordered a crate opened to verify that the contents did indeed agree with the label. Some captains appeared to be afflicted with a strange nervous disorder as this went on. Confusion reigned at the docks where newly arrived ships were tied-up. Merchants' agents tried to beat custom officials aboard for a private word with captains while whenever the officers turned their backs, sailors attempted to slip onto the dock and do business with the sharks come to fleece those too eager from weeks at sea to seek out better prices elsewhere. Buyers of the trinkets seamen acquired in foreign realms or made to while away long hours aboard ship provided the wherewithal for a brisk trade with vendors of strong drink or spicy foods much different from bland and monotonous ship's fare. The liveliest traffic was with courtesans of the lower sorts.

Perissa stood on the broad stone quay, examining the *Sea Falcon* where it lay tied fast to one of the multitudinous docks. Although she had never been to sea, no one could grow up in Goedus and not be a fair judge of ships. A small black ship lying low in the water, its lean lines and sharply raked twin masts with their lateen sails bespoke its speed and ease of handling. Not a vessel for carrying bulk cargoes, it was instead ideally suited for trading precious goods in dangerous waters, smuggling or with an abnormally large crew going on the account.

Picking up her bundle of spare weapons and clothes, she walked to the foot of the short gangplank. An ill favored, leering otter with teeth yellow where they were not missing, regarded her from where he leaned on the rail above. "Inform your captain that Perissa has arrived."

The watch spat and replied insolently, "Tell'm yerself. I'm no messenger boy fer his doxy."

The leopardess briefly weighed possible reactions. Someone in the crew was certain to test her and she'd have to react swiftly and decisively to let them know that she would not tolerate undue familiarity or hazing. Yet this was a small matter and she decided to ignore it. There was no sense so quickly making an enemy over so little. Boarding, she started towards where Connal directed the handful of otters, beavers and squirrels in their preparations for sea. Her rump was pinched, hard. She spun about, dagger in hand as if by magic and slashed across the back of the offending fingers. The otter cried out and clutched his bleeding digits.

Work stopped, faces turned towards them and Connal was at their side. "What happened?" he asked grimly.

"Inform this dung heap that I'm hired as assassin, not ship's whore."

The sailor was ill at ease, shifty eyes unable to meet his captain's foreboding glare. "Honest, Cap'n, all I did was give her a little pinch. What's she expect when she wears trousers that cling to her arse like that? By all the gods, I swear I meant no harm by it."

"But I mean harm by it. My arse is mine alone and no male may lay hand on it without my leave. Do so again and you'll pull your hand back short of fingers!"

"Get your gear and get off," Connal ordered. "You knew I was expecting a bravo and that it'd be a wench. Only a fool would take liberties with such unless he knew beforehand that they'd be well received. And I'll not have a fool aboard." The unfortunate opened his mouth to protest, took another look at his captain's unyielding face, and left to get his things.

"The rest of you get back to work! The tide departs soon and so do we!" He turned to Perissa with a smile and slight bow. "My apologies for that bore's behavior. If you'd like, I'll show you to your cabin now."

The cabin was surprisingly large for a small vessel and luxuriously appointed with a thick carpet, rich hangings on either side of the broad stern window and a table with several chairs. With its fur coverlet and silk pillows, the wide bed was not one for sleeping in alone and she guessed that in port he rarely did so. "This looks to be the captain's cabin."

"The *Sea Falcon* is a small vessel with no room for passenger quarters. This is the only one suitable for a member of the fair sex."

"And the captain, I take it, will also be here?"

The fox grinned winningly. "You cannot expect him to give up his own cabin, can you? The only other one we have is much smaller and will be shared by the mate and our other passenger. I'd not dream of telling them that they must give it up to you and bunk with the crew. And bunking with the crew or sleeping in the hold are your only options other than here."

He was an engaging rogue, handsome and self-assured. She tossed her bundle on the bed and returned his smile. "At least you're giving me the options. This suits me just fine."

Back on deck, Connal was soon pacing about in barely controlled agitation. He would stride to the dockside rail and glare up and down the quay, then it was over to the opposite side where he'd stare fixedly at the water below to see if any of the garbage floating there had begun drifting out on a receding tide. She heard him mutter, "If he causes us to miss the tide, I'll have his guts for a fish line and bait my hook with his liver." Then it was back to dockside to search the crowds with a baleful eye. The crew prudently avoided him in this black mood. He had taken to absent-mindedly drumming his fingers on the railing before his scowl suddenly disappeared and he exclaimed, "At last!"

Perissa examined the crowds in her turn, searching for the one Connal had been awaiting. The brown bear was easily spotted as he towered above all others along the waterfront, nearly seven feet tall with thews to match. A large chest was negligently balanced upon one broad shoulder, steadied by a huge hand. The other hand firmly gripped the arm of an elderly raccoon, more than half dragging him along, heedless of how he must hurry to keep up and equally heedless of his stumbles. The raccoon's difficulties were seemingly not all the result of a vain attempt to match his companion's longer paces. The bear wore typical seaman's garb of leather vest and trousers while the raccoon's tattered robe indicated a professional male fallen upon hard times.

The bear dragged his captive onto the ship. "Here he be, Captain."

Connal glared murderously at the raccoon. The latter tugged at his garment, ineffectually trying to straighten it. The purple staining the fur about his lips bespoke one overly fond of wine. His matted hair and clothes were dirty and his smell was enough to keep the bravo girl at a discreet distance. His attempt at an engaging smile on his befuddled face made him appear even more foolish. "Greetings, Connal. As you can perceive, I've arrived in good time for sailing."

"Only because I sent Tiroc to fetch you. Did you drink it all up or did you manage to purchase some of the items we'll need with the gold I gave you?"

With the unsteady, offended dignity of a drunkard wrongly accused, the old raccoon drew himself up and gestured towards the chest. "'Tis all in there. I bought my apparatus afore I ever bought the first drop of wine."

"That's something at least."

"Ah, you wouldn't perchance have a swallow or two, would you? This great lout wouldn't even let me finish the goblet I had before me, and it was paid for at that!" He was plainly outraged at the shameful waste.

Connal regarded him in disgust. "Get him below and into a bunk, Tiroc. He'll be of no use until he's sober and the palsies have passed. Luckily it'll be some days yet afore he'll be needed." He rounded on the other crewmen. "What are you standing about for, useless as the nipples on your chests? Cast off and make sail! A treasure beckons!" Cheering, the crew ran to their duties.

Perissa joined Connal at the tiller. "Of what use to us is that drunkard?"

"Ryemart will be invaluable; without him we couldn't succeed." Seeing her skeptical look, he said, "Let not his present condition deceive you. Afore he became overly fond of wine he was one of the leading sorcerers in Goedus. Sober, his skills are yet undiminished, and he'll not get a drop of drink until the treasure is in our grasp."

🐾 ☜ 🐾

The *Sea Falcon* entered the Crystal Sea through the narrow break in the isthmus otherwise separating it from the Tirabaedo Sea. The zephyr caught by their sails was just sufficient to glide them across the crystalline ripples. Perissa leaned over a rail, observing the waters over which they sailed. Like the rest, she had adopted less and less clothing as they had sailed south and the heat had grown and now wore only a shirt. She knew the crew was stealing glances at her backside where her garment barely covered her rump and smiled at the thought. They could look all they wanted; only their captain could touch.

It had been an enjoyable voyage for her thus far. She had no duties to perform and could pass the hours as she pleased, almost as if on a holiday she'd never had. Connal made an excellent partner for fencing practice, one who could present her with the challenge she loved. Almost as challenging was letting him win most of the time without realizing she deliberately lost. It was as much to conceal her true skill from the potential foes the crew represented as to assuage his ego. And his reputation as a lover was certainly justified. He was artful, as concerned for her pleasure as his and imaginative. He was also very thorough—his tongue had been everywhere across her body.

Breaking off her reverie, the leopardess returned her attention to the water. Although the shallow sea was as much as twenty fathoms and more deep in places, it was as clear as fine glass, enabling her to discover its ill-hidden secrets. The near invisibility of the water made it easy to fantasize that their vessel was one of the air gliding above the surface of an alien world. Here, too, were deserts of clean, white sands, low mountain ranges of coral and thick forests of seaweed waving in the gentle breezes of the sea's currents. Yet it was a world almost totally devoid of earth-bound fauna, making up for that lack in its multitudes of aerial creatures. Huge schools of fish, some holding thousands of members and the least holding scores, swam through the forests and mountains and across the deserts.

With the bottom everywhere visible, one could certainly see the Sunken Tower if sailing above it. But where to look? The waters were vast as well as shallow and clear. A lifetime could be spent searching and the tower still not be found. How did Connal propose to locate it again? She did not see how he could have marked the spot; as far as she could determine one stretch of water was identical to any other.

"Ryemart!" the captain shouted for the sorcerer. "On deck! 'Tis time you earned your keep!"

Straightening, Perissa turned about. Perhaps some questions were about to be answered, amongst them what black thaumaturgy Ryemart had been engaged in last night. She had awoke just past midnight, preter-naturally keen senses arousing her at the sound of faint, unearthly noises through the thin wall separating his cabin from that she shared with Connal. Leaving her lover asleep, she had armed herself and investigated. From behind his door she had heard him speak in an arcane tongue, a tone she had not heard in his voice previously—strong, confident and commanding. A second voice had answered in the same tongue, a voice sunk in a soul-searing anguish of the spirit. Her fur had fluffed up and her lips had drawn back in a warning snarl at the despair and torment lading that voice. From the crack beneath the door issued a charnel house stench that had her gagging.

Deciding that whatever went on in there was best left undisturbed, she had returned to the captain's quarters. She had opened the stern window and stood there inhaling deep draughts of clean air, the salt tang sud-denly sweet perfume, flushing the sickening odor from her lungs. Unable to compose herself for sleep again, she had spent the night sitting on the window bench, her legs curled beneath her and an arm resting upon the window sash. The hilt of her drawn rapier had never been as much as a foot from her ready left hand. This morning Connal had smiled madden-ingly and refused to enlighten her.

Ryemart arrived on deck dressed in a robe newer and cleaner and richer than any she had seen him wear previously, although still showing signs of mending. His hair and fur were washed and combed. He bore a staff atop which sat a beaver's skull new enough for scraps of scalp and fur to cling to it still. She grudgingly admitted that he looked as compe-tent as Connal had claimed.

"Well?" Connal demanded, fists on hips and legs braced apart as if in readiness for battle.

"Swear it, murderer." The skull's lower jaw moved as it spoke in the doomed tones of the night. "Swear that you will grant me rest."

The crew drew back and exclaimed in dread, even Tiroc the bear mate showing the same signs of fear and loathing. The leopardess, too, had no liking for being involved however slightly with necromancy.

"You've my pledge. Pilot us to the tower and you'll be laid to rest."

"East," it groaned. "Sail east."

"Come about! Lively there!" roared Connal.

A squirrel muttered, "'Tis bad luck, following the dead. Likely he'll lure us onto a reef and have us joining him."

Seeing them hesitate and their fear grow, their captain addressed them scornfully, "You knew Faxx was the key to finding the tower again. How did you believe it would be done if not by using him as our guide? Would you abandon a treasure because you feared someone more than two months dead?"

The bravo girl sighed and drew her rapier. She'd been engaged to back her employer in any confrontation with his crew, no matter the odds. Quelling a mutiny was certainly part of her duties. She moved to his side, her steel reinforcing his words.

"Now come about!"

"You heard the captain! Jump to it or ye'll feel the weight o' my fist landing on yer empty noggins!" Tiroc was the first to decide. His example combined with the potent threat made up the minds of the remainder; they rushed for their stations.

"How did you arrange for our guide?" Perissa asked Connal.

"That's how I marked the spot. When we were sailing these waters on an earlier voyage, I chanced to glance over the side and espied the Sunken Tower. I knew we'd be past afore we could drop sail and we'd not come across it again. Legends tell of those who have beheld it once and never again no matter how long they searched. As you may or may not know, a murder victim has an especial affinity for the place where he met his violent end. No sooner thought than done. I whipped out my dagger and plunged it into the heart of the male beside me. With Ryemart's magic and Faxx's skull I knew the tower could be located anew." He grinned at his quick-wittedness.

She arched an eyebrow inquiringly. "Did the rest of your crew not take it ill that you should murder one of their number?"

"Fortune the Lady was smiling. My victim was the least valuable and least liked male aboard. He was a surly sort and always bickering with the others. The crew had no objection to his death, especially after I explained why I'd done the deed."

"Fortune indeed. The Lady-Bitch appears to smile upon you most times."

"That's because I know how to make a female happy."

"Aye, I can attest to that!" she laughed.

They sailed at the direction of the skull for several hours. Although they did not balk again, the crew continued uneasy, mostly due to the skull rarely being silent. In between issuing sailing instructions, it bewailed its fate, lamenting the agonies suffered by the dead denied peace and informing them of the pale shadow-life they could expect after they'd met their ends. Its groaning tones were as nerve-racking as its subject matter. Perissa sourly reflected that it was singularly loquacious for one of the so-called silent dead. Connal finally grew irked and swore at it, vowing that if it did not keep its teeth together except when giving directions, it'd never be granted peace. If bones could sulk, the skull did so.

Eventually it spoke again. "Close. We're very close. Hurry or we'll sail past it."

"Down sails!" Connal snapped. "We'll use oars the rest of the way. To the bow, Perissa, and sing out when you spy it. Everyone else, take to the sweeps!"

The crew, including captain and sorcerer, took up oars while the leopardess acted as lookout. The *Sea Falcon* crept slowly across the crystalline waters, rising and falling oars propelling it as if it were a titanic water insect and they its legs. They were crawling along the edge of a reef, outlying coral pinnacles and gently swaying seaweed fronds making a tangle of growth in which the sunken tower could remain hidden for centuries. When it appeared suddenly she almost missed it. One moment all she saw was coral and weeds, then the next moment the tower was there below. Constructed of a translucent stone that rendered it next to invisible, it could be seen only from a few dozen feet away. No wonder it was glimpsed for a second and never found again no matter how long the search.

"Hi, here 'tis!"

"Stop oars! Let go the anchor!" The crew abandoned the oars without bothering to ship them and scrambled madly to the side for a look. Connal himself, with Perissa's aid, had to drop the hook.

The crew were jostling one another for the best viewpoint and babbling excitedly. "We've found it! We'll all be rich as kings!" "Gold enough to fill a hundred chests!" "Pearls big as your fist and of the finest luster in all the hues imaginable!" "Bigger yet! I've it on good authority from a cousin who bespoke a savant who read it from a tattered and ancient parchment from just after the time the tower sank!"

"Connal!" a doom-laden voice moaned. "Your oath! Give me release!"

The huge mate's temper flared. "I'll give you release, you croaking crow!" The bear wrenched the skull from the staff and hurled it far from the ship.

It shrieked as it flew out over the sea. "Curse you for your treachery! Curse you and all your fellows! I curse you to—!" It struck the water and sank before it could say more.

"Since he did not complete the curse, we've naught to worry about," the sorcerer reassured them. "Unfinished, it cannot take effect."

"Can you fulfill our pledge to him regardless?" Connal inquired.

"Alas, nay. I require at least part of his remains and now we've none."

"A pity, but he brought it upon himself. Faxx always was unlucky and overly verbose. If he'd kept silent this would not have happened. Conversely, if he'd been concise he'd have completed his curse and would have his revenge."

"Aye," Perissa said with heavy irony, "'Tis a real pity he blathered so."

"Come away from there!" Connal shouted to the crew. "We've work to do; the treasure won't raise itself! Ryemart, ready your other spell. Tiroc, drop a line overboard that we can use as a guide and for hoisting the treasure. Perissa, Yoran, you'll be coming with me."

"And where might that be?"

He grinned. "We'll be diving for the treasure."

The bravo girl was no happier than the otter chosen. "Why us? I'm a poor swimmer and can scarce hold my breath!" The only places for swimming a slum dweller had in Goedus were in the river and harbor filled with garbage and sewage only partially removed by the receding tides. And none were so insane as to actually use them. Since the Guild had only taught her the rudiments, she liked no water deeper than that in a bath.

"Yoran is the best swimmer aboard, and you've been naught save a passenger thus far. 'Tis time you earned your pay! You need not concern yourself with holding your breath; Ryemart will deal with that."

Still unhappy, she felt that her commission's vague terms left her no recourse to argument. "Then I' best go make my preparations."

When Perissa emerged from the cabin later she was totally naked, unless one counted as clothing the scarf knotted about her head to keep her hair out of her eyes or the dagger in its sheath strapped to a thigh. She would not have drawn more than glances in the public baths where more voluptuous figures than her average one would be on display; however, this was not a bathhouse and they were weeks at sea. The crew leered at her, drinking in the sight of her slender figure with its lovely, apple breasts and long, lithe legs.

Connal chuckled. "We'd best get you over the side afore my crew riots. Can you not spare another scarf to tie about your loins?" He and Yoran wore brief cloths about theirs.

"I'll not ruin my clothing with a soak in seawater." With her funds in a sorry state she could not afford to replace any of her garments. After all, every one was silk, including the scarf she did wear. She'd not ruin a second one. "Bad enough my sword and dagger must put up with it; at least they'll be partly protected by the oiling I've given them. Now where is this magic that'll enable us to hold our breaths as long as need be?"

He gestured to where the sorcerer sat cross-legged on the deck, staring at a basin between his knees and muttering. "Not hold our breaths, but actually breathe underwater!"

Perissa went to stand over the old raccoon, scowling down at him. The basin was filled with water and contained three tiny fish.

"As I understand it," Connal continued, "Each fish represents one of us and so long as the spell remains in force, it'll enable us to breathe water as do the fish."

"'Tis singularly unimpressive for so puissant a thaumaturgy."

Ryemart glared up at her. Connal had not allowed him to touch so much as a drop of wine since they'd sailed and he no longer bore a resemblance to the wine-soaked wreck who had boarded weeks earlier. Now he looked as if he might indeed be a competent magician. "This sorcery is not maintained without difficulty, wench," he growled. "Cease dawdling and dive after the treasure."

"Just be certain you do maintain it. I want not to attempt breathing water without its aid."

Connal handed her a pair of wide leather cuffs to which leaden weights were fastened. "Put these about your ankles; they'll overcome your buoyancy and take you straight to the bottom." The otter chosen and he already wore similar ones.

Perissa reluctantly buckled on the weights, concerned that they might work too well at taking her to the bottom. "You go first."

"Is it me or Ryemart's spell you find it so difficult to trust? No matter, I'll gladly lead the way on our grand adventure!" The fox leaped upon the rail, gallantly saluted them with his sword then stepped off, disappearing with a splash.

The bravo girl gestured at Yoran with her rapier, certain that if she left him behind he would neglect to join them. "Now you."

He appeared to briefly consider the support he would receive from his fellows if he should refuse, took another look at her determined face and went over the side. Perissa followed immediately after.

She quickly sank the fifty or so feet, coming to rest on the tower's flat roof where Connal and Yoran awaited. The infamous rogue grinned at her, apparently breathing with ease, the otter grimly holding his breath. She wanted none of that. Should the spell be worthless, she wanted as much time as she could manage to get the weights off. She took a slight, cautious inhalation. There was no sudden, strangling sensation followed by a surge of panic. Connal's grin grew even wider. She breathed out, then in, deeply. There was a feeling of heaviness in her chest, but other than that it was identical to air. After that she ignored the medium and breathed normally.

An otter could hold his breath for a long time, but not forever. Yoran lost control. Dropping his cutlass, he tried to make for the surface, but Perissa and Connal interposed their swords. Given no alternative, he finally gave in. Face tight with barely suppressed terror, he started breathing. When after a few seconds he realized that he was in no danger of drowning an expression of relief comical in its intensity broke over his features.

Connal beckoned imperiously and they followed to where a narrow flight of stairs lead down into the tower. Perissa reflected that that proved the tower had been built on land and later sunk, swimmers having no need for steps. He started down with the bravo girl then the sailor trailing.

The weights about their ankles held their feet down, leaving them upright, so they could walk in a parody of the fashion they would on land. The resistance of the water enforced an exaggerated slowness upon their motions. Fortunately, the water's crystal clarity and the tower's numerous windows admitted sufficient light for their vision, although as they went deeper it gradually grew dimmer and their surroundings took on a faint greenish cast.

''Tis like floating or walking in a dream,' Perissa thought. She would step out, then settle to the step below slow as a dandelion puff falling. In fact, it was too slow. They soon found the best way to progress was by jumping forward over several steps at once and gradually falling to another.

The first floor down was without so much as a clue as to what its purpose had been before the land subsided and the tower sank a millennium ago, barren other than for fish. Their schools swam through the building, darting in and out windows, flying up to the ceiling and spiraling down in streams that almost brushed the floor before spiraling up again, eddies constantly breaking off, briefly going their own way, then curving back to rejoin the main stream. The three moved through living rainbows of blue, green, yellow, red, orange and most especially flashing silver, an ever-changing kaleidoscope. It seemed they could reach out and touch them, but try and the rainbows would swirl away in ever-restless clouds. The only treasure here were the living gems that would quickly die and fade if taken back to their world. Down they went.

The second floor was equally devoid of aught. Perissa saw her companions' faces were as dashed as she felt. Only one floor remained wherein any possible treasure might be found.

Their last hope excited their curiosity and avarice at once. Even after ten centuries it bore signs of occupation, almost as if someone lived there yet. A stone table bore a comb made from the backbone and ribs of a fish and a bronze hand mirror, its handle verdigris while its polished surface was still clean and reflective. Near one wall was a most unusual bed—a huge clamshell, seven feet across, the upper valve forming a partial canopy over the lower. Strung across the opening between the two was a seaweed net, most strands green while others of reddish-brown were woven through them, forming an abstract pattern. Intrigued, they made their dream walkers' way to it. The net was in good repair, a division in it allowing entrance to the bed, and the bottom shell was filled with clean, white sand raked smooth. It seemed impossible for it to have remained thus undisturbed for a thousand years, yet what else could explain it? No fish would have a bed and besides, here alone the schools of fish were absent.

Fascinated by the mystery, they failed to note the long tentacle that emerged from behind the clam and snaked towards them. For the first vital second that Perissa felt it curl around her, she thought that the sailor beside her was taking liberties. Then she realized that no otter's arm felt so cold and boneless. Glancing down, she discovered to her horror the true nature of the embrace. Too late she attempted to propel herself upwards and free. The instant before the tentacle had tightened about her hips.

Connal and Yoran stared aghast at the sight of her in the monstrous embrace and at the sight of more writhing tentacles reaching around and over the shell for them. The sailor stared transfixed in terror too long and a ropy limb snaked about his neck and squeezed. Panicking, he dropped the cutlass that he might have used to cut himself free. Grabbing the tentacle, he vainly tried pitting his strength against the monster's. The tentacle contracted, choking him.

Connal had acted quicker, violently kicking himself upwards. The tentacle groping for him managed to snare only a single leg. He reacted at once, slashing it with his sword, a cloud of blood quickly spreading through the water. Yet it would not release him and continued dragging him towards whatever lurked behind the clam while another reached for him.

Lifted above the shell, Perissa discovered the creature that lay in wait. It was a kraken, albeit an infant one. Even so, its body was as large as an animal ox and an evil intelligence gleamed malevolently in its saucer-like eyes. She silently cursed the water hampering her. Earlier, the slow, languorous motions to which it had limited them had given their adventure a dream-like quality. Now the dream had become a nightmare, one where no matter how fast you ran you could not escape the horror gaining on you. In this case, no matter how vigorously she sliced at the tentacles with the few inches of her blade back of the point that were sharpened, the water's viscosity robbed her efforts of their power and she could not cut through them. The best she could do was fend off others, leaving her no chance of dealing with the one around her hips relentlessly drawing her towards the huge, savage, parrot-like beak that would crush her limbs and rend her flesh.

Yoran had been quickly strangled and now his lifeless body dangled with swollen tongue protruding from a distorted face.

Connal found the water every bit as hampering as the blonde-haired leopardess and he mentally damned it with curses even viler than hers.

The kraken's tough hide added to his difficulties and aside from his first, powerful slash he could inflict no more than shallow cuts and seeming pinpricks. They must strike for its only vulnerable point but she was closer than he and must do the deed.

Perissa saw him signaling frantically, pointing at his eye then at the monster's. She nodded. It took all her courage and determination to steel her nerves and allow herself to be carried unresisting towards that terrible mouth. Try as she might, she couldn't keep from imagining the feel of that horny beak around a leg and the sudden burst of agony as it crunched through as effortlessly as she could bite through a chicken bone. *'At least it isn't a rat,'* she thought relieved, then grinned at the incongruity of her relief. Just before she reached the mouth, she espied the scattered and broken bones of a previous victim. A land fur's skull, arms and rib cage associated with the tailbones of a huge fish solved the mystery of the clamshell bed. One of the rare merfolk had lived here and had died when the kraken arrived.

Closer and closer she was pulled towards the beak awaiting her, a beak that opened and snapped as if already chopping her into pieces, short mouth tentacles waving, ready to feed her bit by bit into the maw waiting to gobble her down. She drew her legs up lest a foot be sliced off. A bare second before the beak had her, her arm shot forward and a foot of steel stabbed through an eye and pierced the brain. Ichor spurted. Another second and she drove her blade into the other evil orb. The kraken exploded into a frenzied spasm of whipping and contracting limbs. She was in danger of being crushed or dashed against a wall. Desperately she sawed at the tentacle prisoning her.

The initial spasm had hurled Connal away, freeing him. He hurried to her aid with the long, slow, gliding steps the water forced. He plunged into the writhing mass, wrapped an arm and legs about the tentacle holding her and sawed at it opposite to where she was cutting. He clung with difficulty to the violently thrashing limb, just as both had trouble retaining their swords as they sliced through it. Both were aided more by the gradually subsiding throes than by their own efforts. At last she was freed from the lifeless monster with no more hurt than a double row of circular bruises about her midsection, sore, but not serious.

The kraken's dying agonies had further crushed and scattered the bones she had spotted so no sense could any longer be made of them. Its throes had also revealed a brass chest tarnished with age. The Treasure of the Sunken Tower was not just a legend after all! The victors grinned at one another and haled it forth from the corner where it had lain hidden for centuries.

It would be impossible to know who had the idea first if in fact they did not think it simultaneously. Still aroused from their battle and near brush with death, heated blood pounding in their veins, it quickly became arousal of a different sort. Words as unnecessary as they were impossible, by mutual consent they let fall the chest and turned to the clamshell. Parting the net, they entered the bed.

It was like making love on a cloud, the buoyant water lifting them up whilst the lead weights around their ankles gave them an anchor point. Entwined to keep from drifting apart, they kissed, lips meeting and opening, their tongues dueling back and forth from mouth to mouth. From nights spent sharing their bed and bodies, each knew what most pleased the other and so sent hands and mouths roaming and caressing. When both were ready they rearranged themselves and joined. They moved together in a leisurely rhythm, their hands still wandering and stroking, slowly climbing the mountain of ecstasy. Nearing the peak, they moved faster and faster until they sprinted the remaining distance. On the summit at last they were as one, together with the gods, briefly mingling their souls as they mingled their fluids. It took them almost as long to descend as they remained intertwined, still kissing and caressing.

It was while they lay thus that Perissa discovered the bed's previous occupant had not slept there alone. Turning her head, she saw they were being spied upon through a window. The bones she'd seen had been heavy, those of a mermale, and now his paramour watched them. She was lovely with the upper body of a seal as slender and supple as an eel, the nipples of her small breasts coral pink and her light green hair a floating nimbus about her head. Her tail was her true glory, its scales iridescent with all the hues of the rainbow and ending in a widespread fan of delicate membrane. For several seconds they stared at one another, the girl of land and the girl of sea, then with a flick of her magnificent tail, the mermaid was gone. The bravo girl decided to keep her a secret to herself, her memory like a rare and exquisite butterfly that a collector was loath to share with his fellows least the fragile wings be damaged from too much handling.

Finally she and Connal parted to return to their world of air, though neither would ever forget their enchanted lovemaking beneath the Crystal Sea.

Back on the tower's roof they tied the line around the chest and signaled for it to be raised. Awaiting the rope's lowering for them, they bent to unfasten the weights about their ankles. Between one breath and the next Perissa found that she could no longer breathe water. The spell was broken! Looking to Connal, she saw that it was the same for him.

Quickly, grimly, fighting down a feeling of suffocation, they tore the weights off. When she made to shoot straight for the surface, he grabbed her arm and shook his head, pointing to the ship's stern. His meaning was clear. With the very real possibility that they had been betrayed, they should enter where they would not be seen.

They swam to the stern, hampered by swords they could not abandon. Luckily, the *Sea Falcon* was built with an overhanging stern. They clung to the rudder, hidden from the view of any above, sucking in deep, refreshing draughts of air, more to be savored than the finest wine.

A window opened. "They're not back here. They must have drowned."

"They might be beneath the stern."

"Would you like to jump in and see? Nay? I thought not. Let's get back on deck; Tiroc wants to sail as quick as we can."

"Lock the window first. That way should they somehow yet live, they'll not gain entry through here."

Perissa and Connal waited a full minute and more, giving the pair ample time to leave before they climbed the rudder to stern windows recessed just sufficiently to give them a precarious perch. "Have you anything with which to pick the lock?" he asked.

In common with many assassins' weapons her rapier was more than it appeared. She pressed a seemingly decorative stud on its guard and pulled a lock pick from its hidden recess.

"A versatile sword you have there," he remarked.

"Aye, it has its uses." Lock picking was naturally taught by the Guild. They were through the window and in the cabin within moments. "How should we go about this?"

"I think just have at them. There's only six."

"Six? I count seven."

"Nay, whatever happened concerning his spell, Ryemart'll not have betrayed us."

Perissa kept her doubts of that to herself, readying her miniature crossbow. While thus engaged, her eye fell upon her tortoise shell comb where it lay, inlaid with silver and garnets. She tossed it out the window. Perchance the finder would know it as her gift to her. He regarded her quizzically, but said nothing.

They cautiously opened the cabin door and peered out onto the deck. The crew was gathered around the chest, the muscular mate straining to break its hasp with a pry bar. Ryemart lay sprawled on the deck, the bowl that was the centerpiece of his spell overturned. Mayhaps there was something to Connal's contention that the sorcerer had been loyal.

It was a longish shot, but one within her capabilities. She took careful aim and caressed the trigger. Set for a delicate pull, it fired almost as quick as the thought came. A squirrel staggered a step, then pitched forward. Before his dumbfounded fellows could comprehend what the small, feathered shaft in his back portended, Perissa and Connal were halfway to them.

Tiroc regained his wits first. "Look to your lives! The captain and his bitch are upon us!"

The sailors' first mistake had been to abandon the watch set against the two before being certain that they were dead. Their second was to think that just because she was female, Perissa was the less dangerous, completely forgetting her calling. Two rounded on her as the other three faced Connal.

One of her opponents hurled a dagger hard and true at her. Her blade knocked it aside with ease, her battle grin wider than usual at the chance to show off her phenomenal reflexes. They were disconcerted, although whether by her obvious joy of battle or the display of her speed, perhaps they could not say themselves and both were dead before they could make up their minds.

The bravo girl was almost at the point of crossing swords with them when a flick of her wrist sent her dagger plunging into the abdomen of her squirrel foe. Both had expected her swordplay to be of the usual sort, rapier and dagger together, and so she had taken them completely by surprise. Her target collapsed, curling about the mortal agony in his belly, screaming.

The beaver barely had time to get his guard up before she was upon him like a whirlwind of steel. She ascertained at once that he was an indifferent swordsfur, no match for her, nor was his cutlass a match for her rapier. Bored, wanting some sort of challenge to demonstrate her skill, she dispatched him with a supremely difficult thrust into his open mouth. She finished the one holding her dagger for her, then spun to see how Connal was faring.

He was hard pressed to keep his life from the three who sought it. He did so by attacking, his blade a whirling, darting serpent of steel striking at them, keeping them off balance. The outcome was never in doubt, though. Soon or late he would make a mistake or they would wear him down and he would die. Even now he was forced to retreat, small step by reluctant step.

She watched only a moment before stepping in, engaging an otter's attention. Connal used the distraction to leave the last crew otter writhing on the deck, bright gouts of blood spurting from a throat grinning red.

"Have you finished your dance with the other two so quickly?" he inquired. "They must have been a sorry pair."

"Aye, they knew not the first thing concerning a lady's entertainment, so I dismissed them. Mayhaps they'll find a less demanding wench in Death's halls!"

Her latest foe was better than her last. The otter at least knew some rudiments of scientific fencing though he relied mainly on muscle, wielding his cutlass like a meat clever while using his dagger to ward off her rapier's scalpel-like precision. It struck her fancy to give him a lesson in swordplay. She showed him how he should attack, in a dozen heartbeats slipping past his defense half as many times, attacking in a different spot with a different ploy each time.

"You gods-cursed slut!" he cried. He launched a desperate assault, slashing and chopping at her, all science fled as fear took control and he strove to overbear her with sheer fury and muscle.

Shaking her head in mock disappointment at his lost finesse, Perissa made her opportunity with a feint. Her rapier was not there to be blocked by his dagger. Instead it shifted its aim and shot forward, needle point splitting his heart.

She turned as Tiroc staggered back from the steel piercing his side. He sat down heavily, his hands trying to staunch the spreading crimson stain.

"You were overlong in finishing," she commented idly.

"Unlike the dolts with whom you dealt, he had some skill. His only virtue it seems, since loyalty was lacking."

"Are you going to leave me thus or are ye going to finish the deed?" The bear spat a bright pink froth of lung blood along with his words.

"And why should we give you the mercy of swift death after you tried drowning us?" his captain scowled at him.

Tiroc turned pleading eyes on the bravo girl. "Wilt ye do it then?"

"Nay, I feel much as he. Furthermore, I'd wager you put the rest up to it."

"Then curse ye both! Which of ye is it that gave the other the pox?" Perissa listened pityingly; he had no imagination whatsoever. Connal's face grew dark. "I warrant it was ye, Connal, I know ye've had it afore! I only wish I could live to see it eat away at—" He broke off and his head flew back with a snapping sound as Connal stepped forward and delivered a powerful kick beneath his chin that broke his neck.

"Ah, he was cleverer than I'd thought. He knew how to provoke me into killing him quickly." He turned to find her sword's point scant inches from his manhood.

"Have you the pox? I swear if you've given it to me, I'll cut it off so you'll never give it to another!"

"Nay, rest assured I'm clean! 'Twas long ago when I was a mere youth! So soon as I realized I had it, I sought out a sorcerer and had it spelled away. I've taken care to be free ever since."

The leopardess searched his face for a lie. A moment passed. Her furious countenance grew calm and her blade no longer threatened. "Aye, I suppose such could happen, especially to a careless youth."

"I'm happy you decided to believe me. A male's as unarmed as he can get without that sword!"

"I'd surely not want that in your case. I'd be loath to forgo your skilled swordplay!"

"You'd not regret the loss near as much as I! Now we'd best see if Ryemart is slain or merely senseless."

Kneeling, they examined him for sign of injury. His slack features were those of one unconscious, not dead. Perissa stiffened, her eyes becoming as hard and cold as green ice. Beside him lay a brown bottle, the smell from its spilled contents revealing the nature of the foul deed done to him.

"Dead drunk! Swilling wine whilst leaving us to drink a sea! Soon 'twill be dead in truth!" she hissed, readying her strangling cord. She slapped his face. "Wake up, sot, so you can feel yourself choking as I did on the water you left me to try and breathe!"

"Nay, stay your hand; 'tis a weakness beyond his control. I share the blame with him. If I'd given him a cup each day rather than naught he might have resisted the temptation."

"He could have been content with just a swallow or two. There was no need to drink himself senseless!"

"It may have been drugged."

"You sound as if he were an old and dear friend for whom one makes allowances," she said accusingly.

"He is." The fox regarded him sadly. "In my younger days he was my father's resident sorcerer. He fought long and hard before a demon thirst we can scarce imagine bested him and he was thrown out. He it was who took me in when my brother inherited all and I was left penniless. I owe him much."

Perissa was scarcely mollified by his explanation. Her own besotted parents' maltreatment of her and her siblings left her with a loathing for drunkards and contempt for their failings. Then she brightened. There was yet the treasure. Mayhaps it would prove as fabulous as legendary hoards were always said to be. "Oh, let the sot sleep it off in peace. Let's examine our prize."

"Aye, and settle the reckoning of your fee."

With the pry bar his crew had been using, Connal broke the corroded hasp fastening the chest. Both bent closer to catch the first gleam of gold and sparkle of jewels. He threw back the lid.

Perissa sucked in her breath. And spat. "Coral!"

"What constitutes treasure differs for different peoples," he remarked philosophically. Taking several pieces, he turned them over, peering closely at them. "The workmanship's superb at least. With my crew dead there's no need to split it with them. The quarter you're due should run to fifty thaels or more."

"Run the race less swiftly; let me see those." She examined them critically. The artistry was masterful, the rings, beads and pendants carved with intricate designs evoking the sea. However, coral jewelry was inexpensive stuff no matter how skillfully crafted. Of that she was a good judge since it was all she could afford for many years.

She tossed them back into the chest except for a ring that struck her fancy. In the form of an octopus, its arms curled around in a wavy pattern to form the band. It would make an excellent memento, conjuring memories of the kraken as it did. "This is all I claim from there. I think the whole would run to fifty thaels or less. I'm due more than a quarter of that for these incidental slayings alone if I choose the set fee and I do."

"I think it may fetch more than you realize. I'd advise taking your share of it." Connal was quite sincere.

The bravo girl regarded him in amusement. She knew the trick of lying sincerely from when she'd begged on the streets as a child. "Nay, I want the pay of which I'm certain."

"As you wish." He shrugged, then grinned. "No harm in trying."

🕸 ∞ 🕸

"It was some hours afore that besotted wizard came around and I'm happy to say he suffered a most appalling headache well into the next day. 'Twas a hard and slow voyage back with just three of us to work the ship and only one a seaman, but as you can perceive, return we did," Perissa concluded the account of her adventure.

She looked very different from the tired and bedraggled leopardess who had left the ship earlier that day with a satisfyingly heavy purse after Connal had paid her the nearly thirty thaels she was due. She had availed herself of the luxury of a lingering soak in a steaming tub in one of the better bathhouses and followed it with a massage from her attendant (female since a bath and massage were all she desired) prior to presenting herself at the guild house.

"A kraken and four slain. A most remarkable achievement for one years your senior. What a pity the vaunted treasure proved so paltry," Ismara remarked. "'Tis well you insisted upon having the option to choose a set fee instead."

The girl basked in the approval of her superior. "What's befallen whilst I've been away?"

"Nige slew Lord Kuris."

"Oh, well done for him!"

"Aye, but luck never attended him and so it was again. He was caught by the guards. They spoke of the battle for days—no dragon defending its hoard could have surpassed his ferocity. He slew or grievously wounded a half-dozen and held the rest at bay. They finally called for crossbows to shoot him down."

"Too bad! Oh, too bad! I'll miss him." Perissa felt genuine regret at the news.

"So will we all."

Journeyfur Alwys, a thin and fussy impala from the guild treasury, contemplated the stacks of shiny yellow coins before him. "I could wish you'd returned with more after a commission lasting more than two months. Still, I suppose it would have been worse if you'd heeded his urging to take a portion of the purported treasure."

"I nearly forgot. There is a small additional return," Perissa said jauntily. She pulled off the coral ring and tossed it to him. "Evaluate that and tell me how much silver I owe the Guild for its half."

A first casual perusal quickly became an intense scrutiny. The impala turned it over slowly, studying its every aspect. "Were there others similar to this?" he inquired quietly.

"How mean you?"

"Were many engraved with maritime motifs, especially waves and octopi?"

"Aye, all as far as I saw." She felt a sickening premonition of disaster.

"Perissa, those are the most common themes of the long-vanished island empire of Vocca. Collectors of antiquities pay well for its art objects. It will take every thael you earned on this commission to pay the Guild's share of this ring. That chest was worth thousands."

Her stricken face quickly became one of anger, lips drawn back to show her fangs and a growl issuing from deep in her throat. "That diseased son of an unnatural coupling between a rat and a toad! I'll have his cods for this!" She sprang to her feet and rushed from the room.

※ ⊙ ※

"Connal, you dung-eating serpent, where are you? You owe me my fair share or that measly thing between your legs you call a sword!" Perissa shouted as she rushed up the *Sea Falcon*'s gangplank.

Her way was suddenly blocked by a very large, young bull gripping a quarterstaff as only one experienced in its use did. "Easy, wench! What business have you here?"

Her reach for her sword was halted by the appearance of three more bulls, equally large, beside the first. The grizzled one leveled a crossbow at her. Her hand dropped to her side.

"As my son so politely asked, state your business," the elder said.

Perissa forced herself to reply calmly. "'Tis a private matter between Connal and myself, if you'd be so good as to inform him I'm here."

"Cap'n Connal? A strange one, he. He'd not been back an hour afore he hired my sons and me to guard his ship and took passage on the next ship to leave port."

The bull and his sons listened to the leopardess admiringly. Even on the docks they'd rarely heard anyone curse so long and imaginatively without once repeating himself.

※

SECRET WEAPON

Once a decade in the valley of mists,
for a weekend and a day,
from dimensions all and worlds afar,
the dragons come to play.

The green valley stretched for miles, nestled cozily amid the snow-capped mountains. It was springtime, and the flowers were in full bloom. The warming breezes from the south brought moisture and life to the land as billowy masses of clouds rolled down from the mountaintop, wetted the earth, then were no more.

There at the edge of the valley sat a small village, empty now. The humanoid villagers had boarded up their buildings before leaving across the peaks for the next valley. There was no sign of life in the hamlet; only reminders that people had been there just a short time ago. Rainbarrels were not yet full of water. Straw still sat in the loft in the stable.

In the center of what could possibly be called Main Street, a green-ish circle of light began to form out of thin air. It shimmered and shook, making the air hum with magic as the portal strengthened, grew to about seven feet across, then let out a bright flash of golden light as it finally reached climax.

A scaly paw, colored silver and with black claws at the tips of the fingers, stepped out from the circle of light. Then another. Then the creature's head and craning neck appeared, to be followed quickly by the rest of its body. It walked out of the disk and into the street. As soon as he was all the way through, he turned his head and spoke a word from some unknown language. The disk promptly vanished, leaving the silver-scaled dragon in the middle of the avenue and looking as much like he belonged there as a fish does on a horse.

Cudd Steamraker unfurled his wings from his back, stretching the muscles into shape once more They were sore from being closed tight for his entire dimension-hopping trip. Cudd hated to dimension-door across the cosmos. It was hard on his wings. He kept going back to the magic books, over and over again, trying to figure out a way to make the door-ways larger. So far, no success. So he travelled only when necessary and worked out the kinks in his wings upon arrival.

A roaring cry from above made him look up. Two dragons, a crimson male and a golden female, circled the hamlet, and called out a greeting to him. He blinked as he watched the pair wheel around in the blue morning sky. "Showoffs," he thought wistfully to himself. "It'll be hours before my wings are back into flying condition again."

As he watched, the golden one turned on a wingtip and left the other behind. Cudd studied her carefully as she spilled her wings, lowered her four legs, and landed almost silently in front of him. There was something very familiar about her.

"So!" she roared. "So, you've returned again, have you?" She stood there, glaring fiercely at him. Where he stood only seven feet tall at his shoulder, she stood about eight. She also wore a breastplate in the front, with a family crest and some ornamental jewelry for effect.

Of course, he thought. It was Fawn. Who else would it be?

"Absolutely," Cudd answered with a nod. He did not smile at her. "Just like I do every 10 years when we have this gathering."

The golden dragoness's eyes squinted, blue lines of fire against her golden eyelids. "We still have some unfinished business from last time, if you'll recall," she said in a menacing voice.

"Oh, come on. I just walked in the door."

"Are you chickening out on me?" she shouted. "What's the matter? Afraid I might hurt you or damage you beyond repair?"

"I'm afraid you'll smother me, yes."

"Come on!" she challenged him, crouched low on all fours, ready to leap at him at the slightest chance. "Come on, mister dragonmage. Let's finish what we started all those years ago!"

"Can't this wait, Fawn?"

"Only if you want me dogging your every step for the rest of the party!"

Cudd sighed, and scratched at the ground with his sharp, black claws. "You're not going to let this go, are you?" He grunted as he watched her shake her triangular golden head in negation. "All right then. Same rules as before?"

"Yes. There are no rules."

"Okay then." In a move so fast that only the quickest eye could have caught it, Cudd thrust his head forward until it touched hers. Then he turned his scaly head to the side...

... and kissed her! Warmly and lovingly he pressed his lips to hers, feeling her do the same. After a couple of seconds, he pulled back again.

"It's good to see you again, Fawn." He smiled at her, wondering what an innocent bystander would think of their unusual way of greeting each other.

"That's not where we left off, Cudd," she jokingly said to him as she rose to her feet again. "But it'll do. For now, that is." She turned her head, and winked a brilliantly blue eye at him.

Cudd smiled and nodded to her. Craning his head about on his long neck, he then looked around the street.

"The locals all left again, I see," he stated matter-of-factly.

Fawn nodded, still gazing at him. "Yes, the same as they have for the last century or so."

"They are probably still scared, after that fight down in the valley."

"It's their own fault," she replied with a huff that let a puff of steam escape from her nostrils. "We were minding our own business, and not bothering them at all."

"But they had to send a band of warriors in battle gear to drive us out," he finished for her. "Yeah, I remember that. That was a fun party, wasn't it?"

"I think my favorite moment was when you sat on their wizard to keep him from throwing any spells. I still laugh my wings off when I think about it."

"Well, maybe some day I'll stay behind and talk things out with them. I'll explain that it isn't really necessary to run away every time we come to town, just so long as they leave us alone."

Fawn snorted again. "Yeah, right," she said derisively. "Like you'd stay in one place for any length of time." She then turned around, and began walking down the brick-cobbled trail, heading for the edge of town.

Cudd quickly caught up to her and began walking beside her. He gave her a worried glance. "And what's that supposed to mean?" he asked.

Fawn looked straight ahead, refusing eye contact "What I mean is that it's very hard to be your girlfriend when you're never around. Lately it seems the only time I get to see you is at these gatherings."

"I'm sorry, Fawn."

"I don't want your sorrow. I want your presence."

Cudd nodded slowly as they walked. "Tell you what. After the dance tonight, you and I can fly off to one of the mountaintops together. Then we'll talk about you coming along with me on my travels for a decade or so. Would you like that?"

She chuckled. "Something tells me talk isn't the only thing on your mind."

"Nor yours."

"I didn't say 'no', now did I?" She let out another small laugh, and Cudd felt like a weight had been lifted from his shoulders.

"I guess not," he said as they reached the end of the street. "Oh, by the way. Did you get my message earlier?"

"About the contest?" She turned to him and nodded. "Yes I did. And I passed it along, just like you asked. You're going to enter it again, aren't you!"

"Hey, I won last time," he confidently said as he looked out over the valley before him. "No reason I can't win again."

"This year you'll have some real competition though, Cudd. Launchmolten has entered the contest as well."

"Launchmolten?" Cudd said, puzzling over the name for several seconds before opening his eyes wide. "Crag Launchmolten?"

"Yes, the same. He told me to tell you that he was going to enjoy dethroning you."

Cudd flicked his wings in irritation. "Aw. Crag's just a big blowhard."

"Exactly," Fawn said with a nod. "Like I said, you have some competition this year."

He nodded, then patted the set of bags that were slung across his back. "Well, this year I have a secret weapon," he snickered. "And if Launchmolten is in the contest, I just may need it."

Fawn looked quizzically at his sacks."What?" she asked curiously.

Cudd let out a small laugh. "I'll tell you after the contest. Right now, I'm in the mood for lunch. Have you eaten yet, Fawn?"

"I thought I'd wait till you arrived."

"Well, let's get down to the party then. I could really go for one of Trunksplinter's Sea-serpents-on-a-stick right about now."

🐉 ∞ 🐉

Cudd tried to glide down into the fairgrounds from the village, but his wings weren't quite ready for flight yet so soon after a dimension door spell. So he and Fawn walked side by side down the dirt trail through the pines and meadows. They were quite a pair, gold and silver among the fresh green grasses. Before long they reached the glade at the bottom of the valley, and the lake that had formed there ages ago.

Gathered together throughout the glade were hundreds upon hundreds of dragons of all shapes and sizes. Some were flying above the crowd, taking the shortcut to reach the other side of the fair. Others were gathered around various tables and tents that had been thrown up for the occasion. Small flags flew from the tops of the tents, advertising to flyers-by what could be purchased or bartered for inside. The air was alive with the banter of commerce, the flapping of wings, and the laughter of countless happy souls.

Cudd smiled to himself as he and Fawn took it all in and moved closer. Seeing his friends from long ago running around and having fun, he began to feel less like a dragon-mage who had to scour the universe for lore and magic. The centuries ebbed away from him as he watched his friends and family at play, and he began to feel like a child once again. Fawn chuckled softly to herself as she caught his widening grin out of the corner of her eye.

"I see you can still appreciate a good party," she said as a trio of youngsters rushed past them, wings spread and trying to get off the ground.

Cudd turned his head and watched the children's backs as they rushed uphill. "Do you think we should tell them they'll have better luck running downhill?" he asked.

"Why bother? They'll figure it out eventually."

"True."

"And besides, their parents just may want the little beasts to wear themselves out."

"Heh. I suppose," he said as he craned his neck to look at the wares being sold at one of the tables they were passing. "Say, Fawn, just how much time do we have until the contest starts?"

"Oh, they are still going through the last rounds of the semifinals," she replied, pausing for a second to purchase a frozen treat from nearby vendor. She passed the copper chit and said to the side, "Since you are last year's winner, you are automatically in the finals. Shouldn't be but another 30 minutes or so."

Cudd nodded and reached into the right saddlebag. He pulled out a set of multicolored cylinders. "In that case, I feel like a snack," he told her, and popped six of the things into his mouth. He crunched them noisily for a few seconds before swallowing the entire lot.

"Mmm. Tasty." He reached back with a taloned hand for another one, and offered it to Fawn. "Want one?" he asked.

Fawn studied the metallic thing for a few seconds before shaking her bejeweled head. "No, thanks," she replied. "I'd rather eat stuff I can identify." Saying that, she took a lick at her dessert.

"Okay then," he said with a shrug. "All the more for me." He then gulped down the cylinder in his hand with one chomp.

🌸 ∞ 🌸

About half an hour later, practically every dragon at the fair was gathered around the stone dais at the edge of the lake. The fair seemed to come to a complete halt, and everyone came and formed a half-circle around the garlanded improvised stage.

Cudd glanced at the other contestants standing beside him on the rock. First there was Atara, the pretty but smaller female from the Valley of Forges. How the demure green dragon got all the way to the finals was anyone's guess. Then there was Launchmolten, the huge jet-black dragon who disliked him so much. Cudd had no idea why, but suspected Fawn's affections had something to do with it.

At the end of the lineup was Prag Bloodletter, who got to the finals every year, but never won. Cudd noted the hint of gray along the edges of his sapphire lips. He's getting old, Cudd thought to himself. Pretty soon he won't be able to compete at all. The poor drac already looked exhausted from making it so far. Cudd hoped that when he got as old that he'd be in as good a shape as old Prag.

All at once the audience around him began to shout, roar, and to clap. Cudd turned forward once again and saw this year's Master of Ceremonies climb up onto the rock.

The emcee bowed several times to everyone around him, showing off his pair of championship ribbons from previous contests. The crowd applauded and roared for several minutes as the thin and wiry oriental cloud dragon bowed first to the audience, then to each of the contestants in turn before speaking to the crowd.

"Ladies!" he called out in a booming voice which immediately made the audience quiet down. "Gentlemen, and children of all ages. I'd like to welcome all of you to our 5371st gathering here in the 'Valley of the Mists'. Over the past five millennia, this once-a-decade party has served to keep friends and family in touch with one another, despite distances and differences," he announced to the crowd, holding them in rapt attention. "Before the Great Fair, our kind were scattered to the 12 winds. We rarely saw another of our own species. And as we learned to extend our magical powers and expand into other dimensions, the possibility of extinction loomed in our collective futures.

"But with this meeting site and a reason to collect together, all those fears have melted like snow exposed to Heartfire! No more do we feel alone in the universe. Never again will we need to worry about finding mates or lovers of our own kind." Cudd glanced down as the emcee spoke, and caught Fawn looking up at him, smiling. He gave her a wink, causing her to smile more broadly.

"And now that we are all here," the emcee said with a flourish of his hand, "it is time to pick this year's 'Lord of the Fair.' And how do we do that?" he asked the crowd

"How?!" the audience called back to him in the traditional mass response.

The emcee spread his arms wide to them all. "Other species might choose their leader based on strength or wisdom. Still others might elect their leader by casting votes. But this is only for fun, and such things are not the dragon way. We shall pick our Lord the same way our forefathers did; by choosing the one who can make the valley shake and the waters roil. By finding the one who, deep down, exhibits the best dragon quality that each of us share.

"In other words, the loudest, deepest, and longest belch, wins!"

The audience let out a roar of approval, and the emcee turned around and waved a clawed hand at the elderly dragon at the end of the line. "Okay, everyone, you know the rules. Gas only. If anyone flames, they are disqualified. First up is Prag, a longtime contestant and eternal optimist." Several people in the crowd laughed politely at the joke. Prag nodded to the emcee, turned to the crowd, stretched out his neck and opened his mouth wide.

A gurgling rumble escaped his jaws. He closed his mouth and looked forlornly at the others on the stage, quite embarrased at his pathetic belch. Cudd caught Prag's eye and nodded respectfully to him. The audience broke into polite applause, knowing how exhausted the old-timer must have been and admiring him for sticking it out right to the end.

The emcee took a few steps to the side. "Not a stellar performance," he announced, "but an honorable one. Heaven knows I probably won't be in as good a shape a few centuries from now." The audience's heartfelt continuing applause finally brought a weak smile to Prag's face, and he waved his right wing to them all to show his appreciation.

"Now," he said after waiting for a moment of quiet. "Now it is time for our next contestant. Let's hear from Crag Launchmolten."

Crag frowned and closed his eyes. He clutched his stomach, opened his mouth, and let out a loud belch from the depths of his stomach. It was short, deep, and very very loud. Those standing in the front of the audience flinched and looked away, a sure sign of a winning entry. The noise reverberated through the mountain valley for several moments while Crag turned and gave a smug 'top that' look to Cudd.

The crowd let out a loud whoop! and clapped hands and wings excitedly, quite impressed with Crag's showing. Cudd scratched nervously at the rock's surface. That was going to be one hard one to follow, he knew.

The emcee smiled and nodded his head as he stepped aside again to introduce the next contestant. "Now that's the stuff!" he said. "Very good, Crag. But there are still two more to go. So without any further delay, let's hear from Atara." He gestured with a white wingtip for her to go ahead.

Atara took a step forward and cleared her throat noisily, putting a touch of theater into her performance. She then craned her neck fully forward, and opened her mouth wide.

Her body made a loud obnoxious noise. From the wrong end.

The crowd screamed with laughter and several dragons at the front were literally rolling on the grass. Atara's cheeks blushed cardinal red with embarassment as the flatus echoed for what seemed forever through the valley. She covered her face with her right wing and stepped back to the line next to Cudd. He did his best to keep from laughing, but he could feel the muscles in his face stretching in a broad smile.

The emcee held his nose and moved aside once more, quicker this time. "Oh, my nostrils!" he cried. "That's one for the blooper reels, all right." He started to clap, gesturing for the crowd to join him, which they did. Atara kept her face hidden beneath her wing, and the blush spread all up and down her neck.

"And now," he continued as he reached Cudd. "Now we have our current champion. Let's see if he still has the right stuff, shall we?" Cudd waited a few seconds before stepping forward, letting the anticipation build in the audience first. He then craned his neck out, opened his mouth, and called forth his flame without igniting it.

It was so loud it hurt. The amount of gas built up had swelled his belly, even though he didn't notice it at the time. Now that he was letting it out, his sides rapidly collapsed inward just like a deflating balloon. The belch he made fell somewhere between the decibel range of a foghorn and an atomic bomb. It lasted for seconds, blasting out in fierce gastric intensity and threatening to split his throat. The metal in his stomach rattled in deep resonance with his vocalization.

All at once his gas was spent. He blinked, just as surprised at the intensity as the front row apparently was. They stood there, wings back and mouths hanging open, gawking at him. Finally someone in the back started to clap, and the rest of the crowd joined in with a wave of sound. Cudd glanced to his right as the audience screamed their delight and began chanting his name. He noted Crag looking back at him, unhappy at his loss, but still rather impressed with Cudd's belch.

"Dragons," the emcee loudly announced to the audience. "I think we have a winner. For the second time in a row, our 'Lord of the Fair' is... Cudd Steamraker!" The audience continued to clap as Cudd stepped forward to accept his ribbon from the white dragon. But before the ribbon could be slipped over his head, Cudd leaned back.

"Wait," he told the emcee. "The winner has the honor of chosing who bestows the accolades around his neck. Am I right?"

The emcee nodded, and gave Cudd a sly wink. "Yes, that's true. Did you have somebody in particular in mind to do the honors?"

Cudd looked out into the audience once more, and quickly found Fawn's face. He gestured for her to come up onto the stage.

🐦 ☁ 🐦

The crowd had long since dispersed and gone back to the rest of the fair. Cudd and Fawn stayed behind a bit, rubbing muzzles with folks who were congratulating him and expressing their awe at his winning entry. He talked with everyone who came up to greet him, spending the better part of an hour chatting it up.

Finally, the last of the well-wishers had gone back into the fair in search of other excitement.

Cudd and Fawn were alone, making their slow way across the field, heading themselves for the fairgrounds and the rest of the party.

Fawn tapped his shoulder with her wing. "You know, I never heard you belch like that before."

Cudd nodded, stopped, and turned to look at her. "You're right," he said. "I've never been that loud."

"Does your win have anything to do with that secret weapon you were talking about earlier?"

Cudd reached around to the satchels across his back, stuck a hand in and pulled out another group of small metal cylinders. With a smirk, he presented them to Fawn, who leaned back on her rear legs and regarded the mysterious devices curiously, turning them over in her hands.

"What are they?" she finally asked.

"Something the locals make on some planet called Earth," he explained to her. "I think they call it 'Root Beer', if I'm not mistaken."

🔶

MERCY TO THE CUBS:
A TALE OF THE FURKINDRED

Chas. P.A. Melville

Even the nocturnal citizens of City were absent from the streets that night, all but the hardiest driven into the warmth of their dens by the harsh and bitter winter winds of the new year. Snow fell in a dizzy swirl, painting the twisting alleys in swashes of white and shadowy blues. A fine powder covered the trash bins and filthy building walls with the clean freshness of winter. Here and there an otherwise dark corner was grudgingly illuminated by warm light spilling out from the occasional window.

Retuf buried his face deeper into his fine woolen cloak and wrapped himself tighter yet in an effort to keep warm. The wind picked up again, whipping his tail about and propelling him further into the maze of enclave neighborhoods where, to his dismay, the distinguishing marks and road signs were hidden by the heavy snow. Only the odd scent-marking not yet obliterated by the snowfall, or the lone furkin out on some errand would alert him whether he were on the right roads or not. Foxtown, weaseltown, squirreltown, badgertown... the only location in City where the many furs would congregate according to their own species (except for the Preserve, of course, where the four-leggers dwelled), in order to pursue familial and cultural matters not possible within the normal multi-species environs.

He finally found the scent-marker he had been searching for—thank Wula it hadn't completely vanished yet! He followed it into a *cul-de-sac* where a somber wooden door awaited. His hurried, shivering knock was answered by a large and alarmingly hungry-looking cougar. Glassy eyes in a skeletal face gleamed appraisingly before the scowling cat stepped aside to admit the maned wolf.

Retuf shook himself free of the snowy cold and opened his cloak to make repast of the room's warmth. He greedily gulped in the aroma of the heated interior, catching the familiar scents of those he had come to see. The cougar cast a furtive glance down the alley. Assured that Retuf was alone, the large cat secured the door and motioned the maned wolf into the next room. The stout Kurlanar nodded and followed the lanky feline.

A fire popped and crackled in a small, dirty fireplace, supplying most of the light in the room; a frail oil lamp flickered from its stand upon a small, wooden table, giving what aid it could to its larger cousin. The room itself was stacked high with boxes and crates, most sealed and all tucked against the walls; each case had identifying marks in a code unreadable to Retuf, although he could easily guess what they concealed. Here were the goods and produce that had recently vanished from a dozen or more sites around the docks of City.

Three small figures watched silently from the table, red eyes glittering in the firelight: a ferret in a smart ocean-blue coat decorated with huge brass buttons, a dowdy looking bat draped in an annoyingly loud checker vest, and a chipmunk wearing only a personal pouch strapped about his waist and a heavy woolen scarf around his throat.

"We are honored," greeted the chipmunk in a voice as smooth as a cubling's mane. "How may we serve you, Ambassador Yss? It has been a good many months since you have required our humble services. We have sorely missed your generosity!"

Retuf lowered his ears and bowed respectfully, wagging his tail. There was a snicker from the ferret but the chipmunk rose and solemnly returned the bow. "Ah, Cherikk," Retuf replied. "Honor to your fine house, and to your companions. Indeed, I have missed your gracious company and conversation; I regret that my business affairs have kept me preoccupied. I trust you have been faring well?"

"Well enough. Business has been good, and my mate has produced a litter this past season." Cherikk spread his tiny paws cheerily. "Now I have many mouths to feed."

"Good fortune for you, then!... and unfortunate for me, since your prices will no doubt reflect your new domestic needs."

"No doubt." The chipmunk's beady eyes sparkled with amusement. "But let us see, first. How may we serve you, friend Ambassador?"

Retuf took a seat at the table, towering over all save the cougar, who sat scowling nearby on one of the crates. "I am in need of some items— gifts for some associates of mine—items which I am having difficulty in obtaining. And of course, I recalled the fine service you have rendered me in the past..."

"Of course, Kin Ambassador; and what are these items? I am sure we can arrange something for so valuable a customer of ours."

"I am in need of only three things: first, bananas—at least two cart-loads—"

"Bananas?" The ferret barked a laugh. "What do *you* need with *bananas*?" Cherikk silenced the sailor with an angry glare.

Retuf contemplated the mustelid for a moment. The ferret was the only fur in the room the Kurlanar was unacquainted with; but Cherikk would never allow him to remain if he were not deeply involved with the chipmunk's enterprise in some way. "The bananas are to be a gift to the staff of the embassy of the Trumpet Lord, Arrrungularah. His servants, as is the custom with the elephants, are primarily simian. Bananas are a delicacy among monkeys, but they are rare in our northern markets; the more so with the kraken problem becoming more aggravated these days. I am sure the staff would be most appreciative of such a gift..."

"...And such gratitude would most likely take the form of a confidence revealed, or a sympathetic whisper in the right ear," Cherikk chided the ferret. "Never underestimate the value of any gift, Kafon; I've told you that often enough! And Kin Retuf is a learned fur in the art of gift-giving. I have watched him long and often enough, and have marveled at the proficiency of his talent." There was a genuine admiration in the chipmunk's voice, and Retuf found it difficult to suppress his pride upon hearing it.

Cherikk turned back to his guest. "Two cartloads of bananas, then. What else will you need, my friend?"

"A sculpture... one of those iron workings on display in the Jennoq Quarter? They're made by some Mathokan ferrier, I understand; quite marvelous by all accounts. One of the Panduran delegates has expressed a desire to own such a piece of art—he would even, in his own words, sacrifice his pelt to obtain one!"

"A bold statement for one of the Furkindred!"

Retuf hesitated before continuing. "I realize that there might be some difficulty in obtaining one of these sculptures..."

Cherikk shook his head. "It will be appropriately reflected in the price, Kin Retuf; but I think we will have no difficulty locating one... within our stock."

Retuf nodded understandingly. "The last item is most important, and perhaps the most difficult. There is a Baraslan merchant I should like to put into my debt. He is most influential, and carries much weight with the Barasla delegation. I have spoken long with him on several occasions, and he has been most frank with me. He has indicated that he would put his full support behind me upon some important Congress business, but only for a price. He has heard of my ability to... procure troublesome-to-find merchandise; if I can meet his price, I will earn his undying support!"

"What is his price?"

"Medicine." Retuf shook the last remaining drops of melting snow from his fur. "It would seem that long ago in his youth he traveled to the edge of the Frontier where he spent much time with one of the nomad tribes. I don't know the tale, but apparently he feels a great affection for these furs; or perhaps it is a debt of honor for him. Whatever it may be, they have recently been plagued by a sickness, and they have come to him seeking aid. He, in turn, has come to City with some of his juniors to search for the appropriate medicines while buying goods to ship back home."

"And obviously he has not been able to find what he wants; therefore it is rare or illegal," Cherikk concluded thoughtfully. He sat silently for a long moment thinking to himself. Retuf waited patiently until the chipmunk slid off of his chair and walked into an adjoining room. "I shall return in a moment."

As soon as the chipmunk had vanished from sight, the bat tittered rudely, the sound growing louder as it blossomed into raucous laughter. "What do you find so amusing, M'ful?" snarled the cougar in annoyance.

"Why, Kin Ambassador, of course!" laughed the bat. He loudly gulped down his drink and wiped his mouth on his bright, plaid sleeve. "I'm always touched by his great nobility and honorable intentions! Gifts, gifts, gifts! Not for himself, no! But he still gets himself the bigger prizes, eh?" M'ful guffawed louder, nearly tumbling backwards from his chair.

"You find my actions less than honorable, M'ful?" Retuf glanced disdainfully down at the bulbous figure rolling on the floor. "By obtaining these little favors for such noble furs, I obtain their good will and aid in advancing a motion to investigate allegations of brutal practices in the K'Marr, and in turn obtain both trade and prestige for my people. None of this is for my own sake!" *Unlike your own ambitions*, he thought snidely.

The bat regained his seat and sipped anew at his drink; at Retuf's words, he burbled laughter into his drinking bowl, nearly choking on the liquid. The cougar glared at the bat, then turned away in disgust. The ferret grinned at Retuf, his small, pointy teeth bared. "Nothing for your own sake! My, my! I am impressed! We are *all* impressed! All this *honor*, bought for so little! You are a remarkable bargainer, Kin Ambassador!"

"How do you mean?" Retuf's mane began to bristle, though he kept both ears and voice level.

The ferret waved his hand expressively. "You run such circles sniffing so many tails! Bringing so many good and noble furs into your debt, all for the sake of honor! Yes, I can understand why Cherikk is so fond of you: you are both alike! You scrape and bow so pretty and so humble, anything you please to get what you want. Honor!" He snorted loudly and sneered at Retuf. "Nothing for yourself, my Lord Ambassador? You get plenty! You win the hearts and souls of everyone who looks upon you! *There goes a fine kin, the Lord Ambassador of the Kurene, Maara bless his fine fur!* Yes, that is what you like—the gratitude and praise from your adoring peers! I may be just a poor sailor, but I know your kind, Kin Kurene; I *know* you!"

The ferret again bared his teeth in an unfriendly smile, and bent his head down to lap at his drink again, one eye warily watching Retuf for a reaction. M'ful had ceased his laughing, nervously glancing back and forth between wolf and ferret. The cougar was observing the table with interest, no longer pretending to be cleaning his claws. Retuf was as unmoving as a stone, his face and body revealing nothing. A tense moment passed. Then another.

Retuf laughed suddenly, a sharp bark that startled the trio. The portly Kurlanar moved in a sudden blur. The ferret cursed, dropped his bowl, and grabbed for the firearm strapped to his belt, but he was struck breathless by a blow that sent the weapon clattering across the floor. The bat cried out in a voice that rose so high that it nearly burst Retuf's ears, as he flapped backwards away from the center of confusion.

Retuf grasped the ferret by the throat, baring his own teeth. The ferret twisted, attempting to wriggle free, but at a loud growl from the maned wolf he froze absolutely still. "It is not wise to insult your superiors, Kin Kafon! It is very... impolite!" He released the ferret roughly and returned to his seat at the table. He sat calmly and folded his hands together, composing himself as though nothing had occured. Kafon stood up shakily, coughing and choking, and massaged his throat. "Fortunately for you," continued Retuf, "I consider myself to be a very polite guest. I will not kill you."

The ferret cowered away from Retuf.

Retuf cocked his head thoughtfully. "Not today."

Kafon spat hatefully and spun about to retrieve his weapon. But the cougar was already cradling the firearm in the nook of his arm; he glowered back at the ferret. Kafon began to protest, but caught himself at the sudden return of Cherikk and another maned wolf.

Cherikk stopped, sensing the change in the atmosphere. He twitched his nose inquisitively at the cougar, who nodded reassuringly. The chipmunk frowned at the ferret who shrunk away sullenly; then Cherikk returned his attention to the ambassador.

"I have brought someone who can perhaps supply you with the medicine that you require," Cherikk began, indicating the reluctant figure behind him. Retuf stared at the newcomer in surprise and alarm. His mane rose along his nape and his ears flattened against his skull. "What is he doing here?" Retuf demanded, all cordiality fled from his demeanor. The strange maned wolf cringed, his tail wagging anxiously between his legs. Retuf turned his glare to the chipmunk. "This cur is an exile! He wears no *kenta* or clan sigil; he is a convicted criminal! Why do you bring him to me?"

Cherikk was taken aback for only a moment before regaining his equilibrium. "This is Raggas, who is acquainted with the healing arts; he performs most of our more delicate surgeries as they are required. As for his status, well... my good friend, you must realize that we must make do with whatever we can find!"

Retuf's ease returned reluctantly. Of course they would bring him an outlaw; what else was he expecting? This was a shady business at best, much as he might try to pretend otherwise. Sometimes reality had a nasty bite if one did not watch his tail. Still, the thought of working with an Exile was unnerving—just a little too close to home.

"Forgive me, Cherikk. I forget my place. I would be extremely pleased to hear what advice your healer can offer me." The words were spoken as sincerely as he could possibly manage. But he could not restrain himself from baring his teeth, try though he may.

Raggas stepped forward cautiously, head lowered respectfully and tail wagging pitiably in a frenzy of appeasement. He wore a dingy tunic that still bore the sharp tang of some ointment. "Noble lord," he whimpered, "Cherikk has told me of the sickness and of the medicines you require to cure it. I do have some access to the healer guilds here in City, and can obtain, with some little difficulty, a small amount. If you will but supply me with some minor details—the species and the territories involved, for example—I can then properly prepare the correct dosages and instructions to accompany the cure."

Retuf glowered, but it was a reasonable request. "I will inform Cherikk of the details; you may obtain what you need to know from him."

Raggas bowed lower and stumbled backward towards the door. He turned hastily and nearly fell over himself fleeing from the room. Retuf watched him leave, not speaking again until he was sure the exile had gone. "Raggas," he muttered to himself. He looked at Cherikk, who munched unconcerned upon a chestnut. "I know of this one. He was exiled for killing a cub; I wonder why they did not execute him immediately. You would have such a cur as your physician?"

"He is very skilled; we have certainly never had a better healer in our organization. We do not condemn anyone for their past—not while he still has so much to offer us!"

Retuf snorted rudely, and helped himself to another cup. "Be sure you do not let him treat your litter!" he warned. And he drank the beverage, the hot sweetness coursing down his throat.

🦋 ∞ 🦋

Retuf returned to find the Kurene embassy in a panic. The staff scurried about anxiously, the clipped commands of his denmistress Myrry nipping at their heels. He apprehensively threw his cloak onto a nearby chair and hastened over to the tiny mole, who was dispatching one of their servants to the kitchen. The mole was obviously distressed as she waved her long claws at the departing servant, speeding him along with several sharp words of instruction.

"Myrry!" he barked, "What is happening?" The mole turned to him, her nose quivering nervously.

"Master!" she cried and grasped the sleeve of his robe. "We are having been seeking for you! Come! Come!" She tugged at his arm so fiercely that he nearly toppled forward on top of the squat mole. "Mistress is falling! Very, very ill! Sending Thren for healer, I have! Come!"

But Retuf had shaken loose of his domestic's frantic pulling and was already running up the stairway to the private dens, shoving aside an attendant carrying large bowls of water, very nearly knocking the startled servant down the stairs. He burst into his mate's quarters, heart pounding fearfully.

She lay in a crumpled heap upon the bed, her head lolling limply in the lap of a Kurlanar servant who was desperately dampening Ryla's nosepad with a wet cloth. He lifted Ryla into his arms—Wula bless, but she was so light!—and cradled her to his breast. An eye opened, focused on him for a single lucid moment, then rolled back as the eyelid closed once more.

"No," he whimpered, and licked her nose helplessly.

There was a shadow at the door and he turned to it, holding his mate protectively. Myrry and Thren were there, herding a rumpled Kurlanar in—old Thalyn the *serehn*[1]. Retuf held Ryla out to him. "Help her," he pleaded; his ears, tail, and voice all properly lowered in helplessness and respect.

The M'nsai priest glanced at the stricken female and gruffly motioned for the body to be returned to her bed. Retuf obeyed, setting her down with a tenderness long forgotten, and stepped back as the *serehn* bent over her.

Thalyn gently pulled back one of Ryla's eyelids and examined the eye, then carefully opened her mouth to inspect her teeth and tongue. His free hand gestured in a swift and smooth movement and the female's body radiated a soft glow. A long uncomfortable silence followed before Thalyn turned to the waiting Myrry.

"Go and fetch Forever Hungers from the healer guild—no one else, mind you!—and tell him that Thalyn asks for his assistance. He will come." The old *serehn* met Retuf's frightened stare. "She will live, cub. But we must attend her for awhile longer."

Retuf fell back against the doorframe, nearly collapsing from the relief that swelled over him. The room dimmed and swam about him, and the concerned voices became a blur. She was going to live! He was faintly aware of Myrry taking his arm and leading him back to his study. The little mole murmured something comforting to him, but it was all lost beneath the terrible pounding of his own heart. He closed his eyes and fell into a chair. Retuf dropped his head into his lap and wept from sorrow and relief.

✹ ◠ ✹

"Dosson's Blood!"

Retuf threw the inkwell against the fireplace masonry, snarling furiously as the fragile crystal exploded, showering the comer with ebony droplets.

Thalyn blinked in mild confusion and stepped back from the wake of Retuf's sudden ire.

"I don't understand, *Cafkurra*[2]. I thought the news that Ryla was well would please you."

Retuf swirled to face the old *serehn*, his mane erect and bristling. "I might have known! I might have known this was more of her foolish playacting! Dosson's Blood! but I *believed* that she was dying!"

He threw himself into his chair, the sudden weight nearly collapsing it. "What am I going to do with her?" he growled in a low and miserable voice. "This constant game of hers, her wheedling and whimpering to

[1] A priest of the Kurlanar faith, the *Kurama*.
[2] Ambassador; from the Kurlanar.

return home, is wearing at me! I am growing sick to death of it!" *I really thought she was dying! Ryla, how could you hurt me so?*

Thalyn hobbled across the room to a guest seat and lay himself across its length, sighing audibly as he did so. The elderly priest allowed the ruff of his mane to fall across the vest of his carmine robe in a generous spray of gray and silver fur. "The homesickness is not uncommon to us," he reminded Retuf. "No other fur feels so acutely the call of their homeland as do the Kurlanar. And Ryla has been here for nearly a decade."

"And so have I! You do not see me whimpering like a whipped cur at every turn! Her moaning is just so much otter-play to trick me into returning home with her!"

"No," Thalyn replied quietly. His old, gray eyes studied Retuf closely as he spoke. "She is not faking her condition; that much I can reassure you of. Her attack tonight was quite genuine."

"What do you mean?" Retuf's ears pricked up in alarm. "You said she was well!"

"So she is... well enough for her condition! Forever Hungers and I examined her thoroughly and tended her through the night. She is much stronger now, and has much reason to get stronger in the following months, but her health and stamina are far below what they should be, due to the stress of the homesickess. She will need to recover much of her strength and will in order to heal with the stress of her new burden..."

"New burden?" A pool of ice began to congeal in Retuf's belly. "What are you talking about? Is Ryla well or not? Is she...?" His voice dropped to an incredulous whisper. "Wula bless! Don't tell me she's..."

Thalyn exploded then with joyful laughter. "Yes! By Wula, she is going to have your cub! You're soon to be a father, *Cafkurra*!" With a sudden, unsuspected vitality the old Kurlanar leapt from his seat and danced merrily towards the shocked ambassador, claws clicking a merry tattoo upon the hardwood floor. "Your clan marks another generation with your heir, my young friend! This will certainly please the *cafkurs*[3] back home! A cub in the embassy!" The *serehn* stopped in mid-step and stared unseeing out the window, musing aloud. "Wula bless, but there'll be much to do, won't there? A young one to teach again, dear me! I hadn't thought of that; I do hope that I still have the appropriate texts... *wuf*! What am I saying? His hands won't pop open for a few seasons yet! Or *her* hands for that matter! Or even born yet for several months! Plenty of time to find the books I'll need! Oh, but this is exciting news! I do truly envy you your good fortune, Kin Retuf!"

Retuf sat back stunned. A cub! They were finally going to have a cub after all these years! He grabbed his nearby bowl and gulped down the hot beverage. He fell back in the chair, dropping the bowl to his lap. A cub... but how? When? They had not been the closest of mates in recent years—when did they.. .?

A fragment of memory bubbled up from the wells of his mind: a cold

[3] Clan leaders; from the Kurlanar.

winter's night, not long past... he had been drunk and melancholy, and she, of course, was homesick and also melancholy. Both had sought comfort from their loneliness, first in their singing and then... Why, it had been the very night that old Chur and his coconspirators had approached him about leading the K'marran investigation through the Congress!

"Dosson's Blood!" he whispered in a small voice. He looked up at the happy *serehn*. "Is it true?"

"Oh, no mistake about it! It appears to be coming along quite well, strong and healthy. So far," added Thalyn in a sterner tone.

Retuf shook his head in bewilderment. "What about the Laws?" The Kurene had long maintained strict birth laws dictating when and how often a mated pair could have children.

Thalyn shook his own head in reply, the long mane rippling in waves of silky gray. "Oh, you've no need to be concerned there! The *M'nsai*[4] councils have long ago approved you for a child! In fact, I do believe they were becoming concerned that you hadn't produced one before now." The priest turned to the window and gazed off towards City, continuing to muse. "We shall have to formalize you now, of course; we can perform the ceremony within a few days when Ryla is feeling stronger... and she has already asked for you to come and Recognize the cub..."

The ice in Retuf's stomach grew hard and chill. Recognition was an informal rite, sometimes observed, sometimes not; it merely required the father to come to his mate, to acknowledge and accept the cub as being his. As a ritual, it was primarily a personal reassurance for both that would bind all together.

But the birth of the cub would now signal a permanent change in their mated status. Until this minute, either could have dissolved their union at any time and have been free to choose new mates. Their pairing was a mutually voluntary affair, each held to the other by their free desire to remain. But now, custom and law would bond them permanently together; the ceremony was merely a public announcement of the fact.

He was suddenly stirred by memories of recent years, of their growing estrangement, and of his becoming imprisoned to her constant whining and her growing melancholies. At a time of personal and career growth, he had found that rather than melding together as a pair, they had grown further apart, leaving a cruel and cold void between them. At any time he could have been rid of her by simply announcing their annulment; now it was too late.

"Did you hear me?"

Retuf looked up again, confusion veiling his darker thoughts. "I beg your pardon, *Serehn*?"

Thalyn peered closer into Retuf's eyes, as if he had suddenly noticed something hidden there. "I said, Ryla would like for you to give Recognition; will you come?"

4 The Kurlanar priesthood.

Retuf swallowed nervously. "No! No... not just yet, she... I must let her rest, I think; get her strength back. I will come later."

Thalyn nodded thoughtfully. He took his leave then and closed the door quietly behind him, cutting off the muffled sound of his voice as he numbered off the preparations he must make.

Retuf shot up from his chair and began nervously prowling his study; an overwhelming fear gnawing at his heart. The fact that they had been childless had always left him an exit if ever he chose to use it—and he had quite frankly wondered why it was that Ryla herself had never invoked it—but now he had no such escape. He was forever trapped with the unbearable weight of an unsympathetic, whining female, who very desperately desired nothing less than for him to leave his beloved City and return to a faraway homeland whose very image burned dimly, if at all, within his own breast. He was trapped!

Retuf brooded, his mood becoming darker and fouler. He hunched as he paced, almost seeming to shrivel into the folds of his robe. Abruptly, he stopped in his tracks, jaw open in surprise. A notion: He was trapped only *if* the child was born but, what if... He caught his breath at the thought. Was he really that desperate, to be willing to pay such a monstrous price to remain in his precious City?

To his everlasting shame, he already knew the answer to his own question.

🌼 ⌾ 🌼

"I am in need of some advice. Some... delicate advice."

Cherikk's ears twitched in mild surprise at Retuf's request, the only response his otherwise impassive face betrayed. The chipmunk signed to his companions who immediately stood and left the room. Only the ferret betrayed any curiosity, but was roughly shoved out the door by the lanky cougar. When the two were finally alone in the small, dark room, the chipmunk turned again to the nervous Kurlanar. "What is this 'delicate' advice that you require of me, my friend?"

Retuf hesitated before answering. Did he truly had the nerve to continue? No, the decision was already made, and he always carried through on his decisions. "I have... there is someone who stands in my way; I require that one removed." He stared boldly into the black depths of the chipmunk's fathomless eyes. "I hoped you might have some... suggestions... to aid me."

Cherikk did not respond. Retuf thought he could see an ember kindle within the chipmunk's eyes, small and swirling, an unholy flicker that seemed to beckon to him. He reflexively reached up to grasp the *kenta* that hung beneath his mane. But Cherikk broke the silence, and his hand froze just short of the medallion.

"We don't provide that kind of service, Kin Retuf," the chipmunk replied softly, his hand gestures slight and restrained.

"I am sure that you don't, Kin Cherikk, but I was thinking that your dealings would inevitably bring you in contact with those who were less sagacious in their transactions, and that perhaps you might bring me together with one such. The matter is very important."

"Perhaps."

Cherikk had what he wanted, Retuf knew that very well; they were merely bartering now. Retuf knew the procedure all too well from their previous encounters; only this time the sale item was a far more serious matter.

Cherikk remained both motionless and expressionless. His hands, folded upon the table, parted now and swept gracefully upwards to frame the proper inflections as he somberly chittered, "Who is this person that you need removed?"

The ambassador's mane bristled. "Is it necessary to know?"

The black marketeer shrugged. "It may be. If it is a person of repute or authority, there may be repercussions. A fur would need to be careful. Delicately careful."

Retuf gnawed at a whisker. It was a sensible precaution on Cherikk's part. In order to ensure full participation, he would have to bring the black marketeer further into his confidence. He looked again into the chipmunk's eyes and found a bonfire, hungry and vile, blazing with evil ambition. For the first time in all their dealings, Cherikk was about to obtain an advantage over the Kurlanar, and he was clearly relishing the opportunities it presented.

Retuf reluctantly responded, but only in sign talk, and even then would only indicate that it was a member of his embassy.

Cherikk nodded thoughtfully and closed his eyes, appearing to be asleep. When they reopened, the bonfire had become a conflagration. Cherikk smiled, and Retuf's entire mane stood on end. "Raggas," whispered the chipmunk.

Retuf stared in open-mouthed disbelief. "*Raggas*? The exile?"

"Who better?" Cherikk pushed himself away from the table and dropped to the floor from his chair. "He is a healer with much knowledge of medicines; of how they heal, or kill. And if something *should* go astray, he would be the most obvious one to blame. Wait, and I will fetch him."

Retuf sat alone in the darkened room after Cherikk had left, and pondered the consequences. Yes, Raggas *would* be perfect. It was well known that the exiles were criminal and unstable. He wanted the death to seem natural, but if it should go awry, Raggas would be the perfect fur to take the blame; the ambassador's word against an exile's—he knew whose would be accepted by the Kurlanar. He would first need to set up an alibi, however, perhaps even arrange for Raggas to come to the embassy on some pretext...

Cherikk returned directly with a puzzled Raggas in tow. The exile once more assumed his submissive posture when he saw Retuf, and crouched with his ears back and tail wrapped about his leg. With his eyes lowered, he greeted Retuf deferentially.

Retuf stood and crossed over to Raggas, growling low to remind him who was dominant. "Has Kin Cherikk told you what is required?"

Raggas cringed slightly, but replied in a steady voice, "Only that it was a matter of medicine again, *Cafkurra*."

Retuf glanced at Cherikk, but the chipmunk remained stoic. He was going to allow the ambassador to damn himself before his inferior. Retuf snarled at the exile, and returned to his seat. "I require a medicine, yes. It must be one that will, in ordinary circumstances, heal, but if taken wrongly, will just as easily kill. And it must be untraceable!"

Raggas was startled just enough by the request to forget protocol and look up into the eyes of the ambassador. "For what purpose?"

Retuf was angered by the exile's presumption to look him in the eyes, but Cherikk intervened quickly. "Kin Retuf wishes to remove himself of an obstacle to his continued success. We are both agreed that you have the means to accomplish this."

Raggas looked slowly from one to the other, divining the truth. "No. I am no murderer."

"You killed a cub!" growled Retuf.

"Through negligence! Never through deliberation!" Raggas protested. "I will not kill for you!"

"You will not need to," reassured Cherikk consolingly. "Kin Retuf wishes as few complications to this matter as possible. You shall not be concerned with anything more than supplying our customer with the items he requires to perform the task. What he then does with them is his concern, and not ours."

Raggas stared at his employer doubtfully, apparently wrestling with some inner demon. "Who is it you plan to kill?"

"That is not for you to know!" Retuf barked.

The healer was unmoved. "I must. Who you kill will make a difference in the drugs I must supply you with. Each fur has a different reaction to different types of medicines; some will affect only certain furs, and not affect others at all. Is it a large fur? He may require a heavy dose. Is it a female? Is it in prime health? Has it been ill? Is it a child? All these matter if I am to do my job."

Retuf hesitated. He had not considered this. *He* was not a healer; he had thought that he could simply give Ryla a certain amount of some drug and she would die. Now it was apparent that if the dosage was misjudged she might only become ill and still survive. The job must be performed correctly the first time! Still, he found it difficult to confide to an exile.

When he did not immediately answer the healer's inquiry, the chipmunk turned to Raggas. "The intended victim is the Ambassador's mate, Ryla."

Both Kurlanar gasped in surprise, Raggas from horror, and Retuf from the shock of Cherikk's having known all along. *Dosson's Blood! Is there anything this demon does not know?* Shaking, he once again tried to reach for his *kenta*, a prayer on his lips, but the chipmunk turned back to him once again. The knowing smile on Cherikk's face froze the maned wolf in mid-reach.

"You would kill *family*...?" Raggas stared at Retuf in disbelief. Retuf growled warningly at the exile; *how dare he presume to judge?*

Cherikk once more intervened. "You can now supply Kin Retuf with precisely what he needs, can you not, Kin Raggas?" Raggas did not reply, glaring at the portly ambassador with frank contempt. The chipmunk spoke more harshly. "If you cannot be of service to us, then perhaps we need to review our mutual contract, Kin Raggas?"

The exile blanched and cowered once more. "No, that won't be necessary." He turned to Retuf, once more submissive. "If the *cafkurra* will come with me, I will give him what he needs, and show him how to use it properly."

Retuf relaxed and stood up gruffly. Before following the healer into the back rooms, he turned to Cherikk. "There is still the matter of payment to be settled—" he began, but Cherikk waved him off with a dismissive pass of his hand.

"Oh, no, my friend; there is no payment to be discussed." Cherikk smiled, revealing his tiny, sharp incisors. "Let this be my gift to you, for all your years of being a loyal and faithful customer."

Retuf stared into the blazing inferno of the chipmunk's eyes, and knew that he was lost. Cherikk had at last caught him in his spider's web, and he would never let him go.

🐾 ➝ 🐾

"Three weeks now! Three weeks I have sent messages to the Arbiter, and still she will not respond to my requests for a meeting!" Retuf threw the courier packet upon the low desk in his study. "Her secretary tells me nothing save that the Arbiter is ill following her ordeal at the renderer's, and will be unable to comply with requests for at least another week! Bah!"

He leapt up and paced the room furiously, one hand tugging unconsciously at his *kenta*. "Months of solicitations and debates all snarled up because of that damned raccoon! Security has become lax if she truly was a Mathokan assassin as they claim!"

Thalyn sat calmly, hands folded in his lap. "There is still some doubt that she was truly Mathokan; certainly the Mathokan High Councils have disclaimed her."

"Of course they would! They certainly wouldn't wish to publicly acknowledge that they're busy keeping an intent eye upon Congress activity, in a supposedly neutral arena! It wouldn't be very good relations!" Retuf sniffed and returned to his desk, reopening the packet. "That's unimportant in itself; but the mess left in the wake of that fiasco has left me in a delicate position! At the Brotherhood's request, I've pushed this inquiry into K'Marran butchery against all opposition, and now that we have an opportunity to force a vote for an official investigation, I am left to howl at the moon with no support whatsoever from their precious Baarama!" The disgusted ambassador threw his portly body into his seat, glowering at his reports.

"Have you decided what you will do?"

"Eh?" He looked up to see the *serehn* studying him intently from across the room. "Why, I imagine I'll get the Panduran delegation to aid in persuading Atleki and Copra, but, frankly, without the Arbiter's presence—"

"Actually... I was referring to the cub."

A chill swallowed Retuf whole. "What about the cub?"

Thalyn stood and stretched, his old bones cracking loudly in the quiet of the room. "It has been three days since you learned Ryla was pregnant; in that time, you have not once come to see her. Not to Recognize the cub, not to see if Ryla is well... not to say hello." The old Kurlanar's soft eyes pierced into the ambassador's with an intensity that bore directly into his brain. "There is some concern that you... might not want the child."

A sudden fear stabbed Retuf in the gut. Did the priest suspect something? Had he given himself away in some manner? Worse, could Thalyn have *divined* his intentions? The *M'nsai* were masters of magic; they knew ways of obtaining information from the unseen world. He had foolishly neglected to take the old *serehn* into consideration while making his plans, and now he needed to take extra care while in Thalyn's presence.

"Nonsense!" He snorted and dismissed the suggestion with a barking laugh. "Not want the child? Our firstborn?" He spoke in his most sincere voice. *O, let him believe me!* "No, I have simply been busy with a great many concerns over the past few days, and I thought that Ryla could stand to use the time to recover her health. When she is stronger, I will give Recognition."

"She has been recovering quite well since her collapse," the old *serehn* conceded thoughtfully. "She is much brighter and happier than she has been in months. You may be wiser than I am in what she needs at present. Still, I cannot help but wonder if your presence at her bedside might not speed her recovery further..."

There was a shout outside the door to the study, causing both Kurlanar to start suddenly. Sounds of a scuffle could be heard. The shouting became louder; someone called his name. Then another voice called for silence. Retuf crossed the room and threw open the office door. "What is happening?" he demanded, before freezing with fear, staring into the eyes of the exile, Raggas.

The healer was held by two burly Kurlanar guards, who growled warningly at their captive, their *prochuks* at the ready. One guard, upon seeing the ambassador emerge, dipped his ears deferentially and nodded towards his prisoner. "We spotted him sneaking in through the hedges, *Cafkurra*; he gave us a chase through the grounds before we could catch him. He was determined to get into the embassy."

"Please!" the exile whined pleadingly to the ambassador. "I... I must speak with you urgently! Alone!" he added, glancing nervously at Thalyn.

"Be quiet!" growled the second guard. "Shall we turn him over to the City guard, *Cafkurra*?"

Retuf glared at the exile, barely concealing his fury. "No! I will speak with him in private! Let him go!" He indicated the open study to Raggas, who gratefully slunk inside, not daring to look any of the others in the eye. The first guard watched distrustfully as the healer entered. "Sir, is this wise? I do not trust this *pholarn* alone with you!" *Pholarn*. Outsider. Such was the status of an exile. Retuf nodded reassuringly to his guards. "I will be fine, I think. But stay nearby in case I have need of you!" Both nodded and took their positions just outside the study door.

Thalyn stood in the hallway, thoughtfully scratching his chin. Before Retuf could speak to him, the priest turned to walk back to the staircase. "I suppose I shall look in on Ryla and see how she is faring," he announced in a quiet voice. There was no criticism or reproof in the statement, but Retuf knew it was there all the same.

As soon as the door was sealed, and he could no longer hear the presence of his guards, Retuf turned to Raggas. "Speak!" he growled, huffing back behind his desk.

"I have come to beg you to return the drugs, and to not do this terrible thing." The exile spoke softly and deferentially, but stood openly defiant. Retuf was becoming increasingly irritated by the healer's constant posture of challenge.

"You are no longer concerned with this matter!" growled Retuf, knowing full well that he was lying even as the words flew from him; he intended to frame the healer if necessary, didn't he? That would involve him of a certainty.

"I *am* involved," replied Raggas, unaware that he was echoing the ambassador's thoughts. "By knowingly giving you a weapon, I assist you in your act of murder, if I don't act to prevent you."

"You overstep your bounds!" Retuf was enraged. "How dare you presume—!"

"Your rank means nothing; my lack of it is also meaningless." The exile spoke quietly. "This is a matter of Law, to which we are both subject; even I, a lowly exile."

The sincerity in Raggas' voice shook Retuf. "What do you mean?" he demanded.

"Before my exile, I was both a teacher and a healer in the Kurene, and I performed both jobs with joy and pride. I knew of and taught to the cubs the Laws of the land, and I believed then in their sanctity and power. As I do now." Raggas shifted uncomfortably. "Did Cherikk tell you my story? How I allowed a cub to die?"

"I knew of it."

"I was in charge of a small pack of cubs who had been entrusted to me for learning simple hygiene and speaking lessons. They were young, barely able to walk, having only recently popped their hands. They were a chore, but a joyful one. Always curious, always wandering away while I attempted to teach them some lesson." Sadness permeated the healer's voice. His eyes glazed over as his memories overcame him, but he continued his story.

"One day, one of the cubs wandered away while my back was turned, while I was demonstrating proper speech to another cub. Within moments, I immediately noticed the absence of the cub. It was only a few minutes! But it was already too late. He had found his way into my surgery, and had been playing with the drug vials upon the shelves, thinking he had found some new sweet to drink. I found him, poisoned. I tried everything I could, but the drug was swift and there was no antidote.

"I was careless. On any other day, I would have had that door locked to prevent just such an occurrence; that day, I neglected to do so. The vials should have been placed upon a high shelf; but they were not. I should never have taken my eyes off of any of them; my attention could not be everywhere, but it *should* have been. I was careless, and a cub died because of my carelessness.

"The First Law is *Mercy to the Cubs*; the penalty for the death of a cub is death. But because I was repentant, and it was clear that I had not intentionally caused the death, I was sentenced to exile rather than execution."

Raggas looked up from his reminiscing to stare directly into Retuf's eyes. "I thought the Law to be just, and I did not contest it. I willingly accepted my sentence, hard as it might be. And it has been hard." He turned to the window and gazed out into the chill winter night. "I hear the call of the Kurene, and it boils within my blood: *come home*, it sings, *and shelter in the breasts of my forests and suckle at the teats of my mountains.* But I cannot return, no matter how intense the ache. I also hear the dying coughs of that cub as he writhed on my surgery floor, afraid and never understanding what was happening to him, that he was dying... and that there was nothing I could do to save him."

Raggas broke from his trance and looked again to the silent Retuf. "Neither you nor I are above the Law, *Cafkurra*. It is the Law that unites the Kurlanar, and gives us our strength as a people. It is linked to our hearts, even as the Kurene is... even as the Kurama is."

"You are so fond of the Law," rumbled Retuf, "that you seem to neglect the Second Law: *Each Den unto Its Own!* What happens within my family or Clan is none of your affair, exile or no!"

"The Second Law is overshadowed by the First. But even if it weren't... I have my conscience and the Kurama to consider. Do you know what hold Cherikk has on me? What bargain I have made with that *pholarn screck*?"

Retuf said nothing, his mane bristling; but his curiosity was evident.

"I have no *kenta*. It was taken from me when I was exiled, by the *praka*[5] who escorted me to the Pedesh borders. They told me I was no longer worthy of it. A cub killer is forgiven nothing, allowed less," he said bitterly.

Retuf shivered and raised his hand to his own medallion. A *kenta* was gifted to a Kurlanar upon his coming-of-age, as a sign of his maturity, and a means of spiritual ascension. Without it, he was doomed to climb no further, and if he should die, his spirit would wander forever unfulfilled.

"Cherikk had promised to acquire a replacement for me, a new *kenta*—I made certain to specify that it be new!—in return for my services. In fact, he is to give it to me once this business has been accomplished. You can see, then, that I have a greater deal to gain by your actions than you do!"

"Then why..."

"Because she's pregnant!" Raggas shouted suddenly, throwing himself against the desk and leaning forward to snarl in Retuf's face. The startled ambassador jumped back in alarm. "The gossip has finally reached me, *Cafkurra*: your mate is going to have a cub! If killing her is heinous, killing the innocent unborn is monstrous! I will not take part—I will not allow you to kill them!"

Raggas leaped upon the desk, glaring down at the now frightened Retuf; the healer's eyes were mad, and his lips curled back to display his broken and yellowed teeth, no less menacing for their sad appearance. "If I knowingly allow you to commit murder, then I would indeed be guilty of breaking the Laws! I really would be a cub-killer! And I would no longer be worthy of a *kenta*! Perhaps... perhaps now I will finally redeem myself!"

Snarling, the healer hurled himself at the ambassador. Retuf twisted just enough so that the snapping jaws barely missed his throat. The two fell over the chair and hit the floor with a resounding crash. Retuf immediately swung about and went for Raggas' throat. The two snarled and howled, snapped and bit, clawed and punched, rolling about the floor, filling the air with fur and bits of cloth. Blood dappled the floor in an erratic pattern wherever they passed.

Just as Retuf finally achieved an advantage and was about to press it by tearing out the healer's jugular, he was suddenly stunned by a flare within his brain. When he regained his senses, he was resting upon his chair, a concerned Thalyn hovering over him. "Are you all right?" que-

[5] Kurlanar military/law officials.

ried the *Serehn* worriedly. "I had to stun you both, but wasn't sure how well you would absorb the *mana*..."

Retuf sat up, brushing past the *M'nsai*. The two guards were standing over the slowly recovering Raggas, who weaved drunkenly between them. Blood oozed from a half-dozen gashes, and there was a new tear in his right ear. The guards kept him on his knees by prodding him with their long *prochuks*. Retuf felt a brief, wild exultation, knowing he had won their fight before Thalyn intervened, but quickly restrained himself before signaling to the guards. They hauled the exile to his feet and dragged him to the ambassador.

Retuf leaned forward to growl in Raggas' face; the healer, dazed and beaten, cringed and displayed total submission. "Go back to the *pholarn*, exile!" Retuf snarled. "Never return to the embassy grounds again! Even this small piece of the Kurene is forbidden you! If ever you return, your sentence will be commuted to immediate execution! Do you understand me?"

Raggas raised his ears and forced a low whine. Retuf shot a glance at the two guards who nodded their understanding of the order. Satisfied, he turned away and returned to his chair, becoming aware for the first time of his own wounds received during the brief scuffle. Thalyn, silent throughout the ordeal, motioned to Myrry to bring some bandages and salve.

As the guards led the beaten Raggas away, he stopped and turned back to face Retuf again. Retuf's head snapped up to meet the exile's gaze; there was a deep sadness and genuine pity in the healer's eyes. He let out a weary sigh. *"Speak your Voice when Silence reigns,"* he murmured in an almost inaudible voice. Then, with a meaningful look, *"'Ware the Evil that hides in Good."*

The guards shoved Raggas out the door. Retuf bristled and growled in his throat. Thalyn, unwrapping strips of bandage from a roll, cocked his head at the ambassador. "What," he inquired gently, "was that all about, then?"

Retuf said nothing. Glaring at the *serehn*, he thrust his arm out to be bandaged.

🐾 ⌒ 🐾

Retuf waited until a few hours before dawn, during the sleep time when most of the Kurlanar staff had retired and the nocturnal domestics took care to perform their chores away from the sleeping chambers. He crept cautiously into his mate's den, taking care to make no sound that would alert anyone to his presence. He took pains to close the door silently behind him, and he made sure to step only on the carpeted areas so that his toenails would not click upon the hardwood floor. Even his breathing was quiet and deliberate, not an easy chore for one of his stoutness. For all that, not even a cat could have been more stealthy than he.

Up around the side of the wide, circular bed he crept, the hypodermic in hand, gliding closer to the sleeping Ryla. He knelt next to her and examined her still figure in the dim moonlight that seeped in from outside. Her breathing was quiet and regular, and her appearance was that of a fur who had attained a level of absolute peace with the world. She was, Retuf noted, much happier looking in sleep than she had been awake for the past several years.

He held up the hypodermic to examine the quantity of fluid within its glass chamber. The empty clearness of the drug belied its deathly charm. Raggas had instructed him that it was generally used to stimulate an injured fur when there were signs of heart attack; a stronger dose would over-stimulate, causing the heart to fail prematurely. He would need to inject it directly into an artery—and the healer had shown him how to find the proper artery to inject. If he did it carefully, no one would find the needle mark unless they were specifically searching for it, and there would be no cause to suspect foul play. The death would be accepted as a result of her long stress-induced illness.

Retuf bent over the sleeping Ryla and rolled her gently onto her back. She murmured a sleepy protest and fell silent again, settling once more into a soundless slumber. He brushed apart the mane covering her throat, exposing an area large enough for him to inject the needle. He prepared the instrument and pressed it against her throat. And he hesitated.

He stared down at her, a puzzled ear twitching nervously. Something was amiss with her appearance. What was it? He remained motionless for several heartbeats, struggling to fathom the subtle wrongness of his mate's presence. Then it struck him. She was helpless. Ryla now lay supine, back arched and arms tossed carelessly to either side; her face was calm and passive, eyes closed and ears drooping listlessly. She neither knew nor cared what was happening; she couldn't. She lay totally exposed to the world, unable to prevent even the slightest indignity to her person, let alone any injury or atrocity. Helpless.

The first worms of anxiety tunneled through Retuf's gut. He had never seen Ryla helpless before. It wasn't Ryla's way to be helpless. She had always been the bold one in their youth; no one could approach her unawares or touch her without approval. Even during the years of her homesickness, whenever they needed to medicate her when she became overwrought, it was difficult to get past her defenses.

Except him.

Because she trusted him.

The Kurlanar's hand trembled ever so slightly. Ryla Yss was now helpless, totally vulnerable to the entire world, with only her mate to watch over her—and he came to her in the night with her death in his hand.

His heart was pounding in his ears. He was wasting time! He needed to finish his task quickly and leave, to return to his own den where he would wait to be called for, to be informed of his mate's death. He raised the needle again, but he was trembling so hard that he could not hold the needle steady enough. He accidentally brushed against her head with his hand, and her mane fell back into place, covering the bare patch. Cursing to himself, he reached up to brush the mane back again.

His fingers instead brushed against her muzzle, and he started at the unexpected contact. He looked over at the peacefully sleeping face, and, to his astonishment, realized that even after all these years she was still beautiful.

The needle fell from his shaking hand onto the bed. He quickly snatched it back up again, but was unable to hold it properly. The trembling had become a spasm, and his hands shook violently. He tried furiously for several minutes to steady his nerves, but the shaking only became worse. At last, he uttered a despairing, frustrated whimper, and stormed from the room, leaving his sleeping mate undisturbed.

He rushed down the hallways to his study, no longer mindful of whether or not he was heard by the household. The perfect opportunity— his *only* opportunity—to be rid of Ryla's wretched clinging, and he had *failed*. There would never be a chance such as this! What had happened to him? How could he have fallen apart at such a crucial moment?

He burst furiously into his study, and stopped short in amazement. There in the center of the room was the exile, Raggas, waiting anxiously. He wore bandages over the wounds Retuf had given him, and he cringed slightly at the ambassador's entrance. But he quickly recovered and steeled himself, forcing his ears erect and his tail into a neutral position.

Retuf was too furious to wonder how he had slipped past the guards. He glared at the exile with all of the loathing in his soul. He hurled the hypodermic at the healer's feet. Raggas leapt backwards with a surprised yelp, stared at the hypo, then back to Retuf with puzzlement.

"I couldn't do it!" snarled the ambassador, barely keeping his fury in rein. "I couldn't kill her!" He continued glaring across the room for several moments, and then swept towards the window, brushing brusquely past the bewildered Raggas. "Take it and go!" he gritted through clenched teeth, and turned his back on the healer, gazing out into the snowy world of City's streets. He continued to growl to himself in bitter frustration until he finally heard Raggas' footsteps pass through the doorway and fade into the night.

Abruptly he began to cry, and he fell exhaustedly to his haunches, weeping in loud, gasping sobs and drawn out howls, as all the frustrations of ten long years came out in a deluge of grief and self-pity.

When he had finally exhausted himself, he sat forlornly upon the floor, head in hands, too dazed to think and too weary to care. It was only that he realized that he was not alone.

He turned to slowly to face the patiently waiting *Serehn*. Thalyn had been sitting nearby on the floor, his aged face looking more haggard than ever. The priest reached out to grasp Retuf gently by the shoulder.

"I really think it is time we had a talk," the kindly voice consoled him.

Retuf said nothing, staring sullenly back at Thalyn. He looked away towards the window again.

"You let the exile back in, didn't you?"

"He claimed there was unfinished business between you two. I was curious."

"How long have you been sitting there?"

Thalyn ignored the question. "I have been aware, ever since I began my appointment here two years ago, of the tensions between you and Ryla. I have known of her homesickness, and indeed I sympathize with her greatly, since I have also dreamed of the Kurene of late. It is a heartless siren.

"I have also been aware of your tireless dedication to your post, and your conscientiousness to your duties. You have truly excelled in all that you have done here, for yourself, and for the Kurene. You have harvested honors beyond counting for your clan." Thalyn paused. "Why do you stay?"

"I was in love."

"Not with your mate, you mean."

"No." Retuf sighed and rubbed at his eye. "No, I was in love with City in a way that is hard to explain. There is... a magic to City. It breathes a life of its own, and it sings to me in the racket of its bawling traffic and squabble. It cheers me with its exuberance, amuses me with its rowdiness, caresses me with its intrigue, and excites me with its dangers.

"In the course of my duties, I have found an affinity for the otterplay and squirrel-barter of the Congress; there is more challenge here, in dealing with all of the different furs, than I could ever find in all of the *Cafkurgar* back home. I... I just cannot feel the Kurene in my own heart, as you others do; I cannot imagine a world where a squirrel tree cannot be found at market, or where otters are not raising havoc on a radio, or where the dolphins don't periodically 'swim' into town from the sea!

"Ryla didn't understand that. All she wanted was to go back," he added bitterly.

"I doubt that was *all* she ever wanted," remonstrated the *Serehn*. "If it were, she could have left at any time. You were both childless; she could have annulled your bond at any moment if she so desired. That she didn't should tell you something."

"But now she *will* have a child, and it will no longer matter."

"Do you know why she has asked for you to give Recognition?" The very quiet of the priest's voice stirred a new fear in Retuf's heart, an unsettling he could not identify. The old Kurlanar locked gazes with him, soft grey eyes holding him in place. "Do you know what she would do if you do not accept the child?"

"No," he whispered, his voice as small as a cub's.

"Ryla knows of your feelings for City, for your life and career here. She has always tried to please you in regards to it, and support you, before the homesickness ate her heart." Thalyn cleared his throat and looked away. "She truly believed that you would have been happy with a child..."

"No..." The fear began to swell like a summer storm.

"But if you weren't... if you denied it Recognition..."

"No...!" Retuf crushed his ears flat with his fists, but the horror rushed at him.

"She intended to kill herself... and the cub. She thought this would be the honorable way to release you from your bond, and allow you to find your happiness."

"*No!*" Retuf bounded to his feet, horrified. Ryla kill herself?

Thalyn nodded somberly. "She would never have been happy here, or in the Kurene, without you—despite its claws in our souls." The old gray eyes looked up at him again, burning with a luminosity of softness. "She loves you."

🦋 ∞ 🦋

Retuf returned to Ryla's den, his silent steps far less sinister than before. He stood by her bed and gazed down upon her. There, as he had earlier, he saw the glow of her beauty sculpted gently in the reflected light from the new-fallen snow outdoors, firmed but unstrained by the years of her inner torments. The soft taper of her muzzle, the luxuriousness of her fine, ebon mane, now lightly sprinkled with silver... how had he come to forget the loveliness of her face? He shook his head sadly in self-reproach.

For him! She had remained with him, unwilling to return to their home in the Kurene, for his sake, to aid him with his duties, to be with him—to be a part of him. Until the agony of the homesickness overcame her in the end, and he turned his back upon her. And when she could ignore it no longer and broke down, begging him to return with her, he ignored her and continued with his own plans, heeding her less and less. And still she would not desert him.

He sat next to her upon the bed. *Oh, Ryla!* he wept silently. *Truer to love and den than I! I did not deserve your fidelity, and deserve it far less now.*

He took her hand and held it to his *kenta*, crushing both to his heart. Ryla stirred, awoken by the action, and turned to look at him. There was a moment's confusion in her eyes until she recognized him; a happy glow lit her eyes and she reached for him with her other hand. He took both and nuzzled them affectionately for a moment. Then, he reached out to lay a hand upon her belly, over the unborn cub. *My cub.* Our *cub.*

Solemnly, he looked into her eyes and spoke softly, unable to conceal the happiness and pride that he felt. "Ryla Yss, beloved mate and companion; from this day we are one, bound together by the love that unites us, and sealed forever by the child we have conceived. The mountains I have climbed, the rivers I have swum, the prey I have pursued—these shall be his, and all of the heart of the Kurene shall shed its blessing upon our child. Let our enemies look to their tails, for we are a Family!"

Tears welled in Ryla's eyes and she pulled him down to hug him tightly. His own eyes grew blurry with wetness. How could he have allowed himself to become apart from her? He returned the embrace, holding her tightly. From behind them came the gentle voice of the *serehn*. "You have been heard, Retuf Yss. Ryla is your chosen mate, and the child she bears is yours. It will be recorded in the annals of the Kurene that a new Family has joined the ranks of the Pack. May Wula's watchful eye guide you always!"

Retuf stroked Ryla's mane, nuzzling her, comforting her, sharing her happiness. "A promise, my love," he whispered to her. "We will go home, back to the lands of the Kurene."

Ryla broke the embrace to look into his eyes, astounded, not daring to believe. "Not all at once," he warned, flustering to explain. "There are arrangements to be made, appointments to be cleared, business to be completed... we must wait for a safe period for an ocean crossing... and we must wait until you... well, until you've had the cub..." He paused and looked into the eyes of the one being he knew he could never lie to. "A year, and we shall return; this is my promise to you."

"A year," she said emotionlessly. His ears fell in dismay; was that too long? Would she have a relapse if he made her wait that long?

"I... I think a year would be about right," she said, and her eyes lit up brighter than ever. "It will take that long, I think, for me to make all of the domestic arrangements." She hugged him again, and sobbed from relief and happiness.

Retuf sat there holding her. For a moment, an emptiness opened within him. What would he do without the intrigue of City to engage him? What could possibly take its place? Then he banished the thought from his mind; here, in his arms, was the truly irreplaceable thing in his life... and he had nearly thrown it away! Except for the conscience and actions of an exiled cub killer...

The ambassador remembered something. He broke from his embrace and turned to see the *Serehn* quietly taking his leave of the den. "*Serehn,*" he called. The old priest turned back with an inquisitive cock of his head. "Would you ask Myrry to send for a metalsmith? The finest that we can find in City!" He looked at Ryla, basking in her glow, then beyond her out the window to the faraway Greytowne, where Raggas the healer was returning to his life of exile and shame.

"I wish to have a *kenta* made."

There are two kinds of sins: the sins one remembers and passes along to the generations so that they will be wiser, and the sins one forgets because they are too much for the future to bear.
—Mrrach, First Speaker of the Drrt'noi

Darkness and rain; a cold, wet drizzle that seemed to be a permanent feature of the Misty Lands. Floch gathered her heavy ammeau-pelt cloak around her shoulders and looked backward along the track. The dark mountainsides behind her blended with the coming dusk, and the wind shuddered through the dark pines of the valley. The thick fur that covered her cloak was supposed to be waterproof, but it wasn't equal to the wind and rainstorms here on the high pass of the Tiefie Mountains. She would have to find shelter soon. The Kethturr might live comfortably here, with their thick white pelts and their horn-callused feet and hands, but she was a Drrt'noi; a lowlander, with no underhairs to her tawny pelt. She would be sick from the cold and rain if she didn't find shelter soon. She thumped the sharp iron heel of her walking staff into the soggy ground and half hauled herself up along the pass.

If Covian's directions had been accurate, she should be within a half day's walk of the Buitheon; the temple from which Skaleva took the enchanted sword. It was the deadliest weapon in the Southern Lands, and in the hands of the Champion of all the Drrt'noi, it was a reaping-machine that mowed down armies like the reapers of the Mesa Lands mowed down grass. She had watched from the message-runner's post atop a hill as her liege, Skaleva the Champion, drew the sword and charged the Hathi armies. It was like watching fire consume a grassland. He raged, unstoppable, until the reptilians turned and ran, trampling each other in their desperation to get away from the sword that howled and roared like a demon.

But the blood-drinking sword wasn't sated. What Skaleva had not known; indeed, what the priests had not known was that the thing would turn on friend after no foe was left. Skaleva followed the Hathi as far as he could and then turned and ran after his friends, sword roaring with blood-lust. Only a few of the Drrt'noi fell to the sword before Skaleva collapsed, exhausted. Floch ran up and knocked the sword away from his hand with her staff, and the thing wailed once and then fell silent.

Skaleva, panting, lifted his head briefly. "If I had known..." he whispered, and his eyes were tormented. "How many did I kill, Floch?"

She bowed her head, wanting to lie. "Sixty two. Ikuvi stopped it."

"Ikuvi? The coward?" Her liege's eyes were glazing over.

"Coward no longer. He fell on your sword and knocked it out of your hand." She gestured to the limp shape nearby. Skaleva closed his eyes and lay back limply.

Floch rose and signaled to his camp followers to set up a tent over her liege's inert body and to pile a cairn of rocks over Ikuvi and the sword. She sent a trainee scurrying to fetch the priests and Council. It was time for someone in authority to deal with the sword that Skaleva had stolen from the Buitheon temple. Wheeling, she left the burying and the politics to others. Skaleva's own mage sent a little imp with a message to the priests at Buitheon, offering to give the sword back.

But the priests at the Buitheon didn't seem overly concerned about the loss of the sword. Within days after the message went to the temple, a runner brought back a polite and amused reply which said that the sword belonged to the Drrt'noi now and was theirs to keep. It was of no interest to Buitheon. They did, however, have the sword's scabbard, which was bound with enchantments to make the metallic horror controllable.

The Councilors should have known that nothing good would come from dealing with demonic objects. There was a price for the scabbard, the Buitheon priests said, and named a cost that made the listeners reel. They had no use for gold or treasure, but they did need certain body parts and amulets from the corpse-mound left by the demonic sword—body parts and amulets from both friend and foe of the Drrt'noi. The council, to Floch's horror, agreed to the price.

Because her liege had brought the evil weapon into the land of the Drrt'noi, it fell to Floch, his most senior messenger, to deliver the unwholesome package to the priests at Buitheon. She'd carried heavy packages for Skaleva along the message roads; the weight of the blood price was not that hard to carry. But the repulsive nature of the bundle lay on her soul like a great rock. Floch hoped that the ritual baths and prayers at the end of her journey would be enough to clean the horror from her mind.

She blinked through water-misted eyelashes at the green and gray landscape ahead. A narrow column of pale stone rose toward the sky, pointing like an accusing finger at the rain clouds that hovered a mere hundred feet or so above her head. It was shelter; a ruined one at best, but if none of the beasts of the mountains used it as a lair, she was safe enough there for the night. The tiles had gone from the roof, but enough of the sturdy structure stood that she could find shelter in there.

Kalevi, whispered the old legends, but she ducked her head and marched up the grassy slope. No legend would stand between her and a dry place to sleep.

A quick look around showed that no path led to the door. Nothing was using this tower as a home. She scooped up a huge handful of pine needles in the hem of her soggy cloak and tucked some of the dryer looking branches in with them. Taking a deep breath, she stepped into the cool, dark interior. The world grayed and then focused, as her night vision took over, giving her a good look at the building.

It wasn't much inside, just a rough, leaf-strewn stone floor and a set of winding stairs that curved around a central core, leading up towards the sky. Arrow loops gaped blankly at ten-foot intervals along its moon-pale walls. She climbed as high as the first landing, and glanced out across the valley floor. Nothing moved there. She peered down to the bottom level of the tower where the shadows traced odd patterns in the darkness; shapes that looked like sigils. When she stared at them, using her night vision, they resolved into simple hollows and bumps in the stone. What lay on the floor was not a mage-pattern.

She wasn't superstitious, Floch told herself, but she was cautious. It was caution, she reminded herself, that made her decide to camp out on the first level of the tower instead of on the stone floor below. And the rising hair on the back of her neck was simply caused by her being cold and damp.

And there was nothing, nothing to fear at all from the darkness below her. And the wind was not whispering "Kalevi" out there in the long, lonely sweeps of the High Pass of the Misty Lands.

🐾 ◠ 🐾

She woke as the fire died, startled into wakefulness by something she could not name. The fire had burned into a soft pile of ash, spangled with bright coals. She slid out of the traveling cloak that served as her bed and stood where she could not be seen from the floor below. What awakened her? She opened her mouth and sniffed, tasting the strange tang of the mountain air. There was the cedary burn of the pines and the cold tang of the stones. The fur of her cloak smelled of her own body and over it all was the reek of the fire—and nothing else. Floch fanned her ears forward, listening.

Nothing. Fear was a metallic taste in her mouth. She was a trained Messenger, who had learned to wake quickly and quietly at the slightest movement. There was nothing here—and yet there was something that awakened her.

She put a few resinous twigs on the firecoals and teased the flames into light. She reached for her staff. Steel-tipped and rune-warded, it was a match for many things that a Messenger encountered, from bandits to wandering predators. She shifted it to her left hand and fished a resinous branch out of her firewood pile. She shoved it against the coals and closed her eyes as the branch flared. Lifting her improvised torch high, she leaned and looked down onto the first level of the stone tower.

A pinpoint of light blinked back up at her and then vanished, soundlessly. She gasped, fangs pulling over her lips in a silent hiss, fingers tensing and claws extending. And then the hair on her body lifted, as though by a magnet, bristling against the heavy cloth of her clothing. There had been no movement and no sound, yet she knew as surely as she knew her own name that something very large, heavy, and silent was standing just behind her right shoulder.

She wheeled, flinging her hand out in an almost instinctive swipe, her thick tail curling to counterbalance the awkward move. Nothing. Her arm passed through the air unhindered. There was nothing to be seen—nothing on the stairs above and nothing on the stairs below. Nothing shared the stone landing with her. Through the slit of the tower's loophole she could see the pinpoint lights of the stars winking beyond the trees.

She crouched and backed until the solid bulk of the tower's stone walls stopped her. "Who's here?"

The air rippled briefly, as though dancing in the desert heat. She edged away from the distortion, swinging her heavy staff in a slow arc.

"I am Floch. I travel at the command of my liege, Skaleva, and at command of the Council," she announced, feeling bolder with the iron tip of the staff held in front of her.

"Are you, and do you?" The voice came from just beyond her left shoulder, from the stone wall itself. She shied aside.

"Who are you? Are you Kalevi?"

"No. I am the Eater." There was more than physical hunger in that deep, soft voice. The fur on her arms rose.

"What do you eat?" She had to be careful how she phrased things. The sigils on her staff would tremble if someone were lying to her. She eyed the painted signs closely.

"I eat... words." The designs stayed straight and clear. The invisible being was telling the truth, though the answer was odd.

"Words? Written words on parchment? Books?"

"Stories." The designs on the staff never wavered. Perhaps it would be friendly if she fed it.

"Would you like to hear a story?"

"Oh yes." The sigh whispered around her like the wind. The runes wavered then, not enough to say that there was a lie, but enough to make her wary.

"What happens when the story is told?" She watched the staff.

"Oh, nothing. I listen." The runes flickered like firelight then.

"And what happens when you listen?"

Silence answered her.

She crouched down beside her fire and tossed a small handful of twigs on it. "I heard once of a man who loved riddles," she said, and stopped.

"Yessss?"

"But I daren't tell his story until I know what happens." She tossed another stick onto the fire. "If it causes something bad to happen, then I won't tell the story."

There was a long silence. "I am the Eater of Stories. I... eat the story," was the answer. "The words. They go inside me and the story is no more.

The people cannot tell it because it is as if it does not exist. They forget the story the moment someone finishes telling it to me."

"So if I tell you about my liege, then he will not exist?" She stared hard at the runes on her staff now.

"No. I am the Eater of Stories, not the Eater of Life. But the memory of his deeds and his life will be gone, both the good and the bad. The dead that he killed will still be dead, though no one will remember who killed them. The manuscript rolls that recorded the tales will all crumble to dust. The towns that were sacked and looted will still be in ruins. But none will know how it was done or why it was done." The runes stood straight and true.

"So if I tell you how my liege was disgraced when his sword turned against our people, the memory of that will be gone?"

"Yes. All record of it will be gone. But choose what you tell carefully, for in that tale of a bad time there may be good things that need to be passed along," the Eater of Stories answered.

"So others would not know that at the end, it was the coward named Ikuvi who threw down my liege and saved us all at the cost of his life if I tell you the tale of my liege's shame?"

"No." The voice was like a great sad bell, mourning the loss of something unexplainable.

"Are the things I'm telling you now—are they vanishing, right now?" Floch asked.

There was a long sigh. "No, to feed me you must begin it with the words, 'This is the beginning of the eating,' and end it with 'and this is the end of the eating.' If you don't say that, then the words are just words; shiftings of the air. They don't feed me, but they don't vanish."

"I will tell you a tale, but I must think on what to Say."

※ ∞ ※

In the end, she told the voice all the tired old jokes she could remember; the ones she had heard so often that she hated them. They were tattered and worn; stories that weren't really funny the first time she heard them—stories that grew more irritating the more she heard them. But the great invisible hulk beside her seemed to relish them, chuckling at them as if they were fresh and new. Encouraged, she stretched out the tales a bit, garnishing them with small details. When the bright glitter of the constellation called the Two Daughters sank below the mountain's crest, the voice called a halt to her stories.

"You fed me well," it rumbled softly, "now I will feed you with advice. I can smell the stink of the demon sword of the Buitheons around you, though you do not carry it. I know the reek of the blood price for the scabbard. One of your kind has made a treaty with the Buitheons to buy the scabbard of the demon sword."

"Yes." Floch glanced at the staff. The lines of the runes never wavered.

"What the priests don't tell is that the second time it is unsheathed, it grows thick tentacles that loop around the wrist of the one that carries it. Most think it is a magical glove; a sign that the demon sword provides a magical armor. The victim fights like the very demon-possessed until sundown, protected from harm by the glove and the sword. But when the sun's edge vanishes below the horizon, the tentacle glove wakes. Metallic vines grow from it; vines that bury themselves in the owner's flesh, stabbing and tearing, stripping skin from bone. The champion is flayed alive. This is the way that the sword feeds. It is a most obscene thing. Some brave soul always puts the sword in the sheath and brings the whole thing back to the priests and then the priests bring it to me to un-tell the story of what the sword has done."

"And so no one knows the real price," Floch whispered softly. "And the priests get paid whatever they want."

"They got tired of treasure long ago," the Eater commented.

"And that's why they asked for body parts and amulets as their price?"

"Gold is easy to find. Souls are not. They will stop at nothing," the Eater replied.

"I can—" she began.

"You can do nothing," the Eater answered softly. "If you die before you bring back the scabbard to free your liege from the demon sword, then the land itself will be ravaged. The sword will sing out to anyone near it, calling them to pick it up and begin the bloodshed. Any one will do—adult or child."

She nodded, numbed by a sudden weariness that fell over her like a blanket. A wind whispered around the spirals of the tower's stairwell. "Sleep, messenger of Skaleva the Champion. Nothing more will disturb you tonight." Floch's eyes closed suddenly and she slumped sideways, breathing evenly. Something large and invisible paused to feed a branch to the struggling fire and to tug the cloak over the sleeper before departing on almost-silent feet up the long steps to the top of the tower.

※ ⋙ ※

A week later, a messenger from the Hathi trotted across the meadow in front of the tower that guarded the High Pass, carrying a feathered pouch bound with gold cord and sealed with jade green wax. The Hathi had their fill of war. The Hathi wanted peace—but at their own terms. Their Sacred Messenger carried a letter to the priesthood of the Buitheon, promising the altar stone from the Tura temple and a gift of five hundred bodies in exchange for a weapon to defeat the Drrt'noi.

He paused when he saw the stone tower looming ahead of him. The door gaped unpleasantly at him like a hungry mouth and the mean little eyelike arrow slits stared down the swath of green meadow at him. He looked around carefully. There was a faint trail in the grass, showing where something or someone had run to the tower. Puffing out his breath in a long hiss, he stepped back into the shadows of the pines. If it was games that the watcher wanted, they would have to play the game according to the Sacred Messenger's rules.

Something moved at one of the tower loopholes; a mere glimpse of a golden-skinned figure. The Sacred Messenger blinked his second eyelids down over his large eyes and squinted, telescoping. The shape in the window had the distinctive blunt muzzle of a Drrt'noi.

Drrt'noi meant trouble. Drrt'noi meant treachery. The creature might have noticed him on the mountain behind; might be waiting with a trap. The Sacred Messenger faded back further into the pine forests. Let the Drrt'noi starve and watch. There was more than one way around the mountain and the Hathi were faster than any of the People of the Lands. Once out of range of any arrows, the Sacred Messenger could outrun any message carrier in all the world.

He unpacked his pen case and scribbled a quick note on a folded piece of parchment, showing the layout of the tower and the valley leading up to it. The Negotiator Generals would want to hear about this new deception. It might have occurred to the Drrt'noi to post an ambush on the trails leading to the temple of the Buitheon. He craned his neck back over his shoulder and began a quick sketch of the valley and the tower at its crest.

For a moment, the only thing he heard was the thin scratching of his pen on the parchment. The air grew suddenly quiet; like the silence that falls after the thunder of a carillon of bells, like the silence that anticipates the end of the world. He could hear the Drrt'noi's voice clearly now, across the distance between the pines and the tower.

"...and the Buitheon were powerful priests who ruled a temple set in the middle of the mountains; a place of magic and sorcery, where anything could be gotten at any price, even a demon sword that could destroy armies."

The Hathi looked up, unaware that the parchment in his hands was crumbling into dust, unaware of the crumpling of the fabric of reality. New facts collapsed into the vacuum left by the vanished information.

The Sacred Messenger sighed once as birdsong started up, loud and cheerful. It was a long way to the town of the Kethturr; across the flat saddle of the mountain pass and beyond the village of the strange little people called the Buitheon, who lived at the foot of some splendid temple. The Drrt'noi were killing Hathi people and stealing Hathi land, and his people needed a weapon to stop the gold-furred monsters.

It was a pity that there was no help closer than the land of the Kethturr, thirty thousand paces and more beyond the village of the Buitheon.

He gulped a handful of berries and began trotting up the long slope past the old stone tower that guarded the flanks of the pass.

The long column of goats wove down through the high pass. Weary and beaten, their march was a retreat. Behind them, the steppes were lost to them. The wolves had won, and now the only goats remaining were behind fences. They would be raised for meat, made into dull, docile slaves. There would be no teaching of language, no music, no art. There would only be birth, fattening, breeding, and early death.

The soldiers among the goats carried dulled weapons and wore dented armor, while their females and their young labored under packs containing the little that they had salvaged. There was no pursuit: the wolves were busy consolidating their victory. The straggling away of a last, lost tribe of goats was of little concern to them.

Down the trail, threading the massive, wind-scoured boulders, the goats sought their way. Below them, a new land came and went, hidden by swift clouds and fog until a rare gap opened to reveal green hills and valleys. There was a beauty to the new land, but none of the goats was able to take it in, for their minds were filled with the bitterness of their defeat.

"Belike the land will be as full of wolves as the land we leave behind," complained one.

"Wolves, yes, or worse. Great cats with patterns painted on their flanks. Or snakes or eels or things with scales."

"Word is spoken of birds, like eagles, great enough to catch us up, two at a time, one in each claw, and bear us away to the feeding."

"I have heard the wolves eat us still living, cutting away part and coming back for more the next day."

"Hist! Is there pursuit?"

A pause, a fearful wait, then the column went on again. The goats, filled with their despair, wandered toward the fair valley. There, they found something more startling than all of their fears could ever prepare them for.

They found no one.

The vales were thick with uncropped grass, and icy snow-melt bubbled down rills and freshets unhindered by dam or weir. No roads cut across the riverside plains. No houses, no huts, no towers, no smithies, no walls, and no sign of the long fences that the wolves crafted to hem the goats in their movements.

"Is this land now ours?" the goats asked, unable to believe that any good could come at the end of so ill a journey. But there was none to gainsay them.

They spread out, then, each family taking a valley, each soldier claiming a mate. The winter was old and spring drew near, and the fodder and the land were rich.

"Wait!" cried ancient Andus, mightiest of the warriors. Many would not wait, but he met them one by one and cracked sense into their heads. He met with the soldiers and brought them around, re-instilling in them the discipline they had lost.

"This land is ours, and each valley belongs to one of you. Each of you may claim a wife. Each of you shall be the founder of a clan, and your line shall grow to glory. But here, where the trail leads from the mountains, we shall raise up a castle. This shall be our defense: it shall be raised high, with walls and towers and weapons. It shall be deep and secure, and we shall fill it with provisions, which always shall be kept fresh, replaced as needed, to withstand siege. It shall be the seat of power, from which all the upper valley is commanded. I shall abide here, and my sons, yet no other land shall I take, and my line shall not be kings over you, but defenders. You shall send me laborers and soldiers."

"Why should we do this that you have said?" asked the soldiers.

"The wolves are there!" pointed Andus. After a moment, he added, "And I am here. Is there any who will stand against me and say otherwise?"

Nartho, a soldier, came forward to challenge him.

"We are free of the wolves now. We can graze here. And if the wolves come, we can go south once more. We cannot fight them; you've seen what happens when we try!"

"You cannot fight them... but now you must fight me."

Andus bent his head and charged. Nartho met him, and the air cracked with the force of their meeting. Nartho was young and Andus old; Nartho was full of his heat and fury, but Andus was cold and watchful. Now it was Nartho's turn to charge. He ran at Andus. Andus wove aside and butted him in the shoulder, spilling him in a tumble upon the rocks. Now Andus stamped about poor Nartho, kicking dirt upon him and jabbing bloodlessly into the ground at Nartho's side with his bronze spear. Nartho cried mercy and fell away, creeping on knees and elbows.

Andus was not challenged again.

"We are weary. We are defeated," the soldiers complained.

Andus nodded solemnly. "I am weary also, but I am not defeated. In two years, the labor will begin. Then you will send me your sons to be stonecutters and spearmen."

When the valley was apportioned, Nartho's clan was derided and sent to a high, reclusive vale at the top of a narrow watercourse.

Many years later, the wolves came.

🐾 ◌ 🐾

Andus IV, Castellan of the New Valley, took in the view over the parapet of his private balcony. Straight below, the walls dropped nearly a hundred feet to the crags and scree: black, broken, rotten rock, treacherous and all but unclimbable. The slope dipped further, until it bottomed out in a gulley, there to reverse and climb steeply once more. There, at a level with the foot of the wall, the Castle Road clung to the far slope.

The castle was master of the road: far beneath Andus' hooves, a long rank of arrow-slits was built into the wall. At a word, a poisonous hail of fire could be unleashed from fixed-bows, weapons much like ordinary bows but hinged and mounted. Andus was well familiar with them; he was familiar with every inch of the castle, every weapon, every storeroom, every bolt and hasp and hinge of every door. The fixed-bows were equipped with a peg-and-hole aiming system, carefully sighted in against marks chiseled into the rocky bank above the road.

Andus looked down, envisioning the slaughter that those bows would make of any enemy who dared to travel the road, seeking to mass against the gates. The castle had many defenses, but none was as fearsome as the killing zone at the castle's fore.

He raised his eyes, following the ridges and folds of the rocky hills, till he came to the bare crags at the top. There, the cold sawtooth rim was blasted free of snow, no matter what the season, by the unending winds funneling up from the valley.

Here and there, giving a hint of color to the sere mountains, the wolves had raised blood-red banners. Wolfen scouts crouched, themselves invisible, grey against grey, fur against stone. They waited, and they watched.

Andus went inside. A short passage led to his quarters, dull and bare, the lodgings of a soldier. There was wealth within the castle—what better place for the clans of the valley to cache their treasuries? But Andus was not a king, and knew he never would be one. The clans would never, as long as he lived, have to come to beg for the return of what was rightfully theirs.

He looked about, seeing memories. Here he had taken his brides; here he had raised his sons and daughters. Here he had nursed his wounds, and here he had waited through the night while his eldest son teetered on the edge of life and death, finally succumbing to his death-wound.

An inner voice recalled him to his duty. He went out into a wider hall, and thence to the central chamber where the fathers of the clans had gathered to confer.

"You are unseemly late, my Lord," a deep, belling voice greeted him as he came in. It was Ulan Nerce, Nerce IV, Lord of Clan Nerce. No one was more close to Andus; no one was more critical.

Andus swiveled his gaze about the room. The clans were all represented. From Nerce, through Cadal and Pernal and Flence, through Donat and Harn and Cielce, down to lowly clan Nartho, represented by the fifth Lord Nartho. The laws of the valley prohibited the attainting of blood, and the sins of the father were not laid upon the head of the son, yet the clan of Nartho was the exception. No one of Nartho was trusted; no one of Nartho was beloved.

"I have no excuse to offer for my late arrival." Andus met the challenging gaze of his oldest friend. "Do you, then, dear Nerce, choose to challenge me? This fine castle can be yours—yours to defend, yours to command—if you only defeat me in single combat. Come, then: show me your horns, else show me your ribs."

Nerce, nettled by Andus' bellicosity, nevertheless squared himself about and displayed his flanks toward Andus. It was an inviting target, and Andus felt the ancient temptation. His head dropped a fraction, but that only, and then he was once more in control of himself.

"Steady, Nerce, old friend. Come back to me. Come." Andus cried a command, and servitors came bearing foodstuffs: cakes pressed of sweet, new grass; flower-scented honey-and-barley comfits; fermented pastes of wheat that produced euphoria and courage, but which, in excess, produced vertigo and foolishness; and other good fodder. But Andus, in his humility, gave the credit for the donation where it belonged.

"This is from Clan Cadal; this is from Clan Cierce. Clan Pernal brings us this. I give thanks for these gifts, and vow the protection of this castle, Castle Andus, in return."

The Lords and Lordlings nodded, satisfied at the formal recognition of the mutual role of protector and protected. Without the provisions they donated, the castle could never withstand a siege; without the protection of the castle's walls, their rich farmlands would fall prey to wolfen pillage.

"This gathering," Andus spoke gravely, "is necessary. The wolves amass their forces. They will soon seek to ravage our valley. Once before, we were defeated by them. A land where once we roamed is now barren to us. The wolves pen our kind, breeding them in cages, feeding upon them as we feed upon grass. The war can never end. Peace can never come upon us. While wolves live, we must war."

"While wolves live, we must fear." It was Nartho, of Clan Nartho, who spoke the unwelcome truth.

"Yes," Andus said, with grave dignity. "We must fear."

"Cielce pledges fifteen warriors."

"Flence pledges fifteen warriors."

"Harn pledges twenty warriors and five hundredweight of dry provisions."

The others chimed in, one by one, until only Nartho remained to be heard from. The silence stretched out, until every head, every eye, every ear was fixed on Lord Nartho.

But Lord Nartho waited, as if the proceedings were not of his concern.

It fell to Andus to force the confrontation.

"Lord Nartho, what do you pledge?"

Nartho stood forward. "I have grievances to present. Until these are resolved, I cannot fix a pledge."

"Name the grievances."

"Harn has occupied certain of my meadows. Cielce has not fulfilled an obligation of wheat. In addition, Cielce has taken away six daughters of Nartho, but there has been no bride-price paid. There are other grievances, but these are the most serious."

Andus shook his head sadly. "Lord Nartho, do you not understand our situation? We are to be enslaved. We are to be eaten."

"I understand all too well. My neighbors among the clans have come to resemble the wolves."

There was a deep gasp from the assembled Lords. That was a blasphemy that was, until this day, unspeakable. The other Lords, great as well as small, jumped up and glared, some grasping at their belts as if to draw weapons. Half a dozen challenges were cried in a single breath.

Nartho seated himself, eyeing his neighbors, his lips twisted in a half-smile of gratification. "You behave like wolves; can that be denied?"

Lord Cielce turned as if to leave the conference. In another moment, all might have been gone save only Andus and Nartho. Andus took the moment the instant before it was lost.

"Halt! You may not leave without my bidding! Is this a conference, or a spring rutting? Do you withdraw, and go to make droppings on the fields and roads, without having agreed or dissented? Is there foam upon your lips and blood on your legs? Is Nartho right? Are we, all of us, more like wolves?"

"You may not speak so, Lord Andus!" bellowed Lord Cielce.

"No! I may not! And you may not leave! Shall we know this as the conference of broken rules?"

"Eject him, or I will not stay."

"Are his grievances justified, or are they not?"

"They are old complaints, satisfied years ago. The wheat was paid, and his daughters left his lands of their own accord. As who would not? They were tired, like as not, of being rutted by their brothers and uncles!"

Nartho's eyes narrowed, but he showed himself their master in self-possession. He waited a time before he trusted himself to answer, and when he did, his words were soft. "There was no bride-price paid, Lord Cielce. That is my grievance."

"And the wheat?" Andus asked.

"It never was given to me. Perhaps it, too, left my land of its own accord."

There was no amusement at this jape; the tensions about the cold stone table were taut as bowstrings, and there was still a danger of violence and stampede.

Andus spoke again. "Lord Harn. The meadows?"

"They were forfeit to my sire, fourteen years ago, in a debt which Nartho defaulted. They were mine to occupy."

"Is there record? I know of no such default."

"It was not a judgement brought to your sire, the third Lord Andus, but a judgement made independently."

"That is your right. I am not your king. I am only your defender." Andus spoke reasonably. "I do not settle disputes unless they are brought to me with the agreement of all concerned." He raised his voice. "Shall that be the case today? Do Nartho, Cielce, and Harn agree to bring me these grievances to be settled?"

"Yes," said Nartho, but "No," said Cielce and Harn.

"Then there is nothing I can do. Lord Nartho, do you pledge a force to help in the defense of the castle?"

Nartho stood and looked about himself, taking in the faces, one by one, of the other Lords. "Yes, Lord Andus. I pledge the full fighting strength of Clan Nartho: seventy and nine warriors, though some are old and some very young, each with a spear and a knife. I pledge further fifty hundredweight of dry fodder... less a measure of wheat which has left my granaries of its own accord."

"Who will guard your lands?" murmured Lord Donat.

"Harn, I think, will guard my lands," responded Nartho. He stood and faced Andus. "Is my pledge acceptable?"

"It is."

"Then the old dispute between the first Lord Andus and the first Lord Nartho is resolved. Defense of the castle is defense of us all, and Nartho will participate whole-heartedly. And now, as a kindness to those who would have me ejected, I will beg this conference's permission to return to my lands. I have a muster to call."

In the silence following this, a distant howling wafted from the crags: wolfen scouts signaling to one another. It was a sound from nightmare, lofty and lonely, faint with distance yet far-carrying. It could have been ten miles away, or at the bottom of the pass where the road crossed to the castle.

No one spoke, but the will of the conference was clear. Nartho bowed and departed.

🐾 👁 🐾

The last of the pledges had not arrived when the storm broke. The wolves sallied from the pass on a moonless night. Shadows within shadows, silent as the clouds that dappled the stars, they came slinking. One moment, the ground was clear; the next, it was alive with movement.

A cry, a shout, the bleating of horns and whistles and the desperate clanking of the bells. Fires leapt up in cressets and lanterns. The whipping sound of bowshots was heard from the walls, along with the ominous hiss of arrows seeking upward from the enemy without.

Andus hurried into his armor, buckling the wood-and-copper pieces on with sleep-thickened fingers, roaring for more torchmen, more bowmen. He shook away the last of the lethargy of sleep and hastened out into the night. A cold wind scurried from the mountains, tossing pennons and cloaks this way and that and making the firelight to jump. Far below, the carpet of wolves looked greater than it was, the wolves and their shadows shifting about in the faint light from the high torches.

"Lord Andus. I yield to you the command of the walls." It was Nartho, standing amid a detail of his relatives.

"Stand to them, then," Andus directed. "Make what light you can. Observe, and direct the fire from below. Was it you who gave the first cry of alarm?"

At that, Nartho hesitated, as if uncertain what answer might serve himself best. The guilty pause was, in itself, an answer: Nartho looked away to the battlements. "No. We were not the first to perceive this threat. One of Cielce, on a lower battlement, gave the cry."

Andus braced Nartho, catching the smaller goat up and pulling him close to his side, turning him by force so that they leaned upon the parapet's cold stones, facing outward into the void. "Look, Nartho. Look. Tell me what you see."

"Darkness. Some movement. Torches. Moving shapes."

"How many shapes do you see?"

Nartho flicked a sharp glance at Andus, then narrowed his eyes and scanned the night. "Dozens. More than half a hundred."

"Those are only the wolves you see. For each, there will be three that you cannot see. Now watch."

Far below, in the roots of the castle, the firing slits had been uncovered. The fixed-bows opened up. Even this high above, so far above that a stone, when dropped, would take a long count of three to fall, the snap of the arrows through the air was loudly heard. The arrows banged forth, striking into the wolves or cracking into the cold stone of the opposite cliff-face. The volume of fire increased steadily as the bowtenders came on station. From the first alarm, surprisingly little time had passed: a youthful goat might only now have clambered up the central stairway from the lowest basement to the highest tower.

"Count them, Nartho. That is your penance for not having seen them. Count them. Make their numbers, now, and, in the morning, go out and make their numbers once more. We must know."

Nartho gave Andus a strange look, but, in a moment, nodded his assent. "I will do as you say, Lord Andus."

The wolves raged and roved. They flung ladders and ropes on high, catching at the stonework with their claws, or mounting in shaking pyramids built up of their own dead. Their howls were sharp with fear and pain. Still and yet, they attacked. They came across the ravine, even when the deadly fixed-bows slaughtered them by tens and dozens. At the last, the wolves screamed in fury right into the firing slits, reaching in with long, lanky, grey-furred arms. Their eyes gleamed with reflected lantern-light.

The slits were too narrow for them to squeeze through, and it was there that the last wolves died. With no remorse in their souls, and remembering the day, long ago when their ancestors had come to the valley, the bowtenders maintained their fire. The bows were as effective at close range as at long, and screams of rage give no protection from razored steel, tall wooden bows, and strong woven bowstrings.

🏹 ∞ 🏹

The second hour of morning had gone before Nartho arrived to report his numbers. Andus received him in the conference hall, where the two made a lonely conversation at one edge of the great table, beneath the high arches of the ceiling.

"Lord Andus: here are my numbers. The wolves, defeated here, numbered more than one hundred and seventy, but fewer than two hundred. We have immured corpses to the number of ninety and four. It is known that more were slain, but their bodies were borne away by their survivors: we number these corpses at between thirty and fifty. Between twenty and six, and seventy and six, may be said to have endured the attack upon these defenses."

Andus nodded. "I accept these numbers. Go, now, and be vigilant upon the walls."

"Lord Andus... I ask you, in humility, do not accept these numbers as a penance, although the counting and carrying of the dead was an evil task. Accept them as your due as commander, and I will accept the task, foul as it was, as my due as a soldier."

Andus was startled by this, for the words sounded of fealty. Moreover, and more troubling, they sounded sincere. Yet Nartho had the knack of giving voice to sincerity even while building lies on lies. With some misgivings, Andus consented. "Very well. It is as you ask."

"Thank you, Lord Andus. There is another thing..." Nartho paused, hesitant to leave. But before Andus could signal permission to speak, Lords Cadal, Donat, and Cielce came hastening into the conference chamber. Andus looked at them, then at Nartho. But Nartho stood away, and turned, marching to fulfill his command. Andus wondered what Nartho might have been prepared to tell him; with irritation quickly hidden, he received the other Lords.

"Lord Andus, the wolves have not left," declared Lord Donat. "Some have gone around to raid into the valley. They will be dealt with by the soldiers whom the clans have retained. Some have gone into the hills again. But they have not gone back up the trail to its top. They amass in the narrows of the pass."

"Many were slain. They will think long before they attack again."

"No, Lord Andus. For we have knowledge of the carcasses which Nartho has accounted for. Have you seen these?"

Andus had not. Nothing would do, then, but for him to rise and travel with the others to a cold room, far below, where the fallen wolves were thrown. The trip down the winding stairways had the feel of nightmare for Andus; a feeling of nausea began to peck at him long before he came within reach of the first scent of death.

A guard had been set upon the door, even though all within were surely dead. The room was darkened, for torches shed heat as well as light, and the bodies already were high and fetid. But in the light of lanterns borne by the Lords at his side, Andus saw the dead wolves, and knew fear. The shifting light lent them animation, and their eyes seemed to blink, their limbs to twitch, their mouths and teeth and pointed ears to quiver.

They were emaciated, their bellies sunken, their fur matted and patchy.

"They starve," Andus said dully.

"There are none of our kind left in the lands behind the mountains," said Lord Cielce, as if only now drawing the unwelcome deduction. "They have eaten all, and now starve. This is only the first wave of the attack, for there must be more. They cannot wait, nor sue for terms, nor do any good thing, but only attack. They must come, *every wolf and all*, and either their kind is lost... or ours is."

"It comes to this, then," murmured the Fourth Lord Andus, eldest grandson of the brave strong goat who had begun the building of the castle. "One or the other must die. There is no other end to this war, but here it ends, and soon."

They made haste to back away from the reeking sepulcher, barring the doors and leaving the guards on duty. The guards, Andus realized, some time after they had climbed back to the conference chamber, were of Clan Nartho.

Plans and preparations were made, and the Lords came and went on their missions. The rest of the day was taken up in the giving and receiving of pledges, for now, none dared stint in the defense of the castle, which was the defense of the valley.

Toward the hour of sunset, a sentry came to Andus, bearing news he would not speak aloud, but only for Andus' ear. Andus took the sentry aside. "What is it? What is so secret a dispatch?"

"There are weapons missing from the stockpiles, Lord Andus. Spears and knives, and small bows with ready quivers of arrows. Someone within the castle has made this raid upon our armories."

"Who?"

"None knows. In the night's battle and arming, anyone could have come. Weapons were issued; there was never thought a need to count."

"Who knows?"

"Myself, some others of the armorers, but we have made a pact to be silent. None else knows."

Andus grinned, but he felt no mirth. "You are wrong. Others know."

"Lord?"

"The ones who stole the weapons know."

"Yes, Lord. What shall we do?"

"Do? What is there to do? Someone within the castle is making league with the wolves. We do not know who they are. But we know who the wolves are. Has anything changed? Prepare the castle for defense."

"Yes, Lord Andus."

The sentry was away, and Andus gave no sign to the other Lords of what he had learned.

※ ☜ ※

That night, the castle withstood its first true assault. The night cracked open with a lightning of surrounding torches, a thunder of wolfen howling, and a bitter hail of hard copper-tipped arrows. The wolves had carved trails into the hills, making their way to natural platforms upon the cliff's brow from which they could send arrows plunging down upon the battlements. Soon, no open place under the sky was safe, and the defenders were forced to shelter within, as if routed by a freezing rain and high winds. The winds bore death, whistling down from the stars with a high whine that the goats could only liken to the ghostly echo of a wolf's howling.

On the ground, the wolves inched forward behind mantlets. These mobile castles protected them from the fixed-bows, and although their sides soon bristled with arrows, they never stopped in their slow advance. Andus ordered fire-arrows employed, but the mantlets never seemed to catch fire or burn. As the wolves drew near, the goats saw, with horror, that the mantlets were padded with hides: caprine hides, still quite recognizable. At the foremost point of each of these war-machines, a goat's head was attached: dead and empty, tongue lolling and lips drawn back obscenely from the teeth, the heads served the wolves as horrid pennons.

The wolves on the ground had bows as well. Their aim was not as fine as the dread mechanical perfection of the fixed-bows, but the wolves made up for this with vigor and elan. Their archers liked to spring forth from cover, wholly exposed, revealing themselves all naked save for charms made of the bones, hooves, and leathered hides of goats. As fast as they were cut down by fire from the castle, they were replaced.

Behind the firing slits, new killing zones were defined, areas in which the wolves, at last, had learned to reach.

Andus was called high and low, tending to each crisis in turn. The wolves cast up grapnels and scaling ropes, and Andus rushed to repel them. The wolves slipped down into the ravines and took to chiseling at the foundation stones of the castle, and Andus told off a detachment to drop weighted darts upon them, ending that strategem. The wolves, wearing strange winglike vanes of fabric, leaped from the high crags in a frenzied effort to sail down upon the castle's battlements, and Andus, in horror, saw them nearly succeed.

"To me! Reserves! Sentries! Form on me!" Andus was the first out onto the blood-slick roofs, where broken arrows lay scattered, as broken branches lay strewn after a high wind. Thirty wolves had made their landing safely, followed by another ten or twenty who had been injured upon landing. Many more had fallen short or to the side or had landed with great force, now to lie dying or dead or hurt beyond the power to move.

The thirty advanced against Andus. Andus never looked to see if his reserves had answered his call: now the blood was hot in his eyes. The enemy—the hated enemy of his kind for untold generations—had set foot upon his stronghold. He would have charged had he been alone and they had twice their numbers.

Atop the castle, the air was still. The archers in their crags rested their bows, for there could be no gain in firing into melee. But they watched, their cold eyes shining high in the darkness: new, cold constellations of hungry winter stars.

Andus led, and others followed. Lords Cielce and Harn answered him, armed with sword and spear. Lord Donat came, a light dueling axe in either hand, and several of his sons came with him. They formed up, pausing only to arrange themselves in order, although Andus and those nearest him never paused at all in their charge. Then the goats charged the wolves, and the battle upon the roofs was joined.

On the flank, teetering at the very verge of the hundred-foot drop to the ravine, Lord Nartho took his stand. The fighting there was the most dangerous, for there was no leeway. Yet he fought as fiercely as Andus. His eldest sons were with him, although most of the rest of his force were behind the arrow-slits, working the deadly bows.

Andus was a whirlwind, cleaving the wolves' line, scattering them, lashing left and right with his sword. Cielce and Harn jumped forward to cover his flanks. Then, for a time, the three were surrounded by the wolves, and the fight was close-pressed. Nartho, too, struggled against the force of the attackers.

Even starving, ill-led, and mad with battle-fury, the wolves were the greater warriors. Their assault was a blur, their strokes long and crafty and deadly.

Andus took a wound upon his shoulder, nearly dropping his sword. He switched from right to left, and fought on. Cielce evaded a long cut, yet backed into a short one, and fell to the bloodied stones with a long copper knife dangling from his shoulder, dangerously close to his neck. Only Harn stood by Andus now, while the rest of the defending force struggled to come to their succour.

Nartho, seeing Cielce fall, cried aloud, and his energies were redoubled. He fought wildly, almost wolf-wildly; he fought with a desperate fury which none, even the enemy, could match.

Then it was that Nartho's strategy was vindicated: he and his sons, having lived all their lives in their high, rocky valleys, were sure of hoof upon the tilted, dampened stones. They had made themselves familiar with each stone, each ledge, each cornice and crenellation. They engaged the wolves, cutting at them with swords, killing few but pushing many back. In that night of battle, upon the edge of the parapet, there was no room to give. With horrid cries, long and woeful, the wolves fell and were lost.

Nartho and his sons burst upon the wolves around Andus. They made hammer-and-tongs, crushing the wolves and slaughtering them. The roofs were secure.

"Now!" Andus cried. "Back! Back to safety!"

His warnings were not an instant too soon, for the wolfen archers in the crags, seeing their assault failed, took up their bows again and made the roofs unlivable.

Yet far below, the wolves who pushed their mantlets forward growled in fury, knowing that their own plans were now ruined. For the roofs could not be swept permanently clean, and the goats would have the ability to essay forth, from time to time, to let fall great blocks from above. The mantlets might withstand even the heaviest archery fire from the castle's fixed-bows, but nothing could withstand a quarter-ton stone that has fallen a hundred feet.

The battle raged into the morning and through much of the day, but there was little heart, now, in the wolves' efforts. They had loosed their best stroke, and it had failed. By sundown, when the siege was less than a full day old, the wolves drew back. For some time, they engaged in petty raids, sending parties down the crags to the valley to murder and to burn. But there was no great victory for them in this. The castle had withstood them, and starvation would have the final triumph upon their kind.

🌲 ∞ 🌲

Lord Cielce did not die of his wound, and Lord Harn, though wearied and hurt from a dozen cuts upon his arms and chest, was yet sound. They came to Andus and made their complaints known. Andus sent to summon Lord Nartho. Nartho answered, and found himself once more in the conference chamber, surrounded by the hostility of the others.

"Lord Andus. What is your wish?" he asked.

"Show me your sword."

Most carefully, Nartho drew his weapon and, reversing it, laid it hilt-first upon the stone table in the center of the room.

"My sword, Lord Andus."

"Where did you get it?"

"It was issued me by one of your armories."

"No! Not true! He lies!" the other Lords hissed.

Andus waved them to silence, and stood forward to examine the weapon for himself. He raised his eyes to Nartho. "You lie, Lord Nartho. This weapon was stolen from my armories. It was not issued you, but was part of a reserve."

"With this sword," Nartho said, speaking softly, "I saved your life. This sword was wet with the blood of wolves. Do you begrudge me the use to which I put it?"

"No," Andus said. "In all fairness, I do not. Why did you steal it, then?"

Nartho reached out and took it up again, and, putting the point to the floor, leaned upon it in an easygoing pose. Yet those who watched saw the tension in his frame, and knew that he could leap to the defense—or the attack—in a second.

"Did I steal it?" Nartho shrugged. "Yes. I did. These weapons were stolen from you at my command."

"He admits it!" gasped Lord Cielce. "He admits his treason. He admits his league with the wolves!"

"No!" Then, and only then, did Nartho throw aside his self-restraint. "Never! The wolves are my enemy, and the enemy of all my clan!"

"That much seems true," Andus judiciously admitted. "You and your family slew their share—and more than their share—of the enemy. Tell me that part of the truth you have, until now, hidden from us."

"A traitor is one who puts the enemy's good ahead of his own. If I were a traitor, I would have worked to assist the wolves in their victory. But I did not do this. My treason, my Lords, was this: I fought as hard as I could to defeat the wolves. But, had it fallen out that they had won—had their assault been successful—had the Castle Andus fallen to them—then there were many among the Lords of the clans of this valley who would have died, not from the weapons of the wolves, but from my weapons."

A gasp went up all around the conference room. Nartho stood now, and held his sword before him in low guard. In the entrances to the hall, a number of his clansmen showed themselves, also bearing unsheathed swords.

"I hate the wolves, my Lords. I hate them, and I have fought them, and I have slain them. But you must know that there are others, here, *whom also I hate!* Lord Cielce, who has raided my clan of brides, and Lord Harn, who has occupied my meadows: had it been their night to die, I intended them to die on my swords. The wolves nearly had you, Lord Cielce, and it was my attack that saved your life. But if the wolves had come up over the walls, and if the night were theirs, then you must know that I, and not they, would have stabbed you in the heart."

A cold, furious silence chilled the room.

"Such is the depth of your vendetta?" Andus asked.

"Yes, Lord. But there is more: I have armed my people with these weapons. My clan, back in its valley, is now the most heavily defended of all clans, save only your own, Lord Andus. Certain valleys, which Harn claims as forfeit, are forfeit no longer. And Cielce might find his own daughters to have left him—of their own accord. So the old grievances have found a way of righting themselves after all."

The Lords blustered and stamped, shouting for vengeance, shouting for war. Lords Cielce and Harn approached Lord Andus. "We ask for your support now. We ask for your judgement. This crime cannot go unanswered. How do you say? Will you give us arms also, and help us war against this treasonous Nartho?"

Andus paused for a very long time, then looked about the hall. Gradually, silence fell, as every one and all waited to know what he would say.

"I am not your king," Andus spoke at the last. "I do not settle disputes unless they are brought to me with the agreement of all concerned. Lord Nartho, do you accept my judgement upon you in this case?"

Nartho smiled, most indulgently, and backed away to join his kinsmen at the doorway.

"No, Lord Andus. I will settle my dispute in the same way it was formed."

※

REPAS DU VIVANT

Little pink skulls danced on the shoulders of the gray wolf as she trotted out of the way of a rickety land wagon. The driver, a dusty weasel, tipped his Stetson at her as he barked an apology. Cory DuPlessis, head cook and bottle washer of the tradeship *Tai-Pan*, smiled her pardon at the embarrassed driver. It was too nice a day to be petty. She stopped briefly to adjust the skull-dotted scarf that was threatening to slip from her shoulders.

Cory walked briskly through the streets of Hsstor, the pads of her feet chilled but not unpleasantly so. The breeze that moved through her grey fur carried her breath off in little puffs.

The tiny sun was diamond-bright in a royal blue sky. Pieces of ice still floated in the puddles—all that remained of the hailstorm that had disappeared as quickly as it had arrived. The slender wolf observed the weasel-like natives of Hsstor, who were dashing about in their usual frenetic manner. *The planet's weather was a lot like its people*, she noted. *Frenzied and unpredictable.*

Some of the Hsstorians were in such a hurry that they dropped to all fours and literally bounded through the streets. Aliens were rare to this planet, but the townsfolk barely noticed her. Periodically one or two of them would run up to Cory, give her a cursory inspection, and then dash off without a word. This had taken Cory by surprise at first, but she had gotten so used to the routine that she hardly noticed it anymore.

As she neared the space port, Cory could hear Eli's voice shouting directions to the crew as they off-loaded their unusual cargo. His voice could barely be heard over the mooing and bawling of their shipment. Cory had to suppress a chuckle as she saw the circus the job had become. Eli normally ran a well-organized operation, but he'd never had to move three hundred head of cattle before.

A plague had struck the huge herds of cattle that were the planet's main food source, rendering most of the bulls sterile. The plague had been controlled and the danger was now past, but the Hsstorians had short term needs to deal with. Though they had embryonic stock ready to replace the lost studs, some purists among them would not stand for using artificial insemination to replenish their herds. This emergency was, in fact, the one reason that the *Tai-Pan* was allowed to land on Hsstor: the little natives had imposed a quarantine on their own planet, to protect its young culture from disruptive foreign influences. In fact, the only reason that Marko Rasputin, Captain of the *Tai-Pan*, would allow three hundred head of cattle on his ship was the hope that such an act might lead to longer term trade agreements.

After a great deal of research (and kibitzing from two crewmen who'd seen a couple of Western holos), Eli had designed a sturdy chute to get the cattle from the ship to the port's loading area. His plan was good; unfortunately Eli could not have imagined the beating the chute would take when pounded by nearly a megaton of angry hooves. A section of the wall had collapsed and several of the animals had broken for daylight. It was a comedy of errors, with most of the crew (some of whom had never seen a cow before this trip) helping to control the riot of beef.

Frith was struggling with a make-shift repair, when Bette, a young vixen, came over and asked him something. At this distance, it was difficult to hear what she asked—some question about seeing rain fall up. Cory saw Frith shake his head and shrug. Laughing, Bette replied by leaping into the deep rain puddle next to him. Cory definitely heard the stream of curses coming from the young ferret. It had to have been another of the pun-riddles that Frith and Bette had been playing at for some time now.

"Hello, Frith," Cory said as she passed the damp mustelid.

"Hey, Cory," Frith returned, trying in vain to shake some of the water out of his fur. All Cory heard as she walked out of earshot were some nasty remarks about Bette's ancestry.

Cory shifted the two bags she was carrying long enough to wave to the ship's security chief, Barney. He was gazing out at the impromptu round-up: there was little to threaten the ship as it stood in the muddy field the Hsstorians sometimes used as a "space port."

"Afternoon, Cory!" the hound shouted back. "Is that all you got for supper? That load don't look like it'd feed a mouse, let alone a chow-hound like me!" Behind him she could see Chester screeching atop a runaway bull which was dragging Billy Gasden behind him by the rope tangled around the muddy human's leg.

Cory stopped and smiled back at Barney. "First of all, if the 'mouse' you refer to is Sama, then no, since she out-chows you and Rufus combined. And secondly, no—I'm having the rest delivered. I'm making enough to feed three times our number, which means that—the way our mob eats—there might be enough left to send up to the bridge crew."

The old hound peered more closely at the scarf the wolf was wearing. "Little pink skulls," he observed, "That some kind of fashion statement or what?"

Cory rolled her eyes and sighed. She recited the explanation she gave to everyone else who had already asked. "No, this scarf is a present from my little brother. He has strange tastes, but a good heart and spent a lot of money to send it to me and I'm going to wear it as I please, thank you very much!"

"Dang! Now I owe Gasden ten creds!" Barney groused. "That's exactly what he said you'd say, when I asked."

"Oh, you men!" Cory huffed, feigning anger as she stalked off into the ship. "I'm not even sure if this scarf isn't my own brother's idea of a joke!"

Barney just chuckled and turned back to watch the fun.

As she entered the ship's hold, the sounds of cows and cursing sprang on her, echoing along the metal walls and deck. Ears folded back, Cory hurried out of the cacophony and down to the relative quiet of the galley.

🐾 ∞ 🐾

Captain Marko Rasputin settled comfortably in a chair and took a long sip at the tea Cory had just poured him. His nose took in the spicy smells pouring from the two huge pots that were cooking on the stove. Chia-te, a female hare who sometimes helped Cory in the galley, strained to stir one of the pots. Stan Elkins, the life-support tech who often helped Cory in the galley, had his hands full getting the hold mucked-out. Fortunately, Stan had been saving up a list of crewmen with disciplinary hours owed him. The cheerful hyena was delighted to "supervise" the misery of the fallen.

"So you see, Cory," Rasputin continued, "we need to impress the local delegation if we have any hope of getting an unlimited trade-license out of them. Unfortunately, our little friends are—shall we say, disdainful—of anyone who isn't a full-up carnivore. I need you to fix something that will really impress them, or at least put them in a good mood."

Cory thought about it for a moment, and then replied, "I think I understand." She smiled mischievously at the burly panda and added, "I'll even fix up some fierce-looking veggies for you, Captain."

"Just make sure I don't have to kill 'em first, DuPlessis!" Rasputin chuckled as he finished off his tea.

🐾 ∞ 🐾

"Ah, Cory!" Chia-te exclaimed as she took a deep breath of the steamy air. "You have created essence of the summertime in this meal! You learn this at cook-school?"

Cory smiled back at the hare as Chia struggled to move the bubbling vat of veggies off the stove. "Thank you, Chia. It's a very ancient recipe known as a Basque stew. This was the first meal my mother taught to me."

"Someday maybe you teach me, eh?"

"It would be my pleasure, Chia," Cory replied, taking a dainty taste from one of the pots. "Stan, could you move the meat stew over to the left side of the serving counter?" she gasped as she struggled with the other pot. The panting wolf quickly restrained her tongue before it could loll out her muzzle, while her ears folded back in embarrassment. "And Stan, could you turn the air cooler up a bit?"

"I was just on that, Cory," panted Stan, who had returned to the galley early, while the hold-muckers went to scrub themselves off.

"Right on time we finish!" Chiate chimed in as she looked at the clock.

Almost on her words, a tired and ragged bunch of crew people jostled into the room, a couple at a fast trot, their conversation drowning out even the galley's clatter.

"Hey, Cory, smells great!" exclaimed the burly stallion at the head of the stampede.

"Thanks, Chumly. Okay, people, veggies on the right, meat on the left. Enjoy!" shouted Cory over the din.

"I owe ya' one, Cor!" Eli said as he pulled up the rear of the group. "As soon as some of these lugs caught a whiff of supper, they moved double-time. Even Frith did a little work!"

"Hey-hey-hey! None of that! I worked my butt to a nub out there!" the ferret protested.

Table talk abounded as crewmembers joked about the round-up and made plans for the next day's shoreleave. Bette nudged Frith as she took her dishes to the cleaner.

"Hey, Frith, here's a new one: ever see a match burn twice?" she asked, her green eyes twinkling.

"Dammit, no! Get away from me!" the ferret yelled as he shielded himself with his chair.

"Sheesh, what a grouch," said the vixen as she left.

As Cory had predicted, the huge amount of food disappeared very quickly, and she was barely able to save some for the evening watch. She handed one of the trays to Stan, and as she started to pick up the other one, Barney stopped her.

"Cory, why don't you take a break and eat. I've got to head up to the bridge anyway. The way we're putting this chow away, there wouldn't be anything left for you when you got back."

Smiling gratefully, Cory thanked him and relinquished the tray. She helped herself to a portion of the stew and sat down across from Frith, Chester and Billy Gasden. Frith seemed to be describing a loading accident he had witnessed at the warehouse. *Perhaps sitting here was a mistake*, she thought, but continued eating.

"Y'see, there was this guy directing traffic here, see, and a loader over here moving about ten crates of lead or bricks or something... here, let me show you, this spoon is the loader, and this tomato is the foreman, and suddenly the loader drops his load—plop!—right on the—"

Suddenly a hand reached down and scooped Frith's plate off the table.

"We are NOT amused!" glowered Cory DuPlessis. "I will not allow my cooking to be used as a prop for some gory re-creation!"

"Aw, c'mon Cory! The tomato would've been perfect for..."

"Enough! I do not like you. You'll get no more banana chips from me, young man!"

"No more chips?" Frith moaned, realizing for the first time that she really was offended. "You don't mean that, do you?"

"Yes, I do," said Cory icily as she took the dishes to the cleaner.

"Oh, Cory, we will take care of the K.P.," said Billy as he got up with a gallant flourish. "You cooked. Chester, he and I will clean-up, won't we, Chester?" he said as he hustled Cory out of the galley.

The ringtail had been drowsing in his chair, idly considering seconds. Hearing his name being volunteered woke him right up.

"Dishes?! Oh, Billy—doing dishes makes my fur all kinky..."

"Only your fur? Ho-ho! That is new!" chuckled Billy wickedly.

"Woo-woo," replied Chester, smiling back. "Dishes it is!"

Frith sat hunched in his chair, either sulking or thinking, Gasden couldn't tell.

"'Ey, Frith, if it is forgiveness you want from Cory, why don't you give us some 'elp," Billy said as he handed Chester a plate.

Frith waived him off. "No, I've got to do something really cool to make it up to Cory... really big..."

Chester looked at Gasden and said, "Be afraid. Be very afraid."

"Poor Cory," Billy said, shaking his head.

🐾 ∞ 🐾

Cory entered her cabin and went straight to her small bookshelf. From past experience she knew that it was a bad idea to go to sleep so soon after a big meal. She really should start thinking about the banquet tomorrow, but that could wait. Right now she needed to unwind, and the best way she knew of was in the small book she brought over to her bed. On the faded cover one could just about make out the title, *Alice Through the Looking Glass*. The book had been a favorite of hers since childhood, when her mother first read it to her. She took a cookie from the jar on her nightstand and poured herself a small glass of wine. Yawning, she settled down to read as she nibbled on her simple dessert.

🐾 ∞ 🐾

The next day Cory began to organize the banquet, freed from cooking since most of the crew had been granted shore leave as a reward for the work they did yesterday. She had just returned from ordering the supplies when she discovered Frith in the galley, surrounded with the wires and boards of the ship's cooking center.

"Gah! Frith, what have you done!" Cory gasped as she stood frozen in the doorway.

"Oh. Hi, Cory. I was gonna surprise you, but you're back early," the young ferret said, calmly looking up from the tangle of wires.

"Surprise? What kind of a surprise? I need the cooking unit to prepare tonight's banquet!"

"Oh, hey, no problem-O," Frith said, turning back to his work. "I'll be done in a sec'. You'll like this: I'm gonna make up for last night!"

"Frith, dear, I'm not angry with you anymore. Please put the ovens back together, " Cory pleaded, trying to stay calm. "What in the world *are* you doing," she asked, her curiosity piqued in spite of herself.

"Look, you remember that crazy book you lent me a few months ago? With all the kooky people in it?"

"Yes, of course. *Alice Through the Looking Glass*. I was just reading it last night."

"Right. Well, just for you, Cor, I'm gonna make it so you can re-create all the weird food they ate. Treacle 'n' all that shit. I've crissed the synth wackity-thingie with the main computer core, and crossed the hoobli-joobly output with the mixing chambers and... Voila!" he declared, holding up a tangled ball of wires and circuit boards.

Cory's head was starting to hurt. "Oh, Frith. Please tell me that I will be able to use the ovens now."

"Oh, hey, yeah. Lemme just put this back and—"

Frazzp!

Cory's nose wrinkled from the sharp tang of ozone in the air. She was almost afraid to ask.

In some embarrassment, Frith looked up at the worried wolf.

"Oops."

Cory put one hand over her eyes in resignation.

"'Oops.' 'Oops,' what, Frith?" she said, not daring to look.

"I can fix it," Frith blurted, madly batting out the sparks smoldering in his fur.

"Frith...," Cory threatened.

"I, uh, think I shorted the framblizer. Tina's gonna have a fit."

"Frith, just tell me one thing before you go help McQuarrie down in engineering..."

"But, I'm not going down to—oh, yeah."

"Will the oven still work?"

"Oh, sure," Frith said as he shoveled the mess of wires back into the programming unit. "Te Teko's the one who's got problems. She's been compiling the ship's expenses all morning, and I think I just glitched her program..."

The intercom near the door chimed and Te Teko Bush's strained voice floated out of it.

"Frith? You still down there? Cory?"

"Cory here, Te Teko. What's up?" she answered as Frith started to sidle towards the door.

"If Frith just did what I think he did, you can add puree of ferret to the menu tonight," the normally pleasant comps master growled.

"...Bye Cory I think I just remembered I was gonna meet Chester on planet so I gotta go see *you later*—" said Frith, who transformed into a streak of fur dashing out the door.

"I think you're too late, Te Teko. I tell you what: if my kitchen doesn't work, I'll lend you my blender."

"Thanks, Cory. If you see the little weasel, tell him I'm gonna make him re-enter that data with his pointy little nose."

"I'm sure he suspects something to that effect already. Out," Cory said as she turned back to her beloved kitchen with suspicion.

🦋 ∞ 🦋

The Hsstor delegation was made up of five of the little natives dressed in formal military uniforms and grey berets. They were milling near the dining table in the wardroom as Cory served the aperitif. All were males and acted more like young studs at a bachelor party than officials at a state dinner.

"Ey, Jyaar, look at that, eh? You like 'er? She big enuf for yer!" one of the Hsstor said as Cory served the brandy.

Politely ignoring the comments, Cory turned to the Captain.

"Brandy, sir?" she asked the smartly-dressed panda.

"Thank you, Cory. Sorry about the, um..." he nodded towards the Hsstorians, who were now discussing the logistical problems of tall women in not-so-subtle stage whispers.

"Oh, don't worry about me. I have two brothers, remember?" she assured him.

"I understand. How are you doing? Frith's tampering cause any problems?" Rasputin asked, smiling back at the Hsstorians, who were either toasting him or DuPlessis from across the room.

"So far, so good. I tested the oven with a batch of cookies and they came out just fine. Or so I guess—they disappeared before they were finished cooling, which is usually a good sign."

Rasputin sighed, shaking his head. "I'll have a talk with Chester later. How is tonight's meal going?"

"I'm serving up beef filets to the Hsstorians and something that doesn't look too veggie-like for you and Eli. The veggie dishes are a little hard to distinguish from the meat dishes. Eat only food with olives in it," she warned, before heading back to the galley.

"Excellent, Cory," said Captain Rasputin as he wandered over to the envoys, who were now trading hunting stories with Chance, the *Tai-Pan*'s First Mate. The rangy snow leopard looked relieved as the Captain joined the group.

Rasputin had to resist the urge to crouch his two-meter-plus bulk down when he spoke to the diminutive delegation. The Hsstorians, themselves, seemed not to notice the difference in heights as they chattered away.

"We jus' don' know, Captain Rasputin," said Jyaar-of-the-big-women.

"We very careful 'bout who comes and goes. We want people who understand our culture, our needs."

"I understand what you're saying. However, there are certainly some things that could be of use to you and still not disrupt your culture."

"Yah, some things, that is so. But maybe we do business with farship *Damascus*, eh? Ship is all wolves, like your cook. Now, wolves not Hsstor, but almost as good. They unnerstan' the art of prey, of hunt." The other Hsstor chittered in agreement.

One of the other Hsstor piped in.

"Those wolves, they brought *kintor* to us as gift. Fine thing, like big rat. Good chase, and they make funny sound when kill-bite." Several of the Hsstor proceeded to try and imitate the sound.

"Eurrrgububleble!"

Rasputin looked slightly ill. "I (urp) understand. Would you care for some more brandy before dinner?"

🐾 ∞ 🐾

Back in the galley, Cory was having problems of her own. Still suspicious of Frith's jury-rigging, she kept a close eye on the meal as it cooked. Every time she turned her back on the oven, a small racket would sound inside. As soon as she turned back, the sound stopped. She couldn't figure out what could be making all that noise. When she finally did take the food out, it looked fine, so she tried to forget about it.

Having artfully arranged the entrée on the plates, Cory turned to get a serving tray. As she did so, one of the filets scampered off one of the plates and back onto the cooking pan.

"Brrr," it said, "cold plate!"

Cory whipped around to see who had spoken, but the galley was empty. She did notice that she had forgotten to put one of the filets onto a plate, though she could have sworn she had removed them all. She shrugged.

"I'm too nervous. Everything is going to be fine," she said to reassure herself. Still, something didn't feel quite right.

🐾 ∞ 🐾

"Ah, comes the meat," one of the weasels exclaimed as Cory entered the dining room.

"And the food, too," another said, winking and nudging Jyaar.

Maintaining her composure, Cory began to serve the meal.

"Gentlesirs, this beef is from your own planet, prepared according to an Old Earth recipe. Bon Appetite!"

"Looks pretty good. You got any ketchup?" asked Jyaar.

Wincing, Cory reached into her apron and pulled a bottle out.

"I kind of expected you to ask that," she said, resigned.

Jyarr began to pour the sloppy red sauce over his meat, when it suddenly jumped up and sputtered at him.

"You trying to drown me? Get that crap out of here!" said the steak as it brushed the ketchup off with two spindly arms.

At the same moment, another piece of meat jumped up as a weasel tried to stick his fork into it. It yelped, and stood away from the surprised Hsstor, rubbing its backside. Another filet was introducing itself to Chance.

"Hi, there! I'm Phil. Phil Lay. Pleased to meat you! Get it? *Meat* you? Get it?" said Chance's good-natured entrée. The snow leopard leapt back in his seat as if he'd been bitten.

"Cats. No sense of humor," the steak pouted.

For a moment, there was a shocked silence. The others looked warily down at their own dinners.

Rasputin stared at his veggie-burger, and gingerly poked a fork at it. Nothing happened. Cautiously, he cut a piece off, and when there was no reaction, started to taste it. He froze when the patty opened two blue eyes.

"That'sh the twouble with fileth. They're tho high-sthrung," it lisped.

Captain Rasputin jumped straight out of his chair. Eli pushed his plate away (even as it whispered, "*Rosebud*"), and Chance was looking a little queasy as his filet inquired after his health. Cory, meanwhile, had lost her iron-composure, and stood shocked and unmoving, her eyes as big as saucers.

The Hsstorians looked at each other, at the meat, and back at each other. Then, with a shrill war cry, they tore after the filets, who taunted them even as the weasels hunted them down.

In a daze, the three *Tai-Pan*'ers wandered over to Cory and watched the wild chase which ensued. It was all very surreal. Even as they were being eaten, the prodigal entrees cheerfully continued to insult the diners.

When it was all over, the Hsstorians—out of breath, but clearly pleased—walked over to Rasputin and the others. Jyaar shook the Captain's hand vigorously.

"I think maybe I change my mind. You really do unnerstan' us! Wolves, they have no sense of humor. Ver' serious. You are hilarity! Dinner-food that run away, run away and make the good joke too! Crack us up! I draw up papers tomorrow!"

The Hsstor trade delegation soon left, escorted out by the flustered snow leopard.

Rasputin, Eli and Cory stood in the dinning room, mouths hanging open. An olive ran across Cory's foot, and she jumped, squealing like a cub. The olive leaped onto the table, grabbed a caper and ran off into the hallway. They could hear it promising the caper an evening of romance. Rasputin cleared his throat. Eli started at the sound, then slowly began to relax.

"Congratulations, Marko. You got your trade status," Eli said, looking at the uneasy panda.

"Thanks, I guess," he said, looking over at the wide-eyed wolf next to him. "You okay, Cory?"

"I think so. Yes, I'm fine," Cory said, shaking herself out of her shock, "I think I'll go lie down for a bit."

"Now I know how Alice felt," she mumbled as she walked out of the room and to her cabin...

🐾 👓 🐾

Cory sat bolt upright in her bed. The light was still on, a cookie still on her nightstand. She began to relax.

"A dream! Thank goodness, it had all been a dream."

She took a deep breath, sighed loudly and reached for the cookie, which was no longer there. It was in her closet, criticizing a scarf covered with little pink skulls.

Rolling over, the drowsy wolf murmured to herself.

"Curious..."

🔳

SECTION THREE

LIVING WITHIN:
TRANSFORMATION

FOREWORD BY PHIL GEUSZ

What does it mean to be human? Philosophers have been asking the question for millennia, and in the process have generated far more new questions than they have answers. Even those relatively few answers, however, can't have any real meaning until one of us somehow actually crosses over and becomes *not* human any longer. Then, we can for the first time compare notes in a meaningful way. Do our physical shapes regulate our souls? Is it our five senses and the manner in which they shape our view of the universe that defines our most essential being? Or perhaps it is our brains, and the basic instincts and premises that are hard-wired into them?

What exactly happens, anyway, when you alter a person on a level so fundamental that they literally become something else?

Like the greater tradition of transformational fiction of which it is part, Furry transformational fiction is all about physical and mental change. It's about living in an alternative skin, about growth and about seeing the familiar world around us in a new and different light. It's about exploring new worlds, facing new problems, and discovering new directions in which to grow. And, sometimes, it's about universal truths that apply to all of Earth's children no matter how they struggle and strive to escape their inevitable fates.

We humans are very imaginative creatures; we've been telling each other stories about people being turned into animals since time immemorial. Today, however, as the art of genetic engineering rushes forward, the genre seems to have developed a new poignancy and immediacy. With every new headline, concepts that once seemed very distant and unlikely to affect our daily lives become more and more relevant. Already, a California man has begun the process of doing everything that today's technology allows to turn himself into a tiger. He's had synthetic whiskers permanently implanted into his face, undergone full-body tattooing, and had his teeth sharpened. Soon, he will receive implanted fur. How much longer can it be before science gives us the means to go even further? Perhaps even more to the point, how much longer can it be before some of the boldest of us push on until we begin to explore the true limits of human identity?

We don't have much longer to wait before the line between Furry transformational fiction and fact begins to blur and become indistinct. The one certainty is that as our universe changes we will learn and grow and mature exponentially, seeing through new eyes and thinking with new brains. We will perceive reality in wholly new ways, and shape ourselves into whatever images we see fit. We will master the makeup of our bodies and our minds and, in so doing, achieve ultimate mastery of everything around us. Our posterity will know no limits and accept no boundaries; indeed, the very concepts of limits and boundaries might go the way of bodily humors and phlogistons.

All of this, if the past is any guide, will begin with Furry transformations.

In the meantime, however, until the technology develops just that little bit further we can always speculate about what it might be like to perceive the world around us through a different lens, in the case of these particular stories a rather Furry one. And, perhaps, the fact that we take such pleasure in doing so is the ultimate expression of our humanity.

※

GRADUATION DAY

The phone call had been totally unexpected, as so many calls at the Shelter are. And already it seemed to have gone on forever. I leaned back tiredly in my specially designed seat and sighed deeply. The request was a reasonable one, and even arguably one that fell well within my field. But still...

"Phil, I cannot think of anyone more likely to be able to help these kids," the voice in my left ear said. "We've never met, but you come most highly recommended."

"You're aware that I have no formal training or certifications?" I replied wearily. "A professional association sent me a letter just the other day threatening to take me to court for practicing without a license." That letter had rattled my confidence, badly. Truly, I wanted not to take this particular job, though I could not have told anyone why. "It's really only legal for me to act as a counselor because I do not charge a fee. In fact, technically I am required to have a legal guardian. And wear a leash in public."

This time it was my caller who sighed. "I knew that you were pretty highly morphed. Are you saying that you physically or psychologically can't handle working with a group of SCAB high school kids about to graduate? If that's the problem, then I certainly do understand."

And then who else would take the task on, I asked myself? There weren't too many other counselors out there with my background or experience, I had to admit. These kids were as important as any other potential clients. So why was it that I didn't want to take the job? It was a mystery even to me; how could I possibly explain it to someone else? "No, it's not that I couldn't handle being out of the Shelter for a few days. If you could perhaps make a few special provisions for me..."

"Oh, I assure you that we would be willing to make any sort of reasonable accommodations for you!" Michael gushed.

"Then I'm certain that in theory at least we could work something out. Like I said, it's not being out of the Shelter so much as it is that I generally work with adults. Not children." I felt really bad at turning this guy down. Back in the days before I became a subject-matter-expert on litter boxes, the conversation would have ended much sooner. But ever since SCABS, I find that I have much more trouble with assertiveness.

"And why is that?"

"Well..." There was the fact that kids were loud and rambunctious, not the sort of folks whose company I went in for ever since the poofy-tail thing had happened to me. But that hardly applied in this case; the clients in question here were all non-threatening SCABS types just like me. So what was really, truly keeping me from taking on this job? Finally, painfully, I found the true answer. "It's like this," I explained. "How can I possibly help these kids when I cannot even help myself? I mean, look at me. I live in the West Street Shelter because I have proven to myself and to others that the real world is simply too tough for me. I work for free; my clients are generally too desperate and broke to find someone that really knows what they're doing. Mike, these kids are simply too much like I am! Are you really, truly certain that you want them to look at me and my personal failures and see their own possible futures?"

There was silence on the line for a bit. Then the head guidance counselor for all the City's public schools spoke firmly and with conviction. "Phil. Listen to me. Yes, I want you. Yes, I want you to serve as a role model. Do you have any idea of who gave me your name?"

"No," I replied.

"You wouldn't believe me, then, if I told you. We've never met, but your reputation is spreading fast. And I need you. These kids need you."

Who can argue with kids in need? So I took the job. Of course.

❦ ∞ ❦

Almost immediately, I regretted my decision. There were scheduling difficulties, transportation difficulties, and a date with Clover that simply had to be canceled. In truth the regret was only skin deep, and did not compare with the warm sense of busyness that set in just as soon as I really got down to work. I may not be a genuine counselor, but I do enjoy the illusion that I can help people in need.

There were twenty-eight really tough SCAB cases due to graduate from City high schools on June Fourth. Eighteen were animal-types, of which thirteen were strict herbivores and one was an insect-eating bat— he was lumped in with the herbivores since he seemed to fit in better socially with the plant-eaters. Though of various species and degrees of morph, all of them were experiencing problems with animalistic issues and/or instincts. Because of these special problems, they had been schooled together in a separate program designed around their needs. Of these fourteen students, eight had shown interest in attending either college or a technical school. Therefore, they were not my concern. It was the other six who truly needed help. They had no plans beyond school, no career goals, and no futures laid out. In the past, there had not been special interest taken in kids like these, and the resulting outcomes had been generally bad. Some had found menial work for themselves, while others had been institutionalized or ended up at the Shelter. Almost none, however, could have been said to have "succeeded" in life. It was my job to try and turn those statistics around. At least for these six kids, if no others.

I got started as soon as possible, since graduation day was only three weeks away. These kids had major hurdles to overcome before then, and I didn't have the slightest intention of simply handing out optimistic-looking brochures or something like that. I wanted to see these kids get real, productive lives started, lives filled with dignity and humanity. That meant I had lots of homework to do before ever even meeting them for the first time.

After getting the appropriate permission slips signed, copies of the school records for my six newest clients appeared on my desk early one morning. Thanks to a canceled cage call, I was able to spend most of that same day looking them over. As expected, the news was not good. They would have been an ordinary group of typical non-college bound kids, really, had it not been for the red-jacketed "SCABS" folder that the records came in and the special instructions and files included to aid the staff in dealing with the morphed adolescents.

But such SCABS cases these were! Bobby Rieser's folder, for example, carried a special notation warning of uncontrollable biting when in a feral state. He was therefore required to wear a muzzle at all times while on school property. This must have done wonders for his self-image, I noted. It was rough enough simply trying to grow up while wearing the body of a full-morph woodchuck, wasn't it, without a muzzle on your face to constantly remind you and others that sometimes you were just another biting animal? Bobby was in danger of flunking out, frankly. It was doubtful that he could even graduate with his class. Even if he did, institutionalization seemed a very likely outcome for him. Up until SCABS, he had been a decent if not outstanding student. All that had ended with the big change, though. Part of his troubles had been traced to an incompletely repressed hibernation reflex, and he had performed better once his medications were increased. But the continuing bad marks were considered to be primarily due to ordinary depression.

I rolled my eyes. Only a Norm could have thought it necessary to add such a notation. Duh!

Then there was Johni Redmund, formerly John Redmund. Her file jacket stated in big letters that she was permitted to present herself as a member of either sex at school on any given day as she wished. This was of course due to her SCABS-induced gender dysphoria. The record before me was studded with entries for all sorts of misconduct. Johni had been a troublemaker even while still John, and things had gone south considerably since then. An attached report from a school psychologist noted that Johni had experienced one of the worst possible SCABS situations in that she had been an aggressive "macho" type before her change, but was now too small and frail to be able to physically intimidate others. Her entire psyche had been built around dominance and bullying, but now she had no outlets at all for her anger. I looked more closely at the disciplinary file; sure enough in the months since her bout with SCABS the infractions had gone from fighting and shoving in the hallways to less physical offences like badmouthing teachers and smoking in the bathroom. However, the frequency of her misbehaviors had increased more than enough to compensate. Her psychologist had recommended committing Johni to a SCABS institution for a period of adaptation and rehabilitation. She and her family, however, had flatly refused. Johni was a low-degree sheep-morph, and physically structured in such a way as to make a satisfactory sex-change back to male for her very unlikely in the foreseeable future. She was also quite attractive, which made things all the harder for her. In fact, the report noted, Johni could not convincingly pass as male, though she tried very hard.

Unless I was terribly mistaken, Johni was probably headed for the street at warp speed.

Then there was Billy Winecrest. He had been dead-set on going into the Marines, his counselor noted, until SCABS had made him into a lapine like me. Though he was a jackrabbit instead of a domestic breed of bunny like I was, Billy and I had a lot in common. He could shift to a much more human state than my everyday morphlocked form, but the price was that he had to later revert to feral full-morph form for a long period of time as a tradeoff whenever he did so. The boy was terrified of existing in a feral state, which was natural enough, so he tended to remain physically as much a rabbit as any given situation allowed. That way, at least, he only had to become mentally an animal if frightened or startled. Over the months, his counselor noted, Billy was becoming more and more withdrawn from society. He spent a lot of time grazing in the back yard when he could, and often socialized for hours with true bunnies of various sorts when he thought no one was watching. His parents, who were fairly wealthy, were fighting off the Lapine Colonies successfully for the moment. In my heart, however, I knew it was only a matter of time.

No matter what we did, we were eventually going to lose this one. I'd seen it before, too many times. Damnit.

Rudie Moorhouse was a horse of a different color. Two colors, in fact, since he was a zebra-morph, and as nearly as I could tell from his folder quite an attractive and outgoing one at that. His file was nearly pristine—there were no notations of disciplinary problems or of serious difficulties with animalistic behavior. Rudie was just an ordinary kid, pretty much...

...except that it seemed he had this terrible fear of predator-types. Even common domestic dogs terrified him to no end. It was purely psychological, his doctor had reported; even true zebras were not nearly so pathologically afraid of being eaten. But poor Rudie simply could not even go near anything (except normal humans) that ate meat. If he did, the result was an uncontrollable terror reaction, complete with deep hoofprints in anything and everything around him. And just to make

Rudie more of a challenge for me, he was borderline academically. He always had been, too. Even before SCABS.

Sandy Blankenship had a special sort of problem. As an elephant full-morph, she required customized fixtures and appliances to accomplish even the most basic of tasks. Her dietary requirements kept a cook busy almost full-time, and a special janitor was employed just to deal with Sandy's waste. The burden on the Blankenships' family life was incredible. Though Sandy was generally cheerful on the surface about her situation, sometimes she became severely depressed. Her boyfriend had died of the Flu while she was Changing, her psychologist noted, and she had shown no interest in any sort of companionship since. Vision is not an elephant's strong point to begin with, and Sandy's was even worse than usual. On top of everything else, as it happened, the poor girl was nearly blind. Sandy had attempted suicide twice, the school record noted baldly. A special watch was to be kept at all times.

Last on my list was the group's sole non-herbivore, a bat morph named George Poltava. He was nearly blind, too, even worse off than Sandy was. George could not abide sunlight, and was kept artificially in the dark at all times so that his day-night cycle could be kept in sync with that of the rest of the students. The socialization this provided was considered more important than any possible negative effects on George's health. His sonar was fully functional, but caused disturbing psychological side effects. The boy had long been interested in drawing and painting. Now, he crafted grotesque death's head monstrosities out of clay at every opportunity, identifying them as likenesses of his father or mother, or sometimes a girl he fancied. It was obvious, of course, that what he was shaping was the boney structure that his sonar "saw" most clearly, and that to George these were indeed probably good likenesses. Still, it was very spooky and helped demonstrate just how alien this poor kid's everyday world had become. Even I, heavily altered in many ways myself, shuddered at the same time as I sympathized.

George was becoming increasingly emotionally and socially isolated over time, his unique perceptions and nocturnal nature driving him into a universe of his own. There were few other bat-morphs around to appreciate his art, and George considered them to be every bit as physically revolting as he believed that he himself had become. His sexual standards, according to his doctor, were still entirely human and heterosexual. But he could never, ever truly see a human girl's delicious smile again. Instead, he was condemned only to "echo-sense" a strangely warped skull-thing in place of her face. That was, if he could ever find a woman willing to let him "look" her in the eye without turning away in disgust...

In short, George really, really worried me. What possible hope could I offer a kid in a situation like his?

They all worried me, in fact. And privately Michael had told me that each had pretty much given up even hoping for a future, near as he could tell. That might be the hardest thing of all to overcome. None of my little group had even bothered to fill out any of the standardized vocational surveys. But what could a career counselor worthy of the name do except try? Even if he was really only a phony one? So I got to work, and started making phone calls. The very first was to Michael, of course, to make arrangements to meet my little brood in person.

🦋 ∞ 🦋

The regular school counselors were all very nice to me; one loaned me her office and another drove me to and from the Shelter. Johni Redmund happened to be absent that day, but I was able to spend all the time I wanted with the rest. First up was my zebra boy, Rudie Moorhouse. He was a lot like I had expected, all smiles and stripes on the surface. When he shook my forepaw I noted that his hands were flexible and well-developed, unlike those of so many hoofed SCABs I'd seen. After we introduced ourselves to each other and sat down, I commented on this to him.

"Yeah," he replied. "The doctors keep telling me I'm pretty lucky."

"There's a lot of people like you out there that are living very normal lives," I replied by way of agreement.

"I know," he answered, looking away. "I know a horse-girl in the normal classes who's actually a bit more morphed than I am. But she isn't so afraid all of the time."

"Afraid?" I asked, already knowing what the substance of the reply would be. But I wanted Rudie to explain for himself.

"Well... you're a rabbit, right?"

"Yes."

"And you've gotta know that there's all sorts of things out there that would like to eat you."

Too very true. "Of course. I've even had something try, once."

"Really? Wow! What was it like? What kind of animal?"

My gorge rose in my throat. Eventually I had intended to share this story with Rudie, but not so soon. I wasn't even close to ready yet. But my chance had clearly come. "A Bengal tiger. Full morph."

His eyes widened, and I caught a whiff of terror. "Feral?"

"I thought so at the time. So did everyone else. But no, not feral. A murderer."

"Jeez!" Rudie replied. "What happened?"

"He's dead. I'm not. That's the short version."

Rudie cocked his head, and looked at me strangely. "He's dead? You killed him?"

"More or less. A cop finished him off. Otherwise we'd both be dead."

"But... This was a tiger, right?"

I nodded.

"Full-morph, you said. A full morph tiger?"

"At the time he was, yes." The old memory had me trembling slightly in fear. As long as I lived, I would never, ever get over having been hunted, forget being seen as mere food.

"You killed a tiger? A rabbit killed a tiger?" Rudie's mouth was agape in wonder.

I nodded solemnly. "Being a herbivore does not automatically make you helpless, son. It makes you a target, yes. Some of us more so than others. But helpless, no. Have you ever seen films of lions in the act of hunting?"

"Yeah. They eat, eat..."

"Zebras." I finished for him. "Lions often eat zebras."

Rudie sat silently for a moment, then a tear began tracing its way down his cheek. "I don't want to be eaten!" The words were a cry of anguish, torn from the boy's heart.

You won't be, I wanted to say reassuringly. But in our herbivore hearts we would both have known that this was merely a comforting lie. So instead, I offered truth. "In the films the lions always win, don't they?"

"Yes. Of course." Rudie's shoulders were shuddering, now.

"You know, that's simply not the way it is in real life. Most of the time the zebras get away. Sometimes a lion is even killed by its intended victim. But the nature films usually only show the successful stalks. In point of fact, if we use our minds and behave intelligently we prey species can almost always get away."

My client put his head down on the table and wailed. "But I don't want to be a prey animal at all! I don't want to have to always know where the door is! I don't want to have to worry about being killed and eaten!"

The desk was too wide for me to reach Rudie, so I hopped up on top of it and, scattering papers all the way, crossed over to him. Once there, I gently pawed at his head. "Son," I said. "Son. Look up at me a minute."

He did, tears streaming.

"Son, almost no one wants what SCABS does to them. Almost no one. Do you hear me?"

He nodded.

"We look like animals, some of us SCABs. And some of us have animal-type problems. But we are not animals. We are human beings. Do you know how it is that we can tell for sure?"

"How?" The reply was fierce and almost mocking, bitter as only words that come from a seventeen-year-old boy in tears can be. "How can we tell?"

"Because animals run away from their problems," I explained. "They let events control their lives. But human beings confront things, and use their minds to their advantage. Humans take charge."

The boy stared at me for a moment, then flopped his Virus-elongated head back down onto the desk. His whole body was wracked with sobs. I simply sat there for a time, holding my forepaw on his shoulder. And eventually, the tempest passed. When I thought that the time was right, I spoke again.

"Rudie, I'm going to leave you alone a bit to pull yourself together. Take your time; there's nothing to be ashamed of. SCABS is hard, son, and well worth crying over. But hear one more thing before I go, all right?"

The boy nodded, head still nestled in his striped arms. His fur looked oddly like an old-fashioned prisoner's uniform, I realized suddenly. "I am a career counselor, not a specialist in dealing with terrible fears. But I have the same basic problem as you do, only worse. Agreed?"

Another nod.

"Your fear is rational and reasonable, to one like me. I do understand it, as few others can. Don't ever let anyone tell you that it is wrong for you to be afraid. But, on the other hand you cannot let it run your life. You need to put it into perspective." I paused a bit to let my words sink in before continuing. "Son, I can help you find a good job in the real world. A place where you can be accepted, earn good money, make your dreams come true, even support a family if you wish. That is, I can do these things if you can at least partly master your fear. But if you cannot do this, than I will have to search down a far more limited path. There are jobs for SCABs with behavioral problems out there, but they are few and far between. The pay is generally very, very bad. Some of your classmates are likely to be able to do no better, frankly. But I think that you can."

My words were met only with silence. He was still listening though, I hoped. "I know someone who might be able to help you out a bit, maybe help you develop some confidence. He's a SCAB too—full-morph, in fact. If I leave his name with Mrs. Abraham, will you call him?"

For a moment nothing happened. Then he nodded, barely.

"Good." And with that I left the room, to grant Rudie the dignity of solitude for his tears. After all, every SCAB deserves to be able to weep in private.

※ ⌀ ※

I always need a bit of time to recover from a very emotional session, so I took the opportunity to call my friend Ken Bronski from a phone just down the hall. Luckily he was at his desk.

"Detective Bronski," he answered in that overly gruff voice of his. It sounded more like what you'd expect from a cave bear than from an ostrich.

"Ken, this is Phil," I replied. "I need a favor."

"What can I do for you?" he asked. Ken is a cop first, foremost and always. However, he is a member of the SCAB community too. And as such, he feels obligated to help out when called upon.

I briefed him on Rudie's situation. "I think that most likely he just needs a boost in confidence, Ken. You've studied self-defense as an ostrich, right?"

"The Department required it, Phil. In fact, they had to go all the way to England to find a qualified instructor for me."

"I'm not surprised. Rudie here is no ostrich, I realize. But I figure that the theory will be at least partly the same."

"Mostly the same, in fact," he agreed. "A kick is a kick. Sure, I'll show him a few tricks—hey!"

"Hey what?"

"I just thought of something. Our regular hand-to-hand instructor at the Academy is a Norm, but carries a certificate in SCAB techniques as well. He needed to get it for training SCAB recruits. My problems were beyond him, but I bet that he'd be glad to spend some time with Rudie."

A warm glow spread through me. Good old Ken! "Just be sure and show him what you yourself can do. Part of my goal is to make him understand that even those more heavily morphed than himself can make it in life without too awfully much reason to be afraid."

"Sure thing," Ken agreed. "Give him my pager number, willya? I'm not going to be at my desk very much for the next few days. You wouldn't believe my caseload! But for a SCAB kid, I'll make time."

"Right. By the way, he's especially afraid of lions, I think. He's been watching nature films."

"Those things will shake you up every time, won't they? I'll make sure to show him how to deal with big cats, then, first thing."

"Thanks so very much, Ken!" And I hung up, feeling quite irrationally that somehow everything was going to be all right now. Somehow, Detective Bronski often has that effect on me.

🐾 ☜ 🐾

It was fortunate that my next appointment was with Sandy Blankenship. She could not possibly fit into the borrowed office anyway, so I was able to leave Rudie in peace there while talking to Sandy outside. It was a warm and clear April day, and Sandy's exercise area was fully fenced in. I felt very safe there. Sandy herself, however, appeared to be a bit cramped for space. She was an African elephant, full-morph, with a set of powerful eyeglasses strapped onto her head. Her face was unreadable, of course, but somehow her very posture communicated a sense of resignation that I did not like at all.

"Hello," I introduced myself from the far side of the pen. Her teachers had made it clear that for safety's sake I had to make absolutely certain that Sandy knew where I was at all times. Otherwise, there might be a terrible accident. "I'm Phil, here to talk with you about career options."

Sandy raised her head and squinted at me. "Oh, yes. Mrs. Abraham told me to expect you. I'm on a feeding break, but that's all right. I'm done eating."

She seemed like a sweet girl; though the high-pitched voder-voice sounded very out of place at first coming from a pachyderm's body. My guess was that her original voice had been reconstructed from recordings or memories. Someone had spent a good deal of money on that. Clearly, Sandy had a family that cared.

"Do you sit down?" I asked hesitantly. This was my first experience with an elephant.

The voder giggled nervously. "No, it's too much of an effort to get up again when I do. Sometimes I need to shift my feet around though. Keep clear!"

I only weigh about a hundred pounds these days; Sandy made me feel absolutely tiny. Staying out from underneath her feet was very, very good advice indeed! "I will, I assure you. Tell me, can you see me at all?"

"You're sort of a white blur. Are you wearing white coveralls, perhaps?"

"No, I'm not wearing anything. Take a sniff."

She giggled nervously again, then reached out carefully with her trunk. It tickled, reminding me of a groomer's vacuum as she took in my scent. "You're a rabbit!" Sandy said wonderingly.

"Yes, about three-quarters morphed. I wanted you to know that I understand some of your problems."

"None of our teachers here are SCABs," Sandy commented. "Except Mr. Dawson. And he's a chronomorph. That doesn't help much."

"No," I replied. "I guess it doesn't."

"Not that I think that you'll be able to do a lot for us either. I'll never be able to hold a real job. Or raise a family. Or be normal in any way."

I sighed, very quietly. Elephant ears might be even better than mine, for all I knew. "To a degree you're right, you know. I'm not here to give you false hopes."

Sandy tossed her head in what might have been elephant laughter. "Well, that's a relief, I suppose. Are all rabbits as honest as you?"

Despite myself, I chuckled. "The ones I've met are. You see, we have a great deal of difficulty lying to each other. Our scents do not match our words when we lie, if you know how to read them. The habit of being truthful spills over into our everyday lives."

"How very... sweet! No such luck with elephants, darn it."

"Have you met others?" I was curious.

"Oh, yes!" she replied. "There's a group home for us in Kentucky. I've visited twice—they have to ship me by rail, you know, so I don't get out much. They have a place reserved for me. It's a very nice little stall."

"And is this what you want for yourself?" I asked quietly.

"It's what I have to want, I think. I can't stay at home. I'm destroying my family."

My ears pricked up. "How so?"

"Mom used to be an advertising exec. Now she takes care of me full-time. Dad has to work hours and hours of overtime to take up the financial slack, though he can never quite manage to catch up. I have two younger brothers that my parents virtually ignore. I take up all the time, all the money, all the attention. And I can never amount to anything, no matter what. I can't even be a big sister to my kid brothers! It's such a terrible waste, really."

"Is that why you do not wish to live?" I asked very quietly.

She looked startled for a second, then nodded her huge head slowly. "Yes. I would rather die than destroy my family. There's no reason for me to go on. Not like this."

"I see. Or at least I think I see."

Sandy bristled, her anger finally showing through. "No one can see! Have you ever been a blind elephant?"

"Have you ever been committed and institutionalized?" I retorted, willing myself not to back down, just this once. "I have."

"You... You were committed?" She seemed shocked. It was rare for SCABs to discuss the matter. It was far, far too close to our hearts.

I nodded slowly. "Yes, for almost a year. And they'd have me back, if they could."

She blinked rapidly. "But... That means you have, well—Instincts. Strong ones."

"Right," I agreed. "Just like some of your fellow students here. My basic personality has changed. I am no longer entirely human in my soul."

Sandy cocked her head to one side. "And you come right out and tell me this? You admit it freely?"

"Of course. It is merely the simple truth, the reality that I must live with every single day. Frankly, I think I might rather be a near-blind elephant, given the choice. Not that either of us have one."

"So would I," she admitted sheepishly. "So would I."

"You are very lucky, to still be basically the same person you once were. When you think about it, I mean. You never need question that you are still a human being, deep down."

Her trunk came snaking back over, this time to caress my ears gently. "I'm so sorry for you," she said gently.

"I'm not," I replied seriously. "Honestly. I stay too busy to feel sorry for myself. And rabbits are happy creatures, fundamentally. I find that I'm very easy to please. Most of the time I'm just fine."

"I wish that I could stay busy," Sandy replied sadly. "But there's nothing worthwhile for me to do. I'm just a burden, is all."

Finally she had spoken the words that I had been waiting for. "Sandy, you do not have to be a burden anymore. I can promise you that much."

"What do you mean?" she asked cautiously.

"I can do some checking around, and talk to some old friends. I'll admit that I don't have anything lined up just yet. But one thing I have learned in this business is that there is a future out there for everyone, including elephant full-morphs. My challenge for you is this. If I can find something for you, will you give it a try?"

She pondered for a moment. "I'll not perform in some kind of circus. Or be part of a freak show. The group home would be better than that."

I nodded. "Of course not. I wouldn't ask you to do anything like that. But if the work were meaningful? And if you could really do it?"

"Then I promise to try it. Cross my heart."

My face won't smile anymore, but over the years I have discovered that largely the same effect can be achieved by rocking my ears rapidly forward and back a time or two. I did so. "Great! I'm sure I'll be able to come up with something, then." The enthusiasm in my words was genuine. The world is a big place; there are all sorts of odd little nooks and crannies out there to look in. I'd just have to work at it, was all.

Sandy giggled again. "I won't be holding my breath, Mr. Bunny Rabbit. To be honest, I don't think that you will find a thing."

"Hmm." I thought rapidly for a moment. "Do you like carrots?" I asked. My nose had already told me the answer. She had eaten them quite recently, in fact. Many of them.

"Yes, I do. And I know that you must."

I ear-smiled again. "All right then. I'll bet you one bushel basket of carrots that I can find you a job which you'll like doing more than you would living in that home in Kentucky."

"Just one bushel? That's hardly a snack!"

"For you maybe, little lady. Is it a bet?"

Sandy snickered. "Yeah. I guess."

"Good." And solemnly we shook forelimbs on it. The sight would have been ridiculous, of course, had anyone been looking. But neither of us cared.

🐾 ᴏ 🐾

Next on my list was the woodchuck, Bobby Reiser. I was worried about not having enough time to spend with him before lunch, but our appointment was relatively brief. His father was a barber, he explained, and was going to try and train Bobby to take over his shop someday. They'd just recently begun planning. Grooming was a lot of fun since the Flu, he explained, and I nodded rather enviously. I could think of worse ways to spend my own days; grooming seems to be a common passion with all of us small and furry types. When I asked about custom equipment, Bobby informed me excitedly that his father was already working on obtaining both barbering tools and a special suspended platform that he could work from. I rocked my ears in pleasure at this; not only did Bobby now seem to have a future ahead of him but it also appeared that he had some all-important family support going for him as well. Mentally, I checked him off of my list. It looked as if all would be well with him in any case. Even if he graduated late, his father would still be waiting.

🐾 ∞ 🐾

Lunch was something of an ordeal. I had been informed that the school cafeteria could provide salads, and this was true. But all of them were chef's salads, and had ham and bologna sitting on top of them. Sure, the revolting stuff could be picked off. The smell remained, however, and turned my stomach utterly. Were I starving, I could have choked the greens down regardless. I was not starving, however. Instead I was merely very, very hungry, which was not nearly incentive enough, not for that! Never, ever expect too much from a school lunch. Otherwise you are certain to be disappointed.

I ate at the faculty table, of course, and was the only obvious SCAB there. The teachers were not too put off by my dining habits, though I got the idea that having a rabbit eat right at their table with them was something of a novelty. Mr. Nogle, a music teacher, was kind enough to carry my tray for me, and Mrs. Ramirez of the Mathematics department was extremely polite. She offered me the parsley from her salisbury steak—it had not gotten any gravy on it. The powerful flavor killed the scent of the meat, and I ate it greedily. After that I downed all the other garnishes at the table too. When I explained what was wrong with my salad everyone was highly sympathetic. They even offered to pick up something for me from the market down the street. But it was too late by then; I was scheduled to see Billy Winecrest, my jackrabbit client, in just a few moments. Still, it was nice to be treated as a fellow professional. Even if I really wasn't.

🐾 ∞ 🐾

I've been around many, many lapine clients, and around even more lapines who were not my clients. Something sort of clicks between we rabbits right away; being social creatures we most often have the ability to "read" each other emotionally without too much difficulty. Billy was no exception. There was not the slightest doubt in my mind that Billy Winecrest was not feeling very happy as he lounged fullmorph in his litterbox with the lights turned out.

I'd had to search him out; Mrs. Abraham had warned me that Billy could not read clocks much of the time. The staff had set up a nice little studying retreat for him off in the corner of an unused classroom. Indeed, they had provided him with everything a rabbit could ask for: litterbox, reading lamp, a few chew toys, a nice "safe" area free from prying eyes.

In fact, it looked so inviting that once I got there I decided to get down on all fours and join him inside.

"May I come in?" I asked formally before entering his territory. He nodded graciously, and I stuffed myself into the limited space up close alongside him. We sniffed at each other a bit in friendly rabbit-fashion, and became comfortable together. Then after a decent interval had passed I spoke again. "I'm Phil, your career counselor. Can you speak in that form?"

Billy seemed to concentrate a second, and the proportions of his skull and neck shifted slightly. After a couple of false attempts, he managed to reply in a voice much like my own. "I can now. Pleased to meet you, sir. I'm sorry that I'm late. They didn't tell me that you were a rabbit too."

"They didn't tell anyone," I observed. "It's not polite to label someone as a SCAB unless there is a good reason for doing so."

Billy nodded. "I hate it when people go out of their way so much for us. It's almost better when they hate me."

It was my turn to nod. I understood exactly what he meant. "Not that too many people hate us rabbits. It's one of the few advantages of the form."

"Actually," Billy corrected me, "I am a hare. The biologists are still arguing about whether we belong in separate genuses or not. But your point is well taken. Why don't you explain it to that Christiasson kid?"

I shuddered. Everyone had heard about that particular hate crime. "You can find plenty of hate in the world, if you look for it. I'll grant you that. But I have found mostly acceptance."

He raised his head. "Acceptance? Tell me, how exactly are you keeping yourself out of the Colonies? My folks are doing it by spending tons of money."

The question hit me like a blow, though it was a subject that I had intended to address before leaving. "Mostly by good luck," I admitted. "And the fact that I have a pension. A means of support, in other words. I'm only a volunteer counselor, you know."

He laid his head down and closed his big eyes. "No, I didn't know that. Not that it matters, particularly. I'll never hold a job."

My ears rose, and I cuffed Billy on the top of the head just a touch roughly with my forepaw, emphasizing my words rabbit-fashion. "Never say never, Billy. At least not around me."

Billy rocked his ears submissively. "I can lie to the doctors. I can lie to my teachers. But I can't lie to you. You know that."

I nodded.

"Don't waste your time on me," he continued. "It's getting harder and harder for me to change shape. And I am going feral for longer and longer afterwards. I'm losing the ability to become partly human. My default form seems to be fullmorph." The jackrabbit sighed. "Though not feral fullmorph, at least."

My ears went limp in sympathy. Damn, but that was bad news! "I'm sorry. I cannot tell you how sorry I am."

He nodded. "That's kinda the final straw, I figure. Once I graduate, I'm gonna tell the folks. That way they can quit spending their retirement money trying to save me. I'm for the Colonies for sure. There's simply no way around it if I'm fullmorph."

I sighed, and snuggled up even closer to Billy. "So you're gonna quit that easy, eh?"

He raised his head, startled. "What do you mean, 'that easy'? My folks and I have fought them off for months! It's been absolutely vicious; they even had me loaded on the truck once before a court order arrived. We've fought hard!"

I nodded. "So far you have indeed fought hard. And I can't lie to you either; I don't think that your chances of winning are all that good. But are you going to go down fighting like a man, or are you going to give up like a warm, fuzzy, dumb little bunny rabbit?"

This time it was Billy who looked as if he'd been slugged in the head. "I, I..." He was silent for a time, then he rolled onto his side. I did the same, and we rubbed up against each other back to back.

"Look," he began again. "We're snuggling like a couple of gay men. Doesn't that bother you?"

"It used to," I admitted. "Before I realized that human perceptions no longer apply in this case."

Billy shook his head violently. "But everyone knows what we are, just by looking! Prey animals, for God's sake! Cute, fuzzy harmless creatures!"

"Right," I replied, as if what he had said was self-explanatory. "That's exactly what we are."

"This is crazy!" he replied.

"But you like it, don't you? You like it a lot, just as I do. You need to snuggle now, Billy. It's how we rabbits interact."

There was another long silence before Billy spoke again. "Then you are saying that we really are just rabbits."

"Of course not," I answered. "We are human beings. But we are rabbits too. And when we behave as such, no one should be surprised. Least of all us."

"But... " Billy hesitated, and I began to wonder if he had received any counseling at all. "Phil, do you make friends with wild rabbits? Ordinary animal-type bunnies? Get to know them? Make friends? Even feel lust for them sometimes?"

I nodded. "Yes. Of course. It's the most natural thing in the world."

Suddenly he pulled away from me. "Then you belong in the Colonies every bit as much as I do, you sick freak!" he wailed.

Rabbits do not weep in the same manner as do humans, and my client was very nearly in fullmorph form. He shuddered violently, and made sad little sounds that would have been almost undetectable to a Norm. There was nothing for me to do but wait until it was over, pondering upon the fact that it surely did seem that I was making an awful lot of people cry today. Eventually he wept himself out, and I sat up quadrupedal fashion to face him, my ears bent over almost double due to the comfortingly low ceiling. "Listen," I began. "There are indeed SCABs who truly belong in the Colonies. The ones who are feral, mostly feral, or even those that go feral unpredictably all arguably belong there for their own good. I can even understand why they want you and me there, though I do not agree with them. I go feral when frightened too, sometimes. But it is not simply because we enjoy lapine company, or have lapine tendencies sometimes. Do you understand?"

He cocked an ear. Clearly, he did not.

I sighed. "You are ashamed of something that is not your fault. It is simply the way that you are made now. If you had had your sex changed by SCABS, would you be ashamed if you began to be attracted to men?"

"Well, no. Of course not. But..."

"No buts. You are physically part jackrabbit. Mostly one, in fact. Why should you be ashamed when you act like one?"

He remained silent, so I reached over and nudged him in the ribs with a forepaw. "You sure look like a jackrabbit to me, Billy. You feel like one, too. " I nudged him again. "This. This is your body from now on, son. It is part of you, and it has its own wants and needs. Like snuggling, for example. Now, do you want to physically socialize some more? Or are you going to spend the rest of your life suffering from lack of attention and denying the obvious?"

He lay still then, and I thought for a moment that I had lost him. But eventually he spoke up again. "What kind of a job do you think that you could find for me?"

I sighed. "Frankly, I don't really know yet. If you are right about becoming morphlocked, then in truth your options are going to be very limited. I'm afraid the Marines are pretty much out of the question, son."

He rocked his ears slightly. "I was just a kid when I wanted that."

For his sake, I hoped that his dream was in fact that easily dismissed, and that he had indeed matured some since then. Not that there was anything wrong with wanting to be a Marine, of course, not at all. But he had been totally fixated upon the single goal, according to his folder. Maturity meant flexibility. "I needed to talk to you a bit, and get to know you in person before I did any serious hunting. However, I can tell you two things right off."

"Yes?" He smelled interested, despite himself.

I groomed a forepaw for a moment before speaking, so as to have time to phrase things just right. "First of all, having any sort of job will do more than anything else I can think of to help your parents keep you free. If that is what you wish."

He nodded. "Our lawyers agree. And the second thing?"

I looked around for something to remove the fur from my tongue, and finally rubbed it off on the rough wooden side of Billy's hideaway. "There's a bit of information that you may want to consider for a while before you report voluntarily for commitment. Did you know that morphlock can be entirely psychological in origin? And curable? You might want to consider talking to your doctor about it. Or, if you don't trust him, I can refer you to one whom you can trust. He's been morphlocked himself, you see."

Then, leaving my client with that little tidbit to gnaw on, I shook myself off and left our safe little haven to go out and face the real world.

🐾 ⌒ 🐾

At that particular moment, of course, the real world that I had to face consisted of my last appointment of the day, a meeting with George Poltava. I was rather looking forward to it, as I had never met a batmorph before. George was sitting alone in the dark when I came in, of course. The room had been fitted with a double-curtain arrangement to keep the sunlight out, and almost right away I had to get down on all fours and navigate by whisker and ear. Certainly it was no darker in George's room than inside a typical burrow, and I was frankly rather proud of being able to find my seat without bumping into anything or even wandering aimlessly around the room.

"Not bad!" George complimented me. I had been just barely able to make out the sharp keening ultrasonic cries by which he had tracked me; in fact, I had sort of homed in on them myself in order to locate my client in the room. "What are you, anyway?" he continued. "I can't get a good echo off of you to save my life." He sounded a little peeved.

"I'm a rabbit morph," I replied, rocking my ears rapidly. "My fur is soft and very, very thick. I'll bet that's why you can't sense me very well."

George shifted in his seat. "A rabbit, eh? Well, at least that explains how you get around so well in the dark. But you're just a blur to me. It's most annoying."

I rocked my ears again. "I can see how it might be. Would you like for me to get under the table or something, where you don't have to look at me? Honestly, it's no trouble. I sit in chairs just to please norms; truthfully, the floor is every bit as comfy." I started to climb down.

George stopped me. "No, no, please don't trouble yourself. It's just that the sensation is... odd."

I chuckled. "Do many SCABs stop by?"

"No, not really. You're almost my very first. And you are the first one that I almost can't see."

I chuckled. "Then you haven't even begun to see strange, son. Trust me on that one." Then we laughed politely together for a moment. When the time seemed right, I spoke again. "I guess that you've been told that I am a career counselor?"

He nodded. "Yes."

"Good," I replied. "I've been looking at your file. You've never expressed any interest in a career, George. Or at least not that anyone's ever taken note of."

There was silence for a minute, and then my client spoke. "What kind of career would you suggest, sir?"

"Phil," I corrected him. "Please, call me Phil."

George nodded obediently. "Yes, sir. Phil, rather. Sorry." I rocked my ears once again encouragingly, and he went on. "Anyway, what sort of thing would you suggest that I look into? Or echo-range into, rather. I haven't done very much genuine 'looking' into anything at all lately." The last words were filled with bitterness.

I pressed my lips together before speaking. "Don't give up so easily, George. Surely you have some sorts of interests. Your records indicate that you are easily bright enough to have gone on into college."

The bat-morph shifted in his seat again, and I wished that I could see. "Sure," he answered cynically. "I could go to college. And major in what? Entomology, perhaps, with a focus on the flavor of night-flying insects? Most of them are pretty nasty-tasting, I can assure you."

I rolled my eyes, confident my client could not detect the gesture. At least the blindness went both ways. "But what options do you have besides getting a job?" I asked. "Do you want to live with your parents forever? Or be institutionalized, perhaps? I find it hard to believe you'd be truly happy as a charity case."

My client made a sharp, nasty barking sound. It took me a moment to recognize it as laughter. "No, I would not be at all happy as a charity case. But then, I'm not very happy as a bat, either. So what I want doesn't seem to matter very much, now does it?"

I looked down at the ground. "George, I'm going to be completely level with you here. Your case is a very, very difficult one. Can you offer me any kind of a lead at all, any sort of clue or direction as to what sort of job you might like to do? I promise to do my best."

The bat-morph stirred once more in his seat. I could quite clearly hear the sheets of featherless skin that made up his useless wings rustling gently in the darkness. "Close your eyes," he said simply.

"What?" I asked. "Why?"

"Close your eyes, Phil. Please? I need to turn on the light to show you something, and I don't want to blind you."

"All right," I agreed, and I heard the scratching of claws against something or another. Then the switch was thrown, and my closed eyelids glowed red.

"Ow!" I heard George complain. "Damnit!" There were more muffled curses after that; clearly he was trying to set up something for me. "All right," he finally said. "You can look now." I opened my eyes—

—and there, two inches in front of my face, hung inverted the most horrible monstrosity I had ever beheld in my life. It had tiny pointed teeth, twisted lips, useless staring eyes, and the nose, the nose, the nose...

My eyes widened in terror. The nose belonged on no living thing!

I screamed in panic, then went totally feral. In my panicked flight I knocked over the lamp, shattering the bulb into a thousand pieces. This only made things worse, as I could no longer see the terrible thing and had to guess at where it was. Finally my little hare-brain remembered the double-curtain trick, and I flashed into the hallway at full speed, bowled over an elderly special-ed teacher, and made straight for Billy Winecrest's little "safe" spot.

And there I hid trembling for the rest of the day, until a more than slightly embarrassed Billy finally managed to calm me down enough to go home.

🦇 ∞ 🦇

I returned the very next day, of course, both to apologize to everyone involved and to finish my business. I'd done serious damage to George's ego already, I feared. At the least I wanted to repair as much as of it as I possibly could, and as soon as possible. The school was kind enough to let me try, and so was George. But it was clear to me that he was very deeply hurt. "I am so sorry, Phil." He began as soon as I entered his cubicle. "Truly I am. I just wanted to show you..."

I shook my head firmly. "No, George. I am the one who should apologize. You had no possible way of knowing about my problems. I should have guessed what it was that you were about to do..."

Both of us sort of trailed off into silence eventually. The situation was very, very awkward. Eventually I broke the silence. "We are both of us SCABs, George. Both of us face very real barriers in life."

"Yes," George acknowledged. "I see that now. But be honest with me, Phil. Would you rather deal with your barriers, or mine?"

Between one thing and another, I could make almost anyone else back down on that particular question. In fact, I had essentially done exactly that with Sandy the elephant yesterday. But I could not in good faith do so with George. Not with the future that he faced. "You win," I replied eventually. "Your case may be beyond me. I admit it."

George took it with good humor. "And we never even got into how I can't sleep unless I hang upside down," he joked, trying to fill in the awkward moment.

I sighed, not caring at all if my client heard me for once. He was facing his fate with dignity and courage. It hurt that I wasn't able to help him. "Just out of curiosity, can I ask a question?"

"Sure, Phil," he replied cheerfully. "Anything at all."

I nodded and rocked my ears. "If I could find you a job, what would you like for it to be? Your dream job, that is."

The boy sat silently for a time before answering. "Dream job? Hmm. I dream a lot, you know. There's not much else for me to do. Mostly about James Bond, I guess."

My face fell. "James Bond?"

"Yep. Old Double-Oh-Seven himself. He always gets the bad guys, always gets the women, always does truly meaningful and important work. And you know what else? He never, ever develops SCABS."

My heart felt like it would rip itself in two. You might as well dream big, I mused, if dreams were all that you could ever have. "Oh god, George! I so wish I could help you!"

"I know," he answered, a sob in his voice. "I know."

Before I could even think about it we were hugging each other, tight. And you know what? It's the most remarkable thing. Bats don't feel ugly. They are actually quite warm and soft, just like the rest of us.

🦇 ∞ 🦇

While at the school anyway I asked about Johni, but she was still out sick. Though I wasn't really looking forward to it, it was absolutely vital that we sit down together very soon. Mrs. Abraham frowned at me when I said so, however. Johni had been missing a lot of school lately, she explained. Most of the faculty believed that she was cutting class. In fact, were it to get much worse her graduation would likely be delayed, perhaps indefinitely. I nodded soberly at this, and made a mental note to check back in a few days. After all, it wasn't like I didn't have enough work to do on the other cases.

Taking on six new clients at once, all of them short-deadline cases, might not have been the brightest thing I had ever done, I very soon realized. But I took the bull by the horns and settled down to a period of twelve-hour workdays. Clover was plenty unhappy about this—heck, I was plenty unhappy about it, too!—but sometimes you just have to do what you have to do.

Bobby Reiser was fairly easy to take care of. I caught a ride over to his father's barber shop and introduced myself. The obvious pride that Bob Sr. displayed while showing me the special haircutting tools he had commissioned and the genuine interest that his customers took in the little suspended platform that Bobby Jr. would someday work from told me all I needed to know. Oftentimes, potential clients prove quite able to solve their problems without me. The best thing for a counselor to do then is butt out. So I took my own advice and did exactly that.

The other cases took more work. I put out feelers to most of the big factories in town, hoping that one or two might be hiring. If so, I could try and work out some sort of arrangement for Rudie and potentially even Johni. Times were tough in manufacturing just then, however, and

I drew nothing but a big blank. So I looked into all sorts of non-public-contact jobs for Rudie; night watchman, telephone operator, greenhouse worker, farmhand. Sadly, no one seemed interested in a SCAB who had even the slightest hint of feral tendencies. I was sitting at my desk one day with my aching head in my paws, trying to brainstorm a new approach, when the phone rang.

It was Rudie. "Phil!" he said excitedly. "Oh, Phil! You'll never guess what!"

"What?" I asked, hoping against hope.

"I rode the bus today. With Ken. And we sat next to a lion-morph! Isn't that just great?"

My ears dropped in relief. I'd begun to get worried. "Yes, Rudie," I answered, "that is wonderful news! Do you think that you have yourself under control now?"

"Ken thinks so, but he says I need to wait a few months to be sure. Besides, I've got to go back to school anyway. All this time up until now it hasn't really mattered much to me, but now I understand why my grades are so important. I've got to do well!"

"Why?" I asked, half-guessing the answer.

"Because Ken says that he can cover the fear-thing with the Police Academy, as long as I really am better now. But the grades, well, I've got to do better with those on my own. And I want to be a cop so bad!"

The rest of the call sort of passed in a sort of pleasant haze. I would have to check in with Ken, of course, to verify that Rudie did indeed have a real chance of making it onto the force. But that was merely a formality. Ken would never mislead a young man about something so important.

Which meant I had two down, four to go.

🐾 ∞ 🐾

Actually, I should really have had only three to go; George Poltava was clearly a hopeless case. I had even given up on him to his face. But somehow, I kept making calls on his behalf. Nothing ever seemed to work out, though. Until something happened one night at the 'Pig'.

I was sharing a drink with Clover, who was doing her best to not hold a grudge against me over my recent work schedule. Almost against my will, I was talking shop with her, something I rarely do.

"You should have seen this poor kid," I was explaining. "There's not a hope in the world for him, of course. God, how I hate it when there's nothing to be done!"

"But you just told me about a half-dozen or more places you've called," she pointed out. "If George is truly a hopeless case, then why are you spending so much time on him?"

I sighed and stared fixedly into our Jack Strafford. "I don't know, honey. It just doesn't feel right to give up. Not this time."

"Then don't." She frowned slightly, thinking hard. "Tell me, have you looked into any research groups?"

I nodded grimly. "Several. All of them require George to be able to fly. Otherwise, they can't use him."

"But that's the closest you've come, right?"

"In short, yes." I sighed again. We were silent for a time.

Then Clover spoke once more. "Well, if you want to hook George up with a research establishment, then why not ask the Federal government for help? They're connected with every university in the country. Surely there's a master list somewhere of who is studying what on a Federal grant."

Later that very night, I e-mailed Congressman Theiu, the only acknowledged SCAB currently elected to Federal office, and outlined my problem. About a week later, I received a very definite, very substantial reply. It came in the form of two rather large federal agents waiting for me outside the door of my office when I arrived there.

They asked me all sorts of questions about George's sonar capabilities, which I had talked up in my letter to Theiu. I explained that I was only a career counselor, and not really qualified to give them the kind of answers they sought. Then the pair politely asked me if they could meet with my client. I was able to arrange an immediate interview, though we generated a lot of raised eyebrows at the school when my companions explained that they were not free to explain precisely which agency of the U.S. Government they represented. Still, their ID's were solid and I vouched for them, so we got in to see George. He was quite excited, and knocked over his lamp again. Fortunately, this time it was not turned on.

The Government types asked George to identify a series of objects held up in the air, which he did without fail. Then they asked him to listen to a recording. I am quite sure that everyone else forgot about my own rather sensitive set of ears, or else they would have kicked me out for this test. As it was, I heard just enough to figure the whole game out. The tape consisted of a series of identical electronic hypersonic cries, much like George's own, and distant, even fainter echoes.

George concentrated for a moment; I could easily picture him cocking his head from side to side as he listened intently. "A round room," he finally said. "The walls are hard, and a bit irregular. Metal cabinets on them, maybe? And in the center is something big and tall. It's round and hard too, like a sort of column... Yes, I have it now. This is a miss—"

"Thank you very much, Mr., er George," the senior of the two government types interrupted hastily. "That's all we needed to see. Or hear rather. I am quite certain that you will be hearing from us again. Soon."

With that, we rather promptly left. Not, however, before I was able to very quietly hum a couple bars of "Live And Let Die" under my breath. I'm quite sure George heard it; he burst out laughing almost instantly.

And crying, too.

The unexpected success with my bat-morph made me all the more anxious to get together with Johni, who I was beginning to think of as my "mystery client." Over and over again she kept missing school on the days when I was scheduled to see her. Finally, with the school's blessing I got Donnie to drive me over to her home. As it turned out, she lived less than a mile from the Shelter.

Her apartment fit right in with the rest of the squalid neighborhood. She lived on the lower floor of a moderately decrepit two-family flat. There was trash scattered all about the place, and young children played out in front unsupervised, dangerously close to moving traffic. I felt Donnie stiffen as we walked up the three steps to the porch. One of them crumbled a bit under his tremendous weight, but he caught himself just in time to avoid a nasty fall.

At least the doorbell worked when we tried it. Though no one answered.

By then, I was becoming angry. And more than a little stubborn, as well. "Donnie," I said, turning to my mute friend, "This is not your affair, and I know you have to get back and open the 'Pig' up. But would you mind if we waited a little bit first? Eventually somebody has got to come along."

He nodded, and wait we did. Sure enough, eventually someone did come along. It was Johni herself. She wasn't trying to pass as male today, I could see. But on the other hand she was certainly trying her best to look "butch", and succeeding. Her wooly hair was short and dyed bright red, looking at first glance almost like a Catholic cardinal's skullcap. The scarlet hair framed a face that was a bit elongated, but was otherwise very human in appearance and even more petite than I had been led to expect. From the neck down she was all chrome jewelry and black leather. Her cigarette would have charmingly completed the ensemble, had it not been for the lost look in her eyes. They didn't look very tough at all.

"Who the hell are you two?" she demanded of us as she strode arrogantly up. "And why are you here?"

"Why do you think we're here?" I asked in return, playing the game.

She frowned menacingly. "Look, I'm gonna call the cops..."

I held up a peacemaking forepaw. "There's no need for that. My name is Phil, and your school knows that I'm here. This is my good friend Donnie; he's giving me a ride. I'm your career counselor."

Her eyes rolled up in her head. They were very blue, I noted, almost the same color as mine. "Oh," she said sarcastically. "So it's not enough that I put up with school shit all day; now they've got to start sending more shit directly to my house."

I held my temper. "All I want to do is to help you find a job. That's all. So that you can get your life started after graduation."

"Fuck," she replied with an evil grin, drawling out the word for all it was worth. "There's no one on earth gonna hire me. I'm a fucked up TG animal SCAB."

"I'd bet against that," I replied evenly. "Though I'd also bet against your keeping any job that you might find, if you act like this all of the time."

"Fuck you," she replied evenly. Then with a pretty smile on her face she repeated it again, sweetly this time. "Fuck you. I've always wanted to say that to a school guy. And now we're not in school, so you can't do jack-shit about it. Now, would you care to get your rabbity ass out of my fucking goddamned way, Mister career counselor, so I can get into my goddamned piece-of-shit house?"

Usually I keep a pretty good eye out for what's happening around me. This comes naturally to us prey-species SCABs. Johni, however, was enough to distract even someone as alert to danger as me.

"What did you just say to the nice bunny rabbit?" asked a snarling voice from a few feet away. I whirled around to face it, startled.

"Oh, shit," Johni whispered under her breath. A very large and powerful looking man was purposefully striding up the sidewalk. I was willing to bet that it was Johni's father.

"Come on, little girl," he demanded. "What just came out of your potty mouth?"

"I'm sorry!" she squeaked to the world in general, bending her knees and cringing. "Oh god, I'm so sorry!"

The man curled his lip in contempt. "You bet your sweet curvy little ass that you're sorry! And you're going to be sorrier! Apologize to the bunny."

"Now..." I began, but a single angry glare cut me off.

"I'm sorry, Mr. Bunny Rabbit," she said, her eyes beginning to tear up. "I'm so very sorry."

"Now curtsey to him," the man demanded.

She did so, awkwardly. He made her do it again, more effeminately.

"Goddamn kids." This time he was speaking to Donnie and I. "They don't show no goddamn respect to anyone. She's a SCAB just like you two. And she ought to have been polite."

I nodded, too upset to speak. He hadn't laid a hand on her or Donnie would have intervened, I knew. But the bastard hadn't touched her. Or at least not yet, he hadn't. We had no grounds to make a legal complaint. Later, though, when we were gone...

He smiled a little at my apparent acceptance of his apology. "She used to be my only son. He was a worthless bastard then. Now she's just a worthless bitch. And a sheep-bitch at that." He nudged his daughter with his foot. "Get in the house, ewe! We'll talk more later." She scooted without hesitation, and he smiled at his own joke. "A female sheep is a ewe."

"I know," I replied flatly.

"Well, then..." He seemed disappointed that I had not laughed. "Be seeing you." And with that he strode inside and began shouting curses at everything in his way.

Donnie and I turned to leave. All the kids that had been playing and having fun were gone. We didn't even look at each other all the way back home.

🐾 ⚬ 🐾

The next day, I called again about seeing Johni at school. I was not surprised to discover that she was absent again. But now she was at the very top of my priority list; I tried again the next day. She was finally in, so I arranged to officially meet with her at long last.

I was deeply torn over what to do about Johni. On the one hand, I knew that I was not competent to be a real counselor. What I should certainly have done was to inform the school officials about my suspicions and then simply try to find the girl a job. This was all that I was being asked to do, and as far as my authority extended. If I did this and no more, I could not possibly get into any trouble myself. But Johni's records contained not a peep about suspected child abuse. Even her psychologist hadn't voiced any suspicions about the possibility. This served to make me believe that they were simply incompetent. Over the years, surely someone ought to have put two and two together. My best guess was that somebody or more probably a lot of somebodies had in fact done so, but then decided that it wasn't their job to do anything about it. Or else perhaps they had decided that it was simply easier to pretend not to see. Or maybe they had realized that by doing nothing they could avoid getting into trouble. The idea of following the same sort of strategy made me feel sick. So I compromised with myself. I would talk to Johni exactly one time before reporting anything. And from there I would play things by ear.

When Johni came in and sat down, there was cold silence between us for many long minutes. Her face was clearly swollen under her heavy makeup; was I the only seeing man in the land of the blind? I sat and carefully studied her features, making it obvious that she was not fooling me in the slightest. Silence can be a very powerful motivator. Eventually, Johni spoke. "I fell down the steps, all right?" she muttered, turning away. "Quit staring at me."

"Do you fall down the steps often?" I asked, not altering my gaze a bit.

"My room is upstairs. I got up in the middle of the night to go to the bathroom, and tripped over the dog. All right? Can we drop this?"

"Funny," I replied. "I'd have sworn that your family lived in the lower-floor flat."

There was more silence. It lasted for a very long time before Johni spoke again. "You're just a career counselor, right? What's this to you, anyway? Why can't we just drop it?"

"How many brothers and sisters do you have?" I asked.

"Three sisters."

"That's three good reasons that I can't drop it, then. And you make four, like it or not. Does he beat your mother, too?"

Johni sighed. "She's dead."

"I'm sorry," I replied automatically, though somewhere in my mind a little warning bell began jangling.

"She died when I was eleven. Car wreck. It wasn't his fault. She was driving."

"Hmm. Does he date?"

Johni's jaw clenched, hard. And suddenly I knew what was really wrong with Johni's life. Oh, dear god! The poor kid! I let the subject drop for a bit. "You're right, you know. I am just a career counselor. This is absolutely none of my business."

"Good!" Johni replied forcefully. "Then let's talk about jobs."

"Yes," I replied. "Let's do that. What exactly do you see yourself doing six months from now?"

There was more silence. Then, hesitantly, she answered me. "I can't work. I need to stay at home and help with my sisters. No one will hire me anyway."

"Really?" I asked. "And why wouldn't they hire you?"

"Because I'm a worthless SCAB piece of shit!" she wailed out. And then the tears began. It seemed that all of these SCAB kids could cry forever, once you got them started. If they shared any common trait regardless of species or degree of morph, then that was certainly the one.

"You sound just like your father," I replied coldly.

"You leave him the fuck out of this!" Johni screamed, so loudly I feared that someone might come in to see if everything was all right. Which was of course the very last thing that I needed just then.

"Why?" I asked. "Why should I leave him out of it when you aren't? All you're doing is mouthing his words and his feelings. It's him that wants you to stay home, isn't it? It's him that needs to beat you down to nothing. It all started when you were still a boy, didn't it?"

"Shut the fuck up!" she screamed again. "Shut up!"

"Not all of it started back then, maybe. But the beatings and the screaming and the cursing, they've been going on for a very long time. And eating your soul alive."

This time, there was no answer except quiet weeping.

"He's told you that you're a piece of worthless crap so many times that you truly believe it, and that's why you act the part. You used to beat up on others when you were big and strong like your Dad because you never learned that people can relate to each other in any other way.

Now that you're a girl, you're one of the weak. And one so filled with anger that you feel like you're going to burst. Am I on the right track, here?"

Again, my only reply was more sobbing.

I sighed and lowered my ears. "Look, kiddo" I explained. "It's like this. I'm absolutely and for sure going to make a stink about this. There's no way on Earth that you can stop me, so don't even try. There's going to be child welfare people at your house by dark tonight. Do you understand me?"

"No," she murmured. "Please, please don't..." But her words were weak, her protests merely reflex. Listening to her, I was convinced that she sounded more relieved than angry. So I continued right on. "You have a choice to make, Johni. You know what I suspect is going on, but only you and your father know the truth. Any day now you're going to be eighteen. That means that you are about to become legally an adult. It's not fair, I know, but I need for you to start thinking like one just a little bit early. What's going to happen to you and your sisters, if things keep going on like they are?"

She didn't respond, so I reached over and gently touched her arm. "Listen, if a dumb untrained career counselor like me can figure out what's happening here, then you had better believe that a dedicated pro can do it quicker and better. And I'm going to see to it that a dedicated pro is exactly who looks into this. If you work with them, they can protect you. They can end this... this nightmare. But if you insist on fighting them, well, I honestly don't know how things will come out."

Johni looked up at me. Her makeup had run, exposing the black-and-blue wounds that I had known must lie underneath. "Why are you doing this?" she asked, her voice twisted with angst. "Why are you doing this to us?"

The victims of repeated and sustained abuse often become confused about right and wrong, I reminded myself. And there were three other children involved. Even if Johni didn't approve of what needed to be done, someone had to speak up for them. Even if it hurt.

"For your own good." I replied evenly. And that ended our interview. Johni hurled insult after tearful insult at me as I quietly left the room, but I was no longer really listening. I'd already heard all that I needed to hear.

I made the promised phone calls, of course, and spent most of the rest of the day answering questions asked by Family Services officers and school officials alike. One of my connections down at City Hall had seen to it that a good caseworker was assigned. But the school officials really got under my skin. They seemed to think I had somehow invaded their turf, stepped over an invisible line. Their questions grew snootier and snootier until finally I explained in rather pointed words that if they had done their goddamned jobs to start with then I wouldn't have had

to do their work for them. I was pretty upset; it was the most assertive I'd been in years. When I finally left I was certain that there was
no remaining love lost between us. My career in the school system was
over before it had even really gotten started. The only really good thing
that happened all day was that I ran into Mrs. Poltava, George's mother,
at school to pick her son up. She raced over, threw her arms around me
and kissed me right in front of the still-steaming school faculty without
even introducing herself. "Oh!" she said, "Thank you so very, very, very
much!"

When she saw that I was both frightened and more than a little confused, she finally explained who she was. "George has been so very
much happier!" she exclaimed. "He acts like he wants to live again! All
he talks about is how he can have a real life now. You've given us back
our son!" Had it not been for that chance meeting, I would have gotten
very, very drunk that evening. But because of Mrs. Poltava, I was able to
keep right on working.

Which was a very good thing indeed, because otherwise I would
never have found work for my jackrabbit client, Billy Winecrest.

🐾 ∾ 🐾

For Billy, landing any old job "right now" was far more important
than finding him a good job later. After all, by the time "later" rolled
around he almost certainly would have been committed to the Colonies.
My hare-friend and I both understood this clearly, and he said his parents would support anything that I could come up with, one-hundred
percent. Even with this sort of freedom, the task proved to be far harder
than I would have expected. The job market for full-morph lapines is
almost non-existent. But I had to find something! The price of failure for
Billy was simply too great for me to even contemplate giving up. I even
considered trying to persuade his parents to set up a sham corporation
to hire him. They were supposed to be well off, after all. But in the end
such extreme measures proved unnecessary. As it happened, a job offer
came right to me. Literally, it came to me. I was sitting at my desk aimlessly going over and over Billy's file when the phone rang.

"West Street Shelter," I answered.

"Hello. I am looking for a certain Phil Goosz, a lapine SCAB. Is this
him?"

"Yes," I replied, wincing once again at the mangled pronunciation. I
was too tired to try and correct it. "That's me."

"Phil, I'm with the Armstead Corporation here in town. And we are
looking to hire a rabbit."

Never, ever had I gotten a call like this before. "Hire a rabbit? Why?
And how did you get my name?"

"You came up on an Internet search for lapiform SCABs. You're a
career counselor now, aren't you?"

"Yes, a volunteer one. But..."

"Well, we sure won't have any trouble topping those wages then, heh, heh." The man's voice sounded a little strained; I could see that he wasn't very accustomed to casually conversing with SCABs.

I sat up straighter. "Tell me, whatever would you specifically need a rabbit for?"

"Have you ever heard of Huggy Bunny Day Care Centers?"

"Well, yes..."

"We want to make that more than just our name. Our clientele is all upper income—the carriage trade, you understand. The next step up from our child care center is to get a nanny."

"Uh-huh," I replied.

I could almost hear my caller smile. "Well, the latest trend out on the coast is for upper class folks—movie stars and such, you know—to hire SCABs for highly visible positions. SCAB gardeners, SCAB limo drivers..."

I nodded, then spoke aloud. "Yes, I get the picture." None of them had SCAB agents or SCAB doctors or SCAB lawyers though, I was willing to bet. God forbid that we should actually have important jobs!

"Well... Huggy Bunny maintains one day care center in your city. And lapiform SCABs are generally pretty safe to have around kids; we've checked out the condition very thoroughly. We're not even worried about fearful parents—everyone loves rabbits. What would you think about becoming a day-care center team member?"

"Uh..." I replied intelligently, at a total loss for words.

"Now, we understand that physically you have limitations. We're willing to work around them, no matter what they are. In fact, you won't have to do any actual work at all. All we ask is that you sort of lay around, keep an eye on things, and let the kids pet you sometimes. And let the parents see you letting the kids pet you too, of course. That's very important."

"Of course," I answered. "I can see where that part would be very important indeed. Tell me, would you consider a rabbit locked in full-morph form?"

"Are you a full-morph now? I am very sorry to hear that you've gotten worse." He sounded sincere; for the first time I warmed a bit towards him. "Of course we would still consider you. Like I said, we don't need any real work done. And by the way, your voder work is superb."

"Actually," I replied," I'm not using a voder. And I'm very happy doing exactly what it is that I'm doing. But there's this client of mine—"

By the time I was done explaining, my caller was as enthused about Billy Winecrest as he had been about me. I had him call the Winecrest home and give them my name as a reference. By the end of the week, my client was working part time. He was making decent money, too; enough to live on, if he chose. Which was going to give the Colony man absolute fits in court when he tried to prove that Billy couldn't possibly take care of himself out in the real world.

And that suited me just fine. Just fine, indeed.

🐜 ∞ 🐜

It was rather startling next morning to realize that I had only one client remaining in need of my help. It was my elephant-girl, Sandy Blankenship.

I was really sweating her case. Keeping an elephant isn't exactly cheap, and almost by the very nature of things anyone who hired Sandy would most likely have to pony up for room and board as part of the deal. But what could she do that might justify such high upkeep, plus a decent wage? I'd had exactly one idea, and it had taken next to forever to find the information that I needed. In fact, the envelope finally arrived from Zambia on the very last day before graduation. It took me three tries to nibble it open, I was so nervous. Then, it seemed to take an eternity for me to unfold the cursed thing with my nose and paws. Once I managed the feat, however, the contents proved itself well worth the trouble. My heart leapt with joy; Sandy had work, if she wanted it!

I hadn't felt very welcome at school since my confrontation with the faculty over Johni, and so had never returned there. But Sandy's home number was in her folder, and no one complained when I asked her parents for permission to visit Sandy at home. This time Clover served as my chauffeur. We were nearly there when we pulled up next to Sandy at a red light. It had never occurred to me before, but once you gave the matter a little thought it was easy to see that Sandy would just about have to walk to and from school. And, given this fact, it was equally obvious that she was physically too large to use the sidewalk as well. So she strode right down a traffic lane, and obeyed all the traffic rules. The poor lonely girl! My heart went right out to her all over again as we smoothly came to a stop beside her.

I had detected a fetching sense of humor in Sandy when we had talked before, so I stuck my head out of the window and raised my voice a little. "I'll bet that you never have anyone fail to yield the right-of-way, do you?"

She cocked her head, trying to identify the voice. "Phil?" she finally asked.

"The one and only!" I answered her, feeling very good down inside. "And I've got some news for you."

Her eyes widened, comically magnified by the thick lenses. "Oh my!" she whispered. "You're kidding. You've simply got to be kidding!"

Just then the light changed, and the impatient driver behind Clover laid on his horn. Looking irritated, Sandy turned around to face the offending vehicle and trumpeted out her reply. Her roar was literally earthshaking, and I was forced to cower under the seat for a moment until it felt safe to emerge. When I did so, the other car was long gone and there were two long black stripes burned into the pavement where the driver had peeled rubber backing away. I sniffed the air, and detected a faint scent of human urine almost buried in the tire-smell. "You really shouldn't do that, Sandy," I pointed out. "It's not polite."

"What are they going to do, take away my driver's license?" she retorted, tossing her head. "I'm not driving, after all, now am I? And if I use the sidewalks they crack and buckle. It was the Public Works Department that asked me to walk out here in traffic to start with."

I sighed. Unless I missed my guess she wouldn't be in town much longer anyway and it really wouldn't matter. "We'll meet you at your house, then. Okay?"

"Sure thing!" she answered eagerly. "I can't wait!"

When we all finally met up again in the Blankenships' back yard, I asked Sandy's mother to read the letter from Zambia aloud. It stated clearly that the Ecopeace organization was very interested in hiring someone like Sandy to help rear orphaned baby elephants. They had a gang of Norms working on such a project already, but their results were mixed at best. Sandy, they believed, could be the factor that made their operation a success. There, it was pointed out, feeding and housing one more elephant would be a relatively simple matter. The climate was amenable, as well. They would gladly pay not only for the one-time relocation, but for a yearly visit home as well. And the salary wasn't bad, either.

When the letter had been read, there was silence for a bit. Then I asked my client the big question. "Does this sound better than the elephant home in Kentucky, Sandy? If it's not, I am willing to try again, you know."

"I... I..." A big tear rolled down Sandy's cheek. She was speechless, it seemed. My client gently stroked my ears once with her trunk, then stepped across the yard so as to be alone. After a moment or two, her family gathered around her.

Clearly, it was time to leave. So Clover and I did exactly that, very, very quietly.

🐾 ∽ 🐾

And then it was Graduation Day at last.

Michael, the Districts' chief counselor and the man who had talked me into taking on the job, had invited me to the graduation ceremony some weeks before. I'd already promised the kids that I would be there, or otherwise, I would never have set a hindpaw on school district property ever again. The whole Johni thing still rankled, and deeply.

Clover came with me. It was hard for us to find time to spend together, but somehow we had grown closer and closer. As I sat waiting with her, hand-in-paw, I realized perhaps for the first time how very important she had become in my life. There had been women before SCABs, of course. But none like Clover. None at all like Clover.

"Oh!" Clover exclaimed, pulling away her hand. "I almost forgot. This was sitting in the foyer at the Shelter when I picked you up. I bet that someone dropped it when they picked up the mail. It looks important."

So it did, I realized upon closer examination. The letter was from Universal Motors, my previous employer. It was from them that I drew my disability pension. "Excuse, me, dear," I mumbled. Clover understood, and held her peace as I nibbled the envelope open.

The letter was cold and bare. My pension was to be cut off on the grounds that I was no longer disabled. I had proven myself able to work in another field, they claimed, with potential pay equal to or exceeding what I had previously made. As evidence they included a letter from the same professional organization that had been threatening to take me to court for practicing without a license, and copies of signed depositions made on the day that Johni and her sisters had passed into the custody of Family Services. The places where I had described myself as a "career counselor" were highlighted.

Clearly, the whole thing was a put-up job.

I crumpled the paper and sighed. In court I could easily beat this kind of scam and get my pension back. But how long would it take? Months? Years? It wasn't the money so much; Universal Motors still owed me an only slightly lesser retirement pension regardless, and I had saved considerably on my own. In point of fact, if I really needed to I could live off of nothing but interest nearly forever; rabbits were notoriously cheap creatures to keep. However, for some reason the courts considered my partial retirement pension to be an inadequate income, even though it was only a few thousand dollars a year less than full disability. Would the Colonies try for me again, once they got word that my circumstances had changed for the worse?

I sighed. Clover asked if the letter was bad news, and I told her that it was but that I was also not going to discuss it then and there. Not on the kid's big day, at least. She nodded understandingly, then squeezed my forepaw again and held her peace.

Geez, I thought as a new angle on the situation struck home. Could I still afford a family, I asked myself. If I decided that I wanted one, that was?

Just then Michael walked up and took a seat next to me. "Why are you two sitting in back?" he asked us cheerfully. "There's plenty of room close up front."

"It's a rabbit thing," Clover answered for me. The exit was in back, and she knew that I preferred to stay just as close to it as possible.

"Oh," Michael replied, letting the subject drop. He was very polite that way. "I'm glad that you could make it. We need to talk about something, Phil."

Here it comes, I thought. It never rains but it pours. "Yes?" There was ice in my voice, but Michael either could not hear it or, more likely, chose not to hear it.

He cleared his throat before beginning. "I wanted to tell you that your handling of these six cases has been discussed in the highest District circles. And that even the School Board itself has taken notice."

"Yes?" My voice remained hard.

"In this city, we try very hard to work with the SCABS community. You people are the victims of a lot of irrational hate and prejudice, sure enough. But hate and prejudice are not official policy. We want you to succeed, because if you succeed then we all succeed."

I sat silently, and Michael went on.

"Frankly, we gave you our most hopeless cases, and did so far too late in the game. We didn't expect much, if anything. Mostly, to be quite honest, we merely wanted to salve our consciences, to be able to say that at least we had tried to help these kids. Yet not only did you find futures for five of them, you through your actions demonstrated that we ourselves had been severely negligent in the sixth case."

"I did not find five of them jobs," I pointed out. "One of them found their own career. And Ken Bronski helped out with another."

"Hmm. Have it your way, if you insist. I'm not denying you any-thing, not after what you've accomplished here. And in the sixth case, well... I think that you did absolutely the right thing, and so does almost everybody else." The head counselor frowned. "Except for those who actually failed Johni for so many years, of course. They are still rant-ing and raving about how you exceeded your authority. As if that were a more important issue than the well-being of the kids themselves! Frankly, we are currently re-evaluating our psychological screening staff and procedures, Phil. Mostly because of you."

I began to feel a little bit better. Maybe the school system did really care, after all.

Mike smiled and squatted down so that we could talk face-to-face. "Next year, we want you back. Earlier, with more time to work. And as a paid consultant, we hope."

"But— But—"

"I remember what you said about legal issues," Mike said, waving off my objections. "And I've done some checking of my own. As it hap-pens, I am a licensed professional guidance counselor, and my specialty is helping students pick out the right schools. If you start night school next week, you can have a minimal certification in three months. That's enough to practice legally on. With pay." He smiled. "And, the professor there is dying to meet you! He says that he's tried to get you in to teach seminars, for crying out loud! Dr. Stephenson would love to have you as a student!"

I cocked my head to one side. It was true enough that I'd been invited to lecture locally many times. But I had always turned everyone down, including Stephenson. After all, who was I to teach others?

Just then the music started playing, and the fourteen graduating students of the special SCAB program began filing in. "Listen, we can talk more about this later," Michael said, standing up straight. "Or, at least I certainly hope so."

And I surprised myself. "Yes. I think that perhaps we can."

The educator looked relieved. "Good! That's very good! I'll be calling soon." And with that he left to take his seat up front with the faculty, where in a flash of clarity I knew that I would be sitting myself next year. Suddenly the letter from Universal Motors seemed very unimportant, a mere relic of a dead person and a dead past. I'd grown far beyond the childish games of my former employers, I realized rather suddenly. Far, far beyond. And I'd never have to depend upon them again.

More music played, and then the class valedictorian, a college-bound giraffe morph whom I'd never had cause to meet, gave her speech. She spoke of the infinite variety of life, and of the equal variety awaiting each and every one of us in life's experiences. When she was done I slapped my paws together with genuine enthusiasm, though my efforts produced little real sound. Amen, sister, I was thinking, Amen. Infinite variety, infinite experiences, infinite growth for everyone. And then the graduates picked up their diplomas one by one. Some of them walked normally, one of them flew, and poor blindfolded George sort of dragged himself along the central aisle. Still, all of them shared the moment together.

Even Johni was there, I was rather startled to see. It was very surprising indeed when I saw her walking up the center aisle, but I was very pleased nonetheless. She appeared, to my eyes at least, to be more dazed than happy. The girl was drugged to the gills, I supposed. Which at least meant she was finally getting some sort of treatment. The scars of abuse promised to remain part of her psyche for a very long time to come, but perhaps the healing was finally beginning. I wondered if she had ever finally told anyone the truth. For everyone's sake, I truly hoped so. But I would never know.

And then the hats went flying, and the class had officially graduated. Clover leaned over and kissed me. I nibbled back; she giggled. And then it was time to leave.

"What was that letter about, anyway," she asked me on the way out.

"Something that's done and over with," I replied. "And, now that I think about it, not so terribly important after all."

The auditorium was located nearly in the center of the campus, and it was a very long walk to where we had parked. When we finally made it all the way out to Clover's car, we found four overflowing bushel baskets of carrots sitting on the hood waiting for us.

✖

TOP OF THE MOUNTAIN

They say a werewolf sleeps with one eye open, always alert for danger or prey. A werewolf's fine senses can see in the dark, catch the faintest whiff of scent in the most still evening, and can pick up a whisper from a mile away. A werewolf can go from fast asleep to wide-awake faster than any other creature. Certainly, with their sharp teeth and sharper claws, they make a formidable challenge and able hunters, and with their thick fur and padded feet, they can survive environments that humans are best left avoiding.

Nevertheless, all of it is worthless without their fierce intelligence and compassion for humans. One shudders to think where humans would be without their protectors.

Just as werewolves do all things to maximum benefit, so too do they sleep as soundly as a coma, and little except danger can roust them. Since the scent of his twelve-year-old cub registered as neither danger nor prey to Tark or his mate, even assuming they could smell anything under the layers of fur they buried themselves in, they didn't awaken to it.

The night was bitterly cold. A blizzard raged outside. Tark had seen signs of its approach two days before and made plans, but even here, a third of a mile from the mouth of the cave, a draft swirled about the floor.

Lahk's eyes sparkled and his breath came in little puffs as he called softly to his father. The furs did not move. Lahk reached up and took the two-foot wooden grease torch from the wall. He struck flint. The near blackness sprang to light.

The room was sparse and bare. Lahk's father had even pulled the tapestry from the ceiling and the rug from the floor and wrapped them around himself and his mate. Lahk wasn't surprised. This chamber of the cave was too large to be a proper den, and was that much harder to keep warm. It was about eight feet across, roughly round, with cracks in the wall deep enough to hide things. Two iron braziers were the only furnishings, and Lahk touched the torch to each of them to chase the bitter cold from the room.

"Father," he announced again, slightly louder, replacing the torch on its wall bracket. He was always timid about rousting his father, although he stood nearly as tall and could almost beat him at wrestling. He brushed a long lock of silky black hair away from his fire-glittering eyes. He was starting to wish he'd brought a cloak. Finally, he touched the pile of furs with a toe.

A low rumble emerged from under the blankets, and a muzzle going white with age poked out. "You've no business here, cub," it growled, a little angrily. "Go back to your den and sleep. It's cold."

"It's Candyman," said Lahk. "He's in the hall, frozen to the bone and calling your name."

"Candyman?" Tark pushed the blankets away and squinted up at his son. "Are you sure?"

"I'd never mistake his scent," said Lahk. He licked his chops, looking uncomfortable. His tail twitched. "But I didn't approach," he said, nervously. "He smelled bad. He's terrified. I thought he was dying."

"Hardly surprising if he's fool enough to scale the mountain on a night like this," growled Tark, fully awake now that he knew there was danger. "Go to him and bring him to the inner meeting hall. I'll be there in ten minutes. Light the fire and try to make him comfortable."

"Yes, Father." Lahk trotted out, obedient as ever. Tark cried after him, "And pull on a cloak, child! You may have fur, but the best fur has its limits!"

Tark reached into a crack in the wall and pawed out his medicine belt. He fastened it around his waist and over one shoulder like a sash. The mound of blankets moved again. "Tark?" murmured Lasha. "What is it?"

"Nestor's in the outer chamber," grunted Tark, pulling an ornate box out of the hole. He stocked his belt bags. The brazier caught the shine of the four strands of beads in his mane, which rattled against each other as he stooped to tie an ornate bone-handled hunting knife to his thigh. The knife was purely ceremonial, forged eight hundred years ago and no longer bearing anything that would be considered an edge by modern werewolf iron-smithing methods.

"Nestor?" Lasha sat up, clutching the blankets to her bosom. "Is it serious?"

"*I* wouldn't run ten miles through the worst blizzard of the year for a trifle," said Tark, straightening up. His long mane tumbled over his shoulders and most of the way down his back, and the smooth plait of the Warrior-Priest's braid rested against his chest. "Keep warm, love. I might not be back for some time."

Lasha curled up again, worried, but she didn't let her worry prevent her from sleeping. A werewolf is a sensible enough creature to be able to sleep when possible during a crisis. Tark seized his walking stick from its place in the corner and swept his buffalo cloak from the top of the blanket pile, feeling a hint of cold in his paw-tips and muzzle. A werewolf's fur is good for temperatures down to twenty below, which meant that it had to be at least so cold even without the wind. Moreover, of course, any werewolf knows that twenty degrees above zero with a gusting wind is far more dangerous than twenty degrees below without one.

He waddled into the corridor like a furry turtle, weighed down by his cloak and sacraments. It certainly was cold. The walls shone with a thin skin of ice. The air was nose-achingly dry. The dirt under Tark's feet was like stone. Worry burned his heart, but he wasn't worried about cold. He worried about his choices, because he really had no choice left at all.

✻ ∞ ✻

"Candyman?"

Nestor raised his head. He sat huddled in a corner of the chamber, barely shielded from the roaring wind, daring to go no further into the cave. The wind blew drifts of snow into the outer hall, and Nestor's eyes were about as accustomed to the lack of light as they'd get. He may as well have been blindfolded.

"Lahk? Dear God, cub, is that you?"

"Candyman? Can you see me?"

Nestor looked around, squinting as if trying to sharpen his eyes to cut through the darkness. He saw the liquid sparkle of light in the eyes of a wolf and came very close to crying out.

The eyes blinked. Nestor barely made out the shape of the face behind them. He stood up and stumbled towards them, tripped over a rock, and sprawled flat.

He heard footsteps behind him and felt a warm, rough paw take his rabbit-fur mitten. Nestor could smell him now, a warm, rich, almost inviting scent of fur. He wanted so much to wrap himself in such fur right now.

"I lit a torch," said Lahk softly. "There's light farther down the passageway. Hold my tail and watch your step." He put Nestor's hand on the end of his tail, and the young shopkeeper dragged himself wearily to his frostbitten feet and hobbled after the child.

When they'd made their way forty feet down the narrow, slippery passage and there was enough light to see, Lahk hugged Nestor and trotted ahead, standing at one of many forks in the cave and gesturing. "This way, Candyman," he called. "Don't be afraid."

Nestor was. He could do nothing about that. He'd never been in the werewolf's cave and had no idea how to conduct himself, or whether the werewolf would be angry. Nestor intended, after all, to roust him out of bed at this absurd hour and in this terrible weather. He didn't know what else to do, though. He was lost, hurting, freezing cold, and very, very frightened. A small, naked, furry child led him through a maze of twisting, colorless passageway, and Lord, even the child frightened him.

He took comfort from the child leading him, though. Deep down, he knew Lahk loved him and wouldn't dream of hurting him or leading him astray. Lahk was strong, fast, and terribly intelligent, on the threshold of becoming a powerful warrior, and Nestor always gave him meat leftovers at the shop in the village. "Candyman" was Lahk's affectionate name for the one who gave him treats.

That animal-smell, the den-smell, strengthened as the corridor widened and brightened. They turned a corner into a large domed chamber, forty feet across. Pillars of stone reached down from the ceiling and up from the floor. A rippling pool of clear liquid rolled and lapped in the corner. It wasn't water, certainly—water would have frozen. Images of werewolves gazed down at them from every surface, hunting, howling, singing, half-moon, full-moon, no-moon, playing, wrestling, sparring, even mating.

"Did your father paint all this?" asked Nestor, teeth chattering.

"Yes, sir." Lahk lit a second torch and approached the pool. "It took two years. He finished long before I was born. This is a sacred place— Father says one can hear the heartbeat of the mountain itself in here."

He tossed the torch into the pool, which burst into flame. A wave of heat rolled over them and Nestor's half-frozen fingers tore at the laces of his coat, clawing at his frozen clothes to let the heat in.

"Let me help," said Lahk, hooking his claws into the knots. The laces were iron. Snow froze them solid. Lahk pressed his muzzle into Nestor's clothes and chewed at the knots, and the shopkeeper sat patiently on a stone slab while the cub gnawed off his heavy coat and gloves. The room was warm, too warm, by the time Nestor unwound his scarf, and shards of pain stabbed into his hands and feet.

"Take them all off," said a voice from the chamber entrance, and Nestor turned to see Tark padding towards him, hanging up his cloak and shaking down.

The Shaman-Wolf Tark was nearly sixty, and his once jet-black hair was shot with white. His thick fur had dulled to a muted, gentle gray, but he was still impressive for any human to look at. Muscles moved under his fur like kittens playing under a blanket. He was no taller than Nestor's six feet, and the fur gave an illusion of bulk, but all humans were impressed to see a werewolf in the fur, whether for the first time or the hundredth. "All your clothes," insisted Tark. "You don't want to warm up too quickly or start to sweat. Let me see your paws." Nestor offered his hands and Tark examined them. "You didn't wrap your gloves properly," he said. "Your hands are white. The circulation is gone. I can bring it back, but you were lucky to get here so quickly. Another half hour, we'd be discussing how many fingers to take off."

Lahk brought brandy and Nestor gulped at a cupful and nearly spit it out. "Careful," said Tark. "It kicks back. What's this all about, sir?"

"My son," gasped Nestor, tears streaming down his face. "He's worse. Much worse. He can't even cry anymore." He clutched the werewolf's shoulders, but his hands could apply no pressure. "He's so hot!" he cried, tugging at Tark's mane. "He's burning up! I couldn't think of anything else to do!"

"You did the right thing, then, whatever pain you're feeling now," said Tark, helping Nestor lie down. "I'm worried for your son, but right now I'm more worried for you. I won't let you leave until you've recovered."

He and Lahk helped him off with the rest of his clothes. Nestor's skin had turned marble white nearly all over, and a blazing red everywhere else. Tark put a paw to Nestor's chest.

"Gods, you're so cold," he said softly, feeling Nestor's heart pound against his paw pad. "And scared. Lahk, hot water. Blood-warm. No warmer." He took his cloak from the wall while Lahk ran the water pump. Well water, too deep to freeze, poured into a depression not far from the infernal pool. Tark lay down on the slab next to Nestor, draped the cloak over them both, and put his shaggy arm around the shivering shopkeeper.

"I'll need a few minutes to get ready," he said. "Is your son shivering?"

"No," whispered Nestor, scared nearly out of his mind. The arm that restored life to his icy skin felt strong enough to crush him in its hug. "He, he's just having so much trouble breathing. He's hardly eaten in two days."

Tark bit his upper lip. That bought them time, but not much. Nestor's son had a blood-disease that Tark was quite inexperienced with. Nestor was only eighteen when his son was born, his wife even younger, and their shop newly established when Nestor's wife was pregnant. Maybe the youth of the infant's parents, or something else, was the key, but the delivery had been messy, fraught with complications.

Tark held the shivering human against his chest and tried to wring the cold from him, remembering, a year ago, a night less cold and ferocious than this one, mild and still. Tark had given Nestor enough brandy to put him into a stupor too deep to interfere with the werewolf's ministry. Tark's arms were matted almost to the shoulders with blood. He'd brought a small, sickly, premature baby into the world, so small that it didn't even cry.

Tark had never been so frightened. He couldn't even remember now how he'd stopped the bleeding and rousted the baby. He'd stayed with mother and child until the young father woke up from his drunken sleep, and then longer.

For a time during the summer, his regular visits were less and less frequent. The baby held its own. (It was so TINY. Even now, at a year old, it weighed no more than fifteen pounds.) However, with winter came flu, and with flu came pneumonia, and the pneumonia that Tark could have treated easily was complicated by a condition that Tark knew nothing about.

His Alpha once told him that he was the finest medicine man within a thousand miles. Though Tark beamed at the compliment at the time, his consultations with other healers yielded no one who knew about the baby's symptoms. The baby grew ill, smelling rank and sickly, fading day by day until...now.

His paw over Nestor's chest felt the rabbit-rapid heartbeat slowing. Peace, human, he thought. Peace and rest.

"Water's ready, Father," said Lahk.

Tark pulled the blanket off Nestor and helped him into the bath. Nestor cried out as Tark lowered him into the water. "It's hot! It's burning!"

"It's not hot," said Tark. "You're cold. Try to rest now, and Lahk will bring you food later. Lahk, remember what I said, that humans need their food cooked properly?"

"Yes, Father."

"Good, then. It's all settled." Tark took his cloak from the bench and swept it over his shoulders. Nestor sloshed in his bath, hysterical. "Where are you going?" He scrabbled at the edge, still too weak to grasp or clutch. "Wait!" he cried.

"I'm going to the village," said Tark quietly, "to save your son's life."

Unfortunately, he knew that he was lying through his muzzle. He tied his cloak tightly and trotted out of the chamber.

🐾 ∞ 🐾

Tark leaped out of the cave and ran down the slope, his feet beating at the deep snow. Wind screamed at him. He wanted to scream back, but did not intend to waste breath. He had ten miles to go and had to keep moving. He'd wrapped his feet and paws, but despite the cold he had no intention of wrapping his muzzle, and blunting his sense of smell.

He was more frightened than he'd been in all his fifty-nine years. Nestor was more than a friend to him, he was almost a son, and Tark had delivered him as he'd delivered his baby. Nestor had, of course, been a more reasonable birth. His was a mere matter of fourteen hours, hot water, dozens of towels, a shrieking mother, and a broken arm for Tark when the formidable woman had crushed it during a contraction.

He'd watched Nestor grow up, at least as much as Nestor had grown up. He knew that werewolves mature mentally a great deal faster than humans, that his son was somewhat more of an adult than Nestor was. A boy of only eighteen producing a child of his own was next to unthinkable in the human community, and the less-charitable of Nestor's village saw his difficulties as punishment for growing up too fast.

By contrast, Lahk would come into Prime for the first time, probably in the coming Spring, and Tark's only cub would probably make him a grandfather before next winter.

Nestor's young wife was barren now. No more children could grow in her scarred womb. In a way, it was a relief. It meant that she'd experience no more near misses. Nevertheless, it made Nestor all the more desperate to save the one he had now. He and Tark had grown closer as Tark had been a good companion and superlative physician, administering medicines and singing prayers, occasionally sending letters about the baby's condition to other Packs and other healers. A few of Tark's werewolf correspondents had arrived to sniff the baby and check his condition, but they, too, walked away defeated. No one could strengthen the healthy body and help it grow.

Tark scrambled down the hillside, got to the ledge, and leaped into space. He plunged straight down thirty feet and tumbled muzzle-over-tail in the snow. He ran among trees now, thick stands of pine waving at the swirling sky. He ran the next half-mile on all fours, his cloak flapping at his flank like a cape. His chest heaved. He was cold and tired, though he'd never been this tired at this stage of the run. Either he was growing older, or was pushing too hard.

He smelled the smoke of the fires in the village. The ground leveled off and Nestor reared up on his hind legs. He'd been floundering through the snow for an hour, his long cloak heavy and his fur drenched almost to skin, slick against his chest and legs. His muzzle was frozen shut from the moisture he exhaled and fingers of ice glued his hair to his shoulders. The energy of fear only lasts for so long, but Tark was determined not to rest. He'd made this same run in better weather in only twenty minutes. Thirty years ago, he could have done it in ten.

Now he sprang out of the forests and saw the valley spread out below him, the cluster of homes and the rich scent of smoke. It was two hours before dawn. Tark paused, his chest heaving. He sagged to his knees and sat down, wondering if he was going to be sick. The wind was letting up, but snow still swirled from the sky. Within a minute, he was a sparkling white.

He shook down in a miniature blizzard and tumbled down the hill as an avalanche, coming to the roadway in a trot. He didn't want to appear at Nestor's door half-exhausted, but he wasn't sure he had time to reclaim his dignity.

He took a moment to urinate by the side of the road and check his health by its scent and color. He also checked his hands and feet to be sure they were warm, not numb. When he was positive he was only fatigued, he trotted up the roadway and counted houses until he found the right one. He thumped on the door.

Something rattled inside. Tark leaned against the wall and counted snowflakes. The house stood like all the rest—small, wooden, unpainted and nondescript. One wall was stone—that was the pub, with the grocery next to it. Tark made a mental note to stock up on whiskey when he left.

"Werewolf!" The relieved cry came from inside. Someone released the latch, and the heavy door pitched open. Nestor's wife Meris seized Tark by the arm and led him into a small, cozy living room, sparsely furnished but warmed by a raging fire.

Tark dropped to all fours once inside, and got his heaving chest under control. "I came as quickly as I could," he said. "It took over an hour to get down the mountain in this weather."

"My husband?" A note of worry.

"He'll be fine, but he's half frozen and exhausted. He'll stay with us until he recovers."

Meris draped Tark's cloak over a rod by the fire. She was a small woman, though her pregnancy had softened her face and hips. She'd long since recovered fully from Tark's spot surgery, and, for a human, was very beautiful, with wavy blond hair and bright blue eyes, a slightly-too-large nose and, usually, a wide smile. Now, though, her blue eyes sported dark circles and she seemed a hundred years old. She was very, very tired.

Tark accepted a towel and rubbed his long mane and chest with it. He pulled off his boots and gloves and shook slightly, trying to knock the water loose without drenching the room and his hostess. He was soggy and cold, and he didn't want to hold a sick baby when he was soggy and cold.

"I'll need one of his bottles and a large kettle," he said, managing to creditably mask his exhaustion. "May I see him?"

"Yes, of course," said Meris. "He's upstairs. We're trying to bring his fever down, but it's so hard."

"You did right, but now we're going to raise the temperature of the room." He shuddered, slightly, but Meris didn't notice. "I have a few things here that will help," he added, not bothering to tell her that he had no medicine that would save her baby. He could postpone the inevitable only long enough to tell her of the decision he wanted her to make.

He padded up the stairs, leaning a little too heavily on the handrail. The upstairs room was lower than he was tall, and he was already stooped over when he reached down and touched the silent baby in his crib.

The baby was awake, and unafraid, but oh, he smelled so bad that Tark waited for him to blink to be sure he was alive. He looked no more than six months old. His skin was an angry red. His breathing rattled hoarsely in Tark's ears.

A few days, maybe more, he wanted to say. A few days, maybe a week, and the town would hold a funeral. Perhaps the clergyman would let him come if he promised to wear a loincloth this time, and cover up those parts that humans were so offended to see. Perhaps he'd come anyway to pay his respects to the baby and the man who was his father, the man who was like a son to Tark. Whether High and Mighty in his chapel wanted him to or not…

"Do you have the bottle?" he said hoarsely to Meris, who had just come up the stairs. She offered one silently, and he poured some white powder from one of his medicine bags. "Milk," he said, and Meris handed him a heavy jug. Tark filled the baby bottle, shook it well, and gave it to the baby.

He's in no pain, but he's too weak to hold the bottle, he wanted to say. *He's not suffering in his final days, but soon he won't have the strength to pull air into his lungs, and he'll suffocate,* he wanted to say. She deserved to know that her infant was beyond medicine.

He wasn't beyond hope, though. There was but one last decision to make, the Wild card, and the hope that went with it.

The baby's breathing eased and he slipped into sleep. Tark held the bottle a moment longer. "Rinse that thoroughly three times before using it again," he said, handing it to Meris. "I'll be here until morning in meditation. Do you have more wood for the fire?"

"Yes, sir."

"Then put it on. Keep piling it on until the house is so hot you can hardly stand it. Then go to bed, dear. You're so tired."

Meris nodded as if to say, *No way, Werewolf,* but left without saying a word. Tark sat cross-legged on the floor and rocked the crib gently, singing softly. The song was ancient and beautiful, meant to give comfort to cubs. He'd sung it to Lahk hundreds of times.

Soon the room was very hot, and sweat slicked his back and mane. He dozed softly with his muzzle on his chest until morning.

🐾 ∞ 🐾

"Werewolf?"

Tark grunted. He lifted his muzzle and looked blearily around, trying to figure out why it was so hot in the middle of winter, and why he wasn't in his cave.

A heartbeat later he crouched over the crib, touching the sleeping baby's face. "I think we did well," he said. "He's resting, comfortable, and fed. He'll draw strength from that."

Meris smiled slightly. "You're a brave werewolf and an excellent healer," she said, "but a terrible liar."

"I'm no liar!" Tark drew breath.

"No, you're not. But you're not telling the whole truth. I see it in your eyes, Tark. You werewolves may claim the monopoly on reading people's feelings in their scent, but we humans can be perceptive too, when challenged." She took his paw and kneaded it. "How long?"

Tark shook his head. "Not long," he said softly. "Four days. Maybe five."

"Is there nothing we can do?" And Tark realized from her scent and her eyes that she'd wept.

Tark's eyes moved, only slightly, but Meris saw the cloud pass over him. To Tark's surprise, she seized the braid that hung over his chest and pulled it like a church bell rope. He actually stumbled forwards. "You're hiding something, Werewolf! Is it something I have to do? Is it dangerous? Is that why you're not telling me? Name it, and I'll do it!"

The outburst startled Tark. He discovered, with amazement, that he couldn't disengage the grip from his sacred braid, and his scalp suddenly felt very sore. "Werewolves don't suffer this disease," he said, finally, trying not to yelp with pain or lash out reflexively. "We're immune. I'd have to Change him. He'd become one of us."

She released the braid, and Tark actually staggered back. She sat down, heavily, as the strength went out from her. "It's possible?" she said. "To change someone like that?"

"It's happened," said Tark. "I know a reliable medicine." He took her hand in his warm paws and held it, tenderly. "Sometimes, a human will choose it. Our legends say that we are descended from humans who chose our life. Sometimes, like now, we will Change one in an emergency. My father was a human until a Warrior-Priest Changed him."

"What would you have to do?" Her voice was small.

"Well, I'll do nothing until I consult with my Alpha in the valley on the other side of the mountain. But time is of the essence. Twenty-four hours, give or take, and even that medicine won't save him."

"Then what are you waiting for? Go, werewolf! Run!"

"It's not that simple." Tark stretched a little, his back stiff. "You would have a werewolf for a son. Werewolves born of humans sometimes find it harder to be part of the Pack. They outgrow their differences, but their childhood is confusion. What's more, he would have to be trained in the way of the Pack that Changes him." Tark took a deep breath, and then another. "He would have to come away to the other side of the mountain and live with the Pack. You wouldn't be able to see him again."

Now it was her turn to experience shock and silence. The pause grew longer, until finally she said, "Never?"

"Not never. After twelve, when he comes into Prime, he can do as he pleases with his life—including knowing and loving his parents. But until then..." Tark shrugged. "Never."

"This drastic cure? It's certain?"

"If we're in time, your son would live. *How* he would live is another matter completely. The Pack would be his family, not you or Nestor. He would not know his father and mother, until he turns thirteen. We would even take away his human name and give him one of ours. The Alpha may even choose to keep his heritage a secret, to make his growth and youth easier on him. There's a fair chance you may never see him again, wolf or man."

She looked into the crib, knelt next to it and touched the face of her sleeping son. "Last night I suffered the worst torture of my life wondering what life would be like without you," she said. "I think I could more easily bear such suffering if I knew you were alive, at least. Then I would only be suffering for you."

She rubbed her eyes. "We admire you werewolves, you know, we really do," she said, sniffing. "So much power and compassion."

"Then you agree."

She hugged Tark, tightly, and he hugged back a little clumsily, and she whispered, "Do whatever it takes, whatever you have to, to save my son. With my blessing."

She kissed Tark's cheek. Tark hobbled down the steps on stiff muscles and found his cloak where Meris had left it.

🐾 ∞ 🐾

Tark ran more moderately over the snowy ground now. Two feet of new snow had fallen, but now that he wasn't pelting pell-mell over the ground, he was able to pace himself with a heavy trot that ate the miles eight to the hour. It was desperately cold, cold enough to touch his skin under his fur, so he kept his cloak wrapped tight and cinched with a bit of rope.

His old footprints were still here. Not much snow had fallen after his mad dash last night. He was a bit weary, but not bone weary, and he had a lot of work to do in very little time.

He padded back to his cave only a little over an hour later, into the rich, invigorating smell of blood. He knew his mate and cub had hunted. He hurried to the inner meeting hall, where the smell was strongest. Lasha and Lahk had finished eating, and Lahk was roasting venison for Nestor, who had curled up, naked and sound asleep, near the generous warmth of the infernal pool.

"I hope you saved some for me?" he said softly, hanging his cloak.

"Father!" Lahk leaped up. Nestor shifted where he slept and Tark looked at him, one ear cocked.

"He drank a lot," said Lahk. "When he wakes up he can have this." He held up the stick and turned it over. The venison was turning a healthy pink.

"Good work. I'll see if he's willing to talk."

Lasha looked imploringly at her mate. Tark blinked blankly back at her for a moment, then bowed his muzzle down and shook his head, tail between his knees. The beads in his hair rattled. Lasha crossed her paws over her breasts. "To all the Gods," she said. "What will you do now?"

"What we discussed," said Tark softly. "Nestor, wake up. Nestor?" He shook the human gently. Nestor opened his eyes blearily. Tark was relieved that Nestor's skin was warm to the touch. He sniffed the human, who reeked of brandy. Tark decided to allow the indulgence, in part because it was probably the only way the human would sleep.

"He stinks," said Lahk quietly. "Very badly. Is there anything we can do? Can we spray him?"

"Hush, child! It's not polite to tell a human that he stinks," said Tark. Nestor was still looking gummily at him, but hadn't heard. Tark helped him sit up. "Nestor, this is urgent."

Nestor rubbed his eyes. "What? What is it? Is my boy all right? Did you make him well?"

"I can't," said Tark. "No medicine can. He's dying, my boy. I must ask something very important of you. Your wife has agreed."

🍃 **389**

"What?" Nestor seized Tark's shoulders and tried to shake him, and almost knocked himself over. "What is it? What are you asking?"

"I can cure him. But the only way to cure him is to turn him into a werewolf."

Nestor froze, hands still clutching Tark's shoulders. Then he slowly toppled over to one side and sprawled out on the floor.

🐾 ∞ 🐾

"He's only fainted, but the alcohol is keeping him out," said Tark impatiently, about twenty minutes later. He paced in circles around the infernal pool, his body soaked with sweat. "I can't wait for him to wake up. I must go consult with the Alpha."

"Why?" said Lasha. "Why run another fifteen miles when time is so precious? You have the mother's consent. Once he understands, I'm sure you'll have the father's as well. The Alpha trusts your judgment and you know him better than anyone else does. Every second is crucial. Go to the village and bring the child here, into his father's presence, so they can say goodbye."

"Lasha, please," groaned Tark. "It's hardly so simple."

"Hardly so simple? All you need to do is take the child and perform the rituals, mix medicines, and Change him into a cub, and not only will you save his life, you'll improve its quality a thousandfold. You knew when he was born that he would only survive to be frail, sickly, and weak, always needing someone's care."

"I still need Alpha consent, if nothing else than to bring another member into the Pack. I also need the cooperation of others. We can't do this by ourselves, Lasha."

"Alpha consent?" Lasha looked as if she couldn't believe her ears. "Tark, that's an ancient rule established for when game is scarce! The mountain and its valleys produce enough prey for twice our Pack! Do you really think the Alpha would deny you this, especially since it's an emergency?"

"I'm going," said Tark firmly, grabbing his cloak. "I'll be back by dusk. Plenty of time."

"Tark!" implored Lasha, but Tark just glanced up at her and left. She cursed to herself colorfully, then turned to look at the sleeping Nestor. *Poor man*, she thought. *He's about to lose his only child, one way or another.* She stroked his hair and his face. He moved a little in his sleep and curled up tight.

"He still smells pretty bad," said Lahk. "His food is cooked. What should I do with it?"

🐾 ∞ 🐾

Tark jogged along the path that led around the mountain, to the thick forests in the valley on the other side. The range was beautiful, fifty square miles of forest, most of it never explored by humans. A single road wound through it, and the werewolves protected unwary travelers from highwaymen. The valley's four lakes had frozen enough for a horse to cut across. A river plunged through the deepest part of the valley. It moved fast, and in the spring it bore enough fish to feed three packs.

Seventy werewolves lived in this territory, most with dens, a few with huts, a couple, like Tark, with caves. They hunted the deer, culling the herds that nibbled at the grasses and leaves. They hunted rabbits and birds, such things as they could catch when they were hungry. It hadn't been a harsh winter, but it had been a harsh couple of days, and Tark guessed that most of the werewolves snuggled in their huts, noses buried in their tails, waiting for a break in the bitter cold.

Tark crossed most of the Range without ever seeing another werewolf. It was possible to spend days in the Range and never see another werewolf. Any werewolf, though, could easily follow any of the tracks or scent-scatters. Tark recognized most of them. Their presence said that some of them had been active recently. Probably on their morning hunt. They'd be back in their dens now. That was only sensible.

He hopped a small stream and scrambled up a short banking. The Alpha's den stood less than a quarter mile away. He pointed his muzzle to the wind and howled his long, beautiful, distinctive note, the one that broke slightly in the middle and fell away, not so much dying as departing.

Someone answered the howl a moment later. Tark recognized Rib's long, low, moaning call. Rib was one of the Alpha's hunters, with a loud howl, but not a very attractive one. A throat infection left him without voice for the first twenty years of his life, until Tark administered a special drug to bring it back. He'd also removed Rib's withered tonsils, a nasty, savage operation. Nevertheless, a few weeks later, Rib could make some guttural moans in his throat, and within a year he'd developed a howl...of sorts. Some of the werewolves said it sounded like a baritone cat rubbing itself vigorously with a cheese grater, but at least Rib had voice.

Tark scrambled up the hill and met Rib near the top. Rib was a big fellow, and what he lacked in voice he made up for in strength and skill. Until recently, he couldn't call to share the kill, but now everyone in the Pack knew what a prodigious hunter he'd become. He was quite white, with only dark streaks in his mane, and he sat in the snow chewing a knot out of his tail.

"Ah, Tark," he croaked. "It sounded like you. It's been a while."

Tark shrugged. "I've been in and out of the Range," he said. "My duties to the villagers keep me busy."

"You'd do better to fulfill your duties to your Pack than your pet humans," said Rib, but his tone was good-natured and his eye twinkled. He knew Tark always fulfilled his Pack duties a dozen times over. "You smell awfully tired, friend. What's wrong?"

"One of the villagers has a dying infant. I can't save him as a human, so I want leave of the Alpha to bring him into the Pack."

"Difficult," mused Rib. "Not impossible. Do you know how?"

"I saw it done once, in another Pack," said Tark. "It isn't difficult, but it can be hard on the Helpers."

"I'll be a Helper if I can," volunteered Rib. "If you need it."

"Thanks, Rib." Tark dropped a paw to Rib's shoulder and hugged him. "Always a brother. Is the Alpha in?"

"He's done with his morning meal, so I would think so." Rib licked his chops. "He's been eating well lately."

"A treat for you, I'd imagine," said Tark. The Alpha had no teeth, so Rib chewed his food for him, which meant that Rib tasted the best game in the Pack. "You know you're not to swallow it."

"Oh, a morsel, a morsel," pleaded Rib. "I generally feed him after I've eaten, so I have little appetite anyway." He licked his chops. "Come on, I'll show you in."

🐾 ∞ 🐾

Tark was certain that the Alpha was over a hundred years old. The Pack's most accurate guess was close to a hundred and seven.

He'd been present at Tark's birth, and Tark already thought him an old man over fifty years ago. He rarely emerged from his den now, and never in the winter. He kept den in a small cave with two chambers, where his own father once lived. He'd raised four cubs in this cave.

Now he was small and wizened, with sticklike arms and a rough voice that would have been near inaudible to humans. He was nearly blind, but his ears and nose worked well, and his mind shone with all the intelligence and wit of a century. He knew all his Pack by scent (as all werewolves should, but not all do), and sometimes, through scent, he could guess why they came to see him, so it seemed. He could still walk, a little, and tried as often as he had strength, leaning heavily on a polished walking stick. He had little control over his bodily functions, and his attendants cared for him and kept him clean and fed. He reeked of wisdom and stank of age, and the scent of his den embraced and comforted anyone who visited.

He lay curled up on the bed, holding his yellowing tail in his paws like a cub. He appeared to doze, but when Tark came into the room, he lifted his head a little. The long hair draped over the bed and spilling on the floor shifted slightly. The old man had kicked his blankets away. "Tark?" he said. "Is that you?"

"Yes, Master," said Tark, kneeling next to the bed and taking one of the old wolf's paws. "I'm here."

"Excellent!" The Alpha sat up, a little stiffly. "Would you be so good as to fetch one of the blankets from the floor? I'm perishing with cold."

"Of course, Master," grinned Tark, seizing a thick bearskin and draping it over his beloved Alpha. "How are you feeling today?"

"Oh, tolerable," said the Alpha. "Good to smell another warm body, though. I've been cooped up in here so long, what with the weather and all, that I'm starting to ripen this place quite thoroughly. You think I stink in the summer, try abandoning me in this den for three months. I must escape here. What brings you by?"

"You smell like roses and sunshine to me, Master. I need leave of you to perform the Rite of Change," said Tark, petting his Alpha's head.

"Rite of Change?" The Alpha peered blearily at him, though he could barely make out the shadow of Tark's face. "That's special, boy, but you're our resident healer. You don't need my permission for that. What else troubles you?"

Tark felt silly being called "boy" when he was barely shy of sixty. It made him grin despite himself. "It's an infant, Master. Very sick. The Change is sure to cure him, but…"

"But the law says that a Werewolf must be raised with Werewolves," grunted the Alpha. "What does his family say? Do they consent?"

"The mother does. She's so eager for her son to live that she'll sell her soul if she needs to."

"As any mother would," said the Alpha. "What of the father?"

"He's too drunk. He came to me sick and frozen last night. We gave him brandy, but he drained the bottle dry."

The Alpha grinned toothlessly. "Poor devil. He'll have a headache by now. Last night, with the wind and snow? By the Gods, he must have been near death. So you didn't ask him, then?"

"No, Master. But I know him. I know he'd consent."

"Then the matter is out of our hands," said the Alpha. "You have no need of me. The parents want the child to live and are willing to give him up for it. Get on with it." The Alpha reached out and touched Tark's face. "Help me up, boy," he said. "I'm parched."

"I can get it."

"No, lad, if I stay here much longer I'll grow roots. You must help me up."

So Tark took his Alpha's paws and helped him to his feet. The old man tottered on his own to the water bowl, lowered himself heavily to his knees, and drank from the water bowl near his fire. He lifted his dripping muzzle and looked at Tark. "You want more than my permission," he said. "You want my advice. I can't give you an answer until you give me a question, boy."

Tark bit his lower lip with a probing fang. "I keep thinking of my father. Would he have chosen to Change, if he had the chance? He had some regrets from being made a werewolf instead of being born one. He never knew his human parents. They died by the time he was Prime. Never knew if he had any brothers or sisters. He didn't have family, really, all he had was the Pack."

"I remember," said the Alpha. He sat down on the bed again, but didn't curl up. He only wrapped his bearskin around his shoulders. "I was the one who Changed him. He was no more than four, and I could have been no more than thirty, the young, brash, cocky healer bursting with my abilities as a Warrior-Priest. The ceremony was summer, I remember, and all the Pack came to share blood. The poor lad was practically drenched in it by the time we were finished. He was ill, though, very ill. Probably not so ill as your friends' baby, but we didn't have your head for medicine or prayer in those days.

"Humans hold werewolves in strange regard. We are more than respected, we are almost exalted, and humans sometimes fear things they exalt. We do as we can to help them, we hunt for them when game grows scarce, and we heal them when they are sick. Not all villages are lucky enough to live near a Pack, and our Pack has been reluctant to interfere with humans at all. Those humans are lucky to have you, Warrior-Priest, a shaman and a healer, but they are not of our Pack. We have our own ways, they have theirs.

"Now, it fascinated your grandparents, that their child would grow up to inherit those ways and our birthright. They wondered if perhaps he would be a Warrior-Priest and live the dual life of the hunter-healer, as you did. I think they were eager to get rid of him on that point, as sad as they were that they wouldn't see him until he was grown. However, they had the same plague he did, less advanced. They died a year later, both of them, on the same day.

"I didn't want to tell your father that he was the son of human parents until he was Prime. I even waited a few months, to make sure I wasn't mistaking the scent. Your father had a confused childhood. He dreamed of being human, living in a house, eating cooked food. Wearing clothes, beyond the cloak or blanket or loincloth. Even using money. We lived near no humans at the time, and he'd never met one. He only knew the stories. Did you know that he was once sick after killing a deer? The sickness that they cook out of meat had infected him. It did him no harm, in the long run, of course. I think it came from his mind.

"He didn't WANT to be human. He didn't see it in terms of want or not-want, but he never realized until Prime that he was as werewolf as if he'd never been human. It did affect his childhood. But—" And here, the Alpha beat the important point. "It did not warp him."

"So what should I do, Master?" said Tark, though he knew the answer already. "What will become of the boy once he's a cub?"

"Well, I'd suggest we name him, and present him, and raise him, and when he's ready, we introduce him to his parents. One thing I would do, though, if I had anything to do differently. I would tell him early on that he is the son of humans. He may more easily come to terms with who he is and what he feels if he understands his origin, and that any confusion in his identity isn't permanent." The Alpha curled up. "I probably don't have long to live, boy," he said softly. "As much as I want to see this new cub grow, and watch how he grows, I doubt I'll be alive to do it. You have great responsibilities before you, and with them will come all their burdens. Talk among the Pack is that when I am gone, you will be the new Alpha."

"Yes, that's true," said Tark. "They came last year, when you were sick."

"And you healed me instead." The Alpha twinkled again. "I feel you're keeping me alive just so you can shirk your responsibilities. Nevertheless, you shall be Alpha, and you will have to deal with what I had to deal with—helping raise a confused, uncertain cub." The Alpha touched Tark's face. "No worse than what you've already faced." He kissed Tark's cheek, sniffed his fur, and frowned. "You still smell scared."

"I am scared," said Tark. "Everyone is scared. Nestor is scared, Meris is scared, and my mate is scared. Even my cub is scared. The only one who isn't scared is the baby."

"The baby is the only one who has nothing to lose," grunted the Alpha, flopping back on his mat. "When you go to the Oracle for purification, maybe you should ask it the questions, instead of me."

"The Oracle? It's only stone."

"It's been around a lot longer than I have, and probably answered a lot more questions. Leave me now. I'm very tired."

"Yes, Master," said Tark, standing up. He hesitated at the entrance, one paw on the stone. "Master?"

"Mm?" grunted the blanket.

"Thank you. For everything. For my father."

"Mm."

Tark padded out of the hut. He still felt troubled. The Alpha answered his questions, but Tark knew, deep down, that he couldn't erase the fears.

Rib met him at the outer entrance. "You still look worried," he said. "Was the Alpha ill?"

"Oh, no, nothing like that," said Tark. "I just don't know why I'm the only one hesitant about this. Can I even pull it off? I've never been asked to do it before."

"Well, I know you well enough to guess that you'd probably find it easy," said Rib.

"Would you come with me, to the Oracle?"

"Sure, if my Master no longer needs me," grunted Rib. "Wait here a moment."

※ ◌ ※

A narrow passage into the rock led to the Oracle, an ancient stone monument carved centuries ago when the werewolves first discovered the caves. Now it was their temple to the Gods.

No human would know or understand these Gods if introduced. To a werewolf, God is the connection they share with everything in their environment that reaches out for them and makes them a part of the whole. God is nature in all her beauty and glory and mystery, the life in a tree or a rock or a river. Werewolves worship these things, and came to the Oracle for the love and support of all the spirits who had been, and all that would be.

The Oracle came with no doctrine or dogma, but most werewolves paid their respects by marking at the door and bathing in its spring-fed pool. It was holy ground. Others embroidered the path to meditation, following their own rituals and traditions to focus their minds and prepare their bodies.

Tark and Rib entered the Oracle. Tark lit the braziers while Rib lit the torch, and the room warmed around them. The walls were broad and roughly square, and a thin skin of ice covered the shining pool. The paintings that once inspired Tark's own drawings covered the walls. He touched the figure of a running werewolf. He couldn't tell what it was running towards, or away from.

The rich smell of urine overpowered him. Not a werewolf walked in that didn't mark the doorway. Tark knelt next to the opening and sniffed at the overlapping scent-marks. The youngest was a week old.

Tark rolled into the dirt, pressing his shoulders and back into the dust of the floor and the centuries of scent embedded there. He rolled onto his belly and sat up with the scent of the entire Pack covering him, a heady smell that made him feel a little less isolated. He breathed it in, deep and rich, and added his own mark to the corner. Rib waited until he was done, then rolled in the dirt himself, collecting as many as he could, then added his own distinct mark.

"Don't go in the pool," he warned, watching Tark standing at the edge of the water. "By the Gods, you'll freeze."

Tark didn't listen. His heart ran fast. He felt giddy. Gods and Spirits rallied around him, sharing their courage, telling him what to do.

He took a deep breath and leaped off the rock and into the pool. Ice shards shattered all around him. He disappeared from sight.

Rib leaped to his feet. "Tark!" he cried, a bark that overrode his hoarse voice and emerged as only a whisper. Tark surfaced, gasping, scrambling out of the pool that burned his skin with cold. He shook down, hard, curled up into a tight ball, and shivered. Rib vaulted the pool and knelt over him, throwing both arms around him and hugging tight. "Come on," he said. "Closer to the fire. Hurry."

Warm light bathed Tark's body. "Open up, wolf," said Rib. "Come on, let the warmth in. Bare your chest to the fire."

At last, Rib unraveled him and sat him up. Tark's breathing was almost normal. "I thought my heart would stop," he whined.

"Are you all right? We mustn't leave this room until you're dry."

"I'm fine. I needed it. Trust me, I needed it."

Tark watched while Rib dunked his scalp and paws into the water, a token measure only, and he joined his shining wet companion by the fire and sat down cross-legged. "We shouldn't stay long," said Tark. "There's a life at stake here, and we have only until morning."

He fought the cold, and his shivering. His back, buttocks, and tail felt as if they were freezing despite the warmth of the fire, and he curled up again, knees to his chest, tail between his legs and clutched in his paws. He watched the drifting fire for a while, and Rib gazed into the same dancing flames. Their minds relaxed and their scents deepened as the Spirits around them gathered them up and carried them away.

🦊 ☜ 🦊

Tark dreamed, and in his dream a strapping werewolf who looked like a younger version of him approached, put a paw to his shoulder, and kissed the top of his head. When the werewolf stepped back, Tark recognized his father.

"Are you scared?" his father asked.

"Aye, Father."

"Don't be." Tark's father vanished, leaving him sitting on the hillside. The flowers shone with wild colors, the grass waved verdant green, and the rich smell of spring covered everything like a warm blanket. The first really warm day of the year. The ground squelched and the world was sloppy with mud, but Tark didn't care. He ran down the hill and plunged into the lake, crying out with joy at the icy intrusion into his fur. His father stood on the banking with a towel and his warm arms to embrace him.

A buck protecting its young had killed Tark's father when Tark was about twenty years old. He'd found the body, covered with mud, blood soaking its face and twisting its hair into sticky red whips. His father had been cold. Apparently, he'd tried to crawl back to his cave.

Tark's greatest comfort was the smell of his father's corpse. It wasn't the same rich, wild smell of his father, the smell of his embrace, of the fur on his chest. This rotting-carrion smell had usurped his father's. This hollow husk wasn't his father. His father was someplace else. Tark grieved to see him go, but the pain was eased by the three-day-dead stink of his father's corpse.

He'd dreamed about his father off and on for a few months, then the dreams tapered away.

The corpse looked at him. The smell was carrion, but the eyes twinkled. The sparkling red fur on its face shifted as the corpse spoke.

"You've been thinking about me lately, haven't you?"

Lahk wrestled on the hillside with someone Tark didn't recognize. He watched with interest. Lahk occasionally wrestled other cubs his age, but his ability outstripped theirs. This was a newcomer. Lahk looked older, stronger, heavier in the arms and legs. Taller, certainly. Hard to tell from here, but he *seemed* taller. The other was about Lahk's age, or at least

Lahk's age now, twelve or thirteen summers, with the faint whiff of year-ling just coming into Prime.

Lahk admitted defeat. He crawled away from the stranger, who stood up, and Tark recognized his father.

"Tark!"

"Father?"

"Tark, wake up!"

Tark popped out of his dream and sat up. "How long?"

"Half an hour," said Rib. He took his paw away from Tark's shoulder. "How do you feel?"

"Feel?" said Tark, as if he didn't understand the question. "I'm fine."

"Spread out. It's very hot in here, and you're nearly dry." Rib sat down, paws on his knees, back against the wall. "What did you learn?"

"I saw my father," said Tark. "I think he wanted to tell me he'd approve of what I'm going to do. He's what's had me frightened all the time." He rubbed the fur on his chest. Nearly dry. "I knew he had regrets in his life," he said, softly. "Knowing him was like knowing the baby's future. Nevertheless, he was basically a happy werewolf. He had his family, his Pack, and his cubs. He didn't dwell on a might-have-been. He was proud to be a werewolf and would have had it no other way. His regrets were too few for him to ever want to be human again."

"But you're not afraid anymore," said Rib.

"No, I'm not. Strange, isn't it?"

Rib helped him up, and they padded out of the chamber and into the bright sunlight.

🐾 ⌒ 🐾

Tark stood at the mouth of the cave, holding the baby tight in his arms. Last night's treatment had strengthened the infant. The weather was warmer than it had been during the day, and the child survived the journey to the Mountain. Tark felt very, very good. Redeemed, he thought. Almost reborn.

Meris and Nestor stood with him, lingering in the moment. Soon Tark would take their son inside, and that would be the last they'd see of him. They'd be banned from entering the cave, and the new cub would live his life on the other side of the Mountain, living and learning with his Pack. They'd have to make do with knowing that he was alive, that they had done their best as far as they could, that he was safe and comfortable, and would grow stronger and healthier than if he'd remained a human.

"It's time," said Tark. "It'll be all right, I swear. In a few hours, he'll be a healthy cub with a prosperous future, and the Pack will have a new member. I don't know how much of his life I'll be allowed to share after this, if anything. I doubt I'll be permitted to bring you regular updates. If I am to be Alpha, I can't risk bending the Law."

"We understand," said Nestor. "But, please, what can you tell us now? What will happen now?"

"Now? He'll be taken inside, anointed with my blood and the blood of witnesses, including Lahk and Rib and Lasha, and a few others. We'll pray for him, and sing for him, and when the sun rises, he'll be a were-wolf."

"What will you do then?" said Meris.

"I'm going to take my Alpha's advice, remind him where he comes from and why he was taken away. As he gets older, I hope he'll understand why his life is the way it is. I think I can even improve on the Alpha's plan a little, and forestall the loneliness my father felt."

"What will you change?" Meris sounded dull.

"Well, he won't just be a part of the Pack," said Tark. "He'll live here and be a part of my family. I can't tell him exactly who his parents are, but he'll know he's near them. He won't be allowed to visit the village until he is Prime, but maybe he'll follow in the footsteps of the Warrior-Priests. And maybe, in a dozen or so years, he'll want to know his real parents."

He let Nestor and Meris kiss the baby one last time, then turned and padded into the darkness and the smell of the cave. The couple sat huddled at the mouth of the cave for about half an hour without saying a word, then hiked back down the mountain towards home.

�֎

FIND THE BEAUTIFUL

"Though we travel the world over to find the beautiful, we must carry it with us, or we find it not."
—Ralph Waldo Emerson

Perfect. The night was perfect. A fine drizzle hung in the air, but off to one side of the clouds, the moon shone bright and full, filling the forest with a soft silver haze. Raf picked his way down the trail, without the help of the flashlight in his pocket. He could feel his heart pounding and fingers shaking as he gripped slick wet branches and held them aside. Tonight, surely, he would find a footprint.

Their last five nights at the campground near the International Wolf Center had been either stormy or very dry, and though he had ventured out on the dry nights (his parents wouldn't let him out in a storm, "not in Tornado Alley," they said), he had not known where to look. Besides, even if he had found a footprint, it would probably have been dry and useless.

Today, though, their guide had taken them off the main trails to a deer carcass that had been spotted from the air the previous day. "Wolf kill," he said succinctly, and showed the families who could stand to look the marks left by long, powerful jaws, the torn skin and scattered blood-stains.

"Maybe the wolves are nearby?" Raf's father said, hopeful for a sighting not only for his son's sake, but also because he would hate to have come all the way from Connecticut and not have seen at least one wolf. He had heard and understood numerous warnings that they would probably not see a wolf, and that the guides were instructed to avoid wolves, but that didn't diminish his hope of getting his money's worth.

The guide shrugged, replying with a noncommittal "Could be." Raf's mother gave him an encouraging squeeze, but Raf was absorbed in the kill, the evidence of the wolves' presence almost as thrilling to him as an actual wolf would be. He imagined the pack crowding around the deer: alphas feeding first, subordinates whining for their turn, their interplay and communication.

Others in the tour group were crowding around the deer with him, but their communication was limited to remarks like, "Hey, honey, they've got some teeth, those wolves," and "Such a pretty animal, why do they have to kill it?" Raf stepped back, a bit disgusted at their ignorance. He looked around, away from the deer, and saw the footprints.

He saw them, he was honest enough to admit to himself, because the guide was peering at the bare patch of ground with great interest. Most of the forest floor was carpeted with pine needles, but in this small clearing, an earthy patch held a few pawprints. Raf walked over, leading his parents, and asked the guide, "Are those their prints?" He knew they were, his heart was racing with the certainty of it, but he had to be sure.

The older man knelt down and nodded. He held three fingers over the prints, side by side, and motioned for Raf to look. "Three fingers'll cover a coyote track," he said. "These are too big for 'otes." Raf studied the prints, then looked around, trying to fix the clearing in his mind. His moonlight excursions had already taught him that he could not depend on finding his way back to a particular point, even with the trail, unless he studied it closely. He felt a thrill run through his muscles as he thought about returning that night.

Now he stood on the trail again, and paused uncertainly. The carcass had been... here? A little further down? No, here. He left the trail and walked through the thick brush, his clothes now dripping wet. He felt he could smell the wolves, and knew they were close. He had wanted for so long (well, two years) to be part of their world. The book on his thirteenth birthday, *White Wolf*, had stolen his heart. In the past two years he had devoured every wolf book he could lay his hands on, in love with their sleek forms, their wise and wild eyes, their hard, compact muscles, and most of all, the love they bestowed on each other. To be in a pack was to *belong*, and belonging was not something Raf was very good at, on his own.

Most of his school friends spent the summers dating, lounging by each other's swimming pools, or going out to the beach. Raf had gone a few times, but had always felt distinctly uncomfortable, an outsider. If they could see him now, he thought smugly, they would laugh. Pushing through a wet forest in search of a wild animal? Most of those people would never want to be wet unless they had a swimsuit on, and never want to see anything more wild than the squirrels they exterminated out of their houses every year. Only one of his friends did he consider close: Mark shared his love of wolves, and had traveled with him to the Bronx Zoo many times to see the wolves there, but even Mark would shake his head now. Raf, he'd say, you're off the deep end this time. Wolves are okay, but werewolves? Stories. You don't really believe that stuff, do you?

Oh, yes, Raf breathed silently to himself, as the silvery glistening-wet fur of the deer carcass appeared to him between two branches ahead. I sure do, Mark. And the leap his heart made at the sight of the carcass, the racing of his blood, and the tightening of his muscles, all these were tied up intimately with Raf's deep-rooted belief. He was old enough to understand what he thought of as the truth behind all the werewolf stories he'd read, and young enough to convince himself that so many stories could not be written without some truth, that the legends must have some fact behind them. He had time and again envisioned himself as a wolf, grey fur, white underbelly, bushy tail, standing proudly atop a rock, gazing over the terrain that was his world. The vision had become so real to him that he could not help but believe in it.

The deer's head gazed up at him emptily, its eyes long vanished down some raven's beak. Raf ignored it, looking around for the bare patch of earth, stamping the ground in frustration. He was beginning to get chilly from not moving. When he'd seen the guide stooping over the prints, he'd been standing by the deer's hind legs... but the deer had been moved some, that he could tell right away. Where had it been? He clasped his arms around himself and scanned the area. All the pine needles were disturbed, offering no clue in their random patterns. At least he knew it had been somewhat away from the trail. He stepped over the deer and walked slowly in that direction, scanning the ground for clues, his feet sinking in the spongy floor.

What if it were the wrong carcass? What if he were looking in vain? He shook his head, water flying from his hair. This had to be right. It felt right. Off to his left, a little brighter? He walked towards it, and then was bathed in the bright moonlit mist, in the little clearing. In front of him, the bare patch of earth was rife with pawprints.

Breathing heavily, he fell to his knees beside it, his jeans already so wet that the forest floor seemed only cool, not soaked. He scanned the earth, fingers twitching nervously, looking for the large prints he'd seen earlier. There was one—wasn't it? It had been partially obscured by several smaller tracks. There was not, he saw, even one clear wolf print; each was smudged or marred by other tracks. All of them had collected little pools of muddy water.

Rainwater collected in a wolf's footprint, he said to himself, reciting the phrase so he could be sure there was no mistake. A man who drinks rainwater collected in a wolf's footprint will himself become a wolf. His body thrummed with his excitement and the strength of his faith. He bent down to lap at the water, then stopped, drops splashing from his eyelashes into the mud. Better, he thought, to collect it some other way. He cast about for something to collect the water in, but hadn't thought that far ahead. Hands will have to do, he thought, and then grinned, thinking, but not for long! He shook his hand as dry as he could in the misty drizzle, and pressed it palm up into the mud beside the footprint, letting the precious water dribble into it. Quickly, he raised his hand to his lips, drank, then repeated the gesture in case he hadn't gotten enough. The water was nasty and dirty, leaving his mouth full of grit, but he scarcely noticed. He sat back and undid the top button of his jeans, ready to slip out of them should the change come upon him quickly, feeling alive with a magical tension.

How long would he have to wait? Only a few of the stories he'd read had involved people trying to become werewolves, and they usually found a werewolf to bite them. Much more convenient than this. He rubbed his arms, and then as the moon came out from behind a cloud, he felt a tingling in his mouth. Shivering with excitement now rather than the cold, Raf unbuttoned the top button of his shirt, oblivious to the chill breeze slicing through the trees. He swallowed a couple times, and then felt his throat start to burn where he'd swallowed, the footprint water leaving fiery trails behind it. He had once tried scotch, at a party his father was giving, and the alcohol had seared his throat shut until he was sure he would never breathe again. He was reminded of that now, gagging against the growing constriction, but instead of fading as it had at the party, it spread down his neck, clamping painful fingers around his lungs and heart. Is it the change, or am I having a heart attack? he thought briefly, and then lost that thought as his stomach contorted painfully. His arms and legs spasmed in agonizing synchrony, sending him thrashing into a bush. It's happening, was his last thought, but oh God it hurts…

🐾 ∞ 🐾

He awoke under a brighter moon, warm in a pile of clammy blankets. Blankets? He struggled to get out from under them, not remembering for a moment where he was. Standing beside the sopping fabric, looking at it, he recognized the pattern of the shirt, and the label on the jeans. These were his clothes, though they looked bigger now. He didn't remember taking them off, but he didn't feel naked, either. He noticed then that his nose was much longer, sticking way out in front of him; he could see it clearly, the whiskers and black tip. And then he remembered everything, and with a quick bound he was free of his clothes. Warm! in the chill drizzling night, with his coat of thick fur, and standing on all fours. Four legs, not two! It had really worked! He yelped out his joy, and in the ensuing quiet realized how noisy it had been, how much better he could hear. He heard rustling through the undergrowth as field mice who had stopped at his cry resumed their lonely, frightened searches for food. He heard the low rustle of an owl's wings, the flutter of bats—suddenly a million sounds came to him, each with its own signature that his new body put an image to and his mind named. Lifting his nose, he could smell them, too, especially here where there was food nearby. Cautious, clever bandits—that would be raccoons. Skulking, vicious—opossums. His own kind! a mix of several individual odors, each rich and musky. They must be wolves, two males and three females. And then several larger predators—bears?

Movement at the edge of the clearing caught his eye; he jumped and before he knew it found himself skulking under a bush. Only the wind. He walked out again and felt his tail behind him. Again came that giddy rush of excitement; he'd often dreamed of having a tail, as some people dream of flying, and he knew just what muscles to use to wag it, lift it, curl it under him. To his delight, those muscles worked just as he remembered from his dreams. He wagged his tail experimentally a few times, grinning foolishly, and then ran, stretching his new body out and flying back to the trail. If he didn't think, he found, he instinctively avoided trees and underbrush. How do my legs work? suddenly flashed across his mind, and the minute he wondered, seizing control of them from his instincts, they splayed out under him and he slipped and fell on his side. He stood, wobbling, and just willed himself forward, keeping his mind deliberately away from his legs, just like all the new werewolves did in the good werewolf books. That seemed to work.

Once back on the trail he ran and ran, tail flying out behind him, feeling as light as a feather and full of vibrant energy. Sounds and smells sifted through his mind, some finding associations, some not. He selected a few to turn over in his mind, marveling at the new range of his senses, but mostly he exulted in the play of his muscles, the feeling that he belonged here, in this forest, that he was one of its creatures.

Humans up ahead, he smelled, quite a few. He realized he'd already made it back almost to the campsite, in something less than a quarter of the time it had taken him to walk to the clearing. He grinned, his mouth hanging open, and decided he would give his parents a thrill. The campsite was on a lakeshore, and he remembered that sound carried well over water. He trotted down through some brush to the lakeshore, then away from the campsite until he could see the points of light some hundreds of feet away. Sitting back on his haunches, he pulled together all his joy and excitement, all the energy that made him want to leap and bound until he was exhausted, threw back his muzzle, and let it all out in a glorious howl.

That was the plan, anyway. He had howled in his dreams, even howled during the last five days, trying to get the wolves to answer. The sound he made had all his exuberance in it, but it was nothing like a howl. It was more a sharp scream.

Alarmed, Raf clamped his muzzle shut and looked around. He looked down at himself—white underbelly, dark paws, bushy tail. Was he just a wolf cub, who couldn't howl yet? He did feel small, somehow, and light, but he knew wolves were smaller than humans. Apprehensively, he trotted down to the lake and stood with his forepaws in the water, then looked down into the moonlit, glassy surface.

When the ripples settled, he saw a slender muzzle looking back at him, white underneath and dark on top. Slit-pupiled eyes widened, taking in the large triangular ears and small nosepad.

He was a fox.

Quickly, he jumped back from the water and ran blindly in circles, shaking his head violently. A *fox*?? A slinking, rotten, stinking, common *fox*?? What had gone wrong?

Panting, he finally stopped and slumped to his belly, resting his muzzle on his forepaws. He could smell himself acutely now, a familiar acrid musk, and wondered how he could ever have mistaken that for a wolf's scent. Maybe he could still change to a wolf, he thought desperately, concentrating. There was nothing in the old stories about werefoxes. Maybe this was temporary.

Closing his eyes, he concentrated, but he knew it was useless. Miserably, he suspected that he could only become human again, that the magic had come and gone, leaving him with only that shape and this. How unfair could life get? To be taken so close to his dream, only to be cast into this nightmare. Best to go back to human and never leave that form, to forget this night had ever happened. Only... how was he supposed to change back? He didn't even know where to begin. Maybe he was stuck with this shape until sunup. Or maybe he could change himself, by concentrating.

Wait. Better to return to where he'd discarded his clothes, and try to change there. No sense in running naked through the forest, though he almost preferred that to keeping this ridiculous shape. A smell filtered through to his consciousness, strong and musky, like back at the clearing. A wolf! Elation thrilled him—at least he would get to see one, even if through a fox's eyes. But when he opened his eyes, he found himself looking into the slender muzzle and shining eyes of another fox.

Of course. The scent he'd thought of as 'his kind' back at the clearing must have been foxes. This was a young female, he sensed, curious and a little afraid. He raised his head, the wash of despair stemmed for a moment by some interest. For the vixen was not making a sound, but his eyes followed her head and body's movements, and he understood her as clearly as if she were speaking English.

—Are you hurt?

He shook his head, then saw her puzzled look and realized that the gesture meant nothing to her. Tentatively, he thought, No, and his fox body got to its feet and shook itself, raising its head a bit. This made more sense to her.

—You are alone, she said, nose held high to sniff the air for other scents. He nodded, cursed himself again for his human thoughts, and let the fox in him do the talking.

—Yes, he answered. My parents are gone.

—This is our land, she answered, a little defiantly but with some hesitation. Her scent told him that she was more curious about him than she was afraid or antagonized by his presence. —Didn't you scent that?

—I'm sorry, he said, ducking in a slightly submissive posture. —I will be leaving soon.

He turned to go, but had only gotten a few steps before she darted in front of him, swift and fluid. Despite his disgust, he was beginning to admire her grace. Not as beautiful as a wolf, he told himself. But still...

—Don't you know how to walk quietly? she said, not condescendingly, but wondering, as if he had forgotten how to breathe.

Embarrassed by his inadequacy even as a fox, he hung his head.—My parents... nobody taught me, he said, aware dimly that it translated more closely to 'I am alone and untaught.' in her eyes.

She nodded matter-of-factly, and unmistakably said, —Follow me, and watch. Lightly, almost soundlessly, she stepped away through the underbrush.

He watched her with fox eyes and human understanding, and tried to walk as she did. It didn't help. His ears' sensitivity betrayed his every step, the sounds as loud as firecrackers to him, while the vixen walked nearly silently only a foot in front of him.

She stopped and looked back at him several times, encouraging him to follow, and his spirits began to pick up a bit. He forgot his unhappiness for the moment and devoted all his concentration to walking as quietly as she did.

He was not even close, though he was a good deal quieter than he had been, when she stopped abruptly, neck arched, ears and muzzle focused on a scrubby patch of weeds. He pulled up short, nearly running into her tail. Her whole attention was devoted to whatever was in those weeds; she ignored him completely. Standing straight and tall, he tried to mimic her posture, and listened with all his might to the weeds. Faintly, he could just hear a soft, quiet scraping, the slow movements of some small animal, probably a field mouse.

The vixen tensed and then suddenly pounced into the weeds. He heard a shrill cry, which ended quickly. Involuntarily, he jumped forward an inch in a small imitation of her pounce, both forefeet coming down together. She emerged from the weeds with a small grey and white shape dangling from her mouth. Coming up to him, she dropped it at his feet.

—Can you hunt?

He looked at the mouse, downcast. —I don't think so, he answered miserably.

She stepped forward and lightly brushed her muzzle along his. The contact was warm and friendly, the sensation of her soft, short fur rubbing his sending a happy thrill through him. It was not a sexual feeling, but one of friendship and camaraderie. She barely knew him, but she was taking care of him because they were partners in the wild world, trying to survive together.

As she lifted her head, he realized that his whiskers were giving him as much new sensation as his nose and ears, sensations he had ignored until she intruded on them. With his whiskers, he could feel and sense the air currents around him, and get a very good idea of the shape and texture of things near his head. Further objects were more difficult to discern, but did leave impressions. As the vixen drew her head back from his, he could feel the shape of her muzzle, her warm breath, and her own whiskers exploring him. The nuzzle had been as much to find out about him as to reassure him, he understood. Probably more.

—There's lots of food, she said through his dizzy assimilation of this new world. She nudged the mouse towards him.

Hesitantly, he sniffed the mouse, his whiskers brushing it. It was still warm and bleeding, exuding layers and layers of odors he could barely begin to sort out: the seeds it was eating, its lifeblood, its thick musk... I can't eat a mouse, he told himself, but then immediately thought, why not? Wolves do. He was already salivating, and grabbed the mouse in his jaws. The little crunch it made between his teeth, the warmth flowing over his tongue, all excited him, so that he had to open his mouth and let it go. He picked it up again, letting the taste fill his muzzle and nose, and crunched it several more times before he swallowed it.

He looked up at the vixen. She was watching with amusement, and when he met her eyes, said, —You've never eaten one of those?

Abashed, but less embarrassed, he grinned and answered, —No.

She seemed very interested by this, but didn't say any more, moving instead back down the little path. He followed her, trying to learn to be quieter as he went, but to his mild frustration he did not seem to be able to advance past his initial improvement. She stopped again after several minutes to hunt, and this time emerged with a small, darker animal. It looked a little larger than a mouse, but Raf's human part could not tell much other difference. His nose was going wild, though. This smelled so distinct from the mouse—the musk was softer, the foods around it were different, and it smelled of a different soil.

Excited, he gobbled it up, and closed his eyes happily, savoring the rich taste. —That was great! he said, looking at her. Some instinct clicked in him, and he reared back and playfully pushed at her.

Caught by surprise, she stumbled back and glared at him for a moment before getting a frisky look on her face and running at him, bowling him over and standing on his chest. He felt a little demeaned, but in a very silly way, knowing it was mostly in fun. Leaning up towards her muzzle, he whined at her instinctively, his fox reflexes taking over, and she lowered her muzzle and bared her teeth, whining loudly back. He struggled out from under her and ran, knowing she would follow, his body alive and a-tingle with the excitement of play.

They ran and played for hours, tussling and chasing. He experimented with running flat out, dodging, and wrestling. He learned the very basics of hunting, and pouncing, and how to escape another fox or a human. It was hours later that he noticed the brightening sky, and she began to look apprehensive.

—Time to rest, she said, and took a couple steps away from him.—I should go.

He felt alone and scared, suddenly, and not very wild or foxlike at all. What if he were to sleep somewhere that wasn't safe? He didn't know where any dens were, and didn't know what was safe and what wasn't.

—May I... he paused. —May I come with you? I promise I will leave soon.

She hesitated, then assented with a wave of her tail. He trotted off after her, a little worried about meeting her parents. That made him giggle inside. It wasn't like he was dating her or anything. Then he stopped. His parents. What would they think? But he couldn't go back to them like this. If he didn't change with the sunrise — and he could see now the bright crescent of the sun peeking above the eastern treeline — he hoped he would not change back during the day. The stories all said the change back happened at sunrise, if the werewolf didn't control it at all. Of course, none of the stories had mentioned what happened to him. He shook his head, and decided he would have to trust to fate.

The smell of other foxes grew stronger as he trotted along, leading him to a small hole hidden behind a clump of weeds, on a small hillock. The vixen disappeared into it, signaling for him to wait. A moment later, a dog fox emerged, larger than both him and the vixen, and circled him cautiously, seeming confused.

Finally he stopped and looked straight at Raf, nostrils flared. —You are alone, he said.

Raf kept his tail lowered in the slightly submissive pose he had adopted earlier. —I will leave soon, he said, since that had seemed to reassure the vixen.

The dog fox studied him for a moment longer, then sniffed his nose. Instinctively, Raf opened his mouth slightly and bared his teeth; the other responded in kind, making Raf back up a step. He shut his mouth, and the larger fox did likewise. They regarded each other for several seconds, the dog fox's nostrils widening as he took Raf's measure. Finally, the larger fox turned toward the hole.

—Come on in.

Raf followed the fox into the small tunnel. It opened out into a large hole, but Raf's nose made him wait in the tunnel while it sifted through the odors. Four pairs of eyes watched him, gleaming, from the darkness; their scents were strongest, but behind them were the scents of countless generations of foxes, and even of some other animals: skunk, badger, opossum. The foxes returned here often, but did not live here permanently, and when they were out, they did not begrudge the room to other animals who needed it.

The scents sorted out, he moved in to the crowd of foxes. A father, a mother, and two daughters. They sniffed him, brushed him with their whiskers, and accepted his sniffs and whisker-brushes in return. A couple times, the mother or father growled and bared their teeth at him, but he maintained the proper respectful, submissive pose, and there was no real trouble. Raf felt himself almost trembling happily at the ease with which he was accepted into this small family. There was no fear of strangers, no worry that he would wake up and slaughter them all in the night. They could smell him and know that he was another fox like them, with no greater concern than his own survival. As long as he was not taking food from their mouths, they welcomed him, and he settled warmly into their collective embrace.

He curled up, tail across his nose, next to the vixen he had befriended, and breathed in the scent of warm fur all around him, felt the warm bodies breathing in and out around him, enfolding him. He fell asleep with the thought thrumming through his head that he had never been more comfortable.

🐾 ☁ 🐾

The press of bodies against him woke him. He snapped to attention quickly, all senses alert. The other foxes were stirring, but he counted one missing. The dog fox. A quick sniff in the direction of one of the tunnels (there were several, he now saw) told him that the dog fox was outside. The sounds the other foxes made told him that they were waiting for him to tell them that the coast was clear.

There was a soft call from outside. Raf couldn't interpret it, but the other foxes relaxed, and started to file out of the tunnels. He followed his friend out into a dry red evening. She stretched, and he mimicked her, and it wasn't until he looked around that he realized that the rest of the family had disappeared.

Startled, he turned to ask her where everyone had gone, and was just in time to see her tail disappear into the bush. He ran after her, crashing through the leaves like an elephant, and she turned, annoyance obvious in the tilt of her ears and the set of her shoulders.

—What?

He retreated a step, tail swishing nervously.

—I thought you were leaving, she said.

He had promised to leave. But he'd felt so secure in their den, he'd dreamed that they would accept him and ask him to stay. He pawed the ground, and while he was hesitating, she turned and walked away.

He was stunned. Didn't she feel the same about him as he did for her? The answer crept up and pounced on him, catching him neatly. Of course she didn't. She had her family. Foxes didn't form deep attachments, like wolves, he told himself, but he could hear the false ring to the rationalization. Seeing the fox family, he knew they did. They just had no reason to love him. Still, they had accepted him, and he wanted to leave them—or at least her—with something.

He rushed after her, cutting her off as she had once done to him. She looked annoyed, but also curious.

Thank you, he tried to say, and realized that there were no fox words for that. He stared at her, wanting to hug her, realizing she would not understand. Finally, he simply nuzzled her gently. She nuzzled him back, and he convinced himself that there was more than just ritual to the gesture. With that self-deception, he turned away from her and left.

His throat felt constricted with emotion, but his body refused him the outlet of tears. Foxes didn't cry, it seemed. The feeling faded gradually, but not completely, as he spent hours wandering through the forest. He wondered if he would be alone forever, trapped in a fox's body without even the pretense of a family. He was hungry, too; he hadn't quite gotten the knack of hunting, and after two failed attempts, he gave it up, disgusted with himself.

When he finally found the trail, it was completely by accident. He couldn't mistake the thick human scent, though. It wasn't pleasant, but it was compelling, and he was standing on the trail with his nose raised when he heard a ringing in his ears and felt himself shiver, and knew he was changing back. No, he thought desperately, not yet, but the feeling was overtaking him and he couldn't stop it. Whining, he tucked his head between his forepaws/arms and waited for it to be over.

This change was much less painful. His body expanded, skin tightening and puckering as it pulled the fur back into itself. His stomach twisted again, making him wonder if he were going to be sick, but then the change sped up, as if he were a rubber band snapping back to its original shape. He shook his head and sat, heavy, naked and fully human, on the pine needles of the trail.

Looking around, he was astounded at the colors and shades of the world, and realized for the first time that as a fox, he had seen in black and white. The colors confused him for a moment, but he was slipping back easily into his human patterns and routines. He was acutely conscious, too, of the sharp pine needles on his bare skin, but it took several minutes for him to get up the nerve to stand up. He felt embarrassed and vulnerable as he started walking naked down the trail, and kept covering his crotch with one hand. Geez, how would I explain this, he thought to himself, his cheeks flushed with more than just the chilly night air. He hoped with all his heart that he wasn't walking back towards the camp.

To his relief, he soon found himself on a part of the trail he remembered, and in a few more minutes had found the deer carcass. His clothes lay nearby, under a bush next to a patch of mud. It looked like they hadn't been found, thankfully. Shivering, he pulled on the clothes, and felt immediately better, even though his clothes were cold and damp. At least he felt more human.

Standing up fully dressed, he instinctively lifted his nose to sniff the wind, then hung his head when he could only smell the rich, damp forest. One smell, where there had been thousands. The sounds of the forest reached his ears, but he could only concentrate on a few at a time, and he knew how many he was missing, even if his memory of them was now gone. Slowly, he walked back to the trail, and from there to camp, deep in thought.

※ ∞ ※

"Rafael James, where the *hell* have you been?!"

"I got lost, okay?" Raf answered petulantly, sullen in the face of his father's bright red anger, his mother's white pinched worry. "I couldn't find my way back at night, so I slept under a tree. Then I wandered around all day and finally found the trail and just now got back."

"We spent the whole day looking for you. We missed the helicopter ride," his father said, still furious. His mother drew her robe tighter around herself. "They said they saw a pack of wolves."

Raf felt a twinge of disappointment. "Are they going again tomorrow?"

"Maybe," his father said, "but we're not. This was our last day."

"Can't we stay?"

"No. You worried the hell out of your mother and me, wandering off like that, and I'll be damned if we're going out of our way to accommodate your stupidity. This whole damn trip was for you, anyway."

Raf nodded, not as disappointed as he once might have been. "I'm sorry," he said sincerely. "I just wanted to see the wolves." His mind worked quickly. "I thought if I could get back to the deer carcass, I could track them. I was doing it for a while, then I lost the trail and realized I didn't know where I was."

His mother turned to his father and said, "I told you we should have gone back to that deer."

"The guide said they checked it from the air," his father reminded her, seeming a little mollified. "You really were tracking them?"

Raf nodded. "I think so. I kept finding footprints." Only by being good at something did he feel comfortable with his father. Pretending to have successfully tracked wolves at least gave his father something to respect in him.

"Well." The bright red was fading to a more normal shade in his father's face. "Look, let's get some sleep. We've got a long drive in the morning. And no more excursions, now or for the next two weeks once we get home."

"I'm *grounded*?"

"You're lucky it's only two weeks and not the rest of the summer. Now get to bed."

🐾 ∞ 🐾

The rented car hummed over the highway towards the Twin Cities. Raf sat in the back, lost in thought. With the experience of the previous nights behind him, he was beginning to recall some of his dissatisfaction. He had been a fox. Not a wolf, a noble predator, taking down deer. He had hunted mice and voles, vermin. He had not been really a part of any pack. Morose, he wondered if he would ever have another chance to become a real wolf.

Not in Connecticut, that's for sure, he thought, and then another thought: are there foxes in Connecticut? And even if I were a wolf, how many wolves could I find to roam around with, back home? Even if there aren't foxes, at least I'll be able to maybe slip out every now and then, run across a field, hunt a few mice... he realized with a little shock that he was looking forward to that.

Am I more than I was two days ago—or less? At least then, I could pretend that I was a wolf. Maybe, he thought, just maybe, a fox isn't such a bad thing to be. And what if it is? He watched a patch of aspen in the distance, and thought, it's what I am, like it or not. If I'm not happy with it, I'll just be miserable. I can't change it, at least not now, and it wasn't all bad. To his embarrassment, his mouth watered a bit as he recalled the rich and varied tastes of the little rodents he'd hunted.

They approached Minneapolis, having spoken very little among themselves. Raf contrasted this isolated silence to the shared silence of the fox family, who seemed to be so much more together, even when they were just curled up and not speaking. Or was he imagining that, projecting his dreams onto the peace of the foxes? At least he thought his father wasn't angry any more. Anger rarely lasted long beyond the handing down of a punishment, with him. Tentatively, he piped up as they passed the skyscrapers.

"Do we have time to go to a bookstore?"

His father turned to his mother. "When's the flight?"

"Not for another two hours," she replied, checking her watch.

"Sure," his father called back to him. "We'll stop at that mall place that's right by the airport."

In all the vast expanse of the largest mall in the United States, Raf found, there were only two bookstores. He couldn't help but feel there was something wrong with that. In the Nature section of one of them, he found a book titled *Red Fox*, and flipped through it briefly. The prologue was a brief story that took place at the Minneapolis airport. Raf considered that an omen of some sort, and so took the book up to the counter and bought it.

His father glimpsed the book. "Fox? Kinda overloaded on wolves?"

Raf feigned nonchalance. "Nah. I saw a fox while I was lost, and it was neat." His father nodded, a bit bemused, but thinking that at least they wouldn't have to fly halfway across the country to see a fox. Not that an obsession with foxes would make him happier than his son's obsession with wolves, but at least it might cost him less.

On the airplane, Raf took out the book. He looked at the fox on the cover, so different in color and soundless, scentless. He knew it was probably saying something, but he couldn't tell what. The image was flat, with no expression he could read as he could a picture of a human. He stared out the window of the plane, still feeling somewhat torn. I was so sure I'm a wolf, he thought, but this time, when he tried to envision how he would look as a wolf, he saw the fox on the cover of the book.

I can't help what I am, he told himself again. I might as well enjoy it, and get the most out of it.

Raf opened the book and began to read.

LITTLE MONSTER

Tom Turrittin

"Who's next?" asked Dr. Alan Wills, leaning out of his door as Judith checked his appointments.

"Mrs. Green called and canceled Mary's checkup, so I filled it with someone from the Child Welfare Agency who phoned at the last minute. But they haven't—" The receptionist stopped as the front door opened. An unfamiliar woman in her thirties stood in the hall, huffing and puffing, clutching a battered brown folder under one arm and ushering in a nine-year-old boy with the other. "They're just coming in now," Judith corrected, smiling, motioning them to go through to the waiting room.

The woman returned the nod, stopping to catch her breath. The boy held her hand impatiently, looking at the open waiting room door. Suddenly he lunged forward with an expression of determination and curiosity. The unexpectedly strong yank on her arm, like a dog on a leash, pulled the woman rapidly past the front desk.

Dr. Wills stepped back from the door as they entered, not used to seeing an enthusiastic child in his office. He was a dentist that specialized in children who hated dentists. New patients were typically angry, crying, or desperately trying to leave while their parents physically dragged them in. Over the course of three or four visits, he usually managed to change the attitude of even the most difficult child into something positive, or at least workable. Such had been his recent success that a month ago the local newspaper had done a column on him in their 'Careers' section. Since then, he had been inundated by over-protective mothers whose claims to having "problem children" amounted to having kids who ate chocolate bars or were afraid of needles. It had gotten to the point that he could only take new patients by referral. And once again, it looked like the city was still trying to dump dysfunctional orphans on him as if he was a baby-sitter.

"I'm sorry, I don't take new patients—", he began, pausing when she shoved the brown folder at him. Her face was tired and haggard, an expression he had seen on many social workers, while the boy seemed attentive and bright, looking around with a strange fascination, letting go of the woman's hand to explore the waiting room. The dentist glanced at the folder. "Oh, I see, you were referred by Dr. Lyne?" He saw the woman was too out of breath to reply. "Are you all right?"

"Yes... insisted we... run up the stairs..." After a moment she could speak again. "I brought him to see Dr. Lyne yesterday but... John, put that back." John had picked up one of the small potted plants and was smelling it. "...But Dr. Lyne recently had a nervous breakdown and told the Agency that John should come see you." The boy had come back, and was looking up at the dentist with odd, eager blue eyes. She immediately took advantage of the pause, angling towards the door before he could ask anything else. "I'm going to go outside to have a smoke, okay?" The door closed behind her, leaving the dentist and the boy staring at each other.

Alan turned his attention to the file. "Well, John, why don't you go in there to the examination room and take a seat, and I'll be with you in a moment. I'm Dr. Alan Wills, you can call me Dr. Wills or Alan or whatever you'd like. Just let me go over your file so I'll know what work Dr. Lyne has done, and..." he paused, looking at the folder.

Lyne's notes were strange. Not only were they almost completely illegible—vastly different from the neat handwriting in Lyne's other referrals—but it looked as if Lyne, who had seen John a total of five times, had never actually done any dental work, aside from superficial cleaning. Here and there were strange, jagged diagrams in ballpoint pen squeezed into the margins. At the bottom of the last page Lyne had messily scrawled the only phrase he could make out, LITTLE MONSTER, underlined several times for emphasis and then scribbled over frantically.

Alan checked back further. According to the file, John had only been with Lyne for six months. Before that were papers from another dentist named Underwood, who had been John's dentist for several years. Underwood's notes were typical—until six months before the switch to Lyne. Once again the dental work stopped, the number of visits were unusually frequent, and the handwriting became more and more illegible, with similar jagged scribbles dotting the pages. The last page looked as if it had once been half-crumpled and smeared with old, dried bloodstains. He closed the file and poked his head into the reception area. "Judith, have you heard of a Dr. Underwood?"

Judith didn't look up from her typing. "Wasn't he that guy in the suburbs who had two of his fingers bitten off last year?"

Alan glanced at the boy, who had wandered into the examination room, and was poking his head into the waste basket. "John—" the dentist started to say. The boy looked up guiltily, and without being prompted, trotted over to the chair and sat down. Alan shook his head. This was a problem child? "You know," Alan said, entering and closing the door, "I've never met anyone who looks forward to their dental appointment."

"I *like* dentists!" John replied, but Alan knew that most child patients were always a bit nervous. It was mostly a question of how well they could hide it. "Are you a fun dentist?" John asked.

"Well now, that depends what you consider fun," Alan said, picking up his mirror implement. "But if your record is anything to go by, then your teeth are in excellent shape. You'll be out of here in no time."

"Awwww…" the boy frowned, crossing his arms. "That's what Dr. Lyne said when I started to see him, before he got all shaky."

"Shaky?"

"Yeah, like Dr. Underwood. I quit him. He got no fun at all. He was really really mean at the end, too. So I quit him and they took me to Dr. Lyne. He was a lot more nice, but he got scared too easily. I was just trying to have fun… then he'd get all kooky every time I went. Now he's all kooky. I miss going there. He was nice. He gave me sandwiches." As Alan listened to John's bizarre monologue, he watched the boy's face change from anger to disappointment to hope. "You're not going to go all mean or shaky, are you?"

"You'll have to be the judge of that," Alan answered. "I know dentists can be no fun sometimes, but a little discomfort while sitting in a chair for a few minutes is a pretty good deal, when you get to avoid a lot of mouth pain later in life."

"It's not that; I like dentists," John sighed, sinking down in the chair. "It's just… dentists don't like me anymore."

"I like all my patients, and I'm glad to have you aboard," Alan smiled. If John was always this well-behaved, the examination would be a breeze. "Hush now, let's start your checkup. Let me know if you get uncomfortable, okay? Open wide…"

At first John seemed nervous, as if he hadn't been taking care of his teeth, but as the examination proceeded, the dentist discovered that John had the most healthy teeth he had ever seen. Dr. Wills couldn't see anything that needed cleaning. There was no plaque, no tartar, and it looked like John's last fluoride treatment was recent. Even his orthodonture was good. All of his adult teeth had grown in, early for a child his age, and not a single one was misaligned or out of place. In fact, Alan realized with a shock, John's mouth was perfect. Thinking about this, he picked up Lyne's notes again. "…John, your last dental appointment was *two weeks* ago."

"Yeah."

"You're in great shape. I don't think there's anything I need to do, except make a new appointment for you in six months."

"But…" John frowned. "It doesn't feel right."

"What doesn't feel right?"

"My *tooth*."

"Which tooth?" Alan asked. John hadn't shown any signs of pain during the checkup. "Show me where."

"It's…" John started raising his hand to point, but then stopped and looked frustrated. "It's inside, but the tooth's not there." He was searching for words.

"Your wisdom teeth? I'd be surprised if they were giving you trouble, at your age. Here, let me see."

John shrank back from his fingers, closing his mouth. "Um… could you turn off the lights first?" He was looking around the room in detail now, taking it in like he had done to the waiting room earlier.

Alan nodded, "Sure." Obviously he had stumbled onto whatever it was that made John not get along with dentists. Alan had learned that to get an uncomfortable patient to cooperate, he would first have to agree to their rules, their game. Only afterwards, as the game progressed, would the patient agree to a compromise. He turned off the lights.

"Could you close the blinds too?" The room was now dim, lit only by the round lamp over the chair. "Make that a little darker?" Alan did so, bathing the chair in a small circle of light. "Sometimes I can do this when it's bright, but I have to concentrate a lot, and it's hard to keep it," the boy explained. "Okay. This is a lot better, I can show you."

At first Alan thought the room was getting darker. A shadow seemed to pass over the boy, and his features were less distinct. With sudden horror, Alan realized that John's face appeared to be darker because it was growing fur. The boy's eyes pinched shut as he opened his mouth to reveal sharp canines, his face pushing forward into a dog-like muzzle. Alan could not believe what he saw, but neither could he tear his gaze away from the unnatural metamorphosis.

John's eyes re-opened, gold instead of blue, bestial instead of human. Startled by what was seeming less and less like a hallucination, Alan moved back, away from the chair, and could tell that the rest of the boy's body had also changed, even under his now awkward-fitting clothes. Shoes tumbled to the floor as something paw-like writhed inside John's socks. John's hands were like paws too, claws penetrating the chair's upholstery while the boy struggled on his back, a tail snaking out uncomfortably from one of the legs of his shorts. Finally, the transformation complete, a wolf-like creature sat up before him, opening and closing its mouth experimentally, obviously not happy about something. The wolf-boy's gaze focused on the dentist, and uttered a loud growl from his throat.

Alan jumped, bumping unexpectedly against the cold wall behind him. John, if it was John, silently got up from the chair and began to walk closer with a threatening posture. In the darkness, all Alan could see was the boy's animal-shaped silhouette approaching ever nearer, golden eyes gleaming, lit only from behind by the lone, dim light above the chair.

"N-nice wolf…" Alan stammered, inching his way along the wall towards the door, trying not to make any sudden moves. John's growling became louder, and he had gotten close enough that Alan could make out a dog-like smell in the air. "G—good wolf…" The dentist had managed to reach the corner of the room. The door was not far away, along the other wall. Alan raised his arm sideways, not breaking eye contact with the creature, while he fumbled blindly for the doorknob. It was out still of reach. Soundproofing the examination room had been, in retrospect, a bad idea.

For a moment they stared at one another. Alan had a sudden sinking feeling, remembering he had read once that dogs interpreted prolonged eye contact as a sign of aggression. Everything seemed frozen—then everything happened at once. John and Alan leapt simultaneously, one for the dentist's leg, and the other for the door; and both were almost successful. Alan, panicking, tripped over himself. Canine jaws, aiming for his flesh, instead bit into his white smock, pulling, ripping and shredding it wildly.

Fallen, Alan rolled over, kicking desperately, but his feet met with air. The beast had let go of him, and was writhing in pain on the floor, holding his paws to his muzzle and emitting high-pitched whines. Seizing the opportunity, the dentist threw open the door and stumbled into the brightness of the waiting room. "JUDITH!!"

The reception room door opened. For a moment Alan's pride got the better of him, and he felt his face flushing. How could he explain what had happened without sounding insane? Judith looked at her speechless employer and misinterpreted his expression. "Hard case? It's all right, I'll make sure you're not disturbed." She set the lock on the door handle, waved, and closed it behind her. Alan felt his heart sink to his stomach. It wasn't that he couldn't unlock the door from this side; it was that he didn't think he would have time to reach it.

Alan looked back nervously. To his surprise, John was John again, sitting on the floor, looking confused. It was as if nothing had happened. Alan shakily turned back into the room, brushing himself off. He was hoping it was all a dream, a delusion of some sort, but his torn coat spoke otherwise. Something very strange and very frightening was going on. He faced the boy. "*What* was *that?!*"

John stood up, straightening out his clothes. "Whydja open the door? Wolf was just starting to have fun."

"You... attacked me!"

John frowned. "Wolf doesn't attack people, he wants to play! I thought you were going to be a fun dentist."

"John—" Alan began, then stopped, passing his hand over his face and letting out a long, shuddering breath. Stay calm, he told himself. He needed to find out what the hell was going on. Only John could tell him that, and seemed to be acting as if everything was normal. Alan wouldn't get anywhere by being hysterical. He reminded himself that it was his job to *care* for his patient's problems. *Your patient is a werewolf!* screamed part of his mind, but his professional side had regained control. The boy seemed to consider "Wolf" as a separate persona, and hadn't yet learned to either rationalize or control his actions. *Accept and play the patient's game*, he told himself. "All right. Let's... start over. I'm sorry. I didn't know that y—Wolf was trying to play."

"That's okay!" John beamed, hopping back onto the examination chair, ignoring the holes in it.

Alan stood next to him with his mirror, determined not to be fazed by the previous experience. The problem was that he wasn't sure what to do next. *Just pretend he's normal.* "Ready?"

"...Can you turn the lights down again? I... I want to be Wolf." John said.

He's not afraid of dentists, Alan realized, *dentists are afraid of him.* He wondered if anyone else knew about Wolf. Obviously the social worker and the orphanage didn't. "I'll turn down the lights, but... no attacking games, okay?" John looked at him blankly. "Okay?" Alan repeated, trying to hide the squeak in his voice.

"Why don't you want to play with Wolf? He only wants to have fun..." the boy sniffed. "None of my dentists ever want to play with Wolf. I used to turn off the lights, and then they wouldn't come into the room, or they'd try to turn the lights on again. Wolf *never* gets to play..."

Accept. "I *do* want to play with Wolf. But there's a lot of dangerous equipment in here and if Wolf knocks something over..." Alan held the torn part of his coat behind his back. "...He could get hurt. Okay?"

"Okay," John answered, no longer sniffing but not looking entirely happy either.

"Okay." Alan went over to the door and carefully closed it, returning the room to its former darkness. The dimmed lamp still shone above the chair—*like the moon.* He understood now, or at least had a plausible working theory. The boy could only bring on the change with the right amount of light. Maybe living in the city, where lights were on all the time, limited his opportunities.

John closed his eyes, concentrating, and Alan watched the transformation again, this time with less shock and more curiosity. The boy's head became almost completely lupine, the fur black or dark brown. The boy's body was still bipedal, but in an animal way, like when a bear or a squirrel stood, with hunched shoulders. His hands had become large, full paws. Alan looked away from them to see that John had already opened his eyes and was peering at him. Alan could perceive the strong presence of the wolf in their golden sheen, still tinted by the boy's intelligence, but exactly where human ended and animal began, he could no longer tell.

"Hello... Wolf," Alan said cautiously, smiling as much as he could. John's tail thumped against the chair as he tried to wag. "Let's get started with your checkup. Open—" The werewolf's muzzle yawned before him with huge, white, sharp canine teeth. "—not that wide."

"Rrf." The wolf's jaw closed by half, the ends of the black mouth seeming to grin.

"Ready?"

"Rrf." Something didn't feel right. Alan thought the werewolf's eyes were following his hand a little too closely—there was some new game going on. Slowly, carefully, he brought his mirror tool down to the wolf's mouth.

SNAP! Alan pulled it away just in time before the jaws clamped violently shut. "No biting, okay Wolf? No biting. Open…"

John's maw opened once more, wider this time, and the wolf's watchful expression showed every intention of trying to bite again. His eyes were gleeful. As Alan paused, trying to think, John emitted a deep and impatient guttural growl. A basic dental examination had become dangerous. Alan feigned with his hand, the wolf mock-biting the air as the dentist tried to negotiate entry at different angles. *Accept*, he continued to tell himself, but this was ridiculous. Was this how Underwood had lost his fingers?

He put down the mirror. "You really want to bite something, don't you."

The lupine face nodded enthusiastically.

"Me?" More enthusiastic nods. *Offer the patient a compromise.* "What if I give you something else to bite instead, will you promise not to bite me?"

A pause, then a single nod. The boy was still in there, all right. "Okay. Stay there, I'll be right back." The werewolf's face showed a deadly, feral grin at the prospect of whatever game the dentist was playing, and he started to sit up. "No, you *stay*. Stay." He took a rubber glove and some cotton swabs from a drawer, keeping his eyes on his patient the whole time, and squeezed out through the door.

Judith looked up from her desk as Alan walked determinedly past and out into the hallway. A moment later he returned, a glove of blood-soaked cotton in his hand, the side of his coat hideously torn. Judith stared at him.

"I went to Doctor Mullen's office down the hall," he said, something weary in his face.

Judith turned back to her work. *I don't want to know.* "Okay. Tell me when you're done, he's the last appointment today."

Alan willingly re-locked the waiting room door and entered the examination room. In the chair, John stared up at him with big, suspiciously innocent eyes. Alan looked to one side. The waste basket had been knocked over, and the contents scattered about. A small trail of garbage pointed towards the culprit. "Ahem." He picked a piece of dental floss off of the bridge of John's nose. "Here, I brought you something to bite on."

John's ears went from flat to up, and he wolfed the bloody cotton balls into his mouth, chewing rapidly. It was evidently a taste he could savor. Suddenly his head jerked, yowling in anguish and pain. His eyes flashed angrily. Whatever had happened the first time was happening again. This was not play—this was rage. Wolf glared at Dr. Wills with every intention of hurting him.

Alan moved back, barely fast enough before Wolf slid off the chair and tried to bite him. He could feel the moist breath from the werewolf's nose against his knuckles, the sharp fangs missing his hand by less than an inch. The force of the bite caused another howl of pain from the creature, who clutched his muzzle, letting out an intense growl of fury.

Dr. Wills had come to the conclusion that he was probably going to die. He felt pale, feverish, and utterly paralyzed, unable to think of a way to either escape or defend himself. The snarling werewolf took another step towards him... and then suddenly stopped. Moaning, he sat down on the cold linoleum floor and nursed his jaw, whining pitifully.

It took a minute for Alan to come to his senses again. It was Wolf, not John, who needed to see a dentist. *Maybe John likes dentists and Wolf hates them,* Alan thought. A werewolf with tooth problems might hate dentists and want to bite them, but couldn't without experiencing pain, which would make him hate dentists again, and so on. That explained the werewolf's current look of utter and miserable defeat. But Wolf hadn't gotten angry the second time he'd transformed, until he had been given the cotton balls to chew on. Maybe Wolf didn't hate dentists, but had instead reacted instinctively against someone who had caused him pain.

"W—Wolf? Can you understand me?" Dr. Wills stammered. The werewolf stared back at him silently, listening, but gave no indication of sentience. "I'm... I'm sorry. I didn't mean to hurt you. I was only trying to play." Wolf looked away, staring down at the floor, sullen. "Is it—do you have a sore tooth? Is that why you came?" John's formerly vague words were now starting to make a lot more sense. "Would you let me take a look?"

The werewolf's eyes opened wide and he shrank back, ears going flat, agitated.

"Shh, shh..." Alan said, moving carefully, slowly, getting closer. "Wolf... I want you to trust me. I'm not going to hurt you. It was an accident before, I'm sorry. I know better now. I want to help you. Please trust me... I trust you, too. I know you could easily hurt me back if you wanted to." The werewolf had stopped trying to move away, and was looking at him. "Will you let me try to help you?"

A long pause, and then a simple nod, meant that the werewolf had agreed. Silently, he got back into the examination chair, and opened his mouth. Wolf whined slightly when Alan first approached, but remained cooperative and immobile.

Carefully, the dentist picked out leftover pieces of cotton swab. "Okay. We're going to figure out where the problem is together. I saw you holding the right side of your jaw earlier. Which part is it, the upper or lower part?" A whine. "Lower. Okay. Don't worry. I'm going to start touching your teeth very very lightly, starting from the left, one at a time, going across. I'm not going to touch the tooth that hurts, because I want you to let me know when I reach the tooth right *before* the one that hurts."

He didn't have to go far. The werewolf let out a distressed yip as he neared the third premolar. "All right. I'm not going to touch it yet, but don't close your mouth. Does it hurt a lot when you bite on it?" A whine. "What about when you push it forward with your tongue?" Wolf tried. Nothing. "Does it hurt all the time?" A light whine. "Does it ache a little?" John nodded. "Okay. Let me look at the rest of your mouth to compare."

As Dr. Wills examined Wolf's mouth, he felt far less confident about explaining the problem. In wolf form, John's teeth were as improbably perfect as his human form's teeth. Did the transformation process give him the power to heal? John's dental record seemed to confirm this, since neither Underwood nor Lyne had needed to do much work. Yet the boy had continued to visit his dentists. It was obvious he was in some pain, but from what? Wouldn't the transformation cure tooth decay? To make matters worse, unlike a human mouth, John's teeth were not only shaped completely differently, but he had an extra incisor and two extra premolars; as well as a third molar that was only on his lower jaw. *I wish I was a veterinarian*, the dentist thought.

Returning his attention to the problem tooth, Alan spied something wedged in at the base. Using a pair of tweezers, he extracted something which looked suspiciously like a tuft of cat hair. It had certainly not been there before the transformation, and couldn't have come from the waste basket. Could John's transformation take things with it? "John, is the ache still there?" The wolf nodded, his golden eyes sad. "You can relax your mouth for a little while, I have to check something."

Dr. Wills sat at his desk in the corner, going over his thoughts. He leafed slowly through John's records, in reverse this time, back through Lyne, back through Underwood. Their mutually frantic handwriting pointed to when they must have first encountered Wolf. Underwood's earliest notes were smooth, indicating that John had only been a werewolf for the past year.

And then he saw it.

Two years ago, Underwood had given John a filling. A *silver* filling.

He snapped the file closed and stood up. "I think I got it. Open again, please." He leaned down, no longer afraid, peering closely into the wolf's muzzle. Sure enough, inside the premolar, was a dark discoloration. "I'm going to turn the light back up, okay? Slowly." As he did so, John winced, trying to stay in wolf form, but he could not stop himself from becoming gradually more human. Even with the lamp at its brightest, the room was still dim. Alan wondered if some of the wolf remained, a sharpness to the canines, a slight pointedness to the ears.

"Did you find out what's wrong with my tooth?" John asked.

"You've got a silver filling. My guess is you're allergic to it and it's got to come out. Once it's taken out, you should be completely okay after the next time you change, but to get it out I'm going to have to drill. I won't lie to you. It will probably hurt."

"Oh." John shivered. "Wolf won't like that."

"I don't think there's any other way, but the good news is that afterwards, you'll heal and should almost never have to visit the dentist again. Almost." He held up the tuft. "Have you been chasing cats?"

"Um… a little—I mean Wolf has. There's a park behind the orphanage that has lots of trees. Wolf can run around there if the moon's not out and there aren't any car headlights and there's no one around." John looked away uncomfortably. Alan decided it was probably prudent not to ask him how it had happened in the first place. In any case, if one of the few places John could change was at the dentist's, it explained his initial enthusiasm when he arrived. "Are you sure there's no other way to take out the filling?" John asked. "Couldn't you look again? Please?"

"Sure, but I don't think there's any alternative. Maybe I can talk about it with Wolf," he smiled at John. *If Wolf doesn't bite my hand off while trying*, part of his mind said. He'd have to improvise this one. John was pretending that Wolf wasn't him, but it looked like John was still John after the transformation, only with more instincts. "Ready?"

He turned the lamp down very slowly this time, and with fascination observed the transformation going at a much slower pace. It was uncanny the way the jaw stretched, sprouting fur, the nose and lips turning to black. John's teeth spread apart, allowing the extra lupine ones to emerge. He watched as the original human teeth grew or changed shape before his eyes. At one point as the premolar shifted its form, he could see the filling become exposed and then hidden again, until it was absorbed into the tooth itself.

"Hello again, Wolf." The tail didn't wag this time. "I suspect you know the bad news. I wanted to ask you if I could—" Alan paused, unsure how to rationalize dental surgery to a theoretically sentient wild half-human creature. Suddenly, he had an idea. He *had* managed to see the whole filling at one point during the transformation… "Wolf, there may be another way. I'm going to turn up the light again."

"Rrrr?"

"I'm going to see if I can take out the filling while you change, without hurting you. Just relax, if anything starts to hurt, let me know and I'll stop. Here we go."

The werewolf looked unsure, but did not complain as Alan slowly, ever so slowly, brightened the lamp, hoping it was an increase in light which would trigger the change back to normal. Sure enough, the fur and claws began to retract, tail vanishing. The teeth shifted, and the premolar re-opened. Carefully turning the light's dial, Alan let go a deep breath he hadn't realized he was holding in. He could see the whole filling. It wasn't going to get any better.

John gazed up with blue eyes rimmed with gold, dazed, breathing but not moving. Something in his body was making him stay still. Probably a biological precaution to prevent him from hurting his joints in mid-shift, Alan guessed, but there was no way to tell. He had to act fast.

He grabbed a tool with a soft point and tipped it with denture gum.

Carefully, gingerly, he touched it to the filling, first pressing then lifting. An uncomfortable, eerie gargle came from John's throat, neither animal nor human in nature. The filling was loose, but refused to rise any further.

Alan looked at his fingers, his patient, and the filling. From his tools, he took the one with the smallest, thinnest hook at the end. Lifting the filling as much as he dared with the denture gum, he wedged in the hook underneath, to act as a lever. With a swift, decisive motion, he popped out the filling, which fell to the floor several feet away. John screamed unnaturally, and Alan quickly removed his hands from John's muzzle, and fumbled for the lamp's brightness control. In a panic, he turned it down instead of up.

The young werewolf buckled on the chair. A loud, painful howl reverberated around the walls and shook the entire chamber, and then he collapsed. Alan swallowed and stepped back, his heart pounding in his ringing ears. "Wolf? John?" The boy was not moving. Feeling faint, the dentist approached the chair, reaching out with his hand, convinced he had killed his patient.

The beast's eyes snapped open and trapped him in their golden gaze.

Wolf leapt off the chair straight at him. Alan screamed as he threw up his arms, the animal's momentum knocking him to the floor. All he could see were the sharp, gleaming white teeth.

And a sloppy, wet tongue licking crazily at his face. Alan stopped screaming. "What the... ack! Stop that! Down boy, down!" Wolf moved off and bounced up and down on the floor, crazy with joy. Alan stood up, and realized it must have been a success, with the transformation healing the injury now that the silver was gone. "You're okay!" Alan couldn't stop smiling.

Wolf bounced some more and ran around the chair several times in celebration, then skidded to a halt. Sniffing the air curiously, he went over to Alan's briefcase and poked his face into it. A moment later his ears pricked up as he dragged out a paper bag, which he quickly shredded, discovering the grilled chicken wrapped in foil that was left over from Alan's lunch. Alan figured that if Lyne had given the boy sandwiches, the chicken would be a good compensation for the physical hassle the boy had been through today.

As the werewolf tore through the tinfoil, Dr. Wills thought about what had happened. John's wolf personality probably hated Underwood for the silver filling, and Lyne hadn't fared much better. The werewolf didn't react well to pain, which meant it was probably just a matter of time before he or some other dentist would have to deal with this potentially deadly patient again. Everything would be all right as long as Wolf wasn't in pain. And, like all good dentists, Alan knew that having healthy teeth (and uninjured dentists) was a question of *prevention*. "Hsst! John! Don't eat that yet."

"Rrrr?" the werewolf growled quizzically, the wrapped leftovers falling to the floor with a thud.

"This is tinfoil," Alan explained, picking it up. "Do you know what tinfoil is?" The werewolf nodded. "Is tinfoil food?" No response. "No, you know it's not food. I know you like biting things. But if you aren't careful, you'll bite something bad for you and you'll get in a lot of pain again. So when you bite, you make sure it's something good for you, okay?" Wolf nodded sheepishly. "Here." He unwrapped the foil and threw the meat to him. "Don't eat the bones, you might choke on them." Wolf grunted in acknowledgement.

Alan rummaged through his desk drawers. Finding the cat hair meant that there was going to be work to do. He was going to have to teach John, as Wolf, about dental hygiene. Finally he found what he wanted, a stiff toothbrush with wide bristles and a long handle. He waited until the werewolf had finished the chicken before showing it to him.

"This," Alan proffered, "Is yours, Wolf. Your very own special toothbrush from Dr. Alan Wills. Try it out." Wolf took it between his teeth like a stick. "Not like that… like how John brushes his teeth. Hold it between your paws." The boy did, pressing it between the pads on his palms, peering at the dentist skeptically. "You've got little bits of chicken between your teeth," he explained. "Like the cat hair I found earlier. If you're going to eat while you're changed, you have to clean your teeth before you change back. Otherwise little bits of stuff will stay in there and your teeth will hurt."

Grudgingly, Wolf tilted his muzzle side to side and ran his fangs awkwardly over the bristles. *Close, but maybe that's as good as it gets without having opposable thumbs*, thought the dentist. "Good work! If you can, take that toothbrush with you when you're going out to change."

The werewolf snorted. *Yeah, right.*

Alan hrmmed. It was a difficult request to make to a werewolf. He rummaged around in another drawer and brought out a length of string, which he looped into a collar for the toothbrush's handle, and draped it around Wolf's neck. "How about this? You can tuck it under your shirt."

Wolf glared up at him, then down at the collar. He got down on all fours like a real wolf, and shook his shoulders and neck rapidly as if he was drying himself off. The loop slipped off and the toothbrush clattered to the floor.

"All right, forget the toothbrush." Alan frowned. "How about this. Break off the end from one of those chicken bones, but don't swallow it." Wolf trotted over to the pile of bones on the floor, sitting down with his legs tucked under him. Taking one of the longer bones between his forepaws, he snapped off the end with a crack, leaving a sharp point. "Now, pick your teeth with that." This time, the werewolf was much more successful.

"So," Alan concluded, "Like I was saying, if you're going eat when you're Wolf, before you change back, use your claws or find a stick—don't use glass or wire or stuff like that—and pick out anything left between your teeth. And remember to floss, before you change, when you're John. That's all it takes, and I guarantee you'll have healthy teeth for the rest of your life!"

The werewolf didn't seem to share his enthusiasm. Dr. Wills was mildly disappointed but hardly surprised. At least half of his human patients had the same attitude. "I'm going to turn the lights back on, okay?" Wolf snorted again. "Don't be so mopey, you're much better now than when you arrived. I'm glad I made a new friend, but we've gone over your appointment time." The werewolf walked over to him and softly butted him with his forehead as if to apologize, as Alan turned on the lights.

In a moment John was standing before him. "That was great, thanks!" he said. "Wolf likes you too. There's no pain at all anymore! Can I come back here real soon?"

"Like when?"

"In a month?" John asked hopefully.

"You've got the most healthy teeth I've ever seen," Alan argued. "Your next appointment shouldn't be for another six months at least." John went glum. Alan sighed. "All right. Three months, okay?" The nights *were* starting to get longer, he justified to himself, and the werewolf would probably be going out more.

"Okay!" John grinned.

Alan led him back out to reception after he'd put on his shoes. "I'll see you later, John, and don't forget to take good care of those fangs!" He turned to his secretary. "Judith, could you make a follow-up appointment for John in three months, and then bring him back to his social worker outside? Don't worry about closing up, I'll do that today."

"Of course, Dr. Wills. Come on, John, let's go find your guardian."

John waved as he went out the door. "Bye Dr. Wills! Thanks a lot!" A moment later the dentist could hear them running down the stairs.

Dr. Alan Wills sat down at his desk, and added new sheets to John's file. Signing and dating the top, he wrote SIMPLE EXAMINATION, FILLING EXTRACTED, and stopped. Anything he wrote about John's condition would probably sound crazy. He ended up writing EXTREME ALLERGY TO SILVER before getting stuck again.

He stared out the window for a long while, and then took out his personal notebook. "Call vet on dog dental hygiene," he wrote, then "Call zoo/guard dog trainers regarding toys." After another minute of thought he added, "Research occult." He sighed, resting his head in his arms on the table. Lyne's notes lay off to one side. LITTLE MONSTER.

Returning to John's file, Dr. Wills tried to remember the number, position, and shape of John's werewolf teeth. He worked on drawing a picture, until he realized he couldn't remember the details clearly enough. For the first time he noticed how badly his hands were shaking, leaving yet another jagged, incomprehensible diagram in John's notes.

He sighed, opened his filing cabinet, drew out his hidden bottle of scotch, and poured himself a drink.

AFTERWORD AND BIBLIOGRAPHY

BY FRED PATTEN

The first science fiction "fandom" event that I attended was the 1958 World Science Fiction Convention in Los Angeles. I put "fandom" in quotes because the attendance (barely over 300) included an approximately equal mixture of readers, writers, magazine cover artists, editors and publishers; so it was as much a professional trade conference as a gathering of fans. At that time the whole genre was so small that everyone, fans and professionals, accepted that the term "science fiction" encompassed equally stories of futuristic technological and interstellar fantasy, surrealistic literary fantasy, heroic adventure fantasy (Tolkien's *The Lord of the Rings* had just been published, and Fritz Leiber would coin the term "sword and sorcery" the next year), and weird-horror fantasy.

In the almost fifty years since then, there have been increasing arguments, some quite bitter, over whether "science fiction" should rightfully include all these forms of what some call "imaginative literature." Today there are a World Science Fiction Convention, a World Fantasy Convention and a World Horror Convention, with proponents of each who insist that their genre is distinctly different from the others.

So, is there a Furry literary genre, or is this just an affectation of Furry chauvinists? If Furry literature is not a separate genre, in what other genre should it be placed, if any? There are clearly Furry interstellar adventure stories, Furry fantasy stories, and Furry horror stories—not to mention human interest stories as mundane as in any radio/TV soap opera except that the characters happen to be anthropomorphized animals (e.g., Matt J. McCullar's *Fornax* series about the misadventures of five adolescent honey badger sisters trying to establish themselves as a singing group in the sleazy commercial pop music industry). There are even trivialists who would rigidly define and then subdivide the Furry genre. "What is the difference between a werecreature and a Furry (anthropomorphic animal)?", asks *Fang, Claw & Steel* magazine. Answer: If it can transform back and forth between human and animal form it is a werecreature, not a Furry (which is either a nonchangeable anthropomorphized animal like Bugs Bunny, or an animal intelligent enough to deal with humans as equals like Napoleon in *Animal Farm*). Or rather this is one opinion; others may debate it.

If there is a Furry literature, when did it start? Talking animals have been used to make moral points since the days of Aesop's fables 2,600 years ago. The romance of Baron Reynard the Fox in King Lion's court was a popular European satirical parable of the arrogance of the nobility 800 years ago. Talking animals arguably became respectable characters, and distinct individuals, in modern literature when Lewis Carroll created the White Rabbit, the March Hare, the Cheshire Cat, the griffin and the mock turtle, and others in *Alice's Adventures in Wonderland* in 1865. Talking animals in children's literature are a given, but there is little or nothing juvenile in such 20th century novels as Richard Adams' *Watership Down* or William Kotzwinkle's *Doctor Rat* or Kenneth Cook's *Play Little Victims*. We praise the allegorical imagination of George Orwell's 1945 *Animal Farm*, and try to forget about Robert van Genechten's 1937 Dutch *Van den vos Reynaerde, Ruwaard Boudewijn en Jodocus*, a modernization of the Reynard parable in which sinister rhinoceros merchants (whose descriptions draw a blatant parallel between rhinos' horns and Nazi caricatures of Jews' hooked noses) try to corrupt the Animal Kingdom by encouraging interspecies mongrelization (an attack upon Racial Purity) so they can take it over, only to be unmasked by clever Reynard leading the heroic National Socialist animals.

There have always been occasional Furry stories within the s-f genre, dating (for those who stretch the genre far enough back to include Jules Verne and H. G. Wells) to Wells' 1896 *The Island of Dr. Moreau*. Pulp magazine stories of the 1920s and 1930s had lots of Mad Scientists who surgically transferred heads or at least brains between humans and animals (one of the best from a literary standpoint is H. L. Gold's "A Matter of Form", *Astounding Science-Fiction*, December 1938). By the 1940s such authors as Olaf Stapledon and later Cordwainer Smith (Dr. Paul Myron Anthony Linebarger) were more thoughtfully exploring the question: if scientific advances could increase animals' intelligence to the level of humans, how would this affect society? (Required reading: Robert A. Heinlein's "Jerry Is A Man", *Thrilling Wonder Stories*, October 1947; reprinted in numerous s-f anthologies.) During the last sixty years there have been many popular s-f series set upon interstellar worlds inhabited by distinctly Furry aliens (e.g., Poul Anderson's & Gordon Dickson's teddybearlike Hokas; H. Beam Piper's adorably cute Fuzzies; and, okay, George Lucas' Wookies and Ewoks, too); and fantasy novels featuring animals who are as intelligent as humans but are hiding it (Diane Duane's *Cats of Grand Central Station* series) or are living in a separate dimension where civilization includes humans as just one species among many funny animals (Alan Dean Foster's *Spellsinger* novels). There are probably at least a dozen stories per year that qualify as Furry within the s-f and fantasy monthly and quarterly magazines, and the original fiction s-f anthologies. Recently Michael Swanwick's "The Dog Said Bow-Wow" in *Asimov's SF*, November-December 2001, won the 2002 World Science Fiction Convention's Hugo Award in the Best Short Story category.

Exactly when Furry fandom began is a matter for debate, but everyone agrees that one of the most important influences was the bimonthly cartoon fanzine *Vootie*, started in April 1976 in Minneapolis by "The Funny Animal Liberation Front" (Reed Waller and Ken Fletcher). *Vootie* was modeled upon the Underground Comix and college humor magazines of the 1960s and '70s. The Funny Animal Liberation Front only accepted cartoonists as members, and *Vootie*'s contents were not limited to funny animal cartoons although they did include several comic-book stories featuring funny animals in adult situations (Reed Waller's *"Omaha", the Cat Dancer*; Steve Willis' *Morty the Dog*). *Vootie* disintegrated when its editors lost interest in it after issue #37, February 1983. But one of *Vootie*'s last members, Marc Schirmeister, determined to create a new club to replace it. The crucial difference was that his *Rowrbrazzle* (quarterly, with #1 in February 1984) emphasized an interest in talking animals specifically, ranging from funny animals in comic books and animation to literary stories, rather than just raunchy cartoon art. *Rowrbrazzle* was open to writers as well as cartoonists, as long as their stories, essays and art featured animal characters—or were devoted to the social activities of the nascent Furry fandom.

The fandom began when groups of attendees at science fiction conventions and comic book conventions got together to talk about stories with animal characters. This started at the 1980 World Science Fiction Convention in Boston, where Steve Gallacci of Seattle exhibited a painting in the Art Show of an anthropomorphized cat pilot standing next to a highly detailed spacecraft. The combination of a cartoony animal pilot and a high-tech vehicle attracted considerable attention. Gallacci told curious fans that the painting was an illustration for a s-f series he was writing set in a civilization of bioengineered intelligent animal characters. As the fans chatted, many realized that their own favorite s-f stories, comic books, and movies featured talking animals or animallike aliens. Between 1980 and 1985, a slowly growing informal group coalesced at the annual World Science Fiction Conventions, the Comic-Cons in San Diego, and some other s-f and comic book conventions to discuss the new additions to Gallacci's story (which he finally began to self-publish in comic book form in 1984 as *Albedo: Anthropomorphics*), and other new releases of books, movies and comic books with animal characters (e.g., the 1982 Don Bluth animated feature *The Secret of NIMH*).

In July 1985 at the West Coast Science Fantasy Conference (Westercon 38) in Sacramento, California, two Southern California fans, Mark Merlino and Rod O'Riley, decided to formalize the gatherings and start active recruiting by hosting an open party and posting flyers around the convention. Their Furry Parties quickly gave their name to the new fandom. At the Furry Party at the May 1987 BayCon '87 in San Jose, Kyim Granger (Karl Maurer) passed around a sign-up sheet to collect addresses for a newsletter for fans who wanted to keep in touch between conventions. The first issue of Granger's *FurVersion*, dated May 30, 1987 was a mere five-page mailing list so that Furry fans could correspond with each other. With #3, dated July 30, *FurVersion* had expanded to 24 pages of amateur art and the first half of a two-part story by Rod O'Riley. #4, September, was 47 pages of text stories, comic book stories, and single-page art ranging from gag cartoons to serious fine-art graphics. Most subsequent issues until the final #21 were from 50 to 80 pages; #16 was 106 pages. *Rowrbrazzle* had published short stories by then, but *Rowrbrazzle* was an APA whose circulation was limited to its fifty members. *FurVersion* was for sale to the public, and it encouraged amateur authors and artists throughout Furry fandom to contribute.

Whether or not Furry literature can be justified as a genre, there has undeniably been a distinct fandom since the mid-1980s. Gathering at first within science fiction fandom's and comic book fandom's conventions, Merlino and O'Riley organized the first Furry convention, the prototype ConFurence Zero, in Santa Ana, California in January 1989. Attendance was slightly less than 100, but it included fans from throughout the U.S. and Canada and one from Australia. The annual ConFurences (which shifted from January to April in 1999) peaked at around 1,200 attendees in 1998 due to the creation of new, regional Furry conventions in the late 1990s. It was no longer necessary to travel to Southern California to socialize with other Furry fans. Today there are more than a half-dozen established regional annual Furry conventions throughout North America. Two of these, FURther CONfusion in Northern California in January and Anthrocon in Philadelphia in July, have surpassed ConFurence's record and slowly grow larger each year. Anthrocon is currently the largest, with an attendance around 1,600. Europe has had its Eurofurence in Summer since 1995 (current attendance is around 200), usually somewhere in Germany but once each in Sweden and the Netherlands, and 2003's is scheduled in the Czech Republic. Experimental national Furry conventions were first held in 2003 in France and the Netherlands with hopes of making them annual. Great Britain has held informal open "Furry house parties" two or three times a year since 1994 at some fan's home which draw from fifteen to fifty fans from throughout the U.K., and has announced plans to launch an annual formal convention, Britfur, in February 2005. Australia has held similar regional Furmeets (house parties and zoo trips) since around 2000, most frequently in Melbourne, Brisbane and Perth.

Furry fans have been communicating via the Internet since Merlino & Co. started the Tiger's Den electronic bulletin board in 1983 (to January 1996). The number and popularity of Furry BBS's, chat groups, mailing lists, and MUCKs has fluctuated wildly, but one of the oldest and most influential has been FurryMUCK (created in November 1990 by a Furry commune among students at Carnegie-Mellon University, Pittsburgh; relocated to Silicon Valley when most of them graduated and got jobs in the computer industry a couple of years later; still going under new management at www.furry.com/furrymain.html.) The most popular Furry Internet "daily newspaper" is *Flayrah.com: Unusually Good Information* (www.flayrah.com/), created by Jim "Aureth" Doolittle, Chicago, in January 2001. Some other comprehensive Furry information sites and collections of individual web pages are: *Miavir's Treasure Chest of Assorted Furryness* (http://furry.de/miavir/furry.html; created by Deon F. Ramsey, August 1995); *The Furry Resource Page* (www.fur.com/furry/; created by "WhiteFire" in June 1999); *Mongoose.net: The Web's First and Finest Anthroportal* (www.mongoose.net/, created by Robert "The Mystic Mongoose" Armstrong, Mystic, CT, in February 1999); and *FurNation* (www.furnation.com/, created by James A. "Nexxus" Robertson in November 1995). There are a few national websites outside the United States, with Australia's *Www.Furry.Org.Au: Australasia's Premier Furry Resource* (www.furry.org.au/), Brazil's *FurryBrasil* (www.furrybrasil.com.br/), and Italy's *Furry.IT: il portale della comunità furry italiana* (www.furry.it/) standing out for comprehensiveness, clarity, and attractive graphics.

This social group supports its own small-press literature. Furry magazines usually have circulations in the low hundreds, and are published as a hobby activity by an individual or a small club until their interests change or they become unable to continue for personal reasons. Lack of commercial success is seldom a reason, because almost no Furry publishers ever begin with the expectation of making a large profit. (There are edifying horror stories about the naïve few who did.) Most hope to only earn back enough to subsidize their hobby as an amateur editor/publisher. There have been Furry magazines with full-color covers produced at high-quality print shops; those usually disappear after only one or two issues. The longer-running magazines have been modestly printed at local office photocopy shops.

Bibliography/Recommended Reading: Printed Magazines

The following list of Furry small-press magazines is limited to those which have featured significant literary content: short stories, serialized novels, articles, essays, and reviews. There have been long-running magazines which have featured only art, or discussions of the conventions and other social activities within the fandom; but they are excluded as being outside the scope of *Best in Show*. Since most of these magazines are long out of print, and their editor/publishers may no longer have copies and may no longer be at their last-published addresses, addresses are given only for those which are currently published as of mid-2003. The editors' home regions are noted as indicating where some of the creative centers of Furry fandom have been during its development. Write for current prices and ordering information. Some of the publications, as noted, are amateur publishing associations (APAs) which are only available to their members, who must contribute writing or art to the issues.

Alternate Realms. Semiannual. #1, August 1993; final issue #4, January 1995. Editor: Tigerwing Press (D. A. Graf), San Diego.

Anthrolations: The Magazine of Anthropomorphic Dramatic Fiction.

Semiannual; current. #1, January 2000; most recent #6, November 2002. Editor: Jeff Eddy. Sofawolf Press, P. O. Box 8133, St. Paul, Minnesota 55108-0133; http://www.sofawolf.com.

A.P.A. Castlehome. Quarterly. #1, October-December 1994; final issue #12, July-September 1997. NOTE: despite its title, this was a traditional literary magazine and not an APA. Editor: (David) Reese Dorrycott, San Antonio.

The Ever-Changing Palace. Irregular; current. #1, July 1990; most recent #9, April 1999 but #10 is still promised "eventually." NOTE: *The Ever-Changing Palace* is a shared-world magazine, devoted to fan-written stories set in V. M. Wyman's *Xanadu* series. Editor: Lex Nakashima, Los Angeles. Steve Gallacci, P. O. Box 19419, Seattle, Washington 98109

Fang, Claw & Steel: Modern Lycanthrope Review. Semiannual; current. #1, Winter 1997; most recent #17, Summer 2003. Editor: Terry Wessner. *Fang, Claw & Steel,* 576 Elm Road, Stouffville, Ontario, Canada L4A 1W7; http://webhome.idirect.com/~twessner/fcs/fcs.htm

Fantastic Furry Stories: "The Magazine for Thinking Furries." Approximately annual. #1, August 1999; final issue #4, January 2003. Editors: #1 & #3 - #4, Carole Curtis; #2, Mel. White. Shanda Fantasy Arts, P. O. Box 545, Greenbrier, Arkansas 72058; http://www.shandafantasy-arts.net/.

FUR Plus: "Furs with a Difference." Quarterly; current. #1, January 1997; most recent #19, July 2003. NOTE: *FUR Plus* is devoted to stories and art of adult erotic content. Editor: Karl Maurer, San Jose. Fauxpaw Productions, Karl Maurer, PMB 285, 105 Serra Way, Milpitas, California 95035; http://www.fauxpaw.com.

Fur Scene: The Anthropomorphic News Letter. Quarterly. #1, Winter 1994; final issue #11, February 1998. Editor: Martin Dudman, London.

Fur Visions. Quarterly; current. #1, January 1996; most recent #29, July 2003. Editor: Karl Maurer, San Jose. Fauxpaw Productions, Karl Maurer, PMB 285, 105 Serra Way, Milpitas, California 95035; http://www.faux-paw.com.

Furkindred. Irregular. *The Furkindred* was a shared-world project created by Edd Vick and Chuck Melville of Seattle, the publishers of MU Press, one of Furry fandom's first small presses. Their goal was to design an alternate Earth inhabited by intelligent animals, some bipedal and some quadrupedal: the geography, the civilization, the species, the politics. This was the basis for a series of stories by many writers, some in text form and some in comic-book form, to be published in a series of books and a magazine by MU Press. The project got off to a good start with the trade paperback *The Furkindred: A Shared World,* edited by Chuck Melville and Edd Vick; MU Press, July 1991, xvii + 220 pages. It contained stories by 18 authors; ten in text form and eight in comic book form. The magazine began with *The Furkindred #1: Otter Madness,* March 1992; nine stories, divided about equally between text and comic books, totaling 106 pages. The last issue was *The Furkindred #2: Renewal of Porpoise*, December 1992; 144 pages in a trade paperback format again. That was the end of *The Furkindred* as a group project. Some text stories have been published individually in other Furry magazines, and one long comic-book story was published as a single-issue comic book, *The Furkindred: Let Sleeping Gods Lie*, by Dean A. Graf (story) & Terrie Smith (art); MU Press, February 1997, 56 pages.

Furry Press Network. Quarterly. #1, December 1990; final issue #5, December 1991. Editor: Gary Sutton, Baker City, Oregon. The *Furry Press Network* was an APA.

FurryPhile. Quarterly. #1, June 1994; final issue #10, January 1998. Original editor: Brian L. Miller, Biloxi; Editor since #8, June 1997, Bryon L. Havranek, San Diego.

FURtherance. Annual. #1, Summer 1989; final issue #3, Winter 1991. Editor: Runé (Ray Rooney), Philadelphia.

Furthest North Crew. Quarterly; current. #1, July 1992; most recent #45, June 2003. Original Editor: Paul "Growl" Groulx, Frankford, Ontario, to #15, December 1995; Co-editor & Production Manager: John "Sasta" Boulton, Toronto, #16, March 1996 to #22, September 1997; Bryan "Shasticat" Feir, Toronto, #23, December 1997 - current; Co-editor & Treasurer: Niall "Servalkei" MacConnaill, Ottawa; #16, March 1996 - current. *The Furthest North Crew* is an APA. For membership applications: Bryan Feir, 374 Glenholme Avenue, Toronto, Ontario, Canada M6E 3E5; http://fnc.furry.com/

FurVersion. "Monthly." #1, May 1987; final issue #21, November 1990. Editor: Kyim Granger (Karl Maurer), Oakland. NOTE: *FurVersion* was officially monthly, though issues from #13 to #20, March 1990 were closer to bimonthly. A final #21 straggled out in November 1990. By the time Granger admitted that personal considerations made it impossible for him to continue publishing, newer magazines had supplanted it. Issue #22 was prepared but exists in a single prototype copy only, which is sometimes exhibited at Furry conventions. Maurer says that some authors are now embarrassed by their early writings and have threatened to kill him if he lets anyone read their stories in it.

HistoriMorphs. Irregular; current. Most recent #1, July 2001. Editor: Lanny Fields, Seattle. Sofawolf Press, P. O. Box 8133, St. Paul, Minnesota 55108-0133; http://www.sofawolf.com.

Morphic Tales: An Anthropomorphic Anthology. Irregular but only one issue. #1, January 2000. Editor: Jim Doolittle, Chicago.

Mythagoras: The Journal of the MSTF. Quarterly. #1, Spring 1990; final issue #3, Autumn 1990. Editors: Bill Biersdorf & Watts Martin, Tampa. *Mythagoras* (New Series): *New Tales & Animal Legends*. Quarterly but only one issue. #1, Summer 1997. Editor: Watts Martin, Tampa.

North American Fur. Semiannual; current. #1, October 1997; most recent #11, January 2003. NOTE: This is an APA in that contributions are only accepted from members, but copies are sold to the public. Original editor: Paul "Growl" Groulx, Ontario, NY; Editors since #4, April-May 1999: James "Tibo" Birdsall & Dan "Flinthoof" Canaan, Seattle. Jarlidium Press, 2406 SW 308th Place, Federal Way, Washington 98023; http://www.picarefy.com/jarlidium.

PawPrints Fanzine. Semiannual. #1, Winter 1994; final issue #12, Fall 2001. Co-editors: T. Jordan "Greywolf" Peacock & Conrad "Lynx" Wong, San Jose. Copies are still available from: *PawPrints Fanzine*, 101 First Street, PMB 554, Los Altos Hills, California 94022; lynx@purrsia.com.

Refractions: An Albedo Omnibus. Irregular. #1, October 1992; final issue #3, Autumn 1996. NOTE: *Refractions* was a shared-world magazine, devoted to fan-written stories set in Steve Gallacci's *Albedo* series. Editor: Steve Gallacci, Seattle.

Rowrbrazzle. Quarterly; current. #1, February 1984; most recent #78, July 2003. Original editor: Marc Schirmeister, Los Angeles; Editor since #20, January 1989: Fred Patten, Los Angeles. *Rowrbrazzle* is an APA. For membership applications: Fred Patten, 11863 West Jefferson Boulevard, Culver City, California 90230-6322; fredpatten@earthlink.net.

South Fur Lands. Quarterly; current. #1, July 1995; most recent #29, June 2003. Original editor: Jason Gaffney, Brisbane; Editor since #20, March 2001: Bernard Doove, Melbourne. The Chakat's Den, P. O. Box 825, Bayswater, Victoria, Australia 3153; http://www.furry.org.au/sfl/ and sfl@furry.org.au

Steam Victorian. Irregular. #1, Spring 1993; final issue #2, August 1993. Editor: Zjonni Perchalski, San Jose.

Tales of the Tai-Pan Universe (originally *The Tai-Pan*; title changed with #8, March 1995). 3-yearly; current. The project was started in March 1988; issue #1 was published in March 1991; most recent #33, July 2003. NOTE: The Tai-Pan Literary Project is a shared-world series; all stories must be set in the established literary universe, and are edited by a board of Associate Editors for consistency. Original editor: Whitney Ware, Seattle; Editor since #8, March 1995, Gene Breshears, Seattle. Tai-Pan Literary & Arts Project, PMB #532, 6201 15th Avenue NW, Seattle, Washington 98107-2382; http://www.taipanproject.org/

The Tapestry: Anthropomorphic Fiction Anthology. Annual; current. Vol. 1, Summer 2002. Editors: Tanamin M. Wingate and Kishma Danielle. Non Species-Specific Communications, c/o Tanamin M. Wingate, P. O. Box 5692, Fresno, California 93755-5692; thetapestry@attbi.com.

Touch: The Magazine of Fantasy Romance and Erotica. Semiannual. #1, June 1991; final issue #3, August 1992. Editors: Mark Merlino, John Stanley, Rod O'Riley, Anaheim.

Wildlife APAzine. Bimonthly. #1, August 1992; final issue #4, February 1993. NOTE: despite its title, this was a traditional literary magazine and not an APA. Editor: Matthew High, San Antonio.

Yarf!: The Journal of Applied Anthropomorphics. Irregular but approximately quarterly; current. #1, January 1990; most recent #67, April 2003. Editor: Jeff Ferris, San Jose. *Yarf!*, P. O. Box 1299, Cupertino, California 95015-1299; yarf@yarf.furry.com.

Zoomorphica. Quarterly but only one issue. #1, Summer 1992. Editor: Watts Martin, Tampa.

Bibliography/Recommended Reading: The Internet

Mia's Index of Anthro' Stories on *Miavir's Treasure Chest of Assorted Furryness* (http://furry.de/miavir/stories/index.html) is a notably valiant attempt by Miavir to create a complete collection of links, indexed and alphabetized by story and author, to every Furry story posted on the web. The latest posted total is 2,501. However, despite claims of completeness there are many stories that are not included at all. Also, many of the 2,501 links to stories no longer work, due either to technical breakdowns or to authors having removed their stories from the net.

The Transformation Story Archive: The Finest in Transformation Fiction since 1995 (http://tsa.transform.to/), is one of the most complete and complex websites. It is devoted to stories about transformations of (usually) humans in the manner of the Roman myths as put into literary form by Ovid in his *Metamorphoses*, and can include transformations of age, gender, and into objects as well as into animals; but it is one of the largest collections of stories about humans transformed into Furries and how they deal with it. Created by Thomas Hassan in May 1995, it has gone through several changes of administrators, many of whom are known only by their Furry names, as well as spinning off specialized subdivisions. The Archive itself is currently maintained by "J. T. SkunkTaur", and includes both individual stories and shared-world writing projects. The *TSA-TALK* mailing list, "a forum for authors to forge and develop new works involving transformation, as well as a place to discuss transformation in published works, in popular entertainment, and on the Internet", was begun on April 3, 1996, and passed on by Hassan to a triumvirate board on its sixth anniversary, May 1, 2001. The stories on *TSA* are actually posted there, not links to stories posted elsewhere which may no longer be at those sites.

An example that is pertinent to *Best in Show* is that of *The Blind Pig* shared-world series. (See Phil Geusz's "Graduation Day.") The first story, "Tails from the Blind Pig" by Mark R. Van Sciver, was posted on the *Transformation Story Archive* on September 8, 1996. Its final two sentences ("We love good stories. Come by and tell us yours.") were taken as an invitation to other authors to write their own stories in the same setting. Enough did that a separate archive of *TBP* stories was soon created within the *TSA* (http://tsa.transform.to/worlds/tbp/index.html). The *TBP* archive currently contains 63 stories by over twenty authors, ranging from vignettes to almost novel-length. This is not complete; stories are usually posted first on their author's or other websites, and not all have yet been added to the *TSA*. *Mia's Index of Anthro' Stories* lists 146 *TBP* stories, although many of Mia's links to those stories lead to "Not Found" messages.

Another example of shared-world writing projects which is not represented in *Best in Show* but is worth recommending is *Metamor Keep*. The *MK* setting is a sword-&-sorcery world of Medieval knights, warriors, and good wizards battling monsters and evil sorcerers. The Keep is a castle in a valley at the southern end of a mountain pass that is the traditional invasion route from the demon controlled northern Giantdowns; and is the key defensive bottleneck protecting the human southern Midlands. In the setup story by Copernicus, the Keep was subject six years earlier to a particularly vicious siege of demonic warriors led by the sorcerer Nasoj. The Keep won but a parting spell by Nasoj transformed the defenders into (mostly) animal people. Shunned by other humans as freaks, the stories explore how the Keep has evolved into a *de facto* independent duchy of (mostly) Furries. The concept was proposed by "Copernicus" on the *TSA-TALK* forum on November 22, 1997. Enough stories had been written by February 18, 1999 to create *The Metamor Keep Story Archives* (http://transform.to/~metamor/). The *MK* discussion group on the *TSA-TALK* forum split off into its own *Metamor Keep* forum on July 6, 1999. The forum is a private group for *MK* authors only, administered by an editorial board currently headed by Chris O'Kane, but the *Archives* is open for public viewing. At press time it lists 251 stories by 48 authors. The *MK* shared-world series is only one of several accessible through *The Transformation Story Archive*.

BIOGRAPHIES

Brian W. Antoine

Brian Antoine, a 40 something software engineer living in Spokane WA, started writing fantasy stories back in 1992 in a local Usenet newsgroup as a way to relax and have fun with a couple of his friends. A decade later and much to his surprise, he is still having fun at it and still getting comments from readers asking when the next story will be out. Taking the advice that you should write what you know about to heart, his stories are written with himself as one of the central characters and draw on his love of science fiction, his years of fantasy role playing and just about anything or anyone that wanders too close. In addition to his stories, Brian has also created or helped in the creation of public archive sites, Usenet newsgroups and IRC networks specific to the Anthropomorphic Community. He considers this his way of saying thank you to the many friendly and talented people he has had the privilege to meet and work with since that day so many years ago when he discovered a lonely looking comic called *Albedo: Anthropomorphics*. A small number of his stories have been published in amateur publications and all of his publicly released material is available from his personal website at http://www.nas-kan.org/. He may be contacted either by email at briana@nas-kan.org, or via AIM using his on-line handle, UniKyrn.

Gene Breshears

Gene Breshears has been involved in publishing and small press activities (sometimes extremely small press) since the age of 12. He made his first fiction sale at 16 but has since discovered that working as a Technical Writer, Graphic Artist, and Technical Illustrator pays better yet leaves him enough time and energy to pursue his creative interests for fun. Born in a small Oklahoma town that was inexplicably located in northwestern Colorado, he attended 10 different elementary schools in five different states, two high schools in different states, then finally abandoned his family's gypsy lifestyle to finish a bachelor's degree in Mathematics in Seattle—where he settled because he likes the rain. He lives in Seattle with his partner, Michael. In his spare time he writes, composes music, bicycles, raises roses, and is President and Editor-in-Chief of the non-profit Tai-Pan Literary & Arts Project.

Robert K. & Margaret Carspecken

Robert & Margaret Carspecken (R&M Creative Endeavors) are a team of freelance creators who work in a variety of fields from their Ozarks home studio. As writers they work primarily in science fiction, fantasy and illustrated children's stories. As artists they are known for cartooning, comic art, and wildlife art and illustrations. Margaret's cartoon-illustrated cookbook *Sweet Treats* is highly regarded within fandom, as are her many animal-oriented paintings and illustrations. On the Web they are primarily known for their fox-related site (http://www.ozfoxes.com/) and the comic strip *Faux Pas*.

Mick Collins

Mick Collins discovered Furry fandom one day at work in 1991, and his friends have doubted his sanity ever since. When he's not on the road with his band The Dirtbombs, he is a record producer. He lives in Detroit, where, he says, "it's safe."

Jeff Eddy

Jeff is Chief Publisher and Co-Owner (with Tim Susman) of Sofawolf Press, whose product list includes the semi-pro literary magazine *Anthrolations* and the New Tibet shared world paperback *Breaking the Ice*. He secures Saint Paul computer networks to support his expensive small press, Siberian Husky, and bird watching habits.

Phil Geusz

Phil Geusz is the author of several full-length novels and numerous shorts. He is best known within Furry fandom for his involvement with the *Transformation Story Archive*, and resides in Tennessee. Phil cut his literary teeth reading Golden Age science fiction, and he considers the timeless gems of this era to be the taproot of his own personal style. Robert Heinlein is his very favorite author of all time, though he also deeply admires Arthur C. Clarke, Larry Niven and Ray Bradbury. Several of Phil's novels can be found for sale at http://ebooks.xepher.net/.

Ben Goodridge

Ben Goodridge was born in Cold War West Germany to American parents and has lived in Maine for most of his life. He has been writing since he was fourteen and has been published in *The Review: Words and Images* and *Fang, Claw & Steel*. He recently took an English degree from the University of Southern Maine, where he kept a regular column on the weekly student newspaper. He also self-published a zine in 1998 called *Wreck of the Amanda K*. He currently lives in Portland, where he cooks up a storm and writes like a demon while waiting for his big break.

Craig Hilton

Craig Hilton is a busy family doctor who has lived and worked in all points of the compass throughout Australia, and now resides in the state of Victoria. In his spare moments, he enjoys writing, cartooning and art. Born in 1960 in Woomera, South Australia, he grew up in Adelaide and Perth (Western Australia). In medical school, he wrote and drew an annual humorous magazine, *Leechcraft*. Published cartoons have included the newspaper strip *Downunderground*, compiled in 1996 as a book, and *Doc Rat* for two medical magazines. He became known for writing, cartooning and filking in s-f fandom in Australia (1987 Australian S-f Achievement "Ditmar" Award - Best Science Fiction or Fantasy Artist) and later in fanzines internationally. He was a member of *ROWRBRAZZLE* from 1988 and of *Huzzah!* from 1992 until 2000, when his medical career forced a cutback in his time for fiction and art. He also contributed to every issue of *The Ever-Changing Palace*, which ran his series of short stories of the detective rat Whimper.

Brock Hoagland

Brock was born in Detroit, Michigan on December 4, 1950. His father was a career officer in the Air Force so he grew up in several states and spent three years in England as a child. The family finally settled in South Dakota, where he attended high school and college. Dropping out of college, he joined the Navy—it was better than slogging through rice paddies and jungles with an M-16. After serving six years he got out and found a job in a power plant in North Dakota and has been there for more than twenty years. Brock began writing more than forty years ago and has been at it ever since. About ten years ago he began writing anthropomorphic fiction. He has a number of published stories to his credit, mostly in different series about such adventurers as Perissa, Hanno and Loris, and Knight and Mouse. These include several comic-book stories for *Magic Carpet* and *New Horizons*; however, it is text stories that are his first love. He has recently completed a Furry erotic sword-&-sorcery novel, *The Iron Star*, which is about to be published.

Jennie Hoffer

Jennie, aka "Snocat" recently graduated with a BFA in character animation from San Jose State University in Northern CA. She now resides in the Los Angeles area where she works as an animator, illustrator, and character designer for the popular virtual pet website, www.neopets.com. In her free time, she takes on various freelance art jobs, and continues to pursue her goal of a career in feature animation.

M. C. A. Hogarth

M. C. A. Hogarth lives in stormy Florida on a plot of land owned by the neighborhood sandhill cranes. She spends days with databases and telecommunications equipment, and comes home to art sketchbooks and notebooks of poetry and fiction. Her writing has been previously published in venues like *Strange Horizons, Speculations* and the *Leading Edge*. You can learn more at her website, http://www.stardancer.org/ or send her e.mail at mcah@stardancer.org.

Allen Kitchen

Allen Kitchen is an Electrical and Computer Engineer in Houston, Texas where he works for the Space Program building lab equipment to fly on the International Space Station. Long a fan of Science Fiction and Fantasy stories, he joined the Furry fandom and began writing in 1995. He likes broiled steaks, well-built cars, ice-cold beer, and imaginative stories and art. His hobbies include writing, programming, and building shiny machines that scare the neighbors. Allen comes by his insanity honestly; he has small children. This limits the time he has to write, read, or visit. He dreams of the day when he can finally escape the bounds of Earth and travel into space, all in the hope that there he will be able to finally get an uninterrupted nap.

Kim Liu

Kim Liu is a computer professional with the occasional bout of artistic aspirations. Presently in California, he enjoys the warmth but occasionally misses the mountains of his native West Virginia—the obvious combination of living on a volcano is unfortunately not practical as yet.

Watts Martin

Watts Martin has been writing since the late '80s, frequently featuring anthropomorphic animal characters in his works. He created the character of Revar, a vampire bat, whose stories have remained popular for over a decade. A contributor to *The Furkindred, Yarf!, PawPrints, FurVersion, Touch* and other small press publications, Watts also co-created *Mythagoras*, a cardinal "semi-prozine" in the early '90s. Watts is working on a collection of out-of-print old and brand new material for Sofawolf Press. Professionally, Watts has worked in the telecom and web development fields, but he still wants to be a writer when he grows up. He recently moved from Tampa Bay, his home of nearly 30 years, to the San Francisco Bay area.

Elizabeth McCoy

Elizabeth McCoy was born on Guy Fawkes Day, but in the wrong country to have her birthday celebrated with fireworks. For fiction, she has written several Kintaran stories in *PawPrints*, one short-short in Marion Zimmer Bradley's *Sword and Sorceress* #7, and assorted fanfic and Mary-Sues. She has also written assorted material for Steve Jackson Games' *In Nomine* line (and is also its Line Editor), co-authored *GURPS Illuminati University* and *GURPS In Nomine*, and has numerous playtest credits. She lives in the Frozen Wastelands of southern New Hampshire with 1 husband, 1 toddler, 3 cats, 3 fish, and between 3 and 5 Macintosh computers. And a Palm Pilot. Elizabeth would like to thank Steve Jackson for the various *GURPS* books which inspired the Kintarans' background and technology, as well as some of the races, and John Moore, who first came up with the concepts of Unars and Thrals (who probably aren't much like he envisioned them, anymore...).

Chas. P. A. Melville

Chuck Melville was first heard of when he wrote, drew, and self-published one issue of his Furry adventure fantasy comic book *The Champion of Katara* in northwest New York in mid-1987. He promptly moved to Seattle and joined its large Furry community. He served as co-editor (and occasional cover artist) with Edd Vick at MU Press for most of that small press' existence during the 1990s, publishing the continuation of *The Champion of Katara* there. He and Vick co-created the concept of *The Furkindred* and co-edited its three volumes during 1991-'92; his own story "Mercy To The Cubs" was published in *Yarf!* three years later. Chuck was a member of the *ROWRBRAZZLE* apa from 1988 to 1998, where he developed his most popular character, Felicia the enigmatic vixen sorceress, the star of his *chef-d'oeuvre* (to date): the 168-page *Felicia: Melari's Wish* (published as a graphic novel by MU in 1995). Most of Chuck's artistic and literary output for the past few years has appeared in the shared-world project *Tales of the Tai-Pan Universe*. He can usually be found on the staff of Seattle's ConiFur Northwest annual Furry convention.

Kylen Christine Miles

Born and raised in California, her art was inspired by popular animation studios and her love for animals. Her art progressed from hobby to career choice, and she studied and majored in Animation at Loyola Marymount University in Los Angeles, California. Kylen has done freelance work ranging from anthropomorphic magazines and publications to illustrating Sign Language Lesson books and screenplays for films bought by such studios as Paramount Pictures. Currently finishing her college studies, she hopes to eventually work in the American animation industry.

John Nunnemacher

John Nunnemacher graduated with honors from the Graphic Arts program at Moravian College in Pennsylvania. Since then, he has worked a long string of diverse jobs, including serving as Production Manager for a monthly business journal, drawing caricatures in the Florida heat and humidity at SeaWorld, and creating animation and character layouts for projects such as *Dilbert: The Animated Series*, and *Disney's The Tigger Movie*.

Fred Patten

Fred Patten has been a voracious reader of s-f in text, comic book, and cinematic forms since he was nine years old. He joined s-f fandom in Los Angeles while in college in 1960, and was in comic-book fandom from its start a couple of years later. He has been particularly active in Japanese animation (anime) and anthropomorphic (Furry) fandoms since their beginnings. In the latter he was a charter member of the *ROWRBRAZZLE* apa in 1984, and has been its Official Editor since 1989; he has written book reviews of Furry fiction for *Yarf!* since its first issue in 1990; he wrote the annotated *An Anthropomorphic Bibliography* (three editions since 1995); and he led the organization of the Ursa Major Awards for the best in Furry arts & literature in 2001. In the former he was one of the founding members of the Cartoon/Fantasy Organization, the first anime fan club in May 1977. After working for over twenty years as an industrial catalogue librarian, he switched to the new anime industry in 1991 and earns his living there today.

Michael H. Payne

Michael H. Payne has had stories published in magazines ranging from *Asimov's Science Fiction* to *Marion Zimmer Bradley's FANTASY Magazine* to *Tomorrow Speculative Fiction*, stories which can be purchased at http://www.fictionwise.com/eBooks/MichaelHPayneeBooks.htm as ebooks. He won 3rd place in the L. Ron Hubbard's Writers of the Future® Contest for his story "Crow's Curse" (published in *L. Ron Hubbard presents Writers of the Future, vol. VII*; the 1991 annual collection of winners), and a 2003 Ursa Major Award in the Best Short Story category for his story "Familiars" (in *Sword and Sorceress XIX*, edited by Marion Zimmer Bradley; DAW Books, January 2002). His novel *The Blood Jaguar* (Tor Books, December 1998) is apparently still available through amazon.com and other such outlets. His comic strip *Terebinth* appears at www.chimericalcomics.com/terebinth.html and in *Yarf!*, and the stories that he writes and draws about a group of harvest mice show up in the *New Horizons* anthology magazine from Shanda Fantasy Arts. Check out http://www.kuci.org/~mpayne if you feel the need for any more info...

Matt Posner

"The Boar Goes North" and its sequel, "The Furriers" (in *Zoomorphica* #1, Summer 1992), are the culmination of a six-year collaboration between me and writer/editor/publishing maven Watts Martin. Watts and I attended college together, and I supplied a variety of materials for his college publications. I was proud to contribute to his first two for-profit magazines circa 1992, with a pair of stories that cross-pollinated the Furry genre with the post-apocalyptic setting of the *Gamma World* RP game and the gritty action style of Robert E. Howard. Originally from Miami, Florida, I was educated at New College, Florida State, and University of Alabama and now work as a private school teacher and administrator in Long Island, New York.

Axel Shaikman

Axel Shaikman lives in the concrete hell sometimes known as Los Angeles. He spends as much time as possible trying to forget this by hiking the nearby hills with strange people and alien dogs.

Tim Susman

Tim Susman was raised by a family of wild foxes in eastern Pennsylvania. At the tender age of seventeen, he was sent out to find his own territory, and wandered from Pennsylvania to Minnesota. After six years (and ten winters), he kept moving westward, finally settling in California when stopped by the Pacific Ocean. He writes and edits stories, reads and analyzes all kinds of databases, and is a non-practicing certified zoologist. He no longer eats bugs, but still loves chicken.

Todd G. Sutherland

Born in the late 1960s in Nova Scotia, Todd G. Sutherland has enjoyed modest notoriety in the circles of anthropomorphic fandom for both his writing and his artwork. While largely withdrawn from participating in the fandom in recent years, he still enjoys writing and occasionally drawing in anthropomorphic themes, and is proud that his story, "Wings", has been selected for inclusion in this volume.

Jefferson P. Swycaffer

Jefferson P. Swycaffer has been a Furry fan since just about the beginning. He came within a fine camel's hair of naming the genre, referring to it as 'fuzzy fandom' in an article around 1984. He has published nine science fiction novels, four of which have been 'Furry' to one degree or another. In serious fiction, his "Marterly Trilogy" from New Infinities (1988) examined the question of genetically engineered "slave races" and the morality of altering nature to serve mankind. In somewhat less serious work, his latest story was an x-rated crossover with Steve Crompton's "Demi the Demoness." Jefferson is emphatic in considering himself a fan first, and a pro merely as a matter of fortuitous contingency.

Tom Turrittin

Tom Turrittin was born in Toronto in 1972 and has degrees in Anthropology and Library Science. His interests include anthropomorphic stories, the Piltdown Man fossil forgery, improvisational theater, and absurdist comedy. He has recently moved to Winnipeg to explore a potential career as a book cataloguer.

Lawrence Watt-Evans

Lawrence Watt-Evans has been a full-time writer of fantasy, science fiction, and horror for more than twenty years, with more than two dozen novels and a hundred short stories to his credit. He won a Hugo in 1988 for his short story "Why I Left Harry's All-Night Hamburgers," served two terms as president of the Horror Writers Association, and is a lifetime Active member of SFWA. His recent work has focused on epic fantasy, such as the three-volume "Obsidian Chronicles" (*Dragon Weather, The Dragon Society,* and *Dragon Venom,* from Tor Books). He lives in Maryland with his wife, two teenage children, a cat, and a corn snake.

Mel. White

Mel. White (a.k.a. Furrymuck Wizard "K'has") is a practicing Renaissance woman who has vowed to get this shtick right sometime before the turn of the century. Any century. A professional artist and writer, she has done book covers for e-books, drawn comic books and graphic novels, been a book reviewer, created sculptural dolls, written short stories for a number of Martin Greenberg's anthologies as well as for a Mercedes Lackey anthology, been a gardening columnist as well as a professional psychic and professional photographer. In some of her spare time, she composes electronic music (currently available on MP3.COM). A licensed (Pagan) minster, she has also occasionally performed weddings. (And those are just the high points. Really.) Her hobbies include reading, amateur rocketry, and amateur robotics, and an interest in petroglyphs and AmerInd rock art preservation. She's also a Lego junkie.

Conrad Wong

Conrad "Lynx" Wong is a programmer by trade, an artist, writer, and gamer in his spare time. He edited *PawPrints Fanzine*, an anthropomorphic-themed magazine, through 1994 to 2001. His art has received regional convention awards, and been published on comic book covers and in role-playing game books. His writing has appeared in numerous small magazines, though not as yet in a mass-market venue. He has been certified an upstart feline miscreant by his friends since 1990. He is honored that the editors of *Best in Show* have granted him the opportunity to revise 'Painted Memories', which appeared in *PawPrints* #1. The plot has not changed, but hopefully those who have read the previous version will find this one a better read. It has been a pleasure to revisit the Tangled Web universe, and he hopes to find time to write new stories following its worlds and its legends.

Vicky Wyman

Vicky is a third generation artist who has been drawing, sculpting, and writing for over thirty years. In addition to *Xandau* and *Xanadu 2000*, she has written extensively for *Anime House*, *Anime Janai*, *Revision X*, and *Ever Changing Palace*. Her artwork has graced numerous fan publications and gaming materials from several companies, including Avalon and Gamelords.